SHORT STORIES FROM THE LITERARY MAGAZINES

Jarvis Thurston
Washington University and *Perspective* Magazine

Curt Johnson
December Magazine

SHORT STORIES FROM THE LITERARY MAGAZINES

131507

Scott, Foresman and Company

ACKNOWLEDGMENTS

"A Four-Day Wait" by Theodore Bloom, reprinted from the *Quarterly Review of Literature* by permission of Robert Lescher, Literary Agent, and the author.

"Storm Still" by Brock Brower, reprinted from *TriQuarterly* by permission of Robert Lantz-Candida Donadio Literary Agency, Inc. and the author. Copyright © 1967 by Brock Brower.

"Will You Please Be Quiet, Please?" by Raymond Carver, reprinted from *December*, copyright 1966 by Raymond Carver, by permission of the author.

"Love in the Winter" by Daniel Curley, from *The Colorado Quarterly*, Winter 1964, reprinted by permission of John Schaffner, Literary Agent. Copyright © 1964 by The University of Colorado.

"The Son of the Sad Fat Wordman Goes North" by Ralph Dennis, reprinted from *Lillabulero*, Vol. 1, No. 4, 1967 by permission of *Lillabulero* and the author.

"The Guest" by Stanley Elkin, from *Criers and Kibitzers, and Kibitzers and Criers*, by Stanley Elkin, © copyright 1965 by Stanley Elkin. Reprinted by permission of Random House, Inc. and the author. ("The Guest" originally appeared in the *Paris Review* No. 32.)

"Summerfield" by J. M. Ferguson, Jr., reprinted from *Descant* (a publication of the Texas Christian University Press), by permission of the author and the publisher.

"In Line for Lemonade" by Andrew Fetler. This story first appeared in *The Malahat Review* Number One, January 1967. By permission of *The Malahat Review* and the author.

"Second Fiddle" by William Fifield, reprinted from *The Texas Quarterly*, Vol. VIII, Number One, Spring 1965, by permission of The University of Texas and the author.

"A Fable" by Robert Fox, reprinted from *Midwestern University Quarterly*, Volume I, Number 4, copyright 1966 by permission.

"Differences" by Carolyn Gaiser, reprinted from *The Paris Review*, Issue Number 40, Winter-Spring 1967 by permission of *The Paris Review* and the author.

"In the Heart of the Heart of the Country" by William H. Gass, from *In the Heart of the Heart of the Country and Other Stories* by William H. Gass. Copyright © 1967 by William H. Gass. Reprinted by permission of Harper & Row, Publishers and the author. ("In the Heart of the Heart of the Country" originally appeared in the *New American Review*.)

"One of You Must Be Wendell Corey" by Philip L. Greene, reprinted from *Partisan Review*, Spring 1965, Volume 32, No. 3, by permission of the *Partisan Review* and the author.

"The Gesture" by James W. Groshong, reprinted from the *Antioch Review*, Vol. XXIV, No. 4, by permission of the Antioch Press.

"Getting Married" by James B. Hall, reprinted from the *Virginia Quarterly Review*, Summer 1967, by permission of the *Virginia Quarterly Review* and the author.

"On the Island" by Josephine Jacobsen, Copyright © 1965 by *The Kenyon Review*. Appeared originally in *The Kenyon Review*. Reprinted by permission of McIntosh and Otis, Inc. and the author.

"Diseases of the Heart" by Conrad Knickerbocker, reprinted by permission of Robert Lantz-Candida Donadio Literary Agency, Inc. Copyright © 1966 by Conrad Knickerbocker. (Originally published in *The Kenyon Review*, 1966.)

"Why Girls Ride Sidesaddle" by Dennis Lynds, reprinted from *The Minnesota Review*, Copyright 1965, by permission of *The Minnesota Review* and the author.

"The Wrong Silence" by Nancy K. MacKenzie, reprinted from *Prairie Schooner*, Winter 1967-68. Copyright 1967 by the University of Nebraska Press. Reprinted by permission of the author.

"Traven" by David Madden, reprinted from *The Southern Review*, Spring 1968, by permission of the author and the publisher.

"Love Song for Doris Ballinger" by Jack Matthews, reprinted from *The Carleton Miscellany*, Copyright 1968 by Carleton College by permission of the author and the publisher.

"Sticks and Stones" by Leonard Michaels. Reprinted with permission of Farrar, Straus & Giroux, Inc. and the author, from *Going Places* by Leonard Michaels. Copyright © 1964, 1969 by Leonard Michaels. First published in *Massachusetts Review*.

"The Nature of the Task" by Howard Nemerov, reprinted from the *Virginia Quarterly Review*, by permission of the Margot Johnson Agency.

"Humbly, for Fyodor" by Alden Nowlan, reprinted from *Prism International*, Copyright 1967, by permission of the author.

"Where Are You Going, Where Have You Been?" by Joyce Carol Oates, reprinted from *Epoch*, Fall 1966 by permission of Blanch C. Gregory, Inc. and the author. Copyright © 1966 by Joyce Carol Oates.

"Revelation" by Flannery O'Connor, reprinted from *The Sewanee Review*, copyright 1964 by Flannery O'Connor. Reprinted by permission of Harold Matson Co., Inc. and the University of the South.

"The Fat Guy" by Henry H. Roth, reprinted from *December*, Copyright 1964, by permission of the author and the publisher.

"Pluto Is the Furthest Planet" by Abraham Rothberg, reprinted from the *Yale Review*, Copyright 1965 by permission of the author.

"The Autopsy" by David Spriggs, reprinted from *Duel* (formerly *Prism '68)*, Spring 1968, by permission of the author and the publisher.

"The Throughway" by Peter Taylor, reprinted from the *Sewanee Review*, Vol. LXXII, No. 4, Autumn 1964, by permission of the University of the South and the author.

"Reasons I Insist You Call Me By My Right Name" by Gordon Weaver, reprinted from *Latitudes*, Vol. 2, No. 1, Spring 1968, by permission of the author and the publisher.

"The Hotel" by Victor White, reprinted from *Southwest Review*, winter 1965. © 1965 by Southern Methodist University Press, Dallas, by permission of the author and the publisher.

"The Round Brass Elevator" by Joseph Whitehill, reprinted by permission from *The Hudson Review*, Vol. XIX, No. 1 (Spring 1966). Copyright © 1966 by The Hudson Review, Inc.

"Baby, Tonight I Rolled Pinto Lee" by Joy Williams, reprinted from the *Colorado Quarterly*, Copyright 1968 by permission of the author and the publisher.

"The Bride" by Margery Wood, reprinted from *The Carleton Miscellany*, Copyright 1967, Vol. VIII, No. 4, by permission of Carleton College and the author.

"The Tennis Player" by John Zeugner, reprinted from *Perspective*, Copyright 1968 by permission of the author and the publisher.

"Mr. and Mrs. McGill" by George A. Zorn, reprinted from *Perspective*, Copyright 1965 by permission of the author and the publisher.

The editors would like to thank the following people for their help in compiling this book: At the Marvin Sukov Collection at the University of Wisconsin's Memorial Library, Mary Fagerlund, Amy Nickles, Ann Zaeske, Michael Beamis, and, most especially, Felix Pollak, Curator of Rare Books, as well as librarians at the University of Chicago's Harper Library.

The editors also extend their special thanks to James L. Ballard, who provided the photographs for this book.

PREFACE

Teachers of "Modern" literature have become increasingly aware that there is a "Contemporary" literature which needs to become part of the course of study. This contemporary literature that has been accumulating in the last twenty years is not likely to replace what has become recognizable as the modern "classics"—Faulkner, Hemingway, Katherine Anne Porter, Joyce, Lawrence—but it does bear the same relation to the 1970's that the classics once did to the 1950's. It is not unreasonable to assume that some of the writers represented in this anthology will come to occupy reputations that last more than a decade or two.

The stories here are, the editors feel, some of the very finest that have been printed in recent years, in both the better- and the lesser-known literary magazines. A look at the table of contents will reveal names that have come into considerable prominence in the last twenty years—among them Flannery O'Connor, Howard Nemerov, and Peter Taylor—but there are others who have more recently moved into wider circles of recognition—for instance, W. H. Gass, Joyce Carol Oates, Stanley Elkin, and Leonard Michaels—and there are others relatively unknown whose excellence, if one can judge by their stories in this collection, will push them shortly into a wider fame.

Although the contemporaneity of the stories (and the appended Directory of Literary Magazines) will make this anthology useful in classes in the writing of fiction, the editors see it centrally as a text (supplementary, perhaps, to such widely used anthologies as Jarvis Thurston's *Reading Modern Short Stories*, Eugene Current-García and Walton Patrick's *American Short Stories*, and related anthologies by Robert Penn Warren, Richard Poirier, Mark Schorer, Robert Heilman, Ray B. West, Jr., and Arthur Mizener) for all those classes in which the study of the short story needs to take into account the postmodern, and all those classes in close reading and introduction to genres in which the teacher desires fresh and significant material that has not been endlessly scrutinized in print.

CONTENTS

INTRODUCTION

The *modern* short story—with its emphasis on character and interiority and rivaling poetry in its search for the universal in particulars—took its shape from Chekhov, Turgenev, Maupassant, and Flaubert, but flourished in the English language with James, Lawrence, Joyce, Faulkner, and Hemingway. It has thrived particularly in America—one thinks of Katherine Anne Porter, Eudora Welty, Robert Penn Warren, Conrad Aiken, John Steinbeck, and many others of equal merit—even though in the United States the novel, as writers and publishers know, is the only genre which gives its practitioners much of a chance at fame and, perhaps, fortune. The economic pressure on the story writer to become a novelist is considerable, and not uncommonly diverts the talents of writers highly skilled in the shorter form, such as, say, Sherwood Anderson and Katherine Anne Porter but not before they have made a significant contribution as writers of short fiction. The notion, widely held in the United States, that writing short stories is a reasonable apprenticeship for becoming a novelist is reflected in the fact that our laureate novelists began their careers as story writers; this is also true to the present time, as the careers of men such as Saul Bellow, Bernard Malamud, Philip Roth, and J. F. Powers demonstrate; before turning to the novel they wrote excellent stories, and even found themselves possessors of a modest degree of fame.

The notion of serving an apprenticeship in the story still persists, but clearly the possibilities of establishing a reputation as *only* a story writer have decreased. There are two main reasons. One is the death of so many widely circulated, high-paying commercial outlets *(Saturday Evening Post, Collier's, Woman's Home Companion,* for example) which did, during their lives, occasionally publish our Faulkners, F. Scott Fitzgeralds, and Ring Lardners. With the commercial market continuing to narrow, the story writer has found himself recently, in relation to money and public, in a cultural status very familiar to poets, who have long practiced their art entirely apart from commercial pressures or expectancies. Paradoxically, the other reason a story writer finds it difficult to establish a reputation if he remains only a writer of short stories is the increase in the number of noncommercial magazines. In answer to the need of poets and story writers for outlets, the "little magazine" movement (which began in the United States in the period around World War I with magazines such as *Poetry, Little Review, Fugitive,* and *Double Dealer*) has expanded enormously, as the list of magazines consulted in assembling this anthology indicates. Many of these "little magazines," or literary magazines as they are also called, are the direct result of the expansion of university education and the acceptance in the curriculum of courses in the "understanding" and writing of fiction, courses not uncommonly taught by writers themselves: Peter Taylor, Stanley Elkin, Joyce Carol Oates, and Jack Matthews, to mention a few represented in this anthology. When there were fewer little magazines a writer publishing a story, say, in the old *Southern Review* could be reasonably sure he had the attention of most of his fellow writers and most of the readers of very contemporary serious stories. But even though the total audience has increased it is split among many magazines; it no longer focuses on a Big Four or a Big Six. The readers of *Descant* do not overlap those of *Antioch Review.*

Many of the newer magazines are university-based and university-financed; *TriQuarterly Review, Colorado Quarterly,* and *Massachusetts Review,* for example, join company with the older *Antioch Review* and *Sewanee Review.* There are, however, dozens of little magazines in the strict sense of that term—those which not only have small circulations but stagger along independently, from issue to issue, never knowing where money is to be found to pay for printing and postage or for contributions (when contributions are paid for in anything more than author's copies); these include *Latitudes, December,* and *Lillabulero,* which join the older *Perspective* and *Quarterly Review of Literature.* Every year these noncommerical magazines publish dozens of stories that deserve to be rescued from the obscurity of serial publication. A reading of the fiction published in them in the last five years will convince one that the short story is thriving in America as it never has before—and that there are many new names pushing into prominence: Joyce Carol Oates, Leonard Michaels, Raymond Carver, Dennis Lynds, Henry H. Roth, and Joy Williams among them.

Though the editors have chosen the stories in this volume because we thought they were among the very best published in the literary magazines, we have also consciously attempted to select, whenever possible, work by lesser-known authors and from lesser-known magazines. Though some of the authors represented have not produced any bulk of work, their stories suggest they will have more conspicuous futures. But whether by commonly anthologized authors such as James B. Hall or Peter Taylor, or by relative newcomers like John Zeugner or Philip Greene, the stories were chosen ultimately because of their high quality.

We have included one story from *New American Review,* a publication with a readership many times larger than that of the usual little magazine, because it is in spirit and intent a magazine indentifiable with those from which our other selections were made. We intentionally excluded from our survey some magazines that publish good fiction—*The New Yorker, Harper's,* and *Esquire,* for example—because our central purpose is to make more available the excellent work being published in magazines of limited circulation, the magazines which have for many years nurtured, especially in their beginnings, our major writers.

SHORT STORIES FROM THE LITERARY MAGAZINES

A FOUR-DAY WAIT

THEODORE BLOOM from *Quarterly Review of Literature*

The old man clutched the box under his arm. It was wrapped in an old newspaper and an elastic band, and as he walked he plunked the elastic in time to his shambling footfalls. It was the first time he had brought the box. For the last three days he had kept the cigars in his inside coat pocket, but today the old man knew he would make the offer. It was the fourth day. The old man knew he would make the offer today. The other alternative was to keep right on walking, right past Raymond's house and on around the block back to his own room. And there to sit in the big chair and light up. For four days—the cigars inside the box were proof—he had deprived himself. "Damn that Raymond, anyway," the old man thought. "Why couldn't he've left things like they was?"

It was quarter past four, just the right time. If it happened at all, it happened at half-past. That would give the old man fifteen minutes to get around Raymond. Or to give in and make the offer. There was no doubt that it was worth it, but the old man hated to humble himself in front of Raymond. If only he could get Raymond to make an offer first. "Maybe," thought the old man. "Maybe with four Havanas within smoking reach he'll give in. But he's cute, that Raymond. He'll know right off why I'm carrying the box. He'll wait me out."

Raymond's sister answered the door. "Bitch," the old man said automatically to himself. She stood, silent and frowning disapproval, and pointed to Raymond's door. The old man never had been able to stand looking at her crumbling, meaty face. "Just don't work him up," she said. "He's mean enough as it is today." The old man hopped gingerly by her, his eyes turned away and his breath held to keep out the smell of cabbage.

Raymond had the television on. "Come over to watch?"

"How're you feeling today, Raymond?"

"What did you come for? To watch?"

"Might say that," the old man said. "Hmmm. Country Doctor." The old man never had liked that program. He had seen enough doctors to recognize the kind of sweet-talking do-gooder that Country Doctor David Little was. "You might say, Raymond, that I just come a-visiting. You might say that."

"You might say, you might say. You might say that you didn't, either." Sister was right, thought the old man. Raymond was mean today. Four days without a smoke could make a man mean, the old man knew.

"I can go if you want, Raymond," Raymond turned suddenly from the television screen and looked at the old man with a glaze of panic over his rheumy eyes. "It's up to you. I stay or I go?"

"If you had a tee-vee in your room you wouldn't come, would you? Answer me that."

"Don't you worry about that. Where would I get the money for a tee-vee, even if the landlady allowed? Tell me that."

"Landlady don't allow! Landlady don't allow! How you can put up with all those rules is something I don't understand."

"I stand for them the same way you stand for what your sister don't allow. That's how."

"It's not the same," Raymond said. "I'm invalided. She takes care of me. Why aren't you living with that famous son of yours in Boston? Answer me that."

"I choose not to," said the old man. He felt that somehow Raymond did not believe he had a son.

"Well, I choose to live here."

"My son sends me money."

"Why doesn't he buy you a tee-vee?"

"Why doesn't your sister buy you cigars?"

"Keep it up," Raymond warned. "And I'll turn off the tee-vee when you come. See if I don't."

"See if I care."

The old man took off his coat, a shabby red-brown tweed with a belted back, and folded it carefully. He placed it over the back of the chair, then put down the box on the seat. He plunked the elastic. Raymond looked, quickly, then turned back to the screen. Then the old man sat down on the edge of the bed. "What's Doctor Littleberg up to today?"

"Watch and see," Raymond said. He pretended to be lost in the life of the little figures that moved inside the box. He turned up the volume on the control box by his bed. "Buy something?" he asked the old man.

"Is he still trying to get that old bag to give polio shots to her brats?" the old man said. "That's the third week he's been on that."

"What you got in the box?"

"I'd rather see him give her a breast examination, or look for hemorrhoids, or something like that. Hee-hee."

"Someday you'll say that when my sister's listening and it's goodby tee-vee for you. You'll see."

"Look who's acting so innocent, like he only has pure thoughts. I'd like to know how you sleep: hands over or under the covers. Hee-hee."

"Dirty old man," Raymond said. "Keep on like that and I'll turn on the baseball game."

The old man knew he had gone far enough. Now he sat silent and watched Doctor Little run his long-fingered hands through his bush of silvering hair. The obstinate woman had left his office and his blonde nurse had come in through a side door. The old man could not control a soft wolf whistle. He could feel Raymond's discomfort.

The rich basso voice of the screen said: "Laura, we can do no more than pray now." Doctor Little lowered his face into his hands. "Man's work is done in the laboratory, in the operating theater, in the medical schools. If God will give me strength to fight this ignorance, I shall do all in my poor power."

"I know that you will, Doctor," the nurse said, her face trembling either in fear or admiration, the old man could not figure out which.

"Maybe you'll get nursie one of these days, too," the old man said as the voices faded down into the booming upsurge of organ music. The old man glanced at the bedside clock. Another two or three minutes, at the most five. Now was the time to begin. He would have to act fast if it were to be today.

"Did your check come early?" Raymond said.

"For twelve years it's been coming on the third. Now why should it come early this month?"

"I just thought maybe it did. What's in the box? Cigars?"

"If you can tell it's cigars by looking at it, you're a damn sight smarter than I give you credit for."

"I am a damn sight smarter than you give me credit," Raymond said. "Changed your mind about our little deal yet?"

"What deal?"

"You'll give in. I can tell. It's in your eyes."

"We'll see," said the old man, taking momentary strength from the challenge. "The old way was all right. You got your cigars once in a while. Sort of a gift. But now that you want to charge me, Raymond, I'll be damned if I give you a-one."

"Then what do you come around here for, you old buzzard?"

"I happen to have a few extra this week," the old man said, stepping full into his plan of attack. "Fact I smoked two in a row after lunch today, sitting right out in the park. Sweet as could be, smoking away and watching the little girls getting their panties dirty. Havanas. Largos. Hee-hee."

"Lost my taste for them," Raymond said. "Feel better without."

"Sure, you lost your taste for them," the old man said, now leaning close over Raymond's pale face and talking rapidly. "Lost your taste for them fat sweet cigars, for that creamy smoke in your throat. Raymond, you know that cigars is your last joy in life. I'm willing to admit what—"

"—soft, you old fool. You want my sister to hear?"

"Why can't you be honest about it, Raymond. You know you're sorry you started the whole business. Charging me a cigar every time."

"I'm sorry about nothing."

"I'll make you sorry."

"What do you want me to do?" Raymond said. He was docile, nearly beaten now. The old man saw this.

"Let me go for nothing today, like old times. Then maybe I'll bring you one tomorrow. Or the next day. When the spirit hits me. Like old times, though. Or no deal."

"I've been without four days now," Raymond said. "Start me off with one today and I won't ask again. Then it'll be like old times, I promise."

"Hee-hee. Don't have any with me today," the old man said.

"What's in the box?"

"Empty."

"Let me look."

"Empty, I say. Brought it along just to make you drool a little."

"Let me look for myself."

The old man said nothing. In another minute or two it would be time. He knew he did not have the strength to wait another day, to wait until Raymond's submission was complete. When it came time, the old man knew he would give up all four cigars if he had to.

"Raymond?" It was his sister's voice barking through the door. "I'm going to take my bath now. If you want anything, tell *him* to get it for you. Do you hear?"

"I hear," Raymond called back. Then they heard the gurgle of running water. "You win," Raymond said. "I'll let you do it today, and then we'll go back to the old way from now on."

"Only fair," the old man said righteously. "You can't start off by giving a man something for nothing, then when he gets used to it start charging him. Isn't fair that way. No sir."

"Okay, okay. Stop blabbering and get ready."

"Don't worry about that. I'm ready." The old man went to the closet and got the magnifying mirror and set it up in the right place on the bureau. Then he opened the door a bit.

"Not too much, you old fool. You want her to see?"

"Hee-hee." The old man nudged the door open another fraction of an inch.

"You won't forget now," Raymond said. "When you feel like it, you'll bring me one. A Havana. Largo. Maybe tomorrow. You won't forget."

"Won't forget," the old man said. He studied now the angle of the mirror which reflected out the slightly open doorway and down a short hall into the bathroom. Sister always left the bathroom door open when she bathed in case Raymond called for something. The mirror on the medicine cabinet reflected perfectly into the tub.

"She's stopped running the water," the old man said, visibly excited, as he took a seat on the edge of the bed. He polished his glasses on the bed sheet. "Perfect. Perfect. Just like old times. Hee-hee."

"How can you look at her and like it?" Raymond said. He studied a commercial on the television screen. "She's fat as a cow."

"Get more for my money that way," said the old man. "Beginning to fog up now."

"What good it does you is what I'd like to know. You're seventy-five if you're a day. Tell me what good it does you."

"Wouldn't you like to know?" the old man said. "Damn fog. If she'd turn on the cold a minute it'd kill the fog. Fat chance of that."

"How much of it you want, anyway? The fat cow."

"Never get enough. Hee-hee. Never."

"You won't forget the cigars. Next time."

"Maybe."

"What's she doing now?" Raymond said.

"Washing. Hee-hee. Washing right where she oughtn't to."

Raymond flicked a button and picked up the last inning of the ball-game. The old man paid no attention. "Now it's no good anymore," the old man said. "She's all fogged up. Can't see a thing."

"Didn't you get enough?"

"Been four days without."

"What good it does you I'll never know."

"Wouldn't you like to, though," the old man said. "Just wouldn't you." He shut the door with his foot and looked vacantly at the screen, seeing nothing. After a few moments he took his coat up carefully from the chair and unfolded it. "I'll be going now, Raymond." Raymond was silent. He watched a close-up of the pitcher winding-up. The old man put on his coat. He opened the door wide and stumbled forward, a dull grin that Raymond hated on his lips.

"Tomorrow," Raymond called after him. "Maybe tomorrow you'll feel like giving me one. Maybe a Havana largo."

"Maybe. Hee-hee. Maybe not." Then the old man let himself out into the clear May afternoon. Now he would go back to his room and sit in the big chair and think. And rest. And remember.

"He gone yet?" sister called from the bathroom.

"He's gone, all right," Raymond answered. Luckily, the chair was close enough to reach. He took the box wrapped in the old newspaper that the old man had forgot and shook it. He heard movement within. He placed the box beneath the mattress, deep in the center of the bed so that it made a hard and uncomfortable lump under the hollow of his back. He flicked up the sound on the television. His sister, barefoot, her dripping feet making prints on the floor, came into the room.

"He never looked better than he did today," she said, a contented smile nudging back the hang of her jowls. "Best show I've had in months."

"That so."

"Thought he'd bust a blood vessel straining his eyes. Hee-hee."

"You really got him when you washed down there," Raymond said professionally.

"Didn't I, though. My, my. Four days it's been. Didn't know I could go so long."

"I still don't understand what in the world good it does you," Raymond said. "Damned if I do."

"My, my, Raymond. Four days it's been. Think he'll come back tomorrow?"

Raymond watched a batter lift a long fly to center field. His sister let her robe fall open and thrust an expert searching hand behind the pillow and beneath the edge of the mattress. "Didn't he leave you one?"

"No. We're back on the old system. That's the only way he'd do it. Now we have to wait till he feels in the mood."

"I'd sure like one of those Havanas right now," she said. "It would top things off proper, it would." She was dreamy and calm now, the way that Raymond could tolerate her best.

"Why don't you go out and buy us a couple?" Raymond asked.

"What about that parcel he was carrying?"

"Didn't see no parcel," Raymond said. He watched the sides change, the players jog in from the outfield. He turned up the volume and lay back on the hard lump under his back. He would wait until late tonight, until she was asleep. Then he would smoke one. Maybe two. It had been four days. Four days. He didn't know how he had lasted that long.

Storm Still

BROCK BROWER

from *TriQuarterly*

It was sometimes wintry, probably in 1608, at Bankside, and he was clearly at the Globe, among the groundlings, chinned up against the front stage by the pushing of the farrier's apprentice behind him, and the garlic-breathed orangegirl on his right. Robert Armin was playing the Fool. That was why he had come. To see Armin in his motley, coxcomb, and huge ass's ears, the bladder rioting in his lunatic hand. But then Richard Burbage was also acting that afternoon. He was playing Lear. Brilliantly, he thought. "Take heed, sirrah; the whip." The steely core of kingly authority. Lear not yet mad, still regal. He suddenly wanted to tell somebody, anybody how fine an actor Burbage was. He turned smiling to the orangegirl. She smiled back coquettishly. He started to open his mouth to utter some critical *bon mot,* but closed it quickly around her wild kiss. Then she was clinging to him like a daughter. "I cannot heave my heart into my mouth," she cried. "I cannot heave my heart into my mouth, I cannot heave my heart into my mouth, I cannot heave my . . ."

Then everything turned on a great, dizzy wheel, wrenching his attention around to the stage again, away from Cordelia, the orangegirl. He was horrified. Lear *was* whipping the Fool, beating him mercilessly to the cruel, cheek-cracking tune of the thunder. The cannonball rolled back and forth behind the stage, and Armin sang to the beating of the whip.

> He that hath but a tiny little wit,
> > With hey, ho, the wind and the rain,
> > > Must make content with his fortunes fit,
> > > > Though the rain it raineth every day.

The Fool jigged, and the whip cut.

He tried to shout out. The Fool should not be whipped, it wasn't in the play. He started to climb onto the stage. First it grew higher and higher, forcing him down and down as he climbed. Then it collapsed under him. From the three balconies around the octagonal Globe they laughed at him. "But the Fool is *not whipped,"* he shouted at them, almost defensively. "Lear must never do such a thing. Never, never, never, never, never." Then they began to disappear, laughing, behind the rising flames. He saw why the stage had collapsed. It was on fire. The great Globe itself was on fire, burning like a wooden bucket. But that was wrong too. The Globe fire was in 1613. "Stop, stop!" he cried at the flames. "You're too early. Don't burn. Don't whip the Fool. Don't burn. Don't whip the Fool." Then he woke up.

Immediately he felt his old fumbling sense of panic. He'd slipped again in some matter of the play. There was a reference he carelessly hadn't checked all the way back—some date or alternate reading he must look up this very instant, or they were going to catch him out. He knew it was something terribly minor. Some question about the colophon on the Pide Bull Quarto, or a line he'd wrongly attributed to the source play *Leir* or to Holinshed, or even some stupid quibble over the spelling of Cordelia's name. Really that picayune. It didn't affect his main argument in the slightest. But they would crucify him for it, put his whole scholarship in doubt at next spring's meeting, if he didn't find it now and burn it out like a tiny plague spot in his critical acumen.

He knew all this was nonsense, yet he still began shuffling furtively through the papers on his desk to see if he hadn't possibly made a note somewhere, perhaps in the margins of his Spenser. It was one of those involuntary things that had finally become quite voluntary. He needed something to clear his mind when he napped off, and this seemed to do the trick. One of these days, he suspected, he was going to nap off altogether. His mind would simply fail to clear. Last scene of all that ends this strange, eventful history. Second childishness and mere oblivion. But somehow that would be all right too, because, look, he was only here picking over his papers after an insignificant reference. There was nothing really important to get back to. . . .

But he was awake enough now to hear the knock. It was hard to tell whether he was hearing it now, actually at the door, or whether memory was echoing it for him. Such distinctions were becoming difficult for him to make at times. Or just not worth making.

"Yes?" he asked peevishly. He wondered if he wheezed at all. Manly voice, turning to childish treble.

His study door opened part way, and a bearded face cocked around at him, its smile still back in the door's shadow. "Busy?"

This was young Nelson's way of asking permission to come in out of the shadows. For a moment he mused on just leaving him there in the shadows. Forever. Perhaps he would eventually fade into the umbra, pulling his bearded smile in after him, and become a complete shadow, instead of the furtive, diffident half shadow he already was. But oh what silliness, he warned himself, and said pleasantly, "No, no, no. Come in, Nelson. Please."

The young instructor bowed out of the doorway, bringing in a towering pile of corrected blue books. On top of them was the marking book, stretched open to the proper page with a rubber band. Nelson seemed to come bearing them almost like a hecatomb, yet at the same time he managed somehow to be putting them aside—to ask about obviously more important work. "How are you coming along with the old fool?"

He meant Lear, of course. Almost certainly, he meant Lear.

Nelson handed him the pile, which was deceptively heavy. He lifted it the little height onto his desk, straining every chest muscle not to puff.

"All right, my boy," he laughed. "I'm having most of my trouble with the young fool. If I can settle his hash. . . ." He decided he'd better be hospitable. "Can you stay a minute?"

Nelson nodded and slipped over to the other chair by the cold fireplace. On his way he ran his fingers along the books on one shelf. Too lightly, too quickly. Looking for his poems, the older man knew. Feeling for it, actually. An absurdly thin volume, and from the spine, it really was hard to see. A two-dimensional piece of work. If that. It was silly enough to find a scholarly press going in for that sort of publishing, but it was much sillier to have it inspire a beard. An effeminate beard too, he felt, even though it covered those sallow cheeks blackly. A shadow would grow just such a beard. That plushy. His book and his whiskers had both come out far too soon, and that summed up Nelson precisely as far as he was concerned.

Nelson crossed his legs and all his fingers in one nervous motion. "You know," he said, "sometimes I think Shakespeare himself must've been a jester one time or another."

How he hated that kind of remark. Shakespeare was Marlowe, or Bacon, or the Earl of Essex, or the boy who held the horses, and now a Fool. It threw everything out of balance. *The Tragedy of Lear* by Crazy Will.

"Oh?" he said simply.

"Everything he does—well, it has the fool's wit. I was reading an article the other day, sir. You might look at it if you're working on this theme of Folly." He smiled quickly. "I suppose you've got your material down pat as it is, but this man had something really new—I mean, he puts you up against it on a couple of points. Quite up against it."

Nelson had studied a year at Oxford. It had made him an expert at malicious deference. Maddening.

Nelson mentioned where he might find the article. It was in a publication that had not been in existence before his fiftieth birthday. He'd read a few issues, and thought it all nonsense. Then he was flabbergasted to find that he had to suffer a certain amount of condescension for thinking it all nonsense. He kept silent about it nowadays, but he would certainly not read the article.

"Have you been doing anything on *Lear* yourself?" he suddenly thought to ask.

The instructor bowed low before the challenge. "No. Not at all. Nothing on *Lear* itself. I just thought you might like to hear about this man's work. Are those exams all right then?"

"Must be, my boy, if you've done them. You ought to be thanked, of course. It's very pleasant to be left free—"

"Not at all."

Gratitude was the very cup of bitterness sometimes, he thought. But he was too old to be much surprised by the taste. That same taste crept into so many things that were supposed to be ennobling.

"But I'm afraid, sir. . . ."

"You must run along. That it?"

"Yes, I'm afraid."

"Of course. Mustn't keep you. I know better. Thank you again, Nelson. Won't keep you. Must work myself." Sometimes, he calculated, a properly self-effacing old man can lick the pants off any youth for modest demeanor.

Nelson went out, closing the door without a sound, almost as if he didn't want to wake somebody. Maddening.

He leaned back heavily in his chair, lifting the front legs about an inch off the floor, and patted his girth. His Phi Beta Kappa key, comically oversized, topped the hillock like a small tablet of laws. A back leg of the chair suddenly hobbled on its uncertain shank and brought the chair down sharply onto all fours again. The slip shook him for a moment.

So it is all happening to me, he thought. I can't even stay steady in my own chair. I shall simply have to toss up this *Lear* business and seek level ground. Unburthen'd crawl toward death.

That was why he'd asked for young Nelson. Actually asked for him, absurd as that seemed now. So he could gather his thoughts in peace and produce them in final form. Which he hadn't done before, because of the pressure of . . . now, of course, with young Nelson, he'd be able . . . able now, with young Nelson.

Calling him Nelson, that was his first blunder. He'd meant to keep him kindly at a distance by using his last name without the Mister. It would've been just right. Mr. Nelson was too formal, but the last name alone, that set up just the correct balance of friendliness and seniority. Only his name wasn't Thomas R. Nelson. It was R. Nelson Thomas. He must've seen it somewhere on a list as Thomas, R. Nelson, and simply slipped the comma. Bad textual error. Trapped into familiarity. But then he seemed to recall vaguely hearing students call him Mr. Nelson. At least he assumed they were using the Mister. My God, he thought, what has happened to Degree. Take but Degree away and . . . and you get familiarity, and familiarity breeds contempt. He shook his head ruefully. Could he do no better than that innocuous cliche?

He hauled himself out of his chair, away from these thoughts—away from all thinking, in fact—and stood in front of his long, narrow Queen Anne window. Somebody else would have this window all to himself soon, and he'd be outside it. His study was on the first floor of the Library, and the campus was framed before him, cut into neat, rectangular cards by the panes. He'd be out there somewhere. Mostly bare elms, stark in the winter gloom. A five o'clock January gloom. He looked at his watch, a little loose on his wrist now. He should be hearing the Library bells, somewhere in the tower above him, ringing a knell in the gloom. Lights were already dotting on in the buildings behind the elms. The wind was coming up, bringing in the snow again.

Yes, of course, there was snow on the ground. How could he stand there and not think of the snow first thing? The white, even stretch of winter over the earth. Fresh and flocculent yesterday. Old and icy today. The hoary, arthritic, fallen snow. A crust.

Tom's a-cold, he mused. Prithee, Nuncle, be contented; 'tis a naughty night to swim in.

Then he noticed somebody running across the campus towards him, struggling hopelessly with the deep, crusted snow that broke under him at every step. Tom's a-cold, he mused again, looking out at the battling figure. Tom's adrift.

Quite suddenly, he felt himself adrift. His eyes watered and wanted to blink, only ever so slowly. He fought to keep his attention on the figure struggling in the snow, and a sensation of steepness, all about him, grew until he felt he was once again climbing onto the stage in the burning Globe to rescue the Fool. Don't whip the Fool. The whip cut, and the Fool jigged, raising the powdery underdown of snow about him like a rich mist.

He had come nearer the window now. He leaped and pirouetted and somersaulted, playing with the snow as if it were a partner. Bells jingled. He ran to an elm tree, even nearer the window, and passionately kicked it. Immediately he was remorseful and threw his arms around the tree. A long kiss on the icy bark. Then he kicked it and laughed. The bells on his cap trembled. He looked about him inquisitively and discovered the window.

He rushed towards it and pressed his nose moistly against a pane of glass, bordered in frost. His face cocked and bobbed on his nose like the ticking moon in an ancient clock. He grinned and brayed through the glass. He shook his bells, and banged the head of the marotte that he carried against the window. And then his own head. The bells rang. The five o'clock knell rolled through the gloom.

Soberly the old man shook himself, and a certain richness of sensation deserted him. He did blink finally and reassured himself that there was no nose mark on the window pane. Outside, only the gloom. It was the first time in his life he had dozed off still on his feet. Mortifying. He forced himself back to his desk. Work.

I suppose that's really what old age is, he thought. Getting fuzzy about whether you're awake or asleep. When is Lear mad, and when is he sane? He wants to sing like a bird in a cage when he and Cordelia go off to prison. That's mad as much as it is sane. On the heath he wants the storm to strike flat the thick rotundity of the world. That's sane as much as it is mad. What's the difference?

He took the trouble to jot these ideas down in a creaky scrawl, and stuffed the paper in the corner of his blotter. After supper, he'd come back and reread them. He hadn't yet kept his promise to himself to work after supper, but tonight he would.

But already he knew what he really thought of his jottings. If he'd found them in a freshman paper, he'd have put an encouraging remark in the margin, something like, "An interesting approach, but don't rest on it. Sh. certainly intended L.'s madness and sanity to have a distinction. Same with Ham. What is it?" And in a senior thesis, he'd expect a carefully argued answer.

But *was* there an answer? Could any distinction be made between madness and sanity, wisdom and folly, sleeping and waking? He stared at the clutter of papers, the underlined books, the closed Quarto interleaved with ragged notecards, the mere inkblots before him. The impulse to plunge his head into his hands and groan helplessly tugged at his dignity like the impish pluck at the king's sleeve by the court imbecile. What were the lines? "O, let me not be mad, not mad, sweet heaven! Come in," he almost moaned. "Come in, come in, come in."

Then he realized he was saying it, and tried to remember hearing a knock. Yes, most certainly. He could distinctly remember hearing a knock. At his door. So things were back in order again, and he must immediately do the next thing. He reached out to open the door. But his hand bumped the knob long before his grasp closed, and the door moved away from him, a good foot, swinging shut.

For a long moment he did not move his hand. He frowned at the knob, trying to remember many more things, and their proper order. Time ran back and forth in his mind, but he still could put nothing between the last two closings of the study door. It was like that discrepancy in exits he'd once discovered in a bad Jacobean quarto, which forced an important extra character on stage and opened up a wholly new interpretation of the entire scene. That had made his reputation. But this shocked him. It suddenly seemed such a wretched business, trying to think things through, and he decided not to think, only listen. He heard the tunnel echo of his own strained silence, and then deep within it, bells, softened by cap and curled toes, jingling almost in a whisper, and then unmistakably, laughter. Inane laughter.

He whirled around in his chair—too quickly for his age—and a small dizziness seized him, so that the riot of color, the grotesquery, the motley patches of things possible over the chimerical fabric, all assailed his sight at once. Then he was at last able to blink again, and the cowl, braided over with a red coxcomb, dipped toward him in a mocking bow, and the bells on the comb's points shifted. Their fleeting tinkle struck at him, and his old, uncompromising body gave way before the onrush of a deep shudder.

The Fool had his motley feet drawn up in the chair. He was grinning much as he had through the window. With great, friendly inanity. Everything in the room seemed instantly to delight him. His head lolled about on his neck, an imbecile motion exaggerated by the huge ass's ears that flopped from his cowl. When he saw something that had any brightness to it, he pointed his marotte's puppet face toward it, and pretended to whisper violently in the marotte's ear.

The old man's first thought was to rush at the coxcomb and beat him from the room. Never in his life had he felt such savagery rise within him, and he sensed it was all about to burst from him with a leaping howl at the Fool's throat.

But, the Fool abruptly stopped his meandering and rounded his grin on the old man. The grin was even more imbecile. Stupidly loyal, it seemed. The Fool was waiting. Then suddenly he kicked his motley legs with a great mocking jangle of bells, and teased at the old man with groping fingers, daring him to come ahead. Then one finger only crooking at him blackly, like the dead wick in the lamp of reason.

It would kill me. He saw that one fact, and then began to catch hold altogether. Oblivion was smirking at him through a Fool's grin, but he was not going to let loose from the holds of logic and age and certainty. Not yet.

His first thought—his first self-possessed thought—was whether anybody had heard or seen anything. Whether anybody anywhere in the world had heard or seen anything. That he had very nearly attacked the Fool—*admitted him*—filled him with terror. Thoughts carried. Even the silence of the mind was suspicious.

Deliberately he turned back to his desk. He picked up the Pide Bull Quarto and set painfully to work on the storm scene. He courted his powers of concentration, and counted upon them to shut out any other presence that might be—that was how he must think of it, *might be*—near him. Gradually they did. The rollings of the bells and the little chuckles merged with the rising storm outside, and together, close to either side of his window, they passed away, out of his ken.

II

He ate his supper in the upper hall of the undergraduate Commons. He frequently did this for the sake of a change from his quiet widower's meal, served up uneventfully by the bad-tempered housekeeper who had outlived his wife's patience with her. But tonight he wanted something else from the dining hall. Something almost tribal.

He listened gratefully to the tumult of undergraduate cutlery. The meal was eaten out of various triangular, oblong, and serpentine depressions in uniform aluminum trays, collected from a cafeteria line, and the din reminded him of nothing so much as the Roman legionaries going into battle, beating their shields. On top of this, there was the babble of at least two hundred youths, all talking at once, none of them yet sure how his voice should really sound. Bedlam, Jericho. Or a thousand twangling instruments.

It all had a strangely reassuring effect upon him. The noise and liveliness argued against the Fool. When he got back to work, there would only be frost at his window. In a few days he might be able to talk confidently about hallucination, or tricks of the dozing eye, the dream-fondled ear. He tidied his wrinkled mouth with a napkin, took advantage of his age to leave the tray on the table rather than face the confusing actions of the dishwasher's chute, and left the Commons, mantled in an overcoat.

The walk back to his study followed shoveled canyons through the old snow. Within the last hour, they had begun to fill up again with a new undergrowth of flakes. A good way to put it, he thought. It stings your face like nettles, it clings to your clothes like burrs, so why shouldn't it be considered some kind of uncontrollable, prickly weed? The false logic of it pleased him. It kept him warm during the rest of the cold, devious walk, barriered him against the increasing storm that whipped at him devilishly. No matter which way he bent his head, it seemed to strike him on his unprotected side.

He reached the Library. Inside, he stamped his boots in the dark corridor—managed to kick one off, but had to stoop over for the other. He walked briskly down the corridor, congratulating himself on his desire to work after supper. Even if it might be false desire. He unlocked his study door and pushed it open, but it moved too lightly ahead of him, and he caught enough glimpse of haste in the Fool to know he'd just skipped back to the fireplace chair in time.

Disappointed, he told himself. Not surprised. Not afraid. Just disappointed.

He sat down at his desk with his back again to the other chair. He would have to do a little work, make a little progress before he could safely turn around. He did not know where the feeling came from, but he was certain that to work well was his only hope against the Fool's inane grin, his seductive, will-o'-the-wisp bells. The stir of the outside world—the noisy community of the dining hall—he realized now were useless.

He decided to give up the Pide Bull Quarto for the evening, in fact, to turn away from *Lear* itself altogether and read *The Tragecall historie of Kinge Leir and his Three Daughters.* Over the years he'd read the source play in patches, little snippets for his lectures, but he'd never sat down to read the whole play through for itself. He suspected it would be dull, wretchedly jangling, and stupid. In only a few pages he was convinced he was right. But he refused to give in to boredom, to let his mind slip out of its set task. The Fool was seated too near him for that.

The verse trotted along like an old dray. He had to stop reading line by line, and rushed ahead for the sense alone. The play dragged on preposterously. Leir was arrogant, lachrymose, and stupid. Truly stupid.

His patience began to wear. He tried to stifle his irritation, but it grew into a repressed anger. Finally, he yielded to a loss of temper he could hardly understand himself, and flung the book down on his desk. The old fool, he snapped to himself. Yes, precisely. The old fool, because there is no fool worse than Lear without his Fool. And that was Leir.

Suddenly he had the feeling of tottering on the verge of some immeasurably deep but opulent unknown. It was like that quibble that always touched the unsettled edge of his waking, only he felt he was much nearer the instance this time, that it *was* important after all. Terribly important. They were right to catch him up on it. It was a reference he needed to make. Properly. He had to refer back . . . and just as he seemed to have it, something frightened him away from the very thought, and his tottering was all nonsense again.

Behind him, the Fool tittered, and in a rage the old man turned on him. Through the waves of his vision, so tired now, he saw the Fool had taken up a new attitude.

He was sitting straight up in the chair, studiously attending upon a large book in his lap. He was turning the pages as fast as he could with the dexterity of one finger, and keeping time to the flipping of the pages by bobbing his cowled head up and down like a mechanical sage. Yes. Certainly. Quite. True. Most. Likely. Yes. Indeed. Why. Of Course. He was very soon through the book. Immediately he stuffed it back into its place on the shelf, took down another one right next to it, and began the whole burlesque again.

Ignore it, he warned himself. But he watched the bobbing head and the passing pages with utter fascination. He was horrified, but somehow the horror did not reach, could not break in upon the rhythm of the mockery itself. The Fool increased his tempo. The pages beat by as if the book had been blown open, and a shifting wind were leafing through it. The Fool began turning pages either way now, in sharp little gusts of mindlessness. It struck him suddenly that the Fool had probably been hunched over a book, clowning an intelligence this way, all the time he'd been reading *Leir*.

He got to his feet, trembling. But the Fool, the moment he rose, stopped turning the pages and slowly, patiently took up his grin again. The horror at last broke through. For the first time, he really looked into the Fool's face. It was like looking not into a mask, but *out* of one. He was not in front of the Fool's face at all. He was *behind* it, staring out of its vacant eyes and teething its ruthless, dumb, ecstatic grin.

Hastily he piled his papers, closed his books. When he took his overcoat from the hook behind the door, he leaned against the door for just a moment, not realizing that a full minute passed before he pushed away from it again. He left the office, locking it behind him. Then he hurried out of the Library, forgetting his boots in the dark corridor. Once outside, he noticed he'd also forgotten the light in his study. Unless it had been turned on again. He went back for his boots, but decided to leave the light. It would go out when it wanted to.

III

The next afternoon his retirement was announced at the faculty meeting. He came in late, and heard the announcement almost as a surprise, having forgotten that it was to be made.

He looked around at his colleagues, who were clapping tenderly and avoiding his eye. Good night, old prince, he mused foolishly, may flights of angels help you up the stairs. He was amazed at himself. For the past few months, he had been planning how to suppress uncontrollable anger at this inevitable insult to dignity, professionally disguised as a tribute. But listening to the mannerly, almost withdrawn applause around him, he wasn't at all angry. There were so many other furies in his bosom now that he was actually relieved. Good, he thought, they haven't caught me out. They don't know. Then he realized exactly what it was they did not know. That he was suddenly unburdened of them. He had begun an existence which simply did not include them among its cares. Even as he stood among them, reaching for their kind hands, he felt he was setting them aside for good and all.

Nelson was among the first to rush up to him. No longer maddening.

"Congratulations," said Nelson. "Forty-three years. That's a long time."

So it is, he thought. Or said. He wasn't sure which. And forty-three on top of twenty-four makes sixty-seven years' presence of mind, and now I've chucked it all. Don't need it. Wish I'd never had it. Wish I'd never been bothered with it.

He looked carefully at Nelson's face to see if he was possibly saying these things too, not just thinking them. But Nelson's face didn't seem to know either.

"Thank you, Nelson," he made sure to say, not think.

"I wanted to mention to you," Nelson went on, "the light was on in your study this morning. I tried to get in to turn it off, but your door was locked, and I couldn't find the janitor."

It occurred to him that Nelson too said all this without thinking. Or at least without thinking of any of the rich and enchanting possibilities. The scene if they had forced the door and found the Fool asleep at his desk, sprawled out in a garish parody of the pedant adoze over his dry books. The great blot of ink on the end of the Fool's nose, making him look like a broken nib. The marotte stuck into the Variorum like a bookmark, grinning over the binding in a frozen mime of the Contents. For all this, no thought. Of course, Nelson did not have *his* knowledge to go on. But somehow that came off as only another very distinct limitation in Nelson himself. He found it easy to fault him for it and set him aside.

Why, there was even snoring. Great hawking at a burbling lip. A grand test. The Fool curled up in exactly his own napping posture, when he opened the door that morning, pretending the noise of entering had troubled his sleep, bestirring himself with a loud carillon from his cap. He'd really almost laughed out loud, but suddenly sensed the open door behind him. He fell back against it, listening hard for any approaching sound outside in the corridor. God's spies, he thought, it's broad daylight. The Fool chuckled, beaming at him over that great noseblot with blank, uncanny eyes, bright with false sleep, and he felt himself pulled another small tug away from the order of things into the clutter of that merry-andrew gaze.

Perhaps he really ought to tip Nelson off. Perhaps it would be better, even now, if he simply leaned over and whispered, "Look, there's a pest of a fellow in my office. Will you run over and tell him I won't be by today?" Only he knew he would be by, and alone, and all he could bring himself to say was, "Thank you again. Stupid of me. Getting a little careless lately. Need to be watched, don't I?"

An older friend in the English department came up to him then and had the good sense not to congratulate him.

"Working on anything now?" he asked simply.

"Yes. *Lear.* Cleaning up, really. Talked about it enough in my lifetime, haven't I? Never make a book. But a little—a little *opusculum* would do, wouldn't it? For 'A poor, infirm, weak, and despised old man'?"

"Utter nonsense," replied his friend, staring at the floor. "You'd better save a little room in the pasture when they put you out there next spring. I'm afraid they won't give me those extra few years of grace they gave you. I'm not that tough."

"Plenty of room." He wondered if Nelson could see how graciously his friend had turned the compliment. Probably not. But then it really made no difference. They were both foolish even to try. Eptly or ineptly, they stayed nothing by it. They were only tarrying here, all three of them.

"What is it you're trying to do with *Lear?*" his friend asked, bringing back the subject.

"Oh, I'm taking up Folly. Much the same way Erasmus does. Though he's quite wrong about her, you know. She isn't a goddess at all. Only a fool."

"I'm not surprised."

"You would be. I've been spending most of my time lately on the Fool. If you stay with him long enough, he becomes a sort of familiar. A goddess is only a conception. The fool's much more than that." He said all this lightly, edging as near as he dared to his own peccant sense of the matter. The risk was titillating. "I'm really trying to decide just what his existence amounts to."

His friend frowned in a way he quite understood, but Nelson smiled in a way that escaped him. What bit of dried fungi had he managed to fire in that tinderbox this time?

Nelson seemed for a moment to want to hold it all in, but he couldn't resist. "I suppose you might even call him," he said nervously, "the existential fool."

So. That poppycock. When was he going to learn to watch every single word he used in front of this young Holofernes? He felt a wild urge to reach out with grand punctilio and pluck Nelson's velvety beard, but the deepening of his friend's frown kept him off.

"You suppose whatever you wish to suppose, young man," his friend snorted at the instructor, "but remember it's your own tomfoolery." Then he turned back again. "But I must admit I don't quite see what you're driving at either. The Fool's simply a character in the play. His existence is in his role, isn't it?"

And so. More poppycock. This was harder, riskier. "Of course," he agreed affably, "but I'm wondering if that role isn't just a bit wider than you think it is. The Fool is a character in all of sixteenth, seventeenth century life. He has a role even *off* the stage. We find Queen Elizabeth footing the bill for a huge wardrobe of motley. Read the list sometime. The fools Robert Greene, Jack Green, and Mr. Shenstone. An Italian named Monarcho. A little Blackamoor. Thomasina the Dwarf—oh, I'd like to have seen her—and Ipolyta the Tartarian. And Clod. Clod—bless him—Clod is even chided by his Queen for not criticizing her sharply enough. Royal displeasure at his failure to play his role. Not quick enough in his hits upon Glorianna, can you imagine?" He warmed to his own tired lecture style, feeling how safely he could dissemble under its fey pedantry as others gathered around him. "The Fool is with us, you see? With them, I suppose I should say," he added hastily, "but I mean, abroad. That's important. Abroad. As the Lord of Misrule, as the Comte de Permission, guilty of 'Flearing and making of mouths.' He is fed on crow's meat, they say, and monkey flesh. Or he eats only what the dogs have tasted, and so they serve the dogs great delicacies for the Fool's sake. An odd, rarified life, you realize. Terribly indulgent, but at the same time terribly mangy. It says of Will Sommers, for instance, Henry the Eighth's great fool, that he 'laid himself down among the spaniels to sleep' after he'd pleased his Harry with a riddle. A silly riddle at that. Damnably silly. 'What is it that, being borne without life, head, lip, or eye, yet doth run roaring through the world till it die?'"

He looked quickly around him hoping for someone to answer. It was so easy, but they all seemed to give up. He felt the silliness take an oddly dreadful hold upon him, and spoke as lightly as he could.

"'Why, quoth Will, it is a fart.'"

He knew he was the only one laughing—senselessly—yet all their faces were bent up in a way that meant they might be laughing too, if he could only hear them. Desperately he fought his way out of his own shameful laughter.

"The most ridiculous bawdry. Not funny at all. Just not funny. Very weak. Very. But you see—I think we can sense in it—the Fool's familiarity." He wormed loose again. "To an Elizabethan, Jacobean audience. What I mean is, that the Fool might have more reality for these people than Lear, even though they did know kings too. They wouldn't expect to go into the narrow streets at

Bankside and find Lear walking abroad. But they could very well expect to find the Fool. That, actually, is how fools were found. They existed, you see. Naturals.''

He stopped, hoping he was nearer sense now. "Fascinating idea," his friend said, but he knew that was coddling. He must be more careful, he realized, much more careful, even with friends, and this suddenly enraged him.

"Do you know how to pick a fool?" he burst out. "There was one in Germany named Conrad Pocher—the Count Palatine delighted in him—he was considered ripe for the court's pleasure after he hanged a little boy from a tree. Pocher hanged the little boy because the little boy had scabs. It was a joke that Pocher would hang you if you had scabs too. Beware, all you who are scabrous—''

He felt his friend's hand grip his shoulder, as if to pinch off what he was saying. His friend said to him, "I'm afraid I still don't see what you're getting at, but good luck with it anyhow.'' The others hastily agreed.

He closed them out and turned abruptly to Nelson. "I'm letting you take all my classes.''

The surprise of it dropped his friend's hand from his shoulder. But he couldn't bother to care. He went on to Nelson. "I'd appreciate it if you'd do the exam as well. I'm afraid I'm going to want to be left very much alone.''

Now he didn't dare look at his friend. He had as good as abdicated. Nelson was in a fidget of self-effacement. He felt he wouldn't be able to stand that maggoty beard another moment longer. Other friends came up to him. They suggested delicately all the wonderful things he had done in the past, and the long life he had ahead in peace and quiet contemplation. In five more minutes, it was over, and he turned from the scattered gathering, found his coat, and went across the frozen snow that pitched out flat before him like a white heath.

IV

He worked furiously. Every day he was more exhausted, but he fought fatigue with anger, and anger, he found, could keep him going when all his faculties were otherwise ready to fail.

The storm wore on, running in tatters across the stiff snow, almost following his anger. After a ruthless night, it would seem to be dying away, only to regain its ferocity in the late afternoon, cutting icily against the window, closing away what little light there was in the grey sky. But he didn't mind. It kept him alone. He'd taken his card off the door, and nobody bothered him.

The Fool was always decorous. For the most part, he stayed happily in his chair, and thumbed through the books over and over again, timing his flurries to the storm. There were a few pranks. The old man would glance up from his work to find the marotte nodding methodically over his shoulder like a wizened scholar whose head had been shrunk, the Fool pressed right up against the back of his chair. It made him jump, but no more. Or he would come in to find a paper full of meaningless inkblots, almost like writing, lying among his notes. Yet he could never quite be sure it wasn't a scrap he'd used himself to test his pen. The tricks kept him on edge, but they were nothing beside the threat he felt in the Fool's patience. The Fool seemed somehow able to wait without ever losing a moment. Nothing could exhaust his empty loyalty. He was there forever. Or not. It made no difference to him. Only to those in quest of differences.

But he could admit none of this. Not to himself, certainly not to the Fool. Not even by the fleet tribute of another eyeblink that might drop him into an unguarded sleep.

Instead, he settled into a fixed wakefulness, embarking on what he sensed would be some final test of his scholarship. He had already made a beginning, so it was only a matter of shifting his emphasis. Under the pretense of still pursuing his studies of *Lear*—to whom, he wondered, to whom?—he set out to study the Fool himself. He felt certain that if he could only read up on the Fool, chivvy his motley image through the bramble of source material and first mentions and oblique references and analogues, hunt him down like startled sense at bay behind a faulty and obscure text, he would save him. As simple a thing as fixing the Fool's dates properly might trap him, he was half convinced. He was depending upon his last reliable habit of mind. Somewhere among the disputed readings, the incunabula, the endless exegesis, he felt he was bound to come upon the right page. Then, all he would need to do—all he could ever do to end this gest—was somehow to rip out that page.

He began working through the literature. Other scholars had been there before him, but they had no sense of the menace—he could tell that from the bloodless measure they took in their writings—the menace that lay within the sweet hollow of folly. None of them, obviously, had ever kept a fool. Yet any simpleton writing a pet manual, would at least know his German Shepherd or his Siamese or his box turtle. He pushed impatiently through their treacly rationality to the primary sources, testimony from the great warders who had once kept real fools to fondle like favored apes.

He searched constantly for a touchstone. He picked finically even among the original Latinisms in hopes of finding a proper one. *Stultus. Morio. Fatuus. Sannio.* They all fitted, yet none quite, really. He set the legends alongside his own Fool for measure. Til Eulenspiegel, the owl glass, the wise mirror, but still a brute. At Til's graveside, a cord snapped, and his coffin tipped upright into the broken earth. "Leave him as he is, he was strange in this life, he wants to be after his death." So they buried him standing straight up and stole his estate, which proved his last mockery, being only a box of stones. His own Fool could have inherited, yes, easily inherited that owlishness, that false legacy of stones. But much more his own Fool favored Marcolf, the jester who watched Solomon dispense justice to the two women who claimed one child, and as the king calmly lowered the threatening sword to his side again and judged so wisely, jeered at him for trusting a woman's tears. Ah, how that fitted. That exactly, the same jeering laughter that so harrowed him, turning his own subtlety of mind suddenly as luggish as the clapper in a frozen bell.

Yet legend could not satisfy him. Legendary fools were vagrant in time, and his own Fool carried his days upon his back—a hunch to his motley shoulders that meant he stooped under the hour, not under a proverb. He came from a rich period. The old man relished such labor, and early on, among the many sotties he dug up, he found Robert Armin's own *Nest of Ninnies*. The actor-clown's account of the fools of his day. "Simply of themselves without Compound." Just what was wanted—"without Compound"—and reaching into that nest—down among Jemy Camber, the fat fool a yard wide and a nail high, and Jack Oates, eating a hot quince pie while standing in the moat and drinking from it to cool his tongue, and Will Sommers, capping Cardinal Woolsey's rhymes—he felt the quick flutter of his own Fool's ninny soul cross his fingertips.

He reached again, but then drew back quickly from that mock grin, the glissando that ran down the coxcomb bells in chilling welcome.

He pushed deeper into the documents. Account books of royal households, pamphlet Lives of fools, ha' penny street ballads and mock Last Wills & Testaments, extracts from court diaries, an actual letter to James I from his fool away in Spain with Philip II's court. Some of them were on microfilm, and he turned to this newfangled apparatus for momentary escape. He could leave his Fool behind, yet pursue him still, more at his ease, studying the little scrolls as they unrolled beneath the thumbing white light of the scanner. But he soon found this another mockery. The glare of the machine, blowing up the quaint Elizabethan printing into an illusory page pressed without substance against the cold, milky glass, was too much for his weak, old eyes, and somehow for his sense of reality. He could not stand the ghostliness of it. He felt he must be able to turn the actual page, crumble a chip out of its browned edge, smell its acrid, bookish dust, if he were ever going to find it. What was there to tear out here? He hated the skimping artifice that robbed him of the feel of a book, and imagined the scanner as some great Worm that had invested the castle of his learning. Like Spenser's Error, only too uncreatured a thing to spew forth black ink, or disgorge the books it had swallowed. Its only malice, a pale flush of cold light producing an incubus of a page. He knew how ridiculous he was being, possibly senile, and he drove himself to take meticulous notes, as usual. But he only breathed freely again in the staleness of his closed-up study, back within the pied *ambiance* of his Fool.

By then, he had all his facts. He was now thoroughly familiar with, something of an authority on, a good man in the field of. Oh, he understood his own qualifications all too well. It only remained for him to think things through to the entrapment, to perform the sacred rites of abstraction, and in a curious way, he sought to cleanse himself for them. He stripped away his last ragged pretenses to any venerability, all the shoddy of his professorial airs, and bared himself, in all but intellect, for a naked, failing old man.

It ended so many qualms. He could talk to himself freely. He mumbled and muttered as he pleased, and if his mouth grew wet, he wiped it on his sleeve without shame. When he caught the Fool imitating him in some palsied fumble, he hardly cared. Once he watched the Fool's great, dirty tongue loll almost to the floor before he sensed the coldness at his own cheek and brushed away a long, loose string of saliva. Unimportant. All that mattered was the careful tightening of his logic as it closed around the Fool.

"Decide whether natural or artificial," he thought or said or wrote down somewhere. "Could be a mute. Idiot boy sold by a rustic to some great house in exchange for a few acres grazing land free of enclosure. Such happens. But looks brighter than that. Silence too sly. Vacancy too coy. Hidden wits. I see him offering the egg. Like Will Sommers again, asking the King to let him give an egg to every cuckold in England, and permission granted, hands the first egg to Harry himself. What is he here to hand me? What's in his hand? What's in my hand? A page? A page?"

He glanced down at his hand, but there was only the back of it, covered with liver spots, and he realized that the ambuscado, so carefully laid up in his notes, had missed its elusive quarry yet again.

But he started once more, reciting a tale. "Will Sommers loudly broke wind, and glared at the lady by his side. Then he smiled at her and said for all to hear, 'Don't worry. I'll say it was me.' Clever fool. Rich fool. But this is a poor fool. Violent? Often they are insane. No attack yet. But if it comes. . . . Bawdry? A scurrilous fool? Behind that dumbshow, what cess of mind, waiting to pour over me like a chamber pot? Gardyloo!" And then an old man's decrepit giggle, like beans rattling in a bladder, caught him off guard, sucked up from some grossness he'd suddenly remembered from his long study of folly. Again and again, he broke away from that giggle, forcing his way back to the needed date or reference that would repair the break where flatulence and scurrility had escaped from his thinking.

He even allowed himself little threats now. Never quite to the Fool's face, but, "Take heed," he would mumble, "the whip. The whip."

Then suddenly he felt the grip of it in his hand.

Carefully he let go, and gathered up his notecards to give his hands something else to do. He tried to reshuffle them for the hundredth time, but found that they were at last, by some fluke, in a correct order. Irrefutably that order imposed itself upon him. Sequential, exact, conclusive. This time, all his learning told him, there was no escape. Tapping each card nervously on his blotter, searching for error, he tried to think how many days it had been, how many stormy hours had hawked at his chill window to tumble this sudden, random knowledge upon him. He counted slowly—days, hours, cards—and imagined the Fool at his back, counting too, with great pulls at his gross fingers, unable, like himself, to arrive at any sensible number.

But he did not turn around. He saw that he could corner the Fool now with a mere glance, that he could positively identify him beyond any quibble to his colleagues, much more, that he could whip him, rip him out, do with him as he pleased. He had all that certainty, but once again it seemed to be forcing him to the verge of that same opulent unknown over which he had tottered so often, so perilously. . . .

Only now, at the Fool's warning titter, he deliberately stared down into its black gulf. He referred back and back, as far as his mind would take him, and knowledge did not come to him so much as it physically seized him. The brush of the long ass's ears around his own cheeks. The plucking up of his whole spine into a rich, red comb, topped with bells. The whirligig of his coat plaids turning to lozenges. His grip on the whip thinning, loosening to a fragile, foolish hold upon the stick of a marotte. One foot jingled beneath him, and quite suddenly he could feel just where the whip was going to cut.

He did the one thing possible in the moment left before the black gulf itself turned over and sat upon his head for a cap. He jumped into it at last.

"Stay!" he shouted to the Fool. "Stay right here! Right by my side! Right here with me!"

Then he whirled around and doubled over in laughter, jeering widely at the suddenly defeated jangling thing in the chair.

"Right?" he whispered. "Right, right?"

The Fool's vacant stare was afire like a bone pit, but his marotte nodded its eternal grin.

V

He was still laughing when the knock came at his door. Very cautiously he judged his surprise at it. No, it was no longer an interruption of his solitude. It was an intrusion upon their intimacy. The Fool shook both fists as if beating back at the door, letting loose a rage of bells.

"Who is it?" he asked, smiling at the angry Fool.

"Nelson, sir. Are you all right?"

He and the Fool shrugged at each other, both repressing laughter this time. He was still a little bit in awe of his own triumph, the confidence they had so suddenly found in each other. But then why, he wondered, had it taken so long to see what the Fool was there for?

"Sir?"

Young Nelson was anxious. He chortled to himself. The Fool immediately understood him and giggled into his two ass's ears which he had crossed gleefully over his mouth.

"I heard—well, laughing, sir. I just wondered if everything's all right. I thought I heard. . . ." Nelson left off.

He hesitated because he wanted to savor this moment, the superb jest it had finally turned out to be. With this to top it off.

"No, I'm perfectly fine. Excellent fettle." He winked at the Fool. "Come in, if you've a moment."

The door eased open, just far enough for Nelson to squirm around it, braving everything with his shadow first. He nodded from it, smiling, while his eyes flicked nervously around the room. His stare scurried into every corner, and then he flushed, realizing he had absolutely no excuse.

"No, really. Sit down, sit down."

Nelson gratefully moved over to the chair and plumped down in it. The Fool bounced up just in time. He shook his bells angrily, and scowled. The old man chuckled good-naturedly. Nelson joined him in chuckling, out of deference.

"I'm really sorry, sir." He shifted once, twice in the chair. "Honestly, it sounded like you were in here laughing yourself silly."

"No, no. I was just—" How to put it, how to put it? "I've just finished up my work on Lear, you see, and I was having a good laugh over it."

Nelson grew terribly puzzled, but only above the eyebrows. The Fool caught it, and took off this sedate puzzlement with a mock petite frown of his own. An irresistible bit of fleering. Again the old man chuckled, worrying

Nelson into joining him again. The frown looked even more ridiculous over the polite chuckle.

"Oh, I must fill you in," he said. "It's just that this whole business with *Lear* has turned out to be, after all—well, a pretty big joke."

"I'm sorry about that," Nelson said elaborately. "Really very sorry."

He looked at the young instructor sharply. He'd caught something, just for a second. Nelson *was* sorry for him, of course. Flamboyantly sorry. Poor old codger. But there was something more, edging in, smacking distinctly of derring-do. He glanced at the Fool, who was leaning with both elbows on the back of Nelson's chair. The Fool poked two saucy fingers up for ears behind Nelson's head, and blew his lips flatulently.

"But I can see how it might come out that way," Nelson went on. *"Lear* is such a difficult play—and . . . *disappointing,* don't you think?"

Had he jumped? He felt sure the Fool had. But the skittishness was not so much in them, he sensed, as in Nelson. Was he about to skip and run for it on his own?

"Perhaps you've found—" Nelson paused at a near stutter and then hurdled, "what *I've* always found." The Fool stared, and then lifted himself on the chair back, kicking his bells together at the heels in muffled joy. "In the end, it really all comes to nothing, doesn't it? Dr. Johnson may have been right."

"Then you *have* been. . . ."

He saw instantly that Nelson was going to misinterpret him. There would now be a painstaking mending of fences, he could tell, which would only delay the real point. Only the Fool had the patience for it. His greedy eyes puddled, and that same inane grin sank down once more into the vapid face like water crumbling sand.

"No, no," said Nelson, starting in on his fences. "I honestly haven't. I was leaving that all to you. I touch on the play, yes, but only with reference to some work I'm trying to do on the older play. *Leir."* He leaned forward, and for an awful moment the old man thought that from the undermining of the grin, the Fool's face had at last caved in entirely and fallen upon Nelson's own. But then he saw it was only a great, watery leer. "But if you *are* giving up on your own work—I mean, if you're leaving the field free again—and that's the only way I'd want to have it, frankly—I think I might try to treat the two plays together."

"What *exactly* is it you're going to show?" Besides this abruptness, this, this. . . .

"It'll be tough sledding, but I'm pretty clear now that *Leir* is infinitely the better play. At least, in my own mind. You see, sir. . . ."

Then the flights and dips and swoops and long drifts of a young, excited mind swept over him. A swift, ignorant, sweet bird beating its new wings in the heart of an old storm. He listened as carefully as he could, and tried not to look at the Fool. He was afraid that if he did, he would not be able to account for his tears. Why was it so irretrievably sad? All that he heard was challenging and clever and zealous. But it depended upon so many certainties that weren't really there. The dimness, the vagueness, the lack of distinction that blurred every final thought, every last, best guess—he saw that the young man did not even feel their menace. Perhaps, on some midnight balance of his secret fears, Nelson allowed himself to know he might be wrong, but did he ever allow himself to know he might not even be that?

The old man's gaze drifted in mute appeal to the Fool. Then it simply drifted, caught up in the aimless wandering of the Fool's vacuous stare. Just in time, he saw his mistake. He looked quickly away before the Fool had a chance to throw his own lugubriousness back at him, and pulled himself together, alert to danger. He cursed his own stupidity. How very much, he realized bitterly, my very own.

He was losing his Fool.

"Nelson." He said it for once affectionately, as a first name, not a last. "How sure are you of all these things?" He meant the question to be only cautionary, but he could see it had gone hopelessly wrong. Nelson's face hardened a bit, and the gleeful Fool twirled the marotte over Nelson's head, badgering the old man for—what?—simply an old man, what more. He tried to think of a way to make his words less discouraging, less cantankerous. "I mean it all sounds very wonderful, but is this to be a whole-hearted plunge into—" Into what? He knew the word he wanted to use, but also what irreparable damage it would do his little contact with the young man. And whose fault is it, he asked himself, the contact is so little? How very much, he thought bitterly again, my very own.

"A plunge into what, sir?"

A plunge into Folly. That's what he wanted to say. There was the Fool behind the chair, with as large a charter as the wind, to blow on whom he pleased. No man could hold him back. *Numerus stultorum est infinitus.*

"Let me put it this way, Nelson. I can't tell you how to do your work. Nobody can." He stopped helplessly. The Fool had turned and lifted one fat buttock at him, dropping the marotte down between his motley legs. The tiny head wigwagged at him like a phallus with an obscene, upsidedown grin. He forced himself ahead. "Do you have any idea what it's really like to work your way to the limits of something?" Limits? Limits of what? "I don't mean just setting out to settle a moot point. I mean plunging in so far that you can't—can never succeed—succeed in getting out again."

He pressed his hands together for steadiness. He saw the Fool imitate him, turning it into a silly prayerful gesture.

"You're alone. But accompanied. It's funny, but your companions are all there to help you feel alone. Because you don't, you mustn't admit they're there." He smiled. "That's the funny part about it. Once you admit—"

The Fool shook like a Sunday morning of church bells.

"Once you admit—" He looked hard at Nelson. There was nothing in his face but sufferance. Deferential sufferance. "Think of Lear of the heath, Nelson. Who are his companions? Who? The boundaries of his loneliness, really. Aren't they?"

He waited now. The burden was on the other.

"I'm pretty sure of my ground, I think, sir. Others have had the same idea about *Leir,* I'm sure you're aware. Tolstoi, for instance, gave it my interpretation. What I should say is, I'm taking up *his.*"

So the harlequinade will go on, he thought helplessly. He did not even look about for his Fool. He tried to keep his weak eyes fixed on a single, groomed tuft of Nelson's beard.

"I appreciate all your advice, and I'd like to come to you for some help, if that's all right with you. But for the moment. . . ."

He didn't hear the rest. They said things near the door, but to him, it was an absolutely wordless parting. He could not be sure, but he thought that something scuttled hastily between his knees as he shut himself in.

He stepped over to his window. It was still snowing, as if forever. Across the flurry he could see Nelson trudging away. A shadow—only a shadow—scurried and scraped about him in the storm with grotesque, unhallowed gestures. With great pain, he admitted they were gestures of fondness. Finally he thought he saw it leap up on the man's back, like a loving thing, and that bowed his own head to the cold window pane.

He knew. Deserted now, even by his own measure of solitude, he knew what he would never know again. Any boundary to his own loneliness. He supposed, since he was still alive, that he must take this to be wisdom.

WILL YOU PLEASE BE QUIET, PLEASE?

RAYMOND CARVER   from *December*

When he was 18 and left home for the first time, in the fall, Ralph Wyman had been advised by his father, principal of Jefferson Elementary School in Weaverville and trumpet-player in the Elks Club Auxiliary Band, that life today was a serious matter; something that required strength and direction in a young person just setting out. A difficult journey, everyone knew that, but nevertheless a comprehensible one, he believed.

But in college Ralph's goals were still hazy and undefined. He first thought he wanted to be a doctor, or a lawyer, and he took pre-medical courses and courses in History of Jurisprudence and business-law before he decided he had neither the emotional detachment necessary for medicine, nor the ability for sustained reading and memorization in the *Corpus Iuris Civilis*, as well as the more modern tex's on property and inheritance. Though he continued to take classes here and there in the sciences and in the Department of Business, he also took some lower-division classes in history and philosophy and English. He continually felt he was on the brink of some kind of momentous discovery about himself. But it never came. It was during this time, his lowest ebb, as he jokingly referred back to it later, that he believed he almost became an alcoholic; he was in a fraternity and he used to get drunk every night. He drank so much, in fact, that he even acquired something of a reputation; guys called him Jackson, after the bartender at The Keg, and he sat every day in the cafeteria with a deck of cards playing poker solitaire, or bridge, if someone happened along. His grades were down and he was thinking of dropping out of school entirely and joining the air force.

Then, in his third year, he came under the influence of a particularly fascinating and persuasive literature teacher. Dr. Maxwell was his name; Ralph would never forget him. He was a handsome, graceful man in his early forties, with exquisite manners and with just the trace of a slight southern drawl in his voice. He had been educated at Vanderbilt, had studied in Europe, and had later had something to do with one or two literary magazines in New York. Almost overnight, it seemed to him, Ralph decided on teaching as a career. He stopped drinking so much and began to bear down on his studies. Within a year he was elected to Omega Psi, the national journalism fraternity; he became a member of the English Club; was invited to come with his cello, which he hadn't played in three years, and join in a student chamber music group just forming; and he ran successfully for Secretary of the Senior Class. He also started going out with Marian Ross that year; a pale, slender girl he had become acquainted with in a Chaucer class.

She wore her hair long and liked high-necked sweaters in the winter; and summer and winter she always went around with a leather purse on a long strap swinging from her shoulder. Her eyes were large and seemed to take in everything at a glance; if she got excited over something, they flashed and widened even more. He liked going out with her in the evenings. They went to The Keg, and a few other nightspots where everyone else went, but they never let their going together or their subsequent engagement that next summer, interfere with their studies. They were serious students, and both sets of parents eventually gave their approval of the match. They did their student-teaching at the same high school in Chico the next spring, and went through graduation exercises together in June. They married in St. James Episcopal Church two weeks later. Both of them held hands the night before their wedding and pledged solemnly to preserve forever the excitement and the mystery of marriage.

For their honeymoon they drove to Guadalajara; and while they both enjoyed visiting the old decayed churches and the poorly lighted museums, and the several afternoons they spent shopping and exploring in the market-place (which swarmed with flies) Ralph secretly felt a little appalled and at the same time let-down by the squalor and promiscuity of the people; he was only too glad to get back to more civilized California. Even so, Marian had seemed to enjoy it, and he would always remember one scene in particular. It was late afternoon, almost evening, and Marian was leaning motionless on her arms over the iron-worked balustrade of their rented, second-floor *casa* as he came up the dusty road below. Her hair was long and hung down in front over her shoulders, and she was looking away from him, staring at something toward the horizon. She wore a white blouse with a bright red scarf at the throat, and he could see her breasts pushing against her front. He had a bottle of dark, unlabeled wine under his arm, and the whole incident reminded him of something from a play, or a movie. Thinking back on it later, it was always a little vaguely disturbing for some reason.

Before they had left for their six-week honeymoon, they had accepted teaching positions at a high school in Eureka, in the northern part of the state near the ocean. They waited a year to make certain that the school and the weather, and the people themselves were exactly what they wanted to settle down to, and then made a substantial down-payment on a house in the Fire Hill district. He felt, without really thinking about it, that they understood each other perfectly; as well, anyway, as any two people could understand one another. More, he understood himself; his capacities, his limitations. He knew where he was going and how to get there.

In eight years they had two children, Dorothea and Robert, who were now five and four years old. A few months after Robert, Marian had accepted at mid-term a part-time position as a French and English teacher at Harris Junior College, at the edge of town. The position had become full-time and permanent that next fall, and Ralph had stayed on, happily, at the high school. In the time they had been married, they had had only one serious disturbance, and that was long ago: two years ago that winter to be exact. It was something they had never talked about since it happened, but, try as he might, Ralph couldn't help thinking about it sometimes. On occasion, and then when he was least prepared, the whole ghastly scene leaped into his mind. Looked at rationally and in its proper, historical perspective, it seemed impossible and monstrous; an event of such personal magnitude for Ralph that he still couldn't entirely accept it as something that had once happened to Marian and himself: he had taken it into his head one night at a party that Marian had betrayed him with Mitchell Anderson, a friend. In a fit of uncontrollable rage, he had struck Marian with his fist, knocking her sideways against the kitchen table and onto the floor.

It was a Sunday night in November. The children were in bed. Ralph was sleepy, and he still had a dozen themes from his twelfth-grade class in accelerated English to correct before tomorrow morning. He sat on the edge of the couch, leaning forward with his red pencil over a space he'd cleared on the coffee table. He had the papers separated into two stacks, and one of the papers folded open in front of him. He caught himself blinking his eyes, and again felt irritated with the Franklins. Harold and Sarah Franklin. They'd stopped over early in the afternoon for cocktails and stayed on into the evening. Otherwise, Ralph would have finished hours ago, as he'd planned. He'd been sleepy, too, he remembered, the whole time they were here. He'd sat in the big leather chair by the fireplace and once he recalled letting his head sink back against the warm leather of the chair and starting to close his eyes when Franklin had cleared his throat loudly. Too loudly. He didn't feel comfortable with Franklin anymore. Harold Franklin was a big, forthright man with bushy eyebrows who caught you and held you with his eyes when he spoke. He looked like he never combed his hair, his suits were always baggy, and Ralph thought his ties hideous, but he was one of the few men on the staff at Harris Junior College who had his Ph.D. At 35 he was head of the combined History and Social Science Department. Two years ago he and Sarah had been witness to a large part of Ralph's humiliation. That occasion had never later been brought up by any of them, of course, and in a few weeks, the next time they'd seen one another, it was as though nothing had happened. Still, since then, Ralph couldn't help feeling a little uneasy when he was around them.

He could hear the radio playing softly in the kitchen, where Marian was ironing. He stared a while longer at the paper in front of him, then gathered up all of the papers, turned off the lamp, and walked out to the kitchen.

"Finished, love?" Marian said with a smile. She was sitting on a tall stool, ironing one of Robert's shirts. She sat the iron up on its end as if she'd been waiting for him.

"Damn it, no," he said with an exaggerated grimace, tossing the papers on the table. "What the hell the Franklins come by here for anyway?"

She laughed; bright, pleasant. It made him feel better. She held up her face to be kissed, and he gave her a little peck on the cheek. He pulled out a chair from the table and sat down, leaned back on the legs and looked at her. She smiled again, and then lowered her eyes.

"I'm already half-asleep," he said.

"Coffee," she said, reaching over and laying the back of her hand against the electric percolator.

He nodded.

She took a long drag from the cigaret she'd had burning in the ashtray, smoked it a minute while she stared at the floor, and then put it back in the ashtray. She looked up at him, and a smile started at the corners of her mouth. She was tall and limber, with a good bust, narrow hips, and wide, gleaming eyes.

"Ralph, do you remember that party?" she asked, still looking at him.

He shifted in the chair and said, "Which party? You mean that one two or three years ago?"

She nodded.

He waited a minute and asked, when she didn't say anything else, "What about it? Now that you brought it up, honey, what about it?" Then: "He kissed you after all, that night, didn't he? . . . Did he try to kiss you, or didn't he?"

"I didn't say that," she said. "I was just thinking about it and I asked you; that's all."

"Well, he did, didn't he? Come on, Marian, we're just talking, aren't we?"

"I'm afraid it'd make you angry, Ralph."

"It won't make me angry, Marian. It was a long time ago, wasn't it? I won't be angry . . . Well?"

"Well, yes," she said slowly, "he did kiss me a few times." She smiled tentatively, gauging his reaction.

His first impulse was to return her smile, and then he felt himself blushing and said defensively, "You told me before he didn't. You said he only put his arm around you while he was driving."

He stared at her. It all came back to him again; the way she looked coming in the back door that night; eyes-bright, trying to tell him . . . something, he didn't hear. He hit her in the mouth, at the last instant pulling to avoid her nose, knocked her against the table where she sat down hard on the floor. "What did you do that for?" she'd asked dreamily, her eyes still bright, and her mouth dripping blood. "Where were you all night?" he'd yelled, teetering over her, his legs watery and trembling. He'd drawn back his fist again but already sorry for the first blow, the blood he'd caused. "I wasn't gone all night," she'd said, turning her head back and forth heavily. "I didn't do anything. Why did you hit me?"

Ralph passed his open hand over his forehead, shut his eyes for a minute. "I guess I lost my head that night, all right. We were both in the wrong. You for leaving the party with Mitchell Anderson, and I for losing my head. I'm sorry."

"I'm sorry, too," she said. "Even so," she grinned, "you didn't have to knock hell out of me."

"I don't know—maybe I should've done more." He looked at her, and then they both had to laugh.

"How did we ever get onto this?" she asked.

"You brought it up," he said.

She shook her head. "The Franklins being here made me think of it, I guess." She pulled in her upper lip and stared at the floor. In a minute she straightened her shoulders and looked up. "If you'll move this ironing board for me, love, I'll make us a hot drink. A buttered rum: now how does that sound?"

"Good."

She went into the living room and turned on the lamp, bent to pick up a magazine by the endtable. He watched her hips under the plaid woolen skirt. She moved in front of the window by the large dining room table and stood looking out at the streetlight. She smoothed her palm down over her right hip, then began tucking in her blouse with the fingers of her right hand. He wondered what she was thinking. A car went by outside, and she continued to stand in front of the window.

After he stood the ironing board in its alcove on the porch, he sat down again and said, when she came into the room, "Well, what else went on between you and Mitchell Anderson that night? It's all right to talk about it now."

Anderson had left Harris less than two years ago to accept a position as Associate Professor of Speech and Drama at a new, four-year college the state was getting underway in southwestern California. He was in his early thirties, like everyone else they knew; a slender, moustached man with a rough, slightly pocked face; he was a casual, eccentric dresser and sometimes, Marian had told Ralph, laughing, he wore a green velvet smoking jacket to school. The girls in his classes were crazy about him, she said. He had thin, dark hair which he combed forward to cover the balding spot on the top of his head. Both he and his wife, Emily, a costume designer, had done a lot of acting and directing in Little Theater in the Bay Area before coming to Eureka. As a person, though, someone he liked to be around, it was something different as far as Ralph was concerned. Thinking about it, he decided he hadn't liked him from the beginning, and he was glad he was gone.

"What else?" he asked.

"Nothing," she said. "I'd rather not talk about it now, Ralph, if you don't mind. I was thinking about something else."

"What?"

"O . . . about the children, the dress I want Dorothea to have for next Easter; that sort of thing. Silly, unrelated things. And about the class I'm going to have tomorrow. Walt Whitman. Some of the kids didn't approve when I told them there was a, a bit of speculation Whitman was—how should I say it?—attracted to certain men." She laughed. "Really, Ralph, nothing else happened. I'm sorry I ever said anything about it."

"Okay."

He got up and went to the bathroom to wash cold water over his face. When he came out he leaned against the wall by the refrigerator and watched her measure out the sugar into the two cups and then stir in the rum. The water was boiling on the stove. The clock on the wall behind the table said 9:45.

"Look, honey, it's been brought up now," he said. "It was two or three years ago; there's no reason at all I can think of we can't talk about it if we want to, is there?"

"There's really nothing to talk about, Ralph."

"I'd like to know," he said vaguely.

"Know what?"

"Whatever else he did besides kiss you. We're adults. We haven't seen the Andersons in . . . a year at least. We'll probably never see them again. It happened a long time ago, as I see it, there's no reason whatever we can't talk about it." He was a little surprised at the level, reasoning quality in his voice. He sat down and looked at the tablecloth, and then looked up at her again. "Well?"

"Well," she said, laughing a little, tilting her head to one side, remembering. "No, Ralph, really; I'm not trying to be coy about it either: I'd just rather not."

"For Christ's sake, Marian! Now I mean it," he said, "if you don't tell me, it will make me angry."

She turned off the gas under the water and put her hand out on the stool; then sat down again, hooking her heels over the bottom step. She leaned forward, resting her arms across her knees. She picked at something on her skirt and then looked up.

"You remember Emily'd already gone home with the Beattys, and for some reason Mitchell had stayed on. He looked a little out of sorts that night to begin with. I don't know, maybe they weren't getting along . . . But I don't know that. But there were you and I, the Franklins, and Mitchell Anderson left. All of us a little drunk, if I remember rightly. I'm not sure how it happened, Ralph, but Mitchell and I just happened to find ourselves alone together in the kitchen for a minute. There was no whiskey left, only two or three bottles of that white wine we had. It must've been close to one o'clock because Mitchell said, 'If we hurry we can make it before the liquor store closes.' You know how he can be so theatrical when he wants? Softshoe stuff, facial expressions . . . ? Anyway, he was very witty about it all. At least it seemed that way at the time. And very drunk, too, I might add. So was I, for that matter . . . It was an impulse, Ralph, I swear. I don't know why I did it, don't ask me, but when he said, 'Let's go'—I agreed. We went out the back, where his car was parked. We went just like we were: we didn't even get our coats out of the closet. We thought we'd just be gone a few minutes. I guess we thought no one would miss us . . . I don't know what we thought . . . I don't know *why* I went, Ralph. It was an impulse, that's all that I can say. It was a wrong impulse." She paused. "It was my fault that night, Ralph, and I'm sorry. I shouldn't have done anything like that, I know that."

"Christ!" the word leaped out. "But you've always been that way, Marian!"

"That isn't true!"

His mind filled with a swarm of tiny accusations, and he tried to focus on one in particular. He looked down at his hands and noticed they had the same lifeless feeling as they did when he woke up mornings. He picked up the red pencil lying on the table, and then put it down again.

"I'm listening," he said.

"You're angry," she said. "You're swearing and getting all upset, Ralph. For nothing, nothing, honey! . . . There's nothing else."

"Go on."

"*What* is the matter with us anyway? How did we ever get onto this subject?"

"Go on, Marian."

"That's all, Ralph. I've told you. We went for a ride . . . We talked. He kissed me. I still don't see how we could've been gone three hours; whatever it was you said."

He remembered again the waiting, the unbearable weakness that spread down through his legs when they'd been gone an hour, two hours. It made him lean weakly against the corner of the house after he'd gone outside; for a breath of air he said vaguely, pulling into his coat, but really so that the embarrassed Franklins could themselves leave without any more embarrassment; without having to take leave of the absent host, or the vanished hostess. From the corner of the house, standing behind the rose trellis in the soft, crumbly dirt, he watched the Franklins get into their car and drive away. Anger and frustration clogged inside him, then separated into little units of humiliation that jumped against his stomach. He waited. Gradually the horror drained away as he stood there, until finally nothing was left but a vast, empty realization of betrayal. He went into the house and sat at this same table, and he remembered his shoulder began to twitch and he couldn't stop it even when he squeezed it with his fingers. An hour later, or two hours—what difference did it make then?—she'd come in.

"Tell me the rest, Marian." And he knew there was more now. He felt a slight fluttering start up in his stomach, and suddenly he didn't want to know any more. "No. Do whatever you want. If you don't want to talk about it, Marian, that's all right. Do whatever you want to, Marian. Actually, I guess I'd just as soon leave it at that."

He worked his shoulders against the smooth, solid chairback, then balanced unsteadily on the two back legs. He thought fleetingly that he would have been someplace else tonight, doing something else at this very moment, if he hadn't married. He glanced around the kitchen. He began to perspire and leaned forward, setting all the legs on the floor. He took one of her cigarets from the pack on the table. His hands were trembling as he struck the match.

"Ralph. You won't be angry, will you? Ralph? We're just talking. You won't, will you?" She had moved over to a chair at the table.

"I won't."

"Promise?"

"Promise."

She lit a cigaret. He had suddenly a great desire to see Robert and Dorothea; to get them up out of bed, heavy and turning in their sleep, and hold each of them on a knee, jiggle them until they woke up and began to laugh. He absently began to trace with his finger the outline of one of the tiny black coaches in the beige tablecloth. There were four miniature white prancing horses pulling each of the tiny coaches. The figure driving the horses had his arm up and was wearing a tall hat. Suitcases were strapped down on top the coach, and what looked like a kerosene lamp hung from the side.

"We went straight to the liquor store, and I waited in the car till he came out. He had a sack in one hand and one of those plastic bags of ice in the other. He weaved a little getting into the car. I hadn't realized he was so drunk until we started driving again, and I noticed the way he was driving; terribly slow, and all hunched over the wheel with his eyes staring. We were talking about a lot of things that didn't make sense . . . I can't remember . . . Nietzsche . . . and Strindberg; he was directing *Miss Julie* second semester, you know, and something about Norman Mailer stabbing his wife in the breast a long time ago, and how he thought Mailer was going downhill anyway—a lot of crazy things like that. Then, I'll swear before God it was an accident, Ralph, he didn't know what he was doing, he made a wrong turn and we somehow wound up out by the golf course, right near Jane Van Eaton's. In fact, we pulled into her driveway to turn around and when we did Mitchell said to me, 'We might as well open one of these bottles.' He did, he opened it, and then he drove a little farther on down the road that goes around the green, you know, and comes out by the park? Actually, not too far from the Franklins . . . And then he stopped for a minute in the middle of the road with his lights on, and we each took a drink out of the bottle. Then he said, said he'd hate to think of me being stabbed in the breast. I guess he was still thinking about Mailer's wife. And then . . . I can't say it, Ralph . . . I know you'd get angry."

"I won't get angry, Marian," he said slowly. His thoughts seemed to move lazily, as if he were in a dream, and he was able to take in only one thing at a time she was telling him. At the same time he noticed a peculiar alertness taking hold of his body.

"Go on. Then what, Marian?"

"You aren't angry, are you? Ralph?"

"No. But I'm getting interested, though."

They both had to laugh, and for a minute everything was all right. He leaned across the table to light another cigaret for her, and they smiled at each other; just like any other night. He struck another match, held it a while, and then brought the match, almost to burn his fingers, up under the end of the cigaret that protruded at an angle from his lips. He dropped the burned match into the ashtray and stared at it before looking up.

"Go on."

"I don't know . . . things seemed to happen fast after that. He drove up the road a little and turned off someplace. I don't know, maybe right onto the green . . . and started kissing me. Then he said, said he'd like to kiss my breast. I said I didn't think we should. I said, 'What about Emily?' He said I didn't know her. He got the car going again, and then he stopped again and just sort of slumped over and put his head on my lap. God! It sounds so vulgar now, I know, but it didn't seem that way at all then. I felt like, like I was losing my innocence somehow, Ralph. For the first time—that night I realized I was really, really doing something wrong, something I wasn't supposed to do and that might hurt people. I shouldn't be there, I felt. And I felt . . . like it was the first time in my life I'd ever *intentionally* done anything wrong or hurtful and gone on doing it, knowing I shouldn't be. Do you know what I mean, Ralph? Like some of the characters in Henry James? I felt that way. Like . . . for the first time . . . my innocence . . . something was happening."

"You can dispense with that shit," he cut in. "Get off it, Marian! Go on! Then what? Did he caress you? Did he? Did he try to feel you up, Marian? Tell me!"

And then she hurried on, trying to get over the hard spots quickly, and he sat with his hands folded on the table and watched her lips out of which dropped the frightful words. His eyes skipped around the kitchen—stove, cupboards, toaster, radio, coffeepot, window, curtains, refrigerator, breadbox, napkin holder, stove, cupboards, toaster . . . back to her face. Her dark eyes glistened under the overhead light. He felt a peculiar desire for her flicker through his thighs at what she was leading up to, and at the same time he had to check an urge to stand up yelling, smash his fist into her face.

"'Shall we have a go at it?' he said."

"Shall we have a go at it?" Ralph repeated.

"I'm to blame. If anyone should, should be blamed for it, I'm to blame. He said he'd leave it all up to me, I could . . . could do . . . whatever I wanted." Tears welled out of her eyes, started down her cheeks. She looked down at the table, blinked rapidly.

He shut his eyes. He saw a barren field under a heavy, gray sky; a fog moving in across the far end. He shook his head, tried to admit other possibilities, other conclusions. He tried to bring back that night two years ago, imagine himself coming into the kitchen just as she and Mitchell were at the door, hear himself telling her in a hearty voice, O no, no; you're not going out for liquor with that Mitchell Anderson! He's drunk, and he isn't a good driver to boot. You've got to go to bed now and get up with little Robert and Dorothea in the morning . . . Stop! Stop where you are.

He opened his eyes, raised his eyebrows as if he were just waking up. She had a hand up over her face and was crying silently, her shoulders rounded and moving in little jerks.

"Why did you go with him, Marian?" he asked desperately.

She shook her head without looking up.

Then suddenly, he knew. His mind buckled. *Cuckold.* For a minute he could only stare helplessly at his hands. Then he wanted to pass it off somehow, say it was all right, it was two years ago, adults, etc. He wanted to forgive: *I forgive you.* But he could not forgive. He couldn't forgive her this. His thoughts skittered around the Middle Ages, touched on Arthur and Guinevere, surged on to the outraged husbandry of the eighteenth-century dramatists, came to a sullen halt with Karenin. But what had any of them to do with him? What were they? They were nothing. Nothing. Figments. They did not exist. Their discoveries, their disintegrations, adjustments, did not at all relate to him. No relation. What then? What did it all mean? What is the nature of a book? his mind roared.

"Christ!" he said, springing up from the table. *"Jesus Christ.* Christ, no, Marian!"

"No, no," she said, throwing her head back.

"You let him!"

"No, no, Ralph."

"You let him! Didn't you? Didn't you? Answer me!" he yelled. "Did he come in you? Did you let him come in you? That s-s-swine," he said, his teeth chattering. "That bastard."

"Listen, listen to me Ralph. I swear to you he didn't, he didn't come. He didn't come in me." She rocked from side to side in the chair, shaking her head.

"You wouldn't let him! That's it, isn't it? Yes, yes, you had your scruples. What'd you do—catch it in your hands? O God! God *damn* you!"

"God!" she said, getting up, holding out her hands, "Are we crazy, Ralph? Have we lost our minds? Ralph? Forgive me, Ralph. Forgive—"

"Don't touch me! Get away from me, Marian."

"In God's Name, Ralph! Ralph! Please, Ralph. For the children's sake, Ralph. Don't go, Ralph. Please don't go, Ralph!" Her eyes were white and large, and she began to pant in her fright. She tried to head him off, but he took her by the shoulder and pushed her out of the way.

"Forgive me, Ralph! *Please.* Ralph!"

He slammed the kitchen door, started across the porch. Behind him, she jerked open the door, clattered over the dustpan as she rushed onto the porch. She took his arm at the porch door, but he shook her loose."Ralph!" But he jumped down the steps onto the walk.

When he was across the driveway and walking rapidly down the sidewalk, he could hear her at the door yelling for him. Her voice seemed to be coming through a kind of murk. He looked back: she was still calling, limned against the doorway. My God, he thought, what a sideshow it was. Fat men and bearded ladies.

2.

He had to stop and lean against a car for a few minutes before going on. But two well-dressed couples were coming down the sidewalk toward him, and the man on the outside, near the curb, was telling a story in a loud voice. The others were already laughing. Ralph pushed off from the car and crossed the street. In a few minutes he came to Blake's, where he stopped some afternoons for a beer with Dick Koenig before picking up the children from nursery school.

It was dark inside. The air was warm and heavy with the odor of beer and seemed to catch at the top of his throat and make it hard for him to swallow. Candles flickered dimly in long-necked wine bottles at some of the tables along the left wall when he closed the door. He glimpsed shadowy figures of men and women talking with their heads close together. One of the couples, near the door, stopped talking and looked up at him. A box-like fixture in the ceiling revolved overhead, throwing out pale red and green lights. Two men sat at the end of the bar, and a dark cutout of a man leaned over the juke box in the corner, his hands splayed out on each side of the glass.

The man is going to play something. Ralph stands in the center of the floor, watches him. He sways, rubs his wrist against his forehead, and starts out.

"Ralph!—Mr. Wyman, sir!"

He stopped, looked around. David Parks was calling to him from behind the bar. Ralph walked over, leaned heavily against the bar before sliding onto a stool.

"Should I draw one, Mr. Wyman?" He had the glass in his hand, smiling.

He worked evenings and weekends for Charley Blake. He was 26, married, had two children, babies. He attended Harris Junior College on a football scholarship, and worked besides. He had three mouths to feed now, along with his own. Four mouths altogether. Not like it used to be. David Parks. He had a white bar towel slung over his shoulder.

Ralph nodded, watched him fill the glass.

He held the glass at an angle under the tap, slowly straightened it as the glass filled, closed the tap, and cut off the head with a smooth, professional air. He wiped the towel across the gleaming surface of the bar and set the glass in front of Ralph, still smiling.

"How's it going, Mr. Wyman? Didn't hear you come in." He put his foot up on a shelf under the bar. "Who's going to win the game next week, Mr. Wyman?"

Ralph shook his head, brought the beer to his lips. His shoulders ached with fatigue from being held rigid the last hour.

David Parks coughed faintly. "I'll buy you one, Mr. Wyman. This one's on me." He put his leg down, nodded assurance, and reached under his apron into his pocket.

"Here. I have it right here." Ralph pulled out some change, examined it in his hand from the light cast by a bare bulb on a stand next to the cash register. A quarter, nickel, two dimes, pennies. He laid down the quarter and stood up, pushing the change back into his pocket. The man was still in front of the juke box, leaning his weight on one leg. The phone rang.

Ralph opened the door.

"Mr. Wyman! Mr. Wyman, for you sir."

Outside he turned around, trying to decide what to do. He wanted to be alone, but at the same time he thought he'd feel better if other people were around. Not here though. His heart was fluttering, as if he'd been running. The door opened behind him and a man and woman came out. Ralph stepped out of the way and they got into a car parked at the curb. He recognized the woman as the receptionist at the children's dentist. He started off walking.

He walked to the end of the block, crossed the street, and walked another block before he decided to head downtown. It was eight or ten blocks and he walked hurriedly, his hands balled into his pockets, his shoes smacking the pavement. He kept blinking his eyes and thought it incredible he could still feel tired and fogged after all that had happened. He shook his head. He would have liked to sit someplace for a while and think about it, but he knew he could not sit, could not yet think about it. He remembered a man he saw once sitting on a curb in Arcata: an old man with a growth of beard and a brown wool cap who just sat there with his arms between his legs. But a minute later it snapped into his mind, and for the first time he tried to get a clear look at it; himself, Marian, the children—his world. But it was impossible. He wondered if anyone could ever stand back far enough from life to see it whole, all in one piece. He thought of an enormous French tapestry they'd seen two or three years ago that took up one wall of a room in the De Young Museum. He tried to imagine how all this would seem twenty years from now, but there was nothing. He couldn't picture the children any older, and when he tried to think about Marian and himself, there was only a blank space. Then, for a minute, he felt profoundly indifferent, somehow above it, as if it did not concern him. He thought of Marian without any emotion at all. He remembered her as he had seen her a little while ago; face crumpled, tears running off her nose. Then Marian on the floor, holding onto the chair, blood on her teeth: "Why did you hit me?" . . . Marian reaching under her dress to unfasten her garter belt . . . She raises her dress slowly as she leans back in the seat.

He stopped and thought he was going to be sick. He moved off onto the edge of a lawn. He cleared his throat several times and kept swallowing, looked up as a car of yelling teenagers went by and gave him a long blast on their musical horn. Yes, there was a vast amount of evil loose in the world, he thought, and it only awaited an opportunity, the propitious moment to manifest itself . . . But that was an academic notion. A kind of retreat. He spat ahead of himself on the walk and put his heel on it. He mustn't let himself find solace in that kind of thinking. Not now. Not anymore, if he could help it. If he was going to think about it—and he knew he must, sooner or later tonight—he must begin simply, from the essentials: with the fact that his wife had let herself be fucked, yes, fucked, by another man. And this, this he *knew* was evil: he felt it in his bones.

He came to Second Street, the part of town people called Two Street. It started here at Shelton, under the streetlight where the old rooming houses ended, and ran for four or five blocks on down to the pier, where fishing boats tied up. He'd been down here once, two years ago, to a second-hand store to look through the dusty shelves of old books. There was a liquor store across the street, and he could see a man standing outside in front of the glass door, looking at a newspaper.

Ralph crossed under the streetlight, read the headlines on the newspaper the man had been looking at, and went inside. A bell over the door tinkled. He hadn't noticed a bell that tinkled over a door since he was a child. He bought some cigarets and went out again.

He walked down the street, looking in the windows. All the places were closed for the night, or vacated. Some of the windows had signs taped inside: a dance, a Shrine Circus that had come and gone last summer, an election—Vote For Fred C. Walters, Councilman. One of the windows he looked through had sinks and pipe-joints scattered around on a table. Everything dark. He came to a Vic Tanney Gym where he could see light coming under the curtains pulled across a big window. He could hear water splashing in the pool inside, and the hollow echo of voices calling across the water.

There was more light now, coming from the bars and cafes on both sides of the street. More people, groups of three or four but now and then a man by himself, or a woman in slacks walking rapidly. He stopped in front of the window of one place and watched some Negroes shooting pool. Gray cigaret smoke drifted around the lights over the table. One of the Negroes, who was chalking his cue, had his hat on and a cigaret in his mouth. He said something to another Negro, looked intently at the balls, and slowly leaned over the table.

He walked on, stopped in front of Jim's Oyster House. He had never been here before, had never been to any of these places before. Over the door the name was in yellow lightbulbs: JIM'S OYSTER HOUSE. Above the lights, fixed to an iron grill, a huge neon-lighted clam shell with a man's legs sticking out. The torso was hidden in the shell and the legs flashed red, on and off. Ralph lit another cigaret from the one he had, and pushed open the door.

It was crowded. A lot of people were bunched on the floor, their arms wrapped around each other or hanging loosely on someone's shoulders. The men in the band were just getting up from their chairs for an intermission. He had to excuse himself several times trying to get to the bar, and once a drunken woman took hold of his coat. There were no stools and he had to stand at the end of the bar between a coast guardsman and a shrunken-faced man in denims. Neither of them spoke. The coast guardsman had his white cap off and his elbows propped out in front of him, a hand on each side of his face. He stared at his glass without looking up. The other man shook his head and then pointed with his narrow chin two or three times at the coast guardsman. Ralph put his arm up and signalled the bartender. Once. Ralph thought he heard the shrunken-faced man say something, but he didn't answer.

In the mirror he could see the men in the band get up from the table where they'd been sitting. Ralph picked up his glass, turned around, and leaned back against the bar. He closed his eyes and opened them. Someone unplugged the juke box, and the music ground to a stop. The musicians wore white shirts and dark slacks with little string ties around their necks. There was a fireplace with blue gas flames behind a stack of metal logs, and the band platform was to the side, a few feet away. One of the men plucked the strings of his electric guitar, said something to the others with a grin, and leaned back in his chair. They began to play.

The music was country, or western, and not as bad as Ralph had imagined. He raised his glass and drained it. Down the bar he could hear a woman say angrily, "Well there's going to be trouble, that's all I've got to say about it!" The musicians came to the end of the number and swung into another. One of the men, the bass player, came to the microphone and began to sing, but Ralph couldn't understand the words.

When the band took another intermission, he looked around for the toilet. He could make out some doors opening and closing at the far end of the bar, and headed in that direction, staggering a little. Over one of the doors was a rack of antlers. He saw a man go in, and he saw another man catch the door and come out. Inside, waiting in line behind three or four others, he found himself staring at the pencilled picture of a huge pair of female thighs and pubic area on the wall over the pocket-comb machine. Underneath the drawing was scrawled, Eat ME, and a little lower down someone had added Betty M. Eats It—RA 52275. The man ahead of him moved up, and Ralph took two steps forward, his eyes still fastened on the drawing. Finally, he moved up over the bowl and urinated so hard it was like a bolt going down through his legs. He sighed luxuriously when he was through, leaned forward and let his head rest against the wall. His life was changed from tonight on. Were there many other men, he wondered drunkenly, who could look at one singular event in their lives and perceive the workings of the catastrophe that hereinafter sets their lives on a different course? Are there many who can perceive the necessary changes and adjustments that must necessarily and inevitably follow. Probably so, he decided after a minute's reflection. He stood there a while longer, and then he looked down: he'd urinated on his fingers.

He moved over to the wash basin, ran water over his hands without using the dirty bar of soap. As he was unrolling the towel, he suddenly leaned over and put his face up close to the pitted mirror, looked into his eyes. A face: that was all. Hardly even familiar. There seemed nothing fixed or permanent about it. His nose just hung there, occupying a space, spotted with several tiny blackheads he hadn't noticed before. His skin was slightly chapped on the inside of one cheek. His lips . . . like any other lips. Only his eyes under the narrow eyebrows seemed out of the ordinary, like shiny glass objects. They moved as he moved, followed him around the mirror, looked out at him steadily when he looked straight in. He put his finger up to the mirror and touched the glass, moved away as a man tried to get past him to the sink.

As he was going out the door he noticed another door he hadn't seen at the end of a short, narrow corridor. He went over to it and looked through the glass plate in the door at four card-players around a green felt table. It seemed still and restful inside. He couldn't hear anything, and the silent movements of the men appeared languorous and heavy with meaning. He leaned against the glass, watching. One of the men at the table, the man dealing, looked up at him and stared until he moved away. He weaved back to the bar and thought how the scene reminded him of Cezanne's Card-Players. But did it really?

There was a flourish of guitars and people began whistling and clapping. A plump, middle-aged woman in a white evening dress was being helped onto the platform. She kept trying to pull back and was shaking her head and laughing. Finally she took the mike and made a little curtsy. The people whistled and stamped their feet. He thought of the scene in the card room. No, they didn't remind him of the Cezanne; that was certain. He suddenly had an enormous desire to watch them play, be in the same room with them. He could watch, even if he didn't play. He'd seen some empty chairs along the wall. He leaned against the bar, took out his wallet, keeping his hands up over the sides as he looked to see how much he had. He had eighteen dollars—just in case he was asked to play a hand or two. Without thinking anymore about it, he worked his way to the back. Behind him, the woman began to sing in a low, drowsy voice. Ralph stepped into the corridor, and then pushed open the door to the card room.

The man who'd looked up at him was still dealing.

"Decided to join us?" he said, sweeping Ralph with his eyes and looking down at the table again. Two of the others raised their eyes for an instant then looked back at the cards flashing around the table. As they picked up their cards, the man sitting with his back to Ralph, a short, fat man who breathed heavily through his nose, turned around in his chair and glared at him, and Ralph moved back a step.

"Benny, bring another chair!" the dealer called to an old man sweeping under a table that had the chairs turned up on the top.

"That's all right," Ralph said. "I'll just watch a few hands."

"Suit yourself."

He sat down in a chair against the wall, a few feet away from the table. No one spoke. The only sounds were the *clat-clat* of the chips as the men dropped them into the center of the table, and the shuffle and sharp flicking of the cards. The dealer was a large man, 30 or so; he wore a white shirt, open at the collar, and with the sleeves turned back once exposing the forearms covered with black, curling hair. But his small hands were white and delicate-looking, and there was a gold band on his ring finger. Around the table a tall, white-haired man with a cigar, the fat man, and a small dark man with a gray suit and a tie. An Italian, Ralph thought. He smoked one cigaret after another, and when he swallowed, the tie over his Adam's apple moved up and down. The old man, Benny, was wiping with a cloth around the cash register near the door. It was warm and quiet. Now and then Ralph could hear a horn blare out in the street. He drew a long breath and closed his eyes, opened them when he heard steps.

"Want anything to drink?" Benny asked, carrying a chair to the table.

Ralph said he'd have something— bourbon and water. He gave him a dollar and pulled out of his coat. Benny took the coat and hung it up by the door as he went out. Two of the men moved their chairs and Ralph sat down across from the dealer.

"How's it going?" he said to Ralph, not looking up.

For a minute Ralph wasn't sure whether it was directed at him. "All right," he said.

Then, as Ralph watched the other men play their cards, the dealer said gently, still not looking at him, "Low ball or five card. Table stakes, five dollar limit on raises."

Ralph nodded, and when the hand was finished he bought fifteen dollars worth of blue chips.

He watched the cards as they flashed around the table, picked up his as he'd seen the tall, white-haired man do; sliding one card under the corner of another as each card fell face down in front of him. He raised his eyes once and looked at the expressionless faces of the others. He wondered if it'd ever happened to any of them. In half an hour he had won two hands and without counting the small pile of chips in front of him, he thought he must still have fifteen or even twenty dollars.

Benny brought a tray of drinks, and Ralph paid for his with a chip. He took out his handkerchief and wiped the perspiration from his face, aware how tired he was. But he felt better for some reason. He had come a long way since that evening. But it was only . . . a few hours ago. And had he really come so far? Was anything different, or anything resolved?

"You in or out?" the fat man asked. "Clyde, what's the bet, for Christ's sake?" he said to the dealer.

"Three dollars."

"In," Ralph said. "I'm in." He put three chips into the pot. "I have to be going though . . . another hand or so."

The dealer looked up and then back at his cards.

The Italian said: "Stick around. You really want some action we can go to my place when we finish here."

"No, that's all right. Enough action tonight . . . I just have to be going pretty soon." He shifted in the chair, glanced at their faces, and then fixed upon a small green plaque on the wall behind the table. "You know," he said, "I just found out tonight. My wife, my wife played around with another guy two years ago. Can you imagine?'' He cleared his throat.

One of the men snickered; the Italian. The fat man said, "You can't trust em, that's all. Women are no damn good!"

No one else said anything; the tall, white-haired man laid down his cards and lit his cigar that had gone out. He stared at Ralph as he puffed, then shook out the match and picked up his cards again. The dealer looked up again, resting his open hands palms-up on the table.

"You work here in town?" he said to Ralph. "I haven't seen you around."

"I live here. I, I just haven't gotten around much." He felt drained, oddly relaxed.

"We playing or not?" the fat man said. "Clyde?"

"Hold your shirt," the dealer said.

"For Christ's sake," the white-haired man said quietly, holding onto each word, "I've never seen such cards."

"I'm in three dollars," the fat man said. "Who's going to stay?"

Ralph couldn't remember his hole card. His neck was stiff, and he fought against the desire to close his eyes. He'd never been so tired. All the joints and bones and muscles in his body seemed to radiate and call to his attention. He looked at his card; a seven of clubs. His next card, face-up, was an ace. He started to drop out. He edged in his chair, picked up his glass but it was empty.

"Benny!" the dealer said sharply.

His next card was a king. The betting went up to the five dollar limit. More royalty; the Queen of Diamonds. He looked once more at his hole card to see if he might somehow have been mistaken: the seven of clubs.

Benny came back with another tray of drinks and said, "They're closing in ten minutes, Clyde."

The next card, the Jack of Spades, fell on top of Ralph's queen. Ralph stared. The white-haired man turned over his cards. For the first time the dealer gazed straight into Ralph's eyes, and Ralph felt his toes pull back in his shoes as the man's eyes pierced through to, what seemed to Ralph, his craven heart.

"I'll bet two dollars to see it," the fat man said.

A shiver traced up and down Ralph's spine. He hesitated, and then, in a grand gesture, called, and recklessly raised five dollars, his last chips.

The tall, white-haired man edged his chair closer to the table.

The dealer had a pair of eights showing. Still looking at Ralph, he picked ten chips off one of the stacks in front of him. He spread them in two groups of five near the pile at the center of the table.

"Call."

The Italian hesitated, and then swallowed and turned over his cards. He looked at the dealer's cards, and then he looked at Ralph's.

The fat man smacked his cards down and glared at Ralph.

All of them watched as Ralph turned over his card and lurched up from the table.

Outside, in the alley, he took out his wallet again, let his fingers number the bills he had left; two dollars, and some change in his pocket. Enough for something to eat. Ham and eggs, perhaps. But he wasn't hungry. He leaned back against the damp brick wall of the building, trying to think. A car turned into the alley, stopped, and backed out again. He started walking. He went past the front of the Oyster House again, going back the way he'd come. He stayed close to the buildings, out of the way of the loud groups of men and women streaming up and down the sidewalk. He heard a woman in a long coat say to the man she was with, "It isn't that way at all, Bruce. You don't understand."

He stopped when he came to the liquor store. Inside he moved up to the counter and stared at the long, orderly rows of bottles. He bought a half-pint of rum and some more cigarets. The palm trees on the label of the bottle, the large drooping fronds with the lagoon in the background, had caught his eye. The clerk, a thin, bald man wearing suspenders, put the rum in a paper sack without a word and rang up the sale. Ralph could feel the man's eyes on him as he stood in front of magazine rack, swaying a little and looking at the covers. Once he glanced up in the mirror over his head and caught the man staring at him from behind the counter; his arms were folded over his chest and his bald head gleamed in the reflected light. Finally the man turned off one of the lights in the back of the store and said, "Closing it up, buddy."

Outside again, Ralph turned around once and started down another street, toward the pier; he thought he'd like to see the water with the lights reflected on it. He wondered how far he would drop tonight before he began to level off. He opened the sack as he walked, broke the seal on the little bottle, and stopped in a doorway to take a long drink. He could hardly taste it. He crossed some old streetcar tracks and turned onto another, darker street. He could already hear the waves splashing under the pier.

As he came up to the front of a dark, wooden building, he heard someone move in the doorway. A heavy Negro in a leather jacket stepped out in front of him and said, "Just a minute there, man. Where you think you're goin?"

As Ralph tried to move around him, frightened, the man said, "Christ, man, that's my feet you're steppin on!"

Before he could move away the Negro hit him hard in the stomach, and when Ralph groaned and bent over, the man hit him in the nose with his open hand, knocking him back against the wall where he sat down in a rush of pain and dizziness. He had one leg turned under, trying to raise himself up, when the Negro slapped him on the cheek and knocked him sprawling onto the pavement. He was aware of a hand slipping into his pants-pocket over the hip, felt his wallet slide out. He groaned and tried to sit up again as the man neatly stripped his watch over his hand. He kicked the wet sack of broken glass, and then sprinted down the street.

Ralph got his legs under him again. As if from a great distance he heard someone yell, "There's a man hurt over here!" and he struggled up to his feet. Then he heard someone running toward him over the pavement, and a car pulled up to the curb, a car door slammed. He wanted to say, It's all right, please, it's all right, as a man came up to him and stopped a few feet away, watching. But the words seemed to ball in his throat and something like a gasp escaped his lips. He tried to draw a breath and the air piled up in his throat again, as if there were an obstruction in the passage; and then the noise broke even louder through his nose and mouth. He leaned his shoulder against the

doorway and wept. In the few seconds he stood there, shaking, his mind seemed to empty out, and a vast sense of wonderment flowed through him as he thought again of Marian, why she had betrayed him. Then, as a policeman with a big flashlight walked over to him, he brought himself up with a shudder and became silent.

3.

Birds darted overhead in the graying mist. He still couldn't see them, but he could hear their sharp *jueet-jueet.* He stopped and looked up, kept his eyes fixed in one place; then he saw them, no larger than his hand, dozens of them, wheeling and darting just under the heavy overcast. He wondered if they were seabirds, birds that only came in off the ocean this time of morning. He'd never seen any birds around Eureka in the winter except now and then a big, lumbering seagull. He remembered once, a long time ago, walking into an old abandoned house—the Marshall place, near Uncle Jack's in Springfield, Oregon—how the sparrows kept flying in and out of the broken windows, flying around the rafters where they had their nests, and then flying out the windows again, trying to lead him away.

It was getting light. The overcast seemed to be lifting and was turning light—gray with patches of white clouds showing through here and there. The street was black with the mist that was still falling, and he had to be careful not to step on the snails that trailed across the damp sidewalk.

A car with its lights on slowed down as it went past, but he didn't look up. Another car passed. In a minute, another. He looked: four men, two in front, two in the back. One of the men in the back seat, wearing a hat, turned around and looked at him through the back window. Mill workers. The first shift of plywood mill workers going to work at Georgia-Pacific. It was Monday morning. He turned the corner, walked past Blake's; dark, the venetian blinds pulled over the windows and two empty beer bottles someone had left standing like sentinels beside the door. It was cold, and he walked slowly, crossing his arms now and then and rubbing his shoulders.

He'd refused the policeman's offer of a ride home. He couldn't think of a more shabby ending to the night than riding home in the early morning in a black and white police car. After the doctor at Redwood Memorial Hospital had examined him, felt around over his neck with his fingers while Ralph had sat with his eyes closed, the doctor had made two X-rays and then put merthiolate and a small bandage on his cheek. Then the policemen had taken him to the station where for two hours he'd had to look at photographs in large manila folders of Negro men. Finally, he had told the officer, "I'm sorry, but I'm afraid everyone looks pretty much alike right now." The man had shrugged, closed the folder. "They come and go," he'd said, staring at Ralph. "Sometimes it's hard to nail them on the right charge due to lack of proper identification. If we bring in some suspects we'll have you back here to help identify." He stared at Ralph a minute longer, then nodded curtly.

He came up the street to his house. He could see his front porchlight on, but the rest of the house was dark. He crossed the lawn and went around to the back. He turned the knob, and the door opened quietly. He stepped onto the porch and shut the door. He waited a moment, then opened the kitchen door.

The house was quiet. There was the tall stool beside the draining board. There was the table where they'd sat. How long ago? He remembered he'd just gotten up off the couch, where he'd been working, and come into the kitchen and sat down . . . He looked at the clock over the stove: 7:00 a.m. He could see into the dining room table with the lace cloth, the heavy glass centerpiece of red flamingos, their wings opened. The draperies behind the table were open. Had she stood at that window watching for him? He moved over to the door and stepped onto the living room carpet. Her coat was thrown over the couch, and in the pale light he could make out a large ashtray full of her cork cigaret ends on one of the cushions. He noticed the phone directory open on the coffee table as he went by. He stopped at the partially open door to their bedroom. For an instant he resisted the impulse to look in on her, and then with his finger he pushed open the door a few inches. She was sleeping, her head off the pillow, turned toward the wall, and her hair black against the sheet. The covers were bunched around her shoulders and had pulled up from the foot of the bed. She was on her side, her secret body slightly bent at the hips, her thighs closed together protectively. He stared for a minute. What, after all, should he do? Pack his things, now, and leave? Go to a hotel room until he can make other arrangements? Sleep on the extra bed in the little storage room upstairs? How should a man act, given the circumstances? The things that had been said last night. There was no undoing that—nor the other. There was no going back, but what course was he to follow now?

In the kitchen he laid his head down on his arms over the table. How should a man act? *How should a man act?* It kept repeating itself. Not just now, in this situation, for today and tomorrow, but every day on this earth. He felt suddenly there was an answer, that he somehow held the answer himself and that it was very nearly out if only he could think about it a little longer. Then he heard Robert and Dorothea stirring. He sat up slowly and tried to smile as they came into the kitchen.

"Daddy, daddy," they both said, running over to him in their pajamas.

"Tell us a story, daddy," Robert said, getting onto his lap.

"He can't tell us a story now," Dorothea said. "It's *too* early in the morning, isn't it, daddy?"

"What's that on your face, daddy?" Robert said, pointing at the bandage.

"Let me see!" Dorothea said. "Let me see, daddy."

"*Poor* daddy," Robert said.

"What *did* you do to your face, daddy?"

"It's nothing" Ralph said. "It's all right, sweetheart. Here, get down, Robert, I hear your mother."

Ralph stepped into the bathroom and locked the door.

"Is your father here?" he heard Marian ask the children. "Where is he, in the bathroom? Ralph?"

"Mama, mama!" Dorothea exclaimed. "Daddy has a big, big bandage on his face!"

"Ralph," she turned the knob. "Ralph, let me in, please, darling. Ralph? Please let me in, darling, I want to see you. Ralph? Please?"

"Go away, Marian. Just let me alone for a while, all right?"

"Please, Ralph, open the door for a minute, darling. I just want to see you, Ralph. Ralph? The children said you were hurt. What's wrong, darling? . . . Ralph?"

"Will you please be quiet, please?"

She waited at the door for a minute, turned the knob again, and then he could hear her moving around the kitchen, getting the children breakfast, trying to answer their questions.

He looked at himself in the mirror, then pulled off the bandage and tried gently with warm water and a cloth to wipe off some of the red stain. In a minute or two he gave it up. He turned away from the mirror and sat down heavily on the edge of the bathtub, began to unlace his shoes. No cowardly Aegisthus waiting for him here, no Clytemnestra. He sat there with a shoe in his hand and looked at the white, streamlined clipper ships making their way across the pale blue of the plastic shower curtain. He unbuttoned his shirt, leaned over the bathtub with a sigh, and dropped in the plug. He opened the hot water handle, and the steam rose.

As he stood naked a minute on the smooth tile before getting into the water, he gathered in his fingers the slack flesh over his ribs, looked at himself again in the clouded mirror. He started when Marian called his name.

"Ralph. The children are in their room playing . . . I called Von Williams and said you wouldn't be in today, and I'm going to stay home." She waited and then said, "I have a nice breakfast on the stove for you, darling, when you're through with your bath . . . Ralph?"

"It's all right, Marian. I'm not hungry."

"Ralph . . . Come out, darling."

He stayed in the bathroom until he heard her upstairs over the bathroom in the children's room. She was telling them: settle down and get dressed; didn't they want to play with Warren and Jeannie?

He went through the house and into the bedroom where he shut the door. He looked at the bed before he crawled in. He lay on his back and stared at the ceiling. *How should a man act?* It had assumed immense importance in his mind, was far more crucial and requiring of an answer than the other thing, the event two years ago . . . He remembered he'd just gotten up off the couch in the living room where he'd been working, and come into the kitchen and sat down . . . The light ornament in the ceiling began to sway. He snapped open his eyes and turned onto his side as Marian came into the room.

She took off her robe and sat down on the edge of the bed. She put her hand under the covers and began gently stroking the lower part of his back. "Ralph," she murmured.

He tensed at her cold fingers, and then, gradually, he relaxed. He imagined he was floating on his back in the heavy, milky water of Juniper Lake, where he'd spent one summer years ago, and someone was calling to him, Come in, Ralph, Come in. But he kept on floating and didn't answer, and the soft rising waves laved his body.

He woke again as her hand moved over his hip. Then it traced his groin before flattening itself against his stomach. She was in bed now, pressing the length of her body against his and moving gently back and forth with him. He waited a minute, and then he turned to her and their eyes met.

Her eyes were filled and seemed to contain layer upon layer of shimmering color and reflection, thicker and more opaque farther in, and almost transparent at the lustrous surface. Then, as he gazed even deeper, he glimpsed in first one pupil and then the other, the cameo-like, perfect reflection of his own strange and familiar face. He continued to stare, marvelling at the changes he dimly felt taking place inside him.

Love in the Winter

DANIEL CURLEY

from *Colorado Quarterly*

"Look," Ross Taylor said, when at last Grace Martin was really in his car, "instead of dropping off at the station, why don't you ride overland with me as far as Albany or Syracuse and take your train on from there?" He hesitated, appalled at the traps opening out of the simplest words. "The Berkshires will be worth seeing in all this snow, the Mohawk Trail, the Taconic Trail and all," he concluded lamely. He was glad to have got out of that corner without basing his appeal on some assumption either of his overwhelming personal magnetism or of his pathetic loneliness. (It will make the trip more pleasant for you/for me/for both of us.)

"I was hoping you'd say something like that," Grace said. Taylor had been writing the dialogue in his head for the past three days, ever since they agreed it would be convenient for Grace to drive to the station with him when he left to go back to Chicago. He had written that very speech for her, in fact, but now that he actually heard her speaking it, he felt like a vast jellyfish from his throat to his hips.

There was a lot he was supposed to say now, but he forgot it all. "Good," he said, "good." Fortunately Grace had a great many things to say about sending a telegram to excuse her change of plans, and he had to make a great many replies that didn't need thinking about.

So shaken was he, however, by the success of his opening move and even more by his audacity in making it at all that he found himself unable to concentrate on the next moves in his campaign. His mind jumped from one irrelevancy to another, but kept returning to simple wonder that she was there at all.

Why, four days ago, before he had even met her, he despised her. It wasn't enough that she was to be in the Harris' guest room so that he would have to bed down in the study. No, indeed, she had to be a dean of women on top of that, and Taylor was full of the traditional academic contempt for administrators. Of course, he hadn't had much to do with deans of women in recent years, but he remembered the breed well from his days as a young instructor jumping from hick school to hick school. Probably the one where she was dean was just like the lot of them.

His first look at her had shaken him, but he steadied himself while he took off his coat and greeted the Harrises, watching her all the while. She didn't look like a dean of women. That was hard to forgive. In fact, she didn't look like an old school chum of Jean Harris. Obviously, as a spinster dean, she had been able to take care of herself. He compared her quickly with Jean, who was iron gray and almost a nervous wreck, and with his own wife, who was now built like the Hollywood version of a Russian lady truck driver. As he moved closer, he saw that she had black hair and light eyes, a combination that never failed to move him profoundly. He was profoundly moved and despised her the more bitterly for it.

By the time the house had quieted down, however, and he lay on the couch in the study (it was really very comfortable) enjoying a last cigarette, he had so far changed his mind that he was wondering what would happen if tomorrow he found an opportunity to make her one of the vile proposals that had been running through his mind all evening from the very moment they shook hands and their eyes met and she opened with something other than the standard dean of women's gambit: "We'll get along fine—after all we're in the same game." He had been ready for that, but it didn't come, and he soon realized that she was quite incapable of it. At the same time, she was only politely interested in how his paper had gone at the Modern Languages convention that day and didn't pretend ever to have heard of the Finnesburh Fragment or any problems connected with it. She didn't even pretend to be interested. All this without leaving the least doubt that she was very much interested in him.

Before he finally fell asleep that night, he even went so far as to wonder what would happen if he had the courage then and there to pad on bare feet through the dark house and quietly try the knob of the guest room door. He told himself that he read too many dirty books. He reminded himself of the sanctity of his host's house. He reminded himself of his wife and children. He assured himself that he wasn't that kind of man. In short, he did nothing, neither that night nor the two following nights.

Each day he assured himself that he would make a move if he again caught that look that seemed to enter him like an enormous jolt of neat whiskey and explode into fire inside him. Each day he caught the look but did nothing. Well, not exactly nothing. He did check train and plane schedules and find that if she would agree to give up going by way of New York for the sake of seeing some old friends for a few hours between trains, and if she would agree to drive with him as far as Albany, they could manage a night in Albany if she would agree to that. He had it all worked out, but he didn't believe for a minute that he would ever be able to ask her.

And now it was done. They were actually driving together through the snow across Massachusetts. Of course there were still uncertainties, but if he was careful everything would lead where he wanted to go. His heart pounded at the mere idea of closing a hotel room door on himself and a strange woman. Unfortunately he could see only as far as that gesture, and he had no idea what came next. It was like a honeymoon, of course, but he had never had a honeymoon. How do people get over those first minutes alone? How long or how short is it before you can say, For God's sake, let's get to bed? Probably, since they would both know why they were there, it would work out all right, but in his imagination he remained all night with his hand on the doorknob.

With his wife he had never had to confront that problem. It had already been taken care of before they were even introduced. They had waked up in bed together after a party, very publicly compromised. In fact, it was their host's pounding on the bedroom door that awoke them. Their host and hostess had not slept well on the living room couches and were not disposed to let anyone else sleep, especially in their own bed, especially people who, no matter what éclat they had given the party, had caused all kinds of complications by locking themselves in with all the hats and coats.

During the following week, Taylor was at some pains to find out the name of the girl—his host and hostess wouldn't speak to him. But when he found her, she wouldn't speak to him either. At last she consented to a meeting in a public place. One meeting led to another. Taylor began with apology and ended with the offer of his sacred treasure. She hesitated, and Taylor's fate hung in the balance for weeks—why, she scarcely knew him—and all the while they continued to see each other in public places. Taylor was secretly horrified at what had happened, and at the same time he was secretly delighted.

In later years, however, the emotion that drove out all others was regret: regret that he had found the girl and that she had married him, thereby causing him to lose a precious secret that he might otherwise have held with warm pleasure and consolation in marriage with someone else; and regret that all the people who had been at the party had long ago drifted out of his life and there was now no one left to keep the legend alive.

Today with Grace was going to be more like the beginning of a honeymoon, for all day there would be anticipation while they drove together intimately through the snow. The words "A Night of Love" hung in the air before him as solid as if cut out of stone, as brilliant as if floodlighted on a marquee.

The snow continued to fall all day, but the roads were still good. The car was heavy, and the snow treads gave good traction even in the Berkshires. However, everything was taking longer than Taylor had planned. Never had one of those tiny New England states seemed so endless, and it was well after two o'clock when they finally stopped for lunch in Williamstown. They would still get into Albany early enough, but the sense of leisure was being eaten away, and a familiar tension was building up in the back of Taylor's neck.

As soon as they left Williamstown and began climbing the Taconic Trail, Taylor began to be on the lookout for the state line. Not the least of the incidental pleasures of the day was the knowledge that he would be violating the Mann Act. The very thought that he—Ross Taylor, for God's sake—was transporting a woman across a state line for immoral purposes in full defiance of the Federal Government and the Seventh Commandment, at the risk of his loving wife, his gratifying children, his flourishing career—that terrible thought was delicious indeed.

He knew they must be getting close to the line, and he was preparing a light speech about the Mann Act to give himself yet another *frisson* when she said suddenly, "What's that up ahead?"

Engrossed in his fantasy, he had been aware only of the immediate problems of driving, but now he saw two cars standing in the road just about where he imagined the line to be. He automatically slowed and shifted down into second so as not to lose his traction on the hill. "Looks like an accident," he said.

"Oh, I hope not," she said. "I hope no one's hurt."

By then they were close enough to see better. "No," he said, "it's not an accident. The New York plows haven't come this far, and those cars are stuck."

"Do you think we could help them?" she said.

"Not likely," he said. "I'm going to go on through, and we can leave word for the state police at the first town we come to."

"Do you think we should stop and say we'll send help?"

His neck was now so stiff he didn't expect ever to be able to move his head again. "I don't want to lose my momentum," he said, making an effort to control his temper. After all she wasn't his wife even if she did sound like a wife the way she was asking the questions he had resolved not to think about. He made a further effort. "The top of the trail is just beyond the state line. You can see it from here. Up at that bend where the wind has swept the road bare. It's downhill from there. I think we'll be all right."

"I'm sure we will."

Just hearing that was almost reward enough in itself. He had forgotten—if he ever knew—how good it is for a man to hear such things. However, he was by no means sure himself that they would get through, but he knew that their schedule was already so badly out of order that it couldn't stand much more delay.

"We'll be all right," he said again as they left behind the plowed roads and entered the rutted snow of New York State.

She said, "My mother always maintained she could tell the minute she left Massachusetts, but I never believed it until now."

He laughed because just then he was forging past the first of the stuck cars. It was a Model A and was sitting squarely on the road. It hadn't got far, and he would have thought it could be backed out without much trouble. He glanced at the driver, an old woman in a fur coat and fur cap, who smiled at him and waved him on and blew her horn in encouragement as he went past.

The second car was almost at right angles to the road with its rear end against the snow bank to the left. There was room for him to pass, but he was afraid for a minute his wheels were going to start to spin on him as he edged over off the crown of the road, but he shifted down into first and kept going.

Both his shoulders ached now, but he was very conscious of his skill in keeping his wheels under him. "It won't be long now," he said, thinking as he said it only of getting over the mountain but realizing at once that it might be considered a crude allusion. He hoped she knew he couldn't do a thing like that—yes, or she wouldn't be with him at all. Then he hit a snow drift. The car would move neither forward nor back with all his skill. "I guess that's it," he said, and immediately the tension began to be less. "We can be warm here a long time with the heater, and we have the radio if we get bored with each other's company." He flicked the radio on to demonstrate.

"Bored already?" she said.

"Nothing but football," he grunted. Being a husband for twenty years had at least taught him some arts of silence.

"Let's listen to a game for a little," she said. "I don't really feel it's New Year's unless I hear a touchdown or two."

"Any preference?"

"Rose Bowl, of course," she said. "It's more like Santa Claus." She was disappointed, however, to find that Alabama was being beaten in the Rose Bowl. "They're supposed to win," she said. "The Rose Bowl jinx."

They listened for what seemed to him like a long time. Each time he leaned forward to adjust the radio, he was conscious of her nearness, each time he lit her cigarette. The football game did not exist for him. During a time out, she said, "Do you think using the radio like this will run down the battery too much?"

"No, it's all right." He knew he had been a little curt—his wife would have noticed it anyway—so he added with some effort, "Running the motor like this is keeping the battery up." He wasn't sure about that, but he hoped so anyway.

"Perhaps we shouldn't be running the motor so much."

"There's plenty of gas," he said. "I filled it at Williamstown."

"I mean, how about carbon monoxide and all that? I don't think the school would care to have its dean of women found in a parked car on a lonely mountain road."

"It would teach the girls always to be sure a window is open a bit. You'd be a martyr for education."

She laughed, and he felt repaid for the effort, which had been considerable.

"Besides," she said, "it's not really so lonely, not with them." She gestured toward the other cars, but Taylor knew it was the nearer she meant, about twenty yards back down the slope. That car and Taylor's car were both slewed across the highway so that they were at right angles to each other. A man and a woman sat stiffly on the front seat staring through the windshield as if Taylor's car were something in a movie.

If it had not been for those spectators, Taylor would have felt obliged to consider whether this was the time to make his pass. But even so, the light was beginning to fail. The tension in his shoulders was returning. He peered up and down the trail to see if any help was in sight. "Here comes more company," he said, "and by the looks of things he won't get far."

The car he was watching made a fast run up to the unplowed road and plunged in without slackening speed. "I hope he doesn't chew us up, bulling around like that." The car got past the Model A without trouble, but immediately afterward it began to slow so that to get past the second car it had to slow down noticeably. Once it was past, the driver tramped on the gas, and his wheels began to spin. Very shortly he was squarely across the road just behind Taylor's car.

"Well," Taylor said, "this is more like it. I saw that car being worked on where we stopped for gas in Williamstown. Some college boys on their way back to school rammed a bus and smashed in their grill and radiator—Alabama, too, by the way. It looks like a bad day for Alabama all around. But now there'll be plenty of manpower to help get us out of here—according to the mechanic there are supposed to be six of them."

"You aren't going to do anything rash, are you?" Grace said.

"Good lord," he said. "Rash? What do you mean?" He would have known very well what his wife meant, and he was more than a little dismayed by the intimation that even if he was only borrowed for the night he was to be maintained in good condition.

Before she had a chance to answer, the car was surrounded by boys. Taylor rolled down the window to speak to them. "Good afternoon, sir," the nearest boy said. "We thought we'd get organized and get all four cars out of here. We'll start with the first car down the hill. That will give us a better chance to horse the others around as we come down, right? Are you with us?"

"Right," Taylor said and began to roll up his window.

"Just a minute," Grace said. She leaned across Taylor to speak out the window. The boys crowded around for a good look at her. "What my husband means," she said—Taylor was struck dumb and motionless at that, and she was leaning negligently on his knee besides, her hair brushing his cheek. "What he means is that he's with you in spirit, but the fact is that he's ruptured and can't do that sort of work no matter how much he'd like to. You see how it is."

"Sure," said one of the boys who had not spoken before.

"That's tough," said another.

"Of course," said the one who had been spokesman and whom Taylor had privately labeled Fraternity President. "Can we count on you to drive, sir, if we need you, that is, while the rest of us push?"

"Absolutely," Grace said, quickly sensing that Taylor wasn't going to reply. Taylor, in fact, had not heard the question. He was no longer aware even that he was being smothered by her perfume, her hair, her soft weight against him, a death which he had been contemplating with delight all day up to that very moment.

He was not aware of his surroundings even when she had rolled up the window and withdrawn. "I'm sorry," she said, touching his sleeve.

"That's all right," he said automatically. He also performed the gesture of patting her hand without having to return to the full unpleasantness of consciousness.

"I didn't want to do that," she said. "I knew it would hurt you—as if you needed to prove anything to those kids—"

"No, it's really all right, Betty," he said, making an effort to reassure her and turning toward her. He felt as if he had run into something in the dark when he saw that it was not actually his wife who was reading his wife's lines. He remembered vividly that he had called her by his wife's name. "That's done it," he said.

"What?" she said.

"On top of everything else, calling you by the wrong name."

"Don't think about it," she said. "In fact under the circumstances it might even be a sort of compliment, but I really don't mind anyway. I'm the one really who owes you apologies."

"No, no," he said. He had withdrawn from her as far as possible. "You did absolutely the right thing. I shouldn't have forced you to do it. It was nothing but my vanity. You were right about that."

"And men laugh at women for dressing to please other women," she said. He could tell that she would have laughed if he had been able to give her the least encouragement. "What does a thing like that matter?"

This succeeded in diverting his attention but probably not as she had intended to divert it. He wanted to ask her how she knew about that old rupture although he was aware there was only one way she could have heard of it. The whole question of what women talk about among themselves came up before him, and bitterly he faked a quotation he couldn't quite remember. "I had a gossip," he said, "and one friend more/That if my husband had but pissed against a wall/I must have run to tell them of it all."

"Well," she said, "is *that* the Finnesburh Fragment?"

"No," he said, "it's the Wife of Bath, who knew more about men and women than anybody. She had five husbands, you know."

"It's not very nice to have anybody know—" She broke off in some confusion. "When things begin to go wrong," she said, "they just go wrong."

"No," he said, "it will still be all right. Why, they've got one car out already and are working on the next. We'll be back in Williamstown in an hour, and if we have to stay there, why, then, we stay there and leave for Albany very early in the morning." He knew he wasn't being very realistic about it because the Model A had been no trouble at all, but now, with the second car, the boys were already floundering in the snow and showing signs of exhaustion.

"We'll see," she said. "I'd rather be in Albany tonight if possible though."

"We'll do it barring an act of God," he said.

It was very nearly dark when the boys came back to Taylor's car. "Would you mind," the Fraternity President said, "if we get into your car to rest awhile before we tackle our own car? We don't have a heater."

"By all means," Taylor said, "and, look, I've got some whiskey in the trunk. Let me get it."

"We wouldn't say no," said one of the boys who had already climbed into the back seat.

The moment Taylor stuck his head out the door, the wind whipped off his hat. Before anyone could move a step, the hat had sailed down the road, over the snow bank, and out across the valley. Taylor watched it go until it disappeared far below in the snow and dark. "Beautiful," he said. "The most pleasure I've ever had from any hat I've ever owned." His ears felt cold at once, but he thought he was behaving very well. Then he realized that none of the boys had been wearing hats all the while. "Let me get the whiskey," he said.

When he came back with the whiskey, he found the doors closed and the car full. The Rose Bowl game was on again. The Fraternity President was sitting at the wheel. "I thought," the President said, "that you might not mind holding your wife on your lap for a while."

"Oh," Taylor said, "no, of course not."

"Well, I mind" Grace said. "An old married woman like me doesn't get as many chances as all that to sit on young men's laps. You might have asked me. And so, dear, with your permission—"

"Or without it, I dare say," Taylor dared say bitterly.

"Never," she said, laughing. "Now if this gentleman will be so kind as to accommodate me—" She indicated the boy next to her on the seat.

"Speak up, clown," the Fraternity President said.

"Sure," the boy said.

"He says he is honored, madam," the President said.

"Tell him thank you," she said.

"OK," the President said.

"OK," the boy said.

"He says he is quite at your convenience."

She slid onto the boy's lap and the President slid from behind the wheel and Taylor got in out of the cold. He passed Grace the full bottle, out of courtesy, of course, but at the same time he knew he would be able to tell if she was cheating on the drink. Part of his pleasure had been based on the idea of plying her with drink. In fact, that was almost as good as the Mann Act.

She took the bottle and punished it like a man and passed it on, neglecting even the delicacy of a cough and a goddamn, to the boy on whose lap she was sitting. His face had become suddenly very red against the darkness of her coat, and when he drank, he choked and the tears stood in his eyes. He did not omit the goddamn.

The President did not drink but passed the bottle into the back seat, and when it came to him again, he urged it on Taylor as if the bottle had been his own. Taylor felt a stab of irritation and very nearly said, Goddamn it, it's *my* whiskey. But he felt ultimately that he was obliged to demonstrate—if only to himself—the superiority of his manners. He allowed the President to drink last.

"Go, Alabama," the President said as he raised the bottle on high.

"Go, Jinx," the others chorused as if they had been drilled to it.

"It's not too late," the President said. He drank. It was, in fact, much too late. Even Taylor knew it, and he never paid attention to such things as football.

"They're our boys," the others said chorally.

As the second round of drinks began, Grace gave the "Go, Alabama," and was applauded. She asked to be taught an Alabama song and learned with unconvincing difficulty a song that seemed to be mostly about corn likker and arson. At least Taylor was unconvinced although the boys were enchanted.

"Let's go, men," the President shouted, and in very short order, Taylor and Grace were alone in the car while the boys bounded through the snow yelling, "Go, go, go."

"Confess now," Taylor said. "You knew that song."

"Of course," she said. "Even my sweet little freshmen know it. They think it's very daring. We encourage them to think so."

"Apparently the boys are encouraged to think so too," he said, "but I had never heard it."

"Really?" she said. "From the way you were trying to catch my eye, I thought maybe that song was the Finnesburh Fragment."

"Now that you mention it, it is very Anglo-Saxon in mood—a getting drunk, boasting, burning down the mead hall sort of thing."

"Then what were you trying to catch my eye about?"

Taylor had to grope for a moment back to the time when all the boys were in the car. Once they were gone he had forgotten all the irritation they had caused. It infuriated him now that he was unable to cherish a manly anger, and he said with rather more heat than he intended, "I thought you were being pretty hard on the kid under you," he said.

"*I* was being hard on *him*?" she said. "That's a laugh."

"You couldn't see his face," Taylor said. "He was embarrassed. He was very uncomfortable."

"I didn't have to see his face. He was enjoying it all right."

"Christ," Taylor said, "the famous feminine intuition never knows a goddamn thing about what a man enjoys or when or how he enjoys it."

"Well, I'll tell you something," she said. "The famous feminine intuition can tell in a minute who was really being given a hard time."

"Me?" Taylor said. "Don't make me laugh. What's it to me if you want to act like a giddy freshman on her first football weekend?"

"I don't know what it is to you, but you sure are making it something."

"Look here," Taylor said. He could have gone on as far as "if you think for one minute that," hoping for some inspiration before he ran out of words, but he was saved by shouts from the boys, who were having some trouble with their own car.

Their car was stopped further down the slope now and backed into the snow bank. The boys were crowding around the back of the car and looking at something that was hidden from Taylor's car. "It looks as if they have hit something," Taylor said.

"Perhaps someone is hurt," Grace said. One of the boys was already floundering up toward them, and Taylor and Grace were both out of the car when he got there.

"Let me have the whiskey," he panted. Taylor turned to get it. "An accident."

"I'll take it down," Grace said. "I know first aid. Is he badly hurt?"

"Don't know," the boy called back over his shoulder as he ran ahead of them down the trail.

They found that the car had pushed one of the boys into the snow bank and held him there so that he couldn't even move his arms. "Are you in pain?" Grace asked. The boy, who was obviously terrified, shook his head. Grace tried to pass him the bottle but couldn't reach him.

"Here," one of the boys said. He took the bottle and got into the car and, leaning out the window, held it for the imprisoned boy to drink. He drank as if he was very thirsty, and he did not cough and only added goddamn as an afterthought.

"That's the spirit," Grace said.

"Can't you move the car away enough to get him out?" Taylor said.

"We don't know where his legs are," the President said. "We're afraid to spin the wheels."

"Quite," Taylor said to his own surprise, and he lost track of things for a minute until he realized that Americans he knew didn't get into spots like this, but Englishmen were always doing it in novels and movies.

"We're afraid he may be broken up already," the President said in a lowered voice, "but we don't want to upset him more than he is already."

"Just right," Grace said. "How're you feeling, boy?" she called.

The boy in the snow smiled wanly. One of the others called, "Old Horse is resting. He'll take a deep breath in a minute and move it away with his chest." The others laughed very loudly.

"All right," the President said. "Up on the snow bank and let's dig him out."

In ten minutes they had the boy out and were helping him to stand in the road. They were examining him as if he were something they had just unpacked from a crate that had arrived in bad condition. They moved his arms and legs and watched his face for signs of pain. There seemed to be nothing wrong with him although he could scarcely stand and didn't respond to any questions.

"Old Horse is just tired," the President said. Then in a lower voice but still loud enough for the boy to hear he said, "He's been working more than any two of the rest."

"I'll take him up to our car and get him warm," Grace said. "Come along, Horse." She took the boy's arm to lead him away, but he shook off her hand and began to follow the car, which the other boys were moving down the trail back into Massachusetts.

"I hope they come to get us out," Taylor said when he and Grace were back in the warm car.

"Of course, they will," Grace said. "What an idea."

"They're mad I didn't help," Taylor said. "And now this. They'll blame me. You'll see."

"That's all in your mind," Grace said. "Look," she said, "I'm sorry about sitting in that kid's lap. I thought I was playing the old married woman to the hilt. I thought it would amuse you. I thought you'd be as pleased with me as I was."

"I see," Taylor said. "I didn't see then, but I see now. It's really all right. I just wish I could go back over it again and laugh in the right place." He didn't feel at all like laughing as he began to understand the vast sadness of the gap between his game of the Mann Act and her game of the old married couple, but he did feel a new and very different tenderness toward her. He wondered how much of all that she knew. "I really feel as if we have been married for a long long time," he said. Then, carried away, he added what he thought for a moment might not be a lie, "I think really I was upset at the thought we hadn't been."

"Oh, Ross—" she said. She put her hand on his sleeve, but he didn't trust himself to touch her, not there, not then, not any longer.

"It's just too bad," she said.

"Please, don't touch me," he said. His hands clutched the wheel as they had all day.

She withdrew her hand but was still near him on the seat. Then he heard the boys coming up the trail. He hurriedly put his arm around her shoulders and gave her a gentle squeeze. It really was like squeezing a woman he had been married to for a long long time: they had been through a lot together and small signs meant much. When the boys began to appear out of the gloom, he put his hands back on the wheel.

"We'll laugh about this some time," she said.

Taylor was glad it was dark because he wasn't laughing then. He could feel his eyes brimming, and he was afraid the tears would start to shine down his cheeks at any minute. They didn't—not then and not on the long ride up through a corner of Vermont and down to the Albany station and not even at the station where she caught last night's train coming through six hours late—and that at least was something.

He thought about that day on every New Year's for the rest of his life and at strange moments in between, but he never once laughed about it.

The Son of the Sad Fat Wordman Goes North

RALPH DENNIS

from *Lillabulero*

"For instance, Blankbin, the nun, was constantly tormented by the thought of what could have become of that part of Christ which was removed in circumcision."

Psychopathia Sexualis

"The modern tragic hero is a man committed to something which he knows in his own heart to be absurd."

Life, Art and Tragedy
Abraham Burgess

2/1/62

This afternoon . . . late afternoon . . . I married Miss Clarissa Vauxhall Hedgefox in an empty Baptist church just off Franklin Street. A cold rainy Chapel Hill day with the bare dark trees slick with a sugary thin ice. And the coeds walking up and down the street, while Clarissa and I waited under the colonial portico of the church for Reverend Sandwich to arrive, had legs that were roast beef pink with razor burn. Clarissa, huddled against my soaked raincoat, said, "In a few minutes it will be against the law for you to look at other girls." And smiled. I, with a rare show of wit, blew on her glasses until they fogged and asked, "What other girls?"

To be exact, the church was not empty. There were two witnesses as the law requires. Or is it God? One we had not planned upon, a Mrs. Lelia Earp, was in the church already, in answer to the sign on the church lawn, PRAY AGAINST

THE BOMB 9-5, and stayed at our request, crying throughout the service with all the energy and pride of a professional mourner. The second witness was Clarissa's mother, Edna Vauxhall Hedgefox, a thin stately Southern lady who looks at the world through the venom of a single eye, the empty socket of the other eye covered by a white satin eyepatch trimmed with black sequins. Clarissa told me a few days ago, with a certain misplaced glee, that her mother lost the eye on the day Clarissa was conceived: on a hot August noon while her mother and father waited for the tea to steep, on a bed where minutes before the mother had been crocheting lace doilies. It was, according to Clarissa, the high point in their connubial bliss . . . before it vanished forever.

The Reverend Arthur Sandwich. Think of teeth the color and texture of blue cheese. A nose the shape and hue of a dry gourd. A Phi Beta Kappa key worn purposely upside down as a tie clasp. A dog-eared copy of *Fear and Trembling* sticking out of his right suitcoat pocket. And a voice that rattled about in the dry gourd nose, the words like so many seeds, so that I, wanting to treasure every moment of the ceremony, heard none of it.

On the way down the steps, afterwards, Clarissa and I dodged the fluttering scraps of a letter Mrs. Earp threw at us in place of rice, while she shouted, "Have a lot of strong healthy children with good bones." At the bottom step, I turned to catch a scrap of paper, just in time to hear Edna Vauxhall Hedgefox say to the Reverend Sandwich: "Mark my words. The first child is going to be born a little long in the teeth." Which puzzled me until Clarissa explained to me on our wet bridal march to my basement that long teeth are an inherited trait from the Vauxhall side of the family.

It was a whirlwind courtship. Even Clarissa, who is more romantic than I am because she is a woman, could not get over how surprising it was. I had only known her 18 days, having met her for the first time on the afternoon I kept my appointment with Mr. Criscomb of B.B.D. and O. at the Carolina Inn.

FROM THE JOURNAL ENTRY THAT DAY. 1/11/62 EVENING
Mr. Criscomb and I faced each other across a low narrow table, while a younger man, Mr. Browninhouser, sat behind me and to my right taking notes in an ornate leather clipboard.

I am not certain how well I did. It is hard, looking back on the hour, to establish any kind of rules that might help in a judgment of success or failure. But there was one problem, a moment when I failed in the interview protocol. The lighter I had found on the street a week before and had displayed proudly just before we were seated . . . suddenly gave out of fluid and I had brought no matches. Still, doggedly, each time Mr. Criscomb offered me a cigarette from his silver case I whipped out my lighter and grind, grind, grind . . . sparks but no flame. Behind me, the chair squeaked as Mr. Browninhouser leaned forward to register a notation on his clipboard. Each time it sounded like a small ordinary "x." After Mr. Criscomb had lit our cigarettes for the second time, he leaned back in his chair and burped delicately.

"For your personal file," he said.
"Age?" "Thirty-six."
"Occupation?" "Writer."
"Weight?" "Two hundred and forty-seven."
"Height?" "Five-feet-ten."
"And . . ." Mr. Criscomb looked beyond me at the gray winter afternoon.
" . . . and under Other Physical Remarks balding."
Mr. Browninhouser's pen scratched out b-a-l-d and stopped. Only when I
turned in my chair to look at him did he lift his pen once more and add i-n-g.
"Advertising experience?" "None."
"Publication?" "None."
"College degrees and honorary societies?" "None."
"Civic club memberships?" "None."
"Page three." And after Mr. Browninhouser had turned two pages: "Why do
you want to work for B.B.D. and O.?"
"Because you have the best advertising agency in the world."
Mr. Criscomb leaned forward and shook his head.
"Because I like advertising."
Another shake of his head.
"Because I like New York."
"No, the real reason."
"Because I am tired of living in a basement. Because I am tired of being a
failure."
Mr. Criscomb frowned and Mr. Browninhouser, without making a mark, closed
his clipboard with a loud leathery smack. Like two shoes kissing each other.

Later. A strange and wonderful thing happened to me. In front of the Armpit
Cafe, head down, swinging my arms proudly, having decided to make myself
somebody, to work my way up to the office of President of B.B.D. and O., I
bumped into a girl. My body, the part that touched her, felt like a hand that had
pressed an exquisite, ripe plum. Her name, it seems, is Clarissa Hedgefox. A
face with the delicate bones of a small child. And hyperthyroid eyes with the
luminous gleam of stars in moving water . . . Clarissa? I love that part of her at
once, because it is the name of my favorite heroine. But the question is: am I her
Lovelace?

1/12/62
No letter from Mr. Criscomb.
In the evening it sleeted and I decided not to walk to the A and P to see what the
trucks left outside. I might break a leg and I feel I ought to keep myself whole in
case I ever see Clarissa again.

A PROSE POEM FOR CLARISSA
In Catholic folklore/a Saint Teresa pursued by/the hot hound of a young
man,/but loving only God wrote asking/what he loved about her, and he
replied,/"your eyes," plucked them out and sent them/on a silver platter to
him. . . ./And so, Clarissa, if you loved some part/of me . . . my skinny lean
heart . . ./I would tear it out and send it to you/by special messenger.

1/13/62

Today I met Clarissa on the street and in the conversation (I'm not sure how it came up) she said she thought I was handsome.
Even the lion part of me that won't lie, that will not leave me one dream, wants to believe it. And I, standing in front of a mirror like an idiot I knew who stood in front of a mirror and crushed a rose in his right hand and thought, from the reflection, that he crushed the rose in his left hand, say that the reflection lies and I may, after all, be handsome.

1/28/62

Tonight I asked Clarissa to marry me. . . .
As I remember, she said, "I would like to marry a writer and live in a room full of beautiful words."
I said, "Would you?"
She said, "Yes, I'll marry you." And sighed.

2/1/62

The wedding night. Clarissa will not allow me to write about it. I can only say:
1. It was beautiful and holy.
2. She wore a "Vision of Venus" negligee designed by Lili St. Cyr of Hollywood. That it was sheer as a cloud and trimmed with lace.
3. That she does not believe in birth control.
4. That we drank one bottle of champagne.
5. That the object of marriage is to have children.

2/2/62

Today I began a book on Love. My thoughts on love choking me. . . .
To be titled: LOVE IN A SKINNY WORLD.
Excerpts:
page one: "It is not as Plato said, not halves seeking halves, but Wholes and Cripples. Wholes seeking Wholes and Cripples seeking Cripples. A boy I knew who years ago his mother made take toe-dancing (and remained a toe-dancer all his life) married a nice young girl named Emily Dunn and two weeks later his wife ran off with the Bridesmaid . . . but when Wholes marry Wholes it is different . . . ."
page two: "The death of the heart is the beginning of wisdom." *Note:* I wrote it down as it came off the top of my head (as Mr. Criscomb might say) and I left it with the hope that it might assume a meaning.
page 3A: "Married sex . . . and I can speak of it with some authority, with Clarissa's permission . . . is the spasmodic death of the heart with the resulting birth of the soul."
Note: but what does this birth of the soul have to do with wisdom?
page 4: "A man I know spent twenty years worrying about who he was and what he was and what he had to offer a woman if he loved her . . . until he had only the proof of the twenty years of worry to offer: an ulcer and diet of baby food. F. Scott Fitzgerald in his notebooks: 'Action is Character.' What a man does is what he is and what he is is all he can offer. For example: A room full of beautiful words."

2/3/62
We have conceived. Clarissa is certain. A boy, she thinks.

2/6/62
Clarissa saw the doctor today and there is no doubt. Modern methods of detection astound me. Me a father! And Clarissa, knowing more than I do (having counted on nine of my fingers and reached November) tells me that sometimes first children come early, even months early. Which takes, if it happens, some of the worry and waiting out of it.

2/7/62
A light snow as we lay on the bed talking about Jane Austen. A wind that beat against the window like a fist. Then a moment that I will remember as long as I live. My hand was loose and easy across her plum ripe and grape swollen stomach when suddenly, from inside her, something kicked out at me.
Clarissa saw me jerk my hand away. "Your son," she said and laughing at me, "is talking to you."
All night . . . awake or half-awake . . . I waited. Until the alarm clock went off and Clarissa awoke and left for work.
All night . . . and he'd had nothing more to say.

3/2/62
I tell myself that marriage is a series of experiences. One has to be understanding if one can. If it is possible. This afternoon, I was alone, working on LOVE IN A SKINNY WORLD, page 163. I was out of paper and I needed to write down a thought. The thought: "In South Carolina folklore, there is a belief that ghosts, when they leave their graves, step out of their outer skins, fold them neatly over the head stones . . . and then go haunting. The way to get rid of a ghost is to go down to the graveyard and find the right grave stone (and therefore the right outer skin) and salt the inside of the skin. The ghost, returning to the grave just before dawn, steps back into the skin, only to find an agony that he cannot bear. In the same way, the lover has to lose his outer skin and offer himself as a vulnerable being. Only in the trust of his vulnerability can the lover offer himself completely. In the self-protective, the defensive, there is an implied negation."
In the search for paper I opened a suitcase that belonged to Clarissa. It is not a thing I would usually do. Afterwards I was ashamed . . . inside, on top, were three used diaphragms and fifty copies of movie magazines, all dealing with different aspects of the Liz Taylor-Richard Burton affair before the marriage. All dog-eared, with pages turned down here and there and passages underlined in red ink. The sick love, the love out of control, is not what I want. It frightens me to find that Clarissa might have such interests. But she is young and I must try not to wear the outer skin.
I do not understand the three used diaphragms.

4/5/62
The child (my son) seems to have fallen lower. This morning as Clarissa dressed for work I watched her while I pretended sleep. I was reminded of the

beauty of a D. H. Lawrence poem about watching his wife, Frieda, taking a sponge bath. "Dijon Roses"?

It is a different beauty . . . the beauty of the mother-to-be. Both the sexual violence of the wife and the tenderness of the mother-to-be mixed and stirred together. All this beauty for someone who does not, and cannot, deserve it.

7/1/62

I am a father. As of 4:23 this afternoon. A premature boy that weighed ten pounds and 3 ounces. Clarissa is doing well and the boy is beautiful. Very beautiful: he does not look like either of us.

Clarissa wants to call him Boyd Jay after an uncle on her mother's side of the family. Of course I agreed. There will be other sons to name Henry James, Stendhal, and Sherwood Anderson. Daughters to name Emily Bronte and Jane Austen.

A POEM FOR MY SON
Beautiful Child,
Issue of verbal loins:
The word has a truth that
The picture and the rotten heart
Do not.
Find the right noun,
The proper verb
And the object is always truth.

7/23/62

There is a man always around the house when I come home from work. From the job I've taken washing dishes. I will not let this be salt under my skin. It bothers me that he is always wearing a wet suit and an aqualung . . . even if it is not raining outside.

His name is B. J. Frankenhiemer. In my least rational moments, when I fight to keep the salt away, I think of him as the bald-headed fish.

Still, I tell myself that a house full of beautiful words might not be enough for a lively girl like Clarissa. The other 20% has to be freedom.

From LOVE IN A SKINNY WORLD, page 543: "Love is not a trial. Who can be advocates for which side when there is only a middle?"

8/4/62

Clarissa has left me for the scuba diver, B. J. Frankenhiemer. When I came home this afternoon I found Boyd Jay in the crib with three bottles of prepared formula carefully stacked beside him.

And a note from Clarissa pinned on a wet diaper which was hanging on the side of the crib:

"Your love is not enough. Beautiful words suck. The world is full of men and some swim better than others. (You're right: that's a sexual allusion.) Richard Burton is twice the man you are."

Liz Taylor

LT/cvh
cc: Boyd J. Frankenhiemer

The cvh leads me to think that she has gone back to her maiden name. The postscript: "You're fatfatfatfat . . . fat. So there."

At the A and P store, in the Chapel Hill stillness after midnight, a pickup truck unloaded bunches of fresh flowers. Remembering Ezra Pound and his assault on the tulip tree blossoms I ate the petals from a bunch of blue corn flowers so that I could believe that there was something inside of me that was beautiful. And returned home with a gallon of milk and a loaf of warm bread.

Later, stretched out on the bed that was too large for me now, listening to Boyd Jay snore in the crib, emptying my head for the day of camel-sized memories that would not go through the eyes of needles, the lion part of me that has only lied once said: "Finish the ratsuck book."

On page 678 of LOVE IN A SKINNY WORLD, in a shaky Palmer penmanship that would have horrified Miss Emilia Grayson, my sixth-grade teacher, I wrote, "It is all a lie."

8/15/62

This morning when I was paid I offered to work out my two weeks notice. It seemed to be the honorable gesture. The owner, Big Jim Mallard, after looking at Boyd Jay who was asleep on the salad counter with one foot in the lettuce and the other in the chicken salad, said that it was not necessary. It was honorable of me, but not necessary.

At the bus station, with Boyd Jay asleep and bubbling on my shoulder, I told the man at the ticket counter that I was thinking of going somewhere.

"Where?"

Touching my son who must have a good childhood and the best advantages: "Where it snows more than three times a year."

"New York?"

"No." I had heard that the snow in New York is dirty even before it hits the sidewalks.

"Washington? Boston? Cleveland?"

"They don't sound interesting."

A line was forming behind me. "Well, look, when you decide where you want to go. . . ," he broke off as Boyd Jay awoke and turned to look at him. "Where else? Where else?" He seemed to be thinking. "You know, today a kid came in and bought a ticket to New Haven." He leaned across the counter and lowered his voice. "That's where Yale is." A Chapel Hill where it snows more than three times a year?

On the outside chance it might be true I bought the tickets. At the A and P bunches of flowers again. I decided not to eat any of them. It is phony to act like you are beautiful inside when you aren't. . . .

8/16/62

As the bus turned down Franklin Street (settled in for the long ride with the diaper pail between my feet) I saw Clarissa and Boyd J. Frankenhiemer standing in front of the Intimate Bookshop. They were both wearing wet suits and aqualungs. And breathed through snorkels in their rigid mouths. It was not raining at all.

"Wave to your mama, Boyd Jay," I said. "Wave your mama goodbye." But Boyd Jay, either because he didn't want to look or because he doesn't understand English yet, after a casual look at Clarissa, turned instead and waved at me.

THE GUEST

STANLEY ELKIN

from *Paris Review*

On Sunday, Bertie walked into an apartment building in St. Louis, a city where, in the past, he had changed trains, waited for buses, or thought about Klaff, and where, more recently, truckers dropped him, or traveling salesmen stopped their Pontiacs downtown just long enough for him to reach into the back seat for his trumpet case and get out. In the hallway he stood before the brass mailboxed wall seeking the name of his friend, his friends' friend really, and his friends' friend's wife. The girl had danced with him at parties in the college town, and one night—he imagined he must have been particularly pathetic, engagingly pathetic—she had kissed him. The man, of course, patronized him, asked him questions that would have been more vicious had they been less naïve. He remembered he rather enjoyed making his long, patient answers. Condescension always brought the truth out of him. It was more appealing than indifference at least, and more necessary to him now. He supposed he didn't care for either of them, but he couldn't go further. He had to rest or he would die.

He found the name on the mailbox—Mr. and Mrs. Richard Preminger—the girl's identity, as he might have guessed, swallowed up in the husband's. It was no way to treat women, he thought gallantly.

He started up the stairs. Turning the corner at the second landing, he saw a man moving cautiously downward, burdened by boxes and suitcases and loose bags. Only as they passed each other did Bertie, through a momentary clearing in the boxes, recognize Richard Preminger.

"Old man, old man," Bertie said.

"Just a minute," Preminger said, forcing a package aside with his chin. Bertie stood, half a staircase above him, leaning against the wall. He grinned in the shadows, conscious of his ridiculous fedora, his eye patch rakishly black against the soft whiteness of his face. Black-suited, tiny, white-fleshed, he posed above Preminger, dapper as a scholarly waiter in a restaurant. He waited until he was recognized.

"Bertie? Bertie? Let me get rid of this stuff. Give me a hand, will you?" Preminger said.

"Sure," Bertie said. "It's on my family crest. One hand washing the other. Here, wait a minute." He passed Preminger on the stairs and held the door for him. He followed him outside.

"Take the key from my pocket, Bertie, and open the trunk. It's the blue convertible."

Bertie put his hand in Preminger's pocket. "You've got nice thighs," he said. To irritate Preminger he pretended to try to force the house key into the trunk lock. Preminger stood impatiently behind him, balancing his heavy burdens. "I've been to Dallas, lived in a palace," Bertie said over his shoulder. "There's this great Eskimo who blows down there. Would you believe he's cut the best side ever recorded of 'Mood Indigo'?" Bertie shook the key ring as if it were a castanet.

Preminger dumped his load on the hood of the car and took the keys from Bertie. He opened the trunk and started to throw things into it. "Going somewhere?" Bertie asked.

"Vacation," Preminger said.

"Oh," Bertie said.

Preminger looked toward the apartment house. "I've got to go up for another suitcase, Bertie."

"Sure," Bertie said.

He went up the stairs behind Preminger. About halfway up he stopped to catch his breath. Preminger watched him curiously. He pounded his chest with his tiny fist and grinned weakly. *"Mea culpa,"* he said. "Mea booze. Mea sluts. Mea pot. Me-o-mea."

"Come on," Preminger said.

They went inside and Bertie heard a toilet flushing. Through a hall, through an open door, he saw Norma, Preminger's wife, staring absently into the bowl. "If she moves them now you won't have to stop at God knows what kind of place along the road," Bertie said brightly.

Norma lifted a big suitcase easily in her big hands and came into the living room. She stopped when she saw Bertie. "Bertie! Richard, it's Bertie."

"We bumped into each other in the hall," Preminger said.

Bertie watched the two of them look at each other.

"You sure picked a time to come visiting, Bertie," Preminger said.

"We're leaving on our vacation, Bertie," Norma said.

"We're going up to New England for a couple of weeks," Preminger told him.

"We can chat for a little with Bertie, can't we, Richard, before we go?"

"Of course," Preminger said. He sat down and pulled the suitcase next to him.

"It's very lovely in New England." Bertie sat down and crossed his legs. "I don't get up there very regularly. Not my territory. I've found that when a man makes it in the Ivy League he tends to forget about old Bertie," he said sadly.

"What are you doing in St. Louis, Bertie?" Preminger's wife asked him.

"It's my Midwestern swing," Bertie said. "I've been down South on the southern sponge. Opened up a whole new territory down there." He heard himself cackle.

"Who did you see, Bertie?" Norma asked him.

"You wouldn't know her. A cousin of Klaff's."

"Were you living with her?" Preminger asked.

Bertie shook his finger at him. The Premingers stared glumly at each other. Richard rubbed the plastic suitcase handle. In a moment, Bertie thought, he would probably say, "Gosh, Bertie, you should have written. You should have let us know." He should have written! Did the Fuller Brush man write? Who would be home? Who *wouldn't* be on vacation? They were commandos, the Fuller Brush man and he. He was tired, sick. He couldn't move on today. Would they kill him because of their lousy vacation?

Meanwhile the Premingers weren't saying anything. They stared at each other openly, their large eyes in their large heads on their large necks largely. He thought he could wait them out. It was what he *should* do. It should have been the easiest thing in the world to wait out the Premingers, to stare them down. Who was he kidding? It wasn't his forte. He had no forte. *That* was his forte. He could already hear himself begin to speak.

"Sure," he said. "I almost married that girl. Klaff's lady cousin. The first thing she ever said to me was, 'Bertie, they never build drugstores in the middle of the block. Always on corners.' It was the truth. Well, I thought, this was the woman for me. One time she came out of the ladies' john of a Greyhound bus station and she said, 'Bertie, have you ever noticed how public toilets often smell like bubble gum?' That's what it was like all the time. She had all these institutional insights. I was sure we could make it together. It didn't work out." He sighed.

Preminger stared at him, but Norma was beginning to soften. He wondered randomly what she would be like in bed. He looked coolly at her long legs, her wide shoulders. Like Klaff's cousin: institutional.

"Bertie, how are your eyes now?" she asked.

"Oh," he said, "still seeing double." He smiled. "Two for one. It's all right when there's something to look at. Other times I use the patch."

Norma seemed sad.

"I have fun with it," he said. "It doesn't make any difference which eye I cover. I'm ambidextrous." He pulled the black elastic band from his forehead. Instantly there were two large Richards, two large Normas. The Four Premingers like a troupe of Jewish acrobats. He felt surrounded. In the two living rooms his four hands fumbled with the two patches. He felt sick to his stomach. He closed one eye and hastily replaced the patch. "I shouldn't try that on an empty stomach."

Preminger watched him narrowly. "Gee, Bertie, maybe we could drop you some place."

It was out of the question. He couldn't get into a car again. "Do you go through Minneapolis, Minnesota?" he asked indifferently.

Preminger looked confused, and Bertie liked him for a moment. "We were going to catch the Turnpike up around Chicago, Bertie."

"Oh, Chicago," Bertie said. "I can't go back to Chicago yet."

Preminger nodded.

"Don't you know anybody else in St. Louis?" Norma asked.

"Klaff used to live across the river, but he's gone," Bertie said.

"Look, Bertie . . ." Preminger said.

"I'm fagged," Bertie said hopelessly, "locked out."

"Bertie," Preminger said, "do you need any money? I could let you have twenty dollars."

Bertie put his hand out mechanically.

"This is stupid," Norma said suddenly. "Stay *here.*"

"Oh, well—"

"No, I mean it. Stay *here.* We'll be gone for two weeks. What difference does it make?"

Preminger looked at his wife for a moment and shrugged. "Sure," he said, "there's no reason you *couldn't* stay here. As a matter of fact you'd be doing us a favor. I forgot to cancel the newspaper, the milk. You'd keep the burglars off. They don't bother a place if it looks lived in." He put twenty dollars on the coffee table. "There might be something you need," he explained.

Bertie looked carefully at them both. They seemed to mean it. Preminger and his wife grinned at him steadily, relieved at how easily they had come off. He enjoyed the idea himself. At last he had a real patron, a real matron. "Okay," he said.

"Then it's settled," Preminger said, rising.

"It's all right?" Bertie said.

"Certainly it's all right," Preminger said. "What harm could you do?"

"I'm harmless," Bertie said.

Preminger picked up the suitcase and led his wife toward the door. "Have a good time," Bertie said, following them. "I'll watch things for you. Rrgghh! Rrrgghhfff!"

Preminger waved back at him as he went down the stairs. "Hey," Bertie called, leaning over the banister, "did I tell you about that crazy Klaff? You know what nutty Klaff did out at U.C.L.A.? He became a second-story man." They were already down the stairs.

Bertie pressed his back against the door and turned his head slowly across his left shoulder. He imagined himself photographed from underneath. "Odd man in," he said. He bounded into the center of the living room. I'll bet there's a lease, he thought. I'll bet there's a regular lease that goes with this place. He considered this respectfully, a little awed. He couldn't remember ever having been in a place where the tenants actually had to sign a lease. In the dining room he turned on the chandelier lights. "Sure there's a lease," Bertie said. He hugged himself. "How the fallen are mighty," he said.

In the living room he lay down on the couch without taking off his shoes. He sat up and pulled them off, but when he lay down again he was uneasy. He had gotten out of the habit, living the way he did, of sleeping without shoes. In his friends' leaseless basements the nights were cold and he wore them for warmth. He put the shoes on again, but found that he wasn't tired any more. It was a fact that dependence gave him energy. He was never so alert as when people did him favors. It was having to be on your own that made you tired.

"Certainly," Bertie said to the committee, "it's scientific. We've suspected it for years, but until our researchers divided up the town of Bloomington, Indiana, we had no proof. What our people found in that community was that the orphans and bastards were sleepy and run down, while the housewives and people on relief were wide awake, alert, raring to go. We can't positively state the link yet, but we're fairly certain it's something to do with dependency— in league perhaps with a particularly virulent form of gratitude. Ahem. Ahem."

As he lectured the committee he wandered around the apartment, touring from right to left. He crossed from the living room into the dining room and turned right into the kitchen and then right again into Preminger's small study. "Here's where all the magic happens," Bertie said, glancing at the contour chair near Preminger's desk. He went back into the kitchen. "Here's where all the magic happens," he said, looking at Norma's electric stove. He stepped into the dining room and continued on, passing Norma's paintings of picturesque side streets in Mexico, of picturesque side streets in Italy, of picturesque side streets in Puerto Rico, until he came to a door that led to the back sun parlor. He went through it and found himself in a room with an easel, with paints in sexy little tubes, with brushes, with palettes and turpentine and rags. "Here's where all the magic happens," Bertie said and walked around the room to another door. He opened it and was in the Premingers' master bedroom. He looked at the bed. "Here's where all the magic happens," he said. Through a door at the other end of the room was another small hall. On the right was the toilet. He went in and flushed it. It was one of those toilets with instantly renewable tanks. He flushed it again. And again. "The only kind to have," he said out of the side of his mouth, imagining a rental agent. "I mean, it's like this. Supposing the missus has diarrhea or something. You don't want to have to wait until the tank fills up. Or suppose you're sick. Or suppose you're giving a party and it's mixed company. Well, it's just corny to whistle to cover the noise, know what I mean? 'S jus' corny. On the other hand, you flush it once suppose you're not through, then what happens? There's the damn noise after the water goes down. What have you accomplished? This way"—he reached across and jiggled a little lever and then did it a second time, a third, a fourth—"you never have any embarrassing interim, what we in the trade call 'flush lag.'"

He found the guest bedroom and knew at once that he would never sleep in it, that he would sleep in the Premingers' big bed.

"Nice place you got here," he said when he had finished the tour.

"Dooing de woh eet ees all I tink of, what I fahting foe," the man from the Underground said. "Here ees eet fahrproof, air-condizione and safe from Nazis."

"Stay out of Volkswagens, kid," Bertie said.

He went back into the living room. He wanted music, but it was a cardinal principle with him never to blow alone. He would drink alone, take drugs alone, but somehow for him the depths of depravity were represented by having to play jazz alone. He had a vision of himself in a cheap hotel room sitting on the edge of an iron bedstead. Crumpled packages of cigarettes were scattered throughout the room. Bottles of gin were on top of the Gideon Bible, the Western Union blanks. His trumpet was in his lap. "Perfect," Bertie said.

"Norma Preminger could paint it in a picture."

The phonograph was in the hall between the dining room and living room. It was a big thing, with the AM and the FM and the short wave and the place where you plugged in the color television when it was perfected. He found records in Preminger's little room and went through them rapidly. "Ahmad Jamahl, for Christ's sake." Bertie took the record out of its sleeve and broke it across his knee. He stood up slowly and kicked the fragments of the broken recording into a neat pile.

He turned around and scooped up as many of Preminger's recordings as he could carry and brought them to the machine. He piled them on indiscriminately and listened with visible, professional discomfort. He listened to *The New World Symphony,* to Beethoven's *Fifth,* to *My Fair Lady.* The more he listened the more he began to dislike the Premingers. When he could stand it no longer he tore the playing arm viciously away from the record and looked around him. He saw the Premingers' bookcase.

"I'll read," Bertie said.

He took down the Marquis de Sade and Henry Miller and Ronald Firbank and turned the pages desultorily. Nothing happened. He tried reading aloud in front of a mirror. He went back to the bookcase and looked for *The Egg and I* and *Please Don't Eat the Daisies.* The prose of a certain kind of bright housewife always made Bertie feel erotic. But the Premingers owned neither book. He browsed through Rachel Carson's *Silent Spring* with his fly unzipped, but he felt only a mild lasciviousness.

He went into their bedroom and opened the closet. He found a pair of Norma's shoes and put them on. Although he was no fetishist, he had often promised himself that if he ever had the opportunity he would see what it was like. He got into drag and walked around the apartment in Norma's high heels. All he experienced was a pain in his calves.

In the kitchen he looked into the refrigerator. There were some frozen mixed vegetables in the freezer compartment. "I'll starve first," Bertie said.

He found a Billie Holiday record and put it on the phonograph. He hoped that out in Los Angeles, Klaff was being beaten with rubber hoses by the police. He looked up at the kitchen clock. "Nine," he said. "Only seven in L.A. They probably don't start beating them up till later."

"Talk, Klaff," he snarled, "or we'll drag you into the Blood Room."

"Flake off, copper," Klaff said.

"That's enough Klaff. Take that and that and that."

"Bird lives!" Bertie screamed suddenly, invoking the dead Charlie Parker. It was his code cry.

"Mama may have," Billie Holiday wailed, "Papa may have, but God Bless the child who's got his own, who—oo—zz—"

"Who—oo—zz," Bertie wailed.

"Got his own," Billie said.

"I'll tell him when he comes in, William," Bertie said.

He waited respectfully until Billie was finished and then turned off the music.

He wondered why so many people felt that Norman Mailer was the greatest living American novelist.

He sat down on the Premingers' coffee table and marveled at his being alone in so big and well-furnished an apartment. The Premingers were probably the most substantial people he knew. Though plenty of others wanted to, Bertie thought bitterly, Preminger was the only one from the old crowd who might make it. Of course he was Jewish, and that helped. Some Jews swung pretty good, but he always suspected that in the end they would hold out on you. But then who wouldn't, Bertie wondered. Kamikaze pilots, maybe. Anyway, this was Bertie's special form of anti-Semitism and he cherished it. Melvin Gimpel, for example, his old roommate. Every time Melvin tried to kill himself by sticking his head in the oven he left the kitchen window open. One time he found Gimpel on his knees with his head on the oven door, oddly like the witch in Hansel and Gretel. Bertie closed the window and shook Gimpel awake.

"Mel," he yelled, slapping him. *"Mel."*

"Bertie, go way. Leave me alone, I want to kill myself."

"Thank God," Bertie said. "Thank God I'm in time. When I found that window closed I thought it was all over."

"What, the window was closed? My God, was the *window* closed?"

> "Melvin Gimpel is so simple
> Thinks his nipple is a pimple,"

Bertie recited.

He hugged his knees, and felt again a wave of the nauseous sickness he had experienced that morning. "It's foreshadowing. One day as I'm shoveling my walk I will collapse and die."

When the nausea left him he thought again about his situation. He had friends everywhere and made his way from place to place like an old-time slave on the Underground Railway. For all the pathos of the figure he knew he deliberately cut, there were always people to do him favors, give him money, beer, drugs, to nurse him back to his normal state of semi-invalidism, girls to kiss him in the comforting way he liked. This was probably the first time he had been alone in months. He felt like a dog whose master has gone away for the weekend. Just then he heard some people coming up the stairs and he growled experimentally. He went down on his hands and knees and scampered to the door, scratching it with his nails. "Rrrgghhf," he barked. "Rrgghhfff!" He heard whoever it was fumbling to open a door on the floor below him. He smiled. "Good dog," he said. "Good dog, goodog, gudug. guduggudugggudug."

He whined. He missed his master. A tear formed in the corner of his left eye. He crawled to a full-length mirror in the bathroom. "Ahh," he said. "Ahh." Seeing the patch across his eye, he had an inspiration. "Here, Patch," he called. "Come on, Patch." He romped after his own voice.

He moved beside Norma Preminger's easel in the sun parlor. He lowered his body carefully, pushing himself slightly backward with his arms. He yawned. He touched his chest to the wooden floor. He wagged his tail and then let himself fall heavily on one side. He pulled his legs up under him and fell asleep.

When Bertie awoke he was hungry. He fingered the twenty dollars in his pocket that Preminger had given him. He could order out. The light in the hall where the phone and phone books were was not good, so he tore "Restaurants" from the Yellow Pages and brought the sheets with him into the living room. Only two places delivered after one A.M. It was already one-thirty. He dialed the number of a pizza place across the city.

"Pal, bring over a big one, half shrimp, half mushroom. And two six packs." He gave the address. The man explained that the truck had just gone out and that he shouldn't expect delivery for at least another hour and a half.

"Put it in a cab," Bertie said. "While Bird lives Bertie spends."

He took out another dozen or so records and piled them on the machine. He sat down on the couch and drummed his trumpet case with his fingers. He opened the case and fit the mouthpiece to the body of the horn. He put the trumpet to his lips and experienced the unpleasant shock of cold metal he always felt. He still thought it strange that men could mouth metal this way, ludicrous that his professional attitude should be a kiss. He blew a few bars in accompaniment to the record and then put the trumpet back in the case. He felt in the side pockets of the trumpet case and took out two pairs of dirty underwear, some handkerchiefs and three pairs of socks. He unrolled one of the pairs of socks and saw with pleasure that the drug was still there. He took out the bottle of carbon tetrachloride. This was what he cleaned his instrument with, and it was what he would use to kill himself when he had finally made the decision.

He held the bottle to the light. "If nothing turns up," he said, "I'll drink this. And to hell with the kitchen window."

The cab driver brought the pizza and Bertie gave him the twenty dollars.

"I can't change that," the driver said.

"Did I ask you to change it?" Bertie said.

"That's twenty bucks there."

"Bird lives. Easy come, easy go go go," Bertie said.

The driver started to thank him.

"Go." He pushed the man out and closed the door.

He spread Norma Preminger's largest tablecloth over the dining-room table and then, taking china and silver from the big breakfront, laid several place settings. He found champagne glasses and put another record on the phonograph.

Unwrapping the pizza, he carefully plucked all the mushrooms from it ("American mushrooms," he said. "Very square. No visions.") and laid them in a neat pile on the white linen. ("Many mushloom. Mushloom crowd.") He poured some beer into a champagne glass and rose slowly from his chair.

"Gentlemen," he said, "to the absent Klaff. May the police in Los Angeles, California, beat his lousy ass off." He drank off all the beer in one gulp and tossed the glass behind him over his shoulder. He heard it shatter and then a soft sizzling sound. Turning around, he saw that he had hit one of Norma's paintings right in a picturesque side street. Beer dripped down a donkey's leg. "Goddamn," Bertie said appreciatively, "*action* painting."

He ate perhaps a quarter of the pizza before rising from the table, wiping the corner of his lips with a big linen napkin. "Gentlemen," he said. "I propose that the ladies retire to the bedroom while we men enjoy our cigars and port and some good talk."

"I propose that we men retire to the bedroom and enjoy the ladies," he said in Gimpel's voice.

"Here, here," he said in Klaff's voice. "Here, here. Good talk. Good talk."

"If you will follow me, gentlemen," Bertie said in his own voice. He began to walk around the apartment. "I have often been asked the story of my life. These requests usually follow a personal favor someone has done me, a supper shared, a bed made available, a ride in one of the several directions. Indeed, I have become a sort of troubadour who does not sing so much as whine for his supper. Most of you—"

"Whine is very good with supper," Gimpel said.

"Gimpel, my dear, why don't you run into the kitchen and play?" Bertie said coolly. "Many of you may know the humble beginnings, the sordid details, the dark Freudian patterns, and those of you who are my friends—"

Klaff belched.

"Those of you who are my *friends,* who do not run off to mix it up with the criminal element in the far West, have often wondered what will ultimately happen to me, to 'Poor Bertie' as I am known in the trade."

He unbuttoned his shirt and let it fall to the floor. In his undershirt he looked defenseless, his skin pale as something seen in moonlight. "Why, you wonder, doesn't he do something about himself, pull himself up by his bootstraps? Why, for example, doesn't he get his eyes fixed? Well, I've tried."

He kicked off his shoes. "You have all admired my bushy mustache. Do you remember that time two years ago I dropped out of sight for four months? Well, let me tell you what happened that time."

He took off his black pants. "I had been staying with Royal Randle, the distinguished philologist and drunk. You will recall what Royal, Klaff, Myers, Gimpel and myself once were to each other. Regular Whiffenpoofs we were. Damned from here to eternity. Sure, sure." He sighed. "You remember Randle's promises: 'It won't make any difference, Bertie. It won't make any difference, Klaff. It won't make any difference, fellas.' He married the girl in the muu-muu."

He was naked now except for his socks. He shivered once and folded his arms across his chest. "Do you know why the girl in the muu-muu married Randle?" He paused dramatically. *"To get at me, that's why!* The others she didn't care about. She knew even before I did what they were like. Even what *Klaff* was like. She knew they were corrupt, that they had it in them to sell me out, to settle down—that all anyone had to do was wave their deaths in front of them and they'd come running, that reason and fucking money and getting it steady would win again. But in me she recognized the real enemy, the last of the go-to-hell-god-damn-its. Maybe the first.

"They even took me with them on their honeymoon. At the time I thought it was a triumph for dependency, but it was just a trick, that's all. The minute they were married, this girl in the muu-muu was after Randle to do something about Bertie. And it wasn't 'Poor' Bertie this time. It was she who got me the appointment with the mayor. Do you know what His Honor said to me? 'Shave your mustache and I'll give you a job clerking in one of my supermarkets.'

Christ, friends, do you know I *did* it? Well, I'm not made of stone. They had taken me on their honeymoon, for God's sake."

He paused.

"I worked in that supermarket *for three hours.* Clean-shaved. My mustache sacrificed as an earnest to the mayor. Well, I'm telling you, you don't know what square *is* till you've worked in a supermarket for three hours. They pipe in Mantovani. Mantovani! I cleared out for four months to raise my mustache again and to forget. What you see now isn't the original, you understand. It's all second growth, and believe me it's not the same."

He drew aside the shower curtain and stepped into the tub. He paused with his hand on the tap. "But I tell you this, friends. I would rather be a mustached bum than a clean-shaved clerk. I'll work. Sure I will. When they pay anarchists! When they subsidize the hip! When they give grants to throw bombs! When they shell out for gainsaying!"

Bertie pulled the curtain and turned on the faucet. The rush of water was like applause.

After his shower Bertie went into the second bedroom and carefully removed the spread from the cot. Then he punched the pillow and mussed the bed. "Very clever," he said. "It wouldn't do to let them think I never slept here." He had once realized with sudden clarity that he would never, so long as he lived, make a bed.

Then he went into the other bedroom and ripped the spread from the big double bed. For some time, in fact since he had first seen it, Bertie had been thinking about this bed. It was the biggest bed he would ever sleep in. He thought invariably in such terms. One cigarette in a pack would suddenly become distinguished in his mind as the best, or the worst, he would smoke that day. A homely act, such as tying his shoelaces, if it occurred with unusual ease, would be remembered forever. This lent to his vision an oblique sadness, conscious as he was that he was forever encountering experiences which would never come his way again.

He slipped his naked body between the sheets, but no sooner had he made himself comfortable than he became conscious of the phonograph, still playing in the little hall. He couldn't hear it very well. He thought about turning up the volume, but he had read somewhere about neighbors. Getting out of bed, he moved the heavy machine through the living room, pushing it with difficulty over the seamed, bare wooden floor, trailing deep scratches. Remember not to walk barefoot there, he thought. At one point one of the legs caught in a loop of the Premingers' shag rug and Bertie strained to free it, finally breaking the thick thread and producing an interesting pucker along one end of the rug, not unlike the pucker in raised theatrical curtains. At last he had maneuvered the machine into the hall just outside the bedroom and plugged it in. He went back for the Billie Holiday recording he had heard earlier and put it on the phonograph. By fiddling with the machine, he fixed it so the record would play all night.

Bertie got back into the bed. "Ah," he said, "the *sanctum sanctorum.*" He rolled over and over from one side of the bed to the other. He tucked his knees into his chest and went under the covers. "It makes you feel kind of small and insignificant," he said.

"Ladies and gentlemen, this is Graham Macnamee speaking to you from the Cave of the Winds. I have made my way into the heart of this darkness to find my friend, Poor Bertie, who, as you know, entered the bed eight weeks ago. Bertie is with me now, and while there isn't enough light for me to be able to see his condition, his voice may tell us something about his physical state. Bertie, just what *is* the official record?"

"Well, Graham, some couples have been known to stick it out for seventy-five years. Of course, your average is much less than that, but still—"

"Seventy-five years."

"Seventy-five, yes sir. It's amazing, isn't it, Graham, when you come to think? All that time in one bed."

"It certainly is," Graham Macnamee said. "Do you think you'll be able to go the distance, Bert?"

"Who, me? No, no. A lot of folks have misunderstood my purpose in coming. I'm rather glad you've given me the opportunity to clear that up. Actually my work here is scientific. This isn't a stunt or anything like that. I'm here to learn."

"Can you tell us about it, Bert?"

"Graham, it's been a fascinating experience, if you know what I mean, but frankly there are many things we still don't understand. *I* don't know why they do it. All that licit love, that regularity. Take the case of Richard and Norma, for example—and incidentally, you don't want to overlook the significance of that name 'Norma.' Norma/Normal, you see?"

"Say, I never thought of that."

"Well, I'm trained to think like that, Graham. In my work you have to."

"Say," Graham Macnamee said.

"Sure. Well, the thing is, buddy, when I first came into this bed I felt the aura, know what I mean, the *power.* I think it's built into the mattress or something."

"Say."

"Shut your face, Graham, and let me speak, will you please? Well, anyway, you feel surrounded. Respectable. Love is made here, of course, but it's not love as *we* know it. There are things that must remain mysteries until we have more facts. I mean, Graham, checks could be cashed in this bed, for Christ's sake, credit cards honored. It's ideal for family reunions, high teas. Graham, it's the kind of place you wouldn't be ashamed to take your mother."

"Go to sleep, Bert," Graham Macnamee said.

"Say," Bertie said.

Between the third and fourth day of his stay in the Premingers' apartment Bertie became restless. He had not been outside the house since the Sunday he arrived, even to bring in the papers Preminger had told him about. (Indeed, it was by counting the papers that he knew how long he had been there, though he couldn't be sure, since he didn't know whether the Premingers had taken the Sunday paper along with them.) He could see them on the back porch through the window of Norma's sun parlor. With the bottles of milk they made a strange little pile. After all, he was not a caretaker; he was a guest. Preminger could bring in his own papers, drink his own damn milk. For the same reasons he had determined not even to answer the phone when it rang.

One evening he tried to call Klaff at the Los Angeles County Jail, but the desk sergeant wouldn't get him. He wouldn't even take a message.

Although he had not been outside since Sunday, Bertie had only a vague desire to leave the apartment. He weighed this against his real need to rest and his genuine pleasure in being alone in so big a place. Like the man in the joke who does not leave his Miami hotel room because it is costing him thirty-five dollars a day, Bertie decided he had better remain inside.

With no money left he was reduced to eating the dry, cold remainder of the pizza, dividing it mathematically into a week's provisions, like someone on a raft. (He actually fancied himself, not on a raft perhaps, but set alone and drifting on, say, the *Queen Mary*.) To supplement the pizza he opened some cans of soup he found in the pantry and drank the contents straight, without heating it or even adding water. Steadily he drank away at the Premingers' modest stock of liquor. The twelve cans of beer had been devoured by the second morning, of course.

After the second full day in the apartment his voices began to desert him. It was only with difficulty that he could manage his imitations, and only for short lengths of time. The glorious discussions that had gone on long into the night were now out of the question. He found he could not do Gimpel's voice any more, and even Klaff's was increasingly difficult and largely confined to his low, caressing obscenities. Mostly he talked with himself, although it was a real strain to keep up his end of the conversation, and it always made him cry when he said how pathetic he was and asked himself where do you go from here. Oh, to be like Bird, he thought. Not to have to be a bum. To ask, as it were, no quarter.

At various times during the day he would call out "Bird lives" in seeming stunning triumph. But he didn't believe it.

He watched a lot of television. "I'm getting ammunition," he said. "It's scientific."

Twice a day he masturbated in the Premingers' bed.

He settled gradually, then, into restlessness. He knew, of course, that he had it always in his power to bring himself back up to the heights he had known in those wonderful first two days. He was satisfied, however, not to use this power, and thought of himself as a kind of soldier, alone in a foxhole, in enemy territory, at night, at a bad time in the war, with one bullet in his pistol. Oddly, he derived more pride—and comfort, and a queer security—from this single bullet than others might have from whole cases of ammunition. It was his *strategic* bullet, the one he would use to get the big one, turn the tide, make the difference. The Premingers would be away two weeks. He would not waste his ammunition. Just as he divided the stale pizza, cherishing each piece as much for the satisfaction he took from possessing it during a time of emergency as for any sustenance it offered, so he enjoyed his knowledge that at any time he could recoup his vanishing spirits. He shared with the squares ("Use their own weapons to beat them, Bertie") a special pride in adversity, in having to do without, in having to expose whatever was left of his character to the narrower straits. It was strange, he thought seriously, it was the paradox of the world and an institutional insight that might have come right out of the mouth of that slut in Dallas, but the most peculiar aspect of the squares wasn't their lack of imagination or their bland bad taste, but their ability, like the wildest fanatics, like the furthest out of the furthest out, to cling to the illogical, finally untenable notion that they must have and have in order to live, at the same time that they realized that it was better not to have. What seemed so grand to Bertie, who admired all impossible positions, was that they believed both things with equal intensity, never suspecting for a moment any inconsistency. And here was Bertie, Bertie thought, here was Bertie inside their capitol, on the slopes of their mountains, on their smooth shores, who believed neither of these propositions, who believed in not having and in not suffering too, who yet realized the very same pleasure that they would in having and not using. It was the strangest thing that would ever happen to him, he thought.

"Are you listening, Klaff, you second-story fink?" Bertie yelled. "Do you see how your old pal is developing what is called character?"

And so, master of himself for once, he resolved—feeling what someone taking a vow feels—not to use the last of his drugs until the strategic moment of strategic truth.

That was Wednesday evening. By Thursday morning he had decided to break his resolution. He had not yielded to temptation, had not lain fitfully awake all night—indeed, his resolution had given him the serenity to sleep well—in the sweaty throes of withdrawal. There had been no argument or rationalization, nor had he decided that he had reached his limit or that this was the strategic moment he had been waiting for. He yielded as he always yielded: spontaneously, suddenly, unexpectedly, as the result neither of whim nor calculation. His important decisions were almost always reached without his knowledge, and he was often as surprised as the next one to see what he was going to do—to see, indeed, that he was already doing it. (Once someone had asked him whether he believed in Free Will, and after considering this for a moment as it applied to himself, Bertie had answered "Free? Hell, it's positively *loose.*")

Having discovered his new intention, he was eager to realize it. As often as he had taken drugs (he never called it anything but drugs, never used the cute or obscene names, never even said "dope"; to him it was always "drugs," medicine for his spirit), they were still a major treat for him. "It's a rich man's game," he had once told Klaff, and then he had leaned back philosophically. "You know, Klaff, it's a good thing I'm poor. When I think of the snobbish ennui of your wealthy junkies, I realize that they don't know how to appreciate their blessings. God keep me humble, Klaff. Abstinence makes the heart grow fonder, a truer word was never spoken."

Nor did a drug ever lose its potency for him. If he graduated from one to another, it was not in order to recover some fading jolt, but to experience a new and different one. He held in contempt all those who professed disenchantment with the drugs they had been raised on, and frequently went back to rediscover the old pleasures of marijuana, as a sentimental father might chew some of his boy's bubble gum. "Loyalty, Gimpel," he exclaimed, "loyalty, do you know what *that* is?"

Bertie would and did try anything, though currently his favorite was mescaline for the visions it induced. Despite what he considered his eclectic tastes in these matters, there were one or two things he would not do, however. He never introduced any drug by hypodermic needle. This he found disgusting and, frankly, painful. He often said he could stand anything but pain and was very proud of his clear, unpunctured skin. "Not a mark on me," he might say, drinking off a malted into which he had just stirred a bag of heroin and waving his arms like a professional boxer. The other thing he would not do was take his drugs in the presence of other users, for he found the company of addicts offensive. However, he was not above what he called "seductions." A seduction for him was to find some girl and talk her into letting him share his drugs with her. Usually it ended in their lying naked in bed together, both of them serene, absent of all desire and what Bertie called "unclean thoughts."

"You know," he would say to the girl beside him, "I think that if all the world's leaders would take drugs and lie down on the bed naked like this without any unclean thoughts, the cause of world peace would be helped immeasurably. What do you think?"

"I think so too," she would say.

Once he knew he was going to take the drug, Bertie made his preparations. He went first to his trumpet case and took out the last small packet of powder. He opened it carefully, first closing all the windows so that no sudden draft could blow any of it away. This had once happened to a friend of his, and Bertie had never forgotten the warning.

"I am not one on whom a lesson is lost," Bertie said.

"You're okay, Bertie," a Voice said. "Go save France."

He placed the packet on the Premingers' coffee table and carefully spread the paper, exactly like the paper wrapper around a stick of chewing gum, looking almost lustfully at the soft, flat layer of ground white powder. He held out his hand to see how steady it was, and although he was not really shaky he did not trust himself to lift the paper from the table. He brought a water tumbler from the kitchen and gently placed it upside down on top of the powder. He was not yet ready to take it. Bertie was a man who postponed his pleasures as long as he possibly could; he let candy dissolve in his mouth and played with the threads on his tangerine before eating the fruit. It was a weakness in his character perhaps, but he laid it lovingly at the feet of his poverty.

He decided to wait until sundown to take the drug, reasoning that when it wore off, it would be early morning and he would be ready for bed. Sleep was one of his pleasures too, and he approved of regularity in small things, taking a real pride in being able to keep hours. To pass the time until sundown he looked for something to do. First he found some tools and busied himself by taking Norma's steam iron apart. There was still time left after that, so he took a canvas and painted a picture. Because he did not know how to draw he simply covered the canvas first with one color and then with another, applying layer after layer of the paint thickly. Each block of color he made somewhat smaller than the last, so that the finished painting portrayed successive jagged margins of color. He stepped back and considered his work seriously.

"Well, it has texture, Bertie," Hans Hoffman said.

"Bertie," the Voice said suddenly, "I don't like to interrupt when you're working, but it's sundown."

"So it is," he said, looking up.

He went back into the living room and removed the tumbler. Taking up the paper in his fingers and creasing it as if he were a cowboy rolling a cigarette, Bertie tilted his head far back and inhaled the powder deeply. This part was always uncomfortable for him. "Ooo," he said, "the bubbles." He stuffed the last few grains up his nose with his fingers. "Waste not, want not," he said.

He sat down to wait. After half an hour in which nothing happened, Bertie became uneasy. "It's been cut," he said. "Sure, depend upon friends to do you favors." He was referring to the fact that the drug had been a going-away present from friends in Oklahoma City. He decided to give it fifteen more minutes. "Nothing," he said at last, disappointed. "Nothing."

The powder, as it always did, left his throat scratchy, and there was a bitter taste in his mouth. His soft palate prickled. He seized the water tumbler from the coffee table and walked angrily into the kitchen. He ran the cold water, then gargled and spit in the sink. In a few minutes the bitter taste and the prickly sensation subsided and he felt about as he had before he took the drug. He was conscious, however, of a peculiar smell, unpleasant, unfamiliar, nothing like the odor of rotting flowers he associated with the use of drugs. He opened a window and leaned out, breathing the fresh air. But as soon as he came away from the window, the odor was again overpowering. He went to see if he could smell it in the other rooms. When he had made his tour he realized that the stench *must* be coming from the kitchen. Holding his breath, he came back to see if he could locate its source. The kitchen was almost as Norma had left it. He had done no cooking, and although there were some empty soup and beer cans in the sink he knew *they* couldn't be causing the odor. He shrugged. Then he noticed the partially closed door to Preminger's study.

"Of course," Bertie said. "Whatever it is must be in there." He pushed the door open. In the middle of the floor were two blackish mounds that looked like dark sawdust. Bertie stepped back in surprise.

"Camel shit," he said. "My God, how did *that* get in here?" He went closer to investigate. "That's what it is, all right." He had never seen it before but a friend had, and had described it to him. This stuff fitted the description perfectly. He considered what to do.

"I can't leave it there," he said. He found a dustpan and a broom and, propping the pan against the leg of Preminger's chair, began to sweep the stuff up. He was surprised at how remarkably gummy it seemed. When he finished he washed the spot on the floor with a foaming detergent and stepped gingerly to the back door. He lifted the lid of the garbage can and shoved the broom and the contents of the dustpan and the dustpan itself into the can. Then he went to the bathroom and washed his hands.

In the living room he saw the Chinaman. "Jesus," Bertie said breathlessly.

The Chinaman lowered his eyes in a shy, almost demure smile. He said nothing, but motioned Bertie to sit in the chair across from him. Bertie, too frightened to disobey, sat down.

He waited for the Chinaman to tell him what he wanted. After an hour (he heard the chime clock strike nine times and then ten times), when the Chinaman still had not said anything, he began to feel a little calmer. Maybe he's just tired, Bertie thought, and came in to rest. He realized that perhaps he and the Chinaman had more in common than had at first appeared. He looked at the fellow in this new light and saw that he had been foolish to fear him. The Chinaman was small, smaller even than Bertie. In fact, he was only two feet tall. Perhaps what made him seem larger was the fact that he was wrapped in wide, voluminous white silk robes. Bertie stared at the robes, fascinated by the delicate filigree trim up and down their length. To see this closer he stood up and walked tentatively toward the Chinaman.

The Chinaman gazed steadily to the front, and Bertie, seeing no threat, continued toward him. He leaned down over the Chinaman, and gently grasping the delicate lacework between his forefinger and his thumb, drew it toward his eye. "May I?" Bertie asked. "I know a good deal about this sort of thing."

The Chinaman lowered his eyes.

Bertie examined the weird symbols and designs, and although he did not understand them, recognized at once their cabalistic origin.

"Magnificent," Bertie said at last. "My God, the man-hours that must have gone into this. *The sheer craftsmanship!* That's really a terrific robe you've got there. I mean it. Who's your tailor?"

The Chinaman lowered his eyes still further.

Bertie sat down in his chair again. He heard the clock strike eleven and he smiled at the Chinaman. He was trying to be sympathetic, patient. He knew the fellow had his reasons for coming and that in due time they would be revealed, but he couldn't help being a little annoyed. First the failure of the drug and then the camel shit on the floor and now this. However, he remained very polite.

There was nothing else to do, so he concentrated on the Chinaman's face. Then a strange thing happened.

He became aware, as he scrutinized the face, of some things he hadn't noticed before. First he realized that it was the oldest face he had ever seen. He knew that this face was old enough to have looked on Buddha's. It was only *faintly* yellow, really, and he understood with a sweeping insight that original-ly it must have been white, as it still largely was, a striking, flat white, naked as a sheet, bright as teeth, that its yellowness was an intrusion, the intruding yellowness of fantastic age, of pages in ancient books. As soon as he perceived this he understood the origin and mystery of the races. All men had at first been white; their different tints were only the shades of their different wisdoms. Of course, he thought. Of course. It's beautiful. Beautiful!

The second thing Bertie noticed was that the face seemed extraordinarily wise. The longer he stared at it the wiser it seemed. Clearly this was the wisest Chinaman, and thus the wisest man, in the history of the world. Now he was impatient for the Chinaman to speak, to tell him his secrets, but he also understood that so long as he was impatient the Chinaman would *not* speak, that he must become serene, as serene as the Chinaman himself, or else the Chinaman would go away. As this occurred to him the Chinaman smiled and Bertie knew he had been right. He was aware that if he just sat there, deliberately trying to become serene, nothing would happen. He decided that the best way to become serene was to ignore the Chinaman, to go on about his business as if the Chinaman weren't even there.

He stood up. "Am I getting warm?" Bertie asked.

The Chinaman lowered his eyes and smiled.

"Well, then," Bertie said, rubbing his hands, "let's see."

He went into the kitchen to see if there was anything he could do there to make him serene.

He washed out the empty cans of soup.

He strolled into the bedroom and made the bed. This took him an hour. He heard the clock strike twelve and then one.

He took a record off the machine and starting from the center hole and working to the outer edge, counted all the ridges. This took him eleven seconds.

He found a suitcase in one of the closets and packed all of Norma's underwear into it.

He got a pail of water and some soap and washed all the walls in the small bedroom.

It was in the dining room, however, that he finally achieved serenity. He studied Norma's pictures of side streets throughout the world and with sudden insight understood what was wrong with them. He took some tubes of white paint and with a brush worked over the figures, painting back into the flesh all their original whiteness. He made the Mexicans white, the Negroes white, feeling as he worked an immense satisfaction, the satisfaction not of the creator, nor even of the reformer, but of the restorer.

Swelling with serenity, Bertie went back into the living room and sat down in his chair. For the first time the Chinaman met his gaze directly, and Bertie realized that something important was going to happen.

Slowly, very slowly, the Chinaman began to open his mouth. Bertie watched the slow parting of the Chinaman's thin lips, the gleaming teeth, white and bright as fence pickets. Gradually the rest of the room darkened and the thinly padded chair on which Bertie sat grew incredibly soft. He knew that they had been transported somehow, that they were now in a sort of theater. The Chinaman was seated on a kind of raised platform. Meanwhile the mouth continued to open, slowly as an ancient draw-bridge. Tiny as the Chinaman was, the mouth seemed enormous. Bertie gazed into it, seeing nothing. At last, deep back in the mouth, he saw a brief flashing, as of a small crystal on a dark rock suddenly illuminated by the sun. In a moment he saw it again, brighter now, longer sustained. Soon it was so bright that he had to force himself to look at it. Then the mouth went black. Before he could protest, the brightness was overwhelming again and he saw a cascade of what seemed like diamonds tumble out of the Chinaman's mouth. It was the Chinaman's tongue.

Twisting, turning over and over like magicians' silks pulled endlessly from a tube, the tongue continued to pour from the Chinaman's mouth. Bertie saw that it had the same whiteness as the rest of his face, and that it was studded with bright, beautiful jewels. On the tongue, long now as an unfurled scroll, were thick black Chinese characters. It was the secret of life, of the world, of the universe. Bertie could barely read for the tears of gratitude in his eyes. Desperately he wiped the tears away with his fists. He looked back at the tongue and stared at the strange words, realizing that he could not read Chinese. He was sobbing helplessly now because he knew there was not much time. The presence of the Chinaman gave him courage and strength and he *forced* himself to read the Chinese. As he concentrated it became easier, the characters somehow re-forming, translating themselves into a sort of decipherable Chinese script, like the words "Chow Mein" on the neon sign outside a Chinese restaurant. He was breathless from his effort and the stunning glory of what was being revealed to him. Frequently he had to pause, punctuating his experience with queer little squeals. "Oh," he said. "Oh. Oh."

Then it was over.

He was exhausted, but his knowledge glowed in him like fire. "So *that's* it" was all he could say. "So *that's* it. So *that's* it."

Bertie saw that he was no longer in the theater. The Chinaman was gone and Bertie was back in the Premingers' living room. He struggled for control of himself. He knew it was urgent that he tell someone what had happened to him. Desperately he pulled open his trumpet case. Inside he had pasted sheets with the names, addresses and phone numbers of all his friends.

"Damn Klaff," he said angrily. "Damn Second-Story Klaff in his lousy jail."

He spotted Gimpel's name and the phone number of his boarding house in Cincinnati. Tearing the sheet from where it was pasted inside the lid, he rushed to the phone and placed the call. "Life and death," he screamed at Gimpel's bewildered landlady. "Life and death."

When Gimpel came to the phone Bertie began to tell him, coherently, but with obvious excitement, all that had happened. Gimpel was as excited as himself.

"Then the Chinaman opened his mouth and this tongue with writing on it came out."

"Yeah?" Gimpel said. "Yeah? Yeah?"

"Only it was in Chinese," Bertie shouted.

"Chinese," Gimpel said.

"But I could read it, Gimpel! *I could read it!*"

"I didn't know you could read Chinese," Gimpel said.

"It was the meaning of life."

"Yeah?" Gimpel said. "Yeah? What'd it say? What'd it say?"

"What?" Bertie said.

"What'd it say? What'd the Chink's tongue say was the meaning of life?"

"I forget," Bertie said and hung up.

He slept until two the next afternoon, and when he awoke he felt as if he had been beaten up. His tongue was something that did not quite fit in his mouth, and throughout his body he experienced a looseness of the bones, as though his skeleton were a mobile put together by an amateur. He groaned dispiritedly, his eyes still closed. He knew he had to get up out of the bed and take a shower and shave and dress, that only by making extravagant demands on it would his body give him any service at all. "You *will* make the Death March," he warned it ruthlessly.

He opened his eyes and what he saw disgusted him and turned his stomach. His eye patch had come off during the night and now there were two of everything. He saw one eye patch on one pillow and another eye patch on another pillow. Hastily he grabbed for it, but he had chosen the wrong pillow. He reached for the other eye patch and the other pillow, but somehow he had put out one of his illusory hands. It did not occur to him to shut one eye. At last, by covering all visible space, real or illusory, with all visible fingers, real or illusory—like one dragging a river—he recovered the patch and pulled it quickly over one of his heads.

He stood stunned in his hot shower, and then shaved, cutting his neck badly. He dressed.

"Whan 'e iz through his toilette, *Monsieur* will see 'ow much better 'e feel," his valet said. He doubted it and didn't answer.

In the dining room he tried not to look at Norma's paintings, but could not help noticing that overnight many of her sunny side streets had become partial snow scenes. He had done that, he remembered, though he could not now recall exactly why. It seemed to have something to do with a great anthropological discovery he had made the night before. He finished the last of the pizza, gagging on it briefly.

Considering the anguish of his body, it suddenly occurred to him that perhaps he was hooked. Momentarily this appealed to his sense of the dramatic, but then he realized that it would be a terrible thing to have happen to him. He could not afford to be hooked, for he knew with a sense of calm sadness that his character could no more sustain the responsibility of a steady drug habit than it could sustain any other sort of responsibility.

"Oh, what a miserable bastard I am," Bertie said.

In near-panic he considered leaving the Premingers' apartment immediately, but he knew that he was in no condition to travel. "You wouldn't make it to the corner," he said.

He felt massively sorry for himself. The more he considered it the more certain it appeared that he was hooked. It was terrible. Where would he get the money to buy the drugs? What would they do to his already depleted physical resources? "Oh, what a miserable bastard I am," he said again.

To steady himself he took a bottle of Scotch from the shelf in the pantry. Bertie did not like hard liquor. Though he drank a lot, it was beer he drank, or, when he could get them, the sweeter cordials. Scotch and bourbon had always seemed vaguely square to him. But he had already finished the few liqueurs that Preminger had, and now nothing was left but Scotch. He poured himself an enormous drink.

Sipping it calmed him—though his body still ached—and he considered what to do. If he *was* hooked, the first thing was to tell his friends. Telling his friends his latest failure was something Bertie regarded as a sort of responsibility. Thus his rare letters to them usually brought Bertie's intimates—he laughed at the word—nothing but bad news. He would write that a mistress had given him up, and, with his talent for mimicry, would set down her last long disappointed speech to him, in which she exposed in angry, honest language the hollowness of his character, his infinite weakness as a man, his vileness. When briefly he had turned to homosexuality to provide himself with funds, the first thing he did was write his friends about it. Or he wrote of being fired from bands when it was discovered how bad a trumpeter he really was. He spared neither himself nor his friends in his passionate self-denunciations.

Almost automatically, then, he went into Preminger's study and began to write all the people he could think of. As he wrote he pulled heavily at the whiskey remaining in the bottle. At first the letters were long, detailed accounts of symptoms and failures and dashed hopes, but as evening came on and he grew inarticulate he realized that it was more important—and, indeed, added to the pathos of his situation—for him just to get the facts to them.

"Dear Klaff," he wrote at last, "I am hooked. I am at the bottom, Klaff. I don't know what to do." Or "Dear Randle, I'm hooked. Tell your wife. I honestly don't know where to turn." And "Dear Myers, how are your wife and kids? Poor Bertie is hooked. He is thinking of suicide."

He had known for a long time that one day he would have to kill himself. It would happen, and even in the way he had imagined. One day he would simply drink the bottle of carbon tetrachloride. But previously he had been in no hurry. Now it seemed like something he might have to do before he had meant to, and what he resented most was the idea of having to change his plans.

He imagined what people would say.

"I let him down, Klaff," Randle said.

"Everybody let him down," Klaff said.

"Everybody let him down," Bertie said. "Everybody let him down."

Weeping, he took a last drink from Preminger's bottle, stumbled into the living room and passed out on the couch.

That night Bertie was awakened by a flashlight shining in his eyes. He threw one arm across his face defensively and struggled to sit up. So clumsy were his efforts that whoever was holding the flashlight started to laugh.

"Stop that," Bertie said indignantly, and thought, I have never been so indignant in the face of danger.

"You said they were out of town," a voice said. The voice did not come from behind the flashlight, and Bertie wondered how many there might be.

"Jesus, I thought so. Nobody's answered the phone for days. I never seen a guy so plastered. He stinks."

"Kill him," the first voice said.

Bertie stopped struggling to get up.

"Kill him," the voice repeated.

"What is this?" Bertie said thickly. "What is this?"

"Come on, he's so drunk he's harmless," the second voice said.

"Kill him," the first voice said again.

"You kill him," the second voice said.

The first voice giggled.

They were playing with him, Bertie knew. Nobody who did not know him could want him dead.

"Turn on the lights," Bertie said.

"Screw that," the second voice said. "You just sit here in the dark, sonny, and you won't get hurt."

"We're wasting time," the first voice said.

A beam from a second flashlight suddenly intersected the beam from the first.

"Say," Bertie said nervously, "it looks like the opening of a supermarket."

Bertie could hear them working in the dark, moving boxes, pulling drawers.

"Are you folks Negroes?" Bertie called. No one answered him. "I mean I dig

Negroes, man—*men*. Miles. Jay Jay. Bird lives." He heard a closet door open.

"You *are* robbing the place, right? I mean you're actually *stealing,* aren't you? This isn't just a social call. Maybe you know my friend Klaff."

The men came back into the living room. From the sound of his footsteps Bertie knew one of them was carrying something heavy.

"I've got the TV," the first voice said.

"There are some valuable paintings in the dining room," Bertie said.

"Go see," the first voice said.

One of Norma's pictures suddenly popped out of the darkness as the man's light shone on it.

"Crap," the second voice said.

"You cats can't be all bad," Bertie said.

"Any furs?" It was a third voice, and it startled Bertie. Someone flashed a light in Bertie's face. "Hey, you," the voice repeated, "does your wife have any furs?"

"Wait a minute," Bertie said as though it were a fine point they must be made to understand, "you've got it wrong. This isn't *my* place. I'm just taking care of it while my friends are gone." The man laughed.

Now all three flashlights were playing over the apartment. Bertie hoped a beam might illuminate one of the intruders, but this never happened. Then he realized that he didn't want it to happen, that he was safe as long as he didn't recognize any of them. Suddenly a light caught one of the men behind the ear. "Watch that light. Watch that light," Bertie called out involuntarily.

"I found a trumpet," the second voice said.

"Hey, that's mine," Bertie said angrily. Without thinking, he got up and grabbed for the trumpet. In the dark he was able to get his fingers around one of the valves, but the man snatched it away from him easily. Another man pushed him back down on the couch.

"Could you leave the carbon tetrachloride?" Bertie asked miserably.

In another ten minutes they were ready to go. "Shouldn't we do something about the clown?" the third voice said.

"Nah," the second voice said.

They went out the front door.

Bertie sat in the darkness. "I'm drunk," he said after a while. "I'm hooked and drunk. It never happened. It's still the visions. The apartment is a vision. The darkness is. Everything."

In a few minutes he got up and wearily turned on the lights. Magicians, he thought, seeing even in a first glance all that they had taken. Lamps were gone, curtains. He walked through the apartment. The TV was gone. Suits were missing from the closets. Preminger's typewriter was gone, the champagne glasses, the silver. His trumpet was gone.

Bertie wept. He thought of phoning the police, but then wondered what he could tell them. The thieves had been in the apartment for twenty minutes and he hadn't even gotten a look at their faces.

Then he shuddered, realizing the danger he had been in. "Crooks," he said. "Killers." But even as he said it he knew it was an exaggeration. He had never been in any danger. He had the fool's ancient protection, his old immunity against consequence.

He wondered what he could say to the Premingers. They would be furious. Then, as he thought about it, he realized that this too was an exaggeration. They would not be furious. Like the thieves they would make allowances for him, as people always made allowances for him. They would forgive him; possibly they would even try to give him something toward the loss of his trumpet.

Bertie began to grow angry. They had no right to patronize him like that. If he was a clown it was because he had chosen to be. It was a way of life. Why couldn't they respect it? He should have been hit over the head like other men. How dare they forgive him? For a moment it was impossible for him to distinguish between the thieves and the Premingers.

Then he had his idea. As soon as he thought of it he knew it would work. He looked around the apartment to see what he could take. There was some costume jewelry the thieves had thrown on the bed. He scooped it up and stuffed it in his pockets. He looked at the apartment one more time and then got the hell out of there. "Bird lives," he sang to himself as he raced down the stairs. "He lives and lives."

It was wonderful. How they would marvel! He couldn't get away with it. Even the far West wasn't far enough. How they hounded you if you took something from them! He would be back, no question, and they would send him to jail, but first there would be the confrontation, maybe even in the apartment itself: Bertie in handcuffs, and the Premingers staring at him, not understanding and angry at last, and something in their eyes like fear.

SUMMERFIELD

J. M. FERGUSON, JR.   from *Descant*

Life would be easy if we had only to live it. My friend Summerfield once asked me what I meant by that, but we were having a reunion dinner in Juarez at the time and the champagne had gone to our heads, so I never had to explain.

We had grown up together in a little town in West Texas. I no longer had any attachments there—my parents had long since left the region—but after the war I found myself longing for the bright sunlight and an indefinable warmth that I traced to my boyhood years with Summerfield. I sought him first of all my friends after the war, needing the unclouded blue eyes and the shy friendliness I had known so well. Yet I sought in vain, and standing one evening before the house he had lived in I thought how close we had been. Born on the same day, of the same height and slender build, we had sometimes passed for twins, though I had always to acknowledge to myself with a pang of envy that there was something keen and beautiful in his features which I could not find in my own. As boys we wrestled together on the hard loam of the schoolgrounds. Sometimes I won, but sometimes he pinned my shoulders to the frozen ground, and for the life of me I could not throw him over.

It was not surprising he was gone. Everything about the town was changing. New houses were everywhere, and a handful of factories muddied the sky. The town had become a city, and it was two years later when I learned that Summerfield had been living there without my knowing it.

I had by then married the girl we had both been partial to once—though there was never any rivalry between us—and gone off to Southern Colorado to teach in a high school, the profession of my father and the one I had prepared for before the war. It was in the fall of my second year of teaching, when I was attending a convention in El Paso, that I saw him. The circumstances of our meeting and the evening that followed seem almost unreal to me even now.

It was late on a Saturday afternoon and the convention had ended.

Everyone I knew had checked out of the hotel and gone to the airport, but my own plane did not leave until Sunday morning. I pondered what to do with myself, and settled into a chair in the hotel lobby. I thought of the bum on the street who had wanted to make North Carolina, of old men sitting alone in the cafeteria where I had lunched, of the well-dressed man and his wife in the bookstore where I had browsed who made cynical jokes about the president. Three elderly people sitting near me were striking up a conversation about nothing. The lady had laughed at one of the men when he came in wearing the other man's hat.

I got up and went to the hotel bar, looking for convention stragglers like myself. Above the bar a television set was tuned to a late-season football game, and a few men in business suits lounged about watching half-heartedly. People are bored with football, I thought. Even the announcer's voice could tell you this.

Saturday afternoon and depression. I wished then that I had asked the bum from North Carolina to dinner. I went back to my chair in the lobby and watched a group of men standing nearby talking—not polished and not businessmen either, ranchers perhaps. One said in a raised voice, "Glad to have you aboard, Tom," and then they broke up and departed in all directions. In their wake, in that moment, crossing the lobby toward me with top coat in arm and suitcase in hand, emerged a figure I recognized at once as Summerfield. No one had been further from my thoughts at that time, but I would have known that youthful brightness anywhere.

He stopped when he saw me, setting down his luggage deliberately. I got up, and then we met midway, shaking hands, and I found myself looking again into the tanned face and the clear eyes. Yet he was different, and though I have tried to explain it to myself I can't say how. Perhaps the eyes were not as untroubled as I remembered them, perhaps the mouth seemed drawn, or perhaps it was the hair, less fair, retreating vaguely from the forehead. Still, he wore a blue dress shirt and a tweed coat that were becoming to him, and I had to remind myself that he was, after all, as old as I was. He told me he was traveling for a New York dry goods house, and he expected to move up shortly to the main office. I was disappointed. I had expected something nobler of him.

An hour later we were crossing the bridge to Juarez in the autumn twilight. I seemed to recall that it was not the first time we had done this, though I had forgotten or never noticed the way the neon fury of that border city ignited the haze that hung over the river, and how the Rio Grande, feeble and distracted at that point in its course, was barely audible in the din of the young evening. It was Saturday and one saw American servicemen in every block. Proprietors of the little sidewalk shops accosted the tourists and cab drivers on every corner were touting for the brothels. At one corner a man with both legs amputated was selling flowers, scooting about laboriously on a wooden plank mounted on roller skate wheels. "Flores," he called, "flores para su novia."

We shouldered our way into a restaurant, and over dinner he spoke of his marriage with a hint of unhappiness. "It's hard when you're on the road," he complained, and then he warned, with sudden solemnity, "Stay off the road if you can help it." I had the inspiration to order champagne, which turned out to be a bad mistake. Our conversation took a metaphysical turn, and we spoke thickly for awhile of the good life, and then, all judgment gone, we ordered more. I can't remember who suggested it, or whether we just mutely arrived at the same idea, but sometime after that we were in a taxi headed for a brothel. I was betraying my bad Spanish to the driver, and while he humored us, I was aware enough to know that he was hating us all the while.

We crossed the bridge again after midnight, and down on the sand bars of the dark river below us, barefoot and ragged, three Mexican boys were begging pennies. It will seem incongruous, but my moral sense began to stir, for I had never been able to cross back over the bridge with an easy conscience. To toss them pennies, as they expected, seemed haughty, but to give them a dollar only intensified the problem: why not more? Everything? Yet to give them nothing, to ignore them, seemed worst of all. I watched Summerfield.

He paused at the railing, pressed up close to it, and looked down contemptuously. It was some moments before I realized what he was doing, and when I did I could not believe it. That he should be capable of such an act escaped my understanding. No, this was not the boy I had known. We did not need to understand the outburst of invective from below us, and there was such health and fury in it that I later wondered whether there had not been some provident compassion behind Summerfield's gesture after all.

We said goodbye in the hotel lobby. We were sober and sleepy by then, and he seemed sullen and depressed. Until that night I had never imagined him capable of such demeanor. When we shook hands he looked at me for an instant with accusation in his face, and I noticed that his eyes were bloodshot.

That evening seemed like a bad dream to me later. When I wrote to him once at the address he had given me and got no reply, I thought perhaps it had been. And yet after the encounter everything about me changed almost imperceptibly. I was homesick for a boyhood friend and a town which no longer existed, and my wife concluded that my constant references to my past betrayed my unhappiness with my present. All of this confounded me, and added to it I found myself disillusioned with my vocation, the vocation of my father before me. That summer we made the first of a series of restless moves, dragging our newly born son with us. We moved west to Nevada, hoping for a new start.

There were things about the Nevada desert that reminded me of home, yet it was not home, and I had the terrible sensation that I would never find whatever it was I sought. A year went by and we moved again, this time to a California town at the end of the continent. It was an idyllic setting. No one could have asked for more. And yes, for a while we were happy, that summer in a rented house that overlooked the sea. But school started and by late summer the fog was rolling in on us regularly, and to me the whole earth turned foreign.

My disenchantment with my work persisted. It was as if I had nothing to teach, and when I spoke before the class I heard the sound of my own voice.

One day when summer had just come round again I was crossing the highway that ran through the town when the first warmth of the season was reflecting from it. Something about the road and the hot breath of life made me think of smaller towns further inland, burnt-over crossroads in the desert I had passed through in the sundowns of summer, and I had an illusion of freedom such as I imagined hoboes have. I thought of the railroad towns with the names that were magic to me, Rock Island, Ash Fork, Durango, Laramie. Summer and life, and for an instant I felt I had forever with my life.

Since then I see the enormity of the lie that conspired against me, but in that moment I felt I had forever. I crossed a highway, and in that moment, almost unaware, I made my decision. I gave up everything and threw away my life.

I had no desire now to be anything but a wayfarer, a passer-by over the alien earth. I remembered Summerfield and wrote to the company in New York that he traveled for. I was informed that he was no longer with them, but my application was invited. I was hired, and thus it was I found myself about to do what I had thought poorly of my old friend for doing, and I wanted to see him again now that I understood. I was sent to New York for a week of training, and on my last night there I believe I had a glimpse of him.

I spent my free hours walking the sidewalks of the Village, which teemed with people on the August night. A wonderful sense of tolerance was present, such as one refugee might extend to another. I could not help thinking that I was certain to know someone out of the millions of people in the city I walked, and on my last night, crossing a street a block below Washington Square, I almost bumped into him—I'm sure it was he, Summerfield, walking with a woman and both of them dressed rather formally. I called after him and for a moment he turned around. There were people between us by then, but I saw his face. He turned again when he saw me and continued on his way. He did not want to know me. I was just as glad, and I could understand, for I had learned by then to relish the freedom of my loneliness.

I was surprised at the dissipation in his face, and the black formality of his attire did not become him. I suspected that the woman with him was not the wife he had spoken of briefly in Juarez, and I wondered whether he was not divorced.

How shall I describe the subtle changes which took place in me during my first year of traveling? I no longer had to stand before a class and listen to my own voice, and I sank into silence willingly. It was as if a great weight had been lifted from me.

"Something is happening," my wife warned. I had all of Arizona and part of California to travel, but even when I was home I was distant and removed. Again thereafter she would say, "I don't like what's happening to you." I listened silently, knowing I could not explain, nor could she. It was indefinable.

Finally she accused me, perhaps rightly in her way, of being unfaithful. I had not been, unless you consider the peculiar faithlessness of a distracted man. Eventually she left me, taking our young son with her. Separation was what I seemed to want, she contended. I was barely aware of the pleasure I took in my aloneness. It was inevitable that it should be complete.

Some months after our separation something happened to me which I do not yet fully comprehend, a very simple but singular event, which I now believe changed the course of my life again.

I was visiting with my son and we had gone to the beach at San Clemente. It was a Saturday afternoon in late October, near the end of the beach season. The sun was going down and the tide coming in. I held my son's hand as we waded out of the surf, the sun low at our backs, and I looked down and saw our shadows in the swirling water, my own long shadow beside that of the small boy. That was all. It was just an image: two shadows in the surf at sundown. But it was everything, and the image haunted me.

I had a long drive to Flagstaff ahead of me the next morning, and as I drove east into the desert I could feel that something was wrong. I did not know what. Something had crept into the edge of my self-possession and would not leave me.

I had reached Indio and was attempting to banish my uneasiness, and there just beyond the cut-off to Blythe the first hitchhiker appeared, a boy with a wholesome face, a white shirt and tie and a black book which must have been a Bible. Then another, a Negro with a baseball cap who inclined his head toward the car suggestively, and finally another, standing beside the road where it curved to climb up through the sandhills above the valley. As I passed I saw the man throw something—it looked like a bottle—across the road in disgust because I would not stop. I looked closely at the faces whenever I passed them, drawn to them magnetically, and again in my mirror, expecting to see them curse me.

I made Blythe by noon and crossed the Colorado River into Arizona. The sky was clear and the desert was heating up. A flight of birds flushed at the roadside and I winged one of them. Looking back in the mirror I saw it raise its good wing from the pavement the way I imagined a drowning man would clutch at the air with his hand. I wondered how much consciousness a bird possessed, how much light behind the eyes was turning dark and murky.

Then at midafternoon my fanbelt snapped, and I slowed down carefully and limped ten miles into the next town, the little village of Aguila, and pulled into the first service station. A Mexican boy came out to wait on me. Yes, they had a mechanic, and he went to rouse him from a small and weather-beaten house trailer parked in the lot beside the station. He came back directly to say it would be a few minutes. As I waited I wondered what it was that drove a man to live in such an unlikely place, a tradesman with a skill who might have lived elsewhere. And did he live with a wife in his trailer, or was he alone? No, surely he was alone, and surely he was in some kind of exile, in penance, perhaps. I pondered the concept of penance. I do not know why it came to mind.

It was a leafless, sun-baked village, but the first cool wind of the afternoon stirring in the colored pennants strung above the station attracted my attention. When I looked down again a man in dirty coveralls had emerged from the trailer and was walking toward me. All the uneasiness that had plagued me that day raced up my spine. I knew him at once, in spite of all aging, and I think he knew me too, for he hesitated momentarily and then came forward with his face averted.

He raised the hood and worked behind it as behind a shield, but when he finished and brought it down he gave me a momentary glance, calm and direct, which pierced me like a scream. Then without a word he turned abruptly toward his trailer.

The boy came out again and I paid him. I drove out onto the highway half-stupefied, searching for the word that would name what I had seen in the face of Summerfield. For somewhere there was a word I had forgotten or repressed which would name it, and when I finally found it I knew it was the name for all the vague emotions that had haunted me since I had seen my shadow in the surf. And the word was guilt.

As I drove on and the giant saguaro began to beckon, it was my guilt they played upon. They held out thumbs and they accosted like hitchhikers and cab drivers I thought I had forgotten. They appealed like wife and child, or like father or Summerfield they stood accusing. Only the gathering dusk spared me their faces, faces I feared I would meet again in hell, as if forgiving were beyond the nature of things.

I climbed up the first mountain then in the ascent toward Flagstaff. At Peeple's Valley I watched the birds rise slowly from the fields into the October sky. A jet trail hung there in the haze.

Beyond Prescott there is another valley, a great incredible expanse of high plateau which the thin highway crosses on its way to Mingus Mountain. If you happen to hit that stretch of the road alone on a late afternoon, as I have, drive slowly, look perhaps into the eye of the steer that's standing by the roadside, and tell me what you feel. If you say you cannot, then I'll confide I've known the feeling.

But now there was a car ahead of me, a single car with a man and woman sitting close together, and as I drew closer I saw a child, a small boy, standing in the seat between them. They drove along slowly and stared toward Mingus Mountain, and suddenly I was moved by what I saw, by the beholders themselves, by the boy, fair-haired and beloved, who was Summerfield, who was me in my childhood, who stared out and did not know yet what I knew, and who would know only when it was too late to know.

At a little hill blurred with the green of pine and the red of dying oak I pulled the car to the side of the road. I was entering the mountain, and all the mysterious symbols were behind me now. The air was cooling and the sun was dropping, and the jet trail had turned rose in the dying sky. I could smell the pines and see the sunlight catching the hilltop. Then I was running toward it. I was going to climb to it, and I was going to whisper to the sky while it lived, "Summerfield, Summerfield." After that, in the dark, I did not know what I would do, and it did not matter.

No, that was not the end of me. We say we throw our lives away, but go on living. I mended mine as best I could, and managed to reconcile with my wife. I gave up the road, and took a job writing reports for an engineering concern in that expanding West Texas city where we had started out, factories and all.

What else was one to do? I reconciled myself, and did what I should have done no doubt in the first place. In time, perhaps, I'll call it home again.

We'd taken to driving in the suburbs on weekends, looking over the new houses which all looked alike in quest of our new home, and one Sunday afternoon I saw a distracted looking man out walking his dog, a man who looked vaguely familiar.

Yes, that was the last time I saw him. He was standing there on the corner with the dog, holding the leash. We waved and I honked the horn. We did not stop. In the mirror I saw him raise his hand and wave, and then looking after us, somewhat bewildered, he crossed the street with the dog. I believe he recognized us at the last instant, but then you can't be sure about a thing like that.

A mutual friend tells me he is divorced again, and that he works all day behind a desk at a civil service job. I divine that if you could look down on him some evening as he makes his way home through the shadows of that shapeless city, you might see him pounding his breast or tearing his hair. It is the same with him: he is restless and changing still. And in this he will never change.

IN LINE
FOR LEMONADE

ANDREW FETLER

from *Malahat Review*

Alexander Pashkov, a dixie cup in his hand, was moving with the line towards the lemonade bowl in the Young People's Lounge. He had the round face of a tired child, a stubby nose and large dark eyes; on his head a fine mass of black hair which he never managed to part twice in the same place, so that in spite of careful combing he looked unkempt.

He pretended to some knowledge of Moscow, where he was born forty years before, but never mentioned his having been taken to Germany at the age of three, where he grew up. Most of his adult years were spent knocking about among refugees and intellectual flotsam. He studied in Berlin and then in Zurich, where he wrung out a book on the literature of German expatriates. Just before the war he floundered into Paris on his way to America.

There were flocks of homeless birds in those days who knew wars in offing and knew whither to fly. Pashkov was one of them. He came to America and sat out the war and was taken on by Midwestern College. He had at once felt at home in America. Americans are really a homeless people, he reflected, even the wealthy ones. They have a big continent and automobiles. He liked Maplewood as he might have liked a comfortable inn, the trees, the college, and the fashionable Methodist church, a two-million-dollar edifice in which it was a pleasure to make a harmless confession of faith.

In his youth Alexander Pashkov had wanted to become a poet. The ambition in the adolescent grew to shame in the man. He had lived his poetic ambition so intensely, had crowded his wandering years with so much dreaming and so little doing, that now, being settled and nearing forty, he had found it hard to let the poet in him die. He had tried to work, God knows, but nothing came of it. He wrote best in Russian and German, but he had never decided which was *his* language. His good judgment smiled at him in his German attempts and roared at him in the Russian, and so he flung himself back and forth like a madman between two mirrors.

And yet the day came when his poetic ambition died, and it died without pain. It was mercifully killed by honour from an unexpected quarter. A routine academic essay of his on Mayakovsky, appearing in a literary quarterly on the twentieth anniversary of the poet's suicide, attracted attention. Pashkov had a restrained English prose and his fragments of translation from Mayakovsky came off happily. The editor of the periodical flattered himself on having uncovered a new talent.

Pashkov was invited to contribute something more on Soviet literature. He knew the tides of fashion and replied with an appreciation of Yesenin. Although he scarcely knew Yesenin and had in fact come too late to this poet to translate him with sympathy, he received a number of letters from scholars in the land, solicitations from two obscure magazines, and an inquiry from a New York publisher who smelled a market.

At bottom he mistrusted his talent. He stuck to his first editor with a long paper on the Soviet Futurists. He steered clear of Communist ideology so as not to clutter his literary criticism with political comment. Instead of revealing his slippery hold of the subject, his timidity was praised in Letters to the Editor as "masterful detachment," and a student in California wrote in that Pashkov's approach was "the very thing America needs at a time when mad reactionary dogs are running loose in Washington."

Pashkov was in despair. His interest was literary, he disliked and feared politics, and his only wish was to pass unnoticed by the nests of vipers he saw stirring about him. To make matters worse, he could not help cheating a little in his essays, could not resist making small references here and there to poets and schools and "influences" of which he knew nothing. Nobody, he realized gloomily, not even the chairman of his department at Midwestern, saw through his ignorance. That piece on the Futurists had been a risky job. He would be more careful.

He had the good fortune at this time to meet Thomas Eisner, the great translator of Russian classics, who came to Midwestern for two days. At the lecture tea Eisner took Pashkov aside.

"I have read some of your work," the famous personage said in beautiful Russian. "You are not a critic, dear Mr. Pashkov. You are a poet, somewhat like the English Fitzgerald."

Pashkov stared, and the ponderous Eisner smiled down at him and nodded and said, "Yes."

Pashkov wanted to weep, as though his sins had rolled away. Was he to be a poet after all?

He wanted to thank Eisner, but the oracle was too much for him. He pressed Eisner's hand and blushed. He came home in high spirits.

He set to work. A "translator" of poetry? he mused with a smile, working on Blok. For the first time since his youth he felt that he was growing. When he came to Pasternak he was jubilant. He had found himself. He was a sort of Fitzgerald, he reminded himself, and a sort of Conrad who would not have written at all if not in English. As the year passed he became a small name to people who knew what was happening in the world.

He was touched by a desire he had not known. He got the notion of topping his happiness with a pleasant marriage. His success was after all too one-sided, too public, too much like a display that does not satisfy the performer deeply. There would always be work for him, he might even achieve a small place—but he dared think no further. He thought instead of a wife who would fill the vacancy in him.

There was a vacancy in him. He admitted it. Something in him had not been engaged in his work, a part of him had not bitten into Eisner's flattering words, had remained untouched, unexercised, left to rot in his soul, to petrify, to create darkness and frighten him. Alexander Pashkov needed a wife.

For a man who had travelled so much his love life was disappointing. There had been women. In the closing days before the war Paris was enlivened by numerous cross-currents of festive people meeting and parting for the last time. There was dancing and music. He remembered the poet Tagkvist with his fake anecdotes about Lagerlof and Hedin and even Hamsun, his shrill voice above a crowd offering him his mistress for a week. Very drunk for a Swede. Tagkvist ran ahead introducing Pashkov as the celebrated author of "Hesse and Others," which nobody had read, a cheap paperback edition that lay forgotten in the basement of a publisher nobody had heard of. Tagkvist had fashioned this fact into an acceptable calling card for Pashkov. Goodness knows who all was there, in one or another of the whooping holes the Swede dragged him to. Names and self-made names, and always some repulsive Bebert in the company of nonchalant Americans.

Pashkov might have had something to remember had he not disappointed the women. His Napoleonic height was no impediment, they liked him the more for his child's stature and fondled him with the sharp sensuality that makes the corruption of innocents such a pleasure. In bed his small figure, his unkempt hair and big dark eyes made him look like a little boy. But Pashkov allowed the women no fun. He could not help it. He got carried away, he trembled into oblivion and immediately fell to sleep.

Well, he was not a lover. Worse, he had never loved. It was as if his love had been stopped in childhood by some horrid and commonplace experience, and hid itself at every appeal to the man. There was a girl from Cherbourg fell in love with him. Pashkov fled to other arms. Not without melancholy. Why couldn't he love?

If truth must be told, he did not even love his work. He was making an Anthology now. His publisher insisted on something "comprehensive." He would have to include a lot of facetious muck written by order of the Politburo. There were moments of pleasure when a good poem came his way, but he had lost his freedom in the publisher's contract. And Midwestern College expected a "major production." He sent off the manuscript and started to look for a woman he might marry.

How pretty the women here were, how perfectly they dressed. But how unapproachable. A riddle, their infinite care of appearance and icy chastity. Sunday morning he watched them walking under the shade trees, swinging their hips to church, dressed and painted like the more expensive Parisian whores, not too gaudily, not too modestly. They were afraid of something, he thought with satisfaction—afraid of discolouration, of poverty. It was a good fear, it was what attracted Pashkov.

Forty years old. Yes, it was time to settle down. The college humour magazine, *Banana,* had four pages caricaturing members of the faculty. "Guess Who?" There were storks wearing pince-nez, hippopotamuses, gazelles, lions and crows. On the bars in the gymnasium swung a couple of apes, from the English Department emerged a mild-eyed horse. Pashkov found himself and was not displeased. On the Slavonic branch of the Tree of Languages sat a harmless little lemur. The caption read: "One of our lemures?"

He did not know whether *Banana* knew the difference between lemurs and lemures, between the arboreal mammals and the souls of the dead.

One day a religious worker knocked on his door with solicitations for a settlement in the slums. Pashkov gave generously and two months later the same mendicant returned with an appeal for the underfed in Malaya and an invitation to "meet the folks" at the church. A nice quiet woman, flashed through his mind. He had explored the local movie houses and parks, timidly and with a wary eye. The social life of the town was gruesome—in fact, it did not seem to exist. Possibly in the church? Why had he not thought of the church before?

But he had to go to New York just then. The appearance of his Anthology made it necessary for him to attend an autographing party. He put off thinking about a nice quiet woman.

In New York a junior editor showed him the town. The Anthology was selling well enough. Reviews ranged from talk about two great peoples exchanging ideas to the wisdom of knowing one's enemy. Pashkov knew the book was worthless.

"Doesn't Thomas Eisner live in New York?" Pashkov asked his guide.

"Long Island. Would you like to meet him?"

"No, no. I was just wondering. I could not find him in the telephone directory."

"He'd hardly be listed," the young man said. He gave Pashkov a thin smile. "I have his address in my desk. I'd be glad to introduce you."

Eisner had turned down Pashkov's request for a review of his book.

On the morning of his last day in New York Pashkov travelled to Long Island. The house was rather small; it stood on a large lawn; about the house stood a scattering of slender birch trees.

A negress took his name in, came back and ushered him into a large bedroom, where the man sat behind a breakfast tray.

"So good of you to call on me," Eisner said. He offered his hand. "I have a cold."

That beautiful Russian language, Pashkov thought, and felt a vague longing. But he scarcely touched his hand.

"Mary, bring us a chair. Will you have tea, Mr. Pashkov?"

"Thank you, no." He sat on the edge of the chair and leaned forward, clasping his hands.

"No doubt you wonder why I could not review your Anthology," Eisner said.

Pashkov raised a protesting hand, dropped it and wrung his fingers.

"I did look at it. Very nice. But I am terribly busy just now. It appears we live in an age of deadlines. Is it selling well?"

Pashkov nodded.

"You've got to be careful here. Don't let them cheat you. Who is your agent?"

"I have no agent, Mr. Eisner."

"But that's not good. Shall I introduce you to my Zhivchick? Fine business sense. What have you next in mind? What are you working on now?"

Pashkov looked down at his hands. They were moist.

"I have been thinking of Khlebnikov," he said in a small, subdued voice.

"Hm."

"Not so much Khlebnikov's work," Pashkov's voice rose. "I was thinking of his life, his travels."

"What, a biography?"

"Well, not exactly. The typhoid, the army in Persia. A man . . . a poem, in fact, but a biographical, that is, a panoramic . . . ."

Pashkov opened his mouth for air.

"What?"

"After your lecture in Midwestern, if you remember. You said—" He covered his face. "You said I was a poet."

Pashkov waited, but Eisner remained silent.

At last he looked up. Eisner was stirring his tea.

"I've said a great many things, Mr. Pashkov. But one book is nothing to get upset about. We are too impatient with ourselves."

"What shall I do?"

"Work."

"Mr. Eisner," Pashkov said. "Mr. Eisner," he repeated, "is there any hope?"

Eisner hesitated a moment. "You're asking an impossible question," he said. "And after all, what else is there to do?"

Just then Mary knocked on the door. Eisner waved her out but Pashkov had already taken up his coat.

He smiled. "Strange, isn't it, Mr. Eisner, that some people need to be told they are worth something, and others that they are worth nothing."

"I am not sure I understand."

"Perhaps there is nothing to understand."

And so Alexander Pashkov went back to Maplewood with the thought that he must find a woman; a woman not to be distinguished from the smooth cement of those tidy streets, one of the lacquered beauties. To lose himself. And where better than in a two-million-dollar church?

Pashkov went to the Sunday morning service. He had time now, he would explore his adopted country, find his little hole and drop in. He sat in a padded pew somewhat to the side, toward the rear, on the edge of well-dressed worship.

Thereafter he was seen regularly at the Sunday afternoon social in the Young People's Lounge. He was always very polite and everybody liked him.

Americans are quite right, thought Pashkov. They lead the nations, they have the wisdom of babes. They are right for me, he smiled. He did not know whether they were right for themselves. That did not concern him, that was another question.

He held the dixie cup and moved with the line toward the lemonade bowl.

Second Fiddle

WILLIAM FIFIELD from *Texas Quarterly*

They began to walk around the Round Pond. The summer evening haze had thickened, and Kensington Palace, across the Round Pond, was only dimly to be seen—the trees, the bulk of the orangery, veiled in mist, the statue of Queen Victoria as a young girl, filmy and indistinct, a faint, still ghost among the moving ghosts of the people. Near at hand, some boys sailed boats in the concrete shallows, and one, rolling up trouser legs, waded out, and began to scoop up minnows into a bottle.

The girl, once she got started, proved to be a terrific talker. "That was at Srinagar," she said. "Srinagar—when we lived out in Kashmir. Well, it was queer. Daddy sent Mum and me on to the hill station. There was talk that the tribesmen were coming down, out of Afghanistan. So Daddy sent Mum and me off to the hills. And that was how it happened. I must say it was jolly funny, how it all worked out. The house, you see, was lonely way up there. And Mum had the weirdest feeling about it, from the beginning. 'There is something wrong, Jo.' she said. 'Something wrong. Something wrong. Oh, Jo, we should not have come here.' Jo was what she called me. My name is Joanna—have I told you? And your name?"

"Tom."

They had just met. She had come along through the mist, round, red-cheeked, a plump, boyish mite of a girl, with a little cap like a beanie on the back of her head. Seeing Tom, she had signalled with a cigarette—unlit.

"Match?" she'd asked.

"Oh—sure."

And he had lit her cigarette, and they had fallen into step, beginning to walk around the Round Pond.

"Well," she went on, "it was up to Daddy to solve the affair. If you knew him you would understand. He is a huge man—huge—like this—'' She held her hands wide comically, as if embracing a giant. Having indicated the great girth of her father, she brought the hands together with a clap. "He dug it all out, you see, bit by bit. It was not the house, really, that made Mum feel queer—but a room in the house. One room. And Daddy found out, asking about, that a child had been carved up in that room—murdered horribly—cut up into pieces. And then stuffed into a bureau drawer. Quite a frightful case, you know, but long ago. I won't tell you what led people to the bits of body in the drawer . . . in that hot climate.''

"No, don't," Tom said.

"But they were led to the poor little body—or what remained. And then, you see, time passed, and the thing was forgotten. Or people forgot to talk about it. And so Daddy, when he rented the house and sent Mum and me there, knew nothing of it. But then he followed himself, for the days of real heat, and poked about in local rumor—and worked it all out. But the *queer* thing," said Joanna, "was that *Mum* had known from the first. Not what had happened . . . but that something had happened. The horror sat in the air of the room—that was how she expressed it. She had felt the horror the minute she entered the house— sniffed it, like a dog sniffing fresh beef. That was how we found out she was psychic.''

"Psychic?'' asked Tom.

"Yes, she was. And it was jolly funny how it all worked out. Poor old Mum went from one thing to the next—first there was the sense of that hacked-up body, and then the child itself. The child came to her—though I do admit that this was after Daddy had found the story out and Mum knew of it—the child came to her, wailing in the night. Oh, you should have seen Mum, shrieking in the hall, hair starting out as if she were full of electricity, in her flannel nightdress—she wore it however blistering hot it was. And there she was shrieking in the hall, bringing us all stark awake in the middle of the night. 'Oh God, oh God, oh God in heaven,' she shrieked, 'I've seen him! I've seen him!' Of course we thought it was an intruder she had seen. And Daddy—it *was* funny—caught up the nearest thing to hand, a rattan end table, and went rushing about the house, brandishing the insubstantial thing in his hand. But it was the murdered child Mum had seen. The child had touched her with a pathetic hand, and stood, shining a little in the dark, a bit luminous, and said—very pitifully—'Please help me. Please help me.' Coming awake to that, Mum had had a shock."

Tom laughed. "I believe that," he said.

"After that," Joanna went on, "other spirits came. Whole hosts of them. At first only by night, but then in the daytime. 'Whatever—whatever shall I do?' Mum would say. 'They drive me frantic. They give me no peace. Wherever I look, there they are—poking about. Oh, it *is* frightful!'

"Then Daddy—a very practical sort, Tom—said: 'Well, love, since they're about—why not put them to work?'

"'Whatever do you mean?' Mum asked.

"'Just this—' And Daddy said that since the spirits had begun to give her dictation, tell her all sorts of things, she ought to start putting down what they said.

"'You could make a book of it,' he said.

"'But I couldn't pay attention to them—and write things too,' Mum said.

"'Then I will help you,' Daddy said.

"And it *was* jolly funny, Tom. There they were, the two of them, every evening from half past seven till nine—Daddy said that since they were to do it they ought to be sensibly organized and go about it in a practical way—and there they would sit each evening, at the big oak table, with the lamp burning—we didn't have electric light up there. Of course the evening would be ablaze with heat, right then at the height of the Kashmiri summer, and poor Daddy, fairly blooming with the heat, would sit with a handkerchief tucked under his collar to catch the sweat—and he would write down whatever Mum said. And Mum would half lie back in her chair, her eyes closed. The voices would talk to her and she would repeat what they said. That was how her book was written."

"Was it ever published?" Tom asked.

"Oh yes. But it is out of print now."

They went on around the Round Pond. The light was going; the round, tall cone of the bandstand, off toward the spear of the Albert Memorial over the trees, was disappearing. The trees became a field of black, reared in the mist. Then the few swans that shared the Round Pond with the ducks and gulls broke into flight, went up with a great cracking of heavy wings, beat low over the pond, and came down, breasting up curls. The boys who had sailed boats had gone.

"But," said Joanna, "we've talked of no one but me. And you? Why are you in London? You're American, aren't you?"

"Yes," he said.

"Your accent," she laughed. She pretended to chew mush in her mouth. "Americans talk with their throats. They *pinch* the sounds out."

"I'm a student over here," he said.

"Isn't it lonely?"

He was surprised. "It is," he said.

"Oh, London can be a lonely place. I know. I know!"

"Do you still live with your mother and dad?" Tom asked.

"Oh no. I see Mum sometimes. She's a regular practicing medium now."

When it was nearly dark, and their limbs had chilled and stiffened where they sat—where the Round Pond damp and the mist of the evening reached them on a park bench—Tom said, "I'd like to see you again, Joanna."

"Tomorrow? By the Statue of Light and Energy. Just down there. . . ." And she pointed off through the mist.

And at twenty minutes after nine in the morning, when he went expectant and early, she was there before him. It was a fine, clear, bright morning—one of London's redeeming mornings—not a morning wet and grey, or misty, or sulphurous with imprisoned smoke. And this time they turned away from the Round Pond and went down the slope that led them to the little statue of Peter Pan, and then to the Serpentine, neck of water weedy and willowed along the shore. It did not seem that they were in a giant city.

After a while, when they had been together an hour or so, Joanna said, "There is something I'm honor bound to tell you, Tom. I'm married."

He stopped. For a moment he simply looked down from his taller height into her face. And then he lifted her left hand slowly. But there was no ring.

"Separated," she said.

"You don't live with him?"

"No. Have not for long."

"Will you get divorced?"

"He won't."

"Why not?"

"He's a queer sort. A queer sort, Tom."

Tom puzzled his fair brows.

"A queer sort," she said resignedly, and for a third time.

They began to walk on—the path they followed rose toward a cement road through the park, and beyond, on a lane of packed earth, a few early morning riders cantered on horseback.

"I was not always the girl I might have been, Tom," Joanna began. "Perhaps I was put off the track from the beginning—I don't know. Mother grew strange. Very strange. And it seemed to permeate me too. I thought I was becoming psychic, just like Mum. But Mum said—oh, Tom, it was queer—said she *sent* the rays into me. She was able to do strange things. And I became weird too, being around her. And then, Tom, coming home here to England. The change after India . . . you see, I was a rebellious and bad girl. One day I went to Marble Arch—I went there to see if I might meet up with a chap. It was Sunday afternoon—many were gathered listening to the speakers. Well, I met a Welsh boy—red-faced, earnest, inarticulate chap, with the farm sod of Wales still on him. He was a soldier boy—why he was away from home. So he and I walked along together. The speakers were all going it, and there were hundreds about, gawping up and listening to what they said. Then, aways off, out of the press, there was one lone little knot of people, and at the center of it, raised up on his platform, was John."

"John?" asked Tom.

For answer, Joanna only touched the place on the fourth finger of her left hand where a wedding ring might have been. "Yes, John," she said. "Oh, he was astounding. Everyone was nearly transfixed. He was not like the others. He talked in a wild way, like a river foaming out of his mouth, all froth and gleam, all tossing, wonderful, impetuous words—nothing planned, Tom, every sound just let fly to the ear. You did not think he took thought at all, but just spoke, with that marvelous power, a kind of music of conviction, as if the hunger of it sat in his heart, and broke free. But the things he said! Those words of his, all leaping and turning, they were dangerous, Tom. People hardly knew, he held them so rapt. He could have spun them on his tongue, like little, frail threads. But he was subtle and fantastic, a dangerous man. He said the end of history had come. At first you did not understand what he meant—but he meant that all the accumulation of the years, the centuries, was burning up—that our civilization was going to turn into a barbaric fire before our eyes, and everything we knew was going to be consumed. We were going to emerge, those of us left, clean and naked, purged by fire . . . savages, with passions like unguarded flame, and we were going to scourge the earth. He made this *live*, Tom. You did not know what you were hearing, the wild, exalted plan. Well, my Welsh chap, poor dull lad, took exception. He was too dull-witted to understand; to be carried away. He picked out a phrase that seemed to conflict with his soldierly ideals, and put a question. He challenged the phrase. You have been to Hyde Park, Tom? To Marble Arch?"

Tom nodded.

"Then you have seen how the challengers put their questions, taunting and heckling, for the sport, and how the speakers come back, sometimes crossly, sometimes superior, down from the heights of their platforms. But John stopped. He stopped speaking; he stood, hands on the rail of his platform, looking down over the heads to my lad. He just stood, looking, until my poor chap's face burned, went blood red as a harvest moon. Then John started in. He might have had an insect on a pin—as he had my Welsh boy on the spear of his eye, looking at him, never blinking. And with his face pale as ash, drawn, angry, he sent the words dancing and stinging. He wasn't used to being challenged—no one ever challenged him, Tom. I found that out later on. Well, he obliterated my boy. Then the boy and I pushed out of the crowd and went away. But the next Sunday I went back. When John was finished, when it was cold and dark and he had talked on under the circle of light from the park lamp where he put up his platform, until people began to go, worn out by him, or the hour too late, then he said to those who had stayed till the last—'If you want to hear more, I speak each Tuesday and Thursday evening at the International Club of London, Wexley Road.'

"I went there. The International Club of London was all John's affair. It was a miserable little basement, and all the weird people were drawn there, the hopeless lick-and-spittle little shop girls that idolized him, the halfpenny idealists, a few Indians thrown off the tangent by London, some Colonial blacks. We would sit in rows on folding chairs, and in front of us, at his table, with blackboard behind him, scrawled over with his ideas, John would sit—and talk out over us, a little quieter than at the park.

"So," said Joanna, "that was how it began."

"And you married him?" asked Tom.

"The queer thing was that he married me."

"But it didn't work out?"

They had walked a long way—clear to the rim of the park, and the Park Lane traffic shuttled before them.

"No, it didn't work out."

"But why won't he let you go?"

"He says that marriage is a sacramental state. A holy citadel."

"But my God what kind of a marriage—?"

"A spiritual union," smiled Joanna. "It was."

"And you don't see him now?"

"No. Never."

There was a Lyon's tea room on a corner and they crossed and went in. It was a busy, quick-service shop, the tables for eight or ten, no private tables. Their talk, with others pressing close around them, became spasmodic, general. Then eventually they left and went down to the Thames Embankment. The boats hooted on the river, and a big boat, excursion launch, passed on upriver toward Hampton Court or Kew.

"I live in Chelsea," Joanna said. "Would you like to come? I'll make us lunch."

And after that they were always together. She was a vivid girl, a dart of spirit. Her bed-sittingroom in Chelsea had a long slickly waxed hall, and sometimes, in comical exuberance, she would run and slide the length of it, skidding and laughing. Other times she would be pensive. Once she said, "I feel guilty, Tom. Morbidly guilty."

"Why, darling?"

"You're a good boy, Tom. Do you like this duplicity? Coming here like this—slipping in and out. Like a creature doing deeds of blood."

"Don't be romantic," laughed Tom. "There's nothing wrong."

"No . . . nothing wrong. Except that you're not cut out for this. You aren't, Tom."

Another time, when she had talked like this, Tom said, "Talk to him, Joanna. Maybe he'll let you go."

"Would you marry me? Would you? Would you, Tom?"

"If you'd have me."

"If I'd have you. Oh, Tom! Tom!"

But when she had gone to her husband she came back disconsolate.

"It's no good, Tom," she said. "No good. No use. He will never free me. 'As long as each of us shall live,' he said. Oh, he is a terrifying man. He said we had pledged ourselves—and could not break our word."

"You will have to divorce him then," Tom said. "Whether he likes it or not."

"Charging what? Charging what?"

"Well—desertion."

"But we live apart because of me!"

Then one day Tom went to the flat and found it deserted. There had been no forewarning—except that, looking back, he saw Joanna had brooded more and more. It was the first of the month. The flat was empty.

The next morning a letter waited in the pigeonhole at his hotel. "This is best. There is no future. Forget me."—it said. And more—toward the end a torrent. But the envelope bore no return address.

She had left no address with the owners of her flat in Chelsea. Tom tried this and that, the few things he knew of her leading him on, but always to a dead end. He haunted the places where they had been together—the bit of green in St. James's Park near the children's swings, the Thames Embankment. But then he knew he would not find her in that way. She meant to free him of her, and she would not go where he might come looking for her.

London was a giant city, teeming with the impersonal millions who passed along the curving streets, and he might search the throng, the cold white faces, mask-stiffened to contain private thoughts, until his eyes were blind, and never find Joanna. So then, one Sunday, he went to Marble Arch.

He was much as she had said—the man John, her husband. Tom found his platform almost at once. He entered the corner of park at Marble Arch, and walked through the scattering of people that cast about to attach themselves to some listening group. A Negro with strange gloves on his hands, like brown rubber surgical gauntlets, gesticulated and called his charges against Britain in a pinched, penetrating voice. And next beyond, a hulk of man, lumped and determined on his platform, demanded redress of some other wrong done by the empire. Turbans moved here and there in the crowd—motley crowd of London. At the periphery, a little removed and tentative, perhaps because his interest was commercial amid all the mixed idealisms, a Scot in kilts worked at the air bag of his bagpipe, to get what pence and threepenny bits he could. And with the skirl of his music mingled a Salvation Army hymn from a group near the iron railing that closed in the park. Beyond all this, the general welter, John's platform reared up apart.

He was as Joanna had described him, a torch of energy, a torch of words. But Tom, who listened coolly, waiting for the time Joanna had told of when John would finish and he could go to him and ask the question he had come to ask, saw that the hot fire that burned from the man was kindled at some negative center, a center of hate. He was a hater of life—with his wild eloquence of how it would all end in shambles, a crash of smoking destruction out of the spent, dead ashes of which the few chosen would step. The man had contempt for those who listened; he raged down at them as if their upturned faces were the blank faces of sheep—into which he would *strike* intelligence, comprehension. Tom felt as he watched him that he raged down his dangerous, destructive fire—hellfire though blazed from the tongue and gloried with eloquence—felt as he heard him, that the man spoke out of the pit of desperate contempt for the pack in front of him. And once a tell-tale phrase escaped the speaker's lips: "You cannot comprehend—but I tell you—"

He did not get the chance to speak to him then. There were too many adherents.

So the following Tuesday evening Tom went to the meeting place of the International Club of London on Wexley Road. When he came up from the tube station it was to walk into fog, thick and sulphurous. He could not find his way. He choked at the smoke and his eyes burned. A hollow of light stood here and there in the yellow darkness. It was a business section and the window lights were on in some of the shops. But when he would go to one of these pools of light he would find no one of whom to ask directions. Finally he stumbled on a street sign placed up on a house corner. It was dimly legible in the weak rays of a street light. Wexley Road. Shortly Tom found the half basement—meeting place of the International Club of London.

The meeting was nearly over. John sat as Joanna had once described him, arms folded before him on the table at the front of the room. His drawn, pallid face turned slowly from side to side. He did not look around as Tom entered. A few of the adherents looked; frowned their annoyance; looked back to the front.

When the meeting was over a small wooden box was placed on the table. The audience crowded forward, filing past the table. They dropped coins into the wooden box. Most of them bent and held out their right hands. John, still seated, would take a hand—let it shake his. He seemed wearied and emptied.

Tom went to the table last of all. He dropped a shilling into the box. When he simply stood, waiting, John slowly raised his eyes. He turned up a face tiredly—the face of a lonely martyr.

"Yes?" he asked.

"Where is Joanna?"

"Joanna? Oh." The face smiled palely. "Why? Do you know her?"

"I know her."

"Oh. Then are you the man? She has told me. I do not know where she is, my friend," John said. "Perhaps she will come back to you. Have you quarrelled? If so, I am sorry."

The words and tone angered Tom. Suddenly he leaned low over the table. "Where is she?" he demanded. "Where is Joanna?"

"I cannot tell you. I do not know."

Tom would have reached out to shake the man, taking him by the shoulders, to force the truth from him—something in the man's passiveness made him want to use force—but John drew back, though in a curiously submissive way. "That will not help you, my friend," he said. "I do not know where she is. If I hear from her I will let you know. Leave me your address."

Tom turned abruptly and walked out into the night.

Months passed; the university year ended. Tom went home, and there England, London, Joanna faded in his mind. He came back in autumn to resume school again. In a few days it was as if he had not left London. It was home that seemed far away and half forgotten, the vacation period slipping from him, a distant, unreal island in time. Winter came on, and one morning London was mute and smoking in snow. But then in a few days the snow was wet and sooty. In the winter, Tom heard a few times of John. John Howard Clarke was beginning to appear in the papers. He was enlarging his orbit, reaching out into a bigger world.

In the tender and tentative spring, that came slowly that year after the heavy winter, Tom began to walk a few evenings a week to Albert Hall across the park. He still lived in the hotel where he had lived from the first, and from it he would go alone, into the park and past the Round Pond, and then on to Albert Hall.

One evening he sat in the gallery. He had come late, and the standees had crowded into the floor of the hall. Only a few gallery seats remained. He bought one, and climbed the dozens of stairs. Then he came out on the gallery, a lip running almost around the rotunda, very high up—a narrow rim edged by a railing, a single row of straight-backed chairs for seats, and then the carpeted space behind, hardly twenty feet wide, along which young men and women were stretched out, or propped half erect against the wall, their eyes closed, listening. The concert had already begun.

Tom found his chair at the rail and sat. Along the rail many heads were rested on clasped hands. Tom leaned forward too, resting his arms on the rail. Down below, in the body of the hall, most of the seats had been removed. The room thus made for the crowding many was packed with their compact mass. They stood shoulder to shoulder, pressed together. As Tom watched, there was movement sometimes—ripple over the crowd, like a twitch along the hide of an animal.

In front of the standing crowd, there was a barrier. Beyond it there was a low bank of fern. Then the bandstand, like a sea shell of striated gold, began. Its golden fan spread out and up, containing light, beamed from somewhere, containing the many men of the symphony orchestra, seeming small far below. At their front, on a little podium, the conductor stood. Then beside him, when a number had ended and applause had swept around the hall like a dry clacking of reeds, the soloist appeared and took his place on a companion podium, a little lower than the conductor's. The light faded to dimness in the gold shell, and a beam picked out the violinist, a slim, tall man, throwing a shadow much longer than himself diagonally across the cone of light.

It was surprising how the single tones of the violin could rise out of the sound of all the instruments mellow and clear, the others become a thick underscoring, a kind of elemental hum behind the pure, free voice. But suddenly, when the number had gone through its first movement and the second and more impassioned movement had begun, the violinist began to play with crazy speed. Tom had half lost consciousness, listening. But he started, leaning forward. And abruptly many things merged in his startled consciousness. Many around the gallery railing were half standing, brought astonishedly to their feet. And some of those who had been reclining back against the wall were already reaching the railing to press in between the chairs and look below. And below, the whole packed mass of standees was stirring, as its members stood on their toes and tried to see. On the conductor's podium, the conductor himself was seen to falter—then begin to wave his arms almost wildly, to bring the orchestra up to the hastened pace. And all the players were consulting their scores in amazement. In the whole hall, only one individual was undisturbed: Gregor Ravic, the violinist. But then Ravic slowed his playing, making several queer movements up and down, rising onto the balls of his feet and then rocking back on his heels, and then he played normally again.

The concert over, Tom crowded down the stairs with the others. Everyone was excited and chattering about what had taken place; a wind of nervous amusement swept through the crowd.

When he had reached the cement at the side of Albert Hall, Tom saw that great numbers of people were still issuing from the front doors, coming out from the main body of the auditorium. They all moved in one direction, flowing toward the street. But then he saw there was an eddy at the center of the press, for the crowd had to separate and stream around a single individual who stood motionless, facing not toward the street but toward Albert Hall. And when he had pushed his way in at the edge of the crowd he saw that this sole individual was Joanna.

He fought his way to her.

"Joanna!"

She turned her head slowly, seeming dazed.

"Oh . . . Tom."

He took her arm and began to draw her along, going with the flow of the crowd, and hardly noticing in his excitement at finding her after so long that she came almost lifelessly, gazing back abstractedly over her shoulder at Albert Hall.

They moved with the flow of the crowd and could not choose their direction until they had reached the curb. Then Tom, tightening his grip on her arm, guided her across the street through the traffic, and up the flight of steps toward the great iron Albert thirty feet high, seated reflectively in his pagoda amid the symbols of empire—the crossed spears, the iron African shields, the iron elephants. When they had moved a little further on, and neared the brim of the park, where pansy heads were visible in the half dark, and the park lights hung in the gloom along the walk like globes of luminescent fruit, Joanna suddenly started, looked incredulously into his face, and then without a word broke from his grasp on her arm and ran off and vanished into the park.

In the morning there was a note for him in his box at his hotel. Mrs. O'Ryan handed it to him disapprovingly.

"A woman left this for you just now, Tom," she said when he passed on his way to the dining room and breakfast. "A married person. I saw the wedding ring."

Tom walked on, opening his note. Joanna had written to inquire if he was still in the same hotel. "I will leave this for you if you are." She began to apologize for her behavior of the previous evening; she wrote as she had always talked, in the inflated, impetuous way. "How horrid I was. And after so long. Can you ever forgive me? But there is such an utterly incredible explanation." She lived near Queen Anne's Gate—dear Tom—once again domiciled with John.—"Oh, for a long time. Yes, we are back together. That is a story!" She had struck down on the paper with her pen in such a way that it had slightly torn. "Have you heard about the astonishing progress of John? A real figure now. A power in London. Tom," she concluded abruptly as she neared the bottom of the single sheet, "come by and meet him. Could you come to us for dinner? Say, half past seven? Sometimes he comes home late from his great affairs." In a different-colored ink she had added: "I find you are here. Please come tonight." Her handwriting was large and open, but she'd squeezed the address in tiny characters on the margin of the page.

Tom slowly refolded the note. There was an extent of thirty or forty feet across the old-fashioned waxed parquet floor of the residential hotel lounge, and then there were the two glass swinging doors with their frilly dimity curtains, and the dining room beyond. For the most part the residents of the quiet hotel were elderly folk, and retired colonial servants returned after two-thirds of their lives in far places to what they still felt was home. To England. Mr. Hawley, come back to England after forty years overseas, coughed and laughed discreetly, in the manner of one who invites inquiry as to what it is that is amusing. He was seated on the leather sofa at the dining room entrance with the morning paper open across his knees. As Tom was the only one near, it was he whose attention Mr. Hawley must want. Tom looked down inquiringly.

"Look here, Tom, I want you to listen to this." And Mr. Hawley began to read "'An unexplained occurrence took place at Royal Albert Hall last evening. Hurrmph. Sir Arthur Whale conducted the Promenade Concert, interpreting Brahms well in my opinion, Brahms being a composer whose music would seem especially grateful to Sir Arthur—' Hmp." Mr. Hawley broke off. "Eh. Here we are. '. . . when Mr. Gregor Ravic, at this point in playing, unaccountably increased tempo. Interviewed after the concert, he declared that he was unable to explain what had taken place. He had felt a sensation as if he were being lifted in a cloud. He had felt himself all but borne away, and then again put down on his feet. It was during this moment that he played in the unaccountable fashion. He had the sense of being removed from reality for a time. I spoke with Professor M. D. V. Hillary, the well-known authority on psychological disturbances, and he has stated to me that the phenomenon closely resembles that of *petit mal*—in which the individual ordinarily loses consciousness for a short interval, so that the sensation is that a fragment of time has vanished from his life. Professor Hillary states, however, that had Mr. Gregor Ravic actually experienced *petit mal* he ought properly to have fallen down.' Odd, wouldn't you say, Tom?''

Coming out from breakfast, Tom paused to listen to the wireless news. The announcer gave the weather report, then said: "Here is the news. The American Secretary of State has further elaborated his plan for . . . The Queen has this morning returned from Scotland, accompanied by the children. An incident of mental telepathy has occurred at Royal Albert Hall . . .

"Some considerable attention has already been directed upon last evening's event at Royal Albert Hall," he went on, following the political news. "I am now able to tell you what would seem to be the cause of this unusual incident. Three days ago a person ,whose name is for the present being withheld came here to Broadcasting House and asked to see Mr. Glenn, assistant to Mr. Val Gielgud, the well-known producer. This request having been granted, the person in question handed to Mr. Glenn a sealed envelope, asking that the envelope be kept and opened three days later—that is to say, this morning, for, as the person then said, the envelope contained a prophecy which circumstances would have verified between that time and today, and with this in view an advance record was being placed with someone whose report of the fact would be believed. On opening the envelope today, Mr. Glenn has discovered that the event of last night at Royal Albert Hall is accurately foretold. The person writing claims to possess telepathic power, saying such power will be, on the evening of the Ravic concert, projected into the performer Mr. Ravic, and that he will then play at an insanely heightened speed for a few bars, then play normally again. This will not be an instance of hypnotism or any like thing, but a new manifestation, that of sending mental waves in a manner comparable to that of sending waves by wireless."

"Mental waves by wireless," an old lady by the radio said. "Only think!"

That evening Tom went to the address Joanna had given him near Queen Anne's Gate. It was a flat-fronted building rising up sheerly five or six stories from the street. The whole street was shabby and plain. By the door beneath the number where Tom stopped there was a perpendicular row of doorbells set into the fingermarked wood, each bell with a small placard underneath. One placard had written on it in a microscopic hand—"John H. Clarke." Tom rang. In a moment he heard a window thrown up somewhere above, and when he had stepped back from the threshold and looked up he saw Joanna.

"Catch Tom!" she called and dropped some object.

He caught it—it was the front door key, wound up in a sock.

Upstairs, Joanna waited for him in the hall. She said not a word about the previous night, nor mentioned the long time it had been since they had met. She skipped ahead of him into the flat, and it seemed as if time had wheeled back, almost as if they were together again in Chelsea. She seemed her former vivid self. Her cheeks burned with bright dots, not rouge but the native blood, hot with her energy. She had something like a beanie on the back of her head, as the first time he had met her. But this was a formal skullcap of velvet, sewn with sequins. And she had dressed for the occasion. She had on a black, spangled dress. She was plumper than she had been, and the dress was cut low to her full, plump bosom. Over her dress was an apron.

"I was just dishing up. Do come along, Tom. This way. Everything's ready. We can sit and have a drink, and wait for John, Beloved John." And she rattled on as she led him into the living room of the flat—a neat, done-to-order flat, somehow peculiarly seeming unlived-in.

"What will you drink?"

"Whatever you've got," he said.

The whiskey—when it had gone down—seemed to make Joanna even livelier than she had been before, and after a moment, finishing his own drink and putting the glass aside, Tom began to wonder if her excitement was quite natural. Even for Joanna it was extreme. She could not remain still and flew here and there about the room; flew as she had once flown in the old flat in Chelsea with the exuberance and hilarity of being in love. But this elation was different. It was tinged with something negative, and hectic. Once she went to a great heap of folders, leather-bound volumes overflowing the surface of a gate-leg table, and clapped them on the top. Thrusting out a forefinger, she ran a nail straight down the backs, clipping from binding to binding.

"John's clippings! John's speeches," she said. "His great affairs."

"Does he write his speeches, then?" asked Tom, amazed. "I heard him once. It was astonishing enough to think that anyone could talk like that. Spontaneously . . . But to plan out in advance . . ."

"Yes, he is amazing. No, he does not write his speeches out. But you must understand John has become an important man. Famously rising. He blazes away, just as before. The stupefying fact is, as you would know if you lived with him, he doesn't give a thought to what he will say. Write his speeches? No, hardly! The talk lies inside him, ready and molten, all the while. But when he does let it out someone takes down the words in shorthand. You see, he is a famous, important man now."

"Where is he going?" asked Tom. "Parliament?"

Joanna hooted. "Oh, he looks *beyond* Parliament. Parliament? He means to be bigger than that."

"You used to say he was a dangerous man."

"Tom, he is!"

"And where is he going?"

"Wherever he *has* to go. John has no chosen direction; he is driven. Every stage is only the plateau where he rests a moment, but then the thing within him drives him on. How quiet he is! It is because he dare not move, dare not think, or he touches off his power. And then he speaks, and it all gushes forth. Do you suppose he seeks words or makes the effort of speech as many another man must do? Then you understand the true John no more than the others. It is there within him all the time. And it pours out, and he cannot stop it. And all the strange hush and quiet of his manner, Tom, is only to prevent that."

The hall door opened. As footsteps sounded in the entry hall, Joanna said, "Now, Tom, you will witness the pitched battle we call a marriage."

"Why are you back with him?" Tom had time to ask.

"Ah. I fell in love. You must forgive me, Tom. Time passed, and you and I were apart."

"Fell in love with John?"

"No! Scarcely with John."

And it had to rest with that, for John entered. He had a rolled-up newspaper in one hand. Joanna's eyes went to it at once. John smiled and put the hand and paper behind his back.

"Well, here you are, my friend," he said, extending his other hand. "I am glad to see you. I am glad to see you again."

He was gaunter than Tom had remembered. Unlike Joanna, he had not put on flesh. Success had not fleshed him. Nor had he changed his manner of dress. He wore a loose suitcoat, slack on his spare frame. He had on a necktie but his wide shirt collar with long artist's points was open at the throat. There was something careless or indifferent about him, a bohemian air. Within his bohemian attire he was frail and skeletal. Tom remembered, somehow, a description he had read of Savonarola after one of the monk's harangues in the Duomo of Florence—the wild-eyed, emotion-ravished monk weak and nauseated from the strain of his speaking. John suggested the same quality of a frame ravished and consumed from within. He wore a curiously wide-brimmed hat, of some sort of soft moleskin or fur felt. He sailed it wearily onto a table when he had shaken Tom's hand.

"Is dinner ready?" he asked. And even this casual phrase he could fill with a kind of overpowering sadness.

"The terrible meek," thought Tom.

"Come to the table."—Joanna had spoken.

John did not take the server's chair at the table head. This place he gave Tom. He gave it to him with a docile insistence, and placed himself down the table and passively waited to be served.

Joanna was quiet now that her husband was home. A power of passivity flowed from John, that quietened everything. His mouth was large and mobile and almost white, and though he might only be accepting his plate of soup from his wife he infused a tragic hidden meaning even into this. There was a grave kindness about him, as if he were a very old man, as if he had lived and experienced and suffered and could feel nothing but sadness for those who were to follow along the trail. It was some time before Tom felt with a sudden pity how Joanna was trapped in this passivity, her energy strangled.

When the soup course was over he tried to establish a commonplace tone.

"Can I help you, Joanna?" He pushed back his chair.

He carried out some of the dishes, then received plates and bowls from her in the kitchen, which he would carry in to replenish the table where John waited silently alone.

One moment Joanna had the chance or impulse to speak. "This time I mean to marry," she said. "This time it will *not* slip away, as it did with us. I came back to him to force the issue. A long time; and he does not give way. I knew he would never let me go." She handed him plates.

At the table, Tom watched in consternation. For from Joanna's few words, from what he sensed from their small attitudes and expressions, what he thought must be their life began to expand for him. Her flourishes—she gaily flung off her apron before sitting down for the rest of the meal—in John's presence did not seem right, John had the strange muting power of the meek, that ends in stifling all vitality and spontaneous life. She goaded him, Tom thought; but he would not rise and strike. And Tom, within himself, began to feel her desperation.

"Have they released it?" she suddenly asked. Tom had risen to carve the roast, and was stopped still by her tone. For it had darted like the cut of a whip.

John looked up mildly and did not speak.

"*Have* they? You have the paper. It must be in the evening papers!" And she leaned toward her husband, over the table; and Tom thought her eyes flashed with a brimstone fire.

"You ought not to have used my name," John said. But there was no rancor in his tone. The reproach was mildly said, and the words seemed full of sadness.

And then Joanna laughed so harshly and stridently, throwing herself back in her chair, that Tom was appalled. He stood with the carving utensils in his hands, his hands arrested in midair over the brown roast.

"That was the sole reason I did it!" And her voice hissed with such venom that Tom felt frozen by surprise. John only sat quietly, and there was no anger in his eyes. He did not retort; he said nothing.

"I did it so that I could use your name. You understand *why*, do you, John?" She leaned over the table again, her full, heavy bosom in black extended upon the white cloth, her eyes burning into her husband's, and Tom was so astonished at the scene he had no thought of himself—yet stood at the head of the table with the carving knife and fork in his hands, gaping. "You understand why, do you not, John?"

"To humiliate me. I daresay," he replied mildly, in a measured way.

She hooted once. A short sound; which stopped. "Humiliate you? You *court* humiliation. To make you a laughing stock!" Again the shrill sound shut truncatedly off. "To counter you in that way. I mean you shall lose your public, that you shall be burst by pent-up words."

And Tom's astonished mind, so far as it told him anything at all, told him he was at dinner with lunatics. No—told him that this had gone on long. Joanna made a lunge right out onto the table—for John, in his docile way, held up in one hand the newspaper which he had evidently had behind his back, rolled tight in his hand like a runner's baton, and he tantalizingly tilted it back and forth, just a little distance above the napery. "Give it me!" "It says what you wish, Joanna." Dimly, it passed in Tom's mind that he was seeing a lifetime—a lifetime of two people—that he had come into this very late. "I lied. I lied," Joanna whispered. "I told the Press I did it to establish the reality of telepathic power. No, I count on public incredulity at such a thing. And you are linked to me, my famous man."

John merely smiled. And at this little thing Joanna threw back from the table, and sent her chair against the wall with a crash, and stood, trembling and crouched, glaring at him, like an animal at bay. "Why she is mad," thought Tom. As if from a distance, he looked on. "Poor Tom. Poor Tom," someone said. Had someone said poor Tom? No, it was a line from Shakespeare's King Lear. He thought he saw an image lividly printed on his awareness an instant, then gone. It was of someone lashing another with the knout, until a frenzy was reached—in the spasm of which whipper and not whipped dropped down dead. While the submissive lashed one smiled.

And Tom saw that Joanna had turned from John to him. He felt that her eyes fixed themselves upon him. But almost at once, before he could know what response to take, a wondrous peace flowed into him. Or, actually, he began to float. He physically floated into the air, as if buoyed up on a cloud. No . . . he felt the floor under the soles of his feet. Throat of the lamb, came into his mind—as "Poor Tom" the moment before.

It was a moment more curious and strange than any that had preceded it. He was outside it and looking on, interrupted in carving the roast. He knew the utensils were in his hands, but they had no weight. And that hand of his which held the carving knife was his only in such a limited and literal sense. He felt quite freed of responsibility, and full of such peace. Ah, beloved John.

A FABLE

ROBERT FOX from *Midwestern University Quarterly*

The young man was clean shaven and neatly dressed. It was early Monday morning and he got on the subway. It was the first day of his first job and he was slightly nervous; he didn't know exactly what his job would be. Otherwise he felt fine. He loved everybody he saw. He loved everybody on the street and everybody disappearing into the subway and he loved the world because it was a fine clear day and he was starting his first job.

Without kicking anybody, the young man was able to find a seat on the Manhattan bound train. The car filled quickly and he looked up at the people standing over him envying his seat. Among them were a mother and daughter who were going shopping. The daughter was a beautiful girl with blonde hair and soft looking skin, and he was immediately attracted to her.

"He's staring at you," the mother whispered to the daughter.

"Yes, mother, I feel so uncomfortable. What shall I *do*?"

"He's in love with you."

"In love with me? How can you tell?"

"Because I'm your mother."

"But what shall I do?"

"Nothing. He'll try to talk to you. If he does, answer him. Be nice to him. He's only a boy."

The train reached the business district and many people got off. The girl and her mother found seats opposite the young man. He continued to look at the girl who occasionally looked to see if he was looking at her.

The young man found a good pretext for standing in giving his seat to an elderly man. He stood over the girl and her mother.They whispered back and forth and looked up at him. At another stop, the seat next to the girl was vacated and the young man blushed, but quickly took it.

"I knew it," the mother said between her teeth. "I knew it, I *knew* it."

The young man cleared his throat and tapped the girl. She jumped.

"Pardon me," he said. "You're a very pretty girl."

"Thank you," she said.

"Don't talk to him," her mother said. "Don't answer him, I'm warning you. Believe me."

"I'm in love with you," he said to the girl.

"I don't believe you," the girl said.

"Don't answer him," the mother said.

"I really do," he said. "In fact, I'm so much in love with you that I want to marry you."

"Do you have a job?" she said.

"Yes, today is my first day. I'm going to Manhattan to start my first day of work."

"What kind of work will you do?" she asked.

"I don't know exactly," he said. "You see, I didn't start yet."

"It sounds exciting," she said.

"It's my first job but I'll have my own desk and handle a lot of papers and carry them around in a briefcase, and it will pay well, and I'll work my way up."

"I love you," she said.

"Will you marry me?"

"I don't know. You'll have to ask my mother."

The young man rose from his seat and stood before the girl's mother. He cleared his throat very carefully for a long time. "May I have the honor of having your daughter's hand in marriage?" he said, but he was drowned out by the subway noise.

The mother looked up at him and said, "What?" He couldn't hear her either, but he could tell by the movement of her lips, and by the way her face wrinkled up that she said, what.

The train pulled to a stop.

"May I have the honor of having your daughter's hand in marriage!" he shouted, not realizing there was no subway noise. Everybody on the train looked at him, smiled, and then they all applauded.

"Are you crazy?" the mother asked.

The train started again.

"What?" he said.

"Why do you want to marry her?" she asked.

"Well, she's pretty—I mean, I'm in love with her."

"Is that all?"

"I guess so," he said. "Is there supposed to be more?"

"No. Not usually," the mother said. "Are you working?"

"Yes. As a matter of fact, that's why I'm going into Manhattan so early. Today is the first day of my first job."

"Congratulations," the mother said.

"Thanks," he said. "Can I marry your daughter?"

"Do you have a car?" she asked.

"Not yet," he said. "But I should be able to get one pretty soon. And a house, too."

"A house?"

"With lots of rooms."

"Yes, that's what I expected you to say," she said. She turned to her daughter. "Do you love him?"

"Yes, mother, I do."

"Why?"

"Because he's good, and gentle, and kind."

"Are you sure?"

"Yes."

"Then you really love him."

"Yes."

"Are you sure there isn't anyone else that you might love and might want to marry?"

"No, mother," the girl said.

"Well, then," the mother said to the young man. "Looks like there's nothing I can do about it. Ask her again."

The train stopped.

"My dearest one," he said. "Will you marry me?"

"Yes," she said.

Everybody in the car smiled and applauded.

"Isn't life wonderful?" the boy asked the mother.

"Beautiful," the mother said.

The conductor climbed down from between the cars as the train started up, and straightening his dark tie, approached them with a solemn black book in his hand.

Differences

CAROLYN GAISER

from *Paris Review*

The next morning it was cold in the apartment. She sat on the edge of the bed, wrapped in an old plaid bathrobe and warmed her clothes over the electric heater. He was still asleep. Without his glasses, he seemed accessible, someone who could be talked to with understanding, without self-consciousness: his hair curling up into funny ringlets and the lines of his profile imprinting on the air a certain naive justice. A large suitcase lay open on the floor, overflowing with sweaters and socks. She wondered if anyone wore socks in Israel. Probably not.

She was leaning over, a frayed slip dangling from her hands, when he said, "What in Christ's name do you think you're doing?"

"I was just trying to—who'd ever think Rome would get this cold. You know there's something sort of ungraceful about clothes when you're not wearing them? I mean all the straps and hooks and things, they're ungraceful."

That wasn't at all what she meant but she knew it was useless to pursue any discussion that even hinted at the possibility of becoming personal.

"I'm hungry," she said, feeling hunger somehow a safe and noncommittal state of being.

"So am I. We'll go out to eat, all right?"

He got up then and walked into the other room, leaving her alone to adjust to her ungraceful clothes as best she could. She dressed hurriedly, buttoning up the blue woolen suit she had worn the night before and ran to the mirror in the bathroom, hoping that some miraculous transformation might have taken place. It hadn't. She continued to look not the least bit Slavic, eastern European or even faintly Semitic. She was combing her ordinary-colored hair when he came back, dressed with his usual care, the inevitable corduroy vest, the gray suit he'd had made by a Roman tailor. He had his glasses on and also his air of inviolability. She turned away from the mirror.

"Do I look awful?"

"No, of course not. Come on, let's get going. I've got a lot of things to do today."

She followed him into the living room that also served as his studio. It smelled of turpentine and burnt sienna. One of his paintings was standing on the easel, huge and dark with many edges separating, dividing, crossing each other. He had a flair for edges.

She noticed a new book lying on the table next to *Goodbye Columbus* and *Act One—A History of the Italian Jews.* She decided not to mention it and concentrated on putting on her gloves, an apologetic birthday present he'd given her. All his kindnesses were apologies though she could never discover exactly what he was apologizing for.

"Have you got everything?" he asked, holding out her coat for her.

"Yes, everything."

They left the apartment and started down the stairs. There was an old piece of bread somebody had left behind on the landing. She called his attention to it.

"Look," she said, pointing, "just like one of those neorealistic movies, all that's missing is the girl in the black slip standing in the doorway." She didn't feel very clever today. He wasn't amused.

Outside, the little piazza was deserted, except for a group of young Italians in front of the café, leaning against their motorcycles and arguing about something in Roman dialect.

"We'll go to Rosatti's," he said, and they got into the car.

Driving through the morning traffic and then on the road that ran along the river, she looked out the window, concentrating on the moments jerking past; the trees that still in December managed to have leaves, how the sunlight was peculiarly clear today and sharpened everything you looked at until you wanted to blink it back into a more blurring normalcy. He appeared not to notice her silence.

He parked the car at the Piazza del Popolo and they got out and admired the obelisk with that proprietary admiration of people who have lived in a foreign country for more than a year and no longer feel obligated to react to every monument with extravagant enthusiasm.

"It's one of the nicest spots in Rome, you know?" he said.

"It's my favorite piazza."

Having said all there was to say on the subject, they went to have breakfast. The door of Rosatti's had an imposing sign on it, imploring everyone who entered to have a *Buon Natale.* Inside, the café was deserted except for a short man with a hat who leaned against the bar, seemingly hypnotized by the espresso machine. She thought he was probably a literary critic; they were always short and wore hats. It was too early yet for the writers and the painters who came every day for an apéritif before lunch. The cashier contentedly counted up money and the short man continued to stare at the espresso machine.

"Please, can we sit down? I hate standing at the bar," she said.

"All right."

She followed him past a large table displaying stuffed animals with tinsel draped around their necks. She wondered which of the people who came here would ever be tempted to buy a pink giraffe. Certainly not Moravia or Pasolini or any of the other writers who argued at all hours about censorship and the stupidity of the Catholic Church.

He chose a table in the back and they sat down and ordered *capuccino* and a *dolce.*

"Just think," he said, "the day after tomorrow I'll be in Israel working on some kibbutz. Finally, I'm really going to go there."

"Yes, just think." She wanted to look brightly interested but the expression somehow eluded her.

The waiter set down the coffee cups and two dubious buns. She picked one up and began munching on it. She no longer cared what she said.

"What's so great about working on a kibbutz anyhow? All this mysticism about getting your feet in Israeli sand. After all, you are American." She dared him to get angry.

"You don't understand. It means going back to your people, the old traditions, belonging, all that jazz. It means being proud to be a Jew."

"But why should it matter so much? It's people that matter."

She took another bite of the awful bun. It had bits of minced fruit inside, a further affront.

"Because Jews are different. We've always been different and we've suffered for it. You don't know what it's like to be Jewish."

"Oh, yes, I do. I do know what it's like," she said vehemently. "When I was in grammar school practically everybody was Jewish but me, and everybody took lessons: horseback riding and piano and ballet. And I didn't take any lessons at all."

"That's not what I'm talking about."

She went on anyway.

"And everybody lived in marvelous houses with finished basements and they gave parties where you danced and drank cream soda. And in the seventh grade there was a boy I liked named Joel who gave a huge party for his bar mitzvah. Only I wasn't invited. He told me about it afterwards. He said they gave him lots of presents. I remember he was very pleased about the presents."

"It's hard to be a good Jew, to know who you are and stick up for it. Take Maxine, for instance. She's a good Jew, her grandfather was a rabbi and her family sends her religious calendars with all the holidays marked out. She can laugh about the whole thing and she doesn't go to synagogue the way they'd like her to, but she's a good Jew."

She had listened to him so many times before tell her in the same mumbling incoherent way the story of the good Jew and she still didn't know what he meant, except that Maxine was one.

"Yes, of course, Maxine."

"Or me, even. So maybe I haven't seen the inside of a temple for a long time but the holidays, lighting the candles, all that stuff, it gets me. I don't know, it really gets to me." His face had that inspired expression, the one he always had whenever he talked about his people and his tradition and his unique difference.

She carefully put the bun back on the plate and picked up her purse. She mustn't cry here, she simply mustn't. He would be very annoyed. The cashier would stop counting her money. The little man by the espresso machine might even take off his hat in surprise. She mustn't cry.

"Excuse me, I have to go now. I just remembered I have to be some place." She got up abruptly.

"Wait a minute. You haven't finished your coffee. Wait just a minute and I'll drive you home."

"No, it doesn't matter. I'll be all right. Call me before you leave, if you have a chance."

She hurried past the table with the pink giraffe and ran out the door, running down the street toward her pensione, running, not willing to cry yet, waiting until she got home, and it seemed to her that she was running away from the sunlight, the clear peculiar sunlight that sharpened all the edges of things, dividing one from the other, running also from the field of brightness behind her where line after line of young men were bending, cutting, gathering in grain. And working, they sang together, the words strange and proud, they sang and he was there among them singing too, not really knowing the words but he was proud and suntanned like the others. He had his glasses off.

IN THE HEART OF THE HEART OF THE COUNTRY

WILLIAM H. GASS

from *New American Review*

a place

So I HAVE SAILED the seas and come . . .

to B . . .

a small . . .

town fastened to a field in Indiana. Twice there have been twelve hundred
people here to answer to the census. The town is outstandingly neat and shady,
and always puts its best side to the highway. On one lawn there's even a wood
or plastic iron deer.

You can reach us by crossing a creek. In the spring the lawns are green, the
forsythia is singing, and even the railroad that guts the town has straight bright
rails which hum when the train is coming, and the train itself has a welcome
horning sound.

Down the back streets the asphalt crumbles into gravel. There's West-
brook's, with the geraniums, Horsefall's, Mott's. The sidewalk shatters. Gravel
dust rises like breath behind the wagons. And I am in retirement from love.

weather

IN THE MIDWEST, around the lower Lakes, the sky in the winter is heavy and
close, and it is a rare day, a day to remark on, when the sky lifts and allows the
heart up. I am keeping count, and as I write this page, it is eleven days since I
have seen the sun.

my house

THERE'S A ROW of headless maples behind my house, cut to free the passage of electric wires. High stumps, ten feet tall, remain, and I climb these like a boy to watch the country sail away from me. They are ordinary fields, a little more uneven than they should be, since in the spring they puddle. The topsoil's thin, but only moderately stony. Corn is grown one year, soybeans another. At dusk starlings darken the single tree—a larch—which stands in the middle. When the sky moves, fields move under it. I feel, on my perch, that I've lost my years. It's as though I were living at last in my eyes, as I have always dreamed of doing, and I think then I know why I've come here: to see, and so to go out against new things—oh God how easily—like air in a breeze. It's true there are moments—foolish moments, ecstasy on a tree stump—when I'm all but gone, scattered I like to think like seed, for I'm the sort now in the fool's position of having love left over which I'd like to lose; what good is it now to me, candy ungiven after Halloween?

a person

THERE ARE VACANT LOTS on either side of Billy Holsclaw's house. As the weather improves, they fill with hollyhocks. From spring through fall, Billy collects coal and wood and puts the lumps and pieces in piles near his door, for keeping warm is his one work. I see him most often on mild days sitting on his doorsill in the sun. I noticed he's squinting a little, which is perhaps the reason he doesn't cackle as I pass. His house is the size of a single garage, and very old. It shed its paint with its youth, and its boards are a warped and weathered gray. So is Billy. He wears a short lumpy faded black coat when it's cold, otherwise he always goes about in the same loose, grease-spotted shirt and trousers. I suspect his galluses were yellow once, when they were new.

wires

THESE WIRES offend me. Three trees were maimed on their account, and now these wires deface the sky. They cross like a fence in front of me, enclosing the crows with the clouds. I can't reach in, but like a stick, I throw my feelings over. What is it that offends me? I am on my stump, I've built a platform there and the wires prevent my going out. The cut trees, the black wires, all the beyond birds therefore anger me. When I've wormed through a fence to reach a meadow, do I ever feel the same about the field?

people

THEIR HAIR IN CURLERS and their heads wrapped in loud scarves, young mothers, fattish in trousers, lounge about in the speedwash, smoking cigarettes, eating candy, drinking pop, thumbing magazines, and screaming at their children above the whirr and rumble of the machines.

At the bank a young man freshly pressed is letting himself in with a key. Along the street, delicately teetering, many grandfathers move in a dream. During the murderous heat of summer, they perch on window ledges, their feet dangling just inside the narrow shelf of shade the store has made, staring steadily into the street. Where their consciousness has gone I can't say. It's not in the eyes. Perhaps it's diffuse, all temperature and skin, like an infant's, though more mild. Near the corner there are several large overalled men employed in standing. A truck turns to be weighed at the Feed and Grain. Images drift on the drugstore window. The wind has blown the smell of cattle into town. Our eyes have been driven in like the eyes of the old men. And there's no one to have mercy on us.

vital data

THERE ARE TWO restaurants here and a tearoom. two bars. one bank. three barbers. one with a green shade with which he blinds his window. two groceries. a dealer in Fords. one drug, one hardware, and one appliance store. several that sell feed, grain, and farm equipment. an antique shop. a poolroom. a laundromat. three doctors. a dentist. a plumber. a vet. a funeral home in elegant repair the color of a buttercup. numerous beauty parlors which open and shut like night-blooming plants. a tiny dime and department store of no width but several floors. a hutch, homemade, where you can order, after lying down or squirming in, furniture that's been fashioned from bent lengths of stainless tubing, glowing plastic, metallic thread, and clear shellac. an American Legion Post and a root beer stand. little agencies for this and that: cosmetics, brushes, insurance, greeting cards and garden produce— anything—sample shoes—which do their business out of hats and satchels, over coffee cups and dissolving sugar. a factory for making paper sacks and pasteboard boxes that's lodged in an old brick building bearing the legend, OPERA HOUSE, still faintly golden, on its roof. a library given by Carnegie. a post office. a school. a railroad station. fire station. lumber yard. telephone company. welding shop. garage . . . and spotted through the town from one end to the other in a line along the highway—gas stations to the number five.

business

ONE SIDE SECTION of street is blocked off with sawhorses. Hard, thin, bitter men in blue jeans, cowboy boots and hats, untruck a dinky carnival. The merchants are promoting themselves. There will be free rides, raucous music, parades and coneys, pop, popcorn, candy, cones, awards and drawings, with all you can endure of pinch, push, bawl, shove, shout, scream, shriek, and bellow. Children pedal past on decorated bicycles, their wheels a blur of color, streaming crinkled paper and excited dogs. A little later there's a pet show for a prize—dogs, cats, birds, sheep, ponies, goats—none of which wins. The whirlabouts whirl about. The ferris wheel climbs dizzily into the sky as far as a tall man on tiptoe might be persuaded to reach, and the irritated operators

measure with sour eyes the height and weight of every child to see if they are
safe for the machines. An electrical megaphone repeatedly trumpets the names
of the generous sponsors. The following day they do not allow the refuse to
remain long in the street.

my house, this place and body

I HAVE MET with some mischance, wings withering, as Plato says obscurely, and
across the breadth of Ohio, like heaven on a table, I've fallen as far as the poet,
to the sixth sort of body, this house in B, in Indiana, with its blue and gray
bewitching windows, holy magical insides. Great thick evergreens protect its
entry. And I live *in*.

Lost in the corn rows, I remember feeling just another stalk, and thus this
country takes me over in the way I occupy myself when I am well . . .
completely—to the edge of both my house and body. No one notices, when they
walk by, that I am brimming in the doorways. My house, this place and body,
I've come in mourning to be born in. To anybody else it's pretty silly: love. Why
should I feel a loss? How am I bereft? She was never mine; she was a fiction,
always a golden tomgirl, barefoot, with an adolescent's slouch and a boy's taste
for sports and fishing, a figure out of Twain, or worse, in Riley. Age cannot be
kind.

There's little hand in hand here . . . not in B. No one touches except in
rage. Occasionally girls will twine their arms about each other and lurch along,
school out, toward home and play. I dreamed my lips would drift down your
back like a skiff on a river. I'd follow a vein with the point of my finger, hold
your bare feet in my naked hands.

the same person

BILLY HOLSCLAW lives alone—how alone it is impossible to fathom. In the post
office he talks greedily to me about the weather. His head bobs on a wild flood
of words, and I take this violence to be a measure of his eagerness for speech.
He badly needs a shave, coal dust has layered his face, he spits when he speaks,
and his fingers pick at his tatters. He wobbles out in the wind when I leave him,
a paper sack mashed in the fold of his arm, the leaves blowing past him, and
our encounter drives me sadly home to poetry—where there's no answer. Billy
closes his door and carries coal or wood to his fire and closes his eyes, and
there's simply no way of knowing how lonely and empty he is or whether he's
as vacant and barren and loveless as the rest of us are—here in the heart of the
country.

weather

FOR WE'RE ALWAYS out of luck here. That's just how it is—for instance in the
winter. The sides of the buildings, the roofs, the limbs of the trees are gray.

Streets, sidewalks, faces, feelings—they are gray. Speech is gray, and the grass where it shows. Every flank and front, each top is gray. Everything is gray: hair, eyes, window glass, the hawkers' bills and touters' posters, lips, teeth, poles and metal signs—they're gray, quite gray. Cars are gray. Boots, shoes, suits, hats, gloves are gray. Horses, sheep, and cows, cats killed in the road, squirrels in the same way, sparrows, doves, and pigeons, all are gray, everything is gray, and everyone is out of luck who lives here.

A similar haze turns the summer sky milky, and the air muffles your head and shoulders like a sweater you've got caught in. In the summer light, too, the sky darkens a moment when you open your eyes. The heat is pure distraction. Steeped in our fluids, miserable in the folds of our bodies, we can scarcely think of anything but our sticky parts. Hot cyclonic winds and storms of dust crisscross the country. In many places, given an indifferent push, the wind will still coast for miles, gathering resource and edge as it goes, cunning and force. According to the season, paper, leaves, field litter, seeds, snow fill up the fences. Sometimes I think the land is flat because the winds have leveled it, they blow so constantly. In any case, a gale can grow in a field of corn that's as hot as a draft from hell, and to receive it is one of the most dismaying experiences of this life, though the smart of the same wind in winter is more humiliating, and in that sense even worse. But in the spring it rains as well, and the trees fill with ice.

place

MANY SMALL Midwestern towns are nothing more than rural slums, and this community could easily become one. Principally during the first decade of the century, though there were many earlier instances, well-to-do farmers moved to town and built fine homes to contain them in their retirement. Others desired a more social life, and so lived in, driving to their fields like storekeepers to their businesses. These houses are now dying like the bereaved who inhabit them; they are slowly losing their senses . . . deafness, blindness, forgetfulness, mumbling, an insecure gait, an uncontrollable trembling has overcome them. Some kind of Northern Snopes will occupy them next: large-familied, Catholic, Democratic, scrambling, vigorous, poor; and since the parents will work in larger, nearby towns, the children will be loosed upon themselves and upon the hapless neighbors much as the fabulous Khan loosed his legendary horde. These Snopes will undertake makeshift repairs with materials that other people have thrown away; paint halfway round their house, then quit; almost certainly maintain an ugly loud cantankerous dog and underfeed a pair of cats to keep the rodents down. They will collect piles of possibly useful junk in the backyard, park their cars in the front, live largely leaning over engines, give not a hoot for the land, the old community, the hallowed ways, the established clans. Weakening widow-ladies have already begun to hire large rude youths from families such as these to rake and mow and tidy the grounds they will inherit.

people

IN THE CINDERS at the station boys sit smoking steadily in darkened cars, their arms bent out the windows, white shirts glowing behind the glass. Nine o'clock is the best time. They sit in a line facing the highway—two or three or four of them—idling their engines. As you walk by a machine may growl at you or a pair of headlights flare up briefly. In a moment one will pull out, spinning cinders behind it, to stalk impatiently up and down the dark streets or roar half a mile into the country before returning to its place in line and pulling up.

my house, my cat, my company

I MUST organize myself. I must, as they say, pull myself together, dump this cat from my lap, stir—yes, resolve, move, do. But do what? My will is like the rosy dustlike light in this room: soft, diffuse, and gently comforting. It lets me do . . . anything . . . nothing. My ears hear what they happen to; I eat what's put before me; my eyes see what blunders into them; my thoughts are not thoughts, they are dreams. I'm empty or I'm full . . . depending; and I cannot choose. I sink my claws in Tick's fur and scratch the bones of his back until his rear rises amorously. Mr. Tick, I murmur, I must organize myself. I must pull myself together. Mr. Tick rolls over on his belly, all ooze.

I spill Mr. Tick when I've rubbed his stomach. Shoo. He steps away slowly, his long tail rhyming with his paws. How beautifully he moves, I think; how beautifully, like you, he commands his loving, how beautifully he accepts. So I rise and wander from room to room, up and down, gazing through most of my forty-one windows. How well this house receives its loving too. Let out like Mr. Tick, my eyes sink in the shrubbery. I am not here; I've passed the glass, passed second-story spaces, flown by branches, brilliant berries, to the ground, grass high in seed and leafage every season; and it is the same as when I passed above you in my aged, ardent body; it's, in short, a kind of love; and I am learning to restore myself, my house, my body, by paying court to gardens, cats, and running water, and with neighbors keeping company.

Mrs. Desmond is my right-hand friend; she's eighty-five. A thin white mist of hair, fine and tangled, manifests the climate of her mind. She is habitually suspicious, fretful, nervous. Burglars break in at noon. Children trespass. Even now they are shaking the pear tree, stealing rhubarb, denting lawn. Flies caught in the screens and numbed by frost awake in the heat to buzz and scrape the metal cloth and frighten her, though she is deaf to me, and consequently cannot hear them. Boards creak, the wind whistles across the chimney-mouth, drafts cruise like fish through the hollow rooms. It is herself she hears, her own flesh failing, for only death will preserve her from those daily chores she climbs like stairs, and all that anxious waiting. Is it now, she wonders. No? Then: is it now?

We do not converse. She visits me to talk. My task to murmur. She talks about her grandsons, her daughter who lives in Delphi, her sister or her husband—both gone—obscure friends—dead—obscurer aunts and uncles—lost—ancient neighbors, members of her church or of her clubs—passed or passing on; and in this way she brings the ends of her life together with a terrifying rush: she is a girl, a wife, a mother, widow, all at once. All at once—appalling—but I believe it; I wince in expectation of the clap. Her talk's a fence—a shade drawn, window fastened, door that's locked—for no one dies taking tea in a kitchen; and as her years compress and begin to jumble, I really believe in the brevity of life; I sweat in my wonder; death is the dog down the street, the angry gander, bedroom spider, goblin who's come to get her; and it occurs to me that in my listening posture I'm the boy who suffered the winds of my grandfather with an exactly similar politeness, that I am, right now, all my ages, out in elbows, as angular as badly stacked cards. Thus was I, when I loved you, every man I could be, youth and child—far from enough—and you, so strangely ambiguous a being, met me, heart for spade, play after play, the whole run of our suits.

Mr. Tick, you do me honor. You not only lie in my lap, but you remain alive there, coiled like a fetus. Through your deep nap, I feel you hum. You are, and are not, a machine. You are alive, alive exactly, and it means nothing to you—much to me. You are a cat—you cannot understand—you are a cat so easily. Your nature is not something you must rise to. You, not I, live in: in house, in skin, in shrubbery. Yes. I think I shall hat my head with a steeple; turn church; devour people. Mr. Tick, though, has a tail he can twitch, he need not fly his Fancy. Claws, not metrical schema, poetry his paws; while smoothing . . . smoothing . . . smoothing roughly, his tongue laps its neatness. O Mr. Tick, I know you; you are an electrical penis. Go on now, shoo. Mrs. Desmond doesn't like you. She thinks you will tangle yourself in her legs and she will fall. You murder her birds, she knows, and walk upon her roof with death in your jaws. I must gather myself together for a bound. What age is it I'm at right now, I wonder. The heart, don't they always say, keeps the true time. Mrs. Desmond is knocking. Faintly, you'd think, but she pounds. She's brought me a cucumber. I believe she believes I'm a woman. Come in, Mrs. Desmond, thank you, be my company, it looks lovely, and have tea. I'll slice it, crisp, with cream, for luncheon, each slice as thin as me.

more vital data

THE TOWN is exactly fifty houses, trailers, stores, and miscellaneous buildings long, but in places no streets deep. It takes on width as you drive south, always adding to the east. Most of the dwellings are fairly spacious farmhouses in the customary white, with wide wraparound porches and tall narrow windows, though there are many of the grander kind—fretted, scalloped, turreted, and decorated with clapboards set at angles or on end, with stained glass windows at the stair landings and lots of wrought iron full of fancy curls—and a few of these look like castles in their rarer brick. Old stables serve as garages now, and the lots are large to contain them and the vegetable and flower gardens which, ultimately, widows plant and weed and then entirely disappear in. The shade is ample, the grass is good, the sky a glorious fall violet; the apple trees are heavy and red, the roads are calm and empty; corn has sifted from the chains of tractored wagons to speckle the streets with gold and with the russet fragments of the cob, and a man would be a fool who wanted, blessed with this, to live anywhere else in the world.

education

BUSES LIKE great orange animals move through the early light to school. There the children will be taught to read and warned against Communism. By Miss Janet Jakes. That's not her name. Her name is Helen something—Scott or James. A teacher twenty years. She's now worn fine and smooth, and has a face, Wilfred says, like a mail-order ax. Her voice is hoarse, and she has a cough. For she screams abuse. The children stare, their faces blank. This is the thirteenth week. They are used to it. You will all, she shouts, you will all draw pictures of me. No. She is a Mrs.—someone's missus. And in silence they set to work while Miss Jakes jabs hairpins in her hair. Wilfred says an ax, but she has those rimless tinted glasses, graying hair, an almost dimpled chin. I must concentrate. I must stop making up things. I must give myself to life; let it mold me: that's what they say in Wisdom's Monthly Digest every day. Enough, enough— you've been at it long enough; and the children rise formally a row at a time to present their work to her desk. No, she wears rims; it's her chin that's dimpleless. So she grimly shuffles their sheets, examines her reflection crayoned on them. I would not dare . . . allow a child . . . to put a line around me. Though now and then she smiles like a nick in the blade, in the end these drawings depress her. I could not bear it—how can she ask?—that anyone . . . draw me. Her anger's lit. That's why she does it: flame. There go her eyes; the pink in her glasses brightens, dims. She is a pumpkin, and her rage is breathing like the candle in. No, she shouts, no—the cartoon trembling—no, John Mauck, John Stewart Mauck, this will not do. The picture flutters from her fingers. You've made me too muscular.

I work on my poetry. I remember my friends, associates, my students, by their names. Their names are Maypop, Dormouse, Upsydaisy. Their names are Gladiolus, Callow Bladder, Prince and Princess Oleo, Hieronymus, Cardinal Mummum, Mr. Fitchew, The Silken Howdah, Spot. Sometimes you're Tom Sawyer, Huckleberry Finn; it is perpetually summer; your buttocks are my pillow; we are adrift on a raft; your back is our river. Sometimes you are Major Barbara, sometimes a goddess who kills men in battle, sometimes you are soft like a shower of water; you are bread in my mouth.

I do not work on my poetry. I forget my friends, associates, my students, and their names: Gramophone, Blowgun, Pickle, Serenade . . . Marge the Barge, Arena, Uberhaupt . . . Doctor Dildoe, The Fog Machine. For I am now in B, in Indiana: out of job and out of patience, out of love and time and money, out of bread and out of body, in a temper, Mrs. Desmond, out of tea. So shut your fist up, bitch, you bag of death; go bang another door; go die, my dearie. Die, life-deaf old lady. Spill your breath. Fall over like a frozen board. Gray hair grows from the nose of your mind. You are a skull already—*memento mori*—the foreskin retracts from your teeth. Will your plastic gums last longer than your bones, and color their grinning? And is your twot still hazel-hairy, or are you bald as a ditch? . . . bitch . . . . . . bitch . . . . bitch. I wanted to be famous, but you bring me age—my emptiness. Was it *that* which I thought would balloon me above the rest? Love? where are you? . . . love me. I want to rise so high, I said, that when I shit I won't miss anybody.

business

FOR MOST PEOPLE, business is poor. Nearby cities have siphoned off all but a neighborhood trade. Except for feed and grain and farm supplies, you stand a chance to sell only what one runs out to buy. Chevrolet has quit, and Frigidaire. A locker plant has left its afterimage. The lumber yard has been, so far, six months about its going. Gas stations change hands clumsily, a restaurant becomes available, a grocery closes. One day they came and knocked the cornices from the watch repair and pasted campaign posters on the windows. Torn across, by now, by boys, they urge you still to vote for half an orange beblazoned man who as a whole one failed two years ago to win at his election. Everywhere, in this manner, the past speaks, and it mostly speaks of failure. The empty stores, the old signs and dusty fixtures, the debris in alleys, the flaking paint and rusty gutters, the heavy locks and sagging boards: they say the same disagreeable things. What do the sightless windows see, I wonder, when the sun throws a passerby against them? Here a stair unfolds toward the street—dark, rickety, and treacherous—and I always feel, as I pass it, that if I just went carefully up and turned the corner at the landing, I would find myself out of the world. But I've never had the courage.

that same person

THE WEEDS catch up with Billy. In pursuit of the hollyhocks, they rise in coarse clumps all around the front of his house. Billy has to stamp down a circle by his door like a dog or cat does turning round to nest up, they're so thick. What particularly troubles me is that winter will find the weeds still standing stiff and tindery to take the sparks which Billy's little mortarless chimney spouts. It's true that fires are fun here. The town whistle, which otherwise only blows for noon (and there's no noon on Sunday), signals the direction of the fire by the length and number of its blasts, the volunteer firemen rush past in their cars and trucks, houses empty their owners along the street every time like an illustration in a children's book. There are many bikes, too, and barking dogs, and sometimes—hallelujah—the fire's right here in town—a vacant lot of weeds and stubble flaming up. But I'd rather it weren't Billy or Billy's lot or house. Quite selfishly I want him to remain the way he is—counting his sticks and logs, sitting on his sill in the soft early sun—though I'm not sure what his presence means to me . . . or to anyone. Nevertheless, I keep wondering whether, given time, I might not someday find a figure in our language which would serve him faithfully, and furnish his poverty and loneliness richly out.

weather

I WOULD RATHER it were the weather that was to blame for what I am and what my friends and neighbors are—we who live here in the heart of the country. Better the weather, the wind, the pale dying snow . . . the snow—why not the snow? There's never much really, not around the lower Lakes anyway, not enough to boast about, not enough to be useful. My father tells how the snow in the Dakotas would sweep to the roofs of the barns in the old days, and he and his friends could sled on the crust that would form because the snow was so fiercely driven. In Bemidji trees have been known to explode. That would be something—if the trees in Davenport or Francisville or Terre Haute were to go blam some winter—blam! blam! blam! all the way down the gray, cindery, snow-sick streets.

A cold fall rain is blackening the trees or the air is like lilac and full of parachuting seeds. Who cares to live in any season but his own? Still I suspect the secret's in this snow, the secret of our sickness, if we could only diagnose it, for we are all dying like the elms in Urbana. This snow—like our skin it covers the country. Later dust will do it. Right now—snow. Mud presently. But it is snow without any laughter in it, a pale gray pudding thinly spread on stiff toast, and if that seems a strange description, it's accurate all the same. Of course soot blackens everything, but apart from that, we are never sufficiently cold here. The flakes as they come, alive and burning, we cannot retain, for if our temperatures fall, they rise promptly again, just as, in the summer, they bob about in the same feckless way. Suppose though . . . suppose they were to rise some August, climb and rise, and then hang in the hundreds like a hawk through December, what a desert we could make of ourselves—from Chicago to Cairo, from Gary to Columbus—what beautiful Death Valleys.

place

I WOULD RATHER it were the weather. It drives us in upon ourselves—an unlucky fate. Of course there is enough to stir our wonder anywhere; there's enough to love, anywhere, if one is strong enough, if one is diligent enough, if one is perceptive, patient, kind enough—whatever it takes; and surely it's better to live in the country, to live on a prairie by a drawing of rivers, in Iowa or Illinois or Indiana, say, than in any city, in any stinking fog of human beings, in any blooming orchard of machines. It ought to be. The cities are swollen and poisonous with people. It ought to be better. Man has never been a fit environment for man—for rats, maybe, rats do nicely, or for dogs or cats and the household beetle.

A man in the city has no natural thing by which to measure himself. His parks are potted plants. Nothing can live and remain free where he resides but the pigeon, starling, sparrow, spider, cockroach, mouse, moth, fly, and weed, and he laments the existence of even these and makes his plans to poison them. The zoo? There *is* the zoo. Through its bars the city man stares at the great cats and dully sucks his ice. Living, alas, among men and their marvels, the city man supposes that his happiness depends on establishing, somehow, a special kind of harmonious accord with others. The novelists of the city, of slums and crowds, they call it love—and break their pens.

Wordsworth feared the accumulation of men in cities. He foresaw their "degrading thirst after outrageous stimulation," and some of their hunger for love. Living in a city, among so many, dwelling in the heat and tumult of incessant movement, a man's affairs are touch and go—that's all. It's not surprising that the novelists of the slums, the cities, and the crowds, should find that sex is but a scratch to ease a tickle, that we're most human when we're sitting on the john, and that the justest image of our life is in full passage through the plumbing.

Come into the country, then. The air nimbly and sweetly recommends itself unto our gentle senses. Here, growling tractors tear the earth. Dust roils up behind them. Drivers sit jouncing under bright umbrellas. They wear refrigerated hats and steer by looking at the tracks they've cut behind them, their transistors blaring. Close to the land, are they? good companions to the soil? Tell me: do they live in harmony with the alternating seasons?

It's a lie of old poetry. The modern husbandman uses chemicals from cylinders and sacks, spike-ball-and-claw machines, metal sheds, and cost accounting. Nature in the old sense does not matter. It does not exist. Our farmer's only mystical attachment is to parity. And if he does not realize that cows and corn are simply different kinds of chemical engine, he cannot expect to make a go of it.

It isn't necessary to suppose our cows have feelings; our neighbor hasn't as many as he used to have either; but think of it this way a moment, you can correct for the human imputations later: how would it feel to nurse those strange tentacled calves with their rubber, glass, and metal lips, their stainless eyes?

people

AUNT PET'S still able to drive her car—a high square Ford—even though she walks with difficulty and a stout stick. She has a watery gaze, a smooth plump face despite her age, and jet black hair in a bun. She has the slowest smile of anyone I ever saw, but she hates dogs, and not very long ago cracked the back of one she cornered in her garden. To prove her vigor she will tell you this, her smile breaking gently while she raises the knob of her stick to the level of your eyes.

house, my breath and window

MY WINDOW is a grave, and all that lies within it's dead. No snow is falling. There's no haze. It is not still, not silent. Its images are not an animal that waits, for movement is no demonstration. I have seen the sea slack, life bubble through a body without a trace, its spheres impervious as soda's. Downwound, the whore at wagtag clicks and clacks. Leaves wiggle. Grass sways. A bird chirps, pecks the ground. An auto wheel in penning circles keeps its rigid spokes. These images are stones; they are memorials. Beneath this sea lies sea: God rest it . . . rest the world beyond my window, me in front of my reflection, above this page, my shade. Death is not so still, so silent, since silence implies a falling quiet, stillness a stopping, containing, holding in; for death is time in a clock, like Mr. Tick, electric . . . like wind through a windup poet. And my blear floats out to visible against the glass, befog its country and bespill myself. The mist lifts slowly from the fields in the morning. No one now would say: the Earth throws back its covers; it is rising from sleep. Why is the feeling foolish? The image is too Greek. I used to gaze at you so wantonly your body blushed. Imagine: wonder: that my eyes could cause such flowering. Ah, my friend, your face is pale, the weather cloudy; a street has been felled through your chin, bare trees do nothing, houses take root in their rectangles, a steeple stands up in your head. You speak of loving; then give me a kiss. The pane is cold. On icy mornings the fog rises to greet me (as you always did); the barns and other buildings, rather than ghostly, seem all the more substantial for looming, as if they grew in themselves while I watched (as you always did). Oh, my approach, I suppose, was like breath in a rubber monkey. Nevertheless, on the road along the Wabash in the morning, though the trees are sometimes obscured by fog, their reflection floats serenely on the river, reasoning the banks, the sycamores in French rows. Magically, the world tips. I'm led to think that only those who grow down live (which will scarcely win me twenty-five from Wisdom's Monthly Digest), but I find I write that only those who live down grow; and what I write, I hold, whatever I really know. My every word's inverted, or reversed—or I am. I held you, too, that way. You were so utterly provisional, subject to my change. I could inflate your bosom with a kiss, disperse your skin with gentleness, enter your vagina from within, and make my love emerge like a fresh sex. The pane is cold. Honesty is cold, my inside lover. The sun looks, through the mist, like a plum on the tree of heaven, or a bruise on the slope of your belly. Which? The grass crawls with frost. We meet on this window, the world and I, inelegantly, swimmers of the glass; and swung wrong way round to one another, the world seems in. The world—how grand, how monumental, grave and deadly, that word is: the world, my house and poetry. All poets have their inside lovers. Wee penis does not belong to me, or any of this foggery. It is *his* property which he's thrust through what's womanly of me to set down this. These wooden houses in their squares, gray streets and fallen sidewalks, standing trees, your name I've written sentimentally across my breath into the whitening air, pale birds: they exist in me now because of him. I gazed with what intensity. . . . A bush in the excitement of its roses would not have bloomed so beautifully as you did then. It was a look I'd like to give this page. For that is poetry: to bring within about, to change.

politics

SPORTS, POLITICS, and religion are the three passions of the badly educated. They are the Midwest's open sores. Ugly to see, a source of constant discontent, they sap the body's strength. Appalling quantities of money, time, and energy are wasted on them. The rural mind is narrow, passionate, and reckless on these matters. Greed, however shortsighted and direct, will not alone account for it. I have known men, for instance, who for years have voted squarely against their interests. Nor have I ever noticed that their surly Christian views prevented them from urging forward the smithereening, say, of Russia, China, Cuba, or Korea—Vietnam. And they tend to back their country like they back their local team: they have a fanatical desire to win; yelling is their forte; and if things go badly, they are inclined to sack the coach. All in all, then, Birch is a good name. It stands for the bigot's stick, the wild-child-tamer's cane.

final vital data

THE MODERN HOMEMAKER'S Demonstration Club. The Prairie Home Demonstration Club. The Night-outers' Home Demonstration Club. The IOOF, FFF, VFW, WCTU, WSCS, 4-H, 40 and 8, Psi Iota Chi, and PTA. The Boy and Girl Scouts. Rainbows, Masons, Indians and Rebekah Lodge. Also the Past Noble Grand Club of the Rebekah Lodge. As well as the Moose and Ladies of the Moose. The Elks, the Eagles, the Jaynettes, and the Eastern Star. The Women's Literary Club, the Hobby Club, the Art Club, the Sunshine Society, the Dorcas Society, the Pythian Sisters, the Pilgrim Youth Fellowship, the American Legion, the American Legion Auxiliary, the American Legion Junior Auxiliary, the Gardez Club, the What-can-you-do? Club, the Get Together Club, the Coterie Club, the Worthwhile Club, the No Name Club, the Forget-me-not Club, the Merry-go-round Club . . . . . .

education

HAS A QUARTER disappeared from Paula Frosty's pocketbook? Imagine the landscape of that face: no crayon could engender it; soft wax is wrong; thin wire in trifling snips might do the trick. Paula Frosty and Christopher Roger accuse the pale and splotchy Cheryl Pipes. But Miss Jakes, I *saw* her. Miss Jakes is so extremely vexed she snaps her pencil. What else is missing? I appoint you a detective, John: search her desk. Gum, candy, paper, pencils, marble, round eraser—whose? A thief. I can't watch her all the time, I'm here to teach. Poor pale fossetted Cheryl, it's determined, can't return the money because she took it home and spent it. Cindy, Janice, John, and Pete—you four who sit around her—you will be detectives this whole term to watch her. A thief. In all my time. Miss Jakes turns, unfists, and turns again. I'll handle you, she cries. To think. A thief. In all my years. Then she writes on the blackboard the name of Cheryl Pipes and beneath that the figure twenty-five with a large sign for cents. Now Cheryl, she says, this won't be taken off until you bring that money out of home, out of home straight up to here, Miss Jakes says, tapping her desk.
Which is three days.

another person

I WAS RAKING leaves when Uncle Halley introduced himself to me. He said his name came from the comet, and that his mother had borne him prematurely in her fright of it. I thought of Hobbes, whom fear of the Spanish Armada had hurried into birth, and so I believed Uncle Halley to honor the philosopher, though Uncle Halley is a liar, and neither the one hundred twenty-eight nor the fifty-three he ought to be. That fall the leaves had burned themselves out on the trees, the leaf-lobes had curled, and now they flocked noisily down the street and were broken in the wires of my rake. Uncle Halley was himself (like Mrs. Desmond and history generally) both deaf and implacable, and he shooed me down his basement stairs to a room set aside there for stacks of newspapers reaching to the ceiling, boxes of leaflets and letters and programs, racks of photo albums, scrapbooks, bundles of rolled up posters and maps, flags and pennants and slanting piles of dusty magazines devoted mostly to motoring and the Christian ethic. I saw a birdcage, a tray of butterflies, a bugle, a stiff straw boater, and all kinds of tassels tied to a coat tree. He still possessed and had on display the steering lever from his first car, a linen duster, driving gloves and goggles, photographs along the wall of himself, his friends, and his various machines, a shell from the first war, a record of Ramona nailed through its hole to a post, walking sticks and fanciful umbrellas, shoes of all sorts (his baby shoes, their counters broken, were held in sorrow beneath my nose—they had not been bronzed, but he might have them done someday before he died, he said), countless boxes of medals, pins, beads, trinkets, toys, and keys (I scarcely saw—they flowed like jewels from his palms), pictures of downtown when it was only a path by the railroad station, a brightly colored globe of the world with a dent in Poland, antique guns, belt buckles, buttons, souvenir plates and cups and saucers (I can't remember all of it—I won't), but I recall how shamefully, how rudely, how abruptly, I fled, a good story in my mouth but death in my nostrils; and how afterward I busily, righteously, burned my leaves as if I were purging the world of its years. I still wonder if this town—its life, and mine now—isn't really a record like the one of Ramona that I used to crank around on my grandmother's mahogany Victrola through lonely rainy days as a kid.

the first person

BILLY'S LIKE the coal he's found: spilled, mislaid, discarded. The sky's no comfort. His house and his body are dying together. His windows are boarded. And now he's reduced to his hands. I suspect he has glaucoma. At any rate he can scarcely see, and weeds his yard of rubble on his hands and knees. Perhaps he's a surgeon cleansing a wound or an ardent and tactile lover. I watch, I must say, apprehensively. Like mine-war detectors, his hands graze in circles ahead of him. Your nipples were the color of your eyes. Pebble. Snarl of paper. Length of twine. He leans down closely, picks up something silvery, holds it near his nose. Foil? cap? coin? He has within him—what? I wonder. Does he know more now because he fingers everything and has to sniff to see? It would be romantic cruelty to think so. He bends the down on your arms like a breeze. You wrote me: something is strange when we don't understand. I write in return: I think when I loved you I fell to my death.

Billy, I could read to you from Beddoes; he's your man perhaps; he held with dying, freed his blood of its arteries; and he said that there were many wretched love-ill fools like me lying alongside the last bone of their former selves, as full of spirit and speech, nonetheless, as Mrs. Desmond, Uncle Halley and the ferris wheel, Aunt Pet, Miss Jakes, Ramona or the megaphone; yet I reverse him finally, Billy, on no evidence but braggadocio, and I declare that though my inner organs were devoured long ago, the worm which swallowed down my parts still throbs and glows like a crystal palace.

Yes, you were younger. I was Uncle Halley, the museum man and infrequent meteor. Here is my first piece of ass. They weren't so flat in those days, had more round, more juice. And over here's the sperm I've spilled, nicely jarred and clearly labeled. Look at this tape like lengths of intestine where I've stored my spew, the endless worm of words I've written, a hundred million emissions or more: oh I was quite a man right from the start; even when unconscious in my cradle, from crotch to cranium, I was erectile tissue; though mostly, after the manner approved by Plato, I had intercourse by eye. Never mind, old Holsclaw, you are blind. We pull down darkness when we go to bed; put out like Oedipus the actually offending organ, and train our touch to lies. All cats are gray, says Mr. Tick; so under cover of glaucoma you are sack gray too, and cannot be distinguished from a stallion.

I must pull myself together, get a grip, just as they say, but I feel spilled, bewildered, quite mislaid. I did not restore my house to its youth, but to its age. Hunting, you hitch through the hollyhocks. I'm inclined to say you aren't half the cripple I am, for there is nothing left of me but mouth. However, I resist the impulse. It is another lie of poetry. My organs are all there, though it's there where I fail—at the roots of my experience. Poet of the spiritual, Rilke, weren't you? yet that's what you said. Poetry, like love, is—in and out—a physical caress. I can't tolerate any more of my sophistries about spirit, mind, and breath. Body equals being, and if your weight goes down, you are the less.

household apples

I KNEW NOTHING about apples. Why should I? My country came in my childhood, and I dreamed of sitting among the blooms like the bees. I failed to spray the pear tree too. I doubled up under them at first, admiring the sturdy low branches I should have pruned, and later I acclaimed the blossoms. Shortly after the fruit formed there were falls—not many—apples the size of goodish stones which made me wobble on my ankles when I walked about the yard. Sometimes a piece crushed by a heel would cling on the shoe to track the house. I gathered a few and heaved them over the wires. A slingshot would have been splendid. Hard, an unattractive green, the worms had them. Before long I realized the worms had them all. Even as the apples reddened, lit their tree, they were being swallowed. The birds preferred the pears, which were small—sugar pears I think they're called—with thick skins of graying green that ripen on toward violet. So the fruit fell, and once I made some applesauce by quartering and paring hundreds; but mostly I did nothing, left them, until suddenly, overnight it seemed, in that ugly late September heat we often have in Indiana, my problem was upon me.

My childhood came in the country. I remember, now, the flies on our snowy luncheon table. As we cleared away they would settle, fastidiously scrub themselves and stroll to the crumbs to feed where I would kill them in crowds with a swatter. It was quite a game to catch them taking off. I struck heavily since I didn't mind a few stains; they'd wash. The swatter was a square of screen bound down in red cloth. It drove no air ahead of it to give them warning. They might have thought they'd flown headlong into a summered window. The faint pink dot where they had died did not rub out as I'd supposed, and after years of use our luncheon linen would faintly, pinkly, speckle.

The country became my childhood. Flies braided themselves on the flypaper in my grandmother's house. I can smell the bakery and the grocery and the stables and the dairy in that small Dakota town I knew as a kid; knew as I dreamed I'd know your body, as I've known nothing, before or since; knew as the flies knew, in the honest, unchaste sense: the burned house, hose-wet, which drew a mist of insects like the blue smoke of its smolder, and gangs of boys, moist-lipped, destructive as its burning. Flies have always impressed me; they are so persistently alive. Now they were coating the ground beneath my trees. Some were ordinary flies; there were the large blue-green ones; there were swarms of fruit flies too, and the red-spotted scavenger beetle; there were a few wasps, several sorts of bees and butterflies—checkers, sulphers, monarchs, commas, question marks—and delicate dragonflies . . . but principally houseflies and horseflies and bottleflies, flies and more flies in clusters around the rotting fruit. They loved the pears. Inside, they fed. If you picked up a pear, they flew, and the pear became skin and stem. They were everywhere the fruit was: in the tree still—apples like a hive for them—or where the fruit littered the ground, squashing itself as you stepped . . . there was no help for it. The flies droned, feasting on the sweet juice. No one could go near the trees; I could not climb; so I determined at last to labor like Hercules. There were fruit baskets in the barn. Collecting them and kneeling under the branches, I began to gather remains. Deep in the strong rich smell of the fruit, I began to hum myself. The fruit caved in at the touch. Glistening red apples, my lifting disclosed, had families of beetles, flies, and bugs, devouring their rotten undersides. There were streams of flies; there were lakes and cataracts and rivers of flies, seas and oceans. The hum was heavier, higher, than the hum of the bees when they came to the blooms in the spring, though the bees were there, among the flies, ignoring me—ignoring everyone. As my work went on and juice covered my hands and arms, they would form a sleeve, black and moving, like knotty wool. No caress could have been more indifferently complete. Still I rose fearfully, ramming my head in the branches, apples bumping against me before falling, bursting with bugs. I'd snap my hand sharply but the flies would cling to the sweet. I could toss a whole cluster into a basket from several feet. As the pear or apple lit, they would explosively rise, like monads for a moment, windowless, certainly, with respect to one another, sugar their harmony. I had to admit, though, despite my distaste, that my arm had never been more alive, oftener or more gently kissed. Those hundreds of feet were light. In washing them off, I pretended the hose was a pump. What have I missed? Childhood is a lie of poetry.

the church

FRIDAY NIGHT. Girls in dark skirts and white blouses sit in ranks and scream in concert. They carry funnels loosely stuffed with orange and black paper which they shake wildly, and small megaphones through which, as drilled, they direct and magnify their shouting. Their leaders, barely pubescent girls, prance and shake and whirl their skirts above their bloomers. The young men, leaping, extend their arms and race through puddles of amber light, their bodies glistening. In a lull, though it rarely occurs, you can hear the squeak of tennis shoes against the floor. Then the yelling begins again, and then continues; fathers, mothers, neighbors joining in to form a single pulsing ululation—a cry of the whole community—for in this gymnasium each body becomes the bodies beside it, pressed as they are together, thigh to thigh, and the same shudder runs through all of them, and runs toward the same release. Only the ball moves serenely through the dazzling din. Obedient to law it scarcely speaks but caroms quietly and lives at peace.

business

IT IS THE WEEK of Christmas and the stores, to accommodate the rush they hope for, are remaining open in the evening. You can see snow falling in the cones of the street lamps. The roads are filling—undisturbed. Strings of red and green lights droop over the principal highway, and the water tower wears a star. The windows of the stores have been bedizened. Shamelessly they beckon. But I am alone, leaning against a pole—no . . . there is no one in sight. They're all at home, perhaps by their instruments, tuning in on their evenings, and like Ramona, tirelessly playing and replaying themselves. There's a speaker perched in the tower, and through the boughs of falling snow and over the vacant streets, it drapes the twisted and metallic strains of a tune that can barely be distinguished—yes, I believe it's one of the jolly ones, it's Joy to the World. There's no one to hear the music but myself, and though I'm listening, I'm no longer certain. Perhaps the record's playing something else.

ONE OF YOU MUST BE WENDELL COREY

PHILIP L. GREENE   from *Partisan Review*

Lil Wagner's marriage was on the rocks when I first met her. She was at a point where her need for spiritual renewal came from Erich Fromm. "*The Art of Loving*," she said to me with conviction, "if I had known before I met Ben, if I could have talked with my analyst before he went to California. . . ." The Fromm revelation came to me in a surprised voice. Lil's constant seizing of the obvious and investing it with wonder—another secret uncovered to reward her with a new life—kept her in a perpetual cycle of desire, rapt discovery, and flat-eyed disillusionment. Lil was always a cultural idea away. This caused an impasse between her and Ben, who was always on the frontier of an idea. This situation made for a most satisfactory lesion. They knew what was wounding them. Ben was all modernity, in the vanguard of good causes, always in control of the intellectual apparatus rigged for him by the monopolists of the mid-city mind—*Dissent, Commentary,* the *New Leader.* "Can't you see," he said to me once, while Lil was looking vacantly out of the window onto Waverly Place, "that the social mobility of the new class depends on the morality of the cash nexus." Lil said, "Oh, shit," and walked out of the room. Ben stared after her, looked back at me, and went on. "Take Weber's view of the Protestant ethic and update it to give the petite bourgeoisie its function under the new capitalism. What do you have? The little man with just enough illusions to keep him morally bankrupt forever. I mentioned this to my analyst, and do you know what he said? 'Don't you think you're hiding behind all this, Ben?'"

Lil's doctor had called Ben's doctor to discuss a possible separation—this at the suggestion of Lil, who had thrown herself at the mercy of a new idea: why shouldn't the transferents involve themselves directly in the transferers' problems. When Ben found a place on Hudson Street over a wholesale meat market and refused to put a phone in, Lil's mother sent him a telegram: "Lil wants to try again. Please call." Ben called. Possessed with the idea of effecting a moral sacrifice—he wanted it desperately—he persuaded Lil to a reconciliation. That night, Ben told me later with embarrassing ingenuousness, they got into bed, and he couldn't get an erection. He cried. Lil laughed at him, and he hit her in the face, once, a short, open-handed slap. She screamed at him, "You can punch, but you can't screw, you lousy fat louse."

Shortly after that at a gathering at Marsha Weinstein's house she told me in a drawn voice that she had given up sex for yogurt and carrot juice. Marsha, her best friend, was a ballet dancer when she was not working part-time for Secretaries Anonymous. Marsha's three abortions had taken the limber out of her legs, which were running to fat, and she had recommended the Health Shoppe on Madison Avenue right around the corner from her analyst. Lil had decided to move in with Marsha, the reconciliation with Ben a washout. Larry Jonas, Marsha's new man, was in Washington doing a study of pressure groups and would not be back for a while. Larry had been Lil's boy friend, so she felt a vicarious renewal with Larry in staying at Marsha's. Larry had been good to her, but after two years of indecision, she found Ben at a party given by Murray Abramson, whose book, *Existential Psychodynamics,* had stirred the psychological community. Murray had studied at the W. A. White school with Ben before Ben decided to go into his father's medical supply business. Lil told me that Ben was the warmest, brightest, tenderest man she had ever met. "I never knew about social consciousness before I met Ben," she said. Ben had admired Larry's work with the American Civil Liberties Union and knew too that Larry was sleeping with Lil, so that he found the usurpation of Larry's girl a moral problem painful enough to engage him full time. "I knew something was wrong," Lil said, "the night Ben took me home from Murray's party, but he told me later that he was discussing the problem with his doctor. He had a premature ejaculation; he came all over my dress before I had time to take it off. He said the Larry problem was a projection of an infantile regression, a kind of Oedipal return, since he had always thought of Larry as a kind of father figure."

The marriage had gone on like that for four years, deteriorating steadily. Toward the end, I was having dinner at the Cookery with Merle Jonas, Larry's kid brother. We had just come from Max Lerner's third lecture at The New School where Lerner brilliantly illustrated his thesis of the dynamics of American pluralism by showing the bipolar attitude of the nation at large toward abortion, a topic Merle continued with great expertise, over a cookeryburger. "Marsha has had three—one in Jersey, one in Puerto Rico, and one right here on Fifth Avenue. Lerner is right because this problem epitomizes the indigenous moral strength of the American people. In the face of official sanctions against it, there is a remarkable pragmatic will operating."

When Merle told me that Marsha was having some people over and that Lil would be there, I accepted the invitation. I was at loose ends myself and Lil had looked plaintively neurotic the last time I had seen her. I knew that her health-food phase was temporary, and I hoped I might be just the thing to renew her contact with love. She was leaning heavily on her new Frommian world view. Merle had to pick up Tibby Barrett, Lil's old roommate at Oswego State College, who had recently arrived from Goshen and had taken a one-and-a-half on Jane Street just around the corner from the old cat and dog store that was being torn down to make way for a luxury apartment, one of a number around the West Village that were following an artist motif. The Van Gogh and The Rembrandt had already been built. The new one was called The Picasso Arms. Tibby was doing research at *Newsweek*. Merle, who was writing advertising copy, met her for lunch every day in front of the library lions.

When we arrived at Marsha's Lil was sitting on the couch between Murray Abramson and his wife Lisa, who greeted me with a warm voice edged with a Hungarian accent. She was finishing her work at the White school. Murray and Lisa were planning to start a husband-and-wife group therapy experiment. As the husband-and-wife doctor team they would take only husband-and-wife teams as patients. Murray's chapter on existential therapy for marital groups had been published as an article in the *Saturday Evening Post*. When Marsha came in with a tray of stuffed mushrooms she announced that Larry had just called and would be arriving from Washington any minute. Over drinks Lil posed the problem of pre-non-post-extra-marital relations to Murray. Murray, with Lisa counterpointing in soft Hungarian, suggested that behavioral patterns weren't subject to moral judgments, only analysis and clarification. Lil was overwhelmed by the simple logic of Murray's position. Larry arrived, kissed Marsha and Lil, and added that Murray's view could be applied to the law; in fact his trip to Washington had shown that the sociological carry-over into law had in effect reduced the moral difficulties of law immeasurably. Murray said that he didn't think of sex as sociological. "Sociology is what happens after the behaviorists get finished. Understanding human actions, especially group action, is the psychologists' business. The sociologist puts down in his notebook the kind of hors d'oeuvres served in a group. For the sociologist the great question is: are we or are we not a stuffed mushroom group?"

Then Murray introduced a game called "Psychology." "Someone goes out of the room," he explained, "one of the group is 'it,' and the person excluded is called back and must identify the one chosen by a series of associational questions. For example, you might ask: 'If this person was a fruit, what kind would he be, or if he was on a desert island, what five books would he take.' The same question is asked of all, so there are conflicting answers. Through the pattern of responses the person who is 'it' can be guessed."

Everything went along all right until Lil went out. She asked: "If this person was a movie actor who would he be?" Merle was 'it.' Merle is a kind of relaxed kid, Crosbyish, who surprises occasionally with sharp Spencer Tracy-like perceptions. Everybody gave Lil a tough time, saying things like Mickey Rooney, Donald O'Connor, Jack Lemmon, when Lil came out with a crazy remark: "One of you must be Wendell Corey."

That stopped the show. Murray guffawed. "You mean all of us must be Wendell Corey. How is that for a group label?"

Tibby asked in her bright, flat upstate accent, "Who is Wendell Corey?"

"I was 'it,'" said Merle, "and I see myself as Gerard Philipe. Wendell Corey never made love to anybody. Always that sour, pinched face, like he's getting ready to take a crap any minute."

"Maybe that's how Lil sees the world," Murray said, "constipated non-lovers." Murray thought that was funny, but Lisa gave him a stony look.

Lil said, "Actually I don't know why it came to me, but I hear he's a big fairy."

"I saw Jimmy Stewart in Washington," Larry said, "with some finky right-wing group. You know, the Hollywood hero acting out the role of patriot. It made me sick."

"But nobody answered the question," Marsha said. "Who is Merle? I vote for James Mason."

"I hear he is Jewish," Lil said. Murray really broke up on that one.

"What's so funny?" Lil asked. She was beginning to get sore.

Larry said, "Murray has a big anti-Jewish complex. He is the only analyst in New York who refuses Jewish patients. He even married a shikse."

Lisa smiled. "But I really think Jewish. He must be out of luck."

We finally decided that Merle was Anthony Franciosa, and stopped for coffee and cake. Murray picked it up again at the table. "You are not playing the game right. If you want to show what impression people have of others why not ask some dangerous questions. It's only in discomfort that we find emotional truth. Here's one: If somebody was drowning would this person jump in, call for help, or run away? Or, even better, if this person had a perverse habit, what would it be? That's a good one, because the responder would reveal his own tastes in perversion."

Everybody boldly agreed and I felt then that there really was a difference between intellectual life in the city and the wasteland of suburbia. Murray went out to be the guesser, and we decided on Tibby Barrett as "it," since most of us knew her slightly and it would lessen our personal embarrassment. Murray popped the question about perversion and we went around.

Lisa, sitting in Marsha's Saarinen Womb Chair, was first. She blushed a little, thought for a while, and then said: "If this person had a perverse habit, I would say he likes to smell armpits."

"Not much of a perversion," said Murray. "You know what Freud says about the olfactory sense and primitive man's delight in all smells."

"But this is twentieth-century civilized man," said Lisa. "Who today likes to handle and smell his own excretion?"

Larry, who was next, said loudly, "As a matter of fact, that was going to be my statement about our person, that he likes to smell human feces."

Tibby was next. I figured this was pretty rough stuff for a closed-in upstater, but she came out with a lulu. It almost broke up the game. "If this person was a female and had a perverse habit," she said matter-of-factly, "it would be wearing athletic supporters. Jock straps, you know."

"That's nothing more than locker-room transvestitism," said Murray, "but I'll guess it is you Tibby, because everybody else in the room sees you as anal-oriented. You at least know yourself."

"What does that mean?" asked Merle.

"Probably she thinks she harbors homosexual feelings, and the way to defeat them is to talk about them," answered Murray.

At this point, Lil, who had been crouching in the corner of the couch, said, "I think this whole business is perverse. How everybody enjoys it."

"Verbal sublimation may be a way of ridding oneself of a compulsion neurosis toward societally taboo sex feelings," said Lisa.

"But where is love in all this?" asked Lil.

Larry said, "As an old Stalinist friend would say: love is a romantic excrescence of bankrupt bourgeois capitalism."

Everybody laughed, and right in the middle, Tibby farted. "Oops," she said, and before she could blush we doubled up with laughter. Except Lil.

"I think it's a stupid game. Let's talk about something else." But that finished it. We were all ready to go home.

"Now that Larry is back are you going to stay?" I asked Lil. I offered to take her to my place. She agreed and as soon as we got home she showered and went right to sleep. I thought she was faking it, but when I jostled her, she murmured, "Mommy," and began to snore a little.

I told Ben the story some days later. He was back over the meat market on Hudson Street. "You know," he said, "Lil is really all right. I mean that Marsha Weinstein crowd, I hate it." He stared soupily at a glass of warm Scotch. "I read an article in this week's *Reporter* about the fragmented man. This guy said, I think it was Oscar Jones, who wrote that study of the light-skinned Negro as *the* symbol of the alienated man. He's up at Columbia in C. Wright Mills's place. Wasn't that a tragic thing? Anyway, Jones discussed the possibility that we have lost a real work tradition and are seeking substitute gratification through the arts. He calls it cultural tunneling, whereby the true emotions of man, work-directed, have gone underground, so we seek love, not in sex, but in the movies, 'sex's blessed surrogate' he said. Maybe if I make it with Lil again I'll get job satisfaction too. Does that make sense?"

I said that it did, but I wondered why he didn't comment on Lil's sleeping in my bed. I asked him. "Well," he said, "you're no real threat the way Larry Jonas is. I haven't been able to satisfy Lil, so you may be my blessed surrogate."

"But she fell asleep," I said, thinking how nice it would have been to take her in her sleep.

A few days later Ben told me that he and Lil were going to try again and invited me to dinner to celebrate the reconciliation. When I arrived Lil was on the floor in leotards, practicing a leg-raising exercise she learned from Marsha. The "Ode to Joy" was storming out of the record player. Ben was whistling in the bathroom. "I've got a part-time job as a dental assistant," Lil said, as she kept exercising, and then, jumping up, she whispered, "we have decided to try for a baby."

Ben walked in wiping his face with a towel and boomed, "Say, did Lil tell you that we decided to try for a baby." Lil flashed an angry look at him. He went on. "I looked around me, at all the people I know in the Village, and nobody has a family. Maybe they think it's a concession to middle-class attitudes, but it occurred to me that barrenness extirpates life. Listen to the Beethoven. It sings out the triumph of life, but without the child-bearing function man is deracinated, absolutely deracinated. Have a drink."

Lil looked at him, the light going out of her eyes. "Why must you always intellectualize everything. I want a baby because it will be the fruit of me, mine, yours, ours. Don't feelings have a place anywhere?"

"Of course they do. That's what I was trying to say. There must be a return to feeling and away from the highbrow dissection of everything. I can't even read *Dissent* any more. Doesn't Murray say in his book that the existential moment is truly realized in the coital act?"

"Good God, Murray is forty-five years old, Lisa is his third wife, and do you see any kids around the house?"

"What do you know." Ben gulped his drink. "Murray can't have babies, for goodness sake."

"I don't believe it."

"He is sterile. S-T-E-R-I-L-E. Sterile."

I thought of Murray, wavy-haired, graying at the temples, the image of Jeff Chandler, poor guy, as a psychoanalyst. I didn't believe Ben either.

"But he is," Ben said. "He told me so at the White school. Why do you think he was interested in asking those questions about perversity? He is capable of intercourse, but he knows the guilt-anxiety of the act, and he chooses wayward acts as a kind of self-mutilating penance to his libido. I think those were his exact words to me."

Dinner went along aimlessly and I left shortly after. Ben had put on a John Cage record, and Lil was in the kitchen washing the floor. As I closed the door I heard him come into the kitchen. "Come on, Lil, get off the floor."

The next week I met Merle at Lerner's fourth lecture on American pluralism, this time the dichotomy between our Puritan adherence to monogamy on the one hand, and the new culture's rampant extra-maritalism on the other, a split which carried directly into the political arena. Lerner explained that the only way our statesmen could exorcise private guilt is by being supermoral in our foreign policy. He called it the Dulles syndrome. I wanted to pursue the point over a cookery-split, their ice cream special, but Merle broke in. "I wasn't listening. I broke up with Tibby last week."

"You don't look like you're collapsing over it," I said.

"I'm not. I'm puzzled more by an eerie feeling I have. I might as well tell you because you'll find out soon enough. A few days after the break I ran into Lil at the 8th Street Bookstore. She was looking haggard. The thing with Ben was over, but she said what disturbed her was the fact that she had been riding on the wings of a new idea, and her wings had been clipped. She did look like a fallen bird. She wanted a baby. That was the answer. She knew it. She spoke to her doctor and all he could say was, 'Do you really want it?' 'I don't know what I want,' she answered, and he said, 'Tell me what you think.' She talked a lot. She lies down now, you know, but she came out depressed. I told her about Tibby and me, and a strange, desperate look came over her. 'Come up to my place and we'll talk,' she said, and before I knew it, although I really knew it, we were in bed. 'I want a baby. I want a baby,' she kept repeating. She was too hysterical for any honest screwing, and we ended up drinking coffee in the kitchen. The thing that bothers me is that she was Larry's girl for quite a while. I mean, he is my older brother."

I asked him if he wanted the affair, and he shrugged. "Who knows what I want? The thing with Tibby went sour overnight. Really. We didn't even have a fight. She said, 'I'm moving out,' and I said O.K. I'm not like that. I like to analyze a relationship; that's half the fun. But the lights went out, that's all. So I look at Lil. I mean she probably can be good in bed if she works at it. But she is sick. And there is Larry. And maybe Ben with his crazy moral views will get sore. I like Ben. He was the first guy to give me a sense of social consciousness. I spoke to Marsha this morning and she insisted that I see a doctor. So her analyst arranged for an appointment with a man he recommends. Do you know him? Talcott Weingarten. He's a Sullivanian. I thought of going to Murray, but Marsha laughed. 'You are naive, Merle. You don't go to your friends. He knows too much about you.' I thought that was a funny remark, but I let it go."

I called Ben that night. He was back again at Hudson Street, and he had put a phone in, because, he said, "Who am I kidding? Artificial means of severing communications won't work. I have got to make the break from the inside."

"Why are you breaking?" I asked.

"Actually I'm not. As a matter of fact, for the first time in my life I feel a real spiritual renewal. Why don't you come over and see."

When I got to his place I saw demolition notices on all the stores. A new luxury building was going up. This one, a big placard announced, was to be called The Titian Terrace. When I walked in, Tibby was sitting in a sling chair, holding a copy of *Civilization and Its Discontents.* "It's all in here," she said with a straight face. "He says I'm in trouble because I'm using sex as a sublimation for sex." I laughed and Ben greeted me.

"She really means that Freud is a fraud. Tibby is the answer to all neuroses. She is the incarnation of the love instinct."

"You mean the sex instinct," I offered.

"No, the love instinct. Lil didn't have it. I've been looking for the direct woman all my life. Look at her in the flesh." He went to her and kissed her.

"Ben thinks I am the embodiment of Marilyn Monroe and Jean Harlow. He is cute. I think I'm a quiet Bette Davis. Freud says it's a reaction formation. I refuse to accept my image of myself. I think he's cute too."

Ben said, "You see what I mean. She has insight, a native gift. She is the master of the innocuous apothegm. 'He's cute too.' Could Lil ever say anything like that?"

I said I thought she could. But Ben answered that it didn't matter, and launched into a recital of Tibby's virtues, while Tibby kept looking at him with bemused detachment. After the last breakup with Lil, Ben said he felt like committing suicide, but despite his despondency he knew that suicide was a failure of moral commitment. He had gone to the Cedar Street Bar for a drink, and Tibby was sitting at a table in the back. She told him about her break with Merle, and suggested that they try something together. She meant it as a joke, but Ben said why not. Tibby moved in that night, and Ben had his first successful love-making in months.

"Do you know what it is to make real love?" he said. "I told my doctor that it was a bourgeois myth kept alive for the sake of promoting wish-fulfilling fantasies and to keep the advertising business going. Did you see that piece in *Commentary* on 'Eros as Money-Making Myth'? It may be true, but nobody has ever seen the archetypal force of the pure, private act. It is positively prelapsarian." Just then Tibby farted.

"Oops," she said, and I noticed that she had learned not to blush as she had done at Marsha's.

Ben turned on her. "What kind of a stupid thing is that to do?"

"I had gas," Tibby said.

About a month later I met Larry and Marsha coming out of the 8th Street

Playhouse. *Paths of Glory* was playing. "Film-making of the highest order," Larry said, "absolutely devastating exposure of the military mind. But why cast that right-wing bastard Menjou I can't understand." Marsha thought Larry looked like Kirk Douglas without the cleft. We went to the Limelight for capuccino.

"There's Wilder Benjamin, the movie critic of the *Voice*," Marsha said. "Do you know that he was Lil's first boy friend in the Village?"

"Can you believe it," Larry said, "Ben and Lil are together again. Lil's fling with Merle lasted about a week. Merle came to me and told me that my image haunted the bedroom. He couldn't even get an erection."

"And Ben," Marsha added, "had a terrible fight with Tibby. He accused her of lacking any distinction as a human being. He said he couldn't live with a girl so obtuse about the world around her. So Lil and Ben are back together, and they have decided to attend Murray's husband-and-wife therapy team. They are not going to think about a baby for a while. Murray recommended that Lil go back to dancing classes with me in order to get back to her primal self."

Although it was late when I left them, I wandered over to the Cedar Street Bar thinking that despite the problems people seem to have, they were alive to the possibilities of existence. It was almost closing time. Two fairies were standing at the bar having a furious argument. The only other person was Tibby.

She was sitting at the table in the corner, looking disconsolate. "I just broke up with Ben," she said, before I could sit down. I ordered two beers, and after a quiet cigarette I asked her if she would like to stay at my place. She agreed.

THE GESTURE

JAMES W. GROSHONG from *Antioch Review*

Deutlich forgot his apprehensions almost entirely when he saw the girl step through the hole in the side of the plane and start down the ramp in the gray mist. She held her chin very high, long black throat taut, and did not use the handrail. As she came closer he saw that she wore what appeared to be a man's suitcoat, a double-breasted gray pinstripe, above a swirling skirt of bright colors, and cracked shoes with run-over heels. When she paused at the bottom of the ramp he waved, and she came toward him in a long, loose-jointed stride that made him think of the way running animals look in slow motion.

"Eva Mary?"

"Yes." She nodded, unsmiling, and for a moment he held a thin, long-fingered hand.

"I'm Homer Deutlich. Happy you are here."

"Thank you."

"Are you very tired?"

She shook her head. "Only a little bit." Her voice was soft, high-pitched and fluty, each word a distinct act of creation.

"Mrs. Deutlich—Carol—was so busy preparing for you that she decided not to come to the airport."

"I see." Still no smile.

Feeling a little outfaced, he steered her through the crowd and up the steps to the baggage counter, where he acquired two articles resembling suitboxes with rope handles, and then led her down an escalator and to the parking lot. If the girl found anything strange about the escalator she did not say so.

In the freeway traffic he thought of the violence, for her, of the sudden change, and tried questions. Had she been able to see San Francisco through the October fog? Had she been away from Kenya before? Weren't our eucalyptus trees lovely with their ropy strips of bark? She said no to the first two and seemed not to hear the third, sitting hunched over, long satin lids over her eyes, looking, if at anything, at her own sharp knees. He started to ask about her family but realized she was asleep.

For a moment, just after turning into University Avenue, he almost regretted having begun it all by bringing home the brochure for Project Friendship, with its photographs of handsome young Africans and its three-sentence explanation that international understanding was simply a matter of getting to know the people. He had expected Carol to be amused, and a little offended, as he was, by the glibness. But she wasn't. She had sent off a letter the next morning, and within a month or two of negotiation settled on Eva Mary, with whom she proposed to garden and cook and talk and make dresses for six happy American months. He had wanted to object but was always stopped by the brightness in her face, until the brightness gradually warmed him and made him conspire, even happily, with her. But now everything was suddenly translated into the fact of this long thin sleeping girl. . . .

Carol, blonde and glowing, stood waiting on the grass. In the driveway he stopped the car and turned to shake the girl by the shoulder.

Carol brought tea and cake even before he had had time to return to the car for the girl's luggage.

"I know all Africans like tea," she was saying when he returned with the two cardboard packets, "and I hope I'm not wrong about you." This was a Carolean trick: a strong generalization followed by a hint of fallibility. She was apparently quite right, however, about Eva Mary, who seemed grateful for the tea and took the cup, awkwardly, pink showing in the cracks of her knuckles.

"Yes, I . . . like tea." She looked quickly at her hosts with dark round eyes, and then yawned.

"Just sit over here, dear, and have your tea. You must be very tired after such a long trip." Carol guided the girl to a chair by a table at the side of the room.

The African girl's English was clear and correct but so softly spoken that Deutlich found himself leaning forward in his chair.

"Speak up, dear, we can't hear you." Carol was in her League voice. "We are very much interested in everything you have to tell us, you know, but if we can't hear you . . ."

The girl bent over her teacup, apparently studying its insides, and Deutlich could see entirely the hair which covered her head like a tight-fitting cap. Carol somewhere retrieved her knitting and now fussed with it, dropping a ball of white yarn on the floor so that it rolled part way across the floor toward Eva Mary, the slack making a twisting white road that got nowhere before rolling up in itself again. He tried bright comments on the weather in Nairobi, on Jomo Kenyatta, on Tom Mboya. Her reply was a high-pitched giggle.

When she finally put down her cup, Deutlich snatched it, and with the tray and the other two cups almost ran to the kitchen. He had just reached the sink when he heard Carol ask the girl whether she would like to go to the bathroom.

For the moment safe, he plashed about noisily, finding occupation, unnecessarily rinsing the cups, saucers, and creamer before placing them in the top rack of the dishwasher. He even emptied the sugar back in the bin and turned the bowl upside down beside the cups and creamer in the rack. Carol would fill it again in the morning and ask him about it. But now it gave him an extra moment.

The low sound of Carol's voice, then the flute sound, perhaps a laugh, from the African girl, over the flushing of the toilet.

"Homer, Eva Mary would like more tea. She didn't have room before, did you, dear?" Deutlich went to the faucet to fill the kettle.

Soon the girl was sipping noisily at fresh hot tea, long muscular lips folding over the cup's brim.

"Do you like music?"

"Yes, I like to . . . sing." Her mouth hardly moved from the cup, the manner of her reply suggesting that she had merely overheard his question.

"I have heard some records by a South African singer—Miriam something—surname ending with . . . eba, I believe."

More noisy sipping.

"Do you recognize the name?"

"No."

"Very popular, I understand. Made several appearances on American television a year or two ago."

He waited.

"Do you like jazz?"

"Jazz?"

"Our major borrowing from African culture and some say our only distinctive—"

Eva Mary interrupted to ask for more tea.

"—cultural achievement."

He watched the girl stir sugar into the steaming cup.

"Do you have American records at home? Er—gramophone records?"

"Oh yes, we . . ." a long pause, ". . . have American records. The rockend roll we like. What is jazz?"

Carol smiled brightly over his defeat and changed the subject.

"On your papers," she began, "I noticed that your father had a surname different from yours. Are you a stepdaughter?"

"Stepdaughter?" The black hands, momentarily relinquishing the teacup, turned pink palms up on her knees.

"I mean, dear, is he your real father?"

"Oh yes, he is my real father."

"But I don't understand why your name is different from his."

"The tribe gave us names that are different." She spoke the last word in three distinct syllables.

"Oh."

Apparently finished with her tea, the girl suddenly snatched up the morning *Chronicle* from the arm of the sofa and for five minutes appeared absorbed in an account of a municipal election. Then she turned slowly to look at a far corner of the room, and reaching into the front of her dress, scratched vigorously at a hairless armpit and yawned, stretching her mouth tightly away from an infinity of white teeth. Deutlich, rubbing his aching forehead, heard his wife urge the girl into the guest bedroom.

In minutes Carol was back.

"She's already asleep. She was going to sleep in her dress, but I got her my old flannel nightgown and she wore that. Everything she took off badly needs washing."

Shortly before midnight, Deutlich closed his copy of *Emma* and was about to introduce the ritual of going to bed when he looked up to see Eva Mary standing in the hall doorway. Or rather, Carol's flannel nightgown stood there, with Eva Mary's long neck lifting from it like an ebony sculpture. She seemed strangely tall, unaware and uncaring that her slender Masai body did not at all replace the Nordic amplitude of Carol's. A curious angularity in the lower folds of the garment puzzled Deutlich until he reasoned that she was standing on one foot. A moment later she shifted slightly in the doorway and he could see the long pink sole with its deeply curved arch under the lifted hem. As Carol straightened from her doze over a collection of Conrad stories, the girl folded her arms across her breast, dropped the lifted foot, and smiled a lovely white smile. Then she turned and billowed down the hallway like a cloud and was gone.

Deutlich waited for the sound of the closing door before he turned to his wife. When he saw her tears, he quickly crossed to sit by her and took her in his arms.

"What," she wept against his shoulder, "are we ever going to do with that lovely child?"

In a moment before sleeping, Deutlich concluded finally that Carol's were compassionate tears, or, at the very least, the natural consequence, in a woman of an aesthetic experience. Eva Mary *was* a lovely child, and, as a matter of fact, what *were* they to do with her?

Just as the eggs were ready Eva Mary appeared, wearing a red cotton dress crisscrossed with white stripes which gave her the appearance of a wild bird and deepened the red of her protuberant lips. Silently she sat at the place by the window to which she was guided by Carol. Deutlich was hungry and immediately began on the first of his two boiled eggs. As he ate, he watched the girl lift her cup of coffee, taste it, and with an infant's grimace replace it in the saucer. After a moment she reached for a banana from the fruit bowl in the center of the table and, though it was a very large banana, ate it in three bites with sticky, sucking noises.

Carol now lifted a piece of hot toast from the shiny machine at her left elbow, buttered it heavily and spread it thick with raspberry jam. This dripping combination she handed across the table to Eva Mary, who took it hesitantly.

"This is raspberry jam, dear," she said in her best croon. "It is made from a berry we all love. Go on now, dear, it's delicious."

The girl took a compliant nip with her front teeth at the tiniest corner, and with the same grimace placed the toast on her plate beside the untouched egg.

Deutlich quickly spooned up the second egg, and acquiring the remaining piece of toast, ostentatiously buttered it and added a heaping spoonful of jam, which he plastered studiously out to the edges. This he washed down quickly with hot coffee, sensing his own foolishness in hoping that his appreciative gulps would somehow convince the girl of the error of her taste.

But by now she had peeled and eaten a second banana, and it was apparent from her manner that *her* breakfast, at least, was over. To signify the fact she pushed back her chair and slid from it, in the process knocking a pot of wintering geraniums from the sill behind her. The pot shattered to a strew of earthenware shards and black soil. Looking apprehensively at Deutlich, the girl stood erect and folded her long fingers over her diaphragm.

"Oh, that's too bad, dear," said Carol, going for broom and dustpan. "I shouldn't have placed you so near the window. Here. I'll hold the dustpan and you can sweep."

The girl quickly swept the remnants into the dustpan and finished with a series of quick little sweeps to get the dirt that had slipped under the rubber lip of the pan. Carol scrubbed vigorously with a sponge and then stood up.

"I think the roots are all right and we can save the plant. As soon as we clean up the kitchen and get Homer started we can go to the potting shed and see about it. I don't think it will be too cold for us." After smiling at the girl and patting her bare arm, she went off to the garbage can with the dustpan.

Deutlich stood up, swallowing the last of his by now cold coffee, and went to his study for his briefcase. Instead of kissing his wife, he chose to call goodbye through the kitchen door, for it seemed wrong somehow to make a display of kissing before young African innocence. Just why, he was not sure, any more than he was sure why he was vaguely troubled, as he backed his car from the garage, to see through the kitchen window that Eva Mary was already in an apron and collecting plates and silverware for the dishwasher.

For the first two or three weeks Eva Mary was an exciting presence for Carol. Deutlich knew when his wife was acting out of honest affection; and until nearly the end of November there could be no doubt of her honest affection for the African girl. When Eva Mary learned to bake packaged biscuits (which she did quickly and with no apparent sense of accomplishment) Carol kissed her impulsively on the cheek and hugged her strenuously. That evening she bought the girl a transistor radio and thereafter—for a long time—tried to appear undisturbed by the day-long diet of "rockend roll" the noisy little instrument produced, even when Eva Mary chose, as she frequently did, to turn it to its highest volume and dance solemnly, fingers laced behind her head, up and down the living room, as Carol tried to nap in the adjoining bedroom.

During those early weeks Carol's affection showed largely in the giving of gifts. After the radio came a dress with bouffant skirt, white, with matching shoes; a set of scarves in three different colors, with the girl's initials on each; a lacquered box containing lipsticks, eyebrow pencil (Eva Mary's eyebrows were by nature almost invisible), and assorted shades of fingernail polish. But after a trying-on ceremony the clothing remained in her closet untouched, and Carol's offer to do the girl's nails brought only a brief shaking of the small neat head. Carol tried again, this time with two costly woolen dresses. These went to the closet without so much as a trying-on.

Yet if Deutlich read his wife's mind correctly, her real irritation began not with the girl's rejection of the gifts, but with her eating noises, especially with bananas, which remained her staple food. Early in their marriage Deutlich had had to learn to take his soup tepid rather than hot the way he liked it, for Carol could not tolerate sipping sounds and corrected him by thrusting a finger in her ear and frowning. Once, to counter his enthusiasm for a bowl of hot clam nectar, she had even left the table. Now she had begun the same educational program with Eva Mary.

He remembered the first lesson. (It was also, in a way, the last.) As usual, Eva Mary was making the bulk of her meal from the fruit bowl, having put aside a baked potato, porterhouse steak, and green salad, with only a tentative sip or two at a cup of clear soup. As she was about to demolish the latter half of her second banana, Carol took one herself.

"Eva, dear, let me show you how *we* eat a banana. I'm quite sure it is customary in your country to eat noisily to show your appreciation for the food. We like you to show your appreciation, if that's what it is. But here it is not considered nice to eat . . . well, the way you do, with all that noise. Look." Whereupon she ate the banana, slowly, in at least a dozen small bites, chewing daintily and silently, smiling at the girl, who sat impassively watching.

"There! See how easy it is? Now— You try again and this time eat just like an American lady."

Eva Mary did not care for more, and Deutlich left the table to find his pipe.

By the end of November Deutlich had grown accustomed to nightly reviews of Eva Mary's transgressions—never anything serious and mostly affronts to Carol's sense of her own dignity. He listened and sympathized. He knew his wife was trying hard to make the girl happy and comfortable and yet had been given no real reason to believe she had succeeded. The girl loved to cook (largely, he suspected, because she could turn the shiny gold and chromium dials of Carol's elaborate kitchen range) and coddled her little radio, but otherwise she remained imperturbable and preternaturally quiet.

The ultimate rift which Deutlich had feared came in mid-December, when Carol tried what she called "an early Christmas"—a gift of a white purse with shoulder strap and matching coin purse full of substantial coins.

"Thank you I don't like it." She spoke in the detached manner Carol herself might use in rejecting a color card offered her by a paint salesman. But Deutlich knew it was very necessary indeed that Eva Mary like that purse. Therefore, when Carol went to the bedroom he waited until it would not appear that he was rushing, and then he followed her.

When he came in she did not look up and he felt the jumping in his stomach for which she was always in one way or another responsible. He sat on the bed and took her hand, which she immediately withdrew.

"I am exhausted," she said finally, in a carefully controlled voice.

"I'm sorry, Carol. Just stay here. I'll see about supper."

"I don't mean that. I'm exhausted from trying to do and be everything for that girl and I don't get anywhere. I try and try and try . . ." She turned away from him and her shoulders shook.

"Could I be helping more?"

She turned quickly. "You brought her here!"

A retort just now would be catastrophic, though in a quieter time she would find a way of softening, neutralizing, the remark, but without really correcting it. He hoped there was no rebuttal in his face.

"You are away all day and she is here with me. And I try so hard . . ." Her lip trembled. "I try so hard to interest her in things and to do things for her but she is cold about it all. She says nothing but yes, or no, or thank you. She never starts a conversation. She never starts anything—just does what I tell her to do. But if I don't tell her to do things she just sits and looks at the floor. If I ask her to help me with something she at least moves."

He reached for her hand again, and though it did not unfold in his, she did not draw it away, and he was encouraged.

"I know. I have seen it and worried about it but I have never known what to do. The girl has crossed three or four centuries in the last few weeks. I suppose we mustn't ask too much of her."

Carol sat up and put her face so close to his that he was for a moment examining a small clot of mascara in the bunched lashes on her lower left eyelid. "But Homer, is it too much to expect that after crossing those centuries she would at least be a human being? When we are alone I have nothing but a doll. She walks and she sits down and she goes to the bathroom and she eats. But she answers me in monosyllables. It's worse than having no one at all because her being here is such an *enticement.* I want so terribly to be of some use to her but I'm not. I can't talk with her, I can't even find any evidence that she likes being here, that she likes me, or that she has any appreciation for anything—except the stove and that damned radio!"

She blew her nose.

"Not that I expect her to fawn, Homer. But you know what I mean."

He didn't quite, but nodded.

"All I want, Homer, is a *person.*"

Deutlich continued to nod, thinking of Eva Mary on that first night, standing angelic in a white gown, bathing them in that glorious smile.

An hour later he and Eva Mary sat at the kitchen table eating bowls of rice and slivers of cold chicken, the only two foods in addition to bananas that Carol had found the girl willing to eat regularly and with any enthusiasm. Deutlich was now having rice for the third day in succession and chicken for the fourth. From time to time he looked at the girl and she at him and when he tried to smile at her she looked quickly downward. She ate close to the bowl and used her fork chiefly as a paddle, pushing rather than lifting the food. Often a grain or two of rice clung to the corners of her dark red mouth.

She did not ask about Carol's absence from the table.

The next day was Saturday and Deutlich was as usual up early. Carol, though still in bed, was awake; and as he left the bedroom she suggested that he might "talk" to Eva Mary, meaning in effect that he was to ask the girl to change her personality and do it rather quickly. But "talk"? He did not know, any more than Carol, who the girl really was. Or even where the intelligence lay inside all that resistance.

Still in bathrobe and slippers he stepped from the garage into the garden. The air was cold but the sun was bright and he filled his lungs with the crisp air. Before him he saw the sad spectacle of the frost-ruined plants—the tall dahlias, their leaves brown and slimy and flaccid, the wilted chrysanthemums. Only here and there the stocks hinted at further life, in a few delicately colored, tightly rolled buds. He moved from behind a tall thorn bush to get a better look at the stocks; and then he saw the girl. She was crouched before the flower bed, sniffing delicately at a sprig of stock. Her eyes were closed.

Was now the time?

"Good morning, Eva Mary. I . . ."

The girl stood up. In the cold air she wore as usual a bright cotton dress with no sleeves. Silently she handed him the sweet-smelling stem and turned away, walking in long strides to the house. Watching, he absent-mindedly held the buds to his own nostrils.

At breakfast Carol was bright and cheerful, nothing in her manner or appearance suggesting her spasm of the night before. Deutlich took a deep breath when he saw the three bowls of bananas, sliced in a useless attempt to cut down the sound from the girl's eating.

On Christmas morning the girl, with a shy white smile, accepted her gifts— a dozen bandanna handkerchiefs in different colors and a small cardboard box full of costume jewelry—and then went at once to the kitchen, where Deutlich, from his chair in the living room, could see her standing at the sink and hear her humming a high, thin melody of a half-dozen tones in a staccato, repetitive pattern. Opposite him Carol sat with head back, eyes closed, face expressionless.

"Homer, get that girl out of my house!"

He took a deep breath and held it for a moment; but the humming in the kitchen continued.

Crossing the room he took her hand. "Let's go walk in the garden."

She pulled her hand away and turned her face from him.

In the garden he walked alone, watching the heavy dew rapidly soak the edges of his leather slippers. The air was cold, and he shivered.

Carol was now reacting from a deep place he could not reach but only knew about, and the very quietness of her face meant a festering that could infect their lives. The girl must go, and very soon.

But how to do it? He could not look into those quiet eyes and say something brutal—"We don't want you here any more."

What to do?

Two days after Christmas Carol announced, almost formally, with a significant look at Deutlich, that she would be away for dinner—a League dinner, with a business meeting afterward. He and Eva Mary were to have rice, lamb (a recent addition to the girl's acceptable fare), and of course bananas for dessert. He recognized that the crisis had come.

At dinner there was no conversation. The girl sucked noisily at her meat and rice, head low over her plate, sitting up only to drink her tea with long, drawn-out hisses of the kind that made Carol wince.

After her second banana, the girl cleared the table while Deutlich tried to read the evening paper but found his concentration fixed on the clatter of dishes in the kitchen.

At last he heard the hum of the dishwasher and the sound of the clothesbin shutting, which meant that she had disposed of the damp dishcloth with which she had wiped the table—just as Carol had taught her to do. When she came into the living room he was prepared to sound friendly and jocular.

"Eva Mary, I'm going for a walk. Would you like to come?" It was an improvised idea, and as soon as he had spoken he wondered what he would do or say if she said no.

"Yes, I would like to walk."

"It is cold enough for you to wear a coat." She had not understood about winter in California (the pictures they had sent were made in June) and she had not brought a coat.

"You can wear one of Carol's." He brought her one, an old camel's hair Carol had worn at college. It hung on the black girl unevenly and the seams sagged at her shoulders.

He had not thought about a place to go or even a direction. But there was always the bay. The wind would be cold there but she would be warm in the coat.

As they walked silently, smelling the heavy scent of eucalyptus in the crisp air, they began to see the low-flying gulls, and in twenty minutes they were standing on the quay by the yacht harbor. A heavy fog lay over the far shore. He did not try to think of anything to say. Water lapped against the pilings beneath them. Disappearing in the gray mist were the running lights of a small boat. He could feel the beads of fog gathering in his nostrils. Overhead, above the clouds, the Los Angeles plane was putting down for the field to the north where he had gone for Eva Mary two months ago.

As the plane was directly overhead he felt his hand gripped by a smaller hand, cold and shivering.

"Oh, I'm sorry, Eva Mary. I didn't realize you would be so cold. We'll go right home."

The girl did not release his hand, though except for the hand he would have been hardly aware of her being there. She moved beside him like a dancer, gliding over the curbs, slowing or quickening her pace to match his.

He found he was sweating in the cold.

Until they were within sight of the house he tried not to think of what he must do. For the first time since leaving the quay, he looked down at her face, and she smiled. Perhaps they could talk inside the house.

As he helped her out of the coat, she put her arms around him suddenly and laid her head for an instant against his chest.

"I think it is too bad for you that your wife does not have babies."

Then she was in her room and at once he heard the little radio: "Because you're mine—I'll walk the line. . . ."

He started toward the sound, stopped, sat down, and for a long time stared through the window at a pepper tree, ugly in its winter depression.

The next morning at breakfast he had just finished his last cup of coffee and Carol had already moved the toaster from the table to its place in the cupboard when he found Eva Mary looking at him.

"I think I will be going home."

Deutlich put down his cup. Carol turned quickly.

"What's that, dear?"

"I think I will be going home."

At that moment he hated Carol because of the quick light in her face.

"Home? But, dear, we . . ." Occupation with the silverware allowed her to leave the sentence unfinished.

"I would like to go Tuesday. Will arrangements be difficult?"

"Just a clearance from Internal Revenue and, of course, the reservation. Won't you have lots of things to tell your people? Just think . . ."

Deutlich left the table to pack his briefcase for a day at the library, stopping off in the bathroom for aspirin.

Tuesday was New Year's Day and the airport was not crowded. In the long foyer they walked up and down looking at the display cases. Carol was gay. Eva Mary wore the man's suitcoat and her dress with the white stripes.

Then the amplifiers announced the London plane and they went out to it. Carol put a bundle of new magazines in the girl's arms and touched her lips to the dark cheek. Deutlich once more felt the cold hand, and then he and Carol watched as the girl in her long stride crossed the concrete and climbed the ramp toward the hole in the side of what appeared to be the same great aluminum fish that had delivered her in October. She turned and looked back, smiling, long neck raising her chin high, and then the hole closed. Moments later the plane was gone, leaving trails of black smoke.

Carol walked away quickly, ahead of him, and he moved faster to catch up. He expected her to be crying, and she was. Just before he opened the car door for her he looked up again and saw a final glint of metal to the north.

"Do you suppose," she sobbed as she sat down, "she will ever forgive us?"

Getting Married

JAMES B. HALL   from *Virginia Quarterly Review*

I am not pretty, nor was I a very clever girl around boys. On the other hand, I am pleasant, and understanding, and was glad to find I could become very domestic—I mean loving—after I married Burney.

K. O. Burney: not Kenneth, or Karl, but only the initials. After he moved into my father's rental apartment above our garage, Burney once told me he had a brother somewhere in the Armed Forces whose name was O. K. (initials only). How could any mother ever, ever name her two sons K. O. and O. K.? From that remark I understood from the first that his family was not advantaged. I mean less advantaged than my own family.

My father has his own two-chair shop, and was once the Secretary-Treasurer of his fraternal order. Mother is somewhat less social, but she gets what she wants. Mother was working for her beautician's license when she married Daddy. I am the only child, the kind of girl that tried hard in high school, but always got C+. After graduation—as our neighbors said—I was "at home."

"A-what?" was the exact word Burney said the first day I really spoke to him—and got an answer.

He had been in the garage apartment three months, and had paid promptly in cash. Both mother and father thought he was steady, but I must say he kept his own counsel. He was just wiggling out from beneath his 1953 Ford coupe. He was three years older than me, the kind of man who has never thought himself attractive, for he had not helped his best feature. I mean, his hair. It was just a gorgeous, deep copper against the concrete, there in the sunlight.

"Thanks-no."

I had asked, did he want to lay under the car on our old chenille spread, the cement being no doubt very chilly. Yet the way he said "Thanks-no" was neither rude nor common. He simply did not know exactly how to accept little neighborly things.

Logically, even ruthlessly, he began to wipe grease from his hands. He used one little ball of waste, then tossed it aside in a neat pile beside the back step where I sat watching him.

I said my name was Dora, and he looked at me in a very manly way, daring me to flinch: "K. O. Burney, here."

Probably I looked vague, but I said, "How-do-you-do, *Mister* Burney." I certainly was not going to discuss his name, so I asked him about his car.

"Oh, I just want it *right*. I mean. . . ."

It seemed the car leaked oil from the gasket behind the water pump. He hated for something he owned free and clear to be dripping oil all over his half of the garage. "I want things right. That's all."

I thought our first conversation was over, but he surprised me. In the way of shy people—for no real reason—he became suddenly very talkative. I realized he was also a lonely man.

It seemed this particular Ford was not a bad old car. Got him to the Plant, and back. Liked to keep it tip-top, and that's why he owned his own tools. That way you got full value and you didn't have to trade every year for the benefit of Detroit. . . .

Burney nodded his head in a straight line from our back steps in Haskall—near Chicago—towards Lake Michigan, and towards Detroit, beyond. The way he said it, Detroit was a bad city.

"My father says that too,"—and I could have bit my tongue. Really, I wanted to agree with Burney because what he said seemed accurate; I did not want him to think I was playing up to his opinions.

"I doubt it," K. O. Burney said, and picked up all his balls of waste and put them in a little brown paper sack and put the sack in the Ford. You could tell he would throw that sack in a trash barrel at the first service station he saw. His gesture told me that the Glaspys—father *and* daughter—need not worry about trash left around by K. O. Burney.

Still, he had caught me in a little lie, and I felt he was right to do so: Daddy's new Plymouth was parked in our side of the garage.

I changed the subject.

"Electronics," he said, and I understood he was more than a semi-skilled workman at Teletek, our new plant out beyond Sparkman. Even in high school he had realized electronics was an expanding field—so he got into it. And no regrets.

Burney worked at a bench inside, with meters and clips and wires, testing telemetry equipment. His hands were white, with very long supple fingers. Even today he does not realize his long fingers are a great point of his beauty. It's not the sort of thing a new wife can say to someone like Burney—even after dark.

Abruptly, he walked once around the car. He sighted along the door panel—no dents or dings. He sighted back along our driveway towards the street. He got in the car and slammed the door.

"Got to take off," he said, and backed his car very fast all the way to the street. He did not even say goodbye.

That is how we met. I was certain he had no business elsewhere, except to throw away that little brown sack of waste. It was his afternoon off work, and he probably drove around and around by himself until it was time to park somewhere and eat.

My mother was looking down at me from our kitchen window. Behind the pane of glass her lips were saying, "You come in here right now. . . ."

That was a Saturday in spring, two weeks before I graduated from high school.

At first I had no feeling at all about K. O. Burney, except that he was interesting. He had unusual ideas—things he had worked out for himself.

More than once that spring, after he had washed his car on the ramp, we sat in the front seat in plain sight of the kitchen window, and talked. He told me the difference between AM and FM broadcasting, and how radar works, and about the power-pack and the detector stages of ordinary radio and TV sets. I really understood it. I just knew he could have been a wonderful teacher, especially science.

"What I don't like," he said once, "is the way everyone takes a piece of the working man. I *know* that."

Generally, I believed if a man worked and managed well, then he would get ahead.

"Don't believe what they show you on TV," he said, and smiled bitterly. "At war, or at a hanging, it's the working man first."

"Well, help yourself," I said. "You have a union. Don't they have powers?"

That was what my father said, who was never himself a union barber and who did not like to have a union man in the second chair.

"You really think so, Dora?" and Burney lowered his voice. He looked directly at me. "Union big shots are no different from Senators or Generals or Henry Ford in Detroit."

I had never thought that unions might also oppress a working man. Burney was not cynical or bitter, but he was the first person I ever met who knew from real experience how the world runs. And he had other good ideas.

"Those so-called services," and now he looked straight ahead through the clean windshield as though we were going down the road very fast. "Checking accounts. Time payments. Why, working people ought to buy for less. But we pay more, in interest. You figure it out some time. . . ."

"Dora," he said after a little while. "Some things ain't right."

"Aren't."

"Aren't," Burney said, and to this day he has never said that other word in my presence.

For a long time nothing happened, and I do not know exactly what I was thinking.

Then mother was on the ramp, and I rolled down the car window. She was dressed, or at least as much dressed up as she ever gets to go out with father.

"Now *Dor-a.* . . ." Oh, how I knew that tone.

"Your father and me already had our snack but I didn't know you were out here. *With* Mr. Burney, I mean."

Mother smiled very sweetly and said, "Are you sitting for someone?"

Mother knew very well I did not have a baby-sitting job that evening.

"So, why don't you have Mr. Burney take you to 12th and Sparkman. That's the Drive-Inn."

I was so mortified, I could have cried.

"Here's a dollar. Get what you want."

I said nothing at all, but I could have struck her—or something. It was as though Burney wanted to run my errands, or as though he could not possibly have enough money for a Drive-Inn sandwich.

"Also. *We* will be home soon. It's Ladies' Auxiliary."

That was mother's way of saying, "You come straight home, young lady." After all, I was out of high school, even if I had no real job in mind.

But what hurt me most was the look on Burney's face: he had been told to do something unpleasant. Besides, he had never so much as asked me to go for a ride, much less to go on a date.

Nevertheless, Burney took us across town to the place. What else could he do?

The car hop was a boy from my high school class. When he put his head half inside the car, his cheeks seemed to switch from red to white in the neon or the headlight beams of other parked automobiles. When the car hop heard what Burney said, he smirked.

"Now look, Mac," Burney said. The boy was startled. "I said two checks. Separate bills. Now you do that."

The car hop drew back, and suddenly seemed very thin, as though standing sideways in the outside light. "Yes *sir. . . .*"

For the first time I heard Burney's voice of absolute command. I mean he had character. If the car hop had said another word, Burney would have gotten very slowly out of our car—and then I don't know what might have happened.

Actually, Burney did not show bad temper. He was very firm, and he was doing what he thought was the right thing: respecting my mother's wishes.

Oh, I should have made the best of it, too. I should have been more pleasant, but what I ate did not taste good. I could not think of a single thing to talk about. We sat there in silence.

Only after we were driving home, I looked at him sitting beside me.

"I—I guess it just proved you right, Burney."

"How so?"

"Taking advantage of the working man. I am sorry if I spoiled your night out."

"Look," he said, and parked in the front of our curb, but did not turn off the lights or the car motor.

"I'm doing all right. The way things are."

I understood from that only one thing: his job, the apartment, and his future in electronics were the main thing. If he were single-minded about the way he lived, I admired him for that.

"So forget it. Right?"

As I walked in front of his car, through his car lights, I held my head high.

Inside, I went directly to bed. I lay there for a long time and hated my mother. Finally I blamed myself. I should have been more pleasant, and should have made the most of it.

But if that is really what I thought, then why did I cry?

All that summer I was at loose ends. Mother and father would have sent me to beautician's school, but that seemed so common, so unrewarding. We talked about Polly Potter Secretary School, in the fall; in July I interviewed for the Telephone Company. At least we agreed on one thing: I did not want to be an airline hostess. I had no fear of flying, but I did not want to sleep each night in a strange hotel room. Being an only child. I did not want—secretly—to leave home. Not yet.

If Burney were on the night shift, I saw him arrive back at the apartment each day as we were eating breakfast. On collection days, to keep down unnecessary noise, I carried the trash cans farther away from his window. Or at night, if he were off-shift, we sat on the back steps. We talked about everything. He was a great deal more lonely than he, himself, realized. His father was killed in a bulldozer accident, and then his mother lived in Topeka and Wichita and Independence, Missouri. One night he told me he really had dropped out of high school to enlist in the Army for electronic school. Had Burney not told me, I never would have guessed.

In August Burney worked the day shift. He had no idea of stoves or cooking for himself—except from cans. Each Friday I gave his place a good cleaning, and that's what I was doing—his dishes—when I heard his car stop on the ramp below. I heard his feet on the stairs.

By the time Burney came in—and caught me—I had my hands dry. He stood in the door. I had a terrible electric feeling all over my skin. He was very white—pale.

"You're hurt!"

Burney stepped inside. He held out his white, roller-bandaged hand for me to see.

"Bit me," and I realized he was shaken. I smelled the adhesive tape and burn ointment. "Two-twenty volts. When I jerked back, why the wire looped right around my hand and. . . ."

I had just remade his bed. I led him towards it, because he was so pale and weak from the shock. Burney was going to sit down on the edge of the bed, and that made him turn towards me.

I just couldn't help myself. I am not that kind of a girl, but when I saw his hurt, pale face something seemed to shatter inside me—like a blue bowl dropped on tile.

I threw my arms around him. And for the first time I kissed him—just to comfort him. I held him to me and said, "Oh, poor baby. . . ."

That's all I said, and that was exactly the way I meant it. We must have stood there for only a moment—but oh, it was beautiful.

"What do *I see!*"

Mother was standing in his apartment door.

Burney sat down on the edge of his bed. Quickly he hid his bandaged hand behind his back—as though ashamed of his injury.

I never got a chance to explain. Mother was absolute. And terrible.

"I'll tell you what *I* see," she shouted.

She came into his apartment. She looked around, her eye vicious as a bird's. She lowered her voice.

"I *see* a trollop. Also a *man*—old enough *to know better.* I see two sneaks. And I see now what I should ought to have seen beneath my own eyes on my own property all along. . . .   Well Sir?"

I wanted Burney to get up and slap her. But he did not. I wanted him to explain—the way I could not. I wanted anything but silence, and Burney staring at the floor. Perhaps he was in real pain, but he said nothing at all.

Burney held up his bandaged hand, but mother did not notice it. If Burney was pale, mother knew it was guilt, and fear of her.

"So we will just put a stop to this," she said. "You two will be married. Forthwith and notwithstanding. *And* Sunday's the day. And that's *that.*"

Burney slowly got up from the bed. He went to the door of the apartment. I thought he might walk right on out, and down the steps, and go away forever. In my heart I wished he would—almost.

With his head, he gestured to my mother: get out.

"No," he said to me when I began to follow her. "You stay here."

I did what Burney said.

For a while he walked up and down the apartment, his eyes on the floor.

"Now look here: were you in on. . . ." It was the way he had spoken to the car hop so long ago. Burney saw the tears in my eyes. He did not finish what he was thinking.

"Also, the Law. . . ." He probably calculated my age, which was just nineteen. . . .

Burney stopped pacing. For a long time he looked out the window, through the green tree branches, and along the alley to the spread-out city beyond, to the streets he drove so freely on his days off.

Not out of fear, nor out of love exactly, he turned to me.

"Look, Dora. Would you be square with me? And always do the right thing?"

I did not see his face because there were too many tears in my eyes. But I said it, "Yes."

Burney thrust out his good hand. I took his hand in mine—like this—and we shook on it.

If I live to be a hundred, I could never feel more married to anyone than I felt at that moment. There was just a little moment of silence, there beside the sink full of halfwashed dishes, and then Burney took charge.

"You go tell that mother of yours it's all right. . . ."

He faltered just a second, but then he went on in a positive way.

"You tell her we say Sunday. On Sunday we can do the job."

And that Sunday we really did get married in the minister's study, and mother's friends sent some nice banquet flowers, and at home afterwards at the reception all our friends called, and Mrs. McGonigle and others brought silver settings of the same pattern, and two settings of Spode and—from my Aunt Tilly—an electric perc.

Daddy gave us the use of his new Plymouth, and one hundred dollars. That evening we went into Chicago and stayed at a nice Loop hotel until Wednesday. We ate in restaurants, and saw five movies, and it was just wonderful.

I told Burney again and again that this was a real perfect honeymoon—but I guess he knew that too. Only he couldn't talk about it. Not just yet.

We came back to Haskall, Illinois, very much married—and that was that. In many ways it solved a lot of things. Now I did not need any more schooling. Besides, in my heart, I wanted only one thing: to be a good wife to K. O. Burney, and to help us get along. It was my life, and I loved the prospect.

For Burney, it also made a difference. Never before had anyone, in his words, "given a damn about him, just personally." He knew I cared, and that was enough. Besides, he liked the new Plymouth a lot, and though he was too proud to say so, he was impressed by the lovely wedding presents.

In those first days, I found out Burney was not only good, but also a very sensitive person in some ways. Never by word or gesture has he ever mentioned how awful my mother was that day. In fact, he goes out of his way to please her—just as though nothing had happened. I'm very certain mother never told my father anything.

Shortly after the honeymoon, Burney got a single man from Teletek to rent the garage apartment. Through a friend of the McGonigles my mother found us another place, the whole upper floor of a dwelling, "all our own," as she said.

The new place at 231 1/2 really belonged to Mr. McGonigle. We looked at it, but I had no experience with places to live, and had nothing else to suggest. Burney walked through the rooms, and thought a minute, and said, "Right. We're in." For the first time, we moved.

During our first weeks in our new home I came to know what "deepening love" could mean. Not that I pined while Burney was on-shift. I tried to help with little odd jobs, and Burney was pleased when I got full value from our telephone by making calls for a Dance Studio, offering free lessons—a kind of come-on. I used this money to fix up our new apartment. I began with pink curtains in the kitchen, and then made a box spread for our double bed. I bought the paint and painted out the woodwork, one room after the other. Burney was proud of me for doing all of that, especially since I earned the extra money.

Now I think I very probably brought it all on myself.

In redecorating, I finally got around to our living room. 231 1/2 was the upper part of an old house, but in a nice neighborhood. The living room was just awful: flowered wallpaper and a mantel and a fireplace that no longer worked.

First I went to a hardware store demonstration and learned to paint with an antique effect. I began with the mantel, and then did the whole room. In the end, it looked like wood paneling: Old Ivory, with a brushed gold trim that partly followed the moldings. The electrical part was Burney's. He rewired and relocated the lights. It came out just beautiful—and we had done it together.

I did not say so, but now I wouldn't mind at all if people came to see us. Sure enough, some people did call. I gave the girls I still knew from my class a morning coffee. They liked our place and said I was a very lucky girl.

"Yes, yes," I told them, and smiled pleasantly, but I would never, never have said what I felt in my heart.

Then Mr. McGonigle happened to drop in.

He was in the neighborhood, and was looking over all his rental properties. He owned this house, and the M & M Furniture Store, and was important in the church where we were married. He was very pleased the way I had taken over. It was very nice, he thought. Actually, had I but called him, why he might have thrown in all the paint from M & M. He smiled, and gave me a large wholesale-price wink.

When Mr. McGonigle saw our new antique "paneling" in the living room, he whistled. "All hard work." Then at the top of the stairs he said, "All *very* good."

We shook hands, and he went on to inspect the other places he owned.

Because he had approved, I was extra shocked to get the letter. It came the next week, not from Mr. McGonigle, but from his Tax Consultant (and Management Advisor). I think it was a kind of form letter, but it stated the point clearly: because of recent increased property taxes for schools, increased interest rates, and Federal taxes, all McGonigle-owned rental property (no exceptions, please) are hereby raised 12 per cent.

I hid the letter, and waited until after our supper to tell Burney.

"Here's something. . . , " I said. "For us. In the mail."

Burney read it twice.

Then he brought his fist down on the table and everything jumped up and fell back and rattled.

"Not right!" and he swore and swore. "Why these improvements. You did them all. Time *and* materials. Why we improved it 30 per cent, why. . . ."

Finally I said perhaps I could handle it. Mr. McGonigle would probably see our place was a legitimate exception, since we had furnished all the materials when—actually—the landlord should have done that.

No. Burney was absolute. I would not bargain or ask any favors. No wife of his would ever have to do that. "Also," and he glared at me for the first time, "you keep your mother out of this."

Burney came back to it.

"Oh, you might know it. Every time. It's us working people who take the old shaft. Every time."

I did not think of us as working people exactly, but I kept silent.

"You know, Burney," I finally said. "It would cost us much more to move than twelve per cent. Over the whole year, twelve per cent would only be. . . ."

"You just watch us," he said bitterly. Again I saw the isolated, lonely side of his character. I had thought being married might change all of that.

"You just watch us go," he said again. Then more reasonably, "we can't let my wages go for rent, year after year. We should save. While we can."

"But couldn't I work? Some? I could do that. And make up the difference?"

"I want you," and it was final, "home when I get here at night. I mean that's what I like most about being married. I want to know I really do support you."

I said, Yes. Yes. He was a man, and my husband. He had to say what we would do on big things. This was our first big decision. Looking ahead, I did not want our decisions any other way. Besides, I am not a terribly smart woman, and it is best for us if I am pleasant.

"All right, Burn," and although my heart broke a little, I said very evenly, "you look around for us."

Burney did look around. He came up with—oh, I won't say. It was not nice, but it was something we could better afford. It was up four flights of stairs, in the rear; it was much closer to the center of town, but about the same distance from Burney's work.

So we gave McGonigle notice, and the very first people who came to look rented our place—and the woman laughed at me for leaving all my work behind.

Nevertheless, we moved out on a Saturday.

He rented a two-wheeled trailer. I packed all our new things with care, and helped carry boxes up the four flights of stairs. In spite of the neighbors and the noise, I saw that with some paint our new place might not be too bad.

After the final load, we went back to 231 1/2.

I wanted to take one last look, so I got out of the car, and went up the stairs.

Burney was already in the center of the paneled living room—laughing and laughing.

In his hand was a can of spray paint.

All over the kitchen and bath, and all over our antique ivory and gold paneling, Burney had sprayed great, garish crosses of black paint. Everywhere. Everywhere. Even a big X on the bathroom mirror.

"Now let's see," and Burney's voice came back up the stairs. "Let's see how that bites them."

His voice re-echoing filled each room, and every cleaned-out closet became a mouth—*telling, telling*—the mouths of Mr. McGonigle, and his wife, and the lined-up girls of my high school class—and the loudest of them all, my mother. It was Burney's revenge against them all, and in my whole lifetime in all of Haskall, it could never be undone.

That's why I broke down and cried and cried until Burney finally came back and stood for a long time and stared at me.

Then Burney took me by the arm and led me down, down to the parked automobile and the trailer, and to all of the new places we would be going all of the days of my life.

ON THE ISLAND

JOSEPHINE JACOBSEN   from *Kenyon Review*

After dinner the Driscolls sat for a while with Mr. Soo, by the big windows
looking out and down over the bay. There was nothing to close: they were just
great oblong unscreened openings, with all that fantasy of beauty spread
straight before them. Mary had not learned to believe in it, any more than she
had learned to believe that the shadowy, bamboo-furnished, candlelit room
behind them wouldn't be invaded by insects—even perhaps bats, or one of the
host of hummingbirds. For storms, there were heavy shutters. But nothing ever
seemed to come in; only the air stirred, faintly sweet, against their faces and
their flaccid fingers; it grew spicier and more confused with scent as the dark
strengthened.

Mr. Soo, in his impassive and formidable way, seemed glad to have them;
or perhaps he was only acquiescent, in his momentary solitude. The inn was
completely empty except for themselves, Mr. Soo, and the servants. This was
rare, she gathered, even in the off-season she and Henry had chosen—and,
indeed, their room had been occupied, only the day before yesterday, by
another couple. A party of six would arrive after the weekend. Being here alone
was part of their extraordinary luck. It had held for the whole trip: in Port of
Spain they had got, after all, the room facing the Savanna; on Tobago they had
seen the green fish come in, the ones that were bright as fire in the different
green of the water; they had even seen, far off, on the trip to Bird of Paradise
Island, a pair of birds of paradise, dim and quick through a great many distant
leaves, but unmistakable in their sumptuous, trailing plumage.

This still, small place was their final stop before the plane home, and, just
as they had planned it, it was beginning as it would end, hot and green,
unpeopled, radiantly vacant. "It's the closest we'll get to real jungle," Henry
said eagerly. And the jungle was no way away. The inn sheltered in cocoa
bushes, shaded by their immortelles: Mr. Soo's plantation was a shallow fringe
stretching for acres and acres, with the true jungle less than half a mile behind

it. Mr. Soo, she felt sure, had never read one of Henry's books, but obviously was aware of his name, and this perhaps had led him to offer them brandy and sit by them in one of the gleaming, cushioned chairs, as they stared out to the disappearing sea. He did not look to Mary like a man whose pleasure lay in fraternizing with guests. Pleasure? His hair, in short, shining bristles, clasped his head tightly, giving the effect of pulling his eyes nearly shut by its grip. His face was the agreeable color of very pale copper; the mouth straight and thin, the nose fleshy. She and Henry had secretly discussed his age: thirty-eight? forty-four? thirty-seven? In the exhausted light he appeared now almost as though he had been decapitated and then had his head with its impassive face set, very skilfully, back upon his shoulders.

Mr. Soo had been born in Trinidad, but had come here to the island almost fifteen years ago, to raise cocoa. Mary was sure that the friends who had told them about the tiny inn had spoken of a Mrs. Soo, but she was not here and there was no reference to her. Arthur, the major-domo, had said only, "No Mrs. Soo," in response to an inquiry if she were away. Dead? Divorced? A figment of friends' imagination?

"Yes," Henry was saying, "'like it' is too mild; they can't wait to come again. They're very bird-minded."

Mr. Soo looked at him in astonishment. "Your *friends?*"

"Yes. Very. Why?"

"They seemed to me," said Mr. Soo, obviously shocked, "very nice people. Intelligent. Not bird-minded."

Henry now gaped, baffled.

"Bird-*minded,* Mr. Soo," Mary said nervously. "I think you're thinking of how we sometimes say bird-*brained*. Bird-*minded*. It means thinking a lot about birds. Anxious to see new ones, you know."

Mr. Soo still had an offended air. "Very intelligent people," he said.

"Very!" said Henry and Mary simultaneously.

A rush of wings veered past the window, in the new darkness. "Very few here on the island, intelligent people," said Mr. Soo. "Just natives. Blacks."

There was a short pause. A faint yattering, like the rapid clack of unskilled castanets, came dimly from the upper reaches of an invisible tree.

"Haven't you any Chinese or Indian neighbors?" asked Henry, noncommittally.

"Fifteen miles," said Mr. Soo, "is the nearest. I do not like Indians," he added. "But they are civilized. They come from civilized country. On Trinidad, all the shops, the taxis, all mostly Indians. They have an old civilization. Very few criminals. Except when they are drunk. The criminal classes are the blacks. Every week, choppings."

Oh, God, thought Mary, here goes our jungle holiday. Well, she decided immediately, we don't *have* to talk to him; we can go to our room in a minute. She caught Henry's glance, flicked to his wrist.

"Good heavens, it's after 10:00!" he announced like an amateur actor. "If we're going to get up early for the birds . . . ."

Mr. Soo said quickly, "Lots of birds. Even at night. Pygmy owls. They fool the other birds," he explained. "That honey-creeper, green honey-creeper. The pygmy owl fools him. Like this." He suddenly puckered his lips and gave a tremulant, dying whistle; afterward, he smiled at them for the first time. "And you see cornbirds. Tody-tyrants, too. And mot-mots, with long tails . . ." He sketched one with a quick hand on which the candlelight caught jade. "They pull out their own tailfeathers. And the kiskadee. That's French, corrupted French. *Qu'est-ce qu'il dit?* Means, what's that he says. Over and over. The kiskadee."

The Driscolls rose, smiling. Are the birds part of the inn, like the sour-sop drinks and the coconut milk and the arum lilies?—or does he like them? It seemed to Mary that he did.

"There was a bird this morning," she said, "on the piles . . ."

"A pelican," interrupted Mr. Soo.

"No," said Mary rather shortly. "I know pelicans." (For heaven's sake!) "A little boy told me what it was. But I can't remember. Like 'baby' . . ."

Henry and Mr. Soo said simultaneously and respectively, "A *booby!* That's what it was, a booby!" and, "A little boy?"

"The *nicest* little boy," said Mary, answering Mr. Soo. "He showed me the fiddler-crab holes and all the live things growing on the big rock, on the sea side."

"What was his name?" asked Mr. Soo unexpectedly. He had risen, too.

"I haven't an idea," Mary replied, surprised. "No, wait a minute . . ."

"A black boy," said Mr. Soo. "With a pink scar on his cheek."

Mary was not sure why the words she was about to say—*"Victor,* I'm sure he told me"—seemed suddenly inappropriate. In the little silence, Mr. Soo surprisingly bowed. "I am sorry," he said with obvious sincerity. "He is, *of course,* not allowed there. He has been told. This will be the last," he said quickly. "I am *so* sorry."

"Good heavens," said Henry, rather irritably, "he was fine—we enjoyed him. Very much. He was a bright boy, very friendly. He showed us how he would fight a shark—imaginary knife and all, you know."

"He was in the *water?*" said Mr. Soo with a little hiss.

During this contretemps, Arthur had approached; his dark face, lustrous in the candlelight, was turned inquiringly toward them over the brandy decanter.

"No, really, thanks," said Mary. She managed to smile at Mr. Soo as she turned away, hearing Henry say, "We'll be back for breakfast about 8:00," and then his footsteps behind her across the lustrous straw roses of the rug.

Later in the night she woke up. Theirs was the only bedroom in the main building except for Mr. Soo's apartment. Earlier, massed poinsettia, oleander, and exora had blazed just beyond their casement windows in the unnatural brilliance of the raw bulb fastened outside—now, by a round gold moon that was getting on for full, blue and purplish hues had taken over. The bunches of blossom were perfectly still.

She could see Henry's dark head on his pillow; he was spreadeagled with one foot quite out of bed. Very soon, familiar pressure would swallow them. Henry, even here, was immersed in his plots, manipulating shadowy figures, catching echoes of shifting dialogue. It had nothing to do with happiness, or satisfaction, but she knew that increasingly Henry's mind veered from hers, turning in patterns whose skill she admired. Henry believed in his plots. His cause and effect, lovely as graph lines and as clear, operated below all things. This island, which seemed to her full of hints flying like spray, yielded itself to him in information of tensions, feathers, blossoms, crops. More and more, like a god let loose on clay, he shaped and limited. She loved him for this, too: for his earnestness and the perfection of his sincerity; but sometimes now, she knew, her mind seemed to him disorderly and inconsequential, with its stubborn respect for surprises.

A breeze had begun to stir. The blanched crests of blossoms nodded beyond the broad sill and there was a faint rattle of palm fronds. Also, something moved in the thatch.

I will go to sleep if I think of the right things, she said to herself, and she set about remembering the misty horses, galloping easily over the Savanna track in the Trinidad dawn; she'd stood in her nightgown on the balcony to see their lovely, silent sweep. And the fern banks on Grenada: hills of fern higher than towers, deep springing hills of fronded green. And the surf, the terrifying surf, when they'd launched the little boat off Tobago for the trip to Bird of Paradise Island. The turquoise water had broken in a storm of white over the shining dark bodies and laughing faces of the launchers, the boat tipping and rocking, flung crazily upward and then seized again by dripping hands. She'd felt both frightened and happy; Henry had hauled her in and they'd plunged up and down until finally they reached deep water and saw ahead of them, beginning to shape up in the distance, the trees which perhaps sheltered the marvelous birds. "Nothing is known of the breeding-habits of Birds of Paradise," her *Birds of the Caribbean* said. She repeated this, silently, sleepily. Nothing is known of the breeding habits of Birds of Paradise. How nice.

Suddenly, she heard water, a seeping sound—though, on her elbow, she could see it wasn't raining. She swung her feet over the bed, but not to the floor. Luck had been good here, but in the dark she wouldn't walk barefoot and her slippers she kept under the sheet. She felt her way cautiously to the bathroom door. Inside, she lighted a candle—the generator went off at 11:00. The bathroom was immaculate, but water shone by her feet and seeped toward the depression which served as a shower-floor. The toilet was unobtrusively overflowing in a small trickle. Eventually the floor would be covered and water would ooze under the door. What on earth could they do about it tonight, though? Move in with Mr. Soo? She began to giggle faintly. But it was a bother, too; in remote spots things took forever to get themselves fixed. She put Henry's sandals on the window-ledge, blew out the candle, and closed the door softly behind her. Henry hadn't stirred. She got back in bed, thinking: It's a good thing I saw those sandals—they were *in* the water! The words set off an echo: but, as she remembered what it was, she fell asleep.

By morning, the water was in their room, reaching fingers in several directions; the heavy straw of the rugs was brown and dank. When they came out into the pale, fragrant sunlight of the big room, Arthur was throwing away yesterday's flowers from the two big blue vases on the low tables. Henry, dropping his binocular-strap over his head, stopped long enough to report their problem. Arthur looked at them with an expression of courteous anguish and ritual surprise and said that he would tell Mr. Soo.

When they returned two hours later, hungry and already hot, Mr. Soo had come and gone. His small table, with its yellow porcelain bowl filled each morning with arum lilies, was being cleared by Arthur, who brought them a platter of fruit and told them that after breakfast he would transfer them to Mr. Soo's room. They were astounded and horrified in equal proportions. "That's absolutely impossible," said Henry. "We can't inconvenience him like that. Why can't we go down to one of the beach cottages? Or up on the hill?"

Arthur, who at the moment represented all help except the invisible cook, did not say: Because I can't run back and forth and still do everything here. He said instead, "Mr. Soo did tell me to move you after breakfast."

Henry was anxious to talk to Arthur. Wherever they went, he absorbed gestures, words, inflections, as a lock-keeper receives water, with the earnest knowledge of its future use. He was very quick at the most fugitive nuance; later it would be fitted into place, all the more impressive for its subtlety.

Arthur had poured their second cups of coffee. Now he reappeared from behind the red lacquer screen, carrying one of the big blue vases. It was filled high with yellow hibiscus and he set it gently on one of the teakwood stands.

Henry said, in his inviting way, "You do a bit of everything."

Immediately, Arthur came to the table. "Only I am here now," he said. "And the cook. Two boys gone." He held up two fingers. "Chauffeur is gone."

On short acquaintance, Mary did not particularly like Arthur. He had a confidential air which, she noticed, pivoted like a fan. At present it was blowing ingratiatingly on Henry. "Mr. Soo had a lot of trouble with help," said Arthur. Mary saw with a rather malign amusement the guest's breeding struggle with the writer's cupidity. The victory was tentative.

"Now we're upsetting things," said Henry, not altogether abandoning the subject. "It's ridiculous for him to move out of his room for us."

"Won't upset Mr. Soo," said Arthur soothingly. "He can shut the apartment off, sitting room, library. Another bath, too, on the other side. Used to be Mrs. Soo."

Mary could see the waves of curiosity emanating from Henry, but he gallantly maintained silence. "There is a sleep-couch in the sitting room," Arthur went on. "Mr. Soo does want you to be comfortable, and so." He pivoted slightly to include Mary in his range. His eyeballs had crimson veins and he smelled of a fine toilet water. "Mr. Soo is very angry with that boy," said Arthur. "Mr. Soo does tell he: Stay away from my beach, ever since that boy come here."

In spite of herself, Mary said irascibly, "But that's ridiculous. He wasn't bothering anyone."

"Bother Mr. Soo," said Arthur. "Mr. Soo is so angry he went last night to go to see he grandmother. Told he grandmother, that boy does come here again, he beat him."

"May I have some hot coffee, please?" asked Mary.

Arthur did not move. He swept his veined eyes from one to the other. "Mr. Soo does not own that beach," said Arthur. "Can't no mahn own a beach here. Mr. Soo's beachhouse, Mr. Soo's boat, Mr. Soo's wharf. But not he beach. But he don't let no mahn there, only guests."

"Why does he like this beach so much?" said Mary, for it was small and coarse, with plenty of sharp rocks. "The boy, I mean."

"Only beach for five miles," Arthur told her. "That boy, Vic-tor, come with he brother, come to he grandmother. They live topside. Just rocks, down their hill. Very bad currents. Sea-pussy, too. Can't no mahn swim there."

"May I have some hot coffee?" Mary said again.

Arthur stood looking at her. At this moment a considerable clamor broke out in the kitchen behind them. Voices, a man's and a woman's, raised in dispute, then in anger. The woman called, "Arthur! You come here, Arthur!"

Arthur continued to look at them for about two seconds; then, without haste, he went away, walking around the screen toward the kitchen.

"All right, all right," said Henry, answering a look. "But you know perfectly well we can't come here for five days and tell Mr. Soo who he must have on his beach."

"It isn't his beach."

"It isn't ours, either."

Something smashed in the kitchen. A door banged viciously. Outside the window went running easily a tall, big boy. His dark, furious, handsome face glared past them into the room. He dived down the wooden steps past the glade of arum lilies. His tight, faded bluejeans disappeared among the bushes.

"What was *that* in aid of?" said Henry, fascinated.

Arthur appeared. He carried the faintly steaming enamel pot of coffee, and, coming up to them, poured a rich stream into Mary's cup. Then he said: "The big brother of Vic-tor, he's a bad bad boy. Daniel. Same name as the man fought the lion." He bowed slightly, thus reminding Mary of Mr. Soo, turned to the other teakwood stand, lifted the empty blue vase, and went off with it behind the screen.

"'*Fought* the lion'?" said Mary, inquiringly, to Henry.

"Well," said Henry, "I suppose Arthur places him in the lion's den, and then improvises."

That was the last of the excitement. They were transferred quickly and easily from their moist quarters; the toilet was now turned off and not functioning at all. Mr. Soo's room lacked all traces of its owner, unless a second bed could be viewed as a trace. It had a finer view than their abandoned room, looking all the way down the series of log terraces to the small bright, rocky beach.

Greenness took over; the greenness of the shallows of the bay before it deepened to turquoise, of the wet, thick leaves of the arum lilies, soaked each morning by an indefatigable Arthur, of the glittering high palms, and the hot tangled jungle behind the cocoa bushes shaded by their immortelles. Mary had—unexpectedly to herself—wanted to leave before their time was up. She had even suggested it to Henry right after breakfast on that second morning. But Henry wanted to stay.

"It *isn't* Mr. Soo," she said, trying to explain. "It hasn't anything to do with that. It's something else. There're too many vines. Everything's looped up and tangled. The palms rattle against the tin and give me dreams."

"Don't be fey," said Henry rather shortly. "We'll be away from palms soon enough."

Mr. Soo continued cordial in his immobile fashion; he talked to them from his small table when, at dinner, their hours coincided. Once, he had Arthur make them each a sour-sop, cold and lovely as nectar, when they came in brown and sweaty from the beach rocks. But by some obscure mutual assent, there were no more brandies. After dinner, the Driscolls sat on their tiny terrace, watching the moon swelling toward fullness, and drank crème de cacao in tiny gourd cups provided by Arthur. They knew they were destined to share their final hours on, and their first off, the island with Mr. Soo. He too would be on the biweekly plane to Trinidad. Mr. Soo said he was going to Port of Spain to procure plumbing fixtures. Arthur said Mr. Soo was going to procure a number two boy and a chauffeur. Where on earth did Mr. Soo wish to be driven, over the narrow, pitted, gullied roads that circled the island? Through and through his plantation, perhaps. Arthur took no note of coldness in relation to his comments on Mr. Soo; also, Mary felt, the most ardent questioning would have led him to reveal no more than he had originally determined. His confidences went by some iron and totally mysterious auto-decision. She had absolutely no idea how his sentiments stood in regard to his employer.

On their last afternoon, the Driscolls went for a walk. Just before dusk, they decided to go deep along the jungle path. This was the hour for birds; all over the little island they were suddenly in motion. Almost none, except the hummingbirds with which the island fairly vibrated, flew in the golden hot midday, but at dusk the air was full of calls and wings.

Mary and Henry went along the middle ledge, above the arum lilies. Down on the beach, the fiddler crabs would be veering, flattening themselves, then rearing to run sideways, diving down holes into which fell after them a few trembling grains of sand. From here, the Driscolls could only see the white waves, leaping like hounds up at the rocks. They went along slowly, musingly, in the fading heat, up the steep path back of the garden sheds, below the giant saman, the great airy tree with its fringed, unstirring, pendent parasite world. With its colony of toe-hold survivors, it was like the huge rock on the beach, half in the tides, to whose surface clung and grew motionless breathers.

They turned up the small, dusty road toward the solid wave of tree-crests towering ahead. They had been this way twice before; they remembered a goat tethered up the bank at eye-level, a small scrubby cow standing uncertainly in the ditch. They would pass a cabin, half up the slope, with its back to the bay far below, its straw roof smothered under rose-colored masses of coralita. They walked in intimate silence. The road was daubed with the fallen blossoms of immortelles and their winged pods. Once, two laborers passed them, stepping quietly on their tough bare feet, the shadows of leaves mottling their dark erect bodies and bright blue ripped trousers, their machetes in worn scabbards swinging gently from their heavy belts.

Around a curve, they came on a dead, long snake, savagely slashed. Just before their path struck off the road there was a jingle and faint creaking, and around a tangle of scarlet blackthorn rode two native policemen, their caps tilted against the sunset, their holsters jogging their elbows. They pulled their small horses, stained with sweat, into single file; one raised his hand easily in a half-salute and both smiled. These were the first horses the Driscolls had seen on the island and the first police. Of course, there had to be police, but it was strange how out of place they seemed. When the hushed fall of the hoofs in the dust died away it was as though horses and riders had melted.

Later, sitting on a fallen tree in the bush, Mary thought idly about the snake, the laborers, the policemen. Henry had gone further in, but she had felt suddenly that she couldn't walk another step. She sat on ridged strong bark coursed by ants and thought about the policemen, their faces, their small dusty horses, on that peaceful, hot patrol. Surely there must be almost nothing for them to do. And yet the idea of violence, she realized, had come to the air she breathed. Not violence as she knew it in Henry's books, or in the newspapers at home—riot, rape, murder, burglary. This violence seemed a quality of growth—the grip of the mollusks on the wave-dashed rock, the tentacles of the air plants flowering from the clutched saman. It oppressed her with its silence, its lack of argument. Perhaps she responded in some obscure portion of her feminine heart. An ant ran silently and fast over her hand. She shook it off and stared into the green that had swallowed Henry. His preciousness to her appeared not enhanced but pointed up by her sense of the silent violence of growth around her, as if, among the creepers, windfalls, sagging trees, his face, clear to her love, defined itself as the absolute essential. Of the rest, blind accidents of power, and death, and greenness, she could make nothing. Nothing they might do would surprise her.

There was a wild cocoa bush not ten feet away, dropped into this paroxysm of growth, thin, tall, struggling for light. She could see the pendulous gourds in their mysterious stages of ripeness: cucumber green, yellow, deep rose-bronze, and plum-brown. That plum-brown was on the voluptuous poles of the bamboos, the great, breeze-blown, filmy, green-gold stools of bamboo.

She listened for Henry. There was provisional silence, but no real stillness; hidden streams ran with a deep, secret sound in the throat of distant ravines, and the air was pierced and tremulous with birdcalls, flutings, cries, cheeps, whistles, breaks of song; response and request; somewhere away, lower than all the sounds but that of water, the single, asking, contemplative note of the mourning dove.

All at once, there was Henry. When she saw him, she realized that some portion of her had been afraid, as though, like the police on their little horses, he would melt into the greenness for good.

"Did you realize I'd forgotten my binoculars?" he asked, infuriated with his stupidity. "Of all idiotic times!"

Suddenly, she flung herself at him, winding her arms about his neck, linking their legs, covering his face with quick, light kisses. He held her off to look at her, and then folded her tightly in his arms, as though she too had come back from somewhere. "We haven't a flashlight, *either,*" he said, "and, if we don't look out, we'll be plunging about in the dark, breaking everything."

On the way home, they went more rapidly. The birds were almost completely silent. Now and then one would flash in the treecrests far above them, settling to some invisible perch. We've left this island, Mary thought. There came a turning point—on a wharf, on a station platform, in the eyes of a friend—when the movement of jointure imperceptibly reversed. Now they were faced outward—to their suitcases, to their plane, to the Port of Spain airport, to Connecticut and typewriters. Mary began to worry about the dead snake, in the thick dusk; she didn't want to brush against its chill with her bare, sandaled feet. But, when they came to the spot, she saw it at once. It seemed somehow flatter and older, as though the earth were drawing it in.

As they rounded the bend to the final decline, a sound came to them, stopping them both, Mary with her hand digging into Henry's arm. They thought at first it was an animal in a trap, mistreated or dying. It was a sound of unhuman, concentrated, self-communing pain, a dull, deep crying, with a curious rhythm, as though blood and breath themselves caused pain. "What *is* it?" cried Mary, terrified.

"It's a human being," said Henry.

He was right. Drawn close together, they turned the bend in the road, and saw the group from which the sound came: just up the steep slope to their left, in front of the cabin. Raw light from a kerosene lamp on the porch fell on the heads of the men and women, in an open semicircle. Around this space crawled on her hands and knees a woman. Her head was tied in a red kerchief and the light caught her gold earrings. She pounded the earth with her fist, and round and round she crept in short circles.

Dark faces turned in their direction, but the woman did not stop; on and on went the sound. Alien, shocked, embarrassed by their own presence, the Americans hesitated. Then Henry caught his wife's elbow and steered her, stumbling, down the path.

"Oh, Henry, *Henry* . . ." she whispered frantically to his shadowy face. "Oughtn't we to stop? Couldn't we? . . ."

"They don't *want* us!" he hissed back. "Whatever it is, they don't want *us.*"

She knew he was right, but an awful desolation made her stumble sharply again. The sound was fainter now; and then, in a minute or two, gone. Below them, they could see the lightbulb lashed to the trunk of the saman tree, like a dubious star.

Later, Mary was not sure why they said nothing to Mr. Soo. Neither, strangely, did they discuss it between themselves in their bedroom, showering, dressing for dinner. It was as though its significance would have to come later. It was too new, still, too strange; their suspended atmosphere of already-begun departure could not sustain it.

This sense of strangeness, and also, perhaps, the sense of its being their last evening, seemed to constrain them to be more civil to Mr. Soo. Arthur, bringing their Daiquiris, told them there would be a cold supper; the cook was away. His air was apologetic; this was evidently an unexpected arrangement. On the terrace, he set their drinks down on the thick section of a tree bole that served as a stand, and looked through the open casement window into their room, now transforming itself again into Mr. Soo's room: at the open, filled suitcases, the range of empty hangers, the toilet bottles on the dresser.

"You sorry to go?" asked Arthur. "You like it here, and so?"

"Very, very much," said Henry. "We hope we can come back."

"You know, one thing," said Arthur. A gong was struck imperiously. Arthur took his empty tray back through the room. The door closed behind him.

Perhaps it was too late for a more cordial response; perhaps Mr. Soo, too, felt that they were no longer there. Above his arum lilies in their yellow bowl, he was unresponsive. After one or two attempts at conversation, the Driscolls ate their cold supper, talking to each other in tones made artificial by several kinds of constraint. Over coffee, Henry said, "I'd better see him about the bill now—it's all going to be so early in the morning."

Mary waited for him by the huge open window-frames, where they had sat on their first evening, discussing with Mr. Soo their bird-minded friends. The moon, which tonight was going to be purely full, had lost its blemishes of misproportion; it was rising, enormous and perfect, in a bare sky. She could hear very faintly the sound of the tide as she stared out over the invisible bay to the invisible sea.

Behind her, Mr. Soo and Henry approached, their footsteps hushed by the straw, their voices by the silence. Turning, she was confronted by Mr. Soo's face, quite close, and it struck her that the moonlight had drawn and sharpened it, as though it were in pain.

"I hope you and your husband have been happy here," said Mr. Soo.

"Very," said Mary. (Now we're in for a drink, she thought.) "The birds have been wonderful . . ." she began, but Mr. Soo was not listening.

"The driver from the airport will be here at 6:00," he said. He turned and left them, walking slowly over the gleaming rug.

The moon hadn't reached their terrace. Arthur, arriving with the crème de cacao, had to peer at the tree-bole before setting down the little cups. He did not go away, but stood and looked at them. Finally, he said: "Do you remember Vic-tor?"

"Of course," said Henry, and Mary added, "The little boy."

"He's gon," said Arthur.

Henry said with interest, "Gone?"

"Dead, gon." Arthur stood there, holding his tray, and waited for them to speak. When they still did not, he said, "He did go off those high rocks. Back down from he house, those high rocks. He did go to swim in that sea-pussy. Like he grandmother told he not to. He is gon, out to sea; no body. No body a-tall. He was screaming and fighting. Two men fishing, they tried very hard to grab he up, but couldn't never get to he. He go so fast, too fast. They will never have no body—too much current, too many fish. He grandmother told he, but that boy, he gon to swim. He won't even mind he brother, brother Daniel, brought he up," said Arthur, turning away and continuing to talk as he left, "or he grandmother, took he in. The cook is gon," said Arthur, faintly, from the distance. "Now Mr. Soo, Mr. Soo is all alone." The door closed.

Mary got up uncertainly; then she went into the bedroom and began to cry very hard. She cried harder and harder, flinging herself on the bed and burrowing her head in the pillow. She felt Henry's hands on her shoulder blades and told him, "I can't think *why* I'm crying—I didn't even know the child! Yes, he showed me the crabs, but I didn't *know* him! It's not that . . ." She was obsessed by the mystery of her grief. Suddenly, she sat up, the tears still sliding down over her lips. "That was his grandmother," she said.

"It's a pattern," said Henry miserably. "We saw it happen all the way from the beginning, and now it's ended. It had to end this way."

She touched his face. His living body was here beside her. She slid her hand inside his shirt, feeling his flesh, the bones beneath it. The room was filled like a pool with darkness. She ran her finger over his chin, across his lips. He kissed her softly, then more deeply. His strong, warm hand drew her dress apart and closed over her breast.

"I love you," he said.

She did not know when Henry left her bed. She did not, in fact, wake until a sound woke her. Her bed was still in darkness, but the window was a pale blaze from the moon, now high and small. It struck light from the palms' fronds, and against it she saw the figure on the ledge, in the open window. Young and dark and clear, and beautiful as shining carved wood, it looked against all that light, which caught and sparked on the machete's blade. It was gone; she heard a faint thud on the earth below the window. She raised herself on her elbow. In Mr. Soo's moonlit room she stared at Mr. Soo's bed and at what she now made out on the darkening sheet. It was Henry's dark head, fallen forward, and quite separate. His eyes were still closed, as if in an innocent and stubborn sleep.

Diseases of the Heart

CONRAD KNICKERBOCKER

from *Kenyon Review*

Many years ago a Filipino intern sat down at the hospital bedside of Charlie Armbruster the advertising man and asked, "How much each day you drink?"

Looking into the black, bottomless eyes of the young doctor in white who seemed so anxious to begin a cure of the soul, Charlie replied, "Well, um, actually, quite a bit lately. Yes." He could not remember whether Filipino interns meant he was in a good hospital or a bad hospital.

"Every day? Not so good, every day." The intern frowned at the admission sheet in a metal clipboard. Charlie felt his hands trembling as they lay at his sides. His internal medicine man had assured him that he would be admitted with the diagnosis of organic mid-brain disfunction. That way there would be no stigma. They would pump him full of sparine and niacin and maybe the shakes would be reversible and maybe not, but he would have to quit drinking, that's for sure. "Your nerves don't have any lining left on them. You're demyelinated, boy," the fat internist, sighing and cleaning his fingernails, had told him.

Charlie spent two weeks in that hospital. A sheriff's deputy served him the divorce papers, and his psychiatrist came to see him once to tell him that he had to build a new life. Shirley Myre's husband also showed up and sat close to the hospital bed. No hard feelings, Duane Myre had said, but kept opening and closing a small penknife with a blade just long enough, Charlie estimated, to puncture the peritoneum. Shirley had returned to the fold and was now the perfect mother, which meant, no doubt, that after work she and Duane were back at it in the bathroom to get away from the kids, Duane's cigar parked in the soap dish. In the hospital, Charlie dreamed that Shirley was kneeling over him, while outside the car window Orion gleamed cruelly in the winter sky. He would awaken then, the sweat cold on his neck, and remember with panic the telephone conversations they had toward the end after Duane became suspicious. They breathed clouds of moisture into the receivers.

"Now I am touching you there," he would say.

"Yes, yes," she would answer.

"Now I'm——," he said.

"——."

"——!"

After he hung up, he would go over to the window of his office and look through the Venetian blinds. He was always sure someone had been watching, twenty stories up.

The big blowup ended the telephone conversations and everything else. Charlie's wife Isobel had flown down to see her parents in Topeka, and Charlie took Duane and Shirley to a bad, small Italian place on Rush Street, since part of the whole Shirley business had been putting it over on Duane, the dumbest, lardiest insurance agent west of the Hudson. Then they had gone to one of those fake key clubs and Charlie felt up Shirley on the dance floor while Duane sat and drank sixteen bottles of beer. At 3:15 in the morning, parked in front of the Myre apartment on North Sheffield Avenue back of the ball park, Charlie and Shirley had clutched and fumbled while Duane wobbled at the apartment house door, stabbing at it with a key.

Shirley had stuck her tongue in Charlie's ear and groaned, "Oh, God, let's go, *now.*" For months, parked in the dark up in Evanston, huddled under a blanket in the back seat, they had talked of just cutting out, going to New York and starting over. Charlie had begun to feel self-righteous at 3:15 in the morning, that frigid bitch Isobel and her gunboat mother always blabbering about pioneer Kansas stock. He and Shirley finally disentangled and went into the apartment. Duane sat on the sofa waiting, his hand neatly placed on his knees, his eyes glittering.

"Let's have a nightcap, folks," Charlie said, smiling the smile he usually saved for clients. He went to the can, and heard it—whop!—and Shirley, softly to Duane, "You bastard."

Charlie came out zipping up his fly and said, "You can't do that. I love her," and gasped with relief after all the months of sneaking around. He opened a can of Hamm's and drank it in one swallow, happily, waiting to be shot. But Duane just sat there, his eyes shining, and Charlie made a long speech, and Duane, the bonehead, *agreed,* yes, yes, he had been a terrible husband. The upshot was that Shirley said, "You can't leave me here like this," and Charlie took her home. They woke up late the next morning with terrible hangovers and Charlie went into a panic, expecting Isobel's key in the lock at any moment. Shirley lay there crying without a sound—she never made a sound even in the back seat—until he could get her dressed and into a cab. "Let's think this thing over," he had said. She went back to North Sheffield Avenue.

The next day was Monday. He fixed himself two huge Bloody Marys to get to work. He sat in his office sweating, staring at a florid layout, and with a vodka-and-meprobamate lunch, made it until 4:00 o'clock. Shirley called. "He went to work today, but I think he's going to kill us." Then she hung up.

Charlie drank a bottle of Scotch in his apartment that night, listening to Frank Sinatra sing "I Let a Song Go Out of My Heart" over and over again on the phonograph. The next day he went to the bank and closed out his account, $817 in cash. At the office, four telephone messages were waiting, three from the client and one from Shirley. He called her, and she said, "He has promised to kill us for sure." Charlie told his secretary a family crisis had come up and he had to leave immediately for Fort Smith, Arkansas. He called Isobel in Topeka and told her she'd better stay there awhile. She said that was fine; she planned to stay there permanently and he would be hearing from her lawyer. He went to his apartment and got his clothes and picked up Shirley with her clothes and a table radio. They roared east through Chicago's atomic night. He called his psychiatrist from Evansville, Indiana, and the doctor said something about the Mann Act. They drove back to Chicago in silence, sipping from half-pints of Scotch. In a roadhouse near Gary, he discovered that she had actually never had a dry martini. Sometimes she had said, "They *was . . .*"

That was it, the big blowup. Shirley went home to Duane and Charlie stayed drunk for six weeks in a small hotel on Diversey, staring at a cosmic afterbirth pattern on the wall. Finally he called an uncle in Dalhart, Texas, the only remaining member of his family who would speak to him. The old man wired him $300, to be paid back at six per cent interest from Charlie's tiny share in two family gas wells, and he went to the doctor. He had begun to hear organ music outside the hotel window at night.

In the hospital Charlie read two novels a day and occasionally flexed his wrists to see if the shakes were improving. He could never get beyond the first line of the Lord's Prayer, *which* art in heaven, or *who* art in heaven? At first he shared the hospital room with the owner of a Greek candy kitchen who lay there muttering all day. When the confectioner went home, they wheeled in a large man with a handsome, gray, ruined face and set up a screen and oxygen equipment.

A woman showed up and dabbed at her nose, slumped next to the man's bed. "Is it the heart?" she kept asking. "Is it the heart? I had to borrow the taxi fare over here from the girls at the office."

"Oh, God," the man said, and threw his forearm over his eyes.

At night the man snored and broke wind in huge, gut-wrenching bursts, the explosions of a being in grave distress. He was on only 1000 calories a day; yet he shattered and roared, floating on the thin tides of infarcted sleep. Charlie thought of gales and thunder. Was this the true sound of the heart's anguish?

He lay very still when the interns pushed the big niacin needle into his vein, and wished he would die. He listened for the brisk tap of Shirley's heels in the hall outside signaling that she had come to take him away, but the only visitor to the room was the woman who dabbed at her nose and worried about Blue Cross.

"I told that deputy you would jump out of the window if he served that paper on you in here, but you didn't," the fat internist said to him one day. "Now it's time for you to get off your ass and go to work. Quit drinking. Call the AAs."

Charlie read the interns' bulletin board on the way out of the hospital and, from it, located a one-room basement apartment in an older building up near Lincoln Park. He started going to AA meetings, sitting quietly in the back of the room, his hands neatly on his knees, and, by God, didn't take a drink. He landed a temporary job as copywriter in a small shop, and through a screwy piece of luck developed the "Lion's Roar" campaign that put Simpson Oil, then a regional chain, on the map. Little stories about him began appearing in

Advertising Age. Soon he was getting offers from New York. At first he was afraid to think about them, hanging on to his basement apartment and the AA meetings. "Don't let yourself feel anything at first," his alcoholic counselors told him.

When he had been sober a year, it became his turn to speak. "Think," he told the crowd after they had yelled "Hi, Charlie" to him. "Easy does it. First things first," he told them. They clapped and gave him a birthday cake with one candle on it. He found he enjoyed speaking at the meetings. He began to tell the tale of the big blowup, embellishing the call to the psychiatrist and the Mann Act part. They always laughed. At first he told them about the hospital, but as time went on and he became more confident, and the New York offers kept coming in, he condensed that part until it was as if he had never been in the hospital at all. He liked being in a room full of smiling, sober people, prosperous and discreet. Especially he liked knowing that a flaw ran through each one of them from top to bottom. He began to give counsel himself, urging the new members not to permit themselves to feel anything at first.

The big offer came, copywriter on the Toedman Socktane account; Hunsecker, Kadish, Robinson; $18,000 and all the gasoline he could use. "They got good AA in New York, Charlie," the old-timers wheezed over coffee after the meetings. "You can do it, kid. Remember, a day at a time."

"Yeah," Charlie said. "Except the days in New York are longer than other days." They laughed and punched each other on the arm, and for the first time in a long time he thought about a drink. It passed. He found a little apartment with a terrace on East 65th between Lexington and Park. He spent a lot of time prowling for antique pieces. He wanted the place to look 1920 Moderne, in memory of nothing.

At work he stayed to himself and hammered away. They began to call him Ramrod. Instead of griping about creativity with the copywriters in bars, he sided with the research specialists and the account people. He bore down hard on facts and figures. "You're underreached in twenty-three markets, Mr. Cibulski," he would tell the Toedman advertising manager on long distance to Ponca City, Oklahoma. Budgets, reach, markets. Hunsecker, Kadish gave him a $2000 raise. Kadish, who had a Bentley, stopped him in the hall one day and asked him if he was interested in account work. "Hell, yes, Mr. K.," Charlie said.

"You're on, boy," Kadish said and punched him on the arm. He became account executive on Socktane. He heard talk that he was in line for account supervisor. They gave him an office with a view that extended far uptown.

At an AA meeting on East 90th Street, he met a girl who used to drink a quart of rum and take six doridens a day. She had fine blond hair and a year-around tan and her face had no lines, none at all. After an AA meeting one night, he took her to his apartment. She admired the framed photograph of Amos 'n' Andy and his copies of *The Dial* on the coffee table. He left only the Tiffany lamp burning. While they were seated on the sofa drinking espresso, he kissed her on the ear. Her head fell back and her knees relaxed. "Oh, yes, Charlie," she said.

He took off his $200 suit and hung it up. As he lay down beside her, somebody began ringing the doorbell. They said nothing, straining on their elbows, until the ringing stopped. Charlie found that a calling card had been shoved under the door. It said Avon. "It must be a joke," he said, but he no longer knew any jokers.

He lay down again and the telephone rang. It was Isobel, his ex-wife, calling long distance. She was drunk. "Charlie," she said, "I just called to tell you you're a goddamned dirty son of a bitch." She hung up. The girl got dressed and went home. Later he heard that she stayed sober by inducing her AA lovers to start drinking again.

At twilight on the forty-sixth floor, after the last secretary had gone home and no heels clicked in the halls, he drank coffee and stared across the stone frontiers of the island, watching the lights as they came on all the way to the horizon, wondering how fragments of newspaper headlines managed to reach his altitude on the thermal winds of New York. He did his best work then, when he could hear the full electric hum of the building. At that time, as scraps of newspaper blew past his window, the sensation of floating came to him, a feeling that he was drifting far away toward some sunset. He used to feel that way after a pint of Scotch in the Shirley Myre days.

Working in these twilights, he completed a television presentation, the big one, for Toedman. In his old age, Eleazar Ralph Toedman wanted to save the world. Oil and service stations had not been enough. This was to be a dramatic series on the origins of capitalism and the free enterprise system: "Freedom's Fighters, presented by the Toedman Corporation," great moments in the lives of Lorenzo di Medici, John Calvin, Nathan Rothschild, Jay Gould, John D. Rockefeller, Andrew Carnegie, Henry Ford, and other "pioneering giants whose vision enabled America to reach the pinnacle of greatness." The network had enough confidence in the idea to bankroll a $200,000 pilot made in Italy. The message was that without Lorenzo's capitalistic insight, Michelangelo would not have made it. That way you got in culture and money both. Toedman was supposed to be so excited about the idea that he was flying in for the presentation. He almost never came to anyone; they came to him.

On the day of the presentation, Charlie decided to walk to work in order to encourage blood circulation. Waiting for a light on Park, he noticed that on the opposite corner a panhandler had worked his way uptown and was pacing unsteadily back and forth tipping his baseball cap to passers-by. The panhandler looked like Duane Myre, grizzled, a burnt-out cigar butt clenched in the corner of his mouth, fatter, but somehow more shrunken, and now minus an arm, the stub flapping and waving from the sleeve of a filthy blue sports shirt. A cab discharged an elderly lady at Charlie's corner, and he got in and rode the rest of the way.

Kadish and Charlie waited in front of their office building for Toedman's limousine. The old man had flown in via his Jetstar that morning and was coming straight to the agency. The white Cadillac pulled up at last, bearing its small blue fender flags emblazoned with their phony medieval capital Ts. Son and the old man were in the back seat. Son was E. R. Toedman, Jr., a thin-eyed, computerized young man who kept his father from spending too much in behalf of freedom. Willard, the driver-bodyguard, and Son helped the old man from the car. Even though it was a warm day, Toedman was wearing his long black greatcoat with the sable collar and lining.

The old man aimed his famous pale-blue stare at Kadish and Charlie and finally said, "How do." Those were his last words until they were upstairs in the agency auditorium on the forty-sixth floor. Meredith Walters, known as Old Slick, executive vice-president of the network, and a couple of aides were there, but they kept very quiet. Charlie went to the front and began to talk about the program concept and potential audience, referring to charts on an easel.

"No charts," the old man said. "Let's see the show."

Charlie signaled the projectionist and the lights went out. After about five minutes of the pilot, the projector's beam glinted on something in Toedman's hand. It was a flask. The old man was at it again. Cibulski had not said anything about that. A fist began to form in Charlie's solar plexus. The flask glinted again and again.

"God, look at the boobies on that girl," the old man said. "Gawd, luk et thuh *buh*-bees 'n thet gel, hawg fat!" He shook the flask and handed it to Willard. The film ended. The old man stood up and faced toward them, Willard at his side.

"That was a *rough* show," he said. "Awful rough."

They went to the agency dining room for real Oklahoma steaks. "Where are the drinks?" the old man asked. Kadish, whose face now had locked into a half-smile, nodded to the waiter, who opened the bar credenza. For an hour they stood there while the old man drank martini after martini from a highball glass filled with ice. At last they got him to the table.

"My friend Judge Leonard in San Angelo was telling me they got a rape case for damages down there," the old man said. "Seems this mutt got to this fancy poodle owned by a high-toned old widow woman. The widow woman is suing the mutt's owner. Dog rape, what do you think of that? Dawg raip!" he yelled. He fell forward so that his face almost touched the Vichyssoise and began to snore. Son finished his soup and ate his steak in silence while his father slept.

"Dad is tired," Son finally said after he had lined up his knife and fork. "We'd better get him back to the apartment." He and Willard took Toedman by the elbows. In the elevator, the old man pulled himself erect, and by the time they reached the street he was moving under his own power.

A 1948 Chevrolet two-door was double-parked in front of the building, blocking the white Cadillac at the curb. The Chevrolet's door was open and a man's legs dangled from the seat. A few people had gathered around the old car.

"Take care of that, will you, Charlie," Kadish said. Charlie and Willard went over to the Chevrolet. In its rear window was a stuffed tiger, a plastic hula girl, a miniature stop light, and an illuminated sign that was blinking on and off. It said, CAUTION: ELECTRUM DELIVERIES. An old man, lean and deeply tanned, with a great head of white hair, was lying in the front seat, gasping in long shudders. He appeared to Charlie to have come a long distance.

"Get me a little brandy and strychnine, son," the man said in a hoarse whisper.

"You'll be all right," Charlie said. He depressed the clutch and shifted the gear to neutral. He and Willard pushed the car a dozen feet so that the Cadillac could move.

On the curb, Toedman, his arm around Son's shoulder, swayed slightly. Kadish held out his hand. Toedman ignored it and pointed a huge, accusing finger toward Charlie.

"You, boy," the old man said, "you're a flat tire. Down in Ponca City, we'd string you up by the pecker if we could find it. Do you know what we'd call you down in Ponca City? We'd call you a pissant." He and Son got into the back seat, and the old man moved the power window down. He caught them all in his Dutch-blue Eisenhower stare. "Pissant," he said, and the white limousine pulled away, moving smoothly, its flags rippling, past the Chevrolet.

Charlie's eyes had filled with sweat, and the four glasses of tomato juice he had drunk before lunch had begun to turn to burning clay in his stomach. For a moment, he thought he saw Duane Myre strolling across the street, tipping his baseball cap to the crowd, the rum-and-doriden girl clutching the stub of his arm, laughing and gay.

"You look terrible, Charlie," Kadish said, the half-smile still locked on his face. "You'd better go home and lie down. We'll talk about this tomorrow." Charlie nodded to them all. Meredith Walters and his aides had already turned and were walking away, an elegant little cadre amid the Nielsened slobs, their pinstripe backs totally indifferent.

A cop was leaning into the Chevrolet, and Charlie walked in the opposite direction. If the presentation had worked out, he had planned to buy a good used Aston-Martin 2+2 and take blond girls for long rides in Pennsylvania on the weekends. He caught a cab, wondering if newspaper headlines and old fragments of *Advertising Age* were drifting high overhead in that bright sun. When he felt an iron band clang shut around his chest, he slipped to his knees on the floor of the taxi. The gas howled through his intestines, and suddenly he remembered the gray-faced man lying amid tubes and oxygen in his bed those years ago, and the wife who worried about fare to the hospital. It all came back. He remembered Shirley Myre's tongue in his ear. He remembered the roars of the man's body in its wounded sleep. He whimpered. The entire lower half of his body seemed to be turning to gas. As the terrible eructations began, he screamed, "Take me to P. J. Clarke's. Take me to the Gordian Knot. Take me to the Four Seasons. Take me to Malachy's."

"Mal— Mal—" he barked, clutching his stomach. All the lights on Park turned green, and the cab moved gently forward, floating in the twilight that now perpetually bathes that avenue.

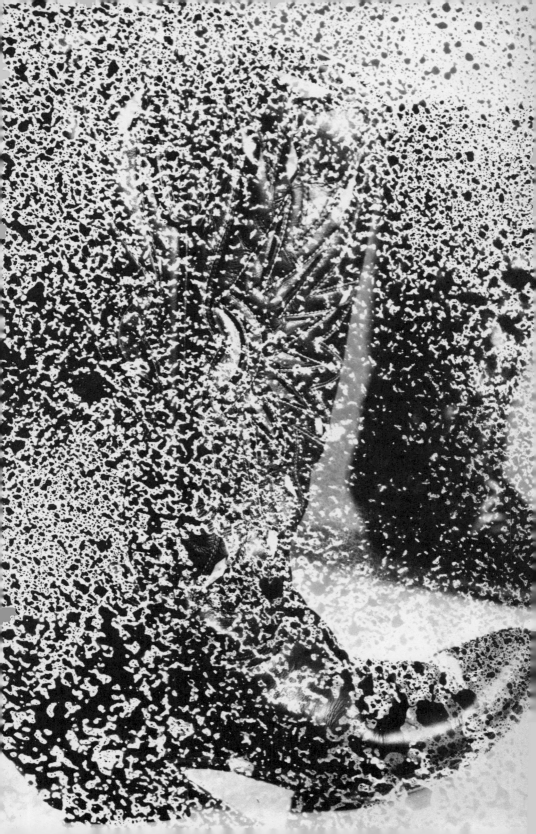

Why Girls Ride Sidesaddle

DENNIS LYNDS

from *Minnesota Review*

He stood in the cabin and held the tube of jelly in his hand. A small, blue tube. He looked at the tube and beyond the tube to the bed. He felt almost old. And it was not that he had already paid for the furniture and the apartment. He would give her the furniture and the apartment, of course, but that was no real loss. It was not even her. Almost old: there was an overtone to that word *old*—an overtone of failure, of ugliness, of finality. The abyss between the dream of eighteen and the reality of thirty-eight. And really not old, simply no longer young.

It had been there in her voice over the telephone—there in the instant of relief he had heard in her voice when he had agreed that Saturday would be better than Friday this week. In three years a man had to learn something about a woman, and he had heard the blue tube in her voice. The tube or something as certain. He had been sure. But to be sure and to know were two different things. Almost the difference between a dream and a reality. The tube of jelly was reality. The bed in the cabin was reality. The sun going down behind the high Catskills across the river was reality.

She would come back to the cabin in less than two hours.

The sun going down behind mountains across a wide river was one of the beautiful moments. A simple moment of sunlight on a river. He stood at the window to look out at the headland near the backwater swamp where they had gone swimming with the late sun on weekends all that summer. The camp and the children behind her for the day, the two of them as alone and happy as children. The two of them in the river, with the reality of land far away across the river where the high Catskills were no more than black shadows. The *high* Catskills. Four thousand feet high. In Wyoming, where he had gone once as a young man, there was flat grassland over eight thousand feet high. All a matter of time and place. The Catskills were old mountains. Four thousand feet is high for old mountains worn down by the river they had held tight when they were young.

Two weeks ago, swimming with her here in the river, he had been young. A day ago. Yesterday, a hot Thursday afternoon in the New York summer. He had been hot, yes, and tired, and perhaps just a little annoyed by the furniture. At thirty-eight, furniture buying had lost some of its thrill, some of its anticipation. Perhaps he had been annoyed, but only a little, and for no more reason than the inconvenience of shopping on a hot day. His coat off in the inertia of a slow afternoon, his feet up on his desk, waiting for her call, and talking of pigeons to his secretary.

"I hate them," his secretary said.

On his window ledge glistened four dusty pigeons the colors of an iridescent rainbow beneath the dust. They picked at the crumbs of refuse on the ledge left from a hundred office lunches. They strutted with bobbing heads. They ate at something deep in their own feathers, oblivious to his eyes as if they owned the city and he were the uninvited guest.

"They're kind of beautiful," he said.

"How can you say that?" his secretary said. "What good are they, Mr. Carlson? They're dirty, they carry disease, they ruin the buildings. They make me sick just to look at them."

Her face was lined with disgust. Miss Schultz was not a pretty woman. Her face was pleasant enough, but it looked as if she had awakened one morning at twenty-one years of age and turned herself to stone. She was in love with him, of course, because he had been in the same office with her for ten years. She had worked for him, waited on him, run his errands, and tried to please him for ten years, and so she was in love with him. There was no other man so fixed and steady in her life.

"All that for a few poor pigeons?" he said.

"I get so mad I shiver," Miss Schultz said.

"I wonder if they would be flattered," he said. "In a way that's a compliment."

"Don't make fun of me," she said. "I can't help it if I hate pigeons."

"I suppose you can't," he said.

"They're not good for anything," Miss Schultz said. "What use are they?"

"None," he said.

"Well then," Miss Schultz said, and she opened her notebook to return to work. "Mr. Friedman wants you to handle the Stone-Webster complaint for Mr. Atkins."

"What's the latest report on Morris?"

"The doctors say there's nothing wrong with his heart at all," Miss Schultz said. "His wife told me. Why does a man like Mr. Atkins think he has heart trouble when he doesn't?"

"Because he wants a bad heart," he said. "It matches his wife's migraine headaches."

"That's cruel."

"But true," he said. "It gives Morris a reason for losing interest in his work. If he just lost interest he'd have to question the whole thing, everything. If he had real heart trouble they would have to retire him for ill-health. This way he keeps his job, I do the work, and everyone is happy. I wonder if he knows how smart it is?"

"You're terrible," Miss Schultz said.

"Just realistic," he said.

It was then that the telephone had rung in the heat of his office. Miss Schultz answered. Her crisp office voice changed. She smiled at the telephone, and yet there was an edge of disapproval in her voice. It was the voice of a woman talking to the lover of a man she knows when she both disapproves of the affair and wishes, in a way, that she were the lover.

"Your fiancée," Miss Schultz said. "On two."

He heard the blue tube in her voice over the telephone almost at once. He could see the tube in her sigh of relief when he agreed that, yes, it might be better if he went up to the cabin on Saturday this weekend.

"I'll be tired to death from the damned counselors' meeting," her distant voice said. "Yes, the meeting is on Friday this week, isn't that too damned much?"

He heard the tube clear in her voice, or something equally certain. Perhaps the man himself was lying there in the bed behind her in the cabin.

"Saturday it is," he said. "I bought the new chairs. That's almost the last. All furnished by Labor Day."

"Are they as nice as they looked?" her voice said. "I can't wait to see them, dear. We'll have a wonderful apartment."

"We will," he said.

He smiled at the telephone as though she could see his face. He knew, even as he smiled, that he would not only go up to the cabin on Friday, but that he would take an earlier train than usual. He did not decide that he would do this, he simply knew that he would do it. It was not that he wanted to go on Friday or wanted to take an earlier train, it was that he had no choice. After she had hung up, he checked the timetable for an earlier train the next day. At five o'clock he asked Miss Schultz to have dinner with him.

"I'd love to, Mr. Carlson," Miss Schultz said.

Miss Schultz was in love with him. She had great hopes. Not hopes for him, for a man, but hopes for them, for a picture. Love for Miss Schultz was not a man, but a fixed picture of a husband and father, a house of her own, and long evenings by the fire with her grandchildren and her comfortable life-insurance income. The man would fit the picture. The man was mutable, but the picture was fixed. He knew all this, and Miss Schultz was not fire to fight fire. Miss Schultz wanted him. Miss Schultz was something he could have if he chose.

The strange thing about doubt is that it is retroactive. Suspicion, even certain suspicion, is like the police searching the past of a captured murderer for other murders. Through dinner with Miss Schultz, and later alone in his new apartment with its new furniture, he tried to find the exact moment, tried to discover the reason by finding the exact moment. A large party less than a year ago. There had been a young man who had admired her knowledge of antiques. That week alone with a woman friend on Fire Island. Perhaps the woman friend had not been a woman. The many nights when she had come home to him very late.

How did a man find the moment, learn—in the maze of three years—the reason? The moment could have been any moment—any smile, any gesture, any person—since the beginning moment, when they had walked in the park on the bank of the river, with the lights of the whole city behind them. The reason could have been on the bank of any river. *I love rivers, Frank. They just keep flowing, you know? It's always the same river, but every second the water is different.* Miss Schultz, playing the coquette but only toying with her food because she was afraid of what might be hidden under the thick sauce, was not a woman who would have liked rivers. Perhaps the reason was hidden in the river itself. If he had looked even at the beginning, he might have seen the reason. But then he had had no reason to look. Now he had to look, had to take an early train on Friday.

Friday was today, and he took a good book to the train with him. At the station he bought a bad magazine. On the train he read neither the book nor the magazine. He never did on trains. He always took the books and the magazines, but he never read them. Outside the window the countryside was always new and fascinating when seen from a moving train, no matter how many times he had ridden the same train. Soon the majestic bulk of Storm King descended into the river. He saw West Point austere on its high bluff across the river. The great river itself was to his left all the long way up to the cabin. The high Catskills, smooth and purple across the river, were like old men brooding in sleep. In the late August evening sun the mountains were smoothed by the soft haze of distance. From the train it seemed that if he reached and touched the mountains they would be as smooth as the green moss that lies close to the ground under the trees. But if he were close, over there beneath the cover of the trees, the mountains would be jagged rocks, sharp cliffs, and tangled underbrush. There would be copperheads curled on rocks.

The smooth surface of time and distance. His own face reflected indistinctly in the train window. His own face and his own life in the window and the distant mountains beyond. So much of a man's life was known, at any given moment, only to him. No matter how much he had told her, she did not know the actual moments of his life. Nor did he really know her life. She could tell him, but he could not know; he could tell her, but she could not see. Time and distance, and it had been a copperhead he had almost sat on the day he and Vinnie had been camping alone in the high Catskills. Twenty years ago. Exactly twenty years ago this year. Two boys of eighteen hiking and sleeping and hiking again in those same mountains. Weary, irritable, dissatisfied, eager, and ambitious boys idealized into simple, happy boys by the smoothing of time. And he had been saved by Vinnie from the bite of a copperhead. No future at all, perhaps, without Vinnie. How fast a man lost touch with his best friend at eighteen. How completely if the year of eighteen was the year before the war, the career, the woman—the holy trinity of here and now. Vinnie somewhere in Brooklyn with his own war, his own career, his own woman. Perhaps there would even be something to say, but who had time for words that might have no value? Twenty years from these mountains across the river as the train moved on toward what he knew he would find at the cabin. A cabin on the river he had rented for her because she liked to be near a river, because she had not worked regularly since they had lived together, and because she wanted to do something useful this summer before they married.

A man lost a friend because he took a different path, because there was time for only one path if a man wanted all that was offered. A man could lose a woman on a different path, too, but that was only one possible reason for losing the woman. A man lost a woman for so many reasons. There might be no reason at all to put a finger on, except another man, and that was not a reason but a result. No reason at all, another man. Yet reason enough, and he would of course give her the furniture. He did not mind the furniture. She could have the furniture and the apartment. It was really her furniture because she wanted it. She needed the furniture. She needed other things, too, the way he needed to take this earlier train on Friday night and not the train on Saturday morning. A matter of time and place.

"Now is the time, young man! Sign here! We must have your signature."

The woman leaned down over him where he sat on the train beside the window. She stood in the aisle and leaned over him. There was a smile on her face, and a long document in her hand. Her face was lined and wrinkled, old and grey-haired, and she peered into his eyes as she thrust her document toward his hands.

"Believe with us, young man," the old woman said. "I have ten signatures. We're going to send it to the President. We must stop the bombs. We're going to send copies to China and Russia. They have a campaign in England, too. If we all understand each other, there will be no bombs."

Her face was so close above him that he could smell the odor of her false teeth. An unpleasant odor, offensive. She blinked her eyes rapidly, nervous. She wore some perfume he did not know. A thick, heavy perfume much too young for her.

"Sorry," he said, "I don't sign petitions."

"If we all work together, we will stop all those bombs!"

"Read some history," a man across the aisle said.

The old woman blinked at the man across the aisle. She walked away down the train aisle. She scuttled away, leaning sideways, smiling as if in a trance, her petition held before her like a shield and a flaming torch combined into one simple talisman.

"They should lock them all up, the stupid idiots," the man across the aisle said. "Damned fools. They're all over the state today. The Governor proclaimed International Brotherhood Week, or some such nonsense. That damned Governor should proclaim Get-To-Work Week, Mind-Your-Own-Damned-Business Week."

"I suppose they don't do any harm," he said. "They mean well."

"Everyone means well," the man across the aisle said.

"Oh, Frank, it's a beautiful sofa! A real antique sofa! You're too nice, and I love you. It means so much to me, a real wonderful sofa of my own. I know it's stupid, it's just a piece of furniture, but it makes getting married seem real. Now I want it, I want us, you know? I do want to get married, I really do. We all need someone, don't we? Something permanent. We'll have a wonderful time together, Frank. We love each other. We even like each other, don't we? We've got a whole lifetime."

Now it was dark in the cabin. He sat on the bed with the blue tube in his hand and listened to the sounds of the night. There were distant voices in the other cabins. On the highway the sound of motors rose and fell. Crickets rasped out their steady noise of late summer, no two crickets playing quite the same note. There was the sound of bullfrogs in the small swamp at the bend in the river near the headland, and the sibilant sound of the flowing river itself. Across the river the mountains hovered unseen and yet somehow squatted heavy on the cabin like old men crouched in a dark corner.

He stood up and turned on the small night lamp next to her bed. The light made the cabin empty, barren. The muddy footprints of the men who had built the cabin were still on the bare boards of the ceiling. He tightened his grip on the tube and, putting it on her chest-of-drawers rather than under the bed where he had found it, walked out of the cabin. He walked through the night to the edge of the river. Across the river the mountains emerged black and high from the night. Behind him the single light in her cabin was like a yellow eye watching him.

He undressed. The river looked cool in the hot night. He laid his clothes neatly on the river bank. Naked, he walked out into the river and began to swim. He was a good swimmer. The current grew stronger as he swam out into the deep river. The moving water was cold. He swam out toward the black mountains on the far side. Great, black mountains. A great, black ram. Othello. . . . *Rather . . . a toad, and live upon the vapour of a dungeon, than keep a corner in the thing I love for others' uses!* Bitch! Whore! Bitch . . . bitch . . . bitch . . . bitch . . .

He turned onto his back to float in the cold stream. The strong current carried him. He saw the headland far off on the shore. He began to swim toward the headland and the small swamp. He swam with the powerful stroke of a good swimmer. The swamp was as dark and solid as a wall in front of him. No light came through the tall, close, towering trees. He swam into the swamp. He changed to a slow sidestroke as he swam into the sounds of crickets and bullfrogs and rustling trees and bullrushes brushed by the moving water. The current of the river carried him on into the swamp. All around him the brittle reeds swished together. The current of the river slackened. On a sudden rush of cold air he smelled the odor of the swamp. The odor of rot. The foul odor of rotting and growing and rotting and growing again. Growing in this dark corner that always ended in the foul odor of stagnation and—finally—in rot.

Around him the whole night moved. The cold of the stagnant water crept through his body. The cold moved up his legs to his chest and reached his chattering lips. The trees leaned over the water ahead of him and behind him. High above him the trees shut out the sky. All around him the water rippled sluggishly through the reeds and lap-lap-lapped at the stumps of dead trees. The current of the river became no current at all. The river no longer moved deep in the small swamp. He stroked slowly ahead deeper into the swamp. The bullrushes and dead tree branches clung to his legs, caught in his hair, brushed his face and eyes. He swam slowly to the right and then slowly to the left. He searched for a path in the swamp, but the rushes touched every part of his body, the dead branches clawed him. Small fish chewed on his toes deep beneath the surface. He kicked out at the small fish. His foot touched a slimy mass hidden below the water. His knees jerked up tight to his chest. His knees jerked up automatically. He strained to force his legs down again. He forced his knees away from his chest, forced his legs down, but the water was thick and slimy, and his feet would not go down. He turned and saw, far off, the faint glimmer of lights in the cabins on the shore. He began to swim toward the lights. The strong current of the river came to meet him. But the river was cold and moving, and he began to shiver. He reached the shore and walked shivering from the river to his neat pile of clothes.

A man stood near his clothes.

"You belong around here, mister?"

"That river's cold," he said.

"Anyone tell you you could swim naked?"

He began to dress. Still wet, he put on his clothes.

"Like you thought you owned the place," the man said. "Naked! You renting one of my cabins?"

"Yes," he said, "I rent one of your cabins."

"I never seen you."

"I rent it for my wife."

"You must be crazy," the man said. "I got decent people living here, family people. I catch you again, I call the cops—you got that?"

The man walked away. An angry man who owned ten cabins on the bank of a river.

When he was dressed, he walked up from the river, passed her still-empty cabin, and walked on to the highway. He crossed the highway to the all-night diner that served food and coffee and beer to passing tourists and to the people who lived in the angry man's cabins. The diner was a favorite spot of the camp counselors. They came from the children at the camp to drink beer at the diner. Soon she would leave the camp and go to the cabin to change for her meeting with whoever the man was. He might be with her. She would find the tube on the dresser. She would know where he was waiting.

"Coffee," he said.

The counterman drew the coffee from a large urn that shone in the light of the diner. At the far end of the long counter three men in work clothes were drinking beer. In a corner booth a father presided angrily over the feeding of his five children while his wife combed her hair. A young boy and a young girl, in the booth farthest from the door, sipped from bottles of beer and giggled at each sip.

"Passing through?" the counterman said.

"Visiting the camp," he said.

"Yeh? We gets all them counselors in here. What a crazy bunch. They laughs all the time, and slops up the beer. They takes care o' kids, then they comes here and drinks like lushes. Catch me sendin' a kid o' mine to one o' them camps!"

"It just doesn't seem right," he said.

"You can say that again. The way they talks, they hates those kids."

"You never can tell, can you?" he said. "Now take my secretary. I've got a secretary who hates pigeons. She hates them so much she nearly froths at the mouth when she talks about pigeons. She really doesn't care about pigeons one way or the other."

The counterman had listened to his secretary story ready to laugh, or agree, or nod wisely. When he had finished telling about his secretary, the counterman was still waiting to react. The counterman was still waiting for the point.

"You have a wife?" he said.

"Who don't?" the counterman said.

"I don't," he said. "That secretary of mine likes me, but she's not my type. I've got a woman, but I've got to let her go. You know *Othello?* It's a Shakespeare play. This Othello killed his wife because she was beautiful, and all his, and he loved her. He didn't kill her because she let another guy play with her, but because she wanted another guy to play with her. She was a beautiful princess. He really killed her because he was an important man. It had nothing to do with love. We don't kill them today, do we? We just walk away."

"I caught my old lady foolin', I'd kill her," the counterman said.

"Of course you would," he said.

"Plenty of fish in the sea," the counterman said. "I'd toss her out on her ass."

"And go catch another fish?"

"What else?" the counterman said.

"Nothing else at all," he said.

She was late. He looked up at the clock behind the long counter. She was already ten minutes later than she should have been. He watched the clock. She was fifteen minutes late. Then twenty minutes late. He ordered another cup of coffee. He drank the coffee and wondered if Morris Atkins could really die of a psychosomatic heart attack. The psychiatrists said a psychosomatic illness was a real illness. But you did not die of a psychosomatic heart, and if you could not die, then it could not be real. It did not work out in practical reality. If Morris did not die, at least he might retire. The two possibilities were the same thing as far as his own career was concerned. Die or retire, the result would be the same for him.

When she came into the diner she walked straight to a rear booth and sat down. The counterman greeted her with a friendly wave. He ordered a cup of coffee for her and a third cup for himself, carrying both cups to the booth. She looked down at the cup of coffee as he placed it before her. She had long red hair and a long smooth neck like a Parisian model. She was tall and slender, with small breasts. They were good, firm breasts. Beneath the loose skirt of her camp uniform her hips were rounded. She was a pretty woman.

"I was trying to think of something," she said. "In the cabin. I couldn't think of anything. The owner said there was a crazy man swimming naked. I didn't have to see the tube."

It was still a part of him, of course. The desire. Desire for her in his belly, in the small of his back where the nerve center was. The desire for this particular woman that was love. The special desire, love, that was for a special woman. It would be part of him for a long time.

"You would think I could find some story," she said. "I could tell you that I let one of the other girls use the cabin, but you wouldn't believe that. You know the brand of jelly I use. You notice those things. I know it's important to you, and I can't think of one good lie."

"Try a reason," he said.

"Reason?" she said. She stirred her coffee. "He's a man in camp, the swimming instructor. You know how much I like to swim. He's young. He's not very good-looking. He's not a patch on you, they never are. He's six years younger, and he's a good swimmer. But it wasn't that. He has a girl down in New York who's six years younger than he is. Sometimes we talked about her. It made me feel like her—young and new. But that's not why either, is it? I don't suppose I can say why. He was here, he wanted me. One night I said, 'Why not?' I suppose he was just something more."

"Was it good? Better than me?"

"After it's over it never seems very much."

"What would you want me to do? Hold his hat?"

"All right," she said.

"Something you could have," he said. "Something more."

"Not much of a reason," she said.

She drank her coffee. She sipped the coffee once and then drained the cup. The coffee was not hot. The counterman was watching them, grinning. The counterman must have seen her in the diner with the swimming instructor. It bothered him, the grin of the counterman. There was no reason why the counterman should bother him. The counterman was not involved. The way the pigeons bothered his secretary for no real reason, or no *true* reason. There was a difference between truth and reality. The petition of the woman on the train was true, but not very real. Someday someone would drop those bombs.

"When I was a boy," he said, "I saw a woman riding a horse. She was riding sidesaddle. I still remember how I stared at her on that shiny black horse. I couldn't understand why she would sit on a horse sideways like that. I imagined all sorts of strange things under that long skirt to make her ride that way. Mysterious things, beautiful shapes. I imagined all kinds of exciting shapes for her body hidden under that long skirt. I was sure that there was something very special under that skirt that made her ride sidesaddle. I must have been almost thirteen when I finally had enough nerve to ask my father about it. I remember how he laughed. He told me that there was nothing under that skirt that made her ride sidesaddle. Women rode that way because it was considered improper for a woman to ride astride. It was just a custom, a rule, and not a custom anyone worried much about anymore. That woman had been riding sidesaddle because someone had told her she should. There was no real reason."

"Why did you come up?" she said. "Why didn't you wait?"

"I had to come up," he said. "I heard him in your voice. I had to take an early train."

"Tomorrow it would have been over, nonexistent."

"As if it had never happened," he said.

"That's the truth, Frank," she said.

"I know it's the truth."

"But you'll leave, walk out?"

"You can keep the apartment and the furniture. They belong to you, you want them. The rent's paid for this month, I'll pay a couple of months ahead so you can get settled down."

"Thank you."

"I don't suppose this was the first time," he said, "and I doubt if it would be the last time. But that's not what I mean. I'd never know, but that's not really important. If I could do it, none of that would matter. If I could say, 'Yes, okay, come on home,' nothing else would really count."

That was true. And he wished with all that he knew he must have inside him somewhere that he could say, "Yes, okay, come on home, I love you." He wished that he could feel it all let go, that he could let go—let all he was or would be go limp and surrender. That was true.

"I'll leave my keys with the landlord," he said.

"All right," she said.

"I'll call," he said. "We'll talk."

"We'll talk," she said.

He left her alone in the booth of the diner. As he went out, she walked to the counter for another cup of coffee. When he passed the diner window, she was back in the booth. He walked the two miles to the railroad station and his train back to New York.

The Wrong Silence

NANCY K. MACKENZIE from *Prairie Schooner*

Milly Tudhope could have told the guard at the gallery that she didn't agree
with him, but she'd smiled and nodded as though she too thought that the two
paintings—of a sixteenth-century Dutchman and his wife—should be hung
together. "One's in this room and one's in the other," he told her. "Why they
dinna hang them together I'll never know." He painted. "I paint mountains," he
said. "I've often thought of copying one of these," and he'd waved at the
medieval faces, "but I've never got aroond to it." He said he'd submitted his
paintings to the Royal Academy for twelve years; his placid chin showed no
resentment when he said he put his rejections down to the fact that it was a
clique.

Now, half an hour later, walking along Sauchiehall Street towards her
room on the other side of Glasgow, she could think of funny words to make his
serious Scottish face change. But when he spoke to her she had been deep in
herself, not expecting to speak again until she went back to work the next day.
It was as though she'd put language away, and being spoken to suddenly had
bewildered her. She might have used gestures. She might have hugged him to
show her interest in the Dali painting in its own little velvet room, but instead
she'd stammered, had looked to see if he was speaking to someone else and had
lost the moment in confusion when she could have spoken to him, perhaps
found a friend. She could have pressed her cheek to his to say let them hang in
different rooms: why should they outstare each other for centuries? She could
have smoothed his bristly hair to say thank you for talking to me, but you see I
need a warning. I need an announcement. I live alone.

She slowed as she approached Mrs. Elders'. She always slowed down. For
this was where her silence had set in, no doubt about that. She always glanced
up at the windows, not expecting anyone to move the curtains but curious to
see if they were still the same. They were the same chocolate brown, with the
lace curtains in between. Someone moved them. She stopped completely,

unable to think and walk at the same time, but then she saw a man's round face look down, yawn and go back. It could hardly have been Mrs. Elders.

She walked on, remembering that it was in the same November weather that she had come to Glasgow from Manchester to look after her aunt—who died too soon to appreciate Milly's care. And then cousins came from all over the north to claim the house, the blankets, the silver, and she had gone to live at Mrs. Elders', unaffected because she was soon to marry Henry Leighton in Kenya—two warm worlds to come alive for when the time came.

Mrs. Elders had greeted her with a knife in one hand and a red pillar-box bank in the other. For a moment she looked at Milly, as though making up her mind forever. Milly looked down, too shy to stare boldly into the older woman's eyes.

"Two guineas a week," Mrs. Elders told her, not opening the door any wider. Her abrupt words were made pleasant by the Scottish accent, disguising the scornful woman Milly later found her to be.

"Oh yes, all . . . ."

"And I never let them for less than three months."

"Oh I shall, I expect to be in Glasgow . . . ."

"And it's three shillings extra for bed linen changed every fortnight."

When Milly did not say anything Mrs. Elders opened the door and showed her the room. It wasn't small; it faced the street and had wooden shutters inside the windows for protection against the north winds, and a fireplace. Milly wished she could say "No thanks, it isn't half good enough for me" but she couldn't. A previous room had been four pounds a week with everything on the electric meter: lights, fire, hot plate, iron. It would have consumed the rest of her salary in shillings to live there, so she nodded at Mrs. Elders.

"Right across the hall is the washroom, next to the kitchen. My bedroom's next to the washroom. Bath's upstairs. Bath night for this room is Wednesday. My sitting room's next door. Here." She opened the door to let Milly see.

Milly looked in, pleased at the show of friendliness. She saw a piano and a television set, armchairs, a heavy table.

"You can use my telephone up to eleven at night. Just put fourpence in this bank. A threepenny bit and a penny will do. That's a convenience. Of course it's harder for me to get the threepenny bit out but I don't mind."

"How thoughtful . . . ."

"When do you want to come?"

"This weekend, if that's all right. I'll give you a check."

"Is it drawn on a local bank? They charge you twopence if it's not."

"It is."

Milly got out her check book and was writing on the hall table when the front door opened and Mrs. Elders greeted someone.

"Oh, it's you, Mr. Dyer. Aren't you home early?"

Milly looked up and saw a red-cheeked young man in a tweed coat glance at her.

"Yes, Mrs. Elders, a trifle, but I thought I'd treat my feet to a rest."

He went past to the stairs and Mrs. Elders followed him. "Mr. Dyer, a wee minute. I wanted to tell you," she lowered her voice slightly, "that it was your bath night yesterday and you left your corn plasters in the soap dish."

Milly heard Mr. Dyer's whispered apology as she finished writing. Then she heard him stumble on the first stair. Mrs. Elders returned cheerfully and took the check.

"Now, Miss . . ." she looked at the name, "not Scots I see. How long will you be wanting the room?"

Milly tried to speak firmly, to keep hold of a sentence until the end. "Only six months. I'm going to Nairobi to be married in June. That is if the room is satis . . . ."

"Married!" Mrs. Elders looked at Milly, as though adjusting her opinion. "Well."

"Good-bye," and Milly left, hoping that she was not going to be cowed by Mrs. Elders.

But she was. The Glasgow accent which made everyone sound alike had not liberalized Mrs. Elders, despite her remark that "I'm not snobbish, but I'm resairved." While Milly unpacked she stood in the door and talked, eyeing the clothes Milly put in the oak wardrobe and darting a look out to watch Mrs. Weir go into the kitchen and Mr. Dyer go out. She came in to help Milly place the suitcase on top of the wardrobe.

"Coal's gone up to 9/2d. Will you still want me to order you any?"

"Yes, please. I like a coal fire sometimes."

"Mrs. Weir will be leaving soon."

"Oh."

"When she goes to hospital. I knew she was pregnant when she came to me for a room. I can always tell by the eyes. It made it difficult, her right eye being off center, but I knew. 'Not in my house,' I said, but she's going to her sister when the baby comes and then her husband's leaving the merchant navy she says."

"I see."

"A slut that girl is. Smokes all day and her pregnant. Lies in bed most of the time—won't read a decent book, just trash. And I won't have anyone wearing bedroom slippers in my kitchen I told her." She looked at Milly and Milly kept her eyes from moving down to the fur slippers she'd put on when she came indoors. Had she worn them to the kitchen yet? She couldn't remember if she had done so when Mrs. Elders was showing her around.

"You haven't met Dr. Coltart, have you?"

"No." Milly moved from foot to foot, waiting for Mrs. Elders to leave.

"The doctor's been with me for five years. She's a university doctor." Mrs. Elders waited.

"How clever."

"And she's county as well," Mrs. Elders added. "That's why she knows so much about horses. She's looking after some horses now for a friend of hers at Milngavie. She comes in to watch the horse jumping on television. You might care to join us some evening."

"Thank you."

"I'll have to cut you off now, Milly. It's away past my tea time." And she went into the kitchen.

Milly learnt like a blind person to know all the footsteps in the house and choose her moments for going across the hall to put the kettle on or into the washroom to wash her clothes. She knew Mrs. Weir's sullen shuffle and banging noises in the kitchen. She knew Mr. Dyer's door-slam before he came downstairs to leave the flat; he never used the kitchen. She knew Dr. Coltart's departure time in the mornings. She got up at 6:30 and Milly heard her stately tread in the hall as though she was thinking, "Now I'll lift this boot and put it down and now this boot and put it down and now I'll smack into the umbrella stand," which she invariably did.

Once, after Mrs. Elders had accused Milly of putting a Canadian quarter into her shilling slot meter, Milly stood in front of the window and watched as Mrs. Elders crossed the road to go to church, holding up her hand to stop the car that was about to get in her way. "You won't do the church much good," she muttered, thinking that the quarter would probably end up in the vicar's collection plate. She moved aimlessly about her room, looked at Henry's picture, asked him why he hadn't written for a week, and sat down morosely in front of the fire. Even though she wanted to wash her hair or clothes or make beans-on-toast in peace she sat and thought of how she had succumbed to Mrs. Elders' arrogance. Typically English, she thought, tell me that certain behavior is in bad taste and I'm crushed. Say that liking fish and chips is common and I'll eat in secret. Tell me, and she looked at Henry's picture again, that someone has a weak chin and I'll stop boasting about him.

She suddenly roused herself and went across to the washroom with a bottle of shampoo. She was supposed to wash her hair only on her bath night but she liked to wash it more often than that. When the water ran cold she didn't even swear. In the kitchen she saw the immerser was switched off; when she opened the door of the boiler she saw that Mrs. Elders had put slabs of slate on top to keep the coal from burning in her absence and heating the water.

"The mean old besom," she said aloud. "The mean Glasgow bitch." She noticed the cobbler's awl on the dresser. That meant Mrs. Elders would come home from church and bang away all afternoon at putting new soles on her laced shoes. Dump her on an island, Milly thought, and she'd tell the natives how to save wood while cooking landladies.

The next evening Milly let herself in as quietly as she could, tiptoeing over to the hall table to see if a letter from Henry was among the display, saw that there wasn't, and was smiling at herself for holding the fish and chip bundle beneath her handbag, when Mrs. Elders came out of the kitchen.

"Oh, Milly, a wee minute. I thought I'd catch you this morning but you ran out."

"Yes?" Milly wondered if the fish smell would make its way out of the *News of the World.*

"The doctor has a holiday next week and won't need to be getting up so early. I wonder if you'd just put her bottle of milk outside her door when you take yours in?"

"Oh well, all . . . ."

"And my leg's been hairting me—it's getting very stiff—so would you take down the rubbish pail in the mornings? It won't be out of your way. Mrs. Weir is supposed to do it but often she forgets until the dustcart's gone by. Just glance in the kitchen to see if it's full."

"If I remember," Milly muttered.

"What? Thank you." Mrs. Elders' tone changed. "How is Henry these days?"

"All right."

"I couldn't help noticing he hasna written to you lately. I trust nothing's wrong in Kenya."

"No, it's just he's not much of a writer . . . ."

"Well, you'd better get your wet coat off. I didn't know it was raining." Her tone changed again. "And Milly, don't fill the kettle so full. It boiled over this morning and put the gas out. It's a terrible waste. I lit it again for you."

Mrs. Elders returned to the kitchen, nodding, it seemed to Milly, at her package of fish and chips. By the time Milly sat down at the fire the chips were limp and the fish batter gluey. She ate them in her fingers without her usual three cups of tea because she could tell Mrs. Elders was still in the kitchen.

The fish and chips were part of her effort to save money. She and Henry had known each other in Manchester but became engaged by letter after he'd been working for ten months in Nairobi. Was Kenya's sun warm? Here she was, shivering, often aching for a real dinner, and yet she wrote calmly every day to Henry about his house hunting, about dresses she'd bought, and post office certificates saved. Henry's letters were brief—about cricket scores in Australia or promotions in his consular office. She memorized names she would know well by this time next year and wondered what Henry did after his office closed. She did not tell him what her evenings were like—bed at nine to save on the electric fire, wearing gloves to hold the book in comfort, hearing Mrs. Elders' cackling laughter at the television programs until she gave an enormous coughing sigh at 10:10 as the news came on, and turned off the set and went her rounds: putting her milk bottle out, turning off the dim hall light, looking into the kitchen, shaking the bank to see if anyone had used the phone, and finally closing her bedroom door as she retired for the night.

The next evening, as Milly looked over the post for the airmail letter from Kenya, she realized that her name was somewhere on the table top. Her glance always slid over all the names so quickly that she could hardly read them. She gripped the table edge with her fingers and forced herself to see that it was indeed her name, but on an overseas cable in a yellow envelope. Numbly she picked it up, and heard Mrs. Elders come up behind her. The front door opened and Mr. Dyer came in.

"Oh there you are, Milly dear," Mrs. Elder said in a new tone Milly had never heard. "There's no mail for you again, Mr. Dyer."

He went past to the staircase.

"The doctor and I are having a scone and a cup of tea, Milly. Why don't you join us?"

Milly had by this time turned the envelope over. "It's for me," she said stupidly.

"Ay, it came about an hour ago."

"It's been opened."

"It never has!"

"Yes."

"It came like that then. Sheer carelessness . . . ."

"What does it say?"

Mrs. Elders was speechless, and Milly took the bad news into her room and slammed the door. She didn't even want to read it. The tears were already there. She dropped her handbag and coat on the floor, kicked off her shoes, and sat heavily in the chair by the unlit fire. Then she read Henry's apology for breaking the engagement.

Since she could not lock the door (only Mrs. Elders' two rooms had keys) she moved the armchair over against it and went to bed, taking off only her skirt. And there under the covers she cried hopelessly until she fell asleep.

After that she didn't talk to anyone. When Mrs. Elders spoke to her she would just nod or shake her head. The day after the telegram came, Mrs. Elders had looked sideways at her as she was filling the teapot and told her about a friend of hers who had been jilted and had sued for breach of promise, and won, but she stopped when Milly just stared. Milly came and went, spending almost every evening in the cinemas in the center of the city, where she sat in the cold, smoky darkness, sometimes staring blindly at the head of the person in front of her, sometimes not hearing the dialogue because she was listening to her own words.

"I hardly dare talk to you whilst you're so wrapped up in your private affairs," Mrs. Elders said to her one evening a few weeks later, "but . . . ."

Milly stopped on her way to her room. She never paused at the hall table any more, and if any letters came for her, after a day or so Mrs. Elders slipped them under her door.

"Well?"

"Well, would you mind popping out again for some milk for Mrs. Weir?" Milly waited.

"A shocking thing happened ten days ago. She had an accident and lost the baby. Yes," as Milly showed her surprise, "you didn't notice, of course, but she's back from hospital today and there's nothing in the house. I cancelled her milk, thinking she'd be going to her sister's, but her sister's in hospital herself so she'd no one to look after her. Dear knows where the husband is, on a high sea somewhere I suppose. She's fair lucky I didn't let her room . . . ."

Milly turned and went towards the door. "One pint should suffice until the milkman comes," she heard as she went down the steps.

When she came back with soup, bread and butter, and milk, Mrs. Elders took them. "She's asleep now, but she'll be awake in an hour or so wanting something. Write down what you paid and I'll tell her . . . ."

"Never mind about that," Milly said, and went to her room.

And then, a week later, Mrs. Elders was gone. That Thursday evening she met Milly in the hall. "Oh Milly, a wee minute. I want to tell you I'm visiting my niece at Bridge of Allan this weekend."

"I see."

"The boiler won't be going but the doctor will start the immerser. You've never taken the rubbish pail down as I asked you to do. Would you do that at least while I'm away? I've been doing it myself these past two weeks, in spite of my hairting leg."

"Very well." Milly felt the first feeling of pleasure since she'd moved in. "When will you be back?"

But Mrs. Elders was too cagey to let her measure out her moments of pleasure. "It's hard to say. My niece never wants me to leave. I always have to remind her that I have a house to look after. But not so long as all that." She nodded and went into her sitting room.

It didn't matter. Even a night and a day of absence would help. She decided she would stay in all day Saturday. She would build a coal fire and get magazines and chocolates and enjoy the solitude. The others wouldn't bother her. No one talked to anyone else, too conscious of how Mrs. Elders talked of each of them.

The house was so quiet when she got there on Friday evening it was like going into the wrong flat. Just as she was going into her room the front door opened and Mrs. Weir came in, puffing slightly from the climb. Milly nodded, uncertain of how to greet her, but Mrs. Weir smiled. "Is she away then?"

"She must be. I'll just look in the kitchen." Milly went across and returned. "Yes, safely straddling the Bridge of Allan."

"Good. I'm dying for a cup of tea. I've been at the pictures all afternoon. I wanted to be out when she left so's I'd get no lecture about taking two baths or using her milk saucepan for soup."

They went to their rooms and reappeared, each carrying a box of matches. Milly put the kettle on and left her matches on the mantel shelf. "I'm always forgetting them when I come in here," she said. "I'll leave them here for once. I'll even let the doctor use them."

"We shouldn't be seeing much of her either, the great clot."

"Why not?"

"One of her horses is cavorting in Mother Goose across in Edinburgh. She'll have to see that it behaves itself. Oh, I'm off to put my slippers on. Mr. Dyer and me suffer from the same complaint—corns."

Milly waited for the kettle to boil, leaning on the kitchen sink to look out the window into lighted rooms across the yard.

"Do you know, the old gossip's left her sitting room unlocked!" Mrs. Weir was back.

"Really?"

"Yes, fancy! She's never done that before. Now we can have a look at the television, play a few hymns."

"You wouldn't!"

"Why not? She goes in our rooms and mucks about with our things. If it hadn't been for her I wouldn't have lost the baby." Mrs. Weir cried for a moment and then wiped her eyes, cheering up again as she put hot water in the teapot.

"How?"

"She kept nagging at me to take down the slops. Said I needed exercise and her leg hurt her. I fell down the steps a week last Monday and all I remember is seeing the postman's face and then the doctor's."

"I'm so sorry." Milly's face flushed as she stopped herself from saying she had been asked to take down the bucket.

"Well, I'm leaving here. It gave my husband a proper scare and his wire this morning says he's coming home for good. Mrs. Elders and me both got wires and we neither of us told the other what they said." She got up and reached down two of Mrs. Elders' cups off the hooks. "These'll do."

Milly moved away from the sink and sat down at the kitchen table. When the outer door opened she sat up straight. "Dr. Coltart!"

"What if it is." But Mrs. Weir stood poised with her hand holding the teapot. At the sound of a cough she relaxed. "It's only Mr. Dyer." She went to the door and called out. "In here, Mr. Dyer, for a cup of tea."

Milly got up to get another cup, suddenly self-conscious and excited, hoping he would turn out to be as friendly as Mrs. Weir. His round red face peered round the door comically, and then he went over to the broom cupboard, opened it, and looked inside.

"You're safe, Mr. Dyer, she's gone and all."

"It's the first time since I've been here then," he said, rubbing his hands together, trying not to smile too broadly. "What did I hear—something about tea? Good evening," he said to Milly, and she smiled.

"You and Mrs. Weir know each other?"

"In a manner of speaking," he replied. "Bill and I worked together before he went to sea. He asked me to keep an eye on her but of course Mrs. Elders wouldn't agree to that. 'I don't allow my gentlemen boarders to go into anyone else's bedroom,' she said, 'including mine.'" Milly laughed. "'If Mrs. Weir needs anything—which she won't—I'll see to it,' she said. And being the cowardly sort, I didn't want her to tell old Bill stories when he came back. When is he coming by the way?"

"Tuesday. He's coming to fetch me out of here and we're going to a council house."

"Isn't that grand?" Mr. Dyer was smiling at Milly, and she agreed it was.

"I'm going to light Mrs. Elders' fire for her," Mrs. Weir said. "Then we can sit in there," and at Milly's alarmed look said, "I'll set it again before Sunday night. She won't come back before then unless her niece gets fed up with her."

"To celebrate," Mr. Dyer announced, and they looked at him, "I believe I'll get some wine and cheese and we can have a little party to ourselves."

Milly smiled and murmured, "How nice." For a second she had thought he was going to suggest fish and chips. This weekend was going to make up for the dreariness of past weekends. Mr. Dyer's name was Charles but everyone called him Chubb, he said, so she and Mrs. Weir, now Joan, did the same. By ten o'clock and the end of the cheese and two bottles of wine he'd asked them both to go to the Trossachs with him the next day. Mrs. Weir said she wanted to pack, but Milly said yes.

And by eleven o'clock they were all ready for a cup of tea so Milly offered to make it. She went out to the kitchen, humming, and slammed the kettle on the gas with a flourish. Then she put her hands over her mouth to keep from laughing. She whirled around the table and out into the hall. The doctor's room was dark; her door was the only one with clouded glass in it so it was always easy to tell if she was in. She's probably cleaning up the stage, Milly thought. She danced back towards the kitchen and idly tried Mrs. Elders' door, feeling sure that even if Mrs. Elders had forgotten to lock her sitting room she would have made sure of the bedroom. But it was unlocked and she pushed it back, curious to see the room Mrs. Elders didn't show her.

It took her half a minute to see that Mrs. Elders was lying on the bed, beneath the window. She was too confused to scream or to react. Slowly it came to her that she was dead. In the light that came from outside, from the moon and two lighted rooms across the way, she could see that the figure, on top of the white coverlet, completely dressed, was motionless. She closed the door quietly and went into the kitchen, where she sat down on a chair.

She could hear Mrs. Weir laughing. She was numb, but aware that the closing of the door had been a decision. Without thinking it through, rather with a jumble of pictures in her mind, she saw the changes that would come if she told the others. Their friendship would be stopped and might not continue. They would have to give up the solitude; the place would be overrun. She remembered the turmoil and excitement when her aunt had died—how she was pushed into the corner and then outside.

When Chubb came into the kitchen she was still sitting at the table, looking at her hands.

"What's up in here? It'll be time for a morning cuppa soon," he said, going over and removing the boiling kettle.

She looked up, unable to mold her face into an expression of any kind.

"It's the wine, isn't it? You're not used to it?"

She nodded.

"Will you feel up to the bus trip tomorrow?"

"Oh yes, yes. I want to get away from Glasgow." She stood up shakily. "But I'd better go to bed now. I'm . . . ."

"Dizzy?"

"Yes. Will you say good night to Joan?"

He stopped her. "You do look queer." She nodded again and he put his arms around her clumsily, patted her head against his shoulder, and kissed her forehead. Her eyes opened in surprise. Then she lifted her face for his kiss and he kissed her shyly. But it was enough. She smiled at him and went to her room.

In bed she wondered how she could sleep, sharing a tomb. Her thoughts flew round and round, overlapped. What was the harm in letting another day go by? If Mrs. Elders had died several months ago no one here would care; they would have forgotten her by this time, would be laughing as they had laughed and joked this evening. But because the death was only hours old their faces and voices would be filled with nervous gloom. She wasn't hypocritical, but something warned her the others were. In fact, as she thought about it, she wouldn't want them to be different. It would make them hard—not that she was callous, no, she knew she wasn't, but she had a sense of justice. Mrs. Elders deserved a cold death. She must have had a stroke; it often happened to older people, and a woman like Mrs. Elders, tightly strapped in by corsets and tight shoes all day and evening, must have been asking for it. The stiff leg had probably been a warning to take herself to the doctor.

She heard Chubb's bed creak in the room above after he'd dropped off his shoes. She finally dozed off, moving uneasily in her sleep, jerking awake early in the morning when the first tram squeaked by the street outside.

But in the bus with Chubb going to the Trossachs she forgot about Mrs. Elders. The day was yellow-cold, with the mountains visible from tip to base, the lochs icy and still. Whenever the bus driver saw something that interested him he leaned back and shouted to the passengers. He stopped the bus for them to look at the poker hanging outside the Bailie Nicol Jarvie Hotel, the poker that had almost hit Rob Roy. When he was out of breath he merely pointed, and all the heads turned.

Chubb held her hand when they were out of the bus. On the drive back to Glasgow she reached out for his. She pretended sleepiness in order to look out the window into the lighted streets, hoping now that Mrs. Weir had discovered Mrs. Elders, or even that the body had been taken away and the shocked talk removed with the relatives so that they could go on without being involved. But she knew once the death was discovered the talk would be only of that. She became aware of harder pressure on her fingers and frowned, wondering what to do. Chubb was squeezing her fingers, pressing them into his thigh. Should she kiss him? she wondered. Would he say something about the future, about love, if she did? In the darkened bus she turned her head slowly towards him, opening her lips, and felt his mouth open even wider over hers, felt him pushing her hand between his legs as his kiss forced her head back towards the window. She fought for breath, gave up, touched tongues with him, and gradually eased him back into his seat.

"People will see," she whispered.

"Later," he said, "in my room?"

She paused, holding his hand between hers, stroking it gently. "I'm very fond of you," she said in a low voice. She laughed a little. "I'm afraid you've guessed."

"Will you come up then?"

She looked out of the window. They were almost at the bus station. "I'd like to make you happy," she said, and saw that this was the wrong thing to say. "It's just that I like you so much," she added quickly. "I don't want you to think I'm that sort."

He put his hand round her neck, pulling her gently towards him. "You're the first lass I've taken to in a long time," he told her. "We might even make a go of it, don't you think?"

"Yes," she said just in time, as the bus pulled up, "Yes, I do, Chubb."

Like his first kiss, it was enough. It was the next step to the words. It would be safe to sleep with him and not expect him to reject her afterwards, as Henry had done before he went to Nairobi. He'd changed his mind again but it hadn't lasted. Chubb would be different. If she could get him to say the word marriage before the game started it would be easy. They could have one or two nights together, and then they would all have to move to other lodgings. Mrs. Weir was leaving in any event; perhaps she and Chubb might even marry right away. She'd take a chance because it was clear he was no risk; he worked steadily; he'd talked about living in the country, of owning a shop . . . .

On their way back to the flat Chubb bought two boxes of chocolates and gave her one, saying the other was for Joan. "We'll have a nice evening by the fire," she said, and he nodded, started to say something, and stopped. And a nice night in bed, she finished for him in her thoughts. On the last landing he stopped and took her in his arms. "Just in case Mrs. Elders is in there," he whispered. "But this is just a beginning for us, isn't it?"

"If you want me," she answered softly.

They stood together, moving slightly, moving into each other, adjusting to hips and knees and when he kissed her his kiss was uncontrolled again. She never would have guessed from his shy politeness over the last weeks and the last day that he was so excitable. She felt his hand slide up under her jumper, his cold hand touch her breast, and she moved as if shocked at his familiarity, so that the nipple moved across his palm. He murmured to her and she started to say something as his mouth met hers. They kissed wet kisses as his hand squeezed her breast and she moved closer into the hardness at his groin. She lost count of time or place; with her eyes closed and all her senses awakened she could only wish that they could lie down on the stone floor and make love and sleep. She had never felt the same desire for Henry; she felt herself swaying; she couldn't bear to open her eyes, but Chubb separated first, leaning against the wall, breathing hoarsely. "What's come over me?" he said. "I'm sorry, Milly, I am."

"I can't imagine how that happened," she said. "It was wonderful." She leaned into him and his arms went around her.

"No, no, we've got to get in," he said. "Later."

When they went in they heard Mrs. Weir singing in the kitchen, which meant Mrs. Elders was still hidden behind her door. Mrs. Weir greeted them and the chocolates with delight. She had prepared shepherd's pie and bread pudding for their supper. "All afternoon I been in here, getting the feel of a proper kitchen. Mrs. Elders always chased me out. When I first came I thought I'd give her a hand, polishing things, but she wouldn't put up with anyone in her kitchen she told me."

"This is all very kind, I must say," Chubb said. He patted her gently on the shoulder, and told her the shepherd's pie made him hungry just to sniff it. "My mum used to make that every Wednesday," he said, turning to Milly, "when we lived in Earnley, in the cottage I was telling you about, the one I'm going to buy back one of these days."

Milly nodded. The smell of the food was making her stomach turn. She felt the bile in her mouth. "Excuse me a minute," she said, and went to the washroom, where she was quietly sick. Then she went to her room and lay down on the bed, her face glistening with sweat. Suddenly it seemed that all the turbulence she had experienced since coming to Mrs. Elders'—the misery, the rage, frustration, spite, and now this sinking desire for Chubb—had gathered into one emotion that surged through her body and left her ill. She knew she could not pretend to discover Mrs. Elders now; she had lived with her death for twenty-four hours. She could not act out shock or respectful horror. It was as though, for her, Mrs. Elders had been dead for six months. She would just have to wait until something happened.

And about three hours later it did. She and Chubb were doing the washing-up after supper while Mrs. Weir warmed her feet on the fender in Mrs. Elders' sitting room. Milly had just hung the dishcloth over the oven door and Chubb was holding her, his hands on her shoulders, smiling. They stood there, their faces a few inches apart, smiling into each other's eyes.

Gradually, at the eerie noise, his fingers tightened on her shoulders and she saw his expression change to listening alertness and alarm. She knew that this was what he saw in her eyes as the croaking groan was repeated, heard faintly in the now silent kitchen. Milly's mouth went dry and she started to shake.

It seemed longer but it was just for a moment that they stood there, only their eyes showing that something had happened. "What . . . ?" he said.

"She's still alive!" she whispered.

"Who?"

She closed her eyes, feeling faint. Suddenly she staggered as his hands released her, almost pushed her.

"Mrs. Elders?"

She nodded, knowing that she had lost her chance for deception. Dimly she realized, as she leaned back against the stove, that there was a rushing about, shouted words on the telephone by Chubb, Mrs. Weir filling a cup with water at the sink, going away with it, the front door opening and Dr. Coltart's heavy voice raised anxiously at the commotion, and finally a pause as all the things were done that could be done. The kitchen door filled with Chubb and Mrs. Weir and Dr. Coltart, moving in a hushed group back from the bedroom.

"She can't last," Chubb said in a low voice and the others murmured. Milly stood apart, unable to look up or join in. The two women must have looked in her direction for Chubb said, "She's stunned, like the rest of us. Leave her be."

"Is she all right?" Mrs. Weir asked, but Chubb did not answer.

"There's the door. It must be the ambulance and the police," and Chubb left, with Mrs. Weir and Dr. Coltart following him.

A doctor came with the quiet-speaking Glasgow police and she went to stand in the hall, forcing herself to look as Mrs. Elders was carried past. A blanket was over her head. Chubb spoke for all of them, saying they understood Mrs. Elders to be visiting her niece, not knowing that a telegram had come Friday morning cancelling the visit. It must have been some time after that that Mrs. Elders lay down to die.

The change Milly predicted overtook them and a death-reverence entered their conversation. Milly looked on, watching them speak as though she was trying to understand what they were saying. Eventually Mrs. Weir and Dr. Coltart grasped the fact that Milly had known about Mrs. Elders; they drew away.

When she went into her room and stood at the window she was still dumb. And when Chubb came in and stood by the door she just turned round and waited. It's not my fault, she thought, but did not speak.

"I don't know what's wrong with you," he said finally, "but there's an inhuman thing you did leaving that poor woman like that. What I wonder is, when did you first think she was dead?"

"Shortly after I came here," she said.

He ran his hand over his head in confusion. "You couldn't have had anything against her. She seemed to like you. I heard her ask you to have tea with her; she never spoke to anyone else like that."

The huge effort it would take to explain kept her silent. She shrugged.

"The poor woman," he said again. "She probably heard everything that went on." He shook his head. "Suppose it had been your mother?"

"Mine died when I was two."

"You're not the only one," he said. "Others have had life as hard."

My thoughts are interesting, she thought. If you knew my thoughts you wouldn't despise me. But she knew if she tried to make words out of them she would fail.

"You see you can't even explain," he said. "You mustn't be like other people, like the rest of us. You can't have any feelings."

She nodded. She was not like them.

"Good-bye," she said.

But of course they were like her—a month or two later. She was just not like them at the time of Mrs. Elders' death. They caught up. They laughed and then forgot Mrs. Elders. But by then Chubb was telling the story—as a story—to another girl and Mrs. Weir was telling it to new neighbors and Dr. Coltart, being county, didn't talk about it at all.

All these thoughts crammed Milly's head as she walked home. Next Sunday she would talk, she would go back to the art gallery and see if the guard could listen. She had to keep looking for the one person who would understand her unspoken language and explain it to her.

TRAVEN

DAVID MADDEN   from *Southern Review*

Did I ever tell you about the time I tried to get my little brother off the Tennessee chain gang? Oh. I did . . . Okay, I *will* tell it again.

I had a wonderful summer all set up. I'd persuaded the parents of this old girl friend of mine from our acting days at the University of Kentucky that while they were "doing" Spain, they'd be smart to let me stay in the house to keep the windows open and exercise the horses. So I had a mansion on River Road all to myself, and I was happy to be back home in Louisville. I was late finishing my master's thesis on Henry James because I had gotten side-tracked by a novel set in Louisville, but Transylvania College hired me with the understanding that I would finish the thesis before September.

The first thing that hit me was my mother. Coming down the gangplank of the Belle of Louisville after a Saturday night excursion, she tripped and broke a leg. So I had to taxi her all over Louisville in the sleek blue, broken-down Buick Streamliner I had bought in San Diego to cross country, because it suddenly hit me that I was getting too old looking to hitch-hike.

We were over at Mam'maw's for Sunday dinner, along with a slew of relatives, when we got this call from Stillwater, in the mountains of Tennessee. It was me that answered.

"Hollis, they gonna throw me on the chain gang," Cody said, in a whine vibrant with outrage.

Hell, it made *me* mad, too. After three years in the federal penitentiary, looks like Tennessee could forgive and forget. But, no, they were out to clear the books of those old charges.

"Prosecuting attorney said he might can drop the charges," said Cody, "if the people I passed them checks on will settle for restitution."

"Hello, Hollis?" somebody said, in a deep, lush drawl, "your brother could use a little he'p." Turned out to be the prosecuting attorney, Jack Babcock. I asked him how much it all came to, and he said, about one thousand dollars. Knowing I couldn't get a spark with two nickels, I said I'd see what I could do.

He said, "One problem."

I said, "What?"

"They all want Cody's ass," he said. "They wanna be able to take a Sunday drive down the highway and see where Cody's cut the grass."

"Didn't I read about some boys on that chain gang that busted each other's feet with sledge hammers because they'd had more than they could take of that kind of life?"

"They run that story all the way up yonder?"

So I asked him what I *could* do, and he said, "Those people he passed the checks on, they're human. Cody says you gonna be a teacher and all—respectable citizen. Maybe if they got a look at his brother and talked to him. . . ."

I said, okay, and told him I'd see him, and got Cody back on to tell him to take it easy, I was on my way. After I hung up, I wondered what the public prosecutor was doing trying to keep Cody off the chain gang. Then I remembered that it was Cody's talent for worming his way into people's confidence that got him in this fix in the first place. A talent trained to performance by our older brother, Traven.

As for the thousand dollars, all I could scrape up was a hundred to show good faith. My folks are all as poor as the corn patches they left behind in the mountain hollers of Eastern Kentucky, so all they could fork over was the gas money. And I was broke, with no money coming in until October when I'd get my first check from Transylvania, and by that time Cody'd have shackle sores on his ankles. Daddy got Momma to turn loose of a dollar, and he threw that in as *his* share.

For the hundred, I crossed over to some kin we have on the other side of the tracks in Louisville. Whiskey kin. Millionaires, with a horse in every derby at Churchill Downs. Kin who left the hills before we did, rich already off moonshine, who bought into whiskey, then bought out the big shareholders. I never cared much for money myself, but I always wanted to meet those Weavers on an equal social basis—they standing on their bank books, me standing on a Pulitzer prize. But now I had to jump the gun, go to them begging, like I was fresh out of the holler. I used my daddy's name to get in the office—it worked like a password on the secretary, who remembered him well—because when *his* daddy was killed in the mines and his momma died of cancer of the breast a year later, daddy lit out for Louisville, and his rich uncle and all the wealthy Weavers took pity, and every time daddy came around the factory, they'd slip him a fiver, but never a job. Daddy has the same arrangement now with the government: it slips him a twenty each week out of sympathy for his chronic failure to find work.

Great uncle Hollis Weaver didn't bat an eye when I told him my daddy named me after him. But when I told him the story of Cody's life, and showed him a picture, which favored daddy—the big Clark Gable ears, the grin that said, "aw, hell, all I need's a few bucks"—it wasn't long before he was taking me on a tour of the distillery, watching me toss down samplers. And when I walked out the gates, I had a check for a hundred.

So four flats and a new carburetor later, I had passed through one of the worst rain storms ever to hit the Cumberland Mountains and was in Sharpsburg, the first town Cody hit, with a list of victims in my pocket.

I parked in front of the Sharpsburg Family Department store, erected 1813, the same feeling in my stomach I had when I played Biff in a college production of *Death of a Salesman.* It didn't take long to see what they'd do to get a little business. They'd even take a check from a stranger passing through. I was tempted to test this impression, but remembered that Cody already had.

Mr. Overby, the proprietor, leaned against the counter under a big spread-eagle fan that hung from the high, pressed-tin ceiling. Mrs. Overby camped by the cash register. As I imagined Cody viewing this little tableaux, *his* thoughts ran through *my* head. Or were they Traven's? Because according to Cody's version, his big damn brother, Traven, was the one got him into this.

Mr. Overby wants to know if he can help me.

"Sir, my name is Hollis Weaver. I'm Cody Weaver's brother."

By the cash register, Mrs. Overby stirs. "And here I was trying to match you up with some folks from around *here,* cause soon's you come in the door, I knew I'd seen a likeness of that face before."

Then Mr. Overby squints against the glare of noon sunlight in the door and walks around me so he can get me in focus, and when he does, he says, "Cody waltzed in here dressed fit to kill and tried on four suits and took one, and cashed a payroll check."

"But I bet you favor your mother," says Mrs. Overby, her black and white polka-dot rayon dress shimmering in the light.

"Folks *say* I do."

"Because I think it was your walk more than your face. Something about the way Cody walked in here made you drop your guard and like him right away."

"I'm after his ass, myself," says Mr. Overby.

"Fred, daddy's old sign's goin back on the wall if you don't curb your tongue."

"Well, it was the biggest I was ever took, and it just scalds my cheeks to think about it."

"I was in the army at the time, sir," I said, "and then I had to go on with my education, and now I'm about to start teaching, or I would have been here sooner to let you know that I'll do everything in my power to pay you back."

"You gonna make a teacher?"

"Yes, ma'am."

Mr. Overby squinted his eyes, suspicious. "That state investigator told me *you* was a con man, too."

"That's Traven, my older brother."

"How come *you* ain't a crook, too?"

I tried hard to fascinate *him* with an answer to a question most people seem to find fascinating.

Then they ask me if I'm a Christian, and when I tell them how I was saved in a tent on sawdust, they invite me to supper.

For such a tacky store, they had a fine modern ranch style house, but what Mrs. Overby puts on the table is good ol' country food.

We're sitting around talking, and glancing at *Gunsmoke,* and I begin to tell about Cody."He's several years younger than I am. Traven's two years older. So while I was looking up to Traven, I was looking down at Cody. Used to have to take care of him while Momma was working in the cigarette factory and Daddy was in the Sahara in the signal corps. We passed most of our lives in movie theatres, soaking up dreams and nightmares.

"What I wanted to tell you is about stopping off in Springfield, Missouri to visit Cody on my way out to get my master's at the University of San Diego. They wouldn't let me through the gate because it wasn't visiting hours, but when I talked with Cody's psychiatric counselor on the phone and persuaded him it would do Cody good to see his brother, he put in a call to the gate. It's one of the biggest federal penitentiaries, where a lot of the mob leaders end up, but it looks like a state university, and Cody was an impressionable pupil.

"Watching the door for Cody to show, I kept seeing him come through all the different doors in all the different places from the time he was nine: the juvenile detention home, the institutions for wayward children, La Grange reformatory, and now here he was in the big time, like the prison where I visited Traven outside Chicago when I was in the army, enroute to Alaska. Well, here come Cody through the door, grinning and waving, and he gives me a shake and a hug, and we talk about old times on the streets of Louisville—the smell of the tobacco factories (which was right there in the Luckies I brought him) and the beer plants, the distilleries, and the big bakeries. Ah, well, let's not go into that. It was just so sad, it hurt all the way to San Diego."

"Let's do with*out Gunsmoke* one night," says Mrs. Overby, twisting the knob. Mr. Overby sunk in his chair like he'd been wounded.

"Anyway, a few months ago, I stopped off in El Reno, Oklahoma where they'd transferred him because they said he was cured of his 'nerves,' as he called it, and ought to learn a trade: how to make brooms. But before he got to fastening on the sweeping part, he flew off the handle and broke some guy's jaw." But I didn't tell the Overbys *why:* the joker wanted to be Cody's buddy after lights out. Cody's got a hair-trigger temper. Good thing the only tools of his trade were a fountain pen and a book of blank checks.

"In El Reno, they had Cody on tranquillizers and it broke me up, because he moved and talked like a zombie. What was worrying him was that Tennessee had a retainer on him for a whole string of checks he passed on his way into Georgia. Straddling the two states was what brought in the F.B.I. Georgia was satisfied with the three years, to cover the one check in Athens. But Tennessee wants to bring him to trial."

What Cody had hoped was that Tennessee wouldn't want to go to the expense of being there at the gate when he stepped out of the federal pen. But on that bright morning, there they stood.

For one thing, Cody wanted to track down Traven and get even with him somehow. Traven had just come out of a Texas prison, full of religion, and somehow he had got hold of a Mack truck and a tent and had gone on a faith-healing tour. I hope he's serious.

"You see, it was my older brother Traven that led Cody astray. How it happened was this: Cody had been out of the reform school for a year and doing all right, playing ball, in fact, and getting scouts interested in his pitching. He had one problem: an eye that was blinking out on him. How did he get *that?* The scar still shows where Traven hit him with a baseball bat when we were little. It was raining outside, so we were doing a dry run in the living room, with me pitching the imaginary ball, Traven at bat, with a real bat, and Cody, age three, catching. Traven swung back and Cody began to scream and hold his head and roll in a spreading puddle of blood. A week later, he slipped while walking a railroad track and broke the stitches. A month later, he fell off his tricycle and busted open the nearly healed wound. So he had a good pitching arm, but one strike against him: a bad eye. And the last I heard he was going deaf in one ear. The prison psychiatrist promised me the chain gang would drive him totally insane."

Mrs. Overby cried and I got to crying, too, and Mr. Overby kept saying, in a friendly way, "I'm gonna have his ass in a sling."

After Mr. Overby had gone to bed, Mrs. Overby told me the story of her life, harping on the theme of childlessness. She made me promise not to write her up in a story.

The next morning, Mr. Overby took me down to his favorite filling station and had them fill me up on his credit card, and as I idled the motor, about to set out for Stillwater, he leaned on the window and said, "You tell that prosecutor, okay, I'll settle for the money, and you tell Cody, it was just that it hurt mine and Mrs. Overby's feelings so much that he'd do us that way, after we took to him the way we did."

In Carsonville, a truck full of fresh peaches was backed up to the curb in front of the courthouse. As soon as I talked with Mr. Crigger, proprietor of the Red Dot Cafe, I was going to get me one of those sweet Georgia peaches from just over the line, maybe two. The waitress behind the counter had a bottom like two clinging halves of a plump peach, and when I see home-made peach cobbler on the menu, I order it first. But what I bit into was Melba peaches from a can. I resisted pointing out the irony of it to the waitress because Mr. Crigger, thin as a hopeless T.B. case, is sitting on a high stool behind the cash register looking right at me. Then he's staring. Then he gets down off the stool and lopes on his long legs out to the sidewalk and crosses the street. I got the funny notion he was going for fresh peaches to make me a decent pie. But a few minutes later, Mr. Crigger comes back and sits down again and does a bad job of acting nonchalant, and a deputy walks in and sits right beside me, no better an actor than Mr. Crigger. The deputy seems aware his performance is weak, but he goes at it with a kind of aw-hell attitude. After I pass him the sugar he asks for and he's got it thoroughly stirred up, he says, "You just passing through?"

I give it to him straight, and he gives Crigger a false-toothed grin. "Hey, Ef, this here's that Cody's brother!"

"Well, 'i God, I tell you, it was that walk that throwed me."

"Ef thought we'd caught you. Hey, Ef, didn't I tell you they had Cody in the Stillwater jail?"

While Crigger leaned against the counter with a gleaming coffee urn behind him, I started in on them. But they were awful cynical and tough. After a while, I wasn't following the waitress' peachy bottom, I was sweating. I felt ashamed, guilty, and cheap, like the time I was twelve, ushering at the Rodeo Theatre and I walked off the job in the middle of the tenth showing of *The Razor's Edge* and struck out for India and ended up in Atlanta, bumming for eating money. It picked up a little when I got to the part Mrs. Overby's tears had cut short: how Traven got Cody *into* this fix.

". . . . so just when Cody got the word that his physical defects ruled him out of a career in baseball, along comes Traven, just finished with a stretch in Montana. Momma's sick and has to have a breast tumor removed. She's in the hospital and it's Mother's Day, which Cody never fails to observe, and she's lying up there worrying how she's gonna pay the bills, and Traven puts his arm around Cody, and starts in on what a hard life he and Cody have given Momma. They owe it to her to take care of those bastards that're worrying her to death with bills." They salute the Mother-flag as I run it up the pole, and I realize I'm consciously trying to manipulate their responses, so when I got the waitress crying and Mr. Crigger said, "Jo Ann, you get back in the kitchen with that bellering! Can't hear what the man's saying," I knew I had them. "So," I says, "he tells Cody about this perfect method of passing checks without getting caught, which he learned from some guy on his cellblock in Montana. He steals a check-making gismo from RCA, and they hit the highway. Traven's method worked fine for Traven. You didn't see *him,* did you, Mr. Crigger? No, he let Cody pass the checks. So Cody spent three years in the pen, hating Traven's guts. Before that, all Cody had done was refuse to go to school (because, as it turned out, he could hardly see or hear) and swipe a few things."

They all shook their heads, and there was good ol' Jo Ann, leaning in the service window, shaking hers.

"Jo Ann was here," said Mr. Crigger, "weren't you, Jo Ann?"

"Yeah, I was here. I been telling you for three years he wasn't a bad kid."

"Cody caught me on a Saturday night just before closing and I just did have the two hundred fifty dollars to break his check," Mr. Crigger reminisced. "Said he had to get on home, 'cause his momma was in the hospital and he'd already missed Mother's Day, and a more pitiful sight, I never—"

"And you fell for it," says the deputy.

"You needn't rub it in."

"What would it have to be 'fore you could smell what it was?"

"Listen," Crigger leaned toward me. "I almost died of the T.B. last winter, and I know what being shut up in a room is, so I say, turn him loose. But not before I see that money. Who needs revenge? I got hospital bills to pay."

The deputy went out with me and leaned on the parking meter while I got started, and as I pulled away, going toward Mt. Galilee, I blinked at the red violation flag under the deputy's elbow.

In Mt. Galilee, twenty miles down the line, I pulled into Pap's Service Station, where Pap's eating his lunch out of a turn-of-the-century lunch pail. I told him I hated to interrupt his lunch but that I was Cody Weaver's brother and wanted to assure him that I'd make good the check Cody passed on him three years ago. He didn't even let me get started on my little softener.

"A body gets what he deserves," says Pap. "Any son-of-a-bitch greedy enough to take in a big check like that from a stranger just for an oil change *ought* to suffer. Well, I did. I suffered two hundred dollars worth, plus the oil, plus the skin off my knuckles where the wrench slipped on that damned oil pan plug. I learned *my* lesson, so I figure he ought to learn *his.*"

"He has been, sir, for three years. And the psychiatrist at El Reno told me that if Cody went on that chain gang, it would kill him, he'd lose his mind." Then I got it in about the threat of mental illness and how Cody was right on the edge now.

"Hell, let him *talk* his way off the chain gang. I never heard such a line as that boy lassoed *me* with, and I ain't about to hear another one such as that, because I ain't sitting still long enough for somebody's brother to get started." I'm leaning against the soft drink box, absorbing the delicate chill through my fanny. I'm about to break the silence by going, when he says, "Come in here grinning like he was my long lost nephew. Why, if he'd wanted to be saddled with it, I bet he could have conned me out of the whole damned filling station, and my uniform throwed in." Then he laughs and slaps his crossed arms, hard, like he's giving himself a friendly whipping. That's where I slipped in with the story of Cody's life, stressing the bad influences, but also the loneliness.

"And talk about filling stations, sir, something about them always drew him to them, I don't know what. Maybe *you* do. Loved to watch the racks go up and shosh down when he's little, and press the button on the air hose. He'd sneak into car junk yards and play all day, trying out the driver's seats and turning the moldy keys and looking through shattered windshields at imaginary six-lane highways. He wandered around a lot, up and down streets and cobblestone alleys of Louisville, alone, looking for buried treasure in the trash cans. And one time I was on a streetcar and I looked out as it turned around at this little park and there he sat on Daniel Boone's head, like a little pigeon."

For some reason, that part of the story got to Pap more than the rest, and he says, "Son, I'll have me a talk with that prosecutor, and if he convinces me that Cody's got it in him to reform himself, I'll drop the charges and settle for restitution. . . . Now sit down and have a big orange with me." He splits his peanut butter and apple jelly sandwich with me, too. Then he points the nozzle of his orange drink at me and asks, "They's just one thing I want to get straight. How come your brothers end up convicts and you turn out a teacher and a story writer?"

I tell him all about it, and he loves it, and skips back in out of the sun from filling up cars to turn me on again. When I told him that a blank page can be just as exciting and alluring as an open road, and, provided that page doesn't bear the name of a bank, you won't end up in a cell, he said, "Son, you a card."

I'm in my car, the motor running, ready to head for Stillwater, and I tell him to keep an eye out for my name as scriptwriter on some TV show, and when I say it might well be a western, he slaps the hood like he's putting the seal of certainty on it. As I'm driving away, he yells, "You get that boy out of there and you bring him by here to see me, you hear?"

Taking the manager of the Western Auto store in Stillwater, where Cody had cashed a check by putting ten dollars down on a plastic rowboat and requested delivery to 2395 Sweetcreek Road, was difficult at first, but once I convinced him that he wasn't the damn fool he apparently thought himself to be for having swallowed Cody's story, it was smooth sailing. Louis Carpetti was a bachelor who had volunteered to take the store in Stillwater and put it back on its feet, but he was homesick for the Bronx, and when I started going over the high moments in several of the Broadway shows of the late forties, he was fighting tears. When I showed up, he was closing the doors, so when we parted, it was in front of the drugstore, where I had a pineapple shake and he had a cherry smash.

By then it was twilight, so I drove around the square and saw the light in the barred windows upstairs over the jailhouse, catty-corner behind the courthouse.

Cody must have been looking and listening for me all day, because just as I shut off the motor, he shows at the window, grinning, barechested, his pants hanging loosely on his hips, his navel black. "Hey, Hollis, where'd you get that carrrrr, good buddy!"

In the soft Tennessee summer twilight, I guess that long baby blue body with the silver trimming looked like what he'd dreamed about in his cell, but in San Diego broad daylight, I got *took* for 500 bucks.

Cody yells, "Come on up, Hollis," like all I had to do was simply walk in, climb up.

On the screened-in porch, a woman in a starched cotton lavender dress sat on a rusty glider, snapping and stringing pole beans, dropping them into a black iron pot clamped between her ankles. On the floor beside the screen sat a girl of about 15 in denim shorts and a pink rayon blouse that had a wide collar, billowed in the sleeves and fastened tight at the wrists. Two top buttons were unbuttoned, showing her white brassiere, and she was bare-foot, but between her legs she was polishing her majorette boots white.

"Majel," the woman says, "if I was you, I'd worry about them white streaks on the porch before your daddy gets back."

Majel hears me shuffling on the steps and looks right up at me over her shoulder, stretching that rayon over her breasts. "Momma, they's a man at the door."

"Looking for the sheriff, ma'am."

"He's wandering over the county som'mers."

"When's visiting hours?"

"Who you looking for?"

"My brother, Cody Weaver."

Majel jerks her head around and looks up at me.

"Majel, it's Cody's brother."

She sees I am.

"You come all the way from Louisville, Kentucky?"

"Yes, ma'am."

"Well, you get yourself in here and go see your brother. That poor thing's been hanging on that window for days. Majel, get up from there and show Cody's brother where to go."

Majel reaches back, pulls herself up by the screen door handle, and starts slapping off down a dark hallway on her bare feet before I can get the screen open. I stepped over the boots and caught up with her.

"I bet you look cute in those majorette boots."

"By god, I better, if I go all the way to Knoxville to compete in that baton twirling convention, by god, I better look cute, and then some."

In the dim hallway, all I can see are her pink rayon blouse and a silver-painted door that she stops at, and when she stands up on tip-toe to reach something on the top ledge of the door, a crescent of pink panties winks at me in the twilight that filters through the bedroom curtains across the hall. Then I smelled her. "I bet you been practicing all day."

"Now, ain't I?"

What she came down from the ledge with was a long key that she shoved into the lock, and like a baton twirler, she gives it a twist and yanks the door open.

She says, "Same key fits the one at the head of the stairs," and before I realize what she's doing, I've got the key in my hand and she's stepping aside for me. "And listen, tell Cody to watch out for my daddy when he whistles while I'm practicing."

"Don't you reckon it preys on their minds to see you leaping around on the lawn in that outfit?"

"Well, ain't it better than nothing? Besides, I gotta practice with a audience, don't I?"

"Why, sure."

I went on up, and there at the barred door stands Cody, posing for the millionth cliché photograph of the prisoner, hands clutching the bars. I unlock the door, step inside, lock it again, and drop the key in my pocket. Cody gives me a big hug and then we shake hands. "Well, Hollis," he says, looking me in the eye, "they really out to get me this time," with that tone of infinite injury. "They jumped me soon's I stepped through the gate at El Reno. Damned man from the T.B.I. and Sheriff Thompson."

"Brought you some stuff," I said, and gave him a bag full of Luckie samplers Momma sent, a pack of Wrigley Spearmint gum, a Milky Way and a *True.*

"Thanks. But I can't hardly read, I'm so nervous." In Springfield and El Reno, he read all the Thomas Wolfe he could round up, because he knew Wolfe was my hero when I was about thirteen, and though I'd switched to Joyce long ago, he always liked to make sentimental allusions to Wolfe. He tried writing, too. War stories, at first, because he'd been in the Marines when he was fifteen and got kicked out, and he thought war stories would sell easy. Later, he wrote some things about kids in trouble and asked me to send them off for him and we'd split the profit, because he knew it would make the best seller list since it was all true.

A fat man wearing nothing but a pair of overalls, his arm in a sling, one eye puffed with mosquito poison, walked around, munching on a Moon Pie, sipping a Dr. Pepper that he tucked under his good arm between sips. Under the windows is a row of cots, and on one of them lies a boy of about nine, on another sits a boy about eleven, who looks at me with mellow curiosity. "Hey, Cody, that your brother?" yells the older one.

"That one shot his mother," Cody tells me, with a melodramatic look. "Yeah, Tom, he's my brother." Then he turns back to me. "Other one's his little brother, Billy."

"You gonna get Cody off the chain gang Mister?" asks Billy.

"I'm gonna try," I say, feeling silly.

"*I* heard they was going to 'lectricute him," says Tom.

"I let him talk that way," Cody says, his voice low, full of long-faced compassion, "to take his mind off what they might do to *him*. She wasn't really his mother—foster mother. She's laying over there in the hospital and they don't expect her to live. See, Tom and Billy's orphans—I mean the court took 'em away from their real mother, who's a two-bit whore in a little town down the mountain. So the county farmed them out to this old man and his young wife that run a chicken farm, and it was like slave labor. They'd get up at five and work till dark, and what they had to eat was scraps when the man and his wife got full. And least little thing, she'd burn'em up with a belt. So finally, Tom got tired of seeing his little brother covered with welts, so he slipped out with the old man's shotgun one evening, and climbed up on the roof of the chicken house, and told Billy to call the woman out, and when she stepped out on the back steps, cussing and wanting to know what he wanted, Tom let her have it."

"Blamed jolt of it nearly flipped me off the roof," says Tom, who's been straining to hear. "I reckon she'll keep her face-slappin' hands *off* my brother."

Cody tosses a Luckie sampler between Tom's legs. Billy jumps up on his cot and dives onto Tom's, grabbing for the cigarettes. Tom holds the pack high over his head. "Ut, ut, ut, watch it, watch it, damn it!" Tom slides off the cot and slaps around on the concrete floor bare-foot, dancing around, holding the cigarettes up out of Billy's reach. "Wait, just a minute, Billy, don't grab. Cody ain't offered *you* nothing."

"Give 'em one," says Cody, watching them closely, smiling.

"Okay, stop, just stop pawing at me a minute," says Tom and starts to take one from the pack but Billy grabs it out of his hands and runs with it and slips in the slime by the open shower stall against the opposite wall before Tom can even get started chasing him.

Tom and Cody laugh, and the man in overalls stops pacing and looks at me. "They ain't no peace and quiet in this place either," he says, like that's what *I* came for.

Billy starts bellering, getting up very slowly, the pack squashed tightly in his little fist, cigarettes strewn around him. "Ha, ha, ha, ha, ha," sings Tom, "lit-tle Billy busted his buh-utt!" Tom laughs so hard he starts to stagger, then tosses himself on the cot and rocks, his feet kicking in the air. Billy cries and picks up each cigarette carefully, looking at his brother between each one. "You better hush," he keeps saying. "Better huh-ush."

Then Billy walks calmly over to the picnic table in the corner and picks up a Dr. Pepper bottle from a Royal Crown bench and whizzes it at the cot and it shatters against the stone wall a foot above Tom's head. I shake the glass off the front of my shirt and it twinkles weakly in the dim light of the three bulbs, speckled with horse flies, that dangle from the ceiling.

Tom, his body frozen in the rocking position, looks at Billy with mock awe and astonishment, then slowly gets up. "All right, by god, all right, by god, now you're going *to get it.*"

"Well . . . . Well . . . . Well . . . . Well, you made me slip and bust my ass, didn't you?"

"I'm gonna beat the living hell out of you," says Tom, spacing each word.

Tom chased Billy for almost five minutes, *all over* the big bull-pen. Watching such a burst of energy was so tiring I had to sit down. The severely carved initials on the top of the school desk I sat on made designs on my buttocks.

"They should-a drowned the little bastards," says the man in overalls, philosophically, "the day they was borned," and he goes into the toilet booth in the far corner, slamming the door. When Billy slams into the partition, the man says, "I'm gonna *kill* me a couple of hellions 'dreckly."

Billy cracks his knee against the iron frame of a cot and doubles over in pain, and Tom catches up with him and starts slapping his head and face. Cody watches every movement, becoming so absorbed his mouth goes slack and his eyes get bleary and then I realize the performance has *me* hypnotized, too.

"I'll kill you, you sonofabitching low-life bastard," says Billy, slugging into Tom. Tom slaps him until his arms weary, and then he walks away, leaving Billy shuddering with screaming on the cot.

"Tom!" a woman calls from out in the yard below.

He goes to the window, panting, red from exertion in the humid air. "Ma'am?"

"Are you beating on Billy again?"

"Yes, ma'am."

"Well, quit it!"

"Yes, ma'am, I will."

Tom had the cigarettes again, lit one, offered Cody one, then me, but I don't smoke, and then he tapped the toilet door. "Hey, Pete, your momma allow you to smoke yet?"

"Better not get close enough for me to smack you."

"She's coming over." He tossed one over the top of the booth.

Billy had stopped screaming at the top of his lungs, and shifted into low.

"Cry baby," says Tom, passing Billy's cot. He lies down on his own and smokes.

Cody was still in a zombie-like state from all the narcotics they had given him at El Reno and from present fear and nervousness. The charm he had turned on his victims was deeply submerged. I told him what I had gotten done that day, and he had a sullen, resentful, bitter word for each of his victims. "Now, Cody, they want to help you. Why shouldn't they want their money, too? *Before,* they were more interested in your hide." When it finally soaked in that their attitude could keep him off the chain gang, he sneered at their gullibility. That annoyed me. I began to defend them. I reminded him of the visit the man from Western Auto had paid him. "He said you just wised off at him." Cody denied it, tried to blame Mr. Carpetti, suggested he and the Judge were friends and out to get him. "He said you called him an s.o.b."

"Liar."

"He said you did, now Cody."

Cody looked shocked. "Would you believe a stranger 'fore you'd believe your own brother?" We were sitting on his cot and he scooted down a little so he could register his shock more dramatically. He wasn't consciously conning me, he was just reaching for the available clichés. If he detected the slightest blood disloyalty—as he did then—he would go into a profound sulk. You could have sliced the silence with a jackknife, until Pete ambles out of the toilet-booth and lies down in the 40 watt light and smokes.

Billy's whimpering. Tom gets up and goes over and sits on Billy's cot and pats him on the shoulder. "Poor ol' Billy, come on, honey, don't cry, come on now. You hear?" He lights a cigarette and leans over and tries to look into Billy's face, stroking him with one hand, offering the cigarette with the other, crooning, "Don't cry, little Billy boy, don't criiiii." Billy pulls the covers over his head. Tom goes back to his cot. From under the covers, Billy says, "Wait'll I tell the judge. I hope they *do* 'lectricute you."

"Didn't I say I was sorry?"

Cody smiles and looks at me. "Who they remind you of?" I pretended not to see it, because I didn't want to go over it. "Me and you, when we was little, and you used to beat hell out of me for something, and then. . . ." That started it. So I sat at the head of his cot, my back against the stone wall, and Cody, half-reclined on the rest of the cot, talked in a resonant, mellow voice about our childhood in Louisville, still pronouncing certain words in the childish way he had. It embarrassed me to listen to it at first, because I am afflicted with a terrible nostalgia. Sometimes I have seizures of nostalgia at night that hurt. One night I was sleeping in the lush grass by the shore under a beached boat in the Russian fishing village of Ninilchik on the Kenai Peninsula in Alaska, and I woke up to take a leak. As I looked across the water at an extinct volcano, bathed in that strange northern light, an intuition of my whole childhood rushed over me. Now I remember that *Alaskan* moment with a strange sadness and melancholy of its own.

Psychiatrists would say we had a traumatic childhood, and I guess the broken home, the bad environment, and all that, had the predictable effect on Traven and Cody, but *I* remember none of it with anything but affection. Traven was nine when Daddy started drinking and staying gone three days at a stretch, so he didn't even have to live through the worst part as a little kid the way Cody and I did. But we were depression babies, and Traven and I had to carry our lunches in a lard pail, with our own milk in a Mason jar, and I guess it was supposed to be humiliating. Traven, anyway, realizing that a boy deserved something better, would steal cans of pineapple from the A & P and at the lunch table he would pull them out and, with a big taunting smile on his face like the Joker in Batman comics, he'd open a can with a little stolen can opener and eat the pineapple and smack his lips while the well-to-do kids watched in envy. Traven takes after my daddy: get what you can out of people with as little effort as possible, but if things go wrong, don't blame anybody, don't feel malice, resentment, or hatred. Daddy took to drink, and Traven took to the con game as ways of dealing with life, and both of them take things as they come. But Cody takes after my mother, seems like.

She had a good life in St. Louis when she was a girl, up till she was about sixteen, then the depression hit my gran-daddy who was doing well in the tree surgery business, and they started going down, and had to return to Louisville, till one day he shot himself, and Momma had to go to work in a cafe, and she met this handsome, soft-spoken easy-going fellow from the mountains, and he turned out not to be much count, so she ended up with the attitude that the world had betrayed her, men in particular. Raised three boys during the depression and the war, while Daddy was in the signal corps, and every chance she could, she played the angle that she was a poor little woman whose husband had more or less deserted her. It just so happens that she did put up a good fight and people admired her for it, and Cody loves her more than anything on earth. Just before he left El Reno, he almost went berserk worrying about her, and they had to let him talk to her on the telephone to pacify him. He was worried about her now because of the broken leg.

Well, the kind of childhood we had, you'd think you'd want to forget, but even when I was six years old, I used to go to sleep after a ritual in two parts: first, I'd review my life until I sensed I was about to go to sleep, then I'd stop, and pick it up the next night like a serial, and then I'd talk to God in a chummy way, and that's how I'd drift off. So Cody in his cell stirred all that up in me.

"And remember that time we went to the show and the ticket man grabbed me as I ran in and ripped my shirt off and you picked up a cigarette butt urn and threatened to frail him? He thought I was going in without a ticket but I was so eager to see the next chapter of Spy Smasher that I just raced on in, and you screamed at him for tearing my only good shirt, and then when I wouldn't leave after the show was over, you started pulling at me and slapping me and I was screaming in the lobby and some man came up and said he was going to beat hell out of you if you didn't quit slapping that sweet little boy—*me.* Ha! Remember?"

I'd never forgotten. I says, "Yeah, and remember," trying to steer him my way, "that creek we always crossed on the way to the show?"

"Yeah. Fartso, the whale."

"The who?" Tom is lying on his stomach, his face propped in his hands, listening to us.

"Hollis used to tell me there was this whale named Fartso—"

"It was Traven told *me.*"

"—that lived in the creek and we'd throw popcorn down to him, and I kept trying to see him. That went on for five years, me believing there really was a whale that would give you presents if you were good."

"Hey, Tom," says Billy, peeling the blanket off his face, "you remember that ghost horse you used to tell *me* about, and you said it was going to come some night and take me and you away from the orphanage?"

"Shhhh," says Tom. "Can't you hear it? He's outsyonder eating Mrs. Thompson's morning glories."

Billy jumps up and leans on the sill and looks out through the bars: "Hey, where? Hey, where at?"

"Ahhhhhh. The springs popping in your cot scared him away."

"You ought to heard the stories Hollis used to tell me and Traven when he was little. We slept in the same bed and we'd get under the quilts and Hollis'd tell us stories about Buck Jones and Zorro and Straight-hair and Fatsy—Laurel and Hardy. They'd forget to put on their clothes in the morning—Straight-hair and Fatsy—and get on the streetcar and these old ladies would say, 'Eow! Butts and do-dos!'"

"Hey, mister, if I turn out the lights, will you tell *us* a story?" Billy's standing up in his cot, looking at me, his eyes bright.

"Yeah, mister," says Tom. "Tell us a story, tell us a story."

"Hate to get started and have to go. It's dark outside, and I reckon they're ready to kick me out."

"Hell," says Tom. "You could sleep *here,* far as that goes. Folks passing through stay the night here all the time. Sheriff Thompson's a good ol' feller."

"Go ahead, Hollis," says Cody. "Tell one, like you used to."

Billy giggles and runs the length of the room, leaping into the air to catch the light cords until all three lights and faces blink out and only the bright moon looks in. The room stinks of stale pee and clogged drains and dirty, fetid clothes and feet and beds, and more than a century of sweat and mustiness, and from the stove below comes the smell of kale simmering and coal smoke. It smells like poverty, lulls me like marijuana—the smell we grew up in.

Says Tom, "Make it a ghost story."

"Ouuuu," says Billy, and jumps over Cody's cot and climbs under the wool blanket with his brother.

"Get ready for bed first."

They shuck off their shorts and snuggle in. Pete's under the covers, too, his back like a wall. Cody smokes Louisville cigarettes and I get set to tell it. I don't know any ghost stories by heart, so I make one up as I go along, about a blood-stained carpet. Billy and Tom are chewing gum, popping and smacking, till I reach a scarey part, and they stop and the gum lolls out on the tip of their tongues in the moonlight. Cody stops smoking, a long ash on his cigarette, and Pete turns over and looks straight at me, his eyes glazed, and in the pause, we hear cars outside in the distance rumble over bridges, and dogs bark, off in the trees.

Near the climax, a key turns in the lock and slowly, responding to the moonlight and the hush and the smell that softened all his movements, the Sheriff walks in. His head bumps a light bulb, and he's slender, a little bent, and wears a gun, slack on his hip. I pause while we watch him amble to the foot of Pete's cot.

"Pete, I been a-lookin' all day fer that gun. I'm wore out."

"Well, Frank, I been studying that over. No use in you hunting and hunting. Hell, I mize well show you where I thew the damn thing."

"Okay, bright and early we'll go out there."

"Shhhhh," says Tom, his finger to his lips. The Sheriff turns slowly and looks at him. "Cody's brother's trying to tell us the finish of a ghost story."

"Well, I *thought* they was somebody sitting in the dark there."

"Let him tell it, Sheriff," says Billy.

"Well, *I* ain't stopping nobody."

But he just sort of dangles there in the moonlight, so I ease back into the story, and the next thing I know, he's sitting on the foot of Pete's cot, listening. Just as the blood-stained Persian rug raises up and smothers the killer, the Sheriff's wife calls up the stairs for him to come to bed.

"You welcome to stay," the Sheriff says, and I say, thanks, and he locks us all in, and as he's going down the stairs, he says, "Goodnight, Baby Jo," and a voice on the other side of the wall calls out, "Goodnight, Sheriff."

"Goodnight, Baby Jo!" yells Billy.

And they all yell goodnight back and forth, and I figure Baby Jo is a Negro.

I took a cot, and Billy was asleep, curled up against his brother, who fell asleep just as I looked his way, and Pete was gone, and Cody, doped with the past, said, "See you in the morning," and I said, "Night," and in a few 'drecklies night was in us all.

Next morning, a backfiring truck woke me, and when I looked out the window, it was a peach truck, so I sneaked down to the square, using the key in my pocket, and got a sack full, and left all but one on the picnic table, and quietly locked Cody in the cell and put the key above the silver-painted door.

The white kitchen door stood open at the end of the hall, and Majel's bending over a round table, taking a last sup of coffee, already setting the cup down as she swings her hip out to miss the curve, and she comes at me fast, the fluffy pompons bouncing on her snow-white boots, the luscious ruffles on her low cut, white cotton, fresh-ironed blouse waving as she bounces, one arm held stiff by a blue suitcase, and I thought she was going to run me down, but she tucks the baton under her arm as she gets to me and gives me a glancing kiss and a flick of her hip as she rushes on, and what she tosses over her shoulder is, "I'd love to give you a *preview*, but I'm about to miss my bus to Knoxville." When I get to the porch screen, she's aiming for the open door of a greyhound, twirling her baton like a buzz saw.

I started out walking to look for the county prosecutor's office. Somebody directed me down a steep hill from the square to an old white, wooden house. Grass stood high in the front yard and grasshoppers flew up as I went along the walk. Two black and white spotted dogs on the porch lifted their heads and started raising hell. A window shoots up to my right and a man sticks out his head, says, "Ace, I reckon you and Hoppy want me to dump another spittoon on your heads! Now hush!" in a voice louder than the dogs. His black-streaked gray hair stirred up on his head, his face red as a beet, his eyes swollen, his lips whitish—the look of him makes me turn away, sure I've got somebody's house, not a lawyer's office, but he says, "What *you* want so early?" and I say, "This where Jack Babcock's office is?"

"It's his bedroom till the office opens. You didn't fiddle around getting here, did you? Cody goes before Judge Stumbo Monday at two."

"Oh, you know who I—"

"With that face and that walk? Swing around the porch to the side door."

He comes to the door in wrinkled trousers and a white shirt open to his navel, showing a hairy pot, and the smell of him hits me below the belt.

"They all described him by his walk, and when I saw him amble into the courtroom with Sheriff Thompson for the indictment, I knew why. Half-cocky, half-friendly, half-better-look-out."

What I walked into was the image of an old-time law office, full of old-fashioned furniture, and what he pointed to when he said, "Sit down, Hollis," was an old cracked-leather couch. I felt Babcock's warm sleep in the seat of my pants. He went into the bathroom.

And when he comes out again, he has on a tie and his hair's combed perfectly, parted almost in the middle, with a wave on one side, and two cups of coffee steam, as if by magic, in his hands. I take one as he blows at his coffee and lets his broad butt and pot belly sink into the leather cushion.

"How's Cody?"

"Well, just waiting, sir."

"Aren't we all!"

I didn't look at him.

"Cody tells me you're a writer."

"I do write, yes, sir."

"Jack. I'm Jack, and you're Hollis, okay?"

"Okay, Jack."

"See all them books that's got you surrounded?"

"Law books?"

"Full, chock full of stories."

So he took me on a two hour tour of legal documents containing vivid testimony concerning various sexual exploits from mere exposure to rape, from 1821 to 1956, and then he shows me a revolver he used on a German prisoner near Buchenwald, and says, "Write a story about *that.*" And running all through it like a thread is Cody, and I imagined not only that Jack had done a production for *him,* but that I was merely an affable stand-in for a re-run.

Then we steered straight onto Cody, with Jack interrogating me about Cody's background, till his eyes were misty. "Steam from the cup," he said, blowing on the cold coffee. "But don't depend on Cody's sad story with Judge Stumbo. The first fact you got to face is that Stumbo's been to the end of the line and come back. The gooks chopped off his son's head in Korea, and if you see a sporty little red Ford convertible, that's all the old man's got left. And second fact is that he's *always* been mean, and he hates my guts almost as much as I hate his."

"Then I'm afraid even to ask you—"

"Asking's free."

"Whether you think he'll let me pay off these people a little at a time through the next year or so out of my teacher's pay."

"Hollis, we may as well kiss Cody goodbye."

When Saturday morning country people started coming in to see him, I told Jack I'd see him later.

By the time I got back up to the top of the hill, I was dizzy with the heat. The sun glanced off cars and pickup trucks parked rib to rib facing the courthouse and in the outer square facing the stores.

As though duty-bound to authenticate the cliché, old men were parked hip to hip on the benches around the courthouse, talking, spitting, whittling, gazing silently out from the hub of law, order, tradition, and sloth, sitting in the cool, under skyscraper oak trees that spread out so lush at the top they covered the clock-face in the tower.

"Hey, there, Weaver, you got any more of them ghost stories?" Through the leaves of a low-hanging, spread-fingered limb of the oak, I saw Sheriff Thompson leaning on the sill of a wide window, smoking, waving. I laughed and waved, and he chuckled and glanced around to someone deep in the cavey-cool and dark of the office and dusted his cigarette on the ground, where no grass grew. His clothes were a little wrinkled and slouchy but he had the ghost of Gary Cooper going for him. Then to his side, suddenly, steps a man in severely ironed and creased khaki uniform, and a glistening leather belt and holster and slick yellow hair give him a corseted look, and he waves me in.

"Come to get your brother off the chain gang. Right?" says the well-groomed cop, as I come in the door.

"To put it subtly, yes."

"I *told* you he was a card," says the Sheriff. "Weaver, this is Mr. McCoy of the Tennessee Bureau of Investigation. Me and him was the ones went to Oklahoma to bring back your brother."

"And me and Cody," says McCoy, "were the ones nursed this old coot back to life. Broke down on us in Kansas City and we had to sit around a hospital room three days before we could come on in."

"Sit around ever' Kansas City bar and strip joint ever was, you mean, while *I* was *dy*ing."

"I never heard *this* story," I says, so they tell it, together, with the precision, pace, and thrust of a duet.

"But my advice to *you,* son," says McCoy "is to turn around and go right back to Louisville. Number One, that brother of yours is a habitual criminal. Guys can murder once, and stop. They can rob and stop, sooner or later. But you take your check passer or a con man, they don't *never* give it up. So you may as well give up on your brother, now as later."

"Well, I think there's hope for Cody. I know what you mean, Mr. McCoy. Traven's like that, but Cody can be saved. Traven can't. Cody's in it out of bewilderment—always getting the world's signals crossed. But Traven's in it for love. And it's the *only* love he knows."

"This your older brother?"

"Yeah."

"Ain't no love 'tween Cody and *him.* That long ride back, all I heard was how Cody was gonna make Traven sorry."

"We all got tickled, thinking up ways he could do it," says the Sheriff, "and it two a.m. on the highway and me sick as a hog in the back seat."

"You know, I once asked Traven, since he never seems to get away with it, why he does it—passes checks and stuff."

"It's the thrill of it," says McCoy.

"That's what *he* said."

"Hell, I didn't have to *ask* him."

"Way *he* put it was, 'You walk into a store and you fox a man into your confidence and you charm the money out of his pocket, and when I walk out,' he says, 'I feel great. It's not the money. Look,' he says, 'I take a chance. When I lose, that's *my* tough luck. Next time, I'll know how to get away with it.' He's never bitter toward—toward you guys, or the people who bring charges, or the prison officials. It's just tough, and that's his attitude."

"I like a guy with a good attitude, don't you, Frank?"

"I pre*fer* 'em."

I didn't go into Cody's attitude, how he's always, since he was little, felt the injustice of it all. Somehow or other, somebody has sold him out, led him astray; it's not his fault; he can't help it; it all started when he was too young to control it. The evidence in his favor is overwhelming. Besides, that's what he's been told all his life. And he believes everything he's told, by this authority and that—by me, and by Traven, and by books, and by ads, slogans, salutes, pledges, promises, all the home truths. But when he rams his hand into one of those Christmas stockings up to the elbow and the smell of what's in it hits him, he gets that look on his face of awed surprise and hurt.

I say, "Another thing about Traven. One time when he was just out, and I was going to the University of Kentucky, we took a ride through the old neighborhood and parked in front of the house, the one out of about twenty-five that we grew up in, where we lived the longest and had the most fun, set between the railroad underpass and the cigarette factory where Momma still works—the house where he broke open Cody's head with a baseball bat (but that's another story)—and I says, 'Well, Traven, I hope you've given it up for good.' 'Hollis,' he says, solemnly, 'I've learned my lesson. I'm through. I'd rather die than go back.' I says, 'You know, Traven, the thing that's always scared me is that when the F.B.I. is tracking you, you might take to a gun, and—' By the red light of the semaphore above us, I saw the hurt look on his face. 'Hollis! You think your own brother'd do a thing like that?' He likes to keep his image in as sharp a focus as the next man.

"At the time, he had a job driving a truck on a run to Texas. It paid well. He even urged me to accept a little loan of twenty bucks. A week later, they caught him smuggling marijuana back over the border."

A Negro boy of about eighteen shows up in the door with a sickle in his hand. "I'm about to cut, Mr. Frank."

"You can't cut those weeds in this heat, Baby Jo." It was the boy the sheriff had spoken to last night as he went down. Turned out, he was an orphan that they let sleep in the jail and do odd jobs.

"I don't mind to cut it, Mister Frank."

"You wait till the sun goes down, you hear?"

"I don't mind to cut it, Mister Frank."

"You want to get a heat stroke?"

"I don't mind it."

"Okay, but when the sun starts to boil, you get in the shade, you hear?" Baby Jo nods and backs out.

Then I ask them if they want to hear a little story about Traven?

"I'd sight rather *hear* about 'em than track 'em down," said McCoy.

"Stick around till dark, and he'll rip off a ghost story for you."

"One time, soon after he was released from prison in—I forgot where— Traven was traveling for a magazine subscription outfit, and he was using the district manager's car, going up and over the hills of North Carolina, and it was late and he was fagged out, and he woke up in a bed, with a state trooper sitting by his side. The threat of the trooper focussed the picture quickly, and behind the trooper he saw his coat hanging on a hook on the open closet door, with a book of phony checks sticking out of his inside pocket. 'Driving a little recklessly, weren't you, Mr. Weaver?' says the trooper, noticing Traven's eyes are open.

"'I guess I was, sir,' says Traven. 'I went to sleep at the wheel. I've been working pretty hard this week and I was trying to get home to my wife and kids.'

"'Know what you mean,' says the trooper. 'I was on the way home to mine, too, just off duty, when I saw you writing your name on the landscape.'

"'Will I be okay?'

"'You *feel* okay?'

"Traven says he feels like he could make it on home. Trooper asks him where he lives, and he says Bristol, Virginia, and the trooper says, 'Oh, yeah,' he had a good buddy, used to be a trooper, running one of those *big* jobs where they're constructing the U.S. interstate highway. 'What's his name?' Traven asks. 'Earl Moretz.' 'Earl Moretz!' says Traven. 'Good drinking buddy of mine. In the V.F.W., right?' Traven asks, because he likes to take risks. 'Yeah,' says the trooper.

"So they chat about good ol Earl Moretz.

"About an hour later, Traven gets ready to leave, and the trooper says, 'Sorry, but I got to take you over to the courthouse and fine you. Serious traffic violation.' 'Sure,' says Traven, and he goes to pay his hospital bill. When the nurse says it's twenty dollars, Traven asks if it's okay to write a check, and she says, no, it's not. But when the trooper, who's known her since she was a baby, says, 'It's okay, he's a friend of Earl Moretz, the check's okay,' she says, 'Then go ahead.' 'Could I make it for a little over the amount,' says Traven, 'so I can gas up my car and get on home?' The trooper says, 'It's okay, isn't it?' and she says, 'I reckon.'

"Then the trooper tells Traven he'll have to sit around the police station until nine o'clock (it's just seven) till the judge comes in. Traven says it's his kid's birthday and he promised him a ballgame, and couldn't the trooper take the check and give it to the judge? Finally, the trooper says okay, but let's see if your car works okay, so he took him over to the filling station, and that pulled in five more guys, and they all had another hour of Earl Moretz, while they got the car to running, and then Traven wrote a check for the trooper to give the judge, and got change from the trooper's own pocketbook, and then wrote a check for fixing the car, and got change, and when he passes the city limits, he has one hundred dollars in cash, and a large charge, and three more years in a North Carolina prison waiting for him."

"And you'll be telling the same story about Cody 'fore long," says McCoy. "What your big brother's got is contagious and your little brother is infected with a full dose of it."

"Cody, hell," says the Sheriff. "What about *this* one? Here I should be out scrounging around a cornfield for that gun Pete used on his wife, and 'stead of that, I'm listening to bedtime stories at high noon."

"What *I'm* trying to figure out is what you doing here in the first place," said McCoy, "less you expect to work on the judge. . . . Hit it, didn't I? Well, forget it, son. You'd have better luck with that statue of Stumbo's great-grandfather about to fall off his horse in front of the courthouse. Am I right, Frank?"

"I'd *swear* to it. *You* all make yourselves at home. I'm riding," says the Sheriff, like it was an all-occasion exit line.

"And not only that, what you got a lawyer for, if you gonna do the tear-jerking on your own?"

"What lawyer?"

"The one up from Florida."

"That's one more than *I* know anything about."

"Maybe your mamma hired him since you left Louisville?"

"Not likely, though to get Cody off that chain gang, she *could* have done *any*thing."

"Well, this lawyer came to see me this morning down in Knoxville where

I'm based, and he was wearing a white Panama suit with a widebrimmed Panama hat, driving a white 1942 Lincoln Mercury Zephyr in mint condition. Fellow with black hair and a mustache and a cigarette holder. And carrying a shiny, shiny briefcase."

"That's pretty good, Mr. McCoy, pretty funny. You're not a bad con man yourself, but you don't expect me to believe anybody'd be seen in public looking like *that,* do you?"

McCoy laughs and slaps me on the shoulder. "You really *are* a card, ain't you?"

In the downstairs hallway of the jailhouse, a young man with numerous little waves in his red hair was talking to the Sheriff's wife. He wore a flowery tie, held a red-leather Bible, and sweat from his armpits molded his white shirt to his ribs. They blocked the silver door, so I stood to the side while they finished talking.

"Way I done, I went up there like I'd just come to see Cody Weaver, because he sent word he wanted a visit from a preacher, but I seen it was a good chance to talk to them *boys.*" He's very solemn, as though standing in a church he's built with his own words. "But I kinda drew them into it, and before I left, I had them all three down on their knees, giving their hearts to Jesus. Sister Edna, it was a blessed thing. If they'd just let Jesus in sooner, maybe none of this misery would have happened."

"Well, law, when kids ain't got no mother. . . ."

She smiled at me, then stepped aside so I could reach the key on the ledge. I went on up, ready to behold an angelic scene—Cody, Tom, and Billy on their knees, sanctified. But before I reached the door, I heard springs bouncing rambunctiously, and then there's little Billy humping his cot sixty miles an hour, yelling, "Give me some poontang! Hey, preacher, get me some poontang, please, preacher!"

Cody and Tom were laughing at him, doubled up on their cots, and Pete is just fading into the toilet booth, slamming the door behind him, disgusted. "Heatherns!"

"Hey Hollis, you missed it, buddy!" says Tom, running to me. He did a perfect imitation of both the preacher, who turned out to be a student from the seminary ten miles down the pike, and of Billy. He acted out the preacher working on Billy for ten sweating minutes, inviting him to get washed in the blood of the lamb, and Billy nodding his head, finally saying, "Yes, sir, preacher, yes, sir, I want to be washed whiter than snow." When he asked Billy if he could get him anything, Billy said, "Please, preacher, all I want is me a red Bible like the one you got." And Tom acted out how Billy, as soon as the preacher shut the door downstairs, yelled out that he'd rather have some poontang.

That got Cody and me into a long story about the three McAnally girls that Traven and Cody and I used to play jungle with back in Louisville down along the Ohio river, and how we'd take turns being Tarzan and Jane and Boy and Cheetah, and how there were always two left out—Cody and Millie, because they were too little. Then Cody told how they would give up and go off and play Tarzan and Jane all by themselves.

Cody was happy with the young preacher's promise to drive fifty miles over to Chattanooga to see Reverend Dunlap, a preacher who used to visit Cody when he was in jail down there, waiting to be picked up by the T.B.I. to stand trial in Nashville years ago. Reverend Dunlap, he was certain, would drive up and try to soften Judge Stumbo.

But when I told him what Jack and the Sheriff and McCoy said about the judge, and when I reviewed the possibilities, he started to cry. Because he had lain on the cot for a week, imagining me driving up to the rescue, getting him out of there.

I lingered with them until almost dark, then I went out and got them some hot dogs and a big orange apiece, and then to pacify Cody, I put in a call to Louisville to see how momma was.

Momma said she was doing okay, except that the cast was heavy and her crutches hurt her, and she wished she could go dancing. Then she asked if I thought she ought to come down to Stillwater. I told her I didn't see that it would do any good. She said, "But don't you think if I come down there on crutches, they'd see how much Cody's mother believed in him, and maybe they'd. . . . Well, you know. . . . " I told her I knew exactly what she meant, but that I had that angle pretty well under control.

I felt guilty locking Cody and the kids in and going to the movies, but I was bone weary, worrying about Judge Stumbo's personality.

I was about to open the door of the screened porch when Mrs. Thompson called to me from inside the house. She held the telephone out to me when I came into the room.

"It's your daddy—long distance from Louisville. Barely make out your name, he's so sloppy drunk."

He was drunker than that. "Hollis" was about all I could make out, and I've had years of practice, trying to net the little silver fish that leap up out of the muddy stream of his drunken gibberish. The penalty for falling for the lovable drunk notion is that you've got to hold still for a lot of unlovely flotsam. As he let it flow, I remembered the bright Sunday morning a cop car pulled up in front of the house next to the cigarette factory and Momma had to take her bathrobe out to it so Daddy could get from the curb to the living room without the neighbors seeing he had on only his shorts and a hangover. The cops had found him under a viaduct, stripped of all but his shorts, into which he had probably peed in fright as they were stripping him. As his voice rose and fell on the phone, crooned and crowed, I remembered the year after he came back from the war and Momma had divorced him as hopeless—the nights when he would stand out in the streets or up on the railroad tracks that rose on a clay bank above our house and call for me. "Hollis! Hey, Hollis! Ho, Hollis! It's you daddy, son!" And Momma'd finally say, "Go out to him, and pacify him, Hollis," and I'd go out at two a.m. to pacify him, and end up gathering material for stories, because as the track chilled my tail, he would tell about the way it was when he served under Patton. He had a theory that Patton was really murdered, because so many people thought he was a sonofabitch, and he'd kill anybody that said he was. Then he'd tell the story about sitting under a tree cutting his toenails with a bayonet and limping quickly over to the aid-tent when he stuck himself, and starting back for his boots just as a mortar shell shivered it to bits, and somehow I always connected that with Patton not being a sonofabitch. He mourned his failure to live up to such luck. "Son," he'd say, "if I could write stories, we'd *all* be rich." Finally, he passed out on the phone, and I hung up, and I drove down to the next town and saw Robert Mitchum in "Thunder Road," about mountain moonshine runners, and it took a while to realize I was seeing a movie instead of more of the real thing, because it seemed such a short leap from Stillwater to moonshine.

Coming back, passing Jack's office, I saw a light in the window, showing through the mist. Craving company, I pulled in the driveway.

The inner door was open, so I saw him through the screen door, feeling behind the law books. He turned with a bottle in his hand, his fingers about to turn the cap, when he saw me, saluted with the bottle. Suddenly, the two bird dogs are at the door, standing rigidly, their noses to the screen, their teeth bubbling with spit. "Ace! Hoppy! Don't you eat that boy! Sit!" They wiggle-backed off and sat, and I went in.

"They tead off at me cause I quit hunting. Have a drink." I did. "Sit down." I sat on the leather couch and he stood in front of me. "So you want to know why I drink. I didn't *used* to drink. Know what I *used* to do when she kicked me out? I'd drive out to that little island in the middle of the intersection of Highway 109 and 54, right under the blinker, and park. Smoke me a cigar in the dark. Then I'd come here and sleep. Some people—well most anybody around *here* would think I was crazy." He took a swig from the bottle. "You know, sitting there, like that, out in the middle of the night, smoking a White Owl. Sometimes at two-thirty in the morning, mist fogging up my windshield, car filling up with smoke. And *drive*—I love to drive at night, you know? Just, by God, drive on down to Atlanta if I have to. Get it out of my damn system. Because if I didn't, I think I'm capable of doing a little harm. That's why I come straight *here* now, and don't go no further, and bring along *these* gentlemen to watch me. *They* know what I'm up to before I do it."

"You're like us, Jack—me and Cody and Traven. Always got to keep moving, us Weavers. Between us, we've covered every town in this country."

"Hell, I rode the rails in the thirties. If I wasn't tied down to the law, I'd walk out. But see, we lost our kid, and we can't have no more, so I got to overlook the way she treats me, don't I? The only thing wrong with *her* is *me*. Now, listen, you the only one I ever told about the traffic island, because you a poet, see, just like me, hell, by God, I'm a poet, too. Hell, look at Edgar Allan Poe. You listening?"

"I'm listening," I said, like it's the first time I ever said that to anybody.

"*I'll* give you something to write about. Hell, I'm a character. Folks all the time say, and not to be funny neither, 'You know something, Jack, you're a real character.' Why, if I was to tell you my life story, you wouldn't believe it."

He told it, and I believed it. Because I had heard it *before*—in Louisville, New York, New Orleans, San Francisco, Denver, Alaska, at sea, enroute to Panama. I reckon some people are born listeners and some are born tellers, and some, like me, are double blessed and damned.

Toward the end, his red face started working and writhing like a can of worms, glistening in the light with sweat, and pretty soon gushing tears and slobber. I was a little uneasy when the bird dogs started thumping and whining, glancing at me like it was *my* fault. Then he went to sleep and I climbed the hill and crossed the square to the jail.

Hanging from a tree near the screened porch below the jail, a truck tire swing looked awful still in the streetlight, and I smelled the juice of the weeds Baby Jo had cut, and the honeysuckle vines clinging to the side of the porch.

As I stepped up to the screen, a voice says, "Look out! Here he comes, with another ghost story," and as he took a draw, the tip of his cigarette lit up the Sheriff's face. I opened the screen and there was somebody sitting with him on the glider, his face, his bare arms and feet pale in the filtered moonlight. "Me and Pete's having us a beer. Old lady's sawing logs, so we thought we'd sneak down a few. Bite the cap off one, Weaver."

"No, thanks, Sheriff."

I fell asleep that night with an image of Majel, sitting on the front seat of that greyhound in her costume, her legs apart, lapping up the miles to Knoxville.

The next day was Sunday, and all I did was sit around the jail with Cody and Billy and Tom and Pete, eating peaches. I got Henry James out of the car and tried to read in him a little just to keep in shape, but the kids kept distracting me with their antics and their wild, rich talk, so, deciding to be one of those on whom nothing, no nothing, was lost, I shut up James. But I couldn't relax, I got worried about the way the judge would react when I offered to pay for crime on the installment plan. So I went out and put through some phone calls to Cody's victims, hoping I could persuade them to agree to that arrangement. I had given them all the impression they would get the full amount tomorrow.

Mr. Overby said he was going to have Cody's ass in a sling, and Mr. Crigger said he had hospital bills to pay, and Pap declared that suffering was good for the soul—look at Job and what it did for him—and he wished it on all his friends, including me. And the Western Auto man said the company expected him to make an example of Cody. Since I'm no good on the telephone, I didn't try any kind of plea.

When I got back at about twilight, Cody was lying on his cot, gazing glassy-eyed at Tom as he chased Billy with an R C bottle, and Pete's bare feet showed below the toilet partition, and from down stairs the aromas of Sunday dinner drifted up.

"I just been laying here worrying about momma," said Cody.

"Well, that's fine. She's probably awake worrying about you. And Traven's probably lying awake trying to figure a way to con somebody out of some change, and that'll be something else to keep Momma awake. String all the nights like this together and what do you get, Cody?"

"What the hell you mean by *that?*"

"Nothing. And don't give me that hurt look. Goodnight."

"Well, by god, you can go off and let them throw me on the chain gang, if *that's* the way you feel about it! Hell, I ain't begging *no* damn body!"

"Shut up and go to sleep," I said, and stormed out of the cell in a huff.

I walked a while, then I drove around town, and I even parked on Jack's traffic island under the blinker, and later passed his place, but the light was out, and then I parked outside the jail and walked some more down the streets of the town, and when I got back to the square the moonlight had soothed my nerves.

On the corner in front of the courthouse, the front of my baby blue Buick streamliner was jacked up over a U. S. mail box, one light smashed, the other glaring at the moon, the four doors slung wide open, a rear tire flat.

When I got up to the cell, Sheriff Thompson was squatting between two cots, petting Tom with one hand and Billy with the other, the two kids lying on their stomachs, the rough blankets over their heads, crying worse than I had yet heard them, and in the past two days they had hurt each other at least twenty times. Cody leaned against the wall, squatting, too, trying to tease Tom, in a sweet way, out of crying. Under the weak electric light, Pete stood, one hand clapped over his mouth. I went up to him and asked him what was going on, and just then somebody kicks me in the tail.The first time in my life anybody *ever* kicked me in the tail. As I turned, thinking it was Cody, Pete let his hand fall from his mouth, and it and his hand were bloody. Pointing his finger at me, the Sheriff says, "And *you* left the damned door open."

"I was mad at Cody, I guess I forgot—"

"And *that* big hog," he says, pointing at Pete, "got mad at the kids and blabbed what I told him. Does it hurt much?"

"Yeah," whines Pete.

"Good."

"What happened, Sheriff?" I ask him, but he turns his back on me and tries to console the kids. Cody came to me and told me that the Sheriff had heard from the hospital that Tom's and Billy's foster mother had died of the gunshot wound, and then Pete, out of spite, told the kids, and said he heard that Judge Stumbo was going to send Tom to prison and Billy to another foster home, so the kids tried to run away in my car.

The racket eased off a little, and I said I'd go sleep in the car.

"No, by god!" says the Sheriff. "You're spending the night in jail!"

After everybody was settled and it got dead quiet, I said, "Cody . . . . Cody . . . . Cody . . . ."

"Yeah, what?"

"I called up all those people a while ago and tried to get them to agree to let me pay them a little each month, but they said they had to have the cold cash tomorrow." He didn't say anything. "Cody . . . . Cody . . . . Cody . . . ."

I wanted to lull him to sleep with a solution, as, in our childhood, I often lulled him to sleep with a story. But I had no solution and he was beyond the consolation of a story. Then I got an idea, a verge-of-sleep idea that blended into a dream. To get the cash to pay off his victims, I could pass some bad checks in Chattanooga. With the completion of my dissertation, I would move progressively into a state of academic rigidity: tenure, marriage, kids, house, new car, the whole show—a bomb. But by passing the checks, I could save my brother, who, it was dead certain, would go berserk, plunge into a deep depression that could get him killed on the chain gang, where there were so many hair-trigger possibilities. And besides, I always wondered what it would be like to have unlimited time to write (and I wondered, too, whether I had my brothers' talent for controlling life, at least for the duration of a con), and as I fell asleep the names of Cervantes, Milton, Dostoyevski, Genet, and other great prison writers chimed in my mind.

But when I woke the next morning, my mind was on the judge. The Sheriff let me out before the others were awake, and I went up and backed my car off the mailbox, then went into the courthouse to work on Judge Stumbo.

The judge's secretary's long black hair, with a pompadour, took me back to the forties. In her blue skirt, white sleeveless blouse, spike heels, and stockings with a lustrous sheen in the dewy morning light, she had a hard-life, country-come-to-town prettiness, and misty eyes. That always does it for *me*—misty eyes.

"I'm Hollis Weaver," I said, as though using a password. It didn't pass with *her*. "Cody's brother."

"Who's Cody?" She lay outside the charmed circle.

"He's to face the judge this morning, and I'd appreciate a chance to talk to him."

"The mood *he's* in, you'll wish you hadn't." Putting it as a challenge that way makes me eager to get to him. But her brassy manner and loud voice, contradicting her misty eyes, make me nervous.

"Is he in there now?" I ask her, looking at the closed door.

"Yes. And be glad *you're* out *here*. Now get out, and I mean that in a nice way, because I'm doing you a favor, Mr.—"

"Weaver. Listen—"

That's just what the judge was doing—listening to her loud mouth. Because the door cracks a foot and he's standing in it, five feet high, with a face that defies description, an expression long ago set in concrete that was beginning now to crack.

"Did you say he was Cody Weaver's brother?" he asks, without, looked like to me, opening his mouth.

"Yes, sir."

"Get out of here," he says to me.

"That's what *I* told him, sir," she says, ripping a sheet from her typewriter.

"But, sir, I must talk to you before two o'clock." Desperate, I blurted out the theme: "The chain gang will kill my brother!"

Judge Stumbo nods from the waist up, his eyelids slam shut three times with gavel-like finality.

"But the prison psychiatrist said—"

"Never *believed* in psychiatrists."

"Please, sir, I'm just trying to be my brother's keeper—"

"You're a fool."

"Well, sir, the nation needs teachers, doesn't it? And I'm trying to become a teacher, but I left off work on my dissertation to come down here to—"

"This nation don't need another educated fool."

"Sir, please, sir, just let me tell you the story of Cody's childhood, and I think you can see—"

"I've heard too *many* stories. Besides, I lack imagination."

"Sir, at least think of my mother—"

"I have no desire to think of your mother."

"Sir, what can I say, what can I do, what can Cody do, to convince you—?"

"He has only to be born again and live his life over in a different way. As it *is,* he goes on the chain gang." The crack closed before I could open my mouth. But then I got to laughing. It was a great line.

"Hey, he's really a very funny judge, isn't he?"

"I thought it was funny, too," she says, throwing her carriage, "first time I heard it."

But when the morning sun hit me in the face on the courthouse steps, I wasn't laughing. I had only five hours to work a miracle. Then, although I had just experienced a failure to the contrary, I realized that my last thin chance was to approach the victims *personally* again, and beg them to accept monthly payments. An even thinner chance on the other side of that was that the judge would accept their decisions.

So I hopped into my Buick, started off and swerved, wobbling, into a service station when I'd forgotten the flat. They patched up the radiator and pounded hell out of a few other places, as if beating the car to submission, and I set out for Sharpsburg with only five dollars left of the hundred I had when I left Louisville. I headed for the other end of the line so I could gauge my time as I worked back toward the deadline at the courthouse.

As I drove along, I half-decided that if I had no luck by the time I got to the third victim, I'd start cashing checks in the next town. Time passed quickly as I imagined the effect of such a move on my life. At least, I could finish the novel I was working on.

Mr. Overby squints against the sunburst where I'm standing in the doorway of his store. He seems puzzled. "He just left," he says.

"Who just left?"

"Your lawyer—Cody's lawyer. Mr. French."

"Huh? Listen, I just came by to talk to you about the money Cody owes you and try—"

"He just paid it off. You s'pose to meet each other here?"

"Hold it, Mr. Overby. What's going on?"

"Mr. French just paid me, see," he says, pulling a check out of his big wallet, thonged to his hip pocket. "And I signed his paper."

"What paper?"

"The affidavit saying I don't want to see Cody prosecuted, I'm satisfied with restitution, plus the interest for three years, like it was a loan. And a big plus feature of the agreement was that I get to keep the money even if Judge Stumbo sentences Cody anyway—which he will."

"So you get your money on the hip and Cody's ass in a sling any way the cookie crumbles, huh?"

"Yeah." He grins, as if delighted with the justice of it all. "Plus, *plus*—I sold him three brand new suits, one his size, and two Cody's size, and about a hundred dollars of this and that."

"What did he look like?"

Then Mr. Overby gives me the exact same description McCoy of the T.B.I. gave me, each item in the same order, right down to the shiny briefcase. "I'm gonna get *me* a briefcase like his," says Mr. Overby.

Then Mrs. Overby comes in and carried on about what a handsome, dashing, though oddly dressed, fellow Mr. French was, and she made me promise to bring Cody by to see her, and I had to promise again not to put her life story in a book.

When I walked into Mr. Crigger's Red Dot Cafe, he's up on that stool smoking a big cigar with a two inch ash.

"You just missed him," he says, and I ask who, and we go through the whole routine, the description of French and all, the gist of which is that Mr. French came in and treated them both to Crigger's best porterhouse steak (since Crigger didn't know what French meant by Chateaubriand), and over their steaks they came to an agreement, and Crigger settled for Mr. French's terms, which were the same as Overby's.

I drove up to the pumps where Pap was white-washing the island. He looks up, double surprised to see me. "I know," I says, "I just missed him."

"By less than five minutes."

"Driving a 1942 white Lincoln Mercury Zephyr in mint condition, right?"

"With brand new rubber all around," he says. "I unloaded four new double-ply nylon tires on him." He gave the island a sloppy slap of white wash.

"Did you get a cigar out of him?"

"Smoke it after lunch. Ought to last the weekend."

I scratched gravel to catch up with Mr. French, but jerked to a stop at the edge of the lot—out of gas. I didn't have any money left. Out of the goodness of his heart, Pap exchanged a tank of gas for my spare tire, my hubcaps, and, since I wouldn't need it without the spare, my jack. He said I looked faint and shouldn't go without my lunch, so he threw in a pack of stale peanut butter crackers that I almost choked to death on before I got to Stillwater.

I had the feeling there wasn't much point in going back, certainly no need to check the Western Auto man. If it was humanly possible, this Mr. French would get Cody off.

In a "no parking" zone in front of the courthouse, aligned with the walkway, was parked the white Lincoln Zephyr. I parked behind it, confident Mr. French would take care of any fines. In front of the drugstore, a greyhound bus was discharging passengers. The driver reached his hand in, and the first thing I saw was a prize-winner's red ribbon bobbing on Majel's breast as she stepped down in her white majorette boots, the pompons swinging. She sees me getting out of my smashed-in Buick and smiles and waves. I wave back, then go on into the courthouse.

The Zephyr, though white, reminded me of the Green Hornet's car in the chapter play Traven took me to see the day Cody was born. Momma wanted us out of the house to spare us the shock of birth. Traven held my hand, and as we went over a bridge, he told me about Fartso the whale, who lived in the creek below. If I threw him a nickle, Traven said, Fartso would tell his gremlins to bring me a Buck Rogers gun. "Give it to me," he said, "and *I'll* throw it in." Later, watching the Green Hornet's car force the bad guy's car to swerve and smash into a gas pump, I wondered for a minute how it was that Traven hugged two bags of popcorn when he had thrown both our nickles into the water. Twenty years later, it suddenly dawned on me.

Dawn's rosy fingers goosed me as I stepped into Judge Stumbo's outer office and saw Traven hefting a dangling lock of the secretary's long black hair that took me back to the forties. As if verifying the testimony of witnesses, Traven's wearing a white panama suit and hat that bring the sunlight indoors, and green-tinted glasses, a mustache, a pink shirt with a white tie, and two-tone, brown and white shoes, and in a chair lies a shiny briefcase with H. F. on the gold clasp. He doesn't see me, and he's saying, "Not many girls can wear such long hair and get away with it, but if you lived in New York, you'd be setting a style, brown eyes." Her misty blue eyes look up at Traven, and she's forgotten, like many other girls, what the hell color her eyes really are, and a feeble smirk is her only attempt to control the situation. I stayed quiet, dangling in the doorway.

I'd come in at the climax, because she gets up and goes into Judge Stumbo's office, and Traven turns and glances right *at* me, as though we had been together all morning and I had just stepped in after a brief trip to the john. So I try to match his cool.

The door opens, and the secretary steps aside to let Traven pass. She leaves the door ajar, so from where I stand, I watch Traven walk up to the desk and put out his hand at such a distance that the Judge has to get up and reach across his desk to shake it. I can't catch all the conversation, but I see the affidavits come out of the shiny briefcase and the Judge take them and peruse them, shaking his head negative.

". . . . willing to pay the court costs," I hear Traven say, his voice becoming louder, stageworthy, as he builds the scene. "I realize that in a case like this the court costs are what some people might regard as exorbitant; nevertheless, we're willing to lay it on the line today, sir. Settle it out of court, if possible."

"Sir, everybody has been at me to handle this case out of court, but I don't handle, sir, and you may as well save your techniques of persuasion until court convenes—in exactly ten minutes. Now, if you'll excuse me . . . ."

I stare at the back of Traven's head as he remains seated, very still, and the judge stares at Traven's face.

"Pardon me for staring, sir," says Traven, "but isn't that—?" Then I see the color photograph of a young man in a Marine uniform. "I *thought* the name was familiar. Judge Stumbo. That name kept nagging at me all the way down the highway. That's Joe, isn't it?"

"Why—yes, but—what's that got to do with Cody Weaver?"

"Nothing, sir," says Traven, rising, still looking at the picture. "Nothing." Then, he jerks himself into a posture of efficiency, puts out his hand so the Judge has to get up again and reach out to it, and as they shake, the Judge says, "Mr. French, what were you about to say?"

"That I knew him. The machine gun—"

"Who told you about Joe?"

"Told *me!* Let me tell *you,* sir. I was there." The Judge's other hand reaches out and the four hands clasp in one fingery knot. "All I got to show is one bullet wound, but poor Joe . . . ."

Then I remember the scar under Traven's shoulder blade. In Texas, a prison guard bent over a water fountain and his pistol fell out of its holster and fired.

"What are you people doing out there?" says the judge. "Mr. Weaver, your lawyer will be with you in a moment." He pushed the door shut. "Now, sir . . . . What did you say your first name was?"

Muffled by the door come a few phrases: ". . . died in my arms . . . . I was delirious at the time. . . . didn't know him well, but . . . . last words were,

'Candyman, Candyman' . . . . That mean anything to you, sir?''

At the word 'Candyman,' the secretary frowns slightly, then, slowly, smiles cunningly, then shrugs, stops pretending to work, and sits with her arms folded, listening with me.

"Candyman Joe's nickname for his father?" I ask.

She smirks and nods her head. "How did *you* know?"

"Imagination," I say, and nod *my* head.

Twenty minutes later, the Judge comes out and says, "Mrs. Harmon, would you please write out a check for a hundred dollars? Mr. French needs some expense money to get back to Florida, and I'm afraid he can't cash a check locally without identification, but they'll cash one with *my* signature on it. And here's his check to cover court costs. We've settled it out of court, so strike Cody Weaver from the docket."

We all shook hands and the Judge hurried out to court, thirty minutes late, content with Traven's promise to return and spend a weekend with him some time.

"Show Mr. French the jail," says Mrs. Harmon to me, smirking.

"If there's a florist in this town," says Traven, posing in the doorway, "expect a dozen roses within an hour."

"I won't hold my breath."

As we're going down the steps toward his car, Traven says, "See you in jail," and I see there's a ticket on my windshield, none on his. I follow in my car, which I want *near* me up to the last minute. In the short drive around the square to the jail, I notice the new tires on Traven's car, the suits hanging neatly in the back, the boxes of other stuff stacked in the seat, and I think of all the checks he passed this morning, and hope each of the receivers got a cigar at least. And then I think, yeah, everybody but me.

By the time I climb out of my wreck of a car and reach the screen porch, Cody is already out there, a grin stretching from one of those big ears to the other, and Sheriff Thompson is folding a piece of paper, probably a note from the judge. And right quick, there's Majel, draped in the doorway, decked in her outfit, the prize winner's red ribbon still dangling, and I see in her eyes, even in the shade of the porch, that when she looks at Traven, she sees Miami in full splendor.

I stayed outside in the broiling sun, while Cody hugs the Sheriff's wife and shakes hands with Thompson. Traven gives the Sheriff a big cigar, then loads his own pearl-handled cigarette holder and feels for matches until the Sheriff lights it for him, then lights his own cigar. They all step out into the sunlight, shaking hands, and Traven even reaches for Majel's, and when her shoulders twitch as if by a small electric shock, I figure he's tickled her palm.

I follow the parade toward the cars, Majel cavorts and tosses her baton into the sun and it spins and sparkles and Cody runs ahead and jumps behind the wheel of that white Lincoln Mercury Zephyr like it was Santa's sleigh.

"Follow *me*," Traven says to me, as he gets in beside Cody. They take off as though they have a motorcycle escort. As, in every sense that matters, they have.

Just before I pull away from the curb, I look up at the window where I first saw Cody two days ago. Behind the silver iron slats stood Tom, his arm around

Billy. They didn't wave. They didn't move.

At the intersection where the caution light blinked in the sun's glare, I took the highway less traveled by, the one that offered a short cut over a curving route to the state line. Traven and his chauffeur, Cody, were borne along in their dreamboat down the super highway toward the horizon.

This was eight years ago, and the last time I saw Cody was when I was in Idaho a few months ago for the world premiere—as the producer called it—of my play *Berserk*. A little theatre group was trying it out for us, and I had gotten leave from the University of Montana (I *didn't* stick at Transylvania after all) to be in on rehearsals. Opening night, a terrific snowstorm hit, and television cameras were set up to shoot first nighters—Boise high society—as they came in out of the blizzard. Three came in and one stepped back to hold the door open for a fourth, and in walked a tuxedo with you-know-who inside, and that grin, transported from the Sheriff's porch.

On camera, Cody was asked why he had made the trip up from Dallas in this terrible blizzard, and he replied, with a jut of his chin and a look of amazement, "Well, you don't think I'd miss my brother's play, do you?" What he missed, of course, was the character *in* the play, who resembled himself—at least in *my* imagination.

He was driving a 1941 green Hudson wasp, one of only 395 that were made that year. Living in the car, he travels all over the United States, constantly on the move, from one brief job to another, living by his wits, but apparently keeping out of trouble. He's been living that way for eight years, and I've taught in almost that many colleges, and he always shows up at least once or twice a year from a thousand miles away, and a few days later, he leaves, usually in a rain or snow storm, and I get a card several days after, saying, "Dear Hollis: Well, I made it to Laredo, okay. On my way to San Diego. All my love, your brother, Cody Weaver." On the back is a color photograph of an Indian in full costume or a buffalo, for my son's sake. And if you'll just be patient, I'm sure Cody will come knocking at that front door before too long.

Since Stillwater, Traven's served three stretches, in California, New Jersey, and Mississippi. But now *he's* going straight, too, living and working in Toronto, where he's married and has a family, and runs a tabernacle of the Holiness church. His wife sings, his little girl shakes the tambourine, and he scorches sinners alive with his visions of hell, and then leaves them in Jordan. Well, who can tell? Maybe, even if it's a con, he does some good.

Because Traven's the oldest rat in the barn. Traven sold us *all* a bill of goods. Not just the judge, the victims, the sheriff, but in the beginning, back home in Louisville—me and Cody. With that Merchant Marine outfit, standing like that at the front door with the September sun around his head, a nimbus of light, evoking far off places, far *out* episodes. I never told you about that? Then listen.

A smoky-red October afternoon. Me and little Cody and Traven playing marbles under the Indian cigar tree with a bunch of tough kids, and somebody says to Traven, "Okay, Big Chief Chew-tabacca, shoot!" and Traven stands up, hitches up his knickers like Humphrey Bogart and spits tobacco juice bulls-eye into the ring and says, "You all take it easy, you hear? I'm going swimming." And we all laugh like hell as he walks down the street past the flood gates, his pockets bulging with marbles, into the autumn sunset, by god.

Thirteen years old at the time, and went off with only a dime to his name. Didn't see him again until a year later, in September, when I looked up from reading Smiling Jack, and there he stood at the screen door with the sunlight behind him and a merchant seaman's cap cocked back to show his pompadour. Says, "Shhhh. Wanna surprise Momma," as if he didn't have twenty more years to do *that* in.

This one ends twenty years later—the summer before my first novel came out—and it'd been eight years since I had seen him last, in Stillwater. He'd just come from working in a Mississippi cotton patch, under the gun. And here *I* was, the first in the family on both sides to graduate from high school and even on through college, and making ten thousand a year teaching at a big university, and a novel coming out, and a clean record in the home-town and the F.B.I. files, and— You know I didn't want to show off and make him feel bad, I wanted to make him feel part *of* it, so here we were: two brothers having a reunion at Mam'maw's house—sort of the home place, you know, because Momma moved all over the city of Louisville when we were little—and Traven was out in the back yard, full of flowers, and he was lolling in the hammock under the mimosa trees, and smoking this fat-assed cigar and wearing the baggy clothes they let him out in. Swinging in that hammock, raising a cloud of Dutch Master, grinning at me.

So I sat in this white kitchen chair Mam'maw'd propped up the curtain stretchers with, and tried to make him feel a part of it all. When I told him about the teaching job, he says, "Listen, kid," in this Yankee accent he picked up and stuck to since his first trip to New York, "what you waste your time teaching English for? Why don't you become a doctor or a lawyer where the *big* money is?" It tipped me off balance, and I made some lame excuses, and he says, "What's this they tell me about you gotta novel going to be published?" "Yeah," I said, and broke out in a face-aching grin. And he says, "Listen, kid, you better watch out for these editors. They'll try to cheat you out of what you got coming to you. *I* know. What you need is an agent."

Well, I was still feeling the reunion scene, so none of this soaked in. I was thinking, here's where I'll make him feel he's a part of it all, and not just a three or four time loser con man fresh out of the pen. He was still kinda thin and hollow-eyed, you know. But 'bout that time, he says, "What's it about?" and I say, "'Bout when I was in the merchant marines." That made him give the hammock a good swing with his dangling foot and look at me squint-eyed through the cigar smoke. "Kid, when were *you* ever in the merchant marines?" Just before they drafted me into the army, I told him, but didn't remind him that I used to send him money orders for stamps and Bull Durham from Savannah and Mobile and Rio, then later from Fort Jackson, nor how he used to sign his letters, "Jesus is the only hope for today's youth," knowing the censors would get it back to the parole officer. I won't stress the fact that *I* believed him. "Whatever made you go in the merchant marines, kid?"

I got choked up a little because I was about to grab him with it. "Well, Traven, remember the time . . . ?" Then I filled him in on our childhood and the time he came back in the merchant seaman's outfit. "And you told me and Cody all about New York and shipping out to Panama and the West Indies.

Remember, Traven? It got Cody to running off from school and taking little trips that finally landed him in a detention home. It stirred up the wanderlust in me, too, but good little ol' Hollis, you know, stayed home, and dreamed about it, and saw movies about it, and wrote novel scenarios projecting himself into it, and read Conrad, and finished high school first. Then I went to New York, worked at the White Tower hamburger joint by night, sat in the union hall in Brooklyn by day, till I finally got out on a ship to India day before Christmas. There was this man on the ship who kind of reminded me of you. In my novel that's coming out, he turns out to be a strange kind of hero, in a bass-ackward way, and I'm his witness."

Traven braked the hammock with his foot, and kept it still, one eye squeezed shut against the smoke from the Dutch Master hanging in the corner of his mouth. Then he gives the hammock a little push, takes a long draw, spews out the smoke, dusts the cigar, and smirks: "Why, kid, I ain't never been in no Merchant Marines."

I heard a mimosa blossom drop. "But—"

"But, hell," Traven said, "I just wore that outfit so I could hitchhike across country easier."

Love Song for Doris Ballinger

JACK MATTHEWS   from *Carleton Miscellany*

As he sipped coffee, his eyes focused upon the front page of a newspaper, held up to conceal the face of the man on the next stool. There was a picture at the top of the page. The portrait of a beautiful, smiling woman.

The picture troubled him. He drank his coffee slowly and shook his head no when the waitress asked if he wanted it warmed up, by which she meant filled.

Then he walked out of Gaetz's, temporarily forgetting the picture, and started back to his office. The snow had stopped falling, and now the sun was out, turning the slushy streets into strips of dented and battered tin, burning fiercely with reflected sunlight.

The thought of the picture came back to him, however, and he decided to stop and buy a newspaper. He paused in the middle of the sidewalk and stared at the woman's face once again, nagged by something trying to move into the face. Then he looked at the caption, hoping that it would prompt his memory and make the face pulse suddenly clear:

MISSING WOMAN SOUGHT

And in the text following was the name, "Doris Jensen," a girl whom he had known as Doris Ballinger years before, in high school. It was impossible for him to conceive of her as missing, because it seemed at that moment that he had not even thought of her as being in any way present since graduating from high school twenty-six years before. How could anyone like that be considered missing? (Or what other state was possible?) How could a Doris Ballinger work her way into a position to be missed?

Now he abstracted himself from the street, letting his distant cold feet find their own way through the melting snow upon the sidewalk. The snow was pock-marked from the heels of pedestrians, each heel print a saucer of cold water . . . tiny puddles that shone like the broken-off bottoms of pop bottles, faintly green with the memory of sand that cheap (or old) glass retains. The sun had not really warmed the air.

Doris Ballinger, he was saying. A man ahead of him turned to the side and spit a gray ghost of phlegm arcing onto the rugged snow tire of a 1965 Buick.

Then he saw her in her last (or at least her most memorable) posture: she stood high upon the stage with her hands folded before her, tiny chin raised and mouth open. As yet, in the arena of his mind, she was silent—as if physically and helplessly waiting for the inventory in the inscrutable memory of a forty-three year old man, who had once (at this precise time of her interruption) been a member of her graduating class.

Because he wanted to be sure this was the authentic and living Doris Ballinger. As the seventeen-year-old girl stood up there on the stage, open-mouthed and paralytic with unreality, he noticed the bulging, muscular calves and the earth-goddess breasts that had impressed him then. Four great physical facts that designated her fate and sometimes turned her cheeks red with shame. For her delicate and fragile spirit was not meant to be saddled so suddenly with such an excess of womanhood and flesh.

Pale blue eyes, perfectly arched, and a beautiful, pious face. Then he remembered even her handwriting, and remembered that she had dotted each of her i's with a meticulous little tear drop. She was a member of student council and the Dolly Madison club, where all the girls sat in a circle in the Home Ec room, doing needle work and sewing, as if preparing for the long matronly years ahead.

An instant's silence, as if time were crouching and hunching its muscles, and then the piercing brilliance of Doris Ballinger's soprano voice, as she hit the high note in *"Spargi d'Amore il Pianto,"* which she sang in Italian, exploding each syllable, so that there were blinks of silence within a single word that someone could have sneezed in.

But no one did, for this was a solemn event, and Doris Ballinger was the most solemn, upright, religious, tender-hearted, big-titted, honorable, dependable, victimized, prudent, judicious, mature, domestic, practical girl in the whole high school. Which was something of a record.

How could a Doris Ballinger disappear?

Contra Naturam. Better contemplate the possibility of a squirrel's attacking cats, or of crab grass being blown into balls of twine and unravelling in the air like dancing, hissing snakes. Better consider the possibility that milk would start oozing from the cracks in brick walls, and the snow that lay upon the distant roofs, as remote and irrelevant as unheard music, might burst forth into black and purple flames, whose smoke was composed of the echoes of lost children, crying.

Because all of these anonymous evenings, when a passing car's horn was blown, interrupting the figures on the television screen (less real than the memory of Doris Ballinger), and interrupting his wife in the kitchen, smearing peanut butter on Ritz crackers and lining up uneven tumblers of cold milk for the kids (so that she would call, "Is that someone honking for us?" and he would call out, "I don't think so," without even looking) . . . all this time, Doris Ballinger was preparing for an exodus. If not her mind, then her great warm breasts—fat kennels of nourishment—or at least her lineman's calves, insidiously preparing for the time they would carry that monumental woman, dismayed, away from whatever destination her eyes thought was before her, waiting.

He stopped, slapped the paper with the back of his hand, and turned around, searching for an interested face. Only an old woman approached him, her cheeks heavily rouged and her legs—as brittle as glass straws—probing her swaddled body forward, her face gazing down from above with alarm.

So, in a vastly different weather—and still damp and warm with the colony of flesh she had borne with her from high school, and the scattering of flowers—so had Doris Ballinger's legs betrayed her; hers, by walking her body out of public life, family life (as from the warmth of a television tube); while this old lady's, by walking her irreversibly into the bewildered suburbs of old age, where a man might turn around, slapping his paper, and say,

"She herself might have been in that car!"

"What is that?" the old lady might ask, looking up; and in looking up step on the edge of an ice saucer, so that the heavy frozen slabs of sidewalk would spit her legs heavenward, and she would fall, cracking like an icicle tightly bundled in furs, while on a distant rooftop a carnivorous squirrel prepares to jump to its death down the back of a dead drummer boy, frozen upright.

Which of course did not happen, and the old lady edged herself sideways (as if the sidewalk were trying to tilt her toward the street, and send her like a bee-bee down the sewer hole; seven old ladies down sewer holes, by tilting the whole town, and the demi-urge wins the game), and cranked herself into the candy store that was exhaling odors of popcorn and caramel over his newspaper.

"I was speaking of Doris Ballinger, who is missing," he continued, now that the lady was inside the candy store, and there was no possibility of a misunderstanding.

Doris Ballinger would of course have been the very one to pass by one's house, her husband pressing the ring of the horn as a dark dog skittered before the headlights, causing one Ritz cracker to wait a fraction of a second longer before being immured in peanut butter.

And at such a time, there would have been no camera, no screen, upon Doris Ballinger, for her husband would have been thinking of his impending lawsuit, concerning title for an apartment building that a corporation he had formed was trying to buy. While Doris Jensen, née Ballinger, sat dreamy and unreal (missing already, in this interval—a preview of coming distractions; for being seen is part of existing)—as the car glided down a residential street (darker than a forgotten canal in Venice), the heater before her knees pouring out a balmy and susurrant stream of warmth upon her magnificent, but aging shins, while somewhere within her expensive hair-do, a nervous seventeen year old girl still stood on a stage, exploding sounds in fabricated Italian over the head of a boy whose name she had forgotten, or would forget.

The back seat was empty.

By this time, he had returned to the office, and the missing girl, who was now a woman, was forgotten, so that she was—without knowing it—further ensconced in mystery, insofar as even her *missing* was now missing, and conceivably, if all those who knew her, or had once known her, forgot about her simultaneously she would have gone up in a puff of smoke, at the end of a frenetic drum roll, the magician's wand scarcely warmed by the muted flash of her exit. So much probity and tenderness excised from the world by an instant's neglect, a second's impiety!

Was this what happened?

Always somewhere in the penumbra of his preoccupations, Doris Ballinger stood waiting, as if for a cue—or else paralyzed by the irrelevance of her presence, until this man brought the camera of his attention around, and at the very instant of its focus upon her raised picnic-ham breasts, her clasped, white-knuckled hands, the explosion of that brilliant soprano, translating melodramatic words about flowers and graves into thrusts of aural needles in the pincushion of a single man's attention.

No music ever dies, and if a pure-hearted girl is ever found to be missing, she must be resuscitated in memory according to the memory of each one who has known her, so that there are these multitudes of girls waiting to rehearse and be heard.

The newspaper story was vague. It gave her age, forty-three, and the business of her husband, real estate; and the fact that the couple had no children. Her husband was referred to as wealthy, and beneath her picture was his. She had presumably been returning from an appointment with her physician, driving her new model Buick alone.

Somewhere, on one snow tire, a silver strand of saliva clung. But of course, that was not so.

What was so, was this. Doris Ballinger was missing long before her husband, the wealthy realtor, reported the fact to the police. Not simply in the sense that she was missing according to him—and worse, unthought of; but missing according to at least one girl standing abandoned on a great stage, before an empty auditorium—the echoes of a foreign song only vaguely transeunt, like the breath of a god no one can quite believe in. Like all of us, Doris Ballinger had abandoned the child she was; and to that child, was missing.

Such might have been the moment of nearest perfection for that strange girl who did not complain, even though she might even then have guessed what awaited her, but stayed nice and kind and thoughtful anyway. This would warm at least one man, twenty-six years later; although it would do no good to what had become of that girl—the frozen corpse in the car, for instance, fallen sideways in a swift gesture of stoney giddiness from a secret aneurysm . . . in a place where the woman it had once been had pulled the car to the side of the road, to let traffic pass. She would not have wanted to disobey the law, or obstruct traffic, while dying.

On the waxed and slippery roof of that handsome new car, a squirrel skated precariously after a fallen hickory nut, while the windblasts from the swift traffic passing by beat like a drum upon the silent upholstery of this car. On the tv screen that evening, a middle-aged woman's picture was flashed briefly before ten thousand faces of local citizens, between the major national news reports and the latest scores of local high school basketball games.

Many who might have recognized her are dead; many who had once known her, did not recognize her because of the passage of time, the metamorphosis of the girl, and the changed name.

Ten thousand more newspapers lay crumpled about, in various rooms and in various postures of disuse. Each one holding Doris Ballinger's face, folded already into the past.

Why didn't she have children? This, too, was a shame.

Snow fell from the roof of the third house down, startling a dog who had just raised its leg to wet into the black shadow of an arbor vitae.

He walked home, slapping the newspaper against his leg as a car turned left at the corner, its headlights gliding over him like the beacon from a lighthouse that was itself sliding carefully and inevitably into blackness.

Beyond this stage, another looms; a dark car is parked crookedly against the curb on a little-travelled road.

Beyond that stage, is a higher one, where a girl stands with her hands folded. There are tears in her eyes, and the world is beautiful and important for her; and she wants, above all, to be loved and to love.

He clears his throat and spits toward a parked car, whose parking lights are on. The parking lights are visible afterthoughts—warm and muted, like congealed globules of chicken fat in a bowl of darker gravy. The car has a cracked left front window; the glass is most essentially itself where it is cracked.

In the distance, one can almost hear a muted drum beat; and if he listens closely, an echo from this beat. A mirror of sound, accepting what it is.

Even farther away than that, a lonely woman suddenly and for no apparent reason, thinks of a boy she once knew years ago; and with a strange wistfulness that she cannot understand or even bother to admit (in the factualness of where she is waiting her turn), and she wonders where he might be waiting, and what coins might be spilling from his hands as he cups them together, lifting water to the doe of her heart, and saying, "Look, I remember. I remember."

STICKS AND STONES

LEONARD MICHAELS

from *Massachusetts Review*

It was a blind date. She met me at the door and smiled nicely. I could tell she was disappointed. Fortunately, I had brought a bottle of bourbon. An expensive brand, though not a penny too much for a positive *Weltanschauung*. I felt disappointed too. We finished the bourbon and were sitting on the couch. She stuttered the tale of her life and named her favorite authors. I'd never met a girl who stuttered. Our hands became interlocked and hot, our knees touched. Both of us were crying. I cried for her. She, moved by my tears, cried for me. Beyond the room, our sobs, and her breaking, retrogressive voice, I heard church bells. I squeezed her hands, shook my head and staggered from the couch to a window. Glass broke, I fainted, and minutes later awoke on a porch just below the window. She was kneeling beside my head, smoking a cigarette. I heard her voice repeating consonants, going on with the story of her life—a bad man, accident, disease. Broken glass lay about me like stars. Church bells rang the hour, then the half hour. I lay still, thinking nothing, full of mood. Cloth moved smoothly across her thighs as she breathed and rocked to the measures of her story. Despicable as it may seem, that made me sexual. I lifted on an elbow. The sight of my face with the moon shining in it surprised her. She stopped telling her story and said, "No, I d-don't want t-to. . . ." Our eyelids were thick with water. We shook like unhealthy, feverish things.

There was a reason for not having called her again. Shame, disgust, what have you? When I saw her in the street I would run. I saw her there often, and I ran hundreds of miles. My legs became strong, my chest and lungs immense. Soon I could run like a nimble dog. I could wheel abruptly, scramble left or right and go for half the day. I could leap fences and automobiles, run from roof to roof, spring deadly air shafts, and snap in middle flight to gain the yard that saved my life. Once I caught a sparrow smack in my teeth and bit off his head.

Spitting feathers and blood, I felt like an eagle. But I was not, and good things, however vigorous, come to an end. At least for me. I was neither Nietzsche, Don Juan, nor Chateaubriand. My name was Phillip. As I resolved to stand and started practicing postures, a friend who knew the girl came and said she wasn't reproachful. I ought to call her on the phone. It didn't sound true, but he insisted. She wanted to see me again, at least as an acquaintance. She would be spared the implications of my flight. I could rest in body and mind. Next time I saw her in the street I ran faster than before, my hair flying, my eyes big. I ran half the day and all that night.

My friend came again. Running alongside, he shouted that he had had her too. We stopped.

"Do you mind?" he asked. It had bothered him so much he couldn't sleep.

"Mind?" I kissed him on the cheek and slapped his back. Was I happy? The answer is yes. I laughed till my sight was bleary. My ribs, spreading with pleasure, made a noise like wheezy old wood. My friend began laughing, too, and it was a conflation of waters, lapping and overlapping.

A crooked nose and small, blue eyes—Henry. A nose, eyes, a curious mouth, a face, my own felt face behind my eyes, an aspect of my mind, a habit of my thought—my friend, Henry. The sight of him was mysterious news, like myself surprised in a mirror, at once strange and familiar. He was tall and went loose and swinging in his stride. Degas dreamed the motion of that dance, a whirl of long bones through streets and rooms. I was shorter, narrower, and conservative in motion. A sharp compliment striking at his side. As Henry was open, I was close, slipping into my parts for endless consultation, like a poker player checking possibilities at the belt. He and I. Me and him. Such opposite adaptations contradict the logic of life, abolish Darwin, testify to miracle and God. I never voiced this idea, but I would think: "Henry, you ought to be dead and utterly vanished, decomposed but for the splinter of tibula or jawbone locked in bog, or part of a boulder, baked, buried, and one with rock." I meant nothing malicious; just the wonder of it.

Now, in company, Henry would grin, expose his dearly familiar chipped front tooth, and whisper, "Tell them how you fell out the window."

"Out the window," people would shout. "You fell out the window? What window?"

I told the story, but declined the honor of being hero. "No, no, not I—this fellow I know—happened to him. Young man out of a job, about my age, depressed about life and himself. You must know the type—can't find meaningful work, spends a lot of time in the movies, wasting . . .

"It was suggested he call a certain girl named Marjorie, herself out of work, not seeing anyone in particular. He asked why out of work. They told him she had had an accident and lived on the insurance payments. Pretty girl? 'Not what you would call pretty. Interesting-looking, bright.' So he called and she said glad to see him, come by, bring something to drink. She had a stutter. It annoyed him, but not so much as her enthusiasm. Anyhow, he was committed. He went with a bottle, and though she was interesting-looking, he was disappointed and began straight in to drink and drink. Perhaps disappointed, too, she drank as fast and as much. The liquor qualified their sense of one another and themselves. Soon they sat on the couch and were full of expectations, drinking, drinking, chatting. He told her about his life, the jobs he had lost, how discontented he felt, and about his one good friend. She followed in a gentle, pleasing way, ooing and clucking. He said there were no frontiers left, nothing for a man to do but explore his own mind and go to the movies. She agreed and said she spent a lot of time just looking in a mirror. Then she came closer and told him about her life. He came closer, too, and fondled her fingertips. She had been raised in an orphanage. He pressed her palms. She had gone to work in a factory. He held her wrists. In an accident at the factory, her leg was bashed and permanently damaged. His hands slid up and down her arms. She limped slightly but the company paid. She didn't mind the limp. He shook his head no. The scars on her face made her look a bit tough; that bothered her. He moaned. She pulled up her dress, showed him the damage, and he began to cry as he snapped it down again. She cried too and pulled it back up. He stumbled from the couch, crying, punching his fists together as he went to the window. Trying to open it he fell through and was nearly killed."

People loved the story and Henry cackled for more.

"You're such a jerk," he said. My heart lunged fiercely with pleasure.

How I carried on. Henry urged me. I carried on and on. Everyone laughed when I fell out the window. No one asked what happened next. Anyhow, the tale of abused and abandoned femininity is pathetic and tediously familiar. Only low, contemptible men who take more pleasure in telling it than doing it would tell it. I stopped for a while after I had a dream in which Henry wanted to kill me.

"Me?" I asked.

"That's right, scum. You!"

Only a dream, but so is life. I took it seriously. Did it warn me of a disaster on the way? Did it indicate a fearful present fact? I studied Henry. Indeed, his face had changed. Never a handsome face, but now, like his face in the dream, it was strangely uncertain, darker, nasty about the edges of the eyes and mouth. Dirty little pimples dotted his neck, and the front chipped tooth gave a new quality to his smile, something asymmetrical, imbecilic and obscene. He looked dissolute and suicidal.

He rarely came to visit me anymore, but we met in the street. Our talk would be more an exchange of looks than words. He looked at me as if I were bleeding. I looked at him quizzically. I looked at him with irony; he returned it with innocence. He burst out laughing. I smiled and looked ready to share the joke. He looked blank, as if I were about to tell him what it was. I grinned, he sneered, he smiled, I frowned, I frowned, he was pained. He looked pained, I looked at my shoes. He looked at my shoes, I looked at his. We looked at one another and he mentioned a mutual friend.

"An idiot," I said.

"A pig."

"Intolerable neurotic."

"Nauseating . . . psychotic."

Then silence. Then he might start, "You know, his face, those weirdly colored eyes . . ."

"Yes," I would say. They were the color of mine. I yawned and scratched at my cheek, though I wasn't sleepy and felt no itch. Our eyes slipped to the corners of the squalid world. Life seemed merely miserable.

Afterwards, alone in my apartment, I had accidents. A glass slipped out of my hand one night, smashed on the floor and cut my shin. When I lifted my pants leg to see the cut, my other leg kicked it. I collapsed on the floor. My legs fought with kicks and scrapes till both lay bleeding, jerky, broken and jointless.

Lose a job, you will find another; break an arm, it soon will heal; ditched by a woman, well

I don't care if my baby leaves me flat,
I got forty 'leven others if it come to that.

But a friend! My own felt face. An aspect of my mind. He and I. Me and him. There were no others. I smoked cigarettes and stayed up late staring at a wall. Trying to think, I ran the streets at night. My lungs were thrilled by darkness. Occasionally, I saw Henry and he, too, was running. With so much on our minds, we never stopped to chat, but merely waved and ran on. Now and then we ran side by side for a couple of hundred miles, both of us silent except for the gasping and hissing of our mouths and the cluttered thumping of our feet. He ran as fast as I. Neither of us thought to race, but we might break silence after some wonderful show of the other's speed and call: "Hey, all right." Or, after one of us had executed a brilliant swerve and leap, the other might exclaim, "Bitching good."

Alone, going at high moderate speed one night, I caught a glimpse of Henry walking with a girl. She seemed to limp. I slowed and followed them, keeping well back and low to the ground. They went to a movie theater. I slipped in after they did and took a seat behind theirs. When the girl spoke, I leaned close. She stuttered. It was Marjorie. They kissed. She coiled slow ringlets in the back of his head. I left my seat and paced in the glassy lobby. My heart knocked to get free of my chest and glide up amid the chandeliers. They seemed much in love, childish and animal. He chittered little monkey things to her. There was a coy note in her stutter. They passed without noticing me and stopped under the marquee. Henry lighted a cigarette. She watched as if it were a spectacle for kings. As the fire took life in his eyes, and smoke sifted backward to membranes of his throat, she asked, "What did you think of the m-m-movie, Hen Hen?" His glance became fine, blue as the filament of smoke sliding upward and swaying to breezes no more visible, and vastly less subtle, than the myriad, shifting discriminations that gave sense and value to his answer. "A movie is a complex thing. Images. Actors. I can't quite say." He stared at her without a word. She clucked helplessly. All was light between them. It rose out of warmth. They kissed.

Now I understood and felt much relieved. Henry cared a great deal about movies and he had found someone to whom he could talk about them. Though he hadn't asked me to, I told my story again one evening in company. My voice was soft, but enthusiastic:

"This fellow, ordinary chap with the usual worries about life, had a date to go to the movies with a girl who was quite sweet and pretty and a wonderful conversationalist. She wore a faded gingham blouse, a flowery print skirt and sandals. She limped a bit and had a vague stutter. Her nails were bitten to the neural sheath in finger and toe. She had a faint but regular tic in her left cheek. Throughout the movie she scratched her knees.

"It was a foreign movie about wealthy Italians, mainly a statuesque blonde and a dark, speedy little man who circled about her like a house fly. At last, weary of his constant buzz, she reclined on a bed in his mother's apartment and he did something to her. Afterwards she laughed a great deal, and, near the end of the movie, she discovered an interlocking wire fence. Taking hold with both hands, she clung there while the camera moved away and looked about the city. The movie ended with a study of a street lamp. It had a powerful effect on this fellow and his date. They fell in love before it was half over, and left the theater drunk on the images of the blonde and the speedy little man. He felt the special pertinence of the movie and was speechless. She honored his silence and was speechless, too. Both of them being consciously modern types, they did the thing as soon as they got to her apartment. An act of recognition. A testimony, he thought, to their respect for one another and an agreement to believe their love was more than physical. Any belief needs ritual; so this one. Ergo, the beastly act. Unless it's done, you know, 'a great Prince in prison lies.' Now they could know one another. No longer drunk, they sat disheveled and gloomy on her living-room floor. Neither looked at the other's face, and she, for the sake of motion, scratched her knees. At last, she rose and went to take a shower. When the door shut behind her, he imagined he heard a sob. He crushed his cigarette, went to the window, and flung himself out to the mercy of the night. He has these awful headaches now and constant back pains."

People thought it was a grand story. Henry looked at me till his eyes went click and his mouth resolved into a sneer.

"Ever get a headache in this spot?" he asked, tapping the back of his head.

"Sometimes," I answered, leaning toward him and smiling.

"Then look out. It's a bad sign. It means you've got a slipped disc and probably need an operation. They might have to cut your head off."

Everyone laughed, though no one more than I. Then I got a headache and trembled for an hour. Henry wanted me to have a slipped disc.

Such a man was a threat to the world and public denunciation was in order. I considered beginning work on a small tract about evil, personified by Henry. But I really had nothing to say. He had done me no injury. My dream, however, was obviously the truth: he wanted to kill me. Perhaps, inadvertently, I had said or done something to insult him. A gentleman, says Lord Chesterfield, never unintentionally insults anyone. But I didn't fancy myself a gentleman. Perhaps there was some aspect of my character he thought ghastly. After all, you may know a person for centuries before discovering a hideous peculiarity in him. I considered changing my character, but I didn't know how or what to change. It was perplexing. Henry's character was vile, so I would change mine. I hadn't ever thought his character was vile before. Now, all I had to do was think: "Henry." Vile, oh vile, vile. It would require a revolution in me. Better that than lose a friend. No; better to be yourself and proud. Tell Henry to go to hell. But a real friend goes to hell himself. One afternoon, on my way to hell, I turned a corner and was face to face with Marjorie. She stopped and smiled. Behind her I could see flames. Fluttering down the wind came the sound of prayer.

There was no reason to run. I stood absolutely rigid. She blushed, looked down and said hello. My right hand whispered the same, then twitched and spun around. It slipped from the end of my arm like a leaf from a bough. She asked how I had. My feet clattered off in opposite directions. I smiled and asked her how she had been. Before she might answer anything social and ordinary, a groan flew up my throat. My teeth couldn't resist its force and it was suddenly in the air. Both of us marveled, though I more than she. She was too polite to make anything of it and suggested we stroll. The groan hovered behind us, growing smaller and more contorted. While she talked of the last few months, I nodded at things I approved of. I approved of everything and nodded without cease until my head fell off. She looked away as I groped for it on the ground and put it back on, shouting hello, hello.

How could I have been so blind, so careless, cruel and stupid? This was a lovely girl. I, beast and fool, adjusting my head, felt now what I should have felt then. And I felt that Henry was marvelous. "Seen any movies lately?" I asked.

She stuttered something about a movie and Henry's impressions of it. The stutter was worse than I remembered, and now that I looked her face seemed thin, the flesh gray. In her effort not to stutter, strain showed in her neck. As if it were my habitual right, I took her hand. She continued to stutter something Henry had said about the movie, and didn't snap her hand back. Tears formed in my nose. "Thank you," I whispered. "F-for what?" she asked. We were near an empty lot. I turned abruptly against her, my lips quivering. She said, "Really, Phillip, I d-don't w-want . . ." With a rapid hand I discovered that she wore no underpants. We fell together. I caught sight of her later as she sprinted into the darkness. Groans issued from my mouth. They flew after her like a flock of bats.

It was a week before Henry came to see me, but I was certain I had heard the bell a hundred times. Each time, I put out my cigarette and dragged to the door, ready for a punch in the face, a knife or a bullet. In the middle of the night, I found myself sitting up in bed, my eyes large and compendious with dark as I shouted, "No, Henry, no." Though I shouted, I had resolved to say nothing or little when he finally came. Not a word would shape my mouth if I could help it. A word would be an excuse. Even self-denunciation was beyond decent possibility. If he flung acid in my face, I would fall and say, "Thanks." If he were out in the hall with a gun and fired point blank into my stomach, I might, as I toppled, blood sloshing through my lips, beg forgiveness. Though I merited no such opportunity, I hoped there would be time for it. If I could, while begging, keep my eyes fixed on him, it would be nice.

After three days passed and he still hadn't come, I thought of hanging myself. I tied a rope to the light bulb, made a noose and set a chair under it. But I couldn't, when I experimented, manage to open the door and then dash to the chair and hang myself without looking clumsy, as if I were really asking to be stopped. On the other hand, I didn't want to practice, become graceful and look effete. I considered poison: open the door, hello, down it goes, goodbye. Or fire: set myself on fire and shrivel, spitting curses on my head.

Despite all this I slept well most of the week, and on several nights I dreamed of Marjorie. We did it everytime. "Is this the nature of sin?" I asked. "This is nature," she said. "Don't talk." I discovered a truth in these dreams: each of my feelings was much like another, pity like lust, hate like love, sorrow like joy. I wondered if there were people who could keep them neat. I supposed not. They were feelings and not to be managed. If I felt bad I felt good. That was that.

The idea made me smile. When I noticed myself smiling, I chuckled a bit, and soon I was cackling. Tears streamed out of my eyes. I had to lie on the floor to keep from sinking there. I lay for a long time digging my nails into my cheeks and thought about the nature of ideas. Pascal, Plato, Freud. I felt kin to men like that. Having ideas, seized as it were. I had had an idea.

When I heard the doorbell I knew immediately that I had heard it. The ring was different from the phony ringing during the week. It was substantial, moral, piercing. It set me running to answer, dashing between tables and chairs, leaping a sofa, lunging down the hall to come flying to the ringing door where I swerved and came back to where I had been. A voice more primitive than any noise the body makes, said:

"Let the son of a bitch ring."

My lips slid up my teeth, my ears flattened to the skull. I found myself crouching. Muscles bunched in my shoulders. I felt a shuddering stiffness in my thighs. Tight as bow strings, tendons curled the bones of my hands to claws. The bell continued to ring, and a hot, ragged tongue slapped across my muzzle. I smelled the sweet horror of my breath. It bristled my neck and sent me gliding low to the ringing door, a noiseless animal, blacker and more secret than night.

Henry out there stood dying in his shoes, ringing in gruesome demise. My paws lifted and lopped down softly. Blood poured me, slow as steaming tar, inevitably toward the door. My paw lay on the knob. It turned. I tugged. Nothing happened. He rang. I shouted, "Can't open it. Give a shove." I tugged, Henry shoved. I twisted the knob and he flung himself against the other side. A panel dislodged. I had a glimpse of his face, feverish and shining. A blaze of white teeth cut the lower half. The door stayed shut. We yelled to one another.

"All right. Give it everything."

"Here we go."

The door opened.

Henry stood in the hall, looking straight into my eyes. The crooked nose, the blue eyes. The physical man. Nothing I felt, absolutely nothing, could accommodate the fact of him. I wondered if it were actually Henry, and I looked rapidly about his face, casting this and that aside like a man fumbling through his wallet for his driver's license while the trooper grimly waits. Nothing turned up to name him Henry. Even the familiar tooth left me unimpressed. Henry's features made no more sense than a word repeated fifty times. The physical man, Henry, Henry, Henry, Henry. Nothing. I wanted to cry and beg him to be Henry again, but only snickered and stepped back. He came inside. I took a package of cigarettes from my pocket and offered it to him. He stared, then shook his head. The movement was trivial, but it was no. No! It startled me into sense. I put the cigarettes back into my pocket and sighed. The breath ran out slowly, steadily, like sand through an hour glass. This was it. He followed with a sigh of his own, then said, "I guess this is it."

"I guess," I murmured, "it is."

"Yes," he said, "it is," and took a long, deep breath, as if drawing up the air I had let out.

I began to strangle. Neither of us spoke. I coughed. He cleared his throat in a sympathetic reflex. I coughed. He cleared his throat once more. I coughed a third time, and he waited for me to stop, but I continued to cough. I was barely able to see, though my eyes bulged. He asked if I wanted a glass of water. I nodded and doubled forward wiping my bulging eyes. When he returned with the water I seized it and drank. He asked if I wanted another glass. I said, "No thanks," coughed again, a rasping, rotten-chested hack. He rushed for another glass. I saw it trembling in his hand. His sleeve was wet to the elbow. "Thanks," I said and seized it.

"Go on, go on, drink."

I drank.

"Finish it," he urged.

I finished it slowly.

"You ought to sit down."

I went to a chair and sat down. My head rolled in a dull, feeble way, and a moment passed in silence. Then he said:

"There has been enough of this."

I stood up instantly.

He looked at me hard. I tried to look back equally hard, as if his look were an order that I do the same. His height and sharp little eyes gave him the advantage. "Yes," I said, shaking my head yes.

"Months of it. Enough!"

"I'm responsible," I muttered, and that put force into my look. "All my fault," I said, force accumulating.

"Don't be ridiculous. I don't blame you for anything. You want to kill me and I don't blame you for that. I'm no friend. I betrayed you."

"Kill you?"

"I came here expecting death. I am determined to settle for nothing less."

"Don't be absurd."

"Absurd? Is it so absurd to want justice? Is it so absurd to ask the friend one has betrayed to do for one the only possible thing that will purge one?"

He moved an inch closer and seemed to be restraining himself, with terrific difficulty, from moving closer.

"Shut up, Henry," I said. "I have no intention of killing you and I never wanted to do such a thing."

"Ha! I see now."

"You don't see a thing, Henry."

"I see," he shouted and slapped his head. "I see why you refuse to do it, why you pretend you don't even want to do it."

He slapped his head again very hard.

"I see, Phillip, you're a moral genius. By not killing me you administer cruel, perfect justice."

"Henry, get a hold of yourself. Be fair to both of us, will you?"

"Don't hand me that liberal crap, Phillip. Don't talk to me about fair. You be fair. Do the right thing, the merciful thing. Kill me, Phillip."

I started backing toward the door, my hands stuffed deep between my lowest ribs. Henry shuffled after me, his little eyes wild with fury and appreciation. "No use. I will follow you until you show mercy. I will bring you guns and knives and ropes, vats of poison, acids, gasoline and matches. I will leap in front of your car. I will . . ."

Whirling suddenly, I was out the door. Henry gasped and followed, tearing for a grip on the back of my head. We went down the night, Henry ripping out fists of my flying hair and jamming them into his mouth so he might choke. The night became day, and day night. These a week, the week a month. My hair was soon gone from the back of my head. When it grew in he ripped it out again. The wind lacerated our faces and tore the clothes off our bodies. Occasionally, I heard him scream, "I have a gun. Shoot me." Or, "A rope, Phillip. Strangle me." I had a step on him always and I ran on powerful legs. Over the running years, they grew more powerful. They stretched and swelled to the size of trees while my body shrank and my head descended. At last my arms disappeared and I was a head on legs. Running.

the nature
of the task

HOWARD NEMEROV from *Virginia Quarterly Review*

Palen's first assignment seemed a simple one, though somewhat demeaning: he was supposed to kill the flies in the room. Not his own room, the one he slept in and to which he was returned at intervals for the other necessities of life, but another room, one which had the appearance of being specially devised, Palen could not quite say for what—not merely as a place in which flies were killed, certainly; but it just had that intentional look, austere and technical. For one thing, it was square, as near as he could tell an exact cube, and unfurnished but for one window, also square and set so high in a corner that nothing could be seen but sky and the tip of a single tree without leaves. The window was divided by iron bars into a lattice of nine equal squares, and by a screen of fine, black mesh beyond the bars, so that the sky, the single tree, the passing cloud, even the occasional bird, appeared superimposed on a graph.

No fly was either visible or audible at first—which was not to say, Palen reminded himself, that there were no flies in the room. For the speckled linoleum of the floor, the pitted acoustical tiles of the ceiling, and the wallpaper, patterned of dark-blue snowflakes ceaselessly failing to fall, offered, probably by design, an ideal camouflage for a quiescent fly—he remembered that flies were said never to sleep, but they sometimes sat still, he was fairly sure of that—who might at any moment reveal himself.

Palen could not help acknowledging a feeling of chagrin about the humble nature of his task—a man need not necessarily be arrogant to consider himself capable of better than swatting flies—but he took this feeling in hand, reminding himself that he had chosen the discipline voluntarily, and so was in a poor position to resent whatever form it took; and seeing, also, that the very lowness and foolishness of the task must probably be by intention, as though testing from the start for the presence of any pride or individual assertiveness to be eradicated. No, he refused to be fooled so easily, refused to be fooled at all; he would stoop his pride to a proper use in the odd situation, if he were put into this cubical world to swat flies, why, he would pride himself upon swatting flies well.

Swatting—it now occurred to him that the conventional weapon for the purpose was not only absent; it had not even been mentioned. The common fly-swatter, a device so primitive it must have appeared at the dawn of history, so inexpensive that even the poorest families might own several, and so selectively efficient an instrument of the human will that not even insecticides could replace it—this instrument was not provided, and its absence gave Palen a moment of regret and even resentment; the fly-swatter he did not have seemed to him not only functional but beautiful as well, so that even the way of passively holding it in expectation would have had an emblematic quality as of the monarch's scepter, once perhaps a mace, and those elegant riding crops that officers used to carry long after their horses had vanished; it would have given an air.

If no fly-swatter, perhaps no fly? Perhaps, and the thought came to Palen as an instant of revelation, he had misinterpreted the problem altogether, and the instruction "to kill the flies in the room" had some allegorical, or even religious sense, as "to destroy the nasty black thoughts that feed on the filth of the self, and whose buzzing has but this one use, that it serves to keep the soul from sleeping in its foulness."

This resolution of the difficulty pleased him at first, but soon began to appear oversimplified. After all, he thought then, even if that is the meaning, it is only the first meaning, the one appearing on the surface; and surely one ought to suspect the obvious and immediate in these matters. On reflection it seemed more likely that the instruction about killing the flies would be a riddle, such as any number of religions had availed themselves of for purposes of instruction, of leading the mind outward from its fixities and falsehoods, and the appropriate reply might be some kind of metaphor—that the flies were thoughts was already a metaphor!—or even an absurdity and a sheer irrelevance, a test of the mind's ability to *leap* . . . where?

In an empty room, Palen now discovered, you cannot leap very far. What was the opposite of a fly? the negation of a fly? In an unfurnished room, even sheer irrelevance is hard to come by, while absurdity, in the confines of a space so like an absence, might well be impossible. But he was to *do* something, of that he felt certain.

Given so sparse a field to choose from, he decided on the snowflakes, and there entered his mind at once a proverb probably psychiatric in origin: he remembered having heard that in some sense to count things was to kill them. So if you equated, by way of axiom, snowflakes with flies, it followed that counting the snowflakes was killing the flies; though that bit of lore about counting summoned up in its wake another, the memory that the Lord God of the Old Testament had set his face obstinately and definitely against numbering and the taking of a census, these newfangled notions probably appearing to Him as unprofitably scientific or even sociological, and somehow bound straight toward idolatry. Still, Lord God, that particular bearded monster from childhood, need not be considered in the present situation. Palen began to number the stars, thinking it best to begin at floor level in a corner and work his way alternately up and down and steadily clockwise around the room. In fact, he now saw, the arithmetic learned in childhood would help him mightily, since the number for one wall would be identical with the number for the opposite wall; while on account of the room's being a cube—one would have to check that also—the other walls might be done by the simple geometrical exercise of subtracting the number of snowflakes contained in the area of window and door.

At this moment he realized that he had no measuring instrument for doing all this, any more than he would have had a fly-swatter had real flies been in question. Palen sighed, feeling a trifle reduced. It would have been so simple, and the calculations themselves, easy as they were, would have afforded him a certain pleasure, not necessarily at his own ingenuity but at the marvelous thing the human intelligence was, with its ability to inherit the thoughts of men long dead. But he would have to count instead. He was thrown back, and probably this too was part of the purpose, upon the self as it was, alone and unaided by the devices of civilization. He was able to count, of course, that was true. But perhaps counting was not a device of civilization, perhaps it was something given? As the mathematicians were accustomed to say, God made the integers, man did all the rest.

Before beginning on the project, though, Palen allowed himself a few minutes of doubt, discouragement, irritable apathy, and cynicism concerning the whole course, however it might go, of what he had let himself in for—"the last expression," he hopefully put it to himself, "of the old, bad, unhappy civilian self." He permitted his memory to rove back over his former life, pausing upon common and familiar pleasures, trivial in themselves, certainly, but supremely important as embodying the one great pleasure of doing what you pleased. And now? Now this—this insensate activity that he was being compelled to do by his own free will: counting the wallpaper, wasn't that proverbially a sign of madness?

After a fit of this indulgence, Palen brought himself up short with the reminder that it had been the former life itself, with its pleasures that never pleased, its hunger-bearing fruits, the ill taste of its satisfactions, that had determined him to the present course. And here he was, ready to break down before the first and doubtless simplest exercise. That would be little faith indeed, for one who had so bravely or foolishly proposed so much, and whose object must be a happiness, even perhaps a power, transcending any possible image that the mind was able to form. So. If it began by counting, he would count.

What he had not counted on, however, was that the work might be not merely difficult, but positively a suffering to body and mind together. It went this way.

Palen knelt down in the corner (image, he remembered, of disgrace and contrition), and pointed to the first, lowest snowflake. Here was already a difficulty, for owing to the nature of wallpaper it happened that some of the flakes on the wall to his left overlapped onto the wall to his right, where he wanted to begin. Well, that was easy enough, he would leave them out, take them last, after making the whole circuit. Only he had to remember that he had taken this decision and not the alternative one to count them first; it was one more thing to remember, and even on account of its simplicity seemed disproportionately a burden. Still, it was decided, and he started counting. But the damnable naturalism of the makers of the wallpaper was such that their snowflakes didn't fall in straight lines, *more geometrico,* but in a helter and a dance; it was distracting, too, that the same impulse to naturalism had made the designer provide several different shapes for his snowflakes, to suggest to the mind the well-known scientific fact that no two snowflakes were alike. Getting used to this circumstance alone made it necessary for Palen to start over several times. But he found in his favor that it was possible, by holding one hand for a boundary marker, so to limit the space under consideration that the small starry shapes formed momentary patterns that could successfully be counted, and if, with patience, he could hold out till he reached a seam—though he dared not look up, he figured that the seam must be not more than a yard away—there would be plain sailing from then on, a matter merely of multiplication. Still, he could have wept for the want of a pencil; how well things would go with a pencil, you would circle the flakes, or even number them, or check them off as you went. . . . The thought made him lose count, and he had to start over.

The practice, however, was definitely bringing about an improvement in his ability, though at the same time fatigue was perceptibly beginning to appear as a factor; something, he observed, that entered his awareness in the form of denial as he said to himself with surprise, "I'm not at all tired yet," and realized it was the cramp in his knees, the ache in his back, the forming of tears in his eyes, that said this. Rising from his knees he stooped, he stood bent over, gradually straightened up, tilted his head back, raised his arm with pointing, counting finger, stood on tiptoe, counting all the while aloud, while the numbers grew monstrous. . . . Because of the cube shape of the room he could not reach anywhere near the ceiling, and up there the stars blinked and occulted before his dazed eyes, his wavering finger, the dizziness of the mind.

And the numbers grew so rapidly, they too were a physical burden to be borne out on the sighing tide of the breath and only to become fully articulate on the last digit. It had seemed so simple at first! Only ten integers to remember, plus one more, the changing first one after every ten; but then, at a hundred, it was two more; and at a thousand three; and when he reached ten thousand. . . .

He did not reach ten thousand, or anything like it. A little flicker of motion at the corner of his eye, of real motion in the midst of that dancing stasis, compelled him to turn his head even as he realized that in doing so he had already lost count and would have to begin again. Looking up and back at the window he saw that while he was engaged in his ordeal the sky had clouded over, and snow had just now begun to fall, a few flakes that even as he stared seemed to increase in number.

Palen sat down—it was not quite that, rather he fell in a sitting position—and put his head in his hands. He shut his eyes, and then rubbed them hard with his knuckles, so that he saw against a burning background a dance of black sparks that even his tears could not quench. These tears were not quite childish tears of outrage and frustration, but neither were they quite the tears of fatigue and strained attention; rather they shared the sponsorship of both, and to Palen this seemed just, correct, and dignified: something that went together in a world where other things did not appear to possess this property.

Thus he sat for some time, though in his changed state of mind the casual "some time" seemed inappropriate though he used it himself. It was more like being in eternity "for some time." It was not only his having been deprived of his watch; he would not in any event have consulted his watch. Alone in the empty room, it came to him to think, "It doesn't count," and "nothing counts." The last especially, perhaps owing to the insoluble ambiguity in the means provided by language for saying it, whatever it was, made an immense, a near absolute, appeal to his feelings; it was at once a mystery and a consolation in the presence of that mystery.

Very gradually, however, Palen came to himself, his thoughts began to sort themselves out in something like reasonable order, and he began in spite of himself to wrestle again with his strange situation. He remembered, to begin with, that the insane business of counting the snowflakes on the wallpaper had been entirely his own invention; nothing in the initial situation as given made him do this, he did it on his own. That was an appalling thought, but yet had a dignity to it if you compared it with the nonsense of numbers he had just put himself through. He had made a mistake, admitted. But even the existence of a mistake proved the existence of a correct solution, or at any rate suggested the likelihood of one.

"All right, I made a mistake, I was wrong. But I am able to acknowledge it." And the thing to do when you perceived that you had made a mistake, as Palen knew even from school days, was to go back along the chain of reasoning—the thread of reasoning, more likely, in this instance—and see just where you made the first step off the true path.

When he attempted to apply this principle, Palen was upset, and even a little frightened, at the spectacle of his own glibness—or the glibness of a mind that moved, it seemed, independently of his will—at getting from here to there. It was even very difficult, at first, to remember what he had started from only a short while ago, the instruction to kill the flies in the room, the relation of that to fly-swatters, the negation of both terms, the translation of that negation in other terms symmetrical with the first . . . leading to the madly irrelevant decision that counting snowflakes on the wall was "the same thing as" killing flies.

Palen believed he had learned something from this sudden and terrible experience—now he looked back upon it he saw how ridiculous and stupid it was, but reminded himself all the same that it had indeed been sudden and terrible. He thought he understood now why the first instruction of the master to the disciple in any mystery had to be a deep and thoroughgoing distrust of the reason—just because it "reasoned" so very well.

The reason's work was so exclusively concerned with single threads isolated from the pattern that finally it took the thread it followed for the whole design. Whereas—

And now he saw. Pattern! Design! how foolish to believe that wallpaper ever came otherwise! He had been pursuing the foolish futility of a savage, or of those half-sophisticated persons who believe that scientific truth emerges of itself out of the collection of large numbers of facts.

The wallpaper—supposing, as he helplessly had to, the wallpaper to be somehow relevant—had a pattern. And perhaps part of his task here (while waiting for those improbable or nonexistent flies) was to elucidate the pattern. Upon this consideration he forced himself to open his eyes, and keep them open although the sight of those dark blue snowflakes made him sleepy almost at once.

Palen advised himself that there was no hurry, not this time. One must just sit and contemplate—sit and stare, would be the better, because the stupider, expression. Under no circumstances was the active intelligence to intervene with its plausible suggestions. After all, it was a point of faith that the assigned task might be very difficult, but not in the nature of things impossible. One must simply sit still. Indeed, that might be precisely the mystical import of an instruction to kill the flies in a room where no flies were: that is, do nothing—the chief recommendation of the great religious of every persuasion from the beginning of the world.

But where—this problem proposed itself inevitably and at once—where did simply looking divide itself from looking and thinking at once? Palen found it impossible not to observe right at the start, for instance, that the seam he had counted on reaching did not exist; the wallpaper went in one unbroken reach from wall to wall and floor to ceiling. Did it possibly go all around the room in a similar manner? He was about to go over to a corner and inspect this more closely, but reminded himself of his very recent decision to sit still: here he was, about to break it almost at once.

And then, this pattern that he intuited, or believed in, or postulated— would it be large or small? How large? How small? At the extreme limits, any two flakes might form a pattern duplicated in any two other flakes; or there might be no repetition whatever over the whole wall, though if that were so one might test the hypothesis that one wall duplicated its opposite, as though it were a mirror.

The mad thought that one of the walls might *be* a mirror hit Palen so suddenly that he shut his eyes tight once again, and kept them that way until reason came to offer the soothing suggestion that Palen too would have to be reflected in such a wall, since he . . . and so on and so on, after the manner of reason.

"—If I exist," said Palen aloud and with an unnecessarily assertive laugh. But he allowed himself to be persuaded all the same into opening his eyes and being reassured, if that was the word, that either he did not exist or one wall was not a mirror; though as to the question of symmetry between one and another wall, that would take patient study which he did not feel quite up to at this time.

Again he was looking, only looking. But from nowhere, and at terrible speed—you could not not have thought it, once you had thought it—there formed in his mind the hypothesis that, on the wallpaper as in nature, there were no two snowflakes alike. At least, Palen could not remember having seen any two alike.

Once opened up, the possible field of this thought appeared to extend indefinitely. Palen had always unthinkingly accepted it as a scientific fact that no two snowflakes were alike; their differences-in-sameness, the elaboration of infinite variations upon the one unpromising hexagonal construction, were always being held up as witness to the unfailing delicacy and artistry, as well as deathly fecundity, of Nature. But now that he thought of this bit of lore, the difficulty or impossibility of ever demonstrating any such thing became for Palen the most obvious and glaring fact in the entire situation; and the well-known scientific fact a piece of preposterous scientific arrogance on the one hand and of gossipy superstition on the other; yet he would have said that he had "always thought" it. Why, even the difficulty of keeping a snowflake unmelted long enough to make possible the gathering of all other snowflakes for purposes of comparison—even the making of an inclusive catalogue—and even that would not account for the snowflakes that had fallen in past winters and were irretrievably gone, the snowflakes of yesteryear—and even this and even that, until Palen realized that he was doing something suspiciously close to counting again, and, with an effort, stopped.

Simultaneously with the conclusion of this meditation he directed his attention outward and realized two things. The snow outside the window had ceased from falling. And somewhere in the room a fly that had been buzzing probably for some time, was buzzing.

Humbly, for Fyodor

ALDEN NOWLAN   from *Prism International*

There were times when he could not believe he would die until he was so old it wouldn't matter. As a child, he had decided for reasons he could no longer remember that his death would occur on August 4, 2004, seven months after his seventy-first birthday. He had written obituaries for the great man he then dreamed of becoming.

CANNES, FRANCE *(AP—Reuters)—Nobel Prize-winning Canadian author and world-famous adventurer Kevin Michael O'Brien died here yesterday. Tributes poured in—*

And in many ways his attitude toward death at thirty-three was no different than it had been at fourteen. Occasionally, like an eclipse of the sun, the shadow of imminent oblivion would cross his consciousness. He would realize suddenly that, in truth, he was going to die, be obliterated, erased, made nothing. And, should the cell madness erupt in another province of his body, his death would come comparatively soon. Yes, he would die and, as his intellect well knew, in the cosmic scheme of things his death would be no more important than the withering of a flower.

Twice in the months since he had learned the nature of his disease, he had wept: once from sheer physical, mental and spiritual exhaustion after his third operation, and once from cowardice. Coming out from under the anesthetic after the final operation on his throat, he had been so unmanned by pain and exhaustion that he had reverted to childhood. He had clung to his wife and pleaded with her not to let them hurt him again. *You won't let them hurt me anymore, Terry? Promise me you won't, Terry.* She had called him *baby* and kissed his forehead and they had given him drugs and, finally, he had slept.

And he had wept when he was returned to hospital for postoperative radiotherapy. He had roamed through hospital corridors half the night, debating whether he should throw himself from a window into the concrete parking lot or steal out of the institution and drown himself in the harbour. What a strange creature is man that the fear of death should provoke thoughts of suicide! He had even contemplated escaping from the hospital, buying a quart of liquor and driving toward Quebec or the United States border—as though in Boston or Montreal he could elude death.

He had wandered all over the hospital and the few nurses and technicians he had met had ignored him; perhaps because he was fully-clothed they mistook him for an employee. At last he had hidden in a closet and wept with self-pity—and the tears had purged him so that next day he was joking with his fellow patients and by the end of the week his reputation as a comedian was so well-established that he felt obligated to be amusing even while suffering through the artificial sunstroke caused by the radiation.

What, after all, was the difference between courage and cowardice? Once in an argument over Ernest Hemingway he had maintained that courage was an artificial virtue, most esteemed in neurotic societies. The man who ran, he had argued, was no worse than the man who stood and fought and chances were he was a good deal wiser. But he had never really believed this. He was so pitifully anxious to appear brave that on the night prior to his operation he had mentally rehearsed how he would behave, even what he would say, in the operating room. *I feel like a bit player on the Dr. Kildare Show,* he had grinned as he sank into the drugged sleep that might end in death. And he had been overjoyed to hear one of the nurses saying: *He's a cool customer; looks as though he could perform the surgery himself.*

It was better to be brave than cowardly (how he loathed the phony connotations that had accrued to the word *brave*) simply because the brave man suffered less than the coward. He was a little proud that he could view the question so pragmatically. *Every man owed God a death.* But it would be insane to run forward to meet death—and that, paradoxically, was what the coward did, what he had done when he had contemplated suicide and an escape that was only suicide prolonged and disguised.

He had learned, also, that such fear was a luxury. Immediately after an operation, when there was danger of internal hemorrhaging and shock and a nurse checked his blood pressure every thirty minutes he hardly thought of such human matters as death. All his wants were animal. There was thirst, for instance. They refused him water. And he realized that never before in his life had he been really thirsty. Hungry, perhaps, but this thirst was worse than any hunger he had known. Afterwards he understood for the first time why the Biblical writers, surrounded by desert, used the thirst for water to represent the ferocity of their desire for God. He understood with shattering clarity what Christ had meant when he said: *I thirst.* Until then, this had been a casual statement like that of a man who goes into a diner and buys a cup of coffee so he'll have a place to sit while he waits for a bus. Now it was as terrible in its pathos as that other cry: *My God, my God, why hast thou forsaken me?* But the latter cry was human; the former reached beyond humanity: a dog no less than a man can go mad with thirst. If he was egotistical enough to identify himself with Christ, he was humble enough to identify himself with his sister's ugly white dog that had to be shot after it was accidentally locked in an unused barn and left there, unfed and unwatered, for weeks. Although, he reflected, that was probably not humility but another form of egotism.

And when he walked for the first time after the first operation, staggering, clutching at the backs of chairs, sliding along the wall like a drunkard, he experienced a sense of triumph that dispelled all fears, as when a man stamps his foot to drive the mice back into their holes. This was one of the most joyously triumphant moments of his life. Gone was the frustration of dropping things and not being able to pick them up; the indignity of being fed and bathed like an infant; the anguish of being unable to raise his hand to drink when, using both hands, he finally succeeded in bringing the glass within inches of his mouth. Had he met death during that walk he'd have spat in his face. He was as contemptuous of death as was Lazarus rising from the tomb.

But now he was out of the vacuum flask that was the hospital. He was at home with his wife and son. In a week or so, the doctor said, he could return to work. There would be tests, of course, endless tests during the next five years. X-rays, blood tests, tests with radioactive iodine. And if he were still alive at the end of five years he would be classified as a five-year survivor, which would mean he had a fair chance of living long enough to die in his sleep of hardening of the arteries. For now, he took books like drugs, watched television, drank beer, smoked cigarettes guiltily, played with his young son, scribbled, went for walks, took drives in the country, even began fooling with watercolours.

On the surface, his life was not very different from what it had always been.

As was suggested in the beginning, a merciful stupidity partially insulated him against the fear of death. He had nightmares every night but he had grown so used to them that they hardly frightened him. He could even smile sardonically at the naïveté of their imagery: as when he dreamt of a gigantic white worm which, upon waking, he assumed to be the Conqueror Worm of Edgar Allan Poe.

Terry wrote to a friend: *Kevin's courage is so great that many people find it disconcerting, even a bit frightening.* Poor, sweet Terry! Never had he loved her more; never had he been less of a lover. Since his discharge from the hospital, they slept in separate beds. When she kissed him he made lame excuses and gently pushed her away. Once when she embraced him she accidentally touched the incisions in his neck and he yelled with pain. *Don't you know better than that, for God's sake?*

He did not want to touch her. Not yet. Because he knew that if life became too sweet he could not maintain his armistice with death.

WHERE ARE YOU GOING,

WHERE HAVE YOU BEEN?

JOYCE CAROL OATES   from *Epoch*

To Bob Dylan

Her name was Connie. She was fifteen and she had a quick nervous giggling habit of craning her neck to glance into mirrors, or checking other people's faces to make sure her own was all right. Her mother, who noticed everything and knew everything and who hadn't much reason any longer to look at her own face, always scolded Connie about it. "Stop gawking at yourself, who are you? You think you're so pretty?" she would say. Connie would raise her eyebrows at these familiar complaints and look right through her mother, into a shadowy vision of herself as she was right at that moment: she knew she was pretty and that was everything. Her mother had been pretty once too, if you could believe those old snapshots in the album, but now her looks were gone and that was why she was always after Connie.

"Why don't you keep your room clean like your sister? How've you got your hair fixed—what the hell stinks? Hair spray? You don't see your sister using that junk."

Her sister June was twenty-four and still lived at home. She was a secretary in the high school Connie attended, and if that wasn't bad enough—with her in the same building—she was so plain and chunky and steady that Connie had to hear her praised all the time by her mother and her mother's sisters. June did this, June did that, she saved money and helped clean the house and cooked and Connie couldn't do a thing, her mind was all filled with trashy daydreams. Their father was away at work most of the time and when he came home he wanted supper and he read the newspaper at supper and after supper he went to bed. He didn't bother talking much to them, but around his bent head

Connie's mother kept picking at her until Connie wished her mother was dead and she herself was dead and it was all over. "She makes me want to throw up sometimes," she complained to her friends. She had a high, breathless, amused voice which made everything she said sound a little forced, whether it was sincere or not.

There was one good thing: June went places with girl friends of hers, girls who were just as plain and steady as she, and so when Connie wanted to do that her mother had no objections. The father of Connie's best girl friend drove the girls the three miles to town and left them off at a shopping plaza, so that they could walk through the stores or go to a movie, and when he came to pick them up again at eleven he never bothered to ask what they had done.

They must have been familiar sights, walking around that shopping plaza in their shorts and flat ballerina slippers that always scuffed the sidewalk, with charm bracelets jingling on their thin wrists; they would lean together to whisper and laugh secretly if someone passed by who amused or interested them. Connie had long dark blond hair that drew anyone's eye to it, and she wore part of it pulled up on her head and puffed out and the rest of it she let fall down her back. She wore a pull-over jersey blouse that looked one way when she was at home and another way when she was away from home. Everything about her had two sides to it, one for home and one for anywhere that was not home: her walk that could be childlike and bobbing, or languid enough to make anyone think she was hearing music in her head, her mouth which was pale and smirking most of the time, but bright and pink on these evenings out, her laugh which was cynical and drawling at home—"Ha, ha, very funny"—but high-pitched and nervous anywhere else, like the jingling of the charms on her bracelet.

Sometimes they did go shopping or to a movie, but sometimes they went across the highway, ducking fast across the busy road, to a drive-in restaurant where older kids hung out. The restaurant was shaped like a big bottle, though squatter than a real bottle, and on its cap was a revolving figure of a grinning boy who held a hamburger aloft. One night in mid-summer they ran across, breathless with daring, and right away someone leaned out a car window and invited them over, but it was just a boy from high school they didn't like. It made them feel good to be able to ignore him. They went up through the maze of parked and cruising cars to the bright-lit, fly-infested restaurant, their faces pleased and expectant as if they were entering a sacred building that loomed out of the night to give them what haven and what blessing they yearned for. They sat at the counter and crossed their legs at the ankles, their thin shoulders rigid with excitement, and listened to the music that made everything so good: the music was always in the background like music at a church service, it was something to depend upon.

A boy named Eddie came in to talk with them. He sat backwards on his stool, turning himself jerkily around in semi-circles and then stopping and turning again, and after a while he asked Connie if she would like something to eat. She said she did and so she tapped her friend's arm on her way out—her friend pulled her face up into a brave droll look—and Connie said she would meet her at eleven, across the way. "I just hate to leave her like that," Connie said earnestly, but the boy said that she wouldn't be alone for long. So they went out to his car and on the way Connie couldn't help but let her eyes wander over the windshields and faces all around her, her face gleaming with a joy that had nothing to do with Eddie or even this place; it might have been the music. She drew her shoulders up and sucked in her breath with the pure pleasure of being alive, and just at that moment she happened to glance at a face just a few feet from hers. It was a boy with shaggy black hair, in a convertible jalopy painted gold. He stared at her and then his lips widened into a grin. Connie slit her eyes at him and turned away, but she couldn't help glancing back and there he was still watching her. He wagged a finger and laughed and said, "Gonna get you, baby," and Connie turned away again without Eddie noticing anything.

She spent three hours with him, at the restaurant where they ate hamburgers and drank Cokes in wax cups that were always sweating, and then down an alley a mile or so away, and when he left her off at five to eleven only the movie house was still open at the plaza. Her girl friend was there, talking with a boy. When Connie came up the two girls smiled at each other and Connie said, "How was the movie?" and the girl said, "*You* should know." They rode off with the girl's father, sleepy and pleased, and Connie couldn't help but look at the darkened shopping plaza with its big empty parking lot and its signs that were faded and ghostly now, and over at the drive-in restaurant where cars were still circling tirelessly. She couldn't hear the music at this distance.

Next morning June asked her how the movie was and Connie said, "So-so."

She and that girl and occasionally another girl went out several times a week that way, and the rest of the time Connie spent around the house—it was summer vacation—getting in her mother's way and thinking, dreaming, about the boys she met. But all the boys fell back and dissolved into a single face that was not even a face, but an idea, a feeling, mixed up with the urgent insistent pounding of the music and the humid night air of July. Connie's mother kept dragging her back to the daylight by finding things for her to do or saying, suddenly, "What's this about the Pettinger girl?"

And Connie would say nervously, "Oh, her. That dope." She always drew thick clear lines between herself and such girls, and her mother was simple and kindly enough to believe her. Her mother was so simple, Connie thought, that it was maybe cruel to fool her so much. Her mother went scuffling around the house in old bedroom slippers and complained over the telephone to one sister about the other, then the other called up and the two of them complained about the third one. If June's name was mentioned her mother's tone was approving, and if Connie's name was mentioned it was disapproving. This did not really mean she disliked Connie and actually Connie thought that her mother preferred her to June because she was prettier, but the two of them kept up a pretense of exasperation, a sense that they were tugging and struggling over something of little value to either of them. Sometimes, over coffee, they were almost friends, but something would come up—some vexation that was like a fly buzzing suddenly around their heads—and their faces went hard with contempt.

One Sunday Connie got up at eleven—none of them bothered with church—and washed her hair so that it could dry all day long, in the sun. Her parents and sister were going to a barbecue at an aunt's house and Connie said no, she wasn't interested, rolling her eyes to let mother know just what she thought of it. "Stay home alone then," her mother said sharply. Connie sat out back in a lawn chair and watched them drive away, her father quiet and bald, hunched around so that he could back the car out, her mother with a look that was still angry and not at all softened through the windshield, and in the back seat poor old June all dressed up as if she didn't know what a barbecue was, with all the running yelling kids and the flies. Connie sat with her eyes closed in the sun, dreaming and dazed with the warmth about her as if this were a kind of love, the caresses of love, and her mind slipped over onto thoughts of the boy she had been with the night before and how nice he had been, how sweet it always was, not the way someone like June would suppose but sweet, gentle, the way it was in movies and promised in songs; and when she opened her eyes she hardly knew where she was, the back yard ran off into weeds and a fence-line of trees and behind it the sky was perfectly blue and still. The asbestos "ranch house" that was now three years old startled her—it looked small. She shook her head as if to get awake.

It was too hot. She went inside the house and turned on the radio to drown out the quiet. She sat on the edge of her bed, barefoot, and listened for an hour and a half to a program called XYZ Sunday Jamboree, record after record of hard, fast, shrieking songs she sang along with, interspersed by exclamations from "Bobby King": "An' look here you girls at Napoleon's—Son and Charley want you to pay real close attention to this song coming up!"

And Connie paid close attention herself, bathed in a glow of slow-pulsed joy that seemed to rise mysteriously out of the music itself and lay languidly about the airless little room, breathed in and breathed out with each gentle rise and fall of her chest.

After a while she heard a car coming up the drive. She sat up at once, startled, because it couldn't be her father so soon. The gravel kept crunching all the way in from the road—the driveway was long—and Connie ran to the window. It was a car she didn't know. It was an open jalopy, painted a bright gold that caught the sunlight opaquely. Her heart began to pound and her fingers snatched at her hair, checking it, and she whispered "Christ. Christ," wondering how bad she looked. The car came to a stop at the side door and the horn sounded four short taps as if this were a signal Connie knew.

She went into the kitchen and approached the door slowly, then hung out the screen door, her bare toes curling down off the step. There were two boys in the car and now she recognized the driver: he had shaggy, shabby black hair that looked crazy as a wig and he was grinning at her.

"I ain't late, am I?" he said.

"Who the hell do you think you are?" Connie said.

"Toldja I'd be out, didn't I?"

"I don't even know who you are."

She spoke sullenly, careful to show no interest or pleasure, and he spoke in a fast bright monotone. Connie looked past him to the other boy, taking her time. He had fair brown hair, with a lock that fell onto his forehead. His sideburns gave him a fierce, embarrassed look, but so far he hadn't even bothered to glance at her. Both boys wore sunglasses. The driver's glasses were metallic and mirrored everything in miniature.

"You wanta come for a ride?" he said.

Connie smirked and let her hair fall loose over one shoulder.

"Don'tcha like my car? New paint job," he said. "Hey."

"What?"

"You're cute."

She pretended to fidget, chasing flies away from the door.

"Don'tcha believe me, or what?" he said.

"Look, I don't even know who you are," Connie said in disgust.

"Hey, Ellie's got a radio, see. Mine's broke down." He lifted his friend's arm and showed her the little transistor the boy was holding, and now Connie began to hear the music. It was the same program that was playing inside the house.

"Bobby King?" she said.

"I listen to him all the time. I think he's great."

"He's kind of great," Connie said reluctantly.

"Listen, that guy's *great*. He knows where the action is."

Connie blushed a little, because the glasses made it impossible for her to see just what this boy was looking at. She couldn't decide if she liked him or if he was just a jerk, and so she dawdled in the doorway and wouldn't come down or go back inside. She said, "What's all that stuff painted on your car?"

"Can'tcha read it?" He opened the door very carefully, as if he was afraid it might fall off. He slid out just as carefully, planting his feet firmly on the ground, the tiny metallic world in his glasses slowing down like gelatine hardening and in the midst of it Connie's bright green blouse. "This here is my name, to begin with," he said. ARNOLD FRIEND was written in tar-like black letters on the side, with a drawing of a round grinning face that reminded Connie of a pumpkin, except it wore sunglasses. "I wanta introduce myself, I'm Arnold Friend and that's my real name and I'm gonna be your friend, honey, and inside the car's Ellie Oscar, he's kinda shy." Ellie brought his transistor radio up to his shoulder and balanced it there. "Now these numbers are a secret code, honey," Arnold Friend explained. He read off the numbers 33, 19, 17 and raised his eyebrows at her to see what she thought of that, but she didn't think much of it. The left rear fender had been smashed and around it was written, on the gleaming gold background: DONE BY CRAZY WOMAN DRIVER. Connie had to laugh at that. Arnold Friend was pleased at her laughter and looked up at her. "Around the other side's a lot more—you wanta come and see them?"

"No."

"Why not?"

"Why should I?"

"Don'tcha wanta see what's on the car? Don'tcha wanta go for a ride?"

"I don't know."

"Why not?"

"I got things to do."

"Like what?"

"Things."

He laughed as if she had said something funny. He slapped his thighs. He was standing in a strange way, leaning back against the car as if he were balancing himself. He wasn't tall, only an inch or so taller than she would be if she came down to him. Connie liked the way he was dressed, which was the way all of them dressed: tight faded jeans stuffed into black, scuffed boots, a belt that pulled his waist in and showed how lean he was, and a white pull-over shirt that was a little soiled and showed the hard small muscles of his arms and shoulders. He looked as if he probably·did hard work, lifting and carrying things. Even his neck looked muscular. And his face was a familiar face, somehow: the jaw and chin and cheeks slightly darkened, because he hadn't shaved for a day or two, and the nose long and hawk-like, sniffing as if she were a treat he was going to gobble up and it was all a joke.

"Connie, you ain't telling the truth. This is your day set aside for a ride with me and you know it," he said, still laughing. The way he straightened and recovered from his fit of laughing showed that it had been all fake.

"How do you know what my name is?" she said suspiciously.

"It's Connie."

"Maybe and maybe not."

"I know my Connie," he said, wagging his finger. Now she remembered him even better, back at the restaurant, and her cheeks warmed at the thought of how she sucked in her breath just at the moment she passed him—how she must have looked to him. And he had remembered her. "Ellie and I come out here especially for you," he said. "Ellie can sit in back. How about it?"

"Where?"

"Where what?"

"Where're we going?"

He looked at her. He took off the sunglasses and she saw how pale the skin around his eyes was, like holes that were not in shadow but instead in light. His eyes were like chips of broken glass that catch the light in an amiable way. He smiled. It was as if the idea of going for a ride somewhere, to some place, was a new idea to him.

"Just for a ride, Connie sweetheart."

"I never said my name was Connie," she said.

"But I know what it is. I know your name and all about you, lots of things," Arnold Friend said. He had not moved yet but stood still leaning back against the side of his jalopy. "I took a special interest in you, such a pretty girl, and found out all about you like I know your parents and sister are gone somewheres and I know where and how long they're going to be gone, and I know who you were with last night, and your best girl friend's name is Betty. Right?"

He spoke in a simple lilting voice, exactly as if he were reciting the words to a song. His smile assured her that everything was fine. In the car Ellie turned up the volume on his radio and did not bother to look around at them.

"Ellie can sit in the back seat," Arnold Friend said. He indicated his friend with a casual jerk of his chin, as if Ellie did not count and she should not bother with him.

"How'd you find out all that stuff?" Connie said.

"Listen: Betty Schultz and Tony Fitch and Jimmy Pettinger and Nancy Pettinger," he said, in a chant. "Raymond Stanley and Bob Hutter—"

"Do you know all those kids?"

"I know everybody."

"Look, you're kidding. You're not from around here."

"Sure."

"But—how come we never saw you before?"

"Sure you saw me before," he said. He looked down at his boots, as if he were a little offended. "You just don't remember."

"I guess I'd remember you," Connie said.

"Yeah?" He looked up at this, beaming. He was pleased. He began to mark time with the music from Ellie's radio, tapping his fists lightly together. Connie looked away from his smile to the car, which was painted so bright it almost hurt her eyes to look at it. She looked at that name. ARNOLD FRIEND. And up at the front fender was an expression that was familiar—MAN THE FLYING SAUCERS. It was an expression kids had used the year before, but didn't use this year. She looked at it for a while as if the words meant something to her that she did not yet know.

"What're you thinking about? Huh?" Arnold Friend demanded. "Not worried about your hair blowing around in the car, are you?"

"No."

"Think I maybe can't drive good?"

"How do I know?"

"You're a hard girl to handle. How come?" he said. "Don't you know I'm your friend? Didn't you see me put my sign in the air when you walked by?"

"What sign?"

"My sign." And he drew an X in the air, leaning out toward her. They were maybe ten feet apart. After his hand fell back to his side the X was still in the air, almost visible. Connie let the screen door close and stood perfectly still inside it, listening to the music from her radio and the boy's blend together. She stared at Arnold Friend. He stood there so stiffly relaxed, pretending to be relaxed, with one hand idly on the door handle as if he were keeping himself up that way and had no intention of ever moving again. She recognized most things about him, the tight jeans that showed his thighs and buttocks and the greasy leather boots and the tight shirt, and even that slippery friendly smile of his, that sleepy dreamy smile that all the boys used to get across ideas they didn't want to put into words. She recognized all this and also the singsong way he talked, slightly mocking, kidding, but serious and a little melancholy, and she recognized the way he tapped one fist against the other in homage to the perpetual music behind him. But all these things did not come together.

She said suddenly, "Hey, how old are you?"

His smile faded. She could see then that he wasn't a kid, he was much older—thirty, maybe more. At this knowledge her heart began to pound faster.

"That's a crazy thing to ask. Can'tcha see I'm your own age?"

"Like hell you are."

"Or maybe a coupla years older, I'm eighteen."

"Eighteen?" she said doubtfully.

He grinned to reassure her and lines appeared at the corners of his mouth. His teeth were big and white. He grinned so broadly his eyes became slits and she saw how thick the lashes were, thick and black as if painted with a black tar-like material. Then he seemed to become embarrassed, abruptly, and looked over his shoulder at Ellie. "*Him*, he's crazy," he said. "Ain't he a riot, he's a nut, a real character." Ellie was still listening to the music. His sunglasses told nothing about what he was thinking. He wore a bright orange shirt unbuttoned halfway to show his chest, which was a pale, bluish chest and not muscular like Arnold Friend's. His shirt collar was turned up all around and the very tips of the collar pointed out past his chin as if they were protecting him. He was pressing the transistor radio up against his ear and sat there in a kind of daze, right in the sun.

"He's kinda strange," Connie said.

"Hey, she says you're kinda strange! Kinda strange!" Arnold Friend cried. He pounded on the car to get Ellie's attention. Ellie turned for the first time and Connie saw with shock that he wasn't a kid either—he had a fair, hairless face, cheeks reddened slightly as if the veins grew too close to the surface of his skin, the face of a forty-year-old baby. Connie felt a wave of dizziness rise in her at this sight and she stared at him as if waiting for something to change the shock of the moment, make it all right again. Ellie's lips kept shaping words, mumbling along with the words blasting in his ear.

"Maybe you two better go away," Connie said faintly.

"What? How come?" Arnold Friend cried. "We come out here to take you for a ride. It's Sunday." He had the voice of the man on the radio now. It was the same voice, Connie thought. "Don'tcha know it's Sunday all day and honey, no matter who you were with last night today you're with Arnold Friend and don't you forget it!— Maybe you better step out here," he said, and this last was in a different voice. It was a little flatter, as if the heat was finally getting to him.

"No. I got things to do."

"Hey."

"You two better leave."

"We ain't leaving until you come with us."

"Like hell I am—"

"Connie, don't fool around with me. I mean, I mean, don't fool *around*," he said, shaking his head. He laughed incredulously. He placed his sunglasses on top of his head, carefully, as if he were indeed wearing a wig, and brought the stems down behind his ears. Connie stared at him, another wave of dizziness and fear rising in her so that for a moment he wasn't even in focus but was just a blur, standing there against his gold car, and she had the idea that he had driven up the driveway all right but had come from nowhere before that and belonged nowhere and that everything about him and even about the music that was so familiar to her was only half real.

"If my father comes and sees you—"

"He ain't coming. He's at a barbecue."

"How do you know that?"

"Aunt Tillie's. Right now they're—uh—they're drinking. Sitting around," he said vaguely, squinting as if he were staring all the way to town and over to Aunt Tillie's back yard. Then the vision seemed to get clear and he nodded energetically. "Yeah. Sitting around. There's your sister in a blue dress, huh? And high heels, the poor sad bitch—nothing like you, sweetheart! And your mother's helping some fat woman with the corn, they're cleaning the corn— husking the corn—"

"What fat woman?" Connie cried.

"How do I know what fat woman, I don't know every goddam fat woman in the world!" Arnold Friend laughed.

"Oh, that's Mrs. Hornby. . . . Who invited her?" Connie said. She felt a little light-headed. Her breath was coming quickly.

"She's too fat. I don't like them fat. I like them the way you are, honey," he said, smiling sleepily at her. They stared at each other for a while, through the screen door. He said softly, "Now what you're going to do is this: you're going to come out that door. You're going to sit up front with me and Ellie's going to sit in the back, the hell with Ellie, right? This isn't Ellie's date. You're my date. I'm your lover, honey."

"What? You're crazy—"

"Yes, I'm your lover. You don't know what that is but you will," he said. "I know that too. I know all about you. But look: it's real nice and you couldn't ask for nobody better than me, or more polite. I always keep my word. I'll tell you how it is, I'm always nice at first, the first time. I'll hold you so tight you won't think you have to try to get away or pretend anything because you'll know you can't. And I'll come inside you where it's all secret and you'll give in to me and you'll love me—"

"Shut up! You're crazy!" Connie said. She backed away from the door. She put her hands against her ears as if she'd heard something terrible, something not meant for her. "People don't talk like that, you're crazy," she muttered. Her heart was almost too big now for her chest and its pumping made sweat break out all over her. She looked out to see Arnold Friend pause and then take a step toward the porch lurching. He almost fell. But, like a clever drunken man, he managed to catch his balance. He wobbled in his high boots and grabbed hold of one of the porch posts.

"Honey—?" he said. "You still listening?"

"Get the hell out of here!"

"Be nice, honey. Listen."

"I'm going to call the police—"

He wobbled again and out of the side of his mouth came a fast spat curse, an aside not meant for her to hear. But even this "Christ!" sounded forced. Then he began to smile again. She watched this smile come, awkward as if he were smiling from inside a mask. His whole face was a mask, she thought wildly, tanned down onto his throat but then running out as if he had plastered make-up on his face but had forgotten about his throat.

"Honey—? Listen, here's how it is. I always tell the truth and I promise you this: I ain't coming in that house after you."

"You better not! I'm going to call the police if you—if you don't—"

"Honey," he said, talking right through her voice, "honey, I'm not coming in there but you are coming out here. You know why?"

She was panting. The kitchen looked like a place she had never seen before, some room she had run inside but which wasn't good enough, wasn't going to help her. The kitchen window had never had a curtain, after three years, and there were dishes in the sink for her to do—probably—and if you ran your hand across the table you'd probably feel something sticky there.

"You listening, honey? Hey?"

"—going to call the police—"

"Soon as you touch the phone I don't need to keep my promise and can come inside. You won't want that."

She rushed forward and tried to lock the door. Her fingers were shaking. "But why lock it," Arnold Friend said gently, talking right into her face. "It's just a screen door. It's just nothing." One of his boots was at a strange angle, as if his foot wasn't in it. It pointed out to the left, bent at the ankle. "I mean, anybody can break through a screen door and glass and wood and iron or anything else if he needs to, anybody at all and specially Arnold Friend. If the place got lit up with a fire honey you'd come running out into my arms, right into my arms and safe at home—like you knew I was your lover and'd stopped fooling around. I don't mind a nice shy girl but I don't like no fooling around." Part of those words were spoken with a slight rhythmic lilt, and Connie somehow recognized them—the echo of a song from last year, about a girl rushing into her boy friend's arms and coming home again—

Connie stood barefoot on the linoleum floor, staring at him. "What do you want?" she whispered.

"I want you," he said.

"What?"

"Seen you that night and thought, that's the one, yes sir. I never needed to look any more."

"But my father's coming back. He's coming to get me. I had to wash my hair first—" She spoke in a dry, rapid voice, hardly raising it for him to hear.

"No, your daddy is not coming and yes, you had to wash your hair and you washed it for me. It's nice and shining and all for me, I thank you, sweetheart," he said, with a mock bow, but again he almost lost his balance. He had to bend and adjust his boots. Evidently his feet did not go all the way down; the boots must have been stuffed with something so that he would seem taller. Connie stared out at him and behind him Ellie in the car, who seemed to be looking off toward Connie's right, into nothing. This Ellie said, pulling the words out of the air one after another as if he were just discovering them, "You want me to pull out the phone?"

"Shut your mouth and keep it shut," Arnold Friend said, his face red from bending over or maybe from embarrassment because Connie had seen his boots. "This ain't none of your business."

"What—what are you doing? What do you want?" Connie said. "If I call the police they'll get you, they'll arrest you—"

"Promise was not to come in unless you touch that phone, and I'll keep that promise," he said. He resumed his erect position and tried to force his shoulders back. He sounded like a hero in a movie, declaring something important. He spoke too loudly and it was as if he were speaking to someone behind Connie. "I ain't made plans for coming in that house where I don't belong but just for you to come out to me, the way you should. Don't you know who I am?"

"You're crazy," she whispered. She backed away from the door but did not want to go into another part of the house, as if this would give him permission to come through the door. "What do you. . . . You're crazy, you . . ."

"Huh? What're you saying, honey?"

Her eyes darted everywhere in the kitchen. She could not remember what it was, this room.

"This is how it is, honey: you come out and we'll drive away, have a nice ride. But if you don't come out we're gonna wait till your people come home and then they're all going to get it.''

"You want that telephone pulled out?'' Ellie said. He held the radio away from his ear and grimaced, as if without the radio the air was too much for him.

"I toldja shut up, Ellie,'' Arnold Friend said, "you're deaf, get a hearing aid, right? Fix yourself up. This little girl's no trouble and's gonna be nice to me, so Ellie keep to yourself, this ain't your date—right? Don't hem in on me. Don't hog. Don't crush. Don't bird dog. Don't trail me,'' he said in a rapid meaningless voice, as if he were running through all the expressions he'd learned but was no longer sure which one of them was in style, then rushing on to new ones, making them up with his eyes closed, "Don't crawl under my fence, don't squeeze in my chipmunk hole, don't sniff my glue, suck my popsicle, keep your own greasy fingers on yourself!'' He shaded his eyes and peered in at Connie, who was backed against the kitchen table. "Don't mind him honey he's just a creep. He's a dope. Right? I'm the boy for you and like I said you come out here nice like a lady and give me your hand, and nobody else gets hurt, I mean, your nice old bald-headed daddy and your mummy and your sister in her high heels. Because listen: why bring them in this?''

"Leave me alone,'' Connie whispered.

"Hey, you know that old woman down the road, the one with the chickens and stuff—you know her?''

"She's dead!''

"Dead? What? You know her?'' Arnold Friend said.

"She's dead—''

"Don't you like her?''

"She's dead—she's—she isn't here any more—''

"But don't you like her, I mean, you got something against her? Some grudge or something?'' Then his voice dipped as if he were conscious of a rudeness. He touched the sunglasses perched on top of his head as if to make sure they were still there. "Now you be a good girl.''

"What are you going to do?''

"Just two things, or maybe three,'' Arnold Friend said. "But I promise it won't last long and you'll like me that way you get to like people you're close to. You will. It's all over for you here, so come on out. You don't want your people in any trouble, do you?''

She turned and bumped against a chair or something, hurting her leg, but she ran into the back room and picked up the telephone. Something roared in her ear, a tiny roaring, and she was so sick with fear that she could do nothing but listen to it—the telephone was clammy and very heavy and her fingers groped down to the dial but were too weak to touch it. She began to scream into the phone, into the roaring. She cried out, she cried for her mother, she felt her breath start jerking back and forth in her lungs as if it were something Arnold Friend were stabbing her with again and again with no tenderness. A noisy sorrowful wailing rose all about her and she was locked inside it the way she was locked inside this house.

After a while she could hear again. She was sitting on the floor with her wet back against the wall.

Arnold Friend was saying from the door, "That's a good girl. Put the phone back."

She kicked the phone away from her.

"No, honey. Pick it up. Put it back right."

She picked it up and put it back. The dial tone stopped.

"That's a good girl. Now you come outside."

She was hollow with what had been fear, but what was now just an emptiness. All that screaming had blasted it out of her. She sat, one leg cramped under her, and deep inside her brain was something like a pinpoint of light that kept going and would not let her relax. She thought, I'm not going to see my mother again. She thought, I'm not going to sleep in my bed again. Her bright green blouse was all wet.

Arnold Friend said, in a gentle-loud voice that was like a stage voice, "The place where you came from ain't there any more, and where you had in mind to go is cancelled out. This place you are now—inside your daddy's house—is nothing but a cardboard box I can knock down any time. You know that and always did know it. You hear me?"

She thought, I have got to think. I have to know what to do.

"We'll go out to a nice field, out in the country here where it smells so nice and it's sunny," Arnold Friend said. "I'll have my arms tight around you so you won't need to try to get away and I'll show you what love is like, what it does. The hell with this house! It looks solid all right," he said. He ran a fingernail down the screen and the noise did not make Connie shiver, as it would have the day before. "Now put your hand on your heart, honey. Feel that? That feels solid too but we know better, be nice to me, be sweet like you can because what else is there for a girl like you but to be sweet and pretty and give in?—and get away before her people come back?"

She felt her pounding heart. Her hand seemed to enclose it. She thought for the first time in her life that it was nothing that was hers, that belonged to her, but just a pounding, living thing inside this body that wasn't really hers either.

"You don't want them to get hurt," Arnold Friend went on. "Now get up, honey. Get up all by yourself."

She stood.

"Now turn this way. That's right. Come over here to me—Ellie, put that away, didn't I tell you? You dope. You miserable creepy dope," Arnold Friend said. His words were not angry but only part of an incantation. The incantation was kindly. "Now come out through the kitchen to me honey and let's see a smile, try it, you're a brave sweet little girl and now they're eating corn and hotdogs cooked to bursting over an outdoor fire, and they don't know one thing about you and never did and honey you're better than them because not a one of them would have done this for you."

Connie felt the linoleum under her feet; it was cool. She brushed her hair back out of her eyes. Arnold Friend let go of the post tentatively and opened his arms for her, his elbows pointing in toward each other and his wrists limp, to show that this was an embarrassed embrace and a little mocking, he didn't want to make her self-conscious.

She put out her hand against the screen. She watched herself push the door slowly open as if she were safe back somewhere in the other doorway, watching this body and this head of long hair moving out into the sunlight where Arnold Friend waited.

"My sweet little blue-eyed girl," he said, in a half-sung sigh that had nothing to do with her brown eyes but was taken up just the same by the vast sunlit reaches of the land behind him and on all sides of him, so much land that Connie had never seen before and did not recognize except to know that she was going to it.

Revelation

FLANNERY O'CONNOR

from *Sewanee Review*

The doctor's waiting room, which was very small, was almost full when the Turpins entered and Mrs. Turpin, who was very large, made it look even smaller by her presence. She stood looming at the head of the magazine table set in the center of it, a living demonstration that the room was inadequate and ridiculous. Her little bright black eyes took in all the patients as she sized up the seating situation. There was one vacant chair and a place on the sofa occupied by a blond child in a dirty blue romper who should have been told to move over and make room for the lady. He was five or six, but Mrs. Turpin saw at once that no one was going to tell him to move over. He was slumped down in the seat, his arms idle at his sides and his eyes idle in his head; his nose ran unchecked.

Mrs. Turpin put a firm hand on Claud's shoulder and said in a voice that included anyone who wanted to listen, "Claud, you sit in that chair there," and gave him a push down into the vacant one. Claud was florid and bald and sturdy, somewhat shorter than Mrs. Turpin, but he sat down as if he were accustomed to doing what she told him to.

Mrs. Turpin remained standing. The only man in the room besides Claud was a lean stringy old fellow with a rusty hand spread out on each knee, whose eyes were closed as if he were asleep or dead or pretending to be so as not to get up and offer her his seat. Her gaze settled agreeably on a well-dressed grey-haired lady whose eyes met hers and whose expression said: if that child belonged to me, he would have some manners and move over—there's plenty of room there for you and him too.

Claud looked up with a sigh and made as if to rise.

"Sit down," Mrs. Turpin said. "You know you're not supposed to stand on that leg. He has an ulcer on his leg," she explained.

Claud lifted his foot onto the magazine table and rolled his trouser leg up to reveal a purple swelling on a plump marble-white calf.

"My!" the pleasant lady said. "How did you do that?"

"A cow kicked him," Mrs. Turpin said.

"Goodness!" said the lady.

Claud rolled his trouser leg down.

"Maybe the little boy would move over," the lady suggested, but the child did not stir.

"Somebody will be leaving in a minute," Mrs. Turpin said. She could not understand why a doctor—with as much money as they made charging five dollars a day to just stick their head in the hospital door and look at you—couldn't afford a decent-sized waiting room. This one was hardly bigger than a garage. The table was cluttered with limp-looking magazines and at one end of it there was a big green glass ash tray full of cigaret butts and cotton wads with little blood spots on them. If she had had anything to do with the running of the place, that would have been emptied every so often. There were no chairs against the wall at the head of the room. It had a rectangular-shaped panel in it that permitted a view of the office where the nurse came and went and the secretary listened to the radio. A plastic fern in a gold pot sat in the opening and trailed its fronds down almost to the floor. The radio was softly playing gospel music.

Just then the inner door opened and a nurse with the highest stack of yellow hair Mrs. Turpin had ever seen put her face in the crack and called for the next patient. The woman sitting beside Claud grasped the two arms of her chair and hoisted herself up; she pulled her dress free from her legs and lumbered through the door where the nurse had disappeared.

Mrs. Turpin eased into the vacant chair, which held her tight as a corset. "I wish I could reduce," she said, and rolled her eyes and gave a comic sigh.

"Oh, *you* aren't fat," the stylish lady said.

"Ooooo I am too," Mrs. Turpin said. "Claud he eats all he wants to and never weighs over one hundred and seventy-five pounds, but me I just look at something good to eat and I gain some weight," and her stomach and shoulders shook with laughter. "You can eat all you want to, can't you, Claud?" she asked, turning to him.

Claud only grinned.

"Well, as long as you have such a good disposition," the stylish lady said, "I don't think it makes a bit of difference what size you are. You just can't beat a good disposition."

Next to her was a fat girl of eighteen or nineteen, scowling into a thick blue book which Mrs. Turpin saw was entitled *Human Development*. The girl raised her head and directed her scowl at Mrs. Turpin as if she did not like her looks. She appeared annoyed that anyone should speak while she tried to read. The poor girl's face was blue with acne and Mrs. Turpin thought how pitiful it was to have a face like that at that age. She gave the girl a friendly smile but the girl only scowled the harder. Mrs. Turpin herself was fat but she had always had good skin, and, though she was forty-seven years old, there was not a wrinkle in her face except around her eyes from laughing too much.

Next to the ugly girl was the child, still in exactly the same position, and next to him was a thin leathery old woman in a cotton print dress. She and Claud had three sacks of chicken feed in their pump house that was in the same print. She had seen from the first that the child belonged with the old woman. She could tell by the way they sat—kind of vacant and white-trashy, as if they would sit there until Doomsday if nobody called and told them to get up. And at right angles but next to the well-dressed pleasant lady was a lank-faced woman who was certainly the child's mother. She had on a yellow sweat shirt and wine-colored slacks, both gritty-looking, and the rims of her lips were stained with snuff. Her dirty yellow hair was tied behind with a little piece of red paper ribbon. Worse than niggers any day, Mrs. Turpin thought.

The gospel hymn playing was, "When I looked up and He looked down," and Mrs. Turpin, who knew it, supplied the last line mentally, "And wona these days I know I'll we-eara crown."

Without appearing to, Mrs. Turpin always noticed people's feet. The well-dressed lady had on red and grey suede shoes to match her dress. Mrs. Turpin had on her good black patent leather pumps. The ugly girl had on Girl Scout shoes and heavy socks. The old woman had on tennis shoes and the white-trashy mother had on what appeared to be bedroom slippers, black straw with gold braid threaded through them—exactly what you would have expected her to have on.

Sometimes at night when she couldn't go to sleep, Mrs. Turpin would occupy herself with the question of who she would have chosen to be if she couldn't have been herself. If Jesus had said to her before he made her, "There's only two places available for you. You can either be a nigger or white-trash," what would she have said? "Please, Jesus, please," she would have said, "just let me wait until there's another place available," and he would have said, "No, you have to go right now and I have only those two places so make up your mind." She would have wiggled and squirmed and begged and pleaded but it would have been no use and finally she would have said, "All right, make me a nigger then—but that don't mean a trashy one." And he would have made her a neat clean respectable negro woman, herself but black.

Next to the child's mother was a red-headed youngish woman, reading one of the magazines and working on a piece of chewing gum, hell for leather, as Claud would say. Mrs. Turpin could not see the woman's feet. She was not white-trash, just common. Sometimes Mrs. Turpin occupied herself at night naming the classes of people. On the bottom of the heap were most colored people, not the kind she would have been if she had been one, but most of them; then next to them—not above, just away from—were the white-trash; then above them were the home-owners, and above them the home-and-land owners, to which she and Claud belonged. Above she and Claud were people with a lot of money and much bigger houses and much more land. But here the complexity of it would begin to bear in on her, for some of the people with a lot of money were common and ought to be below she and Claud and some of the people who had good blood had lost their money and had to rent and then there were colored people who owned their homes and land as well. There was a colored dentist in town who had two red Lincolns and a swimming pool and a farm with registered white-face cattle on it. Usually by the time she had fallen asleep all the classes of people were moiling and roiling around in her head, and she would dream they were all crammed in together in a box car, being ridden off to be put in a gas oven.

"That's a beautiful clock," she said and nodded to her right. It was a big wall clock, the face encased in a brass sunburst.

"Yes, it's very pretty," the stylish lady said agreeably. "And right on the dot too," she added, glancing at her watch.

The ugly girl beside her cast an eye upward at the clock, smirked, then looked directly at Mrs. Turpin and smirked again. Then she returned her eyes to her book. She was obviously the lady's daughter because, although they didn't look anything alike as to disposition, they both had the same shape of face and the same blue eyes. On the lady they sparkled pleasantly but in the girl's seared face they appeared alternately to smolder and to blaze.

What if Jesus had said, "All right, you can be white-trash or a nigger or ugly"!

Mrs. Turpin felt an awful pity for the girl, though she thought it was one thing to be ugly and another to act ugly.

The woman with the snuff-stained lips turned around in her chair and looked up at the clock. Then she turned back and appeared to look a little to the side of Mrs. Turpin. There was a cast in one of her eyes. "You want to know wher you can get you one of themther clocks?" she asked in a loud voice.

"No, I already have a nice clock," Mrs. Turpin said. Once somebody like her got a leg in the conversation, she would be all over it.

"You can get you one with green stamps," the woman said. "That's most likely wher he got hisn. Save you up enough, you can get you most anythang. I got me some joo'ry."

Ought to have got you a wash rag and some soap, Mrs. Turpin thought.

"I get contour sheets with mine," the pleasant lady said.

The daughter slammed her book shut. She looked straight in front of her, directly through Mrs. Turpin and on through the yellow curtain and the plate glass window which made the wall behind her. The girl's eyes seemed lit all of a sudden with a peculiar light, an unnatural light like night road signs give. Mrs. Turpin turned her head to see if there was anything going on outside that she should see, but she could not see anything. Figures passing cast only a pale shadow through the curtain. There was no reason the girl should single her out for her ugly looks.

"Miss Finley," the nurse said, cracking the door. The gum-chewing woman got up and passed in front of her and Claud and went into the office. She had on red high-heeled shoes.

Directly across the table, the ugly girl's eyes were fixed on Mrs. Turpin as if she had some very special reason for disliking her.

"This is wonderful weather, isn't it?" the girl's mother said.

"It's good weather for cotton if you can get the niggers to pick it," Mrs. Turpin said, "but niggers don't want to pick cotton any more. You can't get the white folks to pick it and now you can't get the niggers—because they got to be right up there with the white folks."

"They gonna *try* anyways," the white-trash woman said, leaning forward.

"Do you have one of those cotton-picking machines?" the pleasant lady asked.

"No," Mrs. Turpin said, "they leave half the cotton in the field. We don't have much cotton anyway. If you want to make it farming now, you have to have a little of everything. We got a couple of acres of cotton and a few hogs and chickens and just enough white-face that Claud can look after them himself."

"One thang I don't want," the white-trash woman said, wiping her mouth with the back of her hand. "Hogs. Nasty stinking things, a-gruntin and a-rootin all over the place."

Mrs. Turpin gave her the merest edge of her attention. "Our hogs are not dirty and they don't stink," she said. "They're cleaner than some children I've seen. Their feet never touch the ground. We have a pig-parlor—that's where you raise them on concrete," she explained to the pleasant lady, "and Claud scoots them down with the hose every afternoon and washes off the floor." Cleaner by far than that child right there, she thought. Poor nasty little thing. He had not moved except to put the thumb of his dirty hand into his mouth.

The woman turned her face away from Mrs. Turpin. "I know I wouldn't scoot down no hog with no hose," she said to the wall.

You wouldn't have no hog to scoot down, Mrs. Turpin said to herself.

"A-gruntin and a-rootin and a-groanin," the woman muttered.

"We got a little of everything," Mrs. Turpin said to the pleasant lady. "It's no use in having more than you can handle yourself with help like it is. We found enough niggers to pick our cotton this year but Claud he has to go after them and take them home again in the evening. They can't walk that half a mile. No they can't. I tell you," she said and laughed merrily, "I sure am tired of buttering up niggers, but you got to love em if you want em to work for you. When they come in the morning, I run out and I say, 'Hi yawl this morning?' and when Claud drives them off to the field I just wave to beat the band and they just wave back." And she waved her hand rapidly to illustrate.

"Like you read out of the same book," the lady said, showing she understood perfectly.

"Child, yes," Mrs. Turpin said. "And when they come in from the field, I run out with a bucket of icewater. That's the way it's going to be from now on," she said. "You may as well face it."

"One thang I know," the white-trash woman said. "Two thangs I ain't going to do: love no niggers or scoot down no hog with no hose." And she let out a bark of contempt.

The look that Mrs. Turpin and the pleasant lady exchanged indicated they both understood that you had to *have* certain things before you could *know* certain things. But every time Mrs. Turpin exchanged a look with the lady, she was aware that the ugly girl's peculiar eyes were still on her, and she had trouble bringing her attention back to the conversation.

"When you got something," she said, "you got to look after it." And when you ain't got a thing but breath and britches, she added to herself, you can afford to come to town every morning and just sit on the Court House coping and spit.

A grotesque revolving shadow passed across the curtain behind her and was thrown palely on the opposite wall. Then a bicycle clattered down against the outside of the building. The door opened and a colored boy glided in with a tray from the drug store. It had two large red and white paper cups on it with tops on them. He was a tall, very black boy in discolored white pants and a green nylon shirt. He was chewing gum slowly, as if to music. He set the tray down in the office opening next to the fern and stuck his head through to look for the secretary. She was not in there. He rested his arms on the ledge and waited, his narrow bottom stuck out, swaying slowly to the left and right. He raised a hand over his head and scratched the base of his skull.

"You see that button there, boy?" Mrs Turpin said. "You can punch that and she'll come. She's probably in the back somewhere."

"Is thas right?" the boy said agreeably, as if he had never seen the button before. He leaned to the right and put his finger on it. "She sometime out," he said and twisted around to face his audience, his elbows behind him on the counter. The nurse appeared and he twisted back again. She handed him a dollar and he rooted in his pocket and made the change and counted it out to her. She gave him fifteen cents for a tip and he went out with the empty tray. The heavy door swung to slowly and closed at length with the sound of suction. For a moment no one spoke.

"They ought to send all them niggers back to Africa," the white-trash woman said. "That's wher they come from in the first place."

"Oh, I couldn't do without my good colored friends," the pleasant lady said.

"There's a heap of things worse than a nigger," Mrs. Turpin agreed. "It's all kinds of them just like it's all kinds of us."

"Yes, and it takes all kinds to make the world go round," the lady said in her musical voice.

As she said it, the raw-complexioned girl snapped her teeth together. Her lower lip turned downwards and inside out, revealing the pale pink inside of her mouth. After a second it rolled back up. It was the ugliest face Mrs. Turpin had ever seen anyone make and for a moment she was certain that the girl had made it at her. She was looking at her as if she had known and disliked her all her life—all of Mrs. Turpin's life, it seemed too, not just all the girl's life. Why, girl, I don't even know you, Mrs. Turpin said silently.

She forced her attention back to the discussion. "It wouldn't be practical to send them back to Africa," she said. "They wouldn't want to go. They got it too good here."

"Wouldn't be what they wanted—if I had anythang to do with it," the woman said.

"It wouldn't be a way in the world you could get all the niggers back over there," Mrs. Turpin said. "They'd be hiding out and lying down and turning sick on you and wailing and hollering and raring and pitching. It wouldn't be a way in the world to get them over there."

"They got over here," the trashy woman said. "Get back like they got over."

"It wasn't so many of them then," Mrs. Turpin explained.

The woman looked at Mrs. Turpin as if here was an idiot indeed but Mrs. Turpin was not bothered by the look, considering where it came from.

"Nooo," she said, "they're going to stay here where they can go to New York and marry white folks and improve their color. That's what they all want to do, every one of them, improve their color."

"You know what comes of that, don't you?" Claud asked.

"No, Claud, what?" Mrs. Turpin said.

Claud's eyes twinkled. "White-faced niggers," he said with never a smile.

Everybody in the office laughed except the white-trash and the ugly girl. The girl gripped the book in her lap with white fingers. The trashy woman looked around her from face to face as if she thought they were all idiots. The old woman in the feed sack dress continued to gaze expressionless across the floor at the high-top shoes of the man opposite her, the one who had been pretending to be asleep when the Turpins came in. He was laughing heartily, his hands still spread out on his knees. The child had fallen to the side and was lying now almost face down in the old woman's lap.

While they recovered from their laughter, the nasal chorus on the radio kept the room from silence.

> "You go to blank blank
> And I'll go to mine
> But we'll all blank along
> To-geth-ther,
> And all along the blank
> We'll hep each other out
> Smile-ling in any kind of
> Weath-ther!"

Mrs. Turpin didn't catch every word but she caught enough to agree with the spirit of the song and it turned her thoughts sober. To help anybody out that needed it was her philosophy of life. She never spared herself when she found somebody in need, whether they were white or black, trash or decent. And of all she had to be thankful for, she was most thankful that this was so. If Jesus had said, "You can be high society and have all the money you want and be thin and svelte-like, but you can't be a good woman with it," she would have had to say, "Well don't make me that then. Make me a good woman and it don't matter what else, how fat or how ugly or how poor!" Her heart rose. He had not made her a nigger or white-trash or ugly! He had made her herself and given her a little of everything. Jesus, thank you! she said. Thank you thank you thank you! Whenever she counted her blessings she felt as buoyant as if she weighed one hundred and twenty-five pounds instead of one hundred and eighty.

"What's wrong with your little boy?" the pleasant lady asked the white-trashy woman.

"He has a ulcer," the woman said proudly. "He ain't give me a minute's peace since he was born. Him and her are just alike," she said, nodding at the old woman, who was running her leathery fingers through the child's pale hair. "Look like I can't get nothing down them two but Co' Cola and candy."

That's all you try to get down em, Mrs. Turpin said to herself. Too lazy to light the fire. There was nothing you could tell her about people like them that she didn't know already. And it was not just that they didn't have anything. Because if you gave them everything, in two weeks it would all be broken or filthy or they would have chopped it up for lightwood. She knew all this from her own experience. Help them you must, but help them you couldn't.

All at once the ugly girl turned her lips inside out again. Her eyes were fixed like two drills on Mrs. Turpin. This time there was no mistaking that there was something urgent behind them.

Girl, Mrs. Turpin exclaimed silently, I haven't done a thing to you! The girl might be confusing her with somebody else. There was no need to sit by and let herself be intimidated. "You must be in college," she said boldly, looking directly at the girl. "I see you reading a book there."

The girl continued to stare and pointedly did not answer.

Her mother blushed at this rudeness. "The lady asked you a question, Mary Grace," she said under her breath.

"I have ears," Mary Grace said.

The poor mother blushed again. "Mary Grace goes to Wellesley College," she explained. She twisted one of the buttons on her dress. "In Massachusetts," she added with a grimace. "And in the summer she just keeps right on studying. Just reads all the time, a real book worm. She's done real well at Wellesley; she's taking English and Math and History and Psychology and Social Studies," she rattled on, "and I think it's too much. I think she ought to get out and have fun."

The girl looked as if she would like to hurl them all through the plate glass window.

"Way up north," Mrs. Turpin murmured and thought, well, it hasn't done much for her manners.

"I'd almost rather to have him sick," the white-trash woman said, wrenching the attention back to herself. "He's so mean when he ain't. Look like some children just take natural to meanness. It's some gets bad when they get sick but he was the opposite. Took sick and turned good. He don't give me no trouble now. It's me waitin to see the doctor," she said.

If I was going to send anybody back to Africa, Mrs. Turpin thought, it would be your kind, woman. "Yes, indeed," she said aloud, but looking up at the ceiling, "it's a heap of things worse than a nigger." And dirtier than a hog, she added to herself.

"I think people with bad dispositions are more to be pitied than anyone on earth," the pleasant lady said in a voice that was decidedly thin.

"I thank the Lord he has blessed me with a good one," Mrs. Turpin said. "The day has never dawned that I couldn't find something to laugh at."

"Not since she married me anyways," Claud said with a comical straight face.

Everybody laughed except the girl and the white-trash.

Mrs. Turpin's stomach shook. "He's such a caution," she said, "that I can't help but laugh at him."

The girl made a loud ugly noise through her teeth.

Her mother's mouth grew thin and tight. "I think the worst thing in the world," she said, "is an ungrateful person. To have everything and not appreciate it. I know a girl," she said, "who has parents who would give her anything, a little brother who loves her dearly, who is getting a good education, who wears the best clothes, but who can never say a kind word to anyone, who never smiles, who just criticises and complains all day long."

"Is she too old to paddle?" Claud asked.

The girl's face was almost purple.

"Yes," the lady said, "I'm afraid there's nothing to do but leave her to her

folly. Some day she'll wake up and it'll be too late."

"It never hurt anyone to smile," Mrs. Turpin said. "It just makes you feel better all over."

"Of course," the lady said sadly, "but there are just some people you can't tell anything to. They can't take criticism."

"If it's one thing I am," Mrs. Turpin said with feeling, "it's grateful. When I think who all I could have been besides myself and what all I got, a little of everything, and a good disposition besides, I just feel like shouting, 'Thank you, Jesus, for making everything the way it is!' It could have been different!" For one thing, somebody else could have got Claud. At the thought of this, she was flooded with gratitude and a terrible pang of joy ran through her. "Oh thank you, Jesus, thank you!" she cried aloud.

The book struck her directly over her left eye. It struck almost at the same instant that she realized the girl was about to hurl it. Before she could utter a sound, the raw face came crashing across the table toward her, howling. The girl's fingers sank like clamps into the soft flesh of her neck. She heard the mother cry out and Claud shout, "Whoa!" There was an instant when she was certain that she was about to be in an earthquake.

All at once her vision narrowed and she saw everything as if it were happening in a small room far away, or as if she were looking at it through the wrong end of a telescope. Claud's face crumpled and fell out of sight. The nurse ran in, then out, then in again. Then the gangling figure of the doctor rushed out of the inner door. Magazines flew this way and that as the table turned over. The girl fell with a thud and Mrs. Turpin's vision suddenly reversed itself and she saw everything large instead of small. The eyes of the white-trashy woman were staring hugely at the floor. There the girl, held down on one side by the nurse and on the other by her mother, was wrenching and turning in their grasp. The doctor was kneeling astride her, trying to hold her arm down. He managed after a second to sink a long needle into it.

Mrs. Turpin felt entirely hollow except for her heart which swung from side to side as if it were agitated in a great empty drum of flesh.

"Somebody that's not busy call for the ambulance," the doctor said in the off-hand voice young doctors adopt for terrible occasions.

Mrs. Turpin could not have moved a finger. The old man who had been sitting next to her skipped nimbly into the office and made the call, for the secretary still seemed to be gone.

"Claud!" Mrs. Turpin called.

He was not in his chair. She knew she must jump up and find him but she felt like some one trying to catch a train in a dream, when everything moves in slow motion and the faster you try to run the slower you go.

"Here I am," a suffocated voice, very unlike Claud's, said.

He was doubled up in the corner on the floor, pale as paper, holding his leg. She wanted to get up and go to him but she could not move. Instead, her gaze was drawn slowly downward to the churning face on the floor, which she could see over the doctor's shoulder.

The girl's eyes stopped rolling and focussed on her. They seemed a much lighter blue than before, as if a door that had been tightly closed behind them was now open to admit light and air.

Mrs. Turpin's head cleared and her power of motion returned. She leaned forward until she was looking directly into the fierce brilliant eyes. There was no doubt in her mind that the girl did know her, knew her in some intense and personal way, beyond time and place and condition. "What you got to say to me?" she asked hoarsely and held her breath, waiting, as for a revelation.

The girl raised her head. Her gaze locked with Mrs. Turpin's. "Go back to hell where you came from, you old wart hog," she whispered. Her voice was low but clear. Her eyes burned for a moment as if she saw with pleasure that her message had struck its target.

Mrs. Turpin sank back in her chair.

After a moment the girl's eyes closed and she turned her head wearily to the side.

The doctor rose and handed the nurse the empty syringe. He leaned over and put both hands for a moment on the mother's shoulders, which were shaking. She was sitting on the floor, her lips pressed together, holding Mary Grace's hand in her lap. The girl's fingers were gripped like a baby's around her thumb. "Go on to the hospital," he said. "I'll call and make the arrangements."

"Now let's see that neck," he said in a jovial voice to Mrs. Turpin. He began to inspect her neck with his first two fingers. Two little moon-shaped lines like pink fish bones were indented over her windpipe. There was the beginning of an angry red swelling above her eye. His fingers passed over this also.

"Lea' me be," she said thickly and shook him off. "See about Claud. She kicked him."

"I'll see about him in a minute," he said and felt her pulse. He was a thin grey-haired young man, given to pleasantries. "Go home and have yourself a vacation the rest of the day," he said and patted her on the shoulder.

Quit your pattin me, Mrs. Turpin growled to herself.

"And put an ice pack over that eye," he said. Then he went and squatted down beside Claud and looked at his leg. After a moment he pulled him up and Claud limped after him into the office.

Until the ambulance came, the only sounds in the room were the tremulous moans of the girl's mother, who continued to sit on the floor. The white-trash woman did not take her eyes off the girl. Mrs. Turpin looked straight ahead at nothing. Presently the ambulance drew up, a long dark shadow, behind the curtain. The attendants came in and set the stretcher down beside the girl and lifted her expertly onto it and carried her out. The nurse helped the mother gather up her things. The shadow of the ambulance moved silently away and the nurse came back in the office.

"That ther girl is going to be a lunatic, ain't she?" the white-trash woman asked the nurse, but the nurse kept on to the back and never answered her.

"Yes, she's going to be a lunatic," the white-trash woman said to the rest of them.

"Po' critter," the old woman murmured. The child's face was still in her lap. His eyes looked idly out over her knees. He had not moved during the disturbance except to draw one leg up under him.

"I thank Gawd," the white-trash woman said fervently, "I ain't a lunatic."

Claud came limping out and the Turpins went home.

As their pick-up truck turned into their own dirt road and made the crest of the hill, Mrs. Turpin gripped the window ledge and looked out suspiciously. The land sloped gracefully down through a field dotted with lavender weeds and at the start of the rise their small yellow frame house, with its little flower beds spread out around it like a fancy apron, sat primly in its accustomed place between two giant hickory trees. She would not have been startled to see a burnt wound between two blackened chimneys.

Neither of them felt like eating so they put on their house clothes and lowered the shade in the bedroom and lay down, Claud with his leg on a pillow and herself with a damp washcloth over her eye. The instant she was flat on her back, the image of a razor-backed hog with warts on its face and horns coming out behind its ears snorted into her head. She moaned, a low quiet moan.

"I am not," she said tearfully, "a wart hog. From hell." But the denial had no force. The girl's eyes and her words, even the tone of her voice, low but clear, directed only to her, brooked no repudiation. She had been singled out for the message, though there was trash in the room to whom it might justly have been applied. The full force of this fact struck her only now. There was a woman there who was neglecting her own child but she had been overlooked. The message had been given to Ruby Turpin, a respectable, hard-working, church-going woman. The tears dried. Her eyes began to burn instead with wrath.

She rose on her elbow and the washcloth fell into her hand. Claud was lying on his back, snoring. She wanted to tell him what the girl had said. At the same time, she did not wish to put the image of herself as a wart hog from hell into his mind.

"Hey, Claud," she muttered and pushed his shoulder.

Claud opened one pale baby blue eye.

She looked into it warily. He did not think about anything. He just went his way.

"Wha, whasit?" he said and closed the eye again.

"Nothing," she said. "Does your leg pain you?"

"Hurts like hell," Claud said.

"It'll quit terreckly," she said and lay back down. In a moment Claud was snoring again. For the rest of the afternoon they lay there. Claud slept. She scowled at the ceiling. Occasionally she raised her fist and made a small stabbing motion over her chest as if she were defending her innocence to invisible guests who were like the comforters of Job, reasonable-seeming but wrong.

About five-thirty Claud stirred. "Got to go after those niggers," he sighed, not moving.

She was looking straight up as if there were unintelligible handwriting on the ceiling. The protuberance over her eye had turned a greenish-blue. "Listen here," she said.

"What?"

"Kiss me."

Claud leaned over and kissed her loudly on the mouth. He pinched her side and their hands interlocked. Her expression of ferocious concentration did not change. Claud got up, groaning and growling, and limped off. She continued to study the ceiling.

She did not get up until she heard the pick-up truck coming back with the negroes. Then she rose and thrust her feet in her brown oxfords, which she did not bother to lace, and stumped out onto the back porch and got her red plastic bucket. She emptied a tray of ice cubes into it and filled it half full of water and went out into the back yard. Every afternoon after Claud brought the hands in, one of the boys helped him put out hay and the rest waited in the back of the truck until he was ready to take them home. The truck was parked in the shade under one of the hickory trees.

"Hi yawl this evening?" Mrs. Turpin asked grimly, appearing with the bucket and the dipper. There were three women and a boy in the truck.

"Us doin nicely," the oldest woman said. "Hi you doin?" and her gaze stuck immediately on the dark lump on Mrs. Turpin's forehead. "You done fell down, ain't you?" she asked in a solicitous voice. The old woman was dark and almost toothless. She had on an old felt hat of Claud's set back on her head. The other two women were younger and lighter and they both had new bright green sun hats. One of them had hers on her head; the other had taken hers off and the boy was grinning beneath it.

Mrs. Turpin set the bucket down on the floor of the truck. "Yawl hep yourselves," she said. She looked around to make sure Claud had gone. "No. I didn't fall down," she said, folding her arms. "It was something worse than that."

"Ain't nothing bad happen to you!" the old woman said. She said it as if they all knew that Mrs. Turpin was protected in some special way by Divine Providence. "You just had you a little fall."

"We were in town at the doctor's office for where the cow kicked Mr. Turpin," Mrs. Turpin said in a flat tone that indicated they could leave off their foolishness. "And there was this girl there. A big fat girl with her face all broke out. I could look at that girl and tell she was peculiar but I couldn't tell how. And me and her mama were just talking and going along and all of a sudden WHAM! She throws this big book she was reading at me and . . ."

"Naw!" the old woman cried out.

"And then she jumps over the table and commences to choke me."

"Naw!" they all exclaimed, "naw!"

"Hi come she do that?" the old woman asked. "What ail her?"

Mrs. Turpin only glared in front of her.

"Somethin ail her," the old woman said.

"They carried her off in an ambulance," Mrs. Turpin continued, "but before she went she was rolling on the floor and they were trying to hold her down to give her a shot and she said something to me." She paused. "You know what she said to me?"

"What she say?" they asked.

"She said," Mrs. Turpin began, and stopped, her face very dark and heavy. The sun was getting whiter and whiter, blanching the sky overhead so that the leaves of the hickory tree were black in the face of it. She could not bring forth the words. "Something real ugly," she muttered.

"She sho shouldn't said nothin ugly to you," the old woman said. "You so sweet. You the sweetest lady I know."

"She pretty too," the one with the hat on said.

"And stout," the other one said. "I never knowed no sweeter white lady."

"That's the truth befo' Jesus," the old woman said. "Amen! You des as sweet and pretty as you can be."

Mrs. Turpin knew just exactly how much negro flattery was worth and it added to her rage. "She said," she began again and finished this time with a fierce rush of breath, "that I was an old wart hog from hell."

There was an astounded silence.

"Where she at!" the youngest woman cried in a piercing voice. "Lemme see her. I'll kill her!"

"I'll kill her with you!" the other one cried.

"She b'long in the sylum," the old woman said emphatically. "You the sweetest white lady I know."

"She pretty too," the other two said. "Stout as she can be and sweet. Jesus satisfied with her!"

"Deed he is," the old woman declared.

Idiots! Mrs. Turpin growled to herself. You could never say anything intelligent to a nigger. You could talk at them but not with them. "Yawl ain't drunk your water," she said shortly. "Leave the bucket in the truck when you're finished with it. I got more to do than just stand around and pass the time of day," and she moved off and into the house.

She stood for a moment in the middle of the kitchen. The dark protuberance over her eye looked like a miniature tornado cloud which might any moment sweep across the horizon of her brow. Her lower lip protruded dangerously. She squared her massive shoulders. Then she marched into the front of the house and out the side door and started down the road to the pig parlor. She had the look of a woman going single-handed, weaponless, into battle.

The sun was a deep yellow now like a harvest moon and was riding westward very fast over the far tree line as if it meant to reach the hogs before she did. The road was rutted and she kicked several good-sized stones out of her path as she strode along. The pig parlor was on a little knoll at the end of a lane that ran off from the side of the barn. It was a square of concrete as large as a small room, with a board fence about four feet high around it. The concrete floor sloped slightly so that the hog wash could drain off into a trench where it was carried to the field for fertilizer. Claud was standing on the outside, on the edge of the concrete, hanging onto the top board, hosing down the floor inside. The hose was connected to the faucet of a water trough nearby.

Mrs. Turpin climbed up beside him and glowered down at the hogs inside. There were seven long-snouted bristly shoats in it—tan with liver-colored spots—and an old sow a few weeks off from farrowing. She was lying on her side grunting. The shoats were running about shaking themselves like idiot children, their little slit pig eyes searching the floor for anything left. She had read that pigs were the most intelligent animal. She doubted it. They were supposed to be smarter than dogs. There had even been a pig astronaut. He had performed his assignment perfectly but died of a heart attack afterwards because they left him in his electric suit, sitting upright throughout his examination when naturally a hog should be on all fours.

A-gruntin and a-rootin and a-groanin.

"Gimme that hose," she said, yanking it away from Claud. "Go on and carry them niggers home and then get off that leg."

"You look like you might have swallowed a mad dog," Claud observed, but he got down and limped off. He paid no attention to her humors.

Until he was out of earshot, Mrs. Turpin stood on the side of the pen, holding the hose and pointing the stream of water at the hind quarters of any shoat that looked as if it might try to lie down. When he had had time to get over the hill, she turned her head slightly and her wrathful eyes scanned the path. He was nowhere in sight. She turned back again and seemed to gather herself up. Her shoulders rose and she drew in her breath.

"What do you send me a message like that for?" she said in a low fierce voice, barely above a whisper but with the force of a shout in its concentrated fury. "How am I a hog and me both? How am I saved and from hell too?" Her free fist was knotted and with the other she gripped the hose, blindly pointing the stream of water in and out of the eye of the old sow whose outraged squeal she did not hear.

The pig parlor commanded a view of the back pasture where their twenty beef cows were gathered around the hay-bales Claud and the boy had put out. The freshly cut pasture sloped down to the highway. Across it was their cotton field and beyond that a dark green dusty wood which they owned as well. The sun was behind the wood, very red, looking over the paling of trees like a farmer inspecting his own hogs.

"Why me?" she rumbled. "It's no trash around here, black or white, that I haven't given to. And break my back to the bone every day working. And do for the church."

She appeared to be the right size woman to command the arena before her. "How am I a hog?" she demanded. "Exactly how am I like them?" and she jabbed the stream of water at the shoats. "There was plenty of trash there. It didn't have to be me.

"If you like trash better, go get yourself some trash then," she railed. "You could have made me trash. Or a nigger. If trash is what you wanted why didn't you make me trash?" She shook her fist with the hose in it and a watery snake appeared momentarily in the air. "I could quit working and take it easy and be filthy," she growled. "Lounge about the sidewalks all day drinking root beer. Dip snuff and spit in every puddle and have it all over my face. I could be nasty.

"Or you could have made me a nigger. It's too late for me to be a nigger," she said with deep sarcasm, "but I could act like one. Lay down in the middle of the road and stop traffic. Roll on the ground."

In the deepening light everything was taking on a mysterious hue. The pasture was growing a peculiar glassy green and the streak of highway had turned lavender. She braced herself for a final assault and this time her voice rolled out over the pasture. "Go on," she yelled, "call me a hog! Call me a hog again. From hell. Call me a wart hog from hell. Put the bottom rail on top. There'll still be a top and bottom!"

A garbled echo returned to her.

A final surge of fury shook her and she roared, "Who do you think you are?"

The color of everything, field and crimson sky, burned for a moment with a transparent intensity. The question carried over the pasture and across the highway and the cotton field and returned to her clearly like an answer from beyond the wood.

She opened her mouth but no sound came out of it.

A tiny truck, Claud's, appeared on the highway, heading rapidly out of sight. Its gears scraped thinly. It looked like a child's toy. At any moment a bigger truck might smash into it and scatter Claud's and the niggers' brains all over the road.

Mrs. Turpin stood there, her gaze fixed on the highway, all her muscles rigid, until in five or six minutes the truck reappeared, returning. She waited until it had had time to turn into their own road. Then like a monumental statue coming to life, she bent her head slowly and gazed, as if through the very heart of mystery, down into the pig parlor at the hogs. They had settled all in one corner around the old sow who was grunting softly. A red glow suffused them. They appeared to pant with a secret life.

Until the sun slipped finally behind the tree line, Mrs. Turpin remained there with her gaze bent to them as if she were absorbing some abysmal life-giving knowledge. At last she lifted her head. There was only a purple streak in the sky, cutting through a field of crimson and leading, like an extension of the highway, into the descending dusk. She raised her hands from the side of the pen in a gesture hieratic and profound. A visionary light settled in her eyes. She saw the streak as a vast swinging bridge extending upward from the earth through a field of living fire. Upon it a vast horde of souls were rumbling toward heaven. There were whole companies of white-trash, clean for the first time in their lives, and bands of black niggers in white robes, and battalions of freaks and lunatics shouting and clapping and leaping like frogs. And bringing up the end of the procession was a tribe of people whom she recognized at once as those who, like herself and Claud, had always had a little of everything and the God-given wit to use it right. She leaned forward to observe them closer. They were marching behind the others with great dignity, accountable as they had always been for good order and common sense and respectable behavior. They alone were on key. Yet she could see by their shocked and altered faces that even their virtues were being burned away. She lowered her hands and gripped the rail of the hog pen, her eyes small but fixed unblinkingly on what lay ahead. In a moment the vision faded but she remained where she was, immobile.

At length she got down and turned off the faucet and made her slow way on the darkening path to the house. In the woods around her the invisible cricket choruses had struck up, but what she heard were the voices of the souls climbing upward into the starry field and shouting hallelujah.

THE FAT GUY

HENRY H. ROTH   from *December*

The man shuffled his enormous frame into the reasonably comfortable chair, he
nodded to some people at a nearby table although he wasn't sure he knew them.
"Smile anyway, what the hell is it going to cost you," an elderly rum-pot sage
had once advised him. More advice from the good soul long since claimed by
the grave and free of the *tch tch*'s of the A.A.—"A comedian can never be talked
about except nicely, if they think he's gone high hat or he's a chaser or a bum
they won't laugh. Joe E. is the exception, lad, and you quite frankly, ain't." The
funny thing, the crazy thing, it still amazed him, God dammit, everything the
whiskey brain schemed up was right, still right and it had been ten years since
the old bastard had sopped his last shot. "Everybody is scared not to laugh at a
fat man, if a fat man spits on stage it's class, right out of Charley Chaplin, and if
the crowd has gotten down a few drinks even if they're watered they'll love a fat
man to death. I'll tell you why, because they're all afraid they'll turn out like
that fat tub struggling for laughs and money and the sons of bitches pity you;
even the bastard who stiffs the waiter in the Club, will laugh at a year one gag
because he feels sorry. Now kid, if you begin with good material, stick to the
character you are in the monologues, they'll all go to bed with you. That's the
best I can do for you, no legacy, boy, only the truth."

And the truth had worked, first lousy then pretty good and about six
months after his father died, Danny Cracker, a shyster agent and pimp on the
side wrangled him a two-minute monologue shot on TV and from then on it
was uphill in a Jaguar with no pain and plenty of shock absorbers to cushion
any rough spots. When reporters were looking for copy, he said sure it was too
bad his father couldn't have lived to see his great success, but he knew the old

man had never doubted the outcome if instructions were followed. And by now the booze would have been leaking out of his brain and for ten years mom had slept and eaten without worry.

Danny Cracker was all hustle and bluster and could use ten switch blades at the same time, while his father never used the knife. If he couldn't con his man with the soft voice then he figured nothing would do it. "Your old man was a hell of a good agent, the best if he'd have kissed the gals instead of the glass."

Danny added his own frills to the original plan: "You got to think fat and eat fat. In Lindy's you only order desserts, and you do it nice and easy as if you were ordering table d'hote. For breakfast you don't get orange juice or eggs and crap like that but plenty of Danish and Seven-up, for lunch pies and custards, and for supper butter cream cakes and ice cream by the pint."

It was dumb, so dumb they both figured it would work and any rich dessert soon became synonymous with his name, several of the Broadway places named concoctions after him.

His body sagged like a deflated balloon that miraculously retained its air if not the original shape; his feet throbbed continually; it was torture merely to stand and wait for a cab. The adventure of getting in and out of his sports car had become famous bits, his quest for the richest dessert in the world became a classic shaggy dog story. He was 37 years old and the doctor had told him his body was of a man 60 and he used this information in one of his quick opening lines.

"My doctor says I'm 37 and I have the body of a man 67, I don't wanna worry him, but he's wrong, I'm only 27."

His blood was bad.

"I've got the only blood that looks like whipped cream."

His teeth were racked with cavities.

"I can whistle Dixie through any tooth but I'm not practicing with them as soloists. Soon I'm going to have my very own symphony orchestra."

The old bastard had been right, the gags weren't funny but they frightened the people because it might be true; so they didn't laugh like hell but they wriggled happily like they were sitting under a French tickler and they giggled.

Each time he breathed he sighed deeply, it was accepted as part of his equipment, but now he needed the sigh to get out the next breath. He was happy to be in bed and dozing, it was difficult to sleep but he dozed, awoke but went right back to another doze. "Some are Yale men, I'm a doze man."

Though his mother had fussed over him like any other good mother, he was unable to eat a full meal even in secret. His tongue was a mass of jelly, and steak and potatoes were no longer just dirty words, they tasted dirty. He ate food like a bird pecking unhappily until he could get away from the table. In public he snared meringues and banana splits with aplomb and delight although his body shivered perceptibly as the sugar sped through his body. Some reporter had once noticed it and he explained smoothly, "To me it's like getting laid."

And the headline over a byline was "Morty Barton Chooses Custard over Monroe."

Morty was on TV at least ten times a year at five thousand a throw; he worked four clubs a year and demanded and received a minimum of two weeks and fifteen thousand; he did all the charities he was invited to. He was not the funniest, the busiest, or the best in the business but he was among the top ten and that meant at least one hundred thousand a year.

Danny boy had fared so well that he all but relinquished the stable of girls, concentrating only on the "hundred" nighters and now the Cracker hand was reaching out into the legit theater and had sponsored a hit musical. Danny was up there, way up there, and Morty had asked him only last week about the chances of touring with the national show.

"Nah, but you'd be great, kid, better than the joe we got here, but the grind would take the pounds off and what good is a thin comic telling fat jokes?"

"I'll tell skinny ones."

Cracker answered, "There's more fat gags. Look, baby, you feel down I'll get Irene to come over and keep house for you this weekend. She's not busy, the convention was cancelled till next week."

"All right, but then I may lose some weight this weekend."

Danny looked up, "Go easy will you, she said last time you gave her some bruises that lasted a week."

"Who's going to see?"

"Christ, Morty, a guy pays a hundred bucks he wants a clear-skinned babe."

"Okay, okay."

"Oh, one thing more, the B'nai B'rith is having a dinner next week."

"I'm their boy."

"They say you went over the best last year."

"When it's for free it's easier to laugh."

"Something wrong, kid?"

"No. Just worry about me once a year, I'm not smooth skinned but I bruise sometimes, too."

He had wakened early this morning and walked through Central Park and by twelve o'clock when he reached an exit gate he possessed barely enough strength to fall into the cab and mutter to the driver, "Just drive for a few minutes, anywhere." He hadn't seen one damn thing in the park. After five minutes the trees started to swing down at him, a thousand birds alighted on his shoulder and chirped in unison, the singing would not leave his head and he felt he was swimming in a sea of glue. He was vaguely aware of children's laughter, a lion's roar, the taunts of parrots and sounds that crashed and exploded about his fleeing form. He was drowning on land and could not cry out and he looked hopelessly for escape and thank God he found the exit gate. When he finally composed himself and told the cabbie to stop, pivoting on shaky legs, Morty found himself in a strange neighborhood. Entering the first doctor's office he saw, he told the nurse he was ill and the doctor saw him immediately. A young nice-looking boy fresh out of school and with a real interest in his patients. The kid had recognized him and after the examination said, "I saw you last week on TV, you were very good." And then he let Morty have it. Maybe ten years maybe tomorrow, nobody could bear such weight, his heart was exceptionally strong but could not continue to perform as well. "You have an unusually strong body, Mr. Barton, but one day it will rebel and show no more interest in keeping you alive."

This young man was really intelligent and Morty enjoyed listening to his well-chosen words. Morty pointed to huge waxen rolls of fat, "Doc, this is my profession."

The boy was puzzled.

"I'm a fat guy, a fat comic, I must be fat."

"Mr. Barton, your ankles are swollen three times their normal size, you took a walk through the park on a cool day and you thought you were dying, you sweat like a man who's been caged in a steam room for three weeks and your complexion is poor, your hands shake . . ."

Morty waved his hands wildly, "Hey, hey, I thought I was going to live another ten years, better I should lie down and die right now."

The boy smiled, "You might outlive me but I doubt it. You've been lucky, but once your body begins true disintegration, there'll be great pain and far more discomfort."

"Tell it to my agent."

"Get another one."

"He's a friend. Besides, they'd all sing the same tune."

The doctor shook his head.

"It was originally my father's idea. Hey Doc, you should have seen his body. Lean like a fishing rod and his legs worked only on bar whiskey."

The doctor would say no more, Morty felt really sorry for him and as he shook hands goodbye he said he would consider the idea of a diet.

"If you do, Mr. Barton, come back here or see another physician. That excess must come off slowly."

"Don't get excited, Doc. I have to meet my agent at three, I'll tell him and listen to him and remember what you said."

It was two-thirty, the restaurant now was practically empty. Morty beckoned the waiter. "Lover," he said, "cheese cake and cherry coke." "Yes sir," the waiter smiled. He spent the minutes slashing at the cake and hitting his hands weakly on the table. "Performing the fat man's bongo beat," he told the waiter as the plate was taken away.

One thing about Danny Cracker, he was always on time. "For you, baby," Danny once confided, "it means I'm interested. If not, I stay in my place waiting for any excuse so I can lose you." There was Danny and it was two to three. Well, I'm still important to Mr. Cracker, I'm the soup in his cracker, he sang.

"Hi, baby."

"Take a chair or two."

"Irene clean your house good?"

"Spotless, better than any Lewyt."

"Tonight's the night with the Zion crowd?"

"This is it, I'll slay 'em better than Eichmann."

"Hey, none of those."

"Just for us Gentiles."

"Okay, you eat yet, Morty?"

"Just an appetizer."

"Okay, we'll order."

"Danny."

"That damn waiter, what the hell does he think I'm trying to do, pick him up? Turn around, you hump-backed flatfooted . . ."

"Danny."

"Huh, what?"

"You're a sweet kid."

"Shit, now he's going to the men's room."

"Danny, I went to the doctor today."

"Again? You sick? What Ginzburg say?"

"I didn't go to your abortionist."

"You really sick?"

"I took a walk today, it wasn't very long before I was looking for a cemetery. Danny, I couldn't breathe, I couldn't walk or see."

Danny lit a cigar and blew the smoke gently into Morty's face.

"You pass out, kid?"

"No. I got a cab and after awhile I jumped out. It was on the West Side in the eighties or nineties, I don't know."

"That was dumb. Why didn't you go home?"

"I wanted a doc to see me right then. I was scared, Mr. Cracker."

"What'd he say?"

"He said I could die tomorrow."

"So could I, so could anybody."

"But I got a better chance."

"Ginzburg tells me you've got a ticker stronger than an elephant."

"But not the hide of one, I'm carrying too much weight."

"What are you, kid, a jockey or a comedian? Lose a few pounds then."

"This guy wants me to lose more than a few."

"So lose more than a few."

"A hundred pounds, Danny."

Danny put out the cigar. His small pasty face was expressionless, but Morty knew the message had been received, over and out. Danny Cracker had just wasted a two-dollar cigar, he had been struck in a vital spot, the half-smoked cigar being pounded into the ash tray was proof enough of that.

"You told him you'd be back?"

"I told him maybe."

"Look, Morty, you're from the same block, you know what I'm going to say before I start. Your pop was right, I was right, and you was right. If you give away a hundred we'll still be right."

Morty nodded.

Cracker was puzzled, sincerely at a loss. "Everyone will take you the first swing around and the benefits will hold on a little longer but soon nobody will call. You can tell diet jokes, but when you're skinny and normal it don't go . . . then what?"

"I'll become a sick comic."

"Baby, you're sick right now, sicker, sicker than a college ha-ha guy."

They were both silent, Danny plucked another cigar from inside his antelope grey cashmere sports jacket.

"What a hell of an alteration bill you'll have to pay for the old suits."

"I'll burn em, Danny, off with the old on with the new silhouette." He belched. "Every time I belch I smell like a birthday cake."

Cracker smiled faintly. "That's a new one."

"Right off the flab."

"Kid, kid, what a waste."

The waiter appeared and Danny greeted him with applause. The little man ordered shrimp cocktail, chicken soup with rice, club steak, and a side of asparagus. Morty was feeling hungry, for the first time in years he began to be curious as to how things taste.

His mother stopped cooking a few years ago, a maid did everything. The old lady slept and read her paper. Danny bit his lip and turned to him, the waiter smiled anticipating another anecdote. Morty looked at the menu almost smelling the food, he remembered in detail what Danny had ordered and then he felt the menu snatched away. And watching him was a young doctor shocked at the sight of a man whose fat bulged out everywhere. Naked and unable to hide, Morty faced the others with the doctor and he felt the pressure of their interest as if they leveled daggers at him. The doctor's disgust and wish to help, his father's eyes never blinking (I never miss a thing), Danny puffing smoke like a tugboat, and it was Danny's look that entranced Morty. Danny's eyes caressed the fat, loved every ounce, every ripple. And so Morty chose not wisely but for love.

"Yogurt," he ordered.

Danny's eyes sunk, the waiter's mouth was an open pit.

"Yogurt," he repeated, "and three scoops of cherry vanilla in it."

Pluto Is the Furthest Planet

ABRAHAM ROTHBERG from *The Yale Review*

When they first told him, the doctors and then his wife tried to reassure him, but Sanford Tyler was not reassured. Not that he refused to be, but he couldn't for the life of him see that having what Dr. Morrison called cardiac insufficiency was very different from a heart attack. His wife, Viola, tried to explain in her precise, sensible schoolteacher manner that the difference was that he *hadn't* had a heart attack, that he was only forty-three years old and that once he was rested up, he'd be able to go about his normal life again, but Tyler was by no means convinced. In the meantime, however, it was six weeks of bed rest and then six months of no work, no athletics, and of course—Morrison was half-apologetic, but Tyler thought he detected just a shade of relief in Viola—no sex. Viola moved into one of the twin beds in the guest room, and her clothing, cosmetics, and perfumes went with her. She didn't want to disturb him, she said, and she did have to go on with her job, especially now. It was the cool considerateness and the *especially now* that perturbed Tyler most of all.

No one came to visit because the doctors prescribed complete rest and Viola intended to see that their orders were carried out to the letter. There were some phone calls at first, and a flock of manufactured get-well cards, some of them quite funny, Tyler realized, though his sense of humor also seemed to be suffering comic insufficiency, and the baskets of fruits, candy, and flowers from the office made him feel even closer to the grave than he already did. Tyler did try to take some of the calls, but after a very few he found so little to say that he let Viola issue the medical bulletins and was relieved when she gave them on one of the other phones rather than on the one in his bedroom.

Because he was still a partner, Tyler did have to talk to Charlie Carson, but all Charlie told him was that things were running fine, that his work had been divided up among two of the junior partners, under Charlie's watchful eye, and that he was missed. When Tyler tried to press for more specific information on cases under consideration, Charlie hedged so that Tyler stopped pressing him to avoid their mutual embarrassment. Most of the cases he knew were little more than squabbling for money advantage, and he didn't really want to know about them, though when Charlie told him that all the senior partners had agreed to keep him on full salary while he was out, Tyler was genuinely grateful. But instead of being more easy in his mind, Tyler was more and more terrified: it was almost as if he had been left for dead and was watching over a demise that he had carelessly neglected to consummate. He remembered his own adolescent dreams of frustration and grandeur when he'd vividly imagined his own funeral with everyone dissolved in tears while from on high he looked down and enjoyed their anguish, their guilt and remorse. This living experience, however, he found considerably less soul-satisfying.

The first weeks in bed went by slowly, like the ticking of a clock at night, so that soon he lost track of time. He lay in bed looking out of the three squares of window, watching the early autumn skies still stained with summer pink and green daily deepened into dark winter reds and slate-grey. Most of the time Tyler slept, or dozed, a half-waking numbness so restless that it neither gave him a sense of having been gone and come back, nor restored him, and left him limp from nightmares he could not remember. As he drowsed through the days and the fitful noises of his household's routines, or lay awake nights listening to the sounds of his heart beating in his ears and watching the great hump-backed black beast outside his window, pocked with stars, give ground as light scarred its hide and day whipped it back beyond the horizon, two ideas shaped themselves out of the welter of half-formed feelings in which he seemed suspended like a bucket in a well, and gradually they took possession of his mind. The first was a sense of betrayal and the second of isolation; the two were increasingly difficult to separate.

Most of all Tyler felt betrayed by his body, that bag of guts, bone, and muscle that he now was so separated from and tied to. He'd taken good care of it, fed it well, kept it clean and exercised, and unaccountably it had betrayed him. He had to admit that it had taken a beating during the war and immediately afterward when he was working for the partnership, but no more than many others and a good deal less than most. Worse, he felt betrayed by and isolated from other people. Except for an occasional call from Charlie at the office, in which Tyler thought he heard the note of courteous impatience, there were infrequent calls, no visitors, and virtually no mail. Dr. Morrison saw him twice a week but said no more than, "You're doing quite well, Mr. Tyler. You should be up and around very soon," though Tyler suspected that he gave Viola more details, if not much more substance. If he could accept his body's betrayal as an inevitable biological accident, his loneliness was more difficult to deal with.

On the theory that he was sleeping late and not to be disturbed, Viola did not come in to see him in the mornings. From behind his closed bedroom door, he heard her and Mrs. Byrnes get the twins and Eric started to school each morning, and then Viola go off to school herself. After that Mrs. Byrnes brought up his breakfast tray. Eric came home from kindergarten at noon and stayed home for the rest of the day. He'd been warned not to bother Daddy but he came, every day after his lunch, and stood on the landing, not quite silently, casting oblique glances into the bedroom until Tyler called to him. But the boy wouldn't come into the room, or even come near, as if his father had some terrible and contagious disease—mortality, Tyler thought bitterly—that he might pass on to him. "No, Daddy," Eric said, "Mother and Mrs. Byrnes said not to bother you."

"You're not bothering me. I just want to see what you look like," Tyler would reply, trying to keep his voice easy and level. The boy stood there for a while, his hands buried in the pockets of his blue jeans, stretching the red suspenders which held them up and kicking one shoe against the other. Then he'd turn and go slowly downstairs. After a while, Tyler heard him singing or laughing or yelling, and could barely refrain from calling him back.

With the twins it was different, perhaps because they were girls, or simply older. In mid-afternoon, as soon as they got home from school, they came dutifully to see him. They were full of their day and talked a streak of people and places he couldn't identify, and though Janice occasionally stopped Jacqueline long enough to interject footnotes, they never quite clarified matters for Tyler. After about fifteen minutes of turning his head from one to the other, as if he were watching them play tennis—the girls always sat on opposite sides of his bed, as if he might otherwise not know which was which—the silence came, then the look which always prefaced their saying, in unison, that they had homework, or chores, or dates, and had to go.

It saddened Tyler to watch them leave, so much like one another, a biological accident he had had to learn to bear, though Viola had always rather enjoyed it, dressing them alike and pleased by the attention they always attracted together. They were already, though only just thirteen, so much like women with their lipstick and bouffant hairdos. He and Viola had not only quarreled about that but about dates, eye makeup, the length of skirts, and school work, until, as if both facts were conclusive, his wife had informed him that his daughters were both "ladies," and that he was becoming an old puritan. Neither accusation seemed decisive to Tyler, but eventually he had given in on the issues that seemed least appalling—the lipstick and the haircuts.

Viola usually came in shortly after they'd left, kissed him lightly on the forehead, puffed his pillows, straightened his blankets, checked the radiator, and kept up a running commentary about her colleagues that made as little sense to him as had the twins' talk. It surprised him that they had so little to talk about except what he might like for dinner, or whether he felt like having his linen changed, that he endured the stream of talk as trying to make him feel, as she had once put it, still "part of the world." After the first few weeks, he had tried to tell her what he felt, fumbling over the words, like a newly blind man gropingly examining things with still clumsy fingers, and she had robustly advised him to read more, watch the television, and not think so much about himself. He'd be all right, it was all simply a matter of time. But beneath her abrupt impatience he sensed her own fear of understanding what he was telling her, or attempting to: she didn't want to know and so he stopped trying to tell her. Though he did try, he couldn't get to reading any of the books he'd bought and saved against the day when he'd have some free time to read, nor could he bear to watch the portable television set which Mrs. Byrnes and Viola brought up for him and which, eventually, at his urging, they took back downstairs for the twins to enjoy.

Because he disliked having things done for him, after three weeks Tyler began to get up to go to the bathroom and was shocked to see himself in the medicine cabinet mirror. Hollow-eyed, pale, his face seemed a decade older than when he'd last seen it and like the photograph of some remote relative he faintly remembered from his mother's family album years before. It was, he thought, because his hair was uncut, he hadn't shaved, and his beard had sprouted a short, dense, grizzled growth that was largely white and made him look Victorian and patriarchal. When Viola finally persuaded the barber to come by one evening to cut his hair, Tyler was grateful, but he refused to have the beard shaved off; the most he would consent to was having it trimmed to look less ragged. The white in it was as shocking a betrayal as his cardiac insufficiency, the death that lurked beneath the skin, the face beneath the mask, and Tyler tried to recall when his stubble had turned white, but all he could remember was a glistening—that could have been water or lather—as he slid the razor over the black hairs every morning.

The shock was great enough so that on the very same day Tyler picked up the telephone and called half a dozen of those he considered his closest friends, but though they all seemed glad to talk to him, none offered to come to visit, and after the first two or three none could be persuaded to drop in to see him. And no one returned his calls. Tyler even called his brother in Arizona long distance, but Clem was too busy with his seed business and his own family to come East for a stay. At first Tyler tried to apologize for them to himself, explaining that there was that primitive superstition lurking in the soul of man that made him fearful of the sick and the dead, the injured and insulted, almost the way his son Eric seemed to be, as if all those could infect the living and healthy with some disease for which there was no cure. And they were all busy with what Viola called "their own lives." But Tyler felt betrayed all the same and more than ever isolated, and the conclusion that no one gave much of a damn forced itself on him like a persistent tackler who had to be fended off with a wary stiff-arm.

One night, lying half-asleep in the dark, the house sounds downstairs so distant they seemed like echoes from another life, Tyler heard the soft shuffling of his son's feet coming up the stairs, followed by his wife's more definite high heels. They paused in front of his bedroom door and Eric called out, "Daddy?"

"Don't wake your father," Viola cautioned in a hoarse whisper, before Tyler answered, "Yes, Eric."

"I want to read you a story."

"Daddy's tired," Viola insisted. "Some other time."

"Daddy reads stories to me when I'm sick," the boy replied stubbornly. "I want to read him a story when *he's* sick."

"I'd like you to read me a story," Tyler called to him.

"All right," Viola agreed, her reluctance an obvious criticism. "You can read Daddy one story. No more and not too long. I'll go downstairs and help Mrs. Byrnes clean up."

Eric sat in the chair next to his bed and Viola turned the overhead wall lamp down so that a cone of yellow light poured down over him. Then she went out. The boy sat quietly, his profile turned, fair skin and cheeks flushed from washing, his dark eyes downcast beneath the broad, pale forehead. Zipped up in red dentons from shod feet to throat, he seemed as whole and healthy and beautiful as a red apple. When he turned his face and eyes and asked, "Which story do you want, Daddy?", something like a separate and beating heart moved inside Tyler. "Any one you like," he answered. Unable to look into his son's shining face, Tyler focused instead on the small, straight fingers that held the book, thinking idly that children's hands and fingers were so elegant and shapely and yet how few adults had hands even remotely beautiful. Blunted by time, he thought, warped by living, and he lay back on the pillow and buried in it his own long, scarred fingers, the two knuckles broken and improperly reset during the war. Staring at the eroded slice of moon outside, he only half-listened to his son reading about the solar system, carefully pronouncing each word and occasionally stopping to spell one out so that Tyler could quickly fill it in for him. The book was about the earth and the moon, gravity and sunlight, and the sun and the planets, and Eric read a little about each planet, but he was most fascinated by Pluto. "You know, Daddy," he said, looking up and very serious, "Pluto is the furthest planet from the sun. It hasn't got any light or heat because it's so far away, and it hasn't even got any moons of its own like Jupiter or Saturn." He went on reading about Pluto, as Tyler's mind, snagged on the jagged end of that sentence, caught: "Pluto is the furthest planet. . . ."

"Daddy?"

"Yes," Tyler said, forcing himself to pay attention.

"The book says it takes 256 years for Pluto to go around the sun."

Tyler nodded absently.

"Will you be dead then?"

"Yes," Tyler said slowly, "no one lives to 250."

"Not even me?"

"No, Eric, not even you."

"Mrs. Byrnes says that people in the Bible lived until they were 900 years old."

"There were giants in the earth in those days," Tyler declared, and then seeing his son's puzzled face, went on, "Maybe they measured years differently in those days."

Eric paused. "How do they measure years, Daddy?"

Viola came in then. "All right," she said, "to bed now. Daddy'll explain that another time. Say goodnight."

Eric stood up, closed the book and set it carefully on the night table. He walked to the bed, leaned his face down, and kissed Tyler. "Goodnight, Daddy," he said, "I hope you get better," as if that was what they'd been talking about. Then, as if he was embarrassed, the boy rubbed his face. "Your beard sticks like pins, like after a haircut. When are you going to shave it off?"

"I don't know," Tyler said. "I like it. Don't you?"

The boy shook his head.

Later, after the lights were out, Tyler heard the boy call to him and when he answered, Eric said, "You know, Daddy, the book says that from Pluto everything looks little, like stars look to us. Even the sun only looks like a little star from way up there."

"Yes, Eric," Tyler said. "I know." But he didn't ask his son how you could really know what anything looked like to a Plutonian, or to anyone that far out in the solar darkness.

The next morning Tyler got out of bed for the first time since he'd been sick and went to the windows. Breathing deeply, he raised his arms and rotated them, feeling none of the nagging weakness that only two weeks before had made even lifting his head from the pillow a task. It was a late autumn day so cold that the sky was white and so clear that in the distance he could see the pond in the park through the leafless trees. The cold had bronzed the last leaves on the privet hedges and turned rhododendron leaves limp and curled, but the grass was still green, though mottled here and there by bare spots and straw-colored patches. Tyler dressed, his clothes feeling new and clean against his skin, so used had he become to pajamas and a robe. He wasn't yet ready to negotiate the stairs, but he walked around upstairs looking out of the windows, watching Eric across the street on his tricycle with two other children chasing the various trucks and cars that drove lazily down the winding street. With his hooded jacket over his head and his white socks flashing between his shoes and his trousers as he furiously pedalled his bike, Eric looked like one of Snow White's cheerful dwarfs. As Eric raced back and forth, his open mouth streamed small puffs of smoke in the cold air that Tyler tried to make words of and thought, wryly, that it was like trying to decipher Indian smoke signals in the old Western moving pictures.

Though Tyler's routine remained much the same, the days now seemed to go faster as he watched his son through the windows—digging in the sandbox down the street, swinging from the jungle gym in the backyard, playing hide-and-seek with the neighborhood children. The evenings went more swiftly too for now that he was out of bed and had begun to come downstairs to the living room, Eric played long games of dominoes and backgammon with him, cheating outrageously. When Tyler lectured him about it, assuring him that the point was not to win, but to play the game—hearing himself sardonically speak the words that he could neither say with complete conviction nor absolutely reject—and pointing out that Eric could win often and still play fairly, Eric smiled and said, "Yes, Daddy, but I want to win *all* the time"—to which Tyler could give no simple and honest reply.

Viola and the twins badgered the boy for "tiring Daddy out," but Tyler knew that he was drawing strength and vigor from his son, and he thought they knew and were more than a little jealous. As he drew closer to Eric and leaned on him, Tyler was ashamed of it, as if there was something not fair in a grown man taking so much from a small boy, as if their positions were unfairly reversed, but his love for the child rekindled some guttering flame in him, and out of Eric's love for him, and the boy's swift agile running and jumping, his tough, competitive playing—and cheating—at their nightly games, Tyler knew he drew a new will to live. One evening, when Janice made some casual comment about his "heart failure," he brought her up sharply, correcting it to "cardiac insufficiency," and then Jacqueline started to cry and left the room. Later, before he could fall asleep, Tyler wondered if it had made any real difference, and was it worth having hurt the twins' feelings for. Weren't both terms, to reverse them, simply "failures of heart," or was that a simple, verbal ploy to rob the terror of the simple, physical fact of death?

A week later, the first day after the initial six weeks were ended, Tyler decided to go out. He told no one, not even Viola, but he made his mind up that he would surprise Eric by going in Mrs. Byrnes's place to pick him up at school. When he came downstairs and told Mrs. Byrnes, her silence rang louder than spoken disapproval, and he went through the ritual of telling her that he felt fine and was properly bundled up and really quite ready for a short trip outside. But once he opened the door, he forgot her reproving face altogether in the wave of joy that swept over him with the bite of cold air in his nostrils. "It has taste," he said aloud, "it really does," and Tyler found himself gulping air and walking in what was almost a waltz rhythm.

Everything seemed as if he'd been given new eyes. A scarlet cardinal flushed out of a naked giant hickory tree bolted skyward, a squirrel holding a half-eaten green hickory nut in its paws still seemed to be stalking the bird, and then in disappointed joy went from trunk to branch to electric wires, raced across them in staccato dashes like a high-wire specialist, and plunged down an electric light pole to the street and was lost in the underbrush. A little way further Tyler found a robin's nest blown down from a maple by the wind. Wisps of it still clung to the branch, and when Tyler knelt to touch the nest on the ground, astonished at how silky it felt, he stroked it gently, then stood up and stepped around it.

Briskly, Tyler walked toward the school along the park's edge, stopping on the headland less to rest than to admire the green wintry bay which stretched to the next neck of land where white houses and dark roofs, splotched among the trees, looked almost like a New England village but for the enormous spider of silvered water tower hunched above them. Not a boat was in sight on the choppy waves, only a white cloud of gulls wheeled, banked, and then dived for their prey, skimming the surface like mist. Tyler cut through the park, noting the knotted buds of the young trees, a serene and sealed-off preparation for a coming spring, the arrogant evergreen of jack pine, fir, and hemlock, and the older, leafless trees with ravaged trunks and peeling bark, their heavy limbs creaking like old furniture in the light wind. High over them, a lone white gull with black-tipped wings outstretched and unmoving, clearly outlined, sailed, circling.

At the edge of the park, the red-brick school loomed up, a modified English fortress with concrete crenelated battlements and cinquefoil decorations, its shadow casting an ornamental fretwork on the ground. A small group of waiting women huddled together in the ragged patch of sunlight next to the exit, and Tyler, unwilling to join them, stood across the street in the shade, though there, for the first time, he felt the chill wind blowing off the park.

Only minutes later the big metal doors swung open and the children came running out. When he saw Eric, Tyler went quickly across the street but the boy had already turned in the other direction and had his back to him. Tyler walked

up behind him, tapped him on the shoulder lightly and said, "Eric, I'm here."
The boy turned, arms flailing and fists balled, and Tyler felt him beating his
arms and body before he could grab the boy and hold him. "It's me, Eric," he
repeated twice, stupidly.

"Why did *you* come? Why didn't you send Mrs. Byrnes?" the boy shouted.
"You're sick! You're supposed to be home sick!"

Tyler heard the buzz of women's talk behind him and saw the children
turning to stare. "I thought I'd surprise you," he said softly.

"And why don't you shave that silly beard off?" Eric yelled, and then,
before Tyler could catch his breath, ran off.

Suddenly chilled and very tired, and wanting to get away from the
children's and women's eyes, Tyler followed him at a short distance. Not
looking back, Eric now strode along with a dark-haired little girl Tyler
recognized as Alison Cartright, one of the neighbor's children. After they
walked that way for a while, Eric stopped, and both children waited for him to
come up to them. As Tyler approached, he heard his son telling Alison about
his "planet book," how if you blasted off in a speedy rocket you'd be all grown
up by the time you got to Neptune, and more than thirty years old when you
crossed the path of Pluto, the planet that was furthest from the sun.

When Tyler reached them, they stopped talking and Eric took his hand.
Together, they crossed the street, looking carefully both ways for cars, and
walked on toward home.

That evening when Viola returned and Mrs. Byrnes told her he'd gone out,
she came to his room and, with his bedroom door shut "so the children won't
hear," scolded him in a quiet fury for perhaps twenty minutes until finally, in a
voice so cold and final he scarcely recognized it as his own, he stopped her. "I
will go out whenever I please, wherever I please. I don't want to hear another
word—of advice, caution, or complaint from you, or Mrs. Byrnes, or anyone
else. Is that clear?"

"Perfectly," Viola said distinctly. Her mouth, surprised open, repeated in a
whisper, "Perfectly." She stood up, automatically smoothing her skirt and
brushing her hair from her temples, looking at him with eyes so wide with fear
and puzzlement that for an instant he was contrite. Then she left the room.

Tyler lay there for a long time and when Viola sent the twins to ask him if
he wanted any dinner, he said he wasn't hungry. At bedtime, Eric came in
alone to say goodnight, as if nothing at all had happened at the school. The
sight of his fresh, open face made Tyler clutch the boy's shoulders, hold him at
arm's length and look straight into his eyes. "Why did you punch me when I
came to get you at school, Eric?"

The boy's face closed. He looked down, but he didn't answer, and there
was a half-expressed tic-like shrug of his shoulders.

"Did I embarrass you?"

Still no answer.

"Would you like me to pick you up again tomorrow?"

Eric shook his head.

"The day after?"

The boy shook his head again.

Tyler pursued it no further. "Goodnight, Eric," he said, but when Eric moved to kiss him, Tyler almost involuntarily shifted so that his son's lips only grazed his cheek. After the lights were out, Eric called to him in a strange, uncertain voice that Tyler recognized had much in common with the bewildered concern he had read in Viola's face earlier that evening. "Daddy, if you're not sick any more—I mean, if you're feeling better—when are you going back to the office?"

Tyler was silent, thinking that over.

"Daddy?"

"Yes."

"Did you hear me?"

"Yes, Eric."

"What?"

"Yes, I heard you."

"And Daddy?"

"What is it?" Tyler asked, holding down the note of cold irritation in his voice that had crept into his rejoinder to Viola's tirade.

"When you go to the office, shave off that beard, huh?"

When Tyler didn't answer, Eric said, "Please, Daddy?"

"Go to sleep, Eric. We'll see," Tyler replied.

Tyler tossed and turned for a very long time before he fell into fitful dozing, and when he woke with a start, his pajamas pasted to his chest with sweat, his hair, throat and face wet, and even his palms clammy, he remembered the dream he'd been having. Even as he tried to order it in his mind, it began to recede, just as the grey ground mist in the dream itself had been swallowed up by the darkness. For the first time that he could remember, he'd been dreaming about Italy and the war, and someone chasing him across a field. Running, he had been driven breathless across a ravine by machine-pistol fire and into a house, which had sprung up out of the ground. Then an exploding grenade had hurled him through a giant picture painted on a wall.

Closing his eyes and concentrating all his efforts, Tyler tried not to let the dream slip away. *What was that picture?* For a moment, he was sure he was looking right at the Raphael painting of Aeneas carrying old Anchises on his back out of burning Troy, with a woman staring aghast at the flaming chaos behind, and a small boy accompanying them looking up with affectionate anxiety at old Anchises feebly clinging to his son's power. Then, as Tyler fought to bring the blurred painting into focus, it faded and suddenly he remembered, by rote, like a schoolboy, lines he had had to memorize—in Latin and in English—at prep school, lines he had succeeded in learning only with great diligence and the surreptitious aid of a trot. *"Facilis descensus Averni . . ."* he whispered into the dark, silent bedroom, and then he fumbled, and couldn't remember the Latin until, *"Hic opus, hic labor est."* But the English came back whole and in a rush:

The descent to Avernus is easy;
The gate of Pluto stands open night and day;
But to retrace one's steps and return to the upper air,
That is the toil, that the difficulty.

"Sandy?" It was Viola. "Are you all right?" She turned the night-table lamp on and in the light the last indistinct lines of Aeneas and Anchises disappeared. She stood there, nervously knotting the blue sash of her dressing gown, and when he didn't answer, she explained, "You were gritting your teeth and groaning like you were in pain. I could hear you in the next room."

"It's all right, Viola, it was only a bad dream. Go back to sleep."

"Do you want me to put the light out?"

He nodded. After she had turned off the lamp, she asked, so softly he could barely hear her, "Do you want me to stay here with you?"

For a moment Tyler wanted to say that it wasn't necessary, but instead, deliberately, "Sure, why not?"

She was soon asleep by his side, warm and breathing regularly, and he was glad she'd offered and that he had not turned her away. Lying back and knowing now he would be unable to sleep until morning, Tyler thought about Eric's Pluto, and Virgil's, and his own, but he knew that one and all were the same—in Troy then, or here and now—and could not be avoided. He'd gone down and even let his son carry him a little way back, but no more. Eric was too young and too weak to do more, and besides it was asking too much of him, and after all he himself was not quite yet an enfeebled Anchises.

Turning on his side, carefully so as not to wake Viola, Tyler looked out of the window. Morning was still a long way off, but it would come. When it did he was going to get up, get dressed, and go down to the office. He wasn't going to call Charlie to say he was coming, and get no for an answer. And he wasn't going to consult Viola, or Mrs. Byrnes, or the doctors either. Maybe, at first it would only be for a few hours a day, maybe even less, but he would make a beginning, and the first thing in the morning, he thought, rubbing his chin and cheek ruefully, as a starter, and as a favor to Eric for services received, he was going to shave.

THE AUTOPSY

DAVID SPRIGGS
from *Duel*

We waited outside the autopsy room of the Kingston Public Hospital. I had arrived ten minutes early for a business appointment with the doctor. My company had asked me to cultivate this particular doctor because his influence as the island's chief government pathologist would prove useful. The usual buttering had had its effect and finally I had been invited in to watch him perform a post-mortem examination. The old black fellow sat gumming silently on a bench opposite me. I suddenly recognized him.

He was dressed differently than when I usually saw him, which wasn't very often. It was his voice that I knew—I heard it every morning as I lay in bed. This fellow heaved and pushed a damp, decrepit wooden box under which were nailed two pairs of roller skates to give it mobility. He struggled with it up from the harbour where he bought his goods at day-break to the network of streets where I lived. There he made his way about the neighbourhood until the box was empty, or until the heat spoiled his goods. On the hot black macadam he left a trail of drips, a cloudy, smelly mixture of melted ice and fish juice. He was the fish-man.

Every two or three minutes his voice would cry out. The fish-cry was unique, unmistakable amongst the cries of the other vendors. It sounded like a grackle's call, a short blurp followed half a second later by a long, squeezing sound only he was louder and less distinct. I would lie in bed thinking lazily just after waking while his cry receded and grew louder again, and then receded again as he pushed his box up and down the streets. The cry had become an unconscious thing like the ticking of a clock.

The fish-man did not know me and I could observe him without interference since I didn't have to acknowledge him. He was as old in years as he was from wear and tear. His skin was loose and delicate which made it more susceptible to old age. His face was three sets of concentric circles which spread out from his loose, watery eyes and shapeless, toothless mouth. He was bald except for a band of yellow-white hair covering the skin-wrinkles around the back of his head. His hands were oversized, thick and beaten out of shape from laboring with the fish-box. He had discarded his greasy street pants for his Sunday best—a thin, mismatched coat and pants. His feet like two blocks were crammed sockless into polished brown shoes which were mashed and split. He sat blankly staring about, working his mouth as though repeating his fish-cry to himself.

The pathologist arrived. He brushed between us, motioned for me to follow, and entered the autopsy room. The door closed behind us leaving the old man alone.

The peculiar stench of exposed organs permeated the white, sterile autopsy room. There were three porcelain tables, each rising in a solid block from the tiled floor. Each had a slight depression on the top surface which graded slightly towards a drain-hole down which body fluids disappeared. In the middle of the room from the ceiling hung a huge three bladed fan which throbbed slowly providing back-ground noise. The whiteness in the room was marred by a caking of dust which had collected on the greasy surface of the engine casing. Underneath the fan on the middle table lay the large body of a negress.

The attendants had prepared the body for the pathologist by cutting her open from the neck to the pelvis and sawing up through her breast plate so that her rib-cage sprung apart. The lungs, heart, intestines, and liver presented themselves in a delicate array of colour for systematic examination. The scalp was cut and drawn inside out from the back down over the front of the head so that her short fuzzy black hair was cushioned tightly against her hidden face. The skull was severed across the top and the cap hung glistening white down the back of her head like half of a grapefruit almost cut in two.

The doctor lost no time in performing the post-mortem, and little effort was wasted in explaining the procedure. The cause of death was a ruptured aneurysm of the middle cerebral artery which resulted in massive brain hemorrhage. The woman had collapsed in a grocery store and they had pronounced her dead on arrival at the hospital.

I sat waiting opposite the doctor while he wrote up his report on a little desk in a corner of the room. While he was writing, there came a timid knock on the glass pane of the door.

"What is it?" the doctor shouted from his desk. The fish-man opened the door and looked in slowly as though his movements were resisted by the sanctum of the autopsy room. "Are you here to identify the body?" snapped the doctor. The head nodded up and down. The doctor pointed towards the corpse which lay with arms hanging downwards and outwards off the table. The legs were straight and slightly apart with the feet pointing upwards. The fish-man trudged over to the body and looked down at it. His mouth movements stopped and he looked up and down its length.

An assistant appeared in a lab coat from an inner office and came over to the body on the other side, opposite the fish-man. Starting amongst the tuff of curly pubic hair, he began to sew her together with large, continuous, clumsy stitches using a small carpet needle and a double strand of heavy black thread. Half-way up he stopped sewing and pushed the needle a little into her thigh in order to make it handy to reach again. He gingerly took the woman's brains and slipped them into the abdominal cavity along with heart and lungs, all of which had been taken out and sectioned for better examination on a little three-legged side table. The assistant plucked out the needle and finished sewing her up, then left.

I began fumbling about in my brief case. The doctor was still busy writing but after a while my awkwardness made him look up and he realized what was wrong. He strode over to the corpse, covered it up to the neck with a clean cloth, and drew the scalp back over the head while holding the cap in place which stayed put when the skin was drawn over it. The woman's face appeared.

The doctor looked impatiently at the fish-man.

"Yas sah, dat is she sah—dat is mi wife sah!"

The fish-man resumed his gumming, turned himself around and shuffled out leaving the door open. The pathologist slammed it behind him.

Early next morning I lay in bed. The fish-man was there calling out in the streets as usual.

The Throughway

PETER TAYLOR

from *Sewanee Review*

They were a couple who had lived always in the same house since they had first married—not one they owned but one they had been able to rent all through the years. The house was in an old section of the city, the very part of town in which they both had grown up. Once upon a time it had been a fashionable section, of course, but even when Harry and Irene were young people it was considered no more than highly respectable and "comfortable." Yet they had been delighted to go on living there and had taken satisfaction in bringing up their two daughters in the neighborhood where they had themselves been young. When the daughters married and left them to go and live in the suburbs, they were happy to continue living there alone.

Harry's work was nearby. Just two blocks away there was a cluster of stores where Irene liked to do all her shopping for the house. Having everything so close, they had not found it necessary to own a car—not necessary or feasible. Harry's work had never amounted to more than holding down a job at the wire-mesh plant, but living always where they did and as they did, they had never suffered any real hardship. Irene was an excellent manager. As for Harry, there was no kind of repair job about the place that he couldn't do for himself. He even installed a new furnace when the old one wore out. Their contemporaries had all prospered more than they had, of course, and had moved into the newer, fashionable developments farther out in the east end. But these same contemporaries often expressed envy for Harry and Irene's lot in life. Everyone said that they were such sane and sensible and unsuperficial people. . . . In a changing, uncertain world it was good to know a couple who enjoyed such stability.

But this was how it was for Harry and Irene before the unfortunate business about the throughway came up. After that—after it was announced that one leg of the new throughway system, connecting all the outlying sections of the growing city, would come down their very street and require demolition of their entire block—everything seemed different. Through certain connections that Harry had—boyhood friends in high places—he managed to obtain a court hearing in which to make his protest against the route the throughway was taking. From that day, he revealed himself to all his acquaintances as nothing more than a local crank. His friends could no longer enjoy dropping by his house of an evening for a relaxed talk about old times. And from about that time Irene, out of embarrassment perhaps, since she clearly did not share her husband's obsession, began to decline all invitations from even her oldest acquaintances.

Worse still, from that day forward Harry and Irene seemed almost strangers to each other. At times it was difficult for either of them to understand the motive behind anything the other did or said. On the other hand, there were as many times when each would suspect that he or she understood the other's motives only too well! The routing of the new throughway, which was considered to be in the public interest, seemed to have undermined that very serenity for which Harry and Irene were envied. On the day scheduled for their removal from the old house, they met in the downstairs hall not as two who were allied against an intruding world but as two adversaries.

Irene had left her room and come downstairs half an hour before Harry did. Finally she heard him shuffling about on the bare floor in his room and in the upstairs hall. Then she heard him on the stairs. She went into the hall and waited at the foot of the stairs, just outside the living room doorway. He descended the stairs as though he didn't see her there at the bottom. Finally he stopped on the last step and looked over her head into the dismantled living room. "Three moves," he said quietly, smiling faintly, vaguely—still not looking at her, "three moves are equal to one burning. That's how the old saying goes, isn't it?"

Though she stood with her back to the living room, Irene could see its whole jumble and disarray and even the terrible, blank bareness of its walls, all reflected in the wounded-animal look on Harry's face. Why, he looked like a man nearly eighty this morning instead of like one nearly sixty. She kept thinking that somehow she ought to feel guilty about it. But she could not take the blame. She could not find where her fault lay. In his eyes she seemed to see the goldfish bowl on the mantel piece directly behind her—almost literally she felt she could see it—and she saw in the expression about his mouth the canary's cage with its night cover still on to keep the little thing from taking fright when the movers should arrive. And as Harry's eyes roved slowly about the room behind her, it seemed to her that she could even see the drops of cold rain batting against the curtainless, shadeless windows. "I read in the paper recently," she heard him saying now, his eyes still directed toward the living room as though he were speaking to the covered bird cage or the fish bowl, "I read in the paper that one-third of this country's population moves every year."

Suddenly Irene reached out and placed a hand on his sweater sleeve. She left it there a moment, thinking surely it would make him look at her. In that moment it seemed that his not looking at her during the past weeks had been what hurt her most. Presently, in a tone so dispirited and soft that he may not have noticed that she had spoken, she asked, "How can you even want to stay on here?" Then, as though unexpectedly receiving new energy and a new inspiration, she went on, "Why, last winter the water got up in the basement till it ruined those two old chests of drawers you were refinishing. Didn't you even mind that? And, Harry, we are in for another wet, rainy fall. It's hardly September and the rain already coming down like October!"

Still looking past her, as if addressing someone over her shoulder, he said, "That's why I fired up the furnace this morning." As he spoke, the furnace pipes rattled and clanged as though there were a prison riot in progress.

"Yes, and *that* furnace! Listen to it! And you, at your age, down there shoveling coal at five a.m. A *coal* furnace!"

"I don't know why you should disparage the furnace," he said. And now it was as though he were talking to her—or to someone—over the telephone. "It's a good furnace still," he said in a loud, heartfelt tone. "Hardly four years old. Besides, I like knowing there's a real fire down there—not just some gas piped in, and a jet."

He was silent a moment. Then he fixed his eyes on her for the first time. "It isn't natural," he said, "for a woman to care so little about her home."

Except for the tone of his voice when he said that, she might have thought he was out of his senses. And his gaze on her was suddenly so intense and honest she could almost believe that what he said made sense. . . . After a moment she began shaking her head from side to side. That was all she could do now. Here it was Monday morning, the day of the move, and he was still saying that sort of thing to her. What did he mean? And how dare he? It was really too much. He had been no help at all. He had taken no part in the packing or in finding a new place. All week-end he had wandered about the house like a sick animal who only *sensed* there was going to be a change, padding about in his soft-soled slippers, with never a word to anybody, and never once offering to lend a hand. Their two sons-in-law had had to come in and shift the crates and barrels about for her.

At last Harry turned away into the hall. He was heading for the dining room, she guessed—as though they could eat in *there* this morning! "What isn't natural," she began, not knowing what she was going to say, but following after him and determined to say something, "what's not natural is for a *man* to care so much about a house—especially a house that isn't his." She was willing to say the worst kind of thing that might pop into her head this morning if it took that to prevent Harry's falling back into yesterday's silence.

In the dining room doorway he halted again, almost as if he had found her confronting him in that doorway too. Instead, she was so close behind him that when he stopped her nose actually touched the coarse texture of his cardigan. And she didn't need to peer over the stooped shoulders or around his straight-hanging sweater arms to make out what it was he had come up against that stopped him. She knew the kind of disorder the dining room was in. She could see right through him—she could see it with *his* eyes—the dark table laid with cartons of kitchen junk instead of with the china and silver he expected, or wanted to expect. Then for a moment she had a clear vision, *his* vision, of the heavy oak dining table set with their white bone china (which she had used every day since they set up housekeeping, without ever breaking even one cup-handle) and their wedding silver (which she had never spared, never saved for company, but which she had polished every Saturday night and had used and enjoyed every day that came, just the way he wanted her to). The vision of their table all properly set for breakfast with the cut glass sugar bowl and cream pitcher, *his* vision, was so vivid to her that she closed her eyes and kept them closed for a moment, trying to free herself of it. . . . It was never easy for her not to see things the way he saw them or the way he wanted her to see them.

Her eyes were still shut when she heard him suddenly laugh out loud. It wasn't a kind of laughter she had ever thought him capable of. Without opening her eyes she stretched out an arm in her self-imposed darkness, reaching for him with her open hand. But now he was no longer within her reach. It was still worse when she looked. Harry had crossed the room and dropped down into one of the straight chairs at the table, just as though the table were properly set, dropped down into his own chair, and was smiling at her across the litter on the table in that new way he had that seemed even more alien than his laughter.

"Dear Harry!" she said under her breath.

Harry put his two hands on the table and spoke with a casual warmth, as though he were merely asking what favorite dish of his he could expect this morning. "What would you have me care about instead?" he asked. There was something almost chipper in his voice. "That is, if I am not to care about our home." His voice sounded so natural that she forgot all restraint and let her anger come back.

"Why, you ought to care about your work, that's what!" (Now what was she saying to him? she asked herself.)

"I do," he said.

"You never have!"

She wondered at her own fierceness. She was saying things she couldn't have said to him six weeks before—before the hearing and its attendant publicity began. It was as if she had picked up the hateful, insinuating tone of the city officials and the lawyers and mixed it with the rudeness of the reporters. She heard herself, and she wanted to stop her ears to shut out her own voice.

"I've liked my work just as much as any man does," he said. "So leave that out, if you please. Stick to your real complaint, which is that I've liked my home a great deal better than most men do!"

"But this isn't *our* house—or *your* house. It's a house we've *rented*. Our furniture's our only real home, Harry. And we're taking that with us, Harry."

"Oh," he said, "so you hold that against me then, do you—that we've always only rented. Yet you have always maintained you didn't mind." Now it was he who sounded like the lawyers at the hearing.

"You know better, Harry. I haven't minded—not for myself." She had now followed him all the way into the dining room and stood with her hands clasped and resting on the skirt of her starched apron.

"Anyway," he said, "it's a house we've rented long enough to feel pretty much at home in. Thirty-one years. Our children grew up here, Irene. . . . I mean to die here."

"You're still saying that? *Today?*"

Now he had frightened her. Her fright seemed like something new to her, and yet it seemed familiar too. Momentarily she turned her eyes inward and asked herself, had she been frightened of him always? Frightened of dear, gentle Harry? Harry, who had wanted only to have his peace and keep out of the world's way? But yes, that was it. It was not the throughway that was the cause of their distress. It was Harry's drawing away from life. All through the years, really, he had only been waiting for the throughway, even wishing for it in his own way, wanting to be cornered. He simply could not have borne it if they had suddenly rerouted the throughway down some other street than theirs! . . . Again she shook her head. Such thoughts! She pushed one of the straight chairs over opposite him and sat down. "Listen, my husband, my dearest, we've always known we'd have to move some day. We've loved it here, but this neighborhood—this whole end of town—was going down when we married. That's how it happened we were able to rent so cheaply here where we did."

"I wanted to rent here," he said grimly. "It was not just something we could afford—not for me."

"I know."

"I grew up in this end of town, Irene. So did you. Why not die here? Everybody has the right to die where he's—"

"I'm not thinking of dying, Harry!" she cried. It was as though she were fighting off the sudden image of death itself. "And you shouldn't be." Presently she bent forward and narrowed her eyes at him. "I . . . don't . . . believe . . . you . . . are, Harry."

"But I am, somehow," he said.

"Why, I don't care where I die," she said recklessly. Her two plump forearms were planted on the table before her, and she could feel goosebumps rising on them. "Isn't it enough just to go on being alive? No matter where it is? Isn't our love anything at all to you any more?" But at once she felt she had spoken the word "love" exactly as she would have spoken the name of a long dead child. And she was so shocked by what she had said, and how she had said it, that she drew in her breath sharply.

At first Harry didn't seem to have heard her. Then presently he said: "But *here!*" He was smiling that new smile again. His mouth turned up at the corners, like a child's drawing. "*Here* in the end of town where we grew up and have spent our lives! I tell you, I mean to go on firing that furnace of mine to the end, Irene. I've talked myself into a queer corner, I know. I stop sometimes and ask myself why I've done it. But I can't give in. Can't you see?"

Harry got up from his chair and went to the dining room's plate-glass front window. Stripped of its draperies and its net curtains and even its green canvas shade, it was bare like a store window. How efficiently she had *undone* everything, he said to himself. Just as efficiently and economically as she had always *done* everything. He could imagine her saying to herself: Why leave anything behind in a house that is going to be pulled down? She would have soaked the wallpaper off the walls if she had deemed it practical. And she was so sure she could set them up just as cozily somewhere else. It was her great pride that she could make something of nothing. And that was the trouble. She had made their nothing such a great plenty. She had never allowed him to feel poor, to feel himself a nobody. But he had wanted to feel himself a nobody, to know that he was poor. He had needed to need. It seemed to him that from that he would have derived his deepest satisfaction. Long ago, before they were married even, she and he had talked a great deal about "accepting the world." But he saw now how differently they had meant it. When, last year, they had heard the first threats that the throughway might come down their street, he saw that she seemed almost to welcome the idea. He had suspected her at times of having intercourse with the enemy. He smiled at the expression. The enemy, in his mind, had become the old friend from whom he had rented the house these thirty-one years—the old friend at first, that is, then his widow, then his widow's heirs. It seemed possible that Irene might have gone to the heirs and urged them not to fight the plan—to the heirs and perhaps the other property owners too. Her way of accepting the worst was to welcome it, to invite it, to be for it, of it. Just within recent months she had conveniently discovered all that was wrong with the old house and how bad it was for his heart that he had to fire that furnace. Or had she hated every bit of it all along? Was the throughway only what she had been waiting for?

He stood looking out into the rain. The rain seemed to have subsided somewhat. Out in the wet street a car went by, then a truck. But nobody passed on the sidewalk. There wasn't another house in the block that hadn't been vacated. Two across the street had already come down; even the rubble had been cleared away.

Now she moved up beside him at the window. He felt her hand on his sleeve again. "We'd best get a bite of breakfast in the kitchen, Harry," she said. "The vans are due at eight o'clock."

He answered her in a whisper: "They've widened this street every ten years since we've been living here, Irene. The trees went, the grass went next—now the people." While he spoke, a gray cat out in the rain went scurrying along the sidewalk on the other side of the street. "Hurry, puss!" he said in a normal voice. Then he added, "It's a funny thing. I had a dream about a cat last night. I thought I saw a mother cat eating its kittens. . . . We had one who did that when I was a boy."

Irene made no response immediately. The two of them continued to stand at the window, looking out at the empty lots across the street with the gaping holes that had once been basements. Presently her hand fell away from his arm, but he could tell she was still there even before she spoke. "Harry, don't begin again. You've said it all. You've said it to *everybody*. That should satisfy you. The lawyer tried to make you understand, even after the judge couldn't. I thought maybe he had. Till this week-end, I did. You're a man and ought to understand it better than I do. We're out of character in this, both of us. I've never had any thought but to be what you wanted me to be. My one desire in life has been to give in to you—"

"Yes, that's true."

"—and make you comfortable and live within your—within our—means."

"That's true."

"I've never had any thoughts of my own, Harry."

"I know."

"You've always told me what to think, and I've thought it. But, Harry, even I can understand that it's only the property owners who might have stopped the throughway, and they didn't want to. You ought to have known it was hopeless when *they* hung back. Your own lawyer said you ought to have your head examined for making such a useless fuss just because you could. He said so to me, in just so many words. It's nothing to smile over, either—especially not like that. *I'd* think you were crazy too, if I didn't know the truth. It isn't the house, Harry, and it isn't the part of town you care so much about. Why, this part of town's changed beyond recognition. It's the throughway you hate for itself—or love for itself—coming down our street instead of the next street, or the next. You hate it, or love it, because you always knew it or something like it would come, had to come. . . . But it's not our street really, Harry. It's those people's street who owned these old houses if it's anybody's, and they didn't even stand by you when you got it into court."

"Is ownership the only thing in life? Can't you have a right to something without owning it?" He didn't look around at her. He went on looking out the window. Outside the rain had begun to fall more heavily again. "I own nothing," he whispered. "I made up my mind early in life to ask for nothing. I thought that nothing was something they could never take away from me. But now it seems that isn't so. The world today wants your nothing, even. Perhaps it always did."

"Harry, don't begin that again. Not with that smile, anyway. I have to tell you, Harry, it does scare me a little to have you whispering and smiling so strangely. It would scare anyone. It's strange enough seeing the house like this. It's been strange enough living in this empty street all these weeks and months. Oh, you might as well know it now: I've been scared a long time living in this neighborhood."

"You wanted to be scared in this neighborhood. You wanted to want to move."

"Last winter, for instance, when you worked overtime so many nights at the plant, I used to hear noises at these downstairs windows."

"You wanted there to be noises at the windows."

"At least once I *knew* it was someone trying to break in. . . . Don't smile so, Harry. . . . Some nights I almost telephoned one of the girls to send her husband over; but I didn't want to worry them any more than you. Yes, I switched on those outside lights you've put up. I suppose that's all that stopped whoever it was. But I've been scared in the daytime here. For years, Harry. And since all the neighbors left—*such* neighbors as they were, too, toward the last! Oh, Harry, we've always known we'd have to move some time! Even if they'd put the throughway farther east, it wouldn't have been a year before the Negroes would have been in this block. They're already just two doors the other side of the Cass Street intersection."

"I don't mind the Negroes any more," he said.

"I know you don't mind the Negroes. And they'll be everywhere before long. You say it's right. A sign of progress, you say. Well, the throughway is a sign of progress, isn't it? How can you be for progress and against it too?"

"I can, somehow," he said. She parted her lips to speak, but he interrupted. "And I've reached a point where it's no use trying to explain things."

"Then there's no use my saying more," she said resignedly. "It's seven-thirty, Harry. The vans—"

"Forget the vans," he said sharply. He turned his face to her, and they looked deep into each other's eyes for a moment. "The vans aren't coming, Irene," he said finally.

Irene smiled at him with an indulgent expression. "The vans *are* coming, Harry," she said patiently, as though explaining something to a child— explaining it for perhaps the second or third time. "It's all arranged for, dear. They'll be here at eight—rain or shine."

"No," he said. "I telephoned the transfer company from the plant on Friday. The vans aren't coming."

"You *wouldn't* have, Harry!" she wailed.

"I told them their men would have me to deal with if they showed up here."

"Harry, you *didn't!* Not without consulting me! . . . And letting me go through this week-end."

"And you know how they'd feel about dealing with a crazy fellow like me, after all they've seen in the papers."

"Then I've done all I can do in this house, Harry."

"There's not *much* more anyone can do," her husband answered.

"Not *much* more?" she asked, lifting her eyes suddenly to his.

"Not much more," he said.

It was only then she realized how tired she was—not tired from the packing up, or tired even from the incessant ringing of the telephone or the being stopped by strangers on the street or by reporters waiting to take her picture, wanting *her* picture—*hers!*—the last resident, the wife of the man who said the throughway shouldn't come down his street, wanting *her* picture doing *her* last shopping in the old-timey, pint-sized kind of Piggly-Wiggly store that they still had in their neighborhood. She wasn't tired from the aggressive resentment that other people showed for someone who thought he could stop the throughway. No, what she was tired out by was fighting with herself to keep herself from fighting him. All these years, more than anything else, she had wanted him to have his own gentle way in everything, his own peace. That was what she had believed. She had laughed with him whenever he was passed over for promotion at the plant, and said with him, What did it matter? How could it change their life? Didn't they already have their own little niche? But she knew now what it mattered. She knew now that in this day and age either you accepted the world, manifested yourself to the world, let the world have its way with you, or one way or another, sooner or later, directly or indirectly, you must pay its price—your peace. Yes, sooner or later it would come down your street. But, oh, actually she knew now that so far as she was concerned Harry was part of the world, that he was part of what was not her, that is, and knew that in the end everybody was part of it except yourself. Time was when she believed she kept herself from fighting him because it was the womanly, wifely thing to do. Or had she ever believed that, really? Wasn't it that she had really known all along that in his meekness he was far stronger and more willful than she and would never yield an inch to her in any struggle there might ever be between them? His self-righteous withdrawal from the contest of life she saw now not as a negative thing but as a positive force pulling her with it toward a precipice somewhere. But she had had to try to save herself. She could not let him drag her over the precipice. . . . Suddenly she left him at the window, and went hurriedly from the room.

Harry didn't know where she had gone until he heard the rattle of the metal coat-hanger on the floor of the hall closet. It was an unmistakable sound. He reminded himself that she would already have packed up all the wooden coat hangers—they cost *money*—and probably all the wire ones too, except one for his coat and one for hers. And no doubt she had a place reserved in some box or other for those two wire hangers even. No doubt in some box—he thought it before he could stop himself, before he could tell himself that it didn't make sense—no doubt in some box she had a spot reserved for *him*. Perhaps one of those boxes she had been saving in the attic through the years had been for him all along. Ah, the good-natured teasing he had done about her saving habits! It had seemed such a funny little fault for her to have. And in fact it ought to have put the fear of God in him long ago! He ought to have seen it for what it was. While he had been always avoiding the box the world wanted to put him in, she had been preparing one for him in his own attic. All that string and those old papers and boxes had been to wrap *him* in! She had known the day would come. . . . But what nonsense, he said to himself, trying to calm himself. Am I really out of my head? What nonsense. Am I afraid of such a reasonable, sensible, practical soul as Irene? . . . Nevertheless, it was just as well he had cancelled the order for the moving vans. In effect, she had been going to wrap him up and carry him off with the rest of the furniture. Then when she had moved him and the other furniture out, *they* would come and pull the house down. He had watched them tearing down the houses across the street. He had not told her at the time, but that was when he first realized he must do something. It was the wrong way for those old houses to go. There was something indecent about it, with those thugs hired to come in with their crowbars and their cranes and their great, swinging mace-and-chains. It took murderers for that. Of course, as Irene said, they were not *his* houses. No, but you couldn't watch without feeling it. Burning them would have been better—more decent. That's the way such old houses used to go. He could remember when a whole block on Spencer Avenue burned. There had been four houses in that block that were built before the Civil War. At least three generations had lived out their lives there. He remembered too when the old Milton house on Spruce Street burned. That was the house in which his parents had got married. When the block on Spencer Avenue burned, half the town had turned out to see it, and his father had been one of the volunteers who went in to help. When the Milton house burned, he remembered, his mother shed tears. He could remember also when the Dickinson house burned, the house in which his parents happened to be living when he was born. He had been a boy in his teens at the time of those fires. In those days nobody seemed ever to know how fires got started, and he could recall the strange feelings he used to have about it sometimes. . . . He couldn't understand now why he had had such feelings. . . .

Irene came back into the dining room, slowly pulling on her light-weight cloth coat. From the window, he looked at her over his shoulder. "I'm going to one of the girls," she said. "You can find me when you've finally satisfied yourself. I've endured all I can, Harry. The thought of more publicity and more bickering with the city people is more than I can bear. You can do what you will about the furniture." (Suddenly he wondered if she had ever suspected that it might have been he trying to frighten her those nights when she was at home alone. He felt a flash of guilt, just as though it *had* been.) "Everything's packed up except a few dishes and things in the kitchen. I've written down the address of the new place on that barrel by the front door. It's Apartment A. It's on the first floor, Harry, as I've told you. There's a locker room in the basement that will hold all that won't go in the apartment. I've paid a month's rent in advance. . . . I'm going now. There's some breakfast for you in the kitchen if you can eat it."

She turned away abruptly and crossed the hall to the living room. The canary was chirping under its cover. She quickly removed the cover without looking at the bird. She couldn't bear to look at the poor, protected creature, so innocent and unsuspecting. From the mantel she took the package of seed and poured a full measure into the feeder. Replacing the package of seed on the mantel shelf, she glanced at the bowl of fish. The fish had always been considered mostly his. Beside the bowl lay a packet of fish food. It was open at one end, and she could see the white wafers inside. Somehow it looked repulsive to her. She stood gazing at the fish food, and afterward at the four little mottled fish, without ever lifting a hand. I have done all I can do here, she said to herself. It would take all the energy she had to propel herself through the doorway into the hall again and down the hall to the front door. She was not sure even that she could make that journey, but she knew her life depended upon it.

When she reached the center of the hall she saw that Harry had gone back to his chair at the table—the same chair he had sat in earlier. Her empty chair was still opposite him, across the layers of junk. He sat there smiling over at her chair.

"Whatever are you thinking, Harry?" she asked, despite herself. She had hoped to have spoken her last word.

He bent forward, putting his elbows on the edge of the table and resting his chin on the heels of his two hands. "Well, if you must know," he said, "I was thinking of the houses around here I saw burn when I was growing up."

Irene's hand came up to her mouth. Behind her fingers, under her breath, she uttered a little shriek. It was the cry of a small animal suddenly finding itself trapped when it thought it had escaped.

She wasn't even sure whether or not Harry heard her, because simultaneously she heard the radiators in the downstairs rooms begin to thump and wail again. It seemed to her they were shaking the whole house. She saw Harry laugh soundlessly to himself.

"You know the houses I mean," he continued. "The old Milton house that the Thompsons lived in and where my parents were married, the Dickinson house, the houses in that block on Spencer Avenue." He paused and waited for one of the radiators, which had started up again, to become quiet. "It's a strange thing. It used to worry me that they never knew how those fires got started. Somehow I used to wonder if people thought *I* had done it. I even got so I had guilty feelings about it and half imagined that I *had* set the fires."

Slowly Irene's hand fell from her mouth. Her lips parted, but for a moment she was speechless. . . . She saw at last! She understood! It seemed to her that she stood there for five minutes, or even longer, before she could speak or move. Then she said: "Harry, I understand, at last."

He rose from the table and put up one hand as though to ward off a blow. "No," he said. "No, you don't understand one bit!"

"But I do," she said. As she advanced toward him, he sat down at the table again. He tried to smile, but now the smile failed. He was looking at her with open hatred in his face.

"It's no use," he said.

"Harry, my darling, all along you've wanted *everything,* which is what everybody wants—not nothing. But something inside you made you feel that it was wrong."

"You won't ever understand," he said, looking again toward the front window. "You would have understood years ago if you were ever going to. It's not so simple that you can see it in a flash."

"It is. It is. It's just that you don't want me to see," she said furiously, all the tenderness gone from her voice. "You didn't want to see, yourself! But I do see now. And you see it yourself, Harry. Don't try to deceive me. You wouldn't have remembered those fires and how you felt about them except that suddenly you understood."

"No matter how you make me out or how you explain my coming to where I am, it doesn't alter anything," he said.

He rested his head on the chair-back and closed his eyes. "I don't know whether I'm crazy or not. But if I'm not crazy, Irene, we've something worse to face. If I'm not crazy, the rest of the world *is.*" He opened his eyes and managed to smile at her. "It's as though ever since they widened that street out there the first foot—thirty years ago—as though I've known they would go on widening it till some day I wouldn't make sense about it. But there's no use our leaving here, Irene. No matter where one goes—"

Irene stopped listening and began wandering about the room as though she didn't know how to find her way out. She realized that they had only got back to where they began and that understanding didn't help. There was no help for them. She found herself standing in the wide doorway between the dining room and the hall. For a moment she leaned against the door jamb. Then, without consciously resolving to do so, she began letting herself down very easily and slowly to the floor. She sat with her legs spread out before her at such crooked angles that they looked broken. Harry got to his feet and came to her. But when he offered her his hand, she drew away from him.

"Don't do anything. I can't stop you."

"Irene," he said impatiently. It was a tone she had never heard him use with her before. She sat on the floor gazing out into the hall and through the glass in the front door. She heard the clock upstairs striking eight. So the moving men *weren't* coming! And he *was* mad, of course. She couldn't doubt it now. Glancing down at her broken-looking legs, she found it unbearable to think that she would presently have to try to stand on them once more. And in that moment there seemed to pass before her eyes not the whole of her past life but rather the terrible eternity of life there seemed left before her. . . . Finally, as if in a dream, she saw one of Harry's frayed carpet slippers come down on the small area of floor between her own two feet, and then saw the other slipper lifted over her legs as he stepped over her and out into the hall. With her eyes and ears she followed his soft footsteps across the hall to the foot of the staircase and then down alongside the staircase to the door that led to the basement steps. She watched him place his hand on the polished brass knob. "Harry," she said in a hoarse voice, "what is it? What are you going down there for?"

"Nothing," he said, not looking back.

"Harry—"

"What is it?"

"Don't do anything. I can't stop you."

"Ah, Irene, what are you suggesting?" He spoke in the same impatient tone as earlier, and she could see only the back of his head, which he held at an angle, as though straining to hear her. "What is it you wish I would do, Irene?"

"Harry, I'm afraid of you." It was almost a direct appeal to him, he felt.

"You only *want* it to be me you have to be afraid of," he said.

"No, I'm afraid of you."

She sat very rigid, as though hypnotized, and watched him open the door and place one foot on the first step of the basement stairs. Then she watched him begin to lift the other foot off the hall floor. It was as though instead of the length of the hall she were five or six inches from his foot. And as the heel of the slipper left the floor, though not yet the toe, she became aware of the ringing sound. The foot became aware of it too, and the heel returned to the floor. The foot seemed to tell her it was the telephone out there in the back hall. The foot seemed to tell her who the caller would be, told her even before she raised her eyes to meet her husband's. Of course it would be one of the girls! And there was no not answering it. For if they did not answer, then the husband of one of the girls would leap into his car and, travelling the one already completed leg of the throughway, would arrive at their door within a matter of minutes. And if they did answer, it would no doubt bring the same son-in-law, because there would be no concealing that everything had gone wrong. Both of them knew that all decisions were, from that moment, over for them. To answer or not answer the telephone didn't matter. They were two old people who had behaved foolishly or who had almost behaved foolishly, and in the future all important decisions would be made for them. Henceforth they would be watched over and seen after. Henceforth they were in the hands of their children, and both of them asked silently, What other end would *not* have been better—more decent? Across the bare floor of the hall Harry and Irene looked into each other's eyes coldly, indifferently. The past year, the past quarter-hour itself, seemed like a lifetime. And those long, peaceful years they had known together seemed but a short honeymoon at the beginning of their marriage, a brief interlude almost forgotten. . . . Who was that stranger standing awkwardly with one foot on the cellar stair? . . . Who was that odd-looking old woman crouched on the floor? . . . Why, it was she with whom he was trapped by circumstance to end his days. . . . Why, it was he with whom she must live out her life and whom she must no doubt nurse through a prolonged senility. . . . Ah, yes, ah, yes . . . a husband . . . a wife . . . a fellow human creature, anyhow . . . that the world had come in and estranged from one. What matter if it took a quarter of an hour, a year, or a lifetime? . . . They eyed each other with awful resignation.

Reasons I Insist
You Call Me By My Right Name

GORDON WEAVER from *Latitudes*

When I was born, his fourth son, the last of his five children, ten years younger than my closest brother, my father consented to have me named after himself. And so I am Oskar—a name he detested all his life—Oskar Hansen, Jr. I never heard anyone except his children call him anything but Buck. Buck Hansen. *Buck* was engraved on the pocket knife he pared his nails with; *Buck* was stamped in gold on his luggage and his wallet; *Buck* was embossed on his business cards. He called me Sonny, or Sonny Boy.

My mother was his first wife; they divorced after twenty-five years of marriage. In 1953, the summer I was sixteen, I went to visit him on Long Island, where he lived with Irene, his second wife, and one night, shortly before I went back home to my mother, I met his third. Her name then was Lillie Broadfoot.

"This lady you're going to meet," my father said, "is from *Nawth* Carolina, and sometimes her accent is hard to understand. She's one swell hell of a gal though, I'll tell you." He stopped speaking to cough, and when the cough seemed to go deeper in his throat, vibrating and forcing tears from his eyes, he threw his Pall Mall out the driver's wing of the Dodge.

"You mean we're not going to eat clams like you said?" I asked him. I shouldn't have been surprised. He often arranged surprises for his children. When my brother Milt married, he deposited a thousand dollars in a checking account for him, handing him the bank book just as Milt left for the church. When the basketball season ended one year, he gave my brother Len a sum of money, two dollars for every field goal he scored, one for every free throw, calculated from the newspaper box scores. When my oldest brother, Nils, took me camping in Canada two years before, we found our father waiting for us at the canoe outfitters, his gear ready, the boats and packs paid for. When he heard my sister Jane's husband was mistreating her, he mailed her a loaded pistol with instructions to aim for his legs the next time he came home drunk and mean.

We expected surprises from our father. Everyone did from Buck Hansen. "How come we can't get us some clams and beer like you said?" I asked.

"We'll get all the clams you can put away," he said, "we'll take a sackfull home with us, or we can stop somewhere on the Sound on the way back if you want. I had to say something to get us the hell out of the house. Irene doesn't eat clams, and I wanted you to meet Lillie." I checked the shift in tone of his voice. He exhaled heavily, then lit a fresh Pall Mall, and appeared to swell with confidence, straightening his back against the seat, adjusting his bottom a little on the small inflated rubber tube he always sat on when driving. He called it the best friend a man with piles ever had.

I looked straight ahead through the windshield at the rain bouncing off the asphalt road. The delicious smell of cigarette smoke made my mouth water, and I hoped wherever we were going there would be someplace for me to go for a smoke. He knew I smoked, but never mentioned it. I met him halfway by never doing it in his presence.

"You want me to drive for a while?"

"You wouldn't be able to find the way in this weather. You better watch it, you'll wear that license out before it's a year old. Mother doesn't know you drive my car at all, you know." By *mother* he meant his first wife, my mother. He had no children with Irene, who was not much younger than he was.

"You mean," I said as we drove through the rainy night, "Irene isn't supposed to know where we go tonight? About this Lillie person?"

"Lillie Broadfoot's her name. I'd appreciate it, yes, if you'd be content to keep the whole thing to yourself. You see . . ." my father said, and became strained, seeming to sense the weakness of what he said, "it's not really such a joke to say that women—a lot of women anyhow—are better off without knowing everything that goes on in your life. I'm not kidding. It's one thing to lie to a person—a woman—and it's one thing, too, to have to do things a certain way if your life's going to be worth a plugged nickel to you. I guess that all doesn't make much sense to you, huh?"

"I think I get it," I said. "I mean I know what you mean, but I still don't understand it all, exactly why can't we tell her and everything." I wanted to talk, just to keep my mind off wanting a cigarette, and because I didn't want to think about what getting to Lillie Broadfoot's house was going to mean; I knew that if it was anything I could understand, then I was not going to like it much.

"I hope I don't have to draw you a picture about Irene," he said. "I want you to know I plan on getting her to go back to Minneapolis. In New York the only cause for divorce is adultery, but it's only incompatibility in Minnesota. You should understand these things. God, boy, you know Irene."

I knew Irene.

I met her the first time when I was nine or ten, when they still lived in Minneapolis. She was very nice to me, and I think I sensed even then that she worried he would blame her if I was not happy on my visit. We went smelt fishing with a seine, and the next morning she fried the smelt for breakfast, and so when she had an argument over something with my father later that day, and cried, I felt sorry for her.

I heard my father, in the bedroom with her, say sharply, and with a cynical, affected boredom, "Don't start the tears for me. That won't work. That won't work on me. I've seen the waterworks before, remember?" Yet I also admired this harshness in him. I was nine or ten, and it seemed like strength to me. I'd have liked to have been able to do it as well. I doubt if he was ever very gentle or kind to her.

The night I met Lillie Broadfoot, before we left the house, my father and I were sitting on fold-up chairs in front of the television set, built into the living room wall in a Levitt house. Irene was in the kitchen, finishing the dinner dishes, and she came into the living room to check for any dirty glasses or ashtrays. My father had set his beer bottle on the tile floor next to his chair while we watched wrestling from St. Nick's Arena, one of his favorite TV programs. We knew it was a big fake, but we liked it all the same.

"Buck," Irene said, "please don't put your bottles on the floor anymore. It leaves a ring there and I just waxed."

My father lifted the bottle, looked at the wet circle on the tile, and said, "Bushwah!" loudly, setting the bottle of Miller's High Life back down on the floor in the exact spot it had been. When Irene went quickly back into the kitchen and my father was absorbed by the mauling Lennie Montana was giving Rocco at St. Nick's, I put my pop bottle on the floor next to his.

When I was sixteen, the sixteen that I was, I needed strength, any form or symbol of it I could find. But I wasn't always so stupid, at least not when I was less conscious of myself and my father together.

Since he worked twelve hours a day and rode to work in a car pool, I had the Dodge nearly all the time. And because Irene didn't drive, I took her on shopping trips every couple of days. I found myself naturally doing little things for her; carrying the groceries to and from the car, reaching things that were too high on cupboard shelves, as I would have for my own mother at home. She began to ask me what things were my favorites for meals, what subjects I liked in high school, and if I was going to study to be a sales engineer like my father.

"I think he wants me to. I don't know for sure if I want to or not," I told her.

"It's not all just good money," Irene said, "they work terrible hours. Buck works all the time." I think I recognized how lonely she was. When my father surprised her by bringing her a pair of Mandarin-style lounging pajamas home from Manhattan one evening, I stood by, as excited and happy as she, while she opened the box to see what it was. And having shared these short moments of loneliness and routine and happiness with her made it difficult for me to comfortably digest the lie my father told her, the lie about going to eat clams.

"Did you have to lie to her?" I asked my father. I wanted to feel that my cooperation with the lie didn't make me equally its author.

"If you want to call it that," he said without taking his eyes from the rain-washed road, "then I can only say it's necessary sometimes. You're old enough to be aware of a few things. Things aren't always right. You know enough about your mother and me to take things in stride a little better."

"So where does this Lillie Broadfoot come in?" I said.

"Well, I'm going to marry her," he said, "just as soon as I can. That's why I want you to meet her. I guess you ought to be interested in who I'm going to marry."

"Really marry?" I said. I felt suddenly older, as old as my sister Jane or one of my brothers, and yet I knew that I wasn't old enough to know how to say the things I wanted to say and should have said then. If I'd had more courage, I would have asked if this were quite fair to Irene. If I'd understood my own memories of my parents' divorce then, I would have asked where the fairness lay in his treatment of my mother, my brothers and my sister, myself.

"Hell yes," he said. "She's a wonderful gal. She's had her share of troubles, too. She was married to some screwball made her rue the day—she's got a son older than you. I've never seen him. He's down in North Carolina somewhere. I'd give my right arm for her." We didn't speak for a few moments, until he shifted his position on the inflated tube and cleared his throat, changing the sound into a short laugh before he spoke again.

"She was going to marry an Air Force sergeant before I met her. She broke it off after we got together, but he kept pestering her, and one night he showed up at her place with a snootfull. He passed a lot of smart punk remarks, cursed her and one thing led to another, so her landlord there called the cops on him. This fellow that owns the building—Vernon, his name is—he's another one thinks the world of her, too. He and I have a game of cribbage when I come out now and then. Sometimes when Lillie and I watch TV he comes up for a drink and gasses a while with us."

"What about the sergeant?"

"I happened to drop out there just after the cops hauled him off to the lockup. Lillie was crying and what not, and Vernon was burned up, too. He came with me and we went down to the station house."

"In this car? In the Dodge?" I wanted to authenticate it, to know it was real.

"In my car, yes. I got talking with the desk sergeant, and he let me talk to this screwball through the bars of his cell. He's a goddamned dirty-mouthed little wop!" He had a way of saying words like that. In the thick, maddening traffic of New York he rolled down the car window and bellowed at other drivers: *wop,* or *boogie,* or *yid.* It used to paralyze me; it seemed like strength.

"He shot off his mouth, so I asked the cop how much it would cost me to get in the bullpen with the little bastard for five minutes and teach him some manners. 'Oh, come on now,' he says, 'you're too smart a man to want to do a thing like that,' he says. I said, 'Hell, when a man talks to me that way I want some action!'"

"Does he bother her anymore?" I asked. I was sure the little Italian airman didn't. My father's anger could be infectious; he made me feel as if I had just come close to a big fight, a little shaky and disappointed because I hadn't.

"I think he knows better. I'll for damn sure fix his wagon if he does." The rain had about ended. "I'm going to straighten myself out once and for all," he said. "There's not much chance of my finding a little happiness in this world with Irene around my neck."

"She doesn't know anything at all about it?" I said.

"If she doesn't then she's denser than I think she is." He reached out and wiped the mist from the inside of the windshield with the back of his bare hand. "Here we are," he said, slowing and stopping the car.

We got out of the Dodge and walked up to the porch. Beside him in the moist darkness, I admired the resoluteness of my father's bulk. When I was with him there ran hard and fast lines of strength and decision, so imminent and ultimate that a kind of electric crackle seemed to be in the air when he moved and acted. Troublesome, irritating motorists in heavy traffic trembled when Buck Hansen cursed. Men laughed when he joked, and inside the house, there was a woman from North Carolina waiting for him. Fairness, and doubt, and people's small, bruised feelings evaporated around Buck Hansen. He either destroyed them or laughed them away.

I was sixteen, and he was my father.

I squared my shoulders and tried to achieve the skeptical frown he wore when he listened to, looked at, or read of the ostensible principles of other people. There was nothing my father debunked more than a preacher or reformer, a Billy Graham or an Oral Roberts. "Ah, B. S.!" he would say to the television when Norman Vincent Peale smiled and talked softly of sin and virtue.

Then I was introduced to the woman who would later become his third wife.

"This is my youngest boy," he said, a hand on each of our shoulders. "This is Lillie Broadfoot . . . from *Nawth Cara-Linah.*" It was not his robust introduction, as when I had met men he worked with and for, but one muted and gentled, and with only a hint of joking in the parody of her accent.

"Now, Buck," Lillie said, "you've gotta stop kidding me on my accent. I'm so glad to finally get to know you, Oskar—" she pronounced it *Awscore*— "If I stay here in New York long enough I'll just be starting to talk like some Jew woman, and then I'll have another accent you can make fun of me for," she said to my father. And to me, "Your daddy's told me a lot about you. He thinks you're pretty keen, I'll tell you. Come on now, both of you upstairs and sit down." She herded us subtly to the living room, me to an easy chair, my father to a seat on the sofa where he would be beside her when she sat down.

"Now, Buck, you'll have a drink I know, and I've had one but I want another one, too. Was the driving bad in all this rain? I worry about you on the roads in weather like this, you can hardly see. Now what can I fix you, Oskar? Do you like a drink, too, or I have some beer, I think, or some soda pop. Did Buck tell you you all have to drink soda pop? Don't listen to him; you just tell me what you'd like."

I looked at my father for a signal on how to choose, but the nod or wink or narrowed eye and tight lip were not there. He was smiling like a child, his large body sagged in comfort on the sofa, lazily reaching for his Pall Malls in his shirt pocket. The heavy air of Lillie's perfume in the room seemed to have drugged him into a quiet lethargy.

"I'll have a drink also," I said.

"I don't know, he's only sixteen—" he started to say.

"Hush, Buck," Lillie said. She lit his cigarette for him. "I'll be back here in a second," she said, "so just you get homey all you want. And don't you worry about him having a drink, Buck."

"See?" my father said when she was gone to the kitchen, "I'm only happy these days when I'm here, kid."

We all had bourbon and water. She sat next to him, and I watched my father almost obediently float his hand on top of hers. She covered his hand and held it like a sandwich, patting it rapidly and softly, the way a mother pats an infant's back or buttocks.

I didn't believe in her son older than myself. Her hair was jet black, and she was as thin as any female shape that filled my mind in the solitary reveries I conducted when I found the proper times and places to think graphically about sex. The smell of her perfume was as dark as her eyes, with an added dimension not present in the scent women like my mother or Irene dabbed behind their ears and on their wrists before going downtown. She wore large bracelets on both arms that slipped and slid from her elbows to her hands when she moved to smoke and drink and gesture as she talked. She crossed her legs, showing her knees, and she continually bounced the upper leg, nervously and unconsciously, like a young girl.

Beside her, my father seemed drawn down into the stuffing of the sofa cushions. His age seemed to spring out from his limp cheeks and jaw, to roll down from his large stomach, to settle in his mildly swollen ankles. He smoked steadily, and, most surprising, he listened. Lillie Broadfoot was doing most of the talking. I, with contempt for everyone, drank my whiskey quickly and asked for another. She had brought the bottle, ice and water into the parlor with her.

"What is this here, Sonny?" my father asked me.

"Now sit and relax," Lillie scolded him, "leave the boy enjoy himself. Do you like a lot of water, Oskar? That's the trouble with Buck. Your daddy works himself nearly to death, and then doesn't know how to relax. Making good money is one thing, but knowing how to enjoy it is another, just remember that. Buck's tired all the time, and why not when he works twelve hours a day six days a week! Your health is worth a lot more than any money anyone pays you for ruining it." Her stockings and skirt lisped and sighed as she stepped about the carpet on steep heels, fixing my drink.

"It's a rat race," my father said, "that job is a holy rat race."

"What are you planning on doing?" she asked me, "are you going to college soon?"

"I think I'll take up engineering."

"Oh, now you said that because Buck's listening to you. If you really like it, it's what you should do. Life's too short to work at unpleasant work."

"You said a mouthful, Lillie," he said, almost to himself, but I didn't miss it.

"Can I have one of your cigarettes, Lillie?" I said.

"Why, for sure. Do you care if they have filters? I don't like those Pall Malls your daddy smokes. Buck smokes too much." She touched my hand with hers while she gave me a light. My father said nothing, and I enjoyed the smoke. After that, I simply reached over to Lillie's package whenever I wanted one.

"Hey," Lillie said, "before we get too far on here, it's time for Arthur Godfrey."

"We can just talk," my father said; he sounded lost.

"Do you like Godfrey, Oskar?" she asked me, turning on the TV set. "I don't think he's all that funny, but your daddy loves him. I never laugh *that* hard at anybody. Listen, Buck, why don't I give a yell down the stairs to Vernon and see if he wants to come up and see it too? Oh, go ahead, just pretend you were at home," she said to me when she saw me fixing another drink for myself. "I do like that Tony Marvin's voice, though. That's a bedroom voice if I ever heard one." I looked calmly into my father's eyes over the rim of my glass as I tasted my fresh drink. I think he realized that what he had lost was me, even if I didn't.

"That goddamn Godfrey's got a buck for every hair on his head," he said vacantly.

We had a little party. Vernon, the landlord, came upstairs to Lillie's flat to join us, and Lillie mixed some onion chip dip of her own private recipe. Made hungry by the whiskey, I ate a lot of chips, smoked, and watched the TV while they talked and played games of cribbage. He was teaching Lillie the game. Whenever she was sitting by him, he held her hand.

I used the bathroom. It smelled of pine oil air sweetener and colored soap, and while it was neat, it was filled with Lillie's combs, hairnets, shampoos, bottles of perfume and toilet water vials. I surveyed the kitchen on my way out and took a straight gulp of whiskey from a bottle of Waterfill and Frazier. My eyes teared and I felt robbed of breath for a moment, but then it warmly crowded my stomach, lightened my arms and legs. I walked unsteadily into the parlor again, uncertain of how late it was, and spoke to Vernon.

"Do you have an unfiltered cigarette on you?"

"Huh?"

"Will you give me a cig? Please."

"Hey, son," Vernon said, "you look a little green around the gills. Buck, I think you better look after your boy. He should lie down."

"Are you all right, Oskar?" Lillie asked me. I closed my eyes, then felt her warm hand against the cool light sweat on my forehead. I could feel the perspiration forming around my lips and in the hollows of my eye sockets. Voices and textures became swiftly and excruciatingly clear and present to me, as though I were exposed without a skin to blunt the sensations around me.

"Careful. Watch it!" Vernon said.

"He's made himself sick," my father said. Trying to move away, I stumbled.

"Let me. I'll take him, Buck," Lillie said. I felt her long fingernails through my shirtsleeve, heard her spike heels on the kitchen floor, and then opened my eyes to the blinking fluorescence of the frilly bathroom. "Go ahead, honey," she said. "I know you'll feel better."

I very deliberately put my hands on my knees and lowered my head to just above the toilet bowl. Lillie bent with me, next to me, keeping me steady on my feet. "You'll be a new man in a minute," she said to me, and I turned to look at her. I looked straight down her dress, saw her breasts pendant as she bent over to hold me. I looked then, at her breasts, and overcome with her perfume, infected by her almost as my father seemed to be, I retched in great spasms that seemed to threaten to rise and end forever in one supreme convulsion, completely apart from time, or person, or meaning. All the while I was sick, Lillie cooed gently to me to go ahead without fear; it would make me feel better.

I slept all the way home to Levittown in the back seat of the Dodge. Irene had already gone to sleep when we arrived. In the morning, when I got up to have breakfast with my father at six, before he met the car pool, I felt fine.

"How did you like eating clams? Did you ever have any before?" Irene asked.

Looking at my father, I said, "Fine. I liked them okay."

Later that morning, I took the Dodge out and came back with a carton of cigarettes. Irene said nothing when she saw me lighting a cigarette for the first time. Nor did my father say anything that evening, understanding that I had forgotten nothing of last night.

The day after next, my mother called long distance. My father was playing a game of cribbage with Irene. He answered the phone and talked to her for a long time, saying, "Yes, Anne. I realize that. Certainly it's by virtue of your permission. Of course you can talk to him, yes. Yes."

"Hello, Mom," I said.

"Oskar?" she said, metallic over the thousand miles of wire. "I want you to come home, do you understand me? Your father's to put you on a plane not later than the end of this week. Just so you know what I told him. You've had your visit and your trip to New York, and now I want you back here. Have you behaved yourself?"

"Yes, I have."

"Have you had a good time?"

"Sure. I like the motor boat. We've been out on the Sound about every weekend. Fishing for flukes. They're a flatfish. I'll tell you all about it when I get home."

"Well, you remind your father of what I said. I want you home."

"Can you tell me why?" There was a short scratchy silence. My mother was not accustomed to having me ask for reasons.

"Because I don't care to have you around his wife. Is that clear? Is that good enough for you? Because I say so, that's good enough." Then we said goodbye and hung up. Irene tried to appear busy shuffling the cards for another hand of cribbage with my father. She dropped the cards on the floor, and as she was picking them up, he snapped on the TV. The pity of it was, I thought, that unlike my mother, Irene was not a very strong person. I remembered something: trying to amuse myself with a magazine while my parents sat long into an evening at the dining room table, settling claims with the aid of a lawyer; my father saying *Isn't it enough for me to say I'll do everything I can?* My mother, very firm, *You'll do exactly as the law tells you to do, and nothing less!* Irene, I knew, would never fight back.

"Will you get away from the TV?" he said to her, "I can't see through you."

"Aren't we playing cribbage?" she asked unnecessarily.

"Why the hell," he said, "You don't listen when I try to show you how to play your cards. You might as well be playing with a robot. The hell with it. Get away from the TV so I can see," he said viciously.

My father put me on a flight from Idlewild two days later, the earliest reservation he could get. Irene didn't come to the airport, but had taken my hand and said her goodbye at the house when we left, looking more lonely than ever. Her eyes had a marbled look behind her gold-rimmed glasses, and with her pale skin freshened by powder and too much rouge for the occasion, she seemed like someone ready to die, and so prepared to spare the undertaker pains to make her presentable. It made me remember things: *It wasn't dastardly, Anne,* my father said. *Yes, it was dastardly,* she said, *you lied to me and you lied to her.* I remembered my father's face, taut, caught in deception. I pitied Irene very much then, and now, years later, I wonder at my arrogance.

My father kissed me on the cheek. Holding onto his hat to keep it from blowing away in the prop wash, he said, "Goodbye, Sonny Boy."

"Goodbye."

"Say hello to your mother for me. Give everyone my best."

"Say goodbye to Lillie for me." I said, "tell her I'll look her up if I ever get to *Nawth Cara-Linah.*" I remembered my father, years before, rushing stiff-kneed to the mail slot while the postman's ring still echoed, frantic to screen the letters for something from Irene before my mother saw the mail. I tried, there at the airport, to laugh in his face, but I couldn't.

"I guess the only advice you'd take from me would be never to do anything the way I did, wouldn't it," he said. I think he was close to weeping.

"Goodbye, Dad, I'll be seeing you," I said. But I never saw him alive again. The next year he maneuvered Irene to Minnesota, divorced her, married Lillie, and then died very quickly of a heart attack. He smoked too much.

He died broke, which surprised us all, and so, like everyone who knew him and ever loved him, I have only my memories of him. And his name. He was my father, and I have his name.

But nobody ever called me Buck Hansen.

THE HOTEL

VICTOR WHITE   from *Southwest Review*

The Rib Room was still his favorite. That's why he saved it for Sunday dinner.
The Empire Room and the Bagatelle were fine for weekdays, and for the times
he felt frisky and wanted something light, there was the Tao Room.

The new captain remembered and showed him to one of the three tables he
liked best, about the middle of the row against the wall, but a little closer to the
entrance from the bar than to the kitchen end. He slid in on the leather-
upholstered bench.

"Lovely evening, sir," the captain said. "Just like spring."

"Very fine," he agreed.

The room had not yet started to fill up. Most of the people were still
upstairs in the cocktail lounge or out in the bar, from which the subdued
boisterousness of holiday voices drifted in through the wide entrance, where
the maître d'hôtel and the captains and now a group of guests were clustered.
That's why it paid to come early. From where he sat he commanded a view of
the entire room, from a corner of the bar and two of the lanterns hanging from
the oak rafters clear on down to the row of chefs behind the majestic roasts at
the other end. A handsome woman in a vivid green dress emerged from the
group that was being shown to a table just beyond the middle, opposite one of
the great windows. Good legs. Not too slim, but not plump either. Elegant.

A waiter came. Not one he had seen before, but healthy, cheerfully
competent. He asked for another scotch and soda and, as always, ordered
shrimp remoulade and prime ribs, medium rare, on the rare side. People were
beginning to pile in from the bar. Good thing he hadn't lingered any longer
upstairs over his first scotch.

"This table taken?"

He had been so taken up watching the people who were coming in that the man crossing in front of his table—almost bumping against it in his hurry—took him by surprise. Tall, well set up, about sixty, in a Glen plaid just a couple of shades darker than his own.

"No, I don't believe so," he said.

The man tugged irritably at the next table in his effort to slide in behind it.

"I think you'll have to lift one end out," he suggested to the man, who obeyed and slid a little hastily, furtively, and at the same time defiantly in on the bench, then awkwardly pulled the end of the table back into place, leaving it a little crooked.

"I don't need the damn waiters to show me where to sit," the man explained. "Much too cocky anyhow. I want to sit where I want to sit."

"Of course," he said uncomfortably.

There had been something irregular and vaguely shocking to Brian Entwhistle's sense of propriety about the whole procedure. Besides, he liked the feeling of privacy while he ate and gave himself over to the pleasure of watching the people in the room, and the man showed signs of wanting to talk—talk a lot.

"I'm tired of getting pushed around. Girl in Houston got my plane reservations all screwed up last night, so that I had to wait two hours for a plane; then when I got here, they didn't have my reservation here at the hotel, and the place was full, they said. First time that ever happened to me here. Had to go over to the Dunbaugh. I didn't even bother to move over today. Going straight on to New York tomorrow. They don't care how they treat you today."

"I'm sorry you had such a rough time," Brian Entwhistle said. "With so many people moving around, traveling gets pretty scary." But he felt that some equilibrium had been disturbed, some decency violated, and that it was up to him to save the Sunday peace of the evening. Also, it was like defending one's security. He added soothingly, "This is a pretty good place. I've been staying here quite a while and I've found it very nice."

"All the same, these people are cocky. They're all cocky nowadays." The bristling menace in the man seemed to subside. "You living here?"

"Yes. It beats keeping up a house, all the worries about the lawn. Besides, there's always something going on."

"It'd get on my nerves." The man was hopelessly irascible. "Staying in one place, I mean. It gets monotonous."

"No, you'd be surprised. I never have to set foot outside the hotel. Why should I? Everything a fellow could want is right here: barber, doctor, stores, even a gym up on the twenty-sixth floor. I don't even feel tempted to go outside."

"Now, that's something I couldn't do; I've got to keep moving around. Stay in one place and I always get restless. How long you been here?"

He checked himself. That was none of the man's business. Still, he'd better say something.

"Three months. After my wife died, I closed up the house and moved in here."

He ended on a note of finality, full stop, to indicate that the subject had lost its charm for him, that he had had enough conversation anyhow. It struck him that the old fellow's question was just as impertinent as all the questions of the man from the insurance company, who had wanted to know all the why's and wherefore's after Eloise's funeral. As if a heart attack when there had always been a weak heart needed a blueprint, as if he had been responsible for not hearing Eloise when he had had the TV on downstairs until she knocked over the water carafe, as if he hadn't tried every doctor in town before he found one home. It wasn't as if Eloise and he hadn't had a sensible relationship, give and take, and no more getting on each other's nerves after he had once gotten it into Eloise's head that his glands weren't a young man's glands anymore, at least not as far as Eloise had been concerned. After all, he had spared her any hint that it had all become just too familiar, and that her legs and breasts couldn't rouse him the way they had used to do, or the way she had looked when she combed her hair. And it wasn't as if he had needed the insurance money.

Still, he would almost have liked to tell the man what a pleasure it had been, when the suspicious-looking plainclothesmen began to dog his every step and the cops had evidently had warning to watch him, to find a refuge in the hotel. It had been like escaping into another dimension to be here where the doormen were like guardians who kept the policemen and the snoopers out.

The waiter brought his scotch and soda. A likable young fellow, that waiter.

"If it hadn't been for the Rib Room, I'd have left for New York this afternoon. Only decent place to eat in town."

Brian Entwhistle scrutinized the man's face briefly on the pretext of giving a nod of assent. Imperious; self-willed; spoiled. Hardly old enough for second-childhood tantrums. Good tie; good shirt; only the tiny diamond tiepin was a little chichi.

"Yes, it's very pleasant." He managed to make it sound final again, so that the man would realize at last that he had no desire to carry on a conversation. He tasted his scotch and soda and faced away toward the chefs, one of whom was cutting one of those inch-thick juicy slices off a roast. The room was filling up. The woman in the green dress was talking vivaciously to the two men at her table. Even the other woman was laughing at what she said. Charming profile.

The man had not taken the hint. There was always a warning click in his throat just before he started to say something.

"They can have their Queen's Gate Hotels and their Elizabethan Rooms in London. American roast beef if you know where to go for it is as good as any in the world. Not that there are so many good places left. Me, I like the way they do things at the Brown Palace. You ever been there?"

"No, I'm afraid not." He tried to sound as discouraging as possible.

"The San Marco Room. Best lamb anywhere, and I like their creamed finnan haddie for breakfast. And there's the Palace Court in San Francisco. Ever go there, to the Sheraton Palace? They've got a crab salad that's something to write home about. That's a beautiful place anyhow, with those high ceilings and the service they give you. Of course, the Pavilion in New York is always good; when you get a sole there you know it's Channel sole and not catfish. And the Drake in Chicago is tops. Do you know the Drake?"

"Yes," he said. "I know it."

"Place I like, too, is the Old Warsaw in Dallas. They take an entire chicken and cut it up and roast it in wine sauce. Fit for a king."

Was he in for a rundown of famous places to eat? From sheer irritation, he started to drink his scotch and soda much faster than he wanted. The man was one of those lobby chatterers.

A waiter, not his own, came to the man's table. He was grateful for the respite.

"Bring me a dry martini. I mean, dry."

The waiter noted it on his pad, then asked for the rest of the order.

"I'll see what I want later."

"I'm supposed to take the whole order now, sir."

There was the click in the throat, and involuntarily Brian Entwhistle looked at his neighbor. His face had gone several shades of red. There was a second click, a gurgle almost.

"You'll take my order when I get ready to give it to you."

The waiter wasn't flunky enough to accept that without a struggle inside himself, and Brian found himself secretly cheering for him. But the waiter finally said, "Yes, sir," and went toward the bar.

"They're getting fresher all the time. You'd think you were in a hash house. All these places are running down."

A heavy silence settled between them, but he could take little comfort from it. It was a coiled, squirming silence which might explode into more embarrassing communications from his neighbor at any time, and he looked away determinedly at two young women in pink dresses, who might be sisters, at a table with two men and a slightly older woman. Ordinarily, he would have derived pleasure from figuring out what the score was there, but not this time.

A waiter came, but not the same one who had taken the man's order, and with pointed correctness set down a martini before him, then went without saying anything. The man tasted his martini, and Brian Entwhistle had to resist the impulse to ask him whether it was all right. The worst of it was that the man's outburst had created a sort of vacuum which he was almost irresistibly impelled to fill.

It did not stay a vacuum long.

"Place I really liked was the Zaragosana in Cuba. The Morro crab there was something. And I liked the Floradita restaurant in Havana. They'd wonderful seafood there, too. But that's all gone now."

He nodded politely just as his waiter approached with his shrimp remoulade. It gave him the excuse he needed not to appear open to conversation any longer, and he said "Thank you" with extra enthusiasm to the waiter. He busied himself with it immediately. The shrimp was iced just right, and he told himself that the remoulade sauce was delicious, but to his annoyance he did not really enjoy it. He found himself at once eating too fast and trying to make each shrimp last as long as possible. He kept his eyes firmly on the two young women in pink, as if he had recognized somebody at that table, then looked back at the woman in the bright green dress, who was eating oysters and looking up with fetching vivacity every few seconds at the two men who were both talking to her, seemingly teasing her.

There was a shuffle on his left. The waiter who had brought the man his martini had come to the table, pad in hand. There was the click.

"Give me my check. I'm not having anything more here."

"Yes, sir."

"I'm goddam tired of being pushed around. I'm going on to New York." The man had his billfold out, whipped out two dollar bills, and flung them on the table. He started pushing at the end of the table, got out, and stalked away with angular petulance, slowing down with even more petulance when he had to wait for people to get out of his way in the meander between the tables.

Brian Entwhistle fought back a surge of indignation at the discomfort the man's presence had imposed on him, then gave himself up to relief. It was not, however, until the busboy cleared the next table, set two places on it again, side by side, that he felt wholly himself once more. He settled down to his roast beef and enjoyed every bite of it between surveys of the room. The woman in green continued to delight him. He wondered whether her husband appreciated her vivaciousness. That was something Eloise hadn't had—hadn't ever had.

A good-looking couple—thirty-five or thereabouts—were shown to the table the man had had. Husband and wife, obviously. They had agreeable voices and talked of children and of an aunt who sounded as if she was baby-sitting for them, and about skiing in Vancouver. A marriage that looked like a success. He enjoyed them so much that he decided to have coffee down here instead of up in the lounge, as he usually did on Sunday. He smoked one of the three cigarettes he allowed himself after dinner—to hold himself down to a pack. When he had finished the coffee and the cigarette, he signed the check and sauntered upstairs. Up in the lounge, he smoked the second cigarette before he took his constitutional in the promenade. A couple of windows had been changed since Friday; he hadn't noticed yesterday. He watched the Frenchwomen—or Belgians, for all he knew—who were with the large party of manufacturers from the Benelux countries, and was intrigued with their walk again. You could always tell Continental women by their walk. They didn't swing their hips. He sat down opposite the florist's shop, where there was a whole bunch of them—they must have had dinner in the Empire Room—and proceeded to study their walk. They thrust out the tip of their foot, then pulled their body after it, like a man; whereas American women thrust each hip forward and pulled the leg after it. Maybe sexier that way, though one could argue about that. Too much like taking the wraps off a new car model too soon: nothing left to the imagination. They had probably gotten that from the mannequins.

Anyhow, it had been a good evening in spite of that fool. He found he still bore diamond stickpin a grudge for almost spoiling his dinner for him. Damn bore. The hotel was a fine place. Where else could you see a whole bunch of Continentals, talking among themselves as if they were right in Paris or in Brussels? Everything was right here in this haven from the pressures outside. Abundance and convenience—nobody could ask for more.

Time for the Ed Sullivan show. He'd catch it in his own room and order himself a nightcap—brandy maybe, in honor of the Frenchwomen. . . .

That night—it was half past three when he looked at his traveling clock afterward—he was awakened by a key in the lock of his door. He heard the door being opened rather stealthily, saw the light go on, then saw a bellboy stick his head in from the little hall that led past the bathroom. The bellboy said, "I'm sorry, sir," without appearing in the least sorry; in fact, his plump face wore an expression of downright jeering impertinence before he withdrew. Brian Entwhistle got out of bed and this time locked the door on the inside. He did it most nights, but not invariably. It was part of his luxurious sense of security in the hotel that he did not feel it necessary to turn the night latch.

He felt indignant and forgiving at the same time and went back to sleep quite easily. By morning he had almost forgotten the incident, but that evening, and even when he came in during the day, he now made sure that the door was locked. It was no great chore; people were even supposed to do it if they wanted to avoid mistakes, he told himself. After all, it was the first time he had come up against anything less than perfection in the way the hotel was run. It was for that reason that he minded when two nights later he was again awakened by the discreet scraping of a key in the lock. The door stayed locked, of course, and the key was withdrawn, but he found it hard this time to go back to sleep. He thought for a long time about whether it would be better to complain to the bell captain or to the people at the desk.

It was altogether a bad day, the first one he had had in three months. He could not find his silver-handled shaving brush anywhere. He knew he had left it on the chromium shelf below the mirror, where he always put it. He could have sworn he had seen it there on Monday still, even though on Monday as on most weekdays he used the electric shaver. He finally had to use the electric gadget although his bad night had made him feel that he wanted a real shave to get himself awake. He hung the "Do Not Disturb" sign on the door when he went down to breakfast, because he wanted to see the maid to ask her where she had put the brush.

To make things worse, his favorite hostess, who always steered him to one of the little tables by the windows, where he could look out on the avenue, this time took him to a table by the wall. It was almost like a physical hurt that she should have forgotten what he liked. He stopped her and reminded her of his claim to one of the tables by the window. "They haven't been cleared," she said. "I'll have one cleared for you, sir." But there was none of her usual friendliness, none of the near-intimacy there had always been between them, and she looked irritated with him as she took him to a window table. It was true that the table was messy. The two people who had had breakfast here must have been singularly ill-bred, he thought, looking at the litter of toast crumbs and at a large jam stain. Fortunately, there was the avenue to watch.

But while he usually took pleasure in looking out, this time his eyes kept coming back to the messy table and to the busboys who seemed determined to clear every table but his. He wanted his orange juice and coffee. He finally did catch one of the waitresses as she whisked by and got the table cleared and got his coffee, then Kadota figs, since he had changed his mind about the orange juice. Only, everything seemed a little out of kilter today. The service wasn't as good as usual. Part of it was no doubt the fault of his having come down later than usual, so that the waitresses had lost their first bloom of readiness to oblige. It was all the fault of his sleepless night. Gradually, however, as he ate his scrambled eggs and began to enjoy the coffee, he made his peace with the

hotel and everything in it. He decided not to say anything to the bell captain or the desk clerk after all.

He did not linger downstairs, as he usually did, but only stopped long enough to pick up the paper and a package of cigarettes—he bought them by the package because he enjoyed going into the tobacco shop—before he went back upstairs and hung the "Please Clean This Room" sign on the doorknob. He had a long wait. Usually, the maid did his room while he was downstairs for breakfast and took his first stroll of the day into the patio. By eleven she still had not come, although several times he heard the little wagon on which they had the towels and mops bump against something out in the corridor. He wondered whether the "Do Not Disturb" sign had annoyed her and she was getting even with him for upsetting her routine. At twenty after eleven she finally came and immediately wanted to withdraw again when she saw him in the room.

She professed complete ignorance about the brush, although she admitted having seen it on the ledge above the washbasin—"couple of days ago. I don't remember it was there yesterday." He had a feeling that she merely went through the motions of looking for it. And because her indifference irritated him, he started a second thorough search himself and refused to budge from the room while she cleaned. She obviously did not like his being there and suggested at first that she come back in the afternoon, but he pretended to have something wrong with his ankle and explained that he'd have to stay while she was there. When she was through, he gave her a dollar for "looking so hard," although usually he gave her a dollar tip only every two weeks. He did not feel that the dollar reconciled her to his being there.

Nevertheless, he made it a practice now to be in the room when she cleaned. The brush had obviously not vanished into thin air; somebody had taken it, and she was the only one who came into the room. What made him absolutely certain that he had been right was that three days later she suddenly produced the brush, claiming that it had been in the medicine cabinet—which he never used—all along. The brush even had some dried soap on it, and he was sure it was not his own. He used Yardley's, and this was a different scent. He had no intention of using the brush again, and he just barely managed to restrain himself from throwing it into the wastepaper basket before her eyes.

It made him determined to be always there when she cleaned. What made it a nuisance was that after he ran into her in the corridor one morning, so that she realized he could walk perfectly well, she took to making him wait till the afternoon before she showed up. In the meantime, starting just a little before noon everyday, the large suite next to him, which was rarely occupied, seemed to become a hangout for all the maids on the floor. They had the TV on full blast, and above it he could hear their talk and their laughter. Sometimes there were men's voices, too, bellboys, he supposed. He was sure that they had closed ranks against him over the business of the shaving brush and were punishing him.

It kept up day after day. Between noon and two, it sounded like an uproarious party next door. Shortly after two, when the party was evidently over, his maid arrived and always managed to take nearly a whole hour cleaning his room, so that it was always just before the dining rooms closed that he got downstairs to have lunch. The unaccustomed schedule ruined his appetite for dinner, threw his digestion out of kilter. He had to get some soda mints and milk of magnesia at the drugstore in the lobby when he stopped in to look for a new shaving brush.

He knew that, of course, all he had to do was to return to his normal schedule and not be in the room while the racket went on next door, above all, not be in the room while the maid was there; that would solve everything. But his stubbornness was aroused, and besides he was afraid that some of his other things might disappear. He thought for all of one afternoon of asking for the housekeeper and complaining about the goings-on next door; he even thought of going to the manager, but he was vaguely afraid of reprisals. Presently he saw how right he had been. By sheer happenstance he saw a plump, efficient-looking woman with a tag saying "Housekeeper" on her bulging bosom on his way to the elevator and he asked whether the help couldn't hold their—conventions, he called them humorously—in some suite not so close to his room. The next day, shortly after the usual racket began, it suddenly stopped and the TV went off. That night, however, someone again tried to open his door.

It made him jumpy for several days and he never really slept soundly after that. He had to go to the hotel doctor to ask for sleeping pills. Nor was that the end of their reprisals. The evening after the racket stopped, although he had had two cocktails in the lounge, he still did not feel particularly hungry. To get a change, he went into the Rib Room although it was the middle of the week. He got the same table he had had two weeks ago when the disagreeable man had walked out without having dinner, but the table had been occupied and had not yet been cleared. It was just as at breakfast the week before and several times since: the busboys seemed determined to give his table a miss. Nor did the waiters show any interest in him. It troubled him. Were they mistaking him for the man who had been such a nuisance two weeks ago? When the table was finally cleared, he kept wondering all through dinner how he could let the waiters know that he was not the same man, that there was some confusion. He did not enjoy his dinner one bit.

It got worse. He began to feel that he was no longer welcome in any of the dining rooms, and the consciousness of it hurt him. He would have to wait forever before a waiter condescended to come to his table, and even after they had taken his order, they delayed in bringing him anything to eat, until several times he felt ready to get up and go. Only the memory of the other man and the fear of antagonizing the waiters even more kept him from it. Nor did it help when he left larger tips. He had been adding the tip to the check when he signed it; now he several times put a cash tip on the table besides. It did not seem to make any difference. In fact, several times he had noticed something very like a sneer on a waiter's or a busboy's face as they went by—either that, or their expression was one of patronizing indulgence, as if he were something to be put up with and pitied.

It was, he tried to tell himself during his strolls in the promenade or his twice-daily inspection tours of the flowers in the patio, nothing but his imagination. He was exaggerating things. Or he blamed it all on the weather or on the fact that the hotel was so full and the help overworked. But when he was back in one of the dining rooms or upstairs in his own room, the full weight of their disapproval bore down on him again. It was a conspiracy of the help, nothing less. Communism probably. Wasn't the management aware of it? He made a point of watching how the waiters behaved to the other guests. There was no mistaking it, they were singling him out; the other guests were served with an alacrity that mocked their negligence with him. It was a conspiracy but it was directed against him. Several times it occurred to him that somehow the insurance people outside were behind it. They were begrudging him the money they had paid him on Eloise's death. It was a scheme to wear him down.

He had to go to the doctor for a second batch of sleeping pills, which the man was reluctant to give him. The doctor recommended that he get more exercise and lay off coffee in the evening. Only, how could he get exercise if his whole schedule was upset by the dishonest maid and by his insomnia? He didn't even feel like walking. And as for doing without coffee, that would be depriving himself of just one more prop in the shelter he so desperately needed. Just like the cigarettes. He had taken to smoking a great deal more. He often smoked a whole pack in the evening now.

He did not know how close he had been to giving up going into the dining rooms altogether until the upset cocktail. It was in the Empire Room. The waiter in putting down his salad managed to upset his drink, so that half of it ran right down on his trousers. A double calamity, since he had given up sending things down to the cleaner's by the bellboys, so as to avoid having anything to do with them, and had been taking things down himself in an attaché case, one suit at a time, then bringing it up in the elevator in spite of the obvious disapproval with which the bellboys and the elevator boys looked at him. . . . The maître d'hôtel came over to apologize and to explain that the waiter was new and that that was the end of that waiter. He did not believe the maître d'hôtel, or rather he believed him but was sure that the maître d'hôtel did not realize what was going on. He almost felt like enlightening him, telling him that it had nothing to do with the man's being a new waiter. He lingered over his dinner, which he did not enjoy, to give his trousers a chance to dry. The light gray trousers showed the stain from the manhattan when he walked through the lobby, and he felt humiliated.

It made up his mind for him. No more dining rooms. He was through with anything that put him at the mercy of the waiters. He stopped in the liquor store and laid in a supply of Huntley and Palmer biscuits and all sorts of hors d'oeuvres. For breakfast, he dissolved milk chocolate in a glass of hot water. He persuaded himself that he even enjoyed these improvised meals in his room. His self-sufficiency gave him a grim satisfaction: he could hold out indefinitely. He had a feeling at times as if he were besieged in his room. He had got into the habit of locking the door even during the day because one time the maid had come in earlier than usual, just while he was having "lunch."

It worked beautifully for a week; then one day an assistant manager called him on the phone to inquire whether everything was satisfactory. "Just a routine survey of our permanent guests," the suavely solicitous voice explained. There was just the subtlest overtone of something wrong in his inquiry whether he was satisfied with "our cuisine," the faintest and yet unmistakable reference to his eating in his room. The maid must have reported that to the housekeeper. He had to be on his guard. Thereafter, he locked all the food in one of his suitcases and always took the empty cans and wrappings downstairs himself and as inconspicuously as possible disposed of his paper bag in one of the wastepaper baskets in the lobby. He also made a point of lounging conspicuously in the lobby and of strolling in the promenade, although he felt much less like walking than he had formerly.

Then suddenly a major prop was pulled out from under him. He had been convinced that the elevator boys had eyed him with ill-concealed suspicion the first two times he had got into the elevator with a bag of trash. The third time there had been no doubt in his mind: the elevator boy had looked both suspicious and scornful and had barely greeted him. After that he made it a point to climb by the service stair to the nineteenth floor or to go down to the seventeenth or even the sixteenth, so as to throw them off about the floor on which his room was, so that they would not be able to report him to the manager. He was, moreover, sure that they were in on the conspiracy of the bellboys and the busboys and the waiters and the maids. It tickled him that in spite of their conspiracy, he was fooling them. After all, why had a man been given brains except to use them?

But presently he had to admit that they had outwitted him. When he rang for the elevator, not one of the three elevators would stop. They would pointedly stop on the floor above or the floor below, always on the eighteenth floor he saw from the electric signal light, as if to let him know that they were jeering at his attempt to fool them and to let him know that they were on to what he had in the paper bags hidden under his topcoat. He was certain now that they, along with all the other help, were in cahoots with the insurance man and wanted to drive him out of the hotel, out where the insurance man and the police were only waiting for him to come out.

There was only one way left to foil them: he had to use the service stair. But, then, what was wrong with that? It was even exciting. Besides, it was good exercise; just what he needed. He told himself that he was mountaineering the first time he climbed the seventeen flights—thirty-four half-flights—to the eighteenth floor; that afternoon he fueled his zest by thinking of his room as an eyrie, his fortress. But he did not go downstairs after he had had dinner, as he had intended to do.

That night he slept particularly well. It was the exercise, he told himself the next morning and went gaily downstairs. He made three trips down into the lobby that day, although he found that he had to stop and rest every three or four flights and the climb seemed tedious. He had the TV on for only half an hour before he felt himself dropping off to sleep, but he welcomed that: it meant that he would have another night of sleeping like the night before, like a baby.

He slept just like one, too, until he was wrenched out of his sleep by a nightmare in which a gang of hooligans had him cornered on the top of a tower, vicious men who were forcing him over the edge, so that he was hanging on with one hand to the coping, then with the other hand, until he was finally awake. Someone was trying the lock of the door again. It was persecution. For the first time he thought of writing Ralph in Montana. It didn't matter that they hadn't been writing all these years; Ralph was still his friend. If Ralph would come at night in a car, he could escape the insurance man and that conspiracy. In Montana he would be safe. He resolved to write Ralph first thing in the morning. After that, he could neither go back to sleep nor get himself to get up until ten o'clock in the morning.

He had to force himself to go downstairs. The climb back up suddenly seemed staggering. What puzzled him was that this time even going down the stairs was hazardous. He would get dizzy and have to hold on to the concrete wall which served as railing, every few steps. He sat in the lobby for a long time, debating whether to write to Ralph in the writing room or to go upstairs to write; then he remembered that he had forgotten to bring Ralph's address with him and would have to go back to his room in any case. Shortly before noon he started up the thirty-four half-flights. After the first five floors it seemed to him that every step had become an antagonist. He sat down on the steps to rest several times, getting up only when he heard someone coming. Each time, he made an effort to appear nonchalant, to make it seem natural that he was on the service stair at all, and the very effort braced him.

He finally got to the top, but when he was in his room he could only think of lying down, instead of hanging out the "Please Clean This Room" sign and letting the maid come in. He set the traveling clock for two and felt a little better by the time the alarm went off. The maid came after half an hour and cleaned while he wrote to Ralph. At five, he took the letter down to mail—he did not trust the mail chute—and stuck it into the letter box by the Transportation Desk while no one was looking. He bought some Huntley and Palmer biscuits and more smoked oysters and Greek olives and cheese sticks and then started on his climb. This time he did not think he could make it. Several times he felt a violent pain in his chest when he got out of breath. He thought of his climb as a climb up Calvary. The package was like a cross. The last three floors, especially, seemed beyond him. He spent an hour, he was sure, climbing the six half-flights.

He did not feel like eating anything. He poured himself a drink, telling himself it was brandy, which he was as much entitled to as if it had been brought to him by a St. Bernard. He turned on the TV and lay on his bed and lit a cigarette, then another one. He did not look much at the TV, or rather he looked but he hardly saw anything. He wondered how soon Ralph would get here. He better be all ready with a few things in his attache case, just the absolutely necessary things, so that nobody would be suspicious when he went downstairs.

The odd thing was that the cigarette kept tasting viler and viler and that there did not seem to be enough air in the room. He put out the cigarette and forced himself to get up to open the windows, which the management warned should not be opened on account of the air conditioning system.

Even at the window he could not get enough air, and the pain he had felt on the stair was suddenly there again in his breastbone, only much more alarming than before. It probed clear through his chest and was suddenly between his shoulder blades; then, even the tips of his shoulder blades hurt. An excruciating pain. He lay on the bed, sat up, lay down again in an effort to tame the pain.

The pain dominated everything except his fear of the bellboys. He thought angrily that it was the duty of the huge staff of the hotel to come to his aid but that it was no use to appeal to them. There was still the doctor he could call for down at the desk. He picked up the phone, but when no one answered, he lay back again as another spasm of pain gripped him. He finally heard an impatient "Hello, hello! Can we be of service to you?" The irritation in the woman's voice frightened him. They were part of the conspiracy! He managed to slide and tip the telephone back into the cradle before a still fiercer spasm convulsed him on the bed, made him arch his back, to conciliate the pain in his shoulder blades.

"I need help," he managed to think with the small corner of his brain left free by the pain. "They have everything. It isn't fair. . . ."

The Round Brass Elevator

JOSEPH WHITEHILL from *Hudson Review*

Five red-eyed pigeons, beggars and loiterers, waddled away when the thin girl came down the path to the bench in the eucalyptus park. Alert as she came, she saw the young fellow there lick his lips before he raised his head from his textbook. He was, therefore, the one. He smiled and got up. "You're Sally?"

She inspected him while they shook hands and made their presentations. His chin was strong, and his white teeth went well against his Pacific tan, and there was something strange about his soft brown eyes, something both feminine and penetrating. In an instant she saw the strangeness; his eyes were very large, and the lashes, both upper and lower, were dense as mink fur. Sally was unexpectedly pleased. "I'm Sally-right-on-time," she said. "And I guess you're Paul." As they shook hands, she noted that he continued to mark his place in the thick maroon textbook with an inserted forefinger, as though he regarded her presence there as merely momentary. Even when they sat on the bench, half-turned toward each other, he kept his place in the book, holding it on one knee.

With little stumbling or awkwardness, they agreed it had been a fine day for February, not too warm even though there was no breeze off the Bay, but it was a pity the haze hung that way on the water, making it hard to see across. Only now did Sally touch his book with her small blunt fingertip. "You need a book mark or something?"

Paul started and said, "Oh," then opened the book and memorized his page number and closed it again. "I wasn't thinking. That's part of the collegiate habit, I guess." He put the book between them on the bench. "Look, are you hungry yet? I mean, it's only five, but we could eat any time if you were hungry." He blinked slowly, watching her.

He knows about those eyelashes of his, she thought. She laughed and held her little red plastic purse in her lap with both hands. Her fingernails were short because she bit them from time to time. She was thin and very fair, and her light brown hair was strapped back tightly in a ponytail. When she laughed her voice was high and clear, and she showed pink gums and small irregular teeth. "It isn't so nice to tell a fellow that's just asked you out to dinner, but the truth is, I'm hardly ever hungry. Isn't that awful? It's the trouble with working in a bakery. It's so easy in the store to just *piece,* you know? I don't suppose I eat a real meal once a week. I eat a little at a time, like. A Danish for breakfast. Cheesecake, a piece of pie around lunchtime. Coffee going all the time in back. A doughnut here, a crescent there. You know."

Paul got out his cigarettes and shook up several and held the pack out to her.

Sally put his hand back. "You light me one," she said. "That's the friendly way."

Paul smiled. "All right." He put two cigarettes in his mouth and lighted both at once, watching her steadily over the flaming gold lighter. He handed one to her, then asked, "Don't you ever eat any vegetables?"

She laughed again easily, for little reason but her habit of punctuation. "You sound like my sister, she runs the store. She's on me all the time about a balanced diet." Sally leaned forward just a little and, looking into the middle distance, drew carefully on the cigarette. Then she let the smoke out of her mouth and sucked it up her nose. She was eighteen years old. "But my diet suits me, so Sally eats what Sally wants." She watched Paul, thinking, he's *all right.* Not old or fat or stupid or dirty or any other lousy kind of a blind date. She said, "Now let's talk about you." She smiled and drew rapidly on her cigarette several times as if it were going out. She fanned the smoke away and continued, "You said on the phone you knew Charlie Weintraub last year. Old Charlie. . . . *Good* old Charlie. He's back East somewhere now."

"He's in New York, working on a newspaper. He made Phi Beta Kappa while he was here."

"What's that?"

"What? Oh, he didn't tell you. Very modest. That's the honor society for bright guys. He's very bright."

"Well, 'deed he is, I know that. Good old Charlie Weintraub. Funny, he was a senior up here in the college while I was being a senior down in the high school. He had a car. An old station wagon."

"I know. A Buick."

"With a mattress in the back. We used to go to the beach over at Las Piedras and build a fire."

Paul laughed reminiscently. "I was just going to say the same thing. I went over there with him a few times. They don't let you build fires any more. They've got a cop in a jeep with those fat sand tires on it. He's got a spotlight with about a million candlepower. He's a real sadist." Paul stopped suddenly.

Sally said, "He didn't ever mention you to me. . . . Well, we even went up in the mountains once. Where the snow was."

"I never went up in the mountains," Paul said.

"That was a time, all right. Charlie's radiator all froze up and we had to spend the night in one of those ski shanties. If you don't think my sister about had a conniption when we got back in Sunday. . . . Hum, so you went to the beach with him, too. With who else? With anybody else? With girls, I mean?"

"What? Girls?" Paul gave a light laugh but did not look at her. "No. No girls. Just some boys, stag. The Beer, Banjo, and Body-Surfing Society. Just to get away from girls once in a while."

Thoughtfully, Sally said, "No, he didn't tell me about you."

"I really didn't know him all that well. We were sort of casual friends."

Sally changed the subject. "Do you have a car?"

"Sure. I bought Charlie Weintraub's old Buick."

Well, she thought, so that's how it goes. I have now got the picture.

They fell silent, looking straight before them past the scaly, tendoned trees of the eucalyptus grove, over the brow of the hill at the Bay below. A thin yellowish haze hung close to the water. The prison island was just discernible as a tumbled, rude mass surmounted by a blocky, straight-sided mass. The great bridge was somewhere beyond. There was no wind, and the air felt stale to Sally, as if, somehow, it had already been used. The pungent, almost medicinal smell of the trees hung in her throat. She thought, the little question is, what did old Charlie tell this Paul here? Ah, most likely just what old Andrew told old Charlie *last* year. You've got to watch these boys and their mouths. Boys are okay all except for their mouths. Sally smiled out over the dim water of the Bay and said, "So you heard from old Charlie Weintraub. Is he okay? How's he doing? Was it a letter you had from him? Fine. Now, really, ah, Paul. What'd he say about me? Come on."

Paul gave her a long, amused look. Her lips parted a little at the deep beauty of his eyes. "It was a letter," he said. "The other day. He just said I ought to look you up because . . . because he said you're a natural spirit, a sprite, really. I don't want to embarrass you. He said you weren't like all the other girls, all colleged up. He said you were among the few real people."

"Aw."

"Scout's honor. Now, how about we get off old Charlie Weintraub, okay? He's in New York and we're here." Paul stood up to stretch and look around. His madras jacket lay folded on the redwood bench beside his textbook. He wore the common unofficial college uniform of the time: neatly pressed, artificially faded khaki pants with a little cloth belt in the back, and a white dress shirt and a thin black tie. He stretched now by lacing his fingers and winding his wrists with his arms down straight before him, forcing until his knuckles cracked aloud. "Ah." He smiled down at her serenely and turned about to survey the park. "See there, the tower? You can just see the top through the trees over there. You ever been up it?"

"Sure. Lots. You can really see everything from up there." Idly, she picked up his textbook. "*Problems of Overland Transport,* by McGraw Hill." She opened it and bent her head over it. "Jinks but the print's small. What's it about?"

"One of my courses. Transportation. The man who teaches the course wrote the book, so we have to use it."

"This guy Hill?"

"No, that's the publisher. The teacher is Carson. He gets a royalty on the book."

She laid the text aside, finished with it. She sat up straight and smiled willingly. "Did you want to go up in the tower now?"

"Why don't we? We might as well, don't you think? We've got plenty of time to do that and eat too before any of the movies start."

Sally rose from the bench and smoothed her dress, aware that he was watching her brightly, wearing a fixed smile. She tossed her ponytail and bent gracefully to pick up her purse, saying, "Gee, it's a relief to get out of that white uniform. My sis makes us all wear white, even her husband. She runs *him* all right. But a uniform gets pretty dull day after day. You've been in our shop. I remember seeing you a couple times now. But you don't remember me, because of the uniform. See, that's okay with my sis. I'm just a little cuter'n she is, so she's funny about some things. Boy, has *she* put on the pounds this past year!" They started up the path together with the pale red sun at their backs, watching their own long shadows lunge ahead on the brown sickle-shaped fallen leaves and stringy bark shreds. Sally jumped half a step ahead and turned to look closely up at him, showing her pink gums and small teeth in a grin. "Sis did have a fit when I told her I was moving out into an efficiency of my own. She said I wasn't old enough, and all that jazz, but in reality it was simply because she doesn't like to see me free. Me or anybody else in sight. She was already married when she was my age, but I say you're a long time married, so what's the big hurry? I'm having my fun." Sally laughed and gave a little skip of good feeling. She had seen his lovely eyes flick at the mention of her own apartment. She thought, this boy is *all right.* "Where're you from, Paul?"

"Down near San Diego. My father has some laundries down around there."

"Will you go into the laundry business too?"

"I don't know. They make you wear white."

She looked sharply at him and saw he was teasing, so she hit him lightly on the arm. "You," she said, pouting. She scowled so fiercely that she felt her tight hair pull, then she immediately cleared her face; it was work to get her hair back that tight, and there was no point in loosening it with scowling.

The path they followed led around a dense bougainvillaea bush and came out, two steps up, on a large circular plaza of mosaic tiles, in the center of which rose the finger-shape of the great stone tower. A low tile wall circled the plaza, interrupted by openings at the cardinal paths that led away into the park. At each break in the wall were a pair of cast concrete urns planted with fleshy geraniums. Sally climbed onto the top of the wall to stand and look up at the tower. Paul followed her, saying, "This terrace is just about the third the size it ought to be. When you build a tower, you must have an open place where people can stand off and look at it. Look at Rome. Look at Alexandria. Look at Berlin. Paris. You can't even see this thing unless you're practically standing under it."

This tower had been erected by a graduate of the nearby college as a memorial to his father, and was paid for with money inherited from that father. The son had wanted to build it on the campus itself, but the trustees, honest and practical men, could see neither use nor art in it, and turned the money down. The mayor and city council, however, had been happy to coöperate. Their consensus was that the tower would justify its existence by its existence.

Paul said, "Did you know that there's stone in this thing from every state in the Union?"

Sally said, "Not Alaska or Hawaii, I believe." She had read the bronze

tablet let into the side of the tower minutes ago when she had stopped to freshen her face.

"Well, you may not know," Paul continued somewhat stiffly, "that the tower was designed by a mathematician named Fueste. He ordered all the stone precut by means of an algebraic formula that determined the exact curve and taper and slope of every piece, even before the foundation was poured. They didn't really *build* this tower; they assembled it. There weren't enough stone chips left after the job was done to fill your hat. I thought you'd like to know, in case you didn't happen to already."

This boy is sensitive, a little, she thought. Well, we'll take good care of him, won't we, hon? "That's amazing," she said sincerely. He wants to teach, let him teach.

With other strollers, they walked entirely around the great base of the tower, craning up at the top, wondering and remarking at its sheer bulk, and thinking about each other. Back at their starting place they stopped beside the open doorway into the tower to read the bronze tablet bedded into the wall there. Two new priests, young and similar enough to be brothers, were there before them. The priests at once moved a little way aside to make room for everyone to read together.

MARCH 11, 1928

THE OLSON MEMORIAL TOWER, ERECTED
AS A MONUMENT TO THE MEMORY OF
HARNISH L. OLSON BY HIS SON, HARNISH L.
OLSON, JR., AND BY THE OLSON MEMORIAL
FOUNDATION, IS 51 FEET IN DIAMETER AT THE
CROWN, 325 FEET HIGH, AND COST $762,000.00.
THE WALLS ARE FIVE FEET THICK AT THE
BASE AND TWO AND ONE HALF FEET THICK
AT THE CROWN. 7,300 TONS OF STONE, FROM
EACH OF THE FORTY-EIGHT STATES, WERE
USED IN ITS CONSTRUCTION.

"All that money," Sally whispered, holding her cigarette close to her face on the side away from the priests.

From outside, the tower looked quilted, or pied, since the stones were all colors possible—pink and tan and black and green—and no design was apparent in the adjoinment of colors. The blocks near the foot, much initialed, were nearly cubical, presenting outer surfaces more than five feet square. The mortar joints were so thin as to be almost invisible. Standard opinion in the town below was that the tower was a nice execution of a clumsy idea.

As Sally and Paul stood side by side before the bronze tablet, the backs of their hands touched as planned, and remained touching. They smiled at each other and Sally said, "This is fun." She wrinkled her nose at him.

A pair of black wrought-iron gates, curved like the tower wall and elaborately figured with iron ivy, were open and swung back against the sides of the doorway, latched to the wall with long twisted iron hooks. Just inside, on the edge of the interior gloom, was a souvenir case containing postcards and leaflets and miniatures. The case was glassed-over and heavily padlocked. The priests now entered with Sally and Paul; inside, waiting beside the souvenir case, was a couple with two quiet children.

Directly before the doorway, in the very center of the tower, rested the elevator. It was a huge and handsome brass cage, round, with a door that opened on hinges, like the door of a birdcage. Its roof was a black-painted dome, with eave-edges trimmed in bright brass. The sides were polished brass bars, stiffened by a decorative basket work of riveted brass strapping and woven bronze wire. Inside, passing vertically from the roof to the floor, three feet apart and parallel, were two brass pipes, guides for the stationary cables the elevator traveled on. There was a large iron eye-bolt in the center of the roof-dome, between the two stationary cables, into which was shackled the greased wire rope that hoisted the cage. The three cables disappeared into the darkness overhead.

A small toothless man in shirtsleeves who stood inside the elevator said, "We got a load now." Inside with him already were an elderly couple in tourist clothing who stood very close together, as if to take up as little space as possible. The family by the souvenir case filed on, then the two priests. Sally and Paul pushed their cigarettes into the sand pot and followed. The operator held out his hand to Paul. "That's ten cents each."

Paul put his hand in his pocket, saying, "What about them?" He indicated the other passengers.

The operator gave Paul a warm bare smile and said, "The other folks paid already, and these, of course, is clergy."

Paul took Sally by the arm with his free hand. He looked very angry. He said, blinking rapidly, "Wait a minute. There's never been any charge for this elevator before."

The operator, hand still extended, closed his eyes and said, "Expenses."

Paul pulled Sally from the elevator. "Hey!" she cried softly. "Ouch!"

Paul said, "We'll climb it this time by ourselves. Up the stairs."

Altogether politely, the operator said, "Okay," and swung the brass gate shut and latched it. When he turned the control handle the elevator gave a little elastic bounce, then slowly began to rise. The operator produced a flat pint can of liquid polish and a flannel rag stained with long dark marks of verdigris. He showed the can to Paul through the bars and said, "See? Expenses." As the floor of the elevator rose even with Sally's head, she heard the operator say to his passengers in a practiced, mannerly way, "Now just settle back, folks, if you please. The trip up takes twelve minutes." He began shaking the can of polish with an easy wrist-snapping motion. "The reason it takes so long is that there's no counter weights on this type of elevator, so the hoisting machinery up there is geared lower." Then, as Sally and Paul watched the cage climb into the dimness overhead, the operator's hand appeared with the flannel rag between the bars and began vigorous vertical polishing, one bar at a time.

Paul led Sally out into the pale sunshine on the terrace and held both her thin shoulders in his hands. There was no one else in sight, and Sally, mildly frightened, rubbed the place on her arm where he had grabbed her. "Now, listen," he said, "I don't want you to think I'm cheap. I am not cheap. I may be other things, but I am not cheap." He looked around to be sure they were alone.

then took his wallet from his hip pocket. He showed her, besides the smaller bills, two fifties and a beautiful, complex hundred-dollar bill. "There, now. You can see what twenty cents means to me. You'll see. Just you wait till the good dinner you have tonight some place nice. It isn't the twenty cents. It's a matter of principle." His eyes were burning.

"Wow," Sally said, thinking of the money in the wallet. "Okay, okay. We'll walk up."

Paul grinned broadly. "There's a girl." He hugged her quickly with one arm about her shoulders, and he released her so suddenly that when she twisted to free herself she was already free. Annoyed, she fell away and stumbled, then turned the stumble into a light-hearted skip and went back to the tower.

They stood for a moment at the bottom of the spiral stair gathering themselves for the climb. Looking up the long bore of the tower, they saw the cage ascending, outlined by a ring of daylight from the top where the observatory walk was. Scattered up the walls were numbers of narrow vertical slots, or loopholes, that provided the only light to the stairway. Each was just a gap six inches wide in the normal lay of the stones.

The rusty steel treads of the stairway were cross-patterned with sharp little hobs to keep a climber's foot from slipping. There were no risers, just bent-down tread nosings. A solid-looking galvanized pipe handrail, worn to a mottled luster by many hands over the years, was terminated somewhat incongruously at its lower end by a large polished brass finial on the newel pipe. The finial was an urn shape, fluted and hung with ropes of laurel. Sally ran both her hands down it in interest, liking the delicate look of her hands against the heavy brass. "How beautiful! But it ought to be all over jewels. Diamonds and emeralds, see, and big rubies around here." She made as if to cup the urn in her hands—Bathsheba bringing the wine to David—and it moved.

Paul said, "It used to unscrew."

"What?" She drew back her hands.

"Here. Let me see. Sure, it still does, see?" He turned the finial until half an inch of a threaded mounting stud showed beneath its base.

"Put it back," Sally said.

"Here, you want it?" Teasing, Paul unscrewed it a little farther. "You want to take it home?"

"Stop that!" she cried. "Just you put it back the way it was. I ain't kidding, now."

"I see you're not," he said, quickly screwing the finial back down on its seat. "I'm surprised nobody's stolen that before. I'll bet somebody does one of these days."

"Somebody'll be in a real jam, too, if they do. That thing's expensive. . . . What're you looking for?"

Paul was circling the interior of the tower like a dog on a new scent. Then he stopped and said, "Here, this is all right." He three-folded his madras jacket and laid it, with his textbook, behind the souvenir case. "Didn't want to have to carry that stuff up the climb. Would you remind me to get 'em when we come back down? I forget that kind of thing."

"Sure. . . . You want to race to the top?"

"I do not want to race to the top. I want to walk with you," he said, looking closely at her, as though his eyes were windows for her to see into his heart. He took her hand and squeezed it gently and said, "Nah, what I really want to do is hold your hand."

Sally laughed and leaned to pinch his earlobe. His grip was warm and good. She took her hand away and started up the stairs. The treads felt safe under foot, for the sharp points caught the soles of her loafers at every step and made her climbing sure. This was fun enough. He was a nice guy and his good family leaked out all over him. Sally was aware, though not explicitly, of the difference between the Pauls of this world, so secure that they can safely tease about stealing brass ornaments, and the Sallys, who somehow manage to get arrested for doing the same thing. Heigh-ho! The pity of this moment was that if she climbed the tower, she knew, all the freshness of her hot shower and clean underthings would be lost by the time she reached the top.

From below her, Paul said, "Hey, you see what you missed?"

She turned and descended two treads to look. Her eyes were by now adjusted enough to see the square lettering cut into the great black stone:

BASALT
NEW MEXICO
Take my sorrow and make of it a tree.
—René Voisin

"See, you get geology and geography and theology all at once here with your masonry. These nutty things go all the way up. . . . You are a really handsome girl," Paul said. He tilted his head against the wall and looked at her with his eyes snake-fixed, as though his longing made him weak.

"You make a girl blush," she said seriously, and turned to begin climbing again. She wore a blue cotton frock with a full skirt and many sewn-in pleats down the bodice. She knew it swung nicely across her calves as she climbed.

When they had ascended one full turn around the inside of the tower, they reached a little landing fitted with a bench to rest on. In the wall here was a much-defaced stone, striated with pink and tan, that said:

CRAB ORCHARD SANDSTONE
TENNESSEE
The departed has left us hope.
—Edmund Golyer

Paul laughed. "He has also left us his dough."

Sally said, "Listen, I don't think it's right for you to make fun of this stuff. Somebody took it seriously. I think you could be nicer and not laugh."

Paul said, "I'll never laugh again. Remind me."

"Oh, you."

When they had climbed halfway around again, Paul said, "There, the elevator's all the way to the top now, and you can see how far we have to go. Count the landings. Eight more. This is some place." His voice echoed a little. "Listen—" He called down over the rail, "Hoo! Hoo!" The echo was an almost visible elastic thing bouncing up and down the height of the tower.

For rhythm, Sally counted the steps as she climbed, going from one to ten silently, then starting over. When she reached one of the narrow loopholes she stopped counting and paused here to breathe. Looking out the slot, she saw they were just even with the ragged tops of the tallest eucalyptus trees. The view from this side was toward the campus of the college, all white stucco walls and red tile roofs, with arches and deep-set windows and sheltered balconies, in honorable Latin architecture. Beyond were the high green hills of winter. "I get turned around climbing," Sally said. "I thought this was the Bay side."

Paul put his hand softly on her waist. "The Bay side is where the landings are. Let's go."

He led the way this time. Sally followed as closely as she could, for she was beginning to fear the height a little. She stayed close to the wall, and watched the nickel buckle on the cloth belt at the back of his khakis. She also watched the bulge where his wallet was. She could have reached out and touched him. He wore black loafers and bright white socks. Sally thought he was really very trim and clean.

At the far side, on the landing, a tan, cheese-holed stone there was inscribed:

LIMESTONE
KENTUCKY
The leaves fall when it is time.
—Alan Mills

"Just you don't say anything, now," Sally warned him. Paul tipped her a grave salute, then blinked slowly. He sure knows about those eyes, Sally thought.

Five steps higher there was another loophole, one that gave west over the Bay. Sally stood before it resting on her elbows, which were within the narrow opening. Her forearms lay together on the stone sill. "Look," she said, "the mist is all below us here." The brown-yellow haze formed the ground of a sharp horizon, and the hills of the city across the water were clear in the coming sunset. "Looka. You can even see the tops of the bridge towers."

Paul put his arms around her little waist from behind, and leaned against her. She could neither move away from the wall nor free her arms from the tight opening. She stirred politely in welcome, then turned and grinned at him and kissed his jaw. "Not here," she said levelly.

He stepped back at once.

She turned to face him, and held herself where he had touched her, on the ribs below her breasts. Thinking of his good family and the wonderful big money-bills in his wallet, she took his hand and put it on her ribs again. "Feel that there?" she asked. "That way my bottom rib sticks out there?"

He cupped it with his hand. "I do."

"I had rickets when I was a kid. Rickets among other things."

"That's a shame." Paul pulled his hand away. Under his deep stare Sally felt she must have given everything away then, that Paul was looking straight into her soul. "I did not have rickets," he said. "I was very well nourished."

To escape the trap of her embarrassment, she cried, "But I sure can climb, boy! Here we go!" Ignoring the void beside her, she began to run, laughing and jumping up the stairs two at once, her ponytail jouncing. Paul ran too, staying close behind, not trying to touch or catch her. The echoes of their footfalls and her clear laughter tumbled up and down the tower in broken confusion. After two full times around the tower she cried, "Stop!" and backed gasping against the stone wall. Her eyes rolled up quivering under her fair eyelids, and sweat stood on her upper lip. Paul stayed one step down from her, copying her posture, and they panted for a time with their shoulders touching. Before them, hanging free in space, were the two guide cables for the elevator. Sally looked at them idly; they were a place to lodge her eye while she panted. Then she tilted her head and squinted. She watched a minute more, then nudged Paul with her elbow. "Look at that," she whispered. She pointed to the cables.

"What?"

"Watch how those wires move."

"They aren't moving."

"Yes they are," Sally said. "Toward each other, then away from each other. You watch."

After a silence, Paul said, "Okay, I see it now. That's very slow indeed."

Sally said, "It's making me sick."

"Don't get sick," Paul said. "Just don't look at it."

She closed her eyes and nodded forward and shook her head. "Um," she said. When she opened her eyes she saw the rusty steel treads and the empty spaces between them where the risers ought to have been, and her stomach stirred. She put out a hand to the wall and groped with the other for the railing, then Paul's hard arms were around her and her face was in the warm clean smell of his white shirt. She said, "Ah," and rested her head there and let him hold her up. "All that running!" She put her arms about his waist and hooked her thumbs in the little belt at the back of his pants. Waiting for her nausea to fade, she sensed his tension by its contrast with her own limpness. "Look up," she told him. "Can anybody up there see us?"

"No. Just take it easy." He held her a little tighter.

"That's just the point," she said, lifting her head off his chest to look at him. "You take it easy yourself. You're all in a knot." She rapped him lightly in the loins. "Old Charlie Weintraub used to say, 'Stay loose! Get the pores open and stay loose!' That old Charlie. I never will forget him. What a great guy. I hope you're as nice a guy as old Charlie. You do seem like a nice guy."

"I do my best," Paul said. He was scratching her gently between the shoulderblades.

"But you're sarcastic." She spoke into his shirt in total comfort.

After a pause, Paul said, "That comes from living, I expect. Man in the Modern World kind of thing."

"Crap. If you'll excuse the expression." She lifted her head. "Hey, what does this one say?" She was trying to read the inscription on the stone closest to them. Together they moved away and read:

MARBLE

ARKANSAS

Time's guide takes a crooked path,
but he knows the way.

—William Frank

Sally said, "Now that one really does get me. It's got swing, all right, but I don't know what it means. Do you, really?"

Paul's hands moved a little lower on her back. "I think these are all by mystics the family knew. That's what I remember from the booklet they sell downstairs. But no, I don't know what it means either. I don't think it matters. I think they had these stones, and they were pretty big, and 'Arkansas' and 'marble' didn't fill up much of the space, so they put the other matter on. That's my guess, but if you think I'm being irreverent or something, I'll be glad to change my mind. I mean, I want you to be comfortable."

"I am comfortable except when you are being sarcastic. I think sarcastic people are hateful, don't you?" She leaned back to look in his face, to see his eyes again.

"Oh, I think you're absolutely right," he said sincerely.

She laughed and hugged him, then kissed him delicately on the mouth. When she had learned what she wanted to know, she stopped the kiss and said, "Ah there now, you aren't sarcastic at all." When he made as if to kiss her again, she shook her head. "Let me go now, I feel fine. Please let me go now." She kept her head turned away from him, toward the wall. "Listen, Paul, this is the last time I'll ask you. Let me go. . . . Ah!" She arched back and burst fiercely from his restraint and stumbled and fell on the stairs. She stayed where she fell, rubbing one knee, smiling up at him. "There, now," she said. "You'll find out I don't kid around much." Her tone, though breathless, was entirely friendly and conversational. "When I say something, I mean it. Whether it's yes or no. Or if it's maybe, then I say exactly maybe. Remember, pal, I'm not one of your little college girls with seven different ways of not saying what they mean. I know your college girls, all right. I wait on 'em. They make me laugh." Sally was intent on the demonstration of her proof. "I wait on these girls when they come in, and this is God's truth, do you want to know what they talk to me about every time? Every time, this happens. They set up the conversation so it always comes around that I have the opening to say, 'Oh, no, dearie, what you just bought there isn't fattening.' Otherwise, I am invisible to them. So!" she said finally, "when I tell you not now, I mean not now. Period. You'll find that out." She grinned to erase his look of discomfort, to forgive him, and got to her feet.

Too late, Paul tried to help her up. "Did you hurt your knee? Are you hurt?"

Gracefully, she climbed a few steps backward away from him and breathed deeply. She touched her hair with one hand. "No, I'm not hurt. I am just fine." Paul climbed two steps toward her, watching her, and she responded by immediately climbing two more herself, still facing him. She wore a little smile in a clouded expression, deeply interested in his look of lustful concern. She put a steadying hand on his shoulder and talked to him quietly. "You know what old Charlie Weintraub taught me to say, you think I'm so sweet? Stay down there right where you are. Old Charlie taught me to say this, at just the right time: 'I am dirt for you and you are pig for me. I am your warm wet dirt and you are my long-nosed pig. Now you must root in me.' There. That shock you? That's what old Charlie taught me. But right now don't you touch me, Paul." Her pale blue eyes were wide, and her shoulders moved with her breathing. Suddenly she turned and fled up the stairs.

Paul ran after her as before, staying close behind. The tower rang with their footfalls. The whole steel staircase hummed and shook with the force of their climbing. When she was too winded to run anymore, Sally helped herself by hauling on the rail and kept climbing, two treads at a time. She watched the wall to avoid looking into the great depth beside her. She climbed past two more inscribed stones that she did not stop to read. She heard Paul's breathing behind her, and twice she saw his shadow on the stone beside her in the dimness. He said nothing.

At length she heard a murmur of voices from above, and knew the terrible climb was nearly done. She climbed past the bottom-pan of the round brass elevator hanging in its landing dock, then, blinking and smiling in the brightness, she made the last step and leaned panting against the parapet wall. The others who were already there looked at her with warm interest, as if they would like to congratulate so slight a girl who had made so long a climb.

In the center of the round roof where they stood was a large cupola for the elevator and its hoisting machinery. The operator stood in his doorway out of the slanting rays of the sun, looking serenely out at the world.

Paul said, "We ought not to stand still. Our legs'll knot up unless we keep moving. Come on, let's walk around."

Without comment, Sally took his arm and walked beside him, testing their ability to walk well together in promenade. She leaned on him a little, for she did not feel well. Seeing was difficult; the magnificence of the view swam in her eyes. From time to time she had the sense of looking down a long tube with black walls; things in the side of her eye simply disappeared. "Just a minute," she said, and stopped to lean on the stone wall. "That was a long pull. I'm a little dizzy."

"Take it real easy, now. I'll bet there's not many girls who've done that."

There was a light wind coming off the Bay. The flat haze was breaking into patches, and they could see the glittering red track of the sun on the water. Sally turned her hot face slowly from side to side in the wind, her eyes shut against the sun. A line of tears sparkled in her pale lashes.

They were alone on this side of the terrazzo roof; the rest were around the cupola looking at the college and the town and the distant mountains. Sally sensed Paul behind her. She turned and opened her eyes to the white glare off the cupola, and Paul was approaching her with his arms out, imploring.

"No," she said, and skipped away. Trailing her hand along the parapet for guidance, she trotted around the cupola and went to stand beside the two similar young priests. Both looked at her, then at each other, then they leaned on their elbows again and continued to look in the distance, talking very seriously in soft French.

Paul stood at the parapet six feet from her and looked at her. She did not return the look directly; she half-smiled and looked at her fingernails. He signaled for her to come back to him, a simple gesture with one hand on the slanting capstone. She saw the movement but did not acknowledge it. She was tired, and it was pleasant to stand in the shelter of the priests listening to their intense and personal talk, and to feel the last heat of the sun on her back. Also, it was pleasant to run this thing her way as long as possible. It was little enough to ask.

Paul took a sideways step toward her. "Sally." Another step. "Say, Sally." He reached, and took her by the cloth of her sleeve. Sally shrank away, into the nearest priest, and struck down hard at Paul's hand. Everyone on the roof turned at the sound of her slap. Paul's wristwatch flew off, halfway to the cupola, and broke into three golden pieces when it struck the terrazzo. Paul held his wrist against his stomach and said, "God damn!"

The priests said, "Ah, ah!" The one Sally had backed into supported her to keep from falling himself. His hands were thick-fingered and soft. Sally bit her knuckle and watched Paul pick up the parts of his watch. She was scared, and sorry to have caused the general embarrassment. Paul's face was red when he straightened. The priests, who were very little older than Paul himself, watched him in deep disapproval. "Thanks," Paul said nastily to everyone who was watching him. He took the parts of his watch over to a flat place on the parapet and reassembled them. He was tight-lipped, and concentrated on the little task with strong control. He held the watch to his ear, then put it over his knuckles and rotated his wrist quickly several times and listened again. Then he put the watch in his pants pocket.

Sally left the priests and went to Paul, knowing everyone was watching her. I will be swell, she thought. I will be lovely and sweet and swell, but I will let the boy know. He'll get the idea pretty soon. . . . Gaily, for all to hear, she said, "I *told* you it wasn't shockproof!" She added softly, still smiling for everyone, "Listen, I'm awful sorry about that. Give it to me later. I'll get it fixed, okay?"

"There's no need," Paul replied, turning his back to her and looking out across the park.

"But I guess you understand about me now, though, hon. Really, I can't stand to be picked at or pulled on, you know. I get so mad I see red. Even downtown, when I see some stupid mother hauling her kid around by one arm, I get mad. Bunch of kids that grow up with one arm longer than the other. It's an awful shame. I'd like to slap those women silly so they know how it feels. Oh well, I should worry. Right? Nobody pushes little Sally around, right?" Suddenly she felt that Paul was not paying enough attention. He was looking past her now, toward the cupola. Sally made a side step to interpose herself, and continued, still grinning hard, "I think it's wonderful to have an understanding from the very beginning, now, isn't it? That's the way everybody should be, don't you think? Start square. Right?"

Paul looked down at her and smiled suddenly. He held out his hand to her, which Sally, mistaking, took immediately. He shook hers firmly and said, "So long, Sally, it's been very pleasant."

"*What!*"

Paul stepped around her and walked to the brass elevator. He was the last one on. He had been watching the others enter.

Sally followed him halfway, then stopped and turned about and stiffened her arms down at her sides. She lifted her face to the pale sky, lips pressed together, and held her breath while she waited for some sound from the elevator. When none came in several seconds, she surrendered and hurried to the cupola. The cage door was still open. The operator was leaning against the hinge with his arms folded, watching her. His eyes twinkled, and he gummed from time to time.

Sally did not get on the elevator. Putting aside all shame, she said, "Now listen, this is silly. Get off here. I've got to talk to you."

Paul blinked slowly and put his hand in his pocket. He took out his change, picked out one dime, and gave it to the elevator operator.

Sally said, "Please?"

Paul and the operator looked at each other. Then the operator shrugged himself away from the door hinge and said, looking down, "Excuse me, miss." She stepped back in blind obedience. He leaned around the polished brass gate and unhooked it and, entering the elevator, let it close behind him. He latched it shut, checked all his passengers, then turned the control handle. A relay clacked in a metal cabinet and, with a soft hum, the machinery began to let the elevator down. A brief scent of ozone lay behind.

Sally folded her arms tightly and looked away until the black-domed roof of the elevator went below the floor, then she carefully started down the spiral stairway. Four steps down she paused to read a stone that she somehow knew, without surprise, had simply not been there before:

GRANITE
MINNESOTA
*There are very few things in this world
that cannot be improved with either
garlic or butter.*
—Kent Curtis

Sally said softly, "Ah, what's happening?"

As the elevator descended into the dimness of the core of the tower, the glow of its electric light gave the occupants the gilded, holy look of stained-glass people. Sally stared at them as she went down the stairs. At first the elevator gained on her, but she soon learned how to go down the treads two at a time in a regular, accurate movement, with her hand always on the pipe rail, and so managed to catch up what she had lost. Because of the brightness in the cage and the dimness on the stair, she felt unnoticed and unseen. Everyone seemed to have forgotten her. She saw Paul light a cigarette, and called, "Hey! One for me too, how about?" He did not turn. As if to avoid annoying any of his fellow passengers, he blew a plume of smoke away through the bars. Sally ran around and around, repeating her steps exactly to avoid stumbling, staying always level with the brass cage. Soon a harmless, though nasty, disorientation enveloped her; since she remained even with the elevator but was continuously going around it, suddenly in her sight the elevator itself was turning, screwing its way down the bore of the tower. She stopped for several seconds, panting as she held to the sill of one of the narrow loopholes, and her confusion cleared. Outside in the park dusk lay in the feet of the trees, and the water in the fountain pools was black. She began running down again, a little behind the slow elevator. She saw the operator talking to all his passengers. He shimmered slightly in her eyes, and, to her astonishment, she saw that the elevator itself was shimmering too, for it had changed from brass to real gold. The light in the cage, too, was golden, warm and bright, and the people were ruddy and healthy-looking, smiling as they listened to the operator tell a story. The white-haired couple were holding hands. As Sally ran down past the front of the elevator, like a circling moth, she saw Paul scratch his ear while he listened, smiling. Then she saw the operator make a baby-grin and give a little hop and a bow that meant the end of the story, and everyone in the cage laughed, even the children. Sally heard none of this, and reasoned loosely that her own footfalls were overwhelming all other sounds. She was now beginning to tire seriously; she feared her knees might buckle without warning and pitch her down. She depended more and more on the pipe rail that guided her hand. By now her little white socks had run well down into her loafers, and hurt her. She wondered briefly how the hell she had got herself into this. Now she dared a look down over the rail and saw, much to her relief, that the great finial that marked the end of the stairs was just two more turns below. She was ready to slow somewhat. She called loudly across to the elevator, spacing her words to fit between the tread-jolts of her descent, "Listen, Paul, I'm tired out. Wait when you get down, okay? I'll be right there. Just wait, is all, because this is silly and we'll get it straightened out. Okay? Okay?" Then she added quietly to herself, "Okay." Paul had not looked at her. Now he blew a puff of smoke between the bars. In the dead air of the tower, the smoke moved out to let the roof of the elevator go past, then lazily surged back and hung there among the cables. Sally let the elevator go ahead while she stumped on down the stairs in general pain, watching the retreating roof and sliding her hand down the pipe rail. Her mistake was to watch only the elevator, descending below her, so her hand struck the great finial utterly unexpectedly. By quick reflex she grabbed it with both hands as she fell. She swung around it and dangled there for a moment, for, world gone, there was no next step. Making small sounds of effort in her throat, she swung one thin leg back onto the last step and bent herself up to safety. On her knees, she looked weeping up at the solid gold finial she held, and her lips parted at the crowded twinkling beauty of the great jewels that crusted it. So this is how, she thought. This is the way. Dropping her hands, she crawled up three steps and curled herself close against the stone, where the treads were broadest. She pulled her skirt tightly down over her knees. The steel of the tread was moist and cold under her, and the sharp little hobs were real and hurt. This far down in the tower it was now almost dark. *God, what's happened to the door?* Sally swallowed. Peering between the treads she could see far below her a ring of golden light moving slowly down the blank stone bore. After a moment she felt in her waist pocket for her handkerchief. Hunching against the stone, she wet it in her mouth and washed her eyelids. She raised her head when she heard the distant murmur of voices, but they were too far away to understand. Moving carefully to avoid vertigo, she helped herself up the stone wall until she was standing, leaning against it. She took a breath that hurt her ribs terribly, and in one step crossed the stair to the rail, catching it in both hands. Her little plastic purse swung from its strap on her wrist. She looked down over the rail and sighed, for the elevator was now no larger than half a dollar, glowing warmly at the edges. Sally said, "Old Charlie Weintraub wouldn't ever have let something like this go on." Clinging to the rail with both hands, Sally removed her loafers one at a time by scraping the heels against the nosing of the next tread above. Then she put her purse neatly beside her loafers and, in her socks, descended to the bottom tread. She stood there a moment in twisted dignity with one fair hand on the jeweled finial, while with the nail-bit thumb of the other she made crabbed, upward-hooking motions all about the pleated bodice of her dress. Since by now everything seemed so surely planned for her, she sensed that any protest would be useless and embarrassing, yet she did resent with real irritation this unnecessary insult, this hot band of pain that circled her chest now and shrank tighter every moment. *I'm going,* she thought. *You don't have to push. I hate being pushed.* Just as her thin ribs were about to crack, she drew on the courage of her anger and inhaled against this squeezing strap. Something burst softly and let her go. As everything failed but her pride, she smoothed her skirt and stepped off into the abyss.

Paul, who had been standing directly before her, hectoring her with whispered shouts to wake her as he watched her love the finial and go into herself, caught her as she toppled forward, caught her because he could not step back quickly enough to avoid her falling. "Oh, Jesus," he implored, holding her under the arms and looking wildly about at the others for help.

"Just let her down," said the elderly tourist. "No. Not that way. On her back." Then he added, to everyone, "I'm a pharmacist. Uh, from Sioux Falls, South Dakota."

Paul laid Sally in beauty on her back, close to the wall at the foot of the stairs. A little sweat sparkled on her lip and in the fine hair at her temples.

Then, without a word or a look at anyone, Paul straightened and trotted across to the doorway as if never to stop again, yet, once there, he came to a skipping one-legged halt and turned and walked back, loose-limbed and stooping, his feminine eyes starting with an embarrassment lifted to the level of horror.

The two priests conferred softly in French, with swift, sad gestures to each other, then one touched Paul's sleeve and asked, "Was she Catholic?"

Paul twitched and tilted his head as if against a wasp coming in on his quarter. "What? What? No. *Was?*"

The priests looked at each other, then went together to stand by the doorway.

The young couple with the two quiet children had herded them around to the far side of the standing elevator, and busied themselves now with continuous movements of interposition to prevent the children from seeing.

The pharmacist stood beside Sally looking down at her, his lower lip out in sympathy. Hands in his pockets, he jingled his change loudly and went up and down on his toes. Then he kneeled and took her thin wrist in one hand while he fingered for her pulse with the other. His swimming blue eyes went from person to person as if gathering up the loathing in their faces; he looked last at Paul to let him see it all. He laid her arm back on the stone floor and thought a moment on his knees, sitting back on his heels, then he bent far down to lay his ear on her chest. His face reddened at once in this position. He pushed down with his head several times in a snuggling effort to get his ear closer to her heart, and with one big hand he casually tried to push her breast out of the way.

At this, Paul took a quick step forward, then another, just as quick, backward.

Now the pharmacist lifted himself from Sally, pulled down the square tails of his sport shirt, patted the pockets to be sure nothing had fallen out, then covered one of Sally's wide eyes with his hand. He drew it away quickly, watching the eye. He tried this twice, then took a breath and got to his feet. He said to his wife, "I don't know. I think she's gone." To Paul he added with a certain hostile exaggeration, "But I'm not sure. I mean, I'm not a doctor."

Paul's upper lip lifted and drew back from his teeth. He tried to lick it back in place. He stared at the elevator operator, who was dialing a telephone at the souvenir case, then at the two priests, who were now standing spread in the doorway so as to fill it. He was very pale.

"You ought to cover the poor thing," said the pharmacist's wife, speaking to everyone.

"What with, Ethel, what with?" her husband asked, jingling his change again.

Paul spun about clumsily and ran to the souvenir case and bent behind it.

"Hey!" cried the toothless elevator operator across the telephone.

"Just this! Just this!" Paul shook his jacket in the man's face, then carried it to Sally's body. He knelt and slapped her cheek several times tentatively, not hard enough to hurt if she had been alive, and hissed at her, "What'd you have to go and do something *serious* for?" He covered her with his jacket, up to her neck, and got to his feet. At once, with a look of great pain at the others, he fell to his knees again, took up his jacket, and went through all the pockets. Blushing, he removed a notebook, a fine monogrammed handkerchief, a pair of black-framed reading glasses and, with two little clicks, his gold pen and pencil. When he had stowed all these in the pockets of his pants and shirt, he covered Sally again with the jacket, this time including her sweet, fair head.

Baby, Tonight I Rolled Pinto Lee

JOY WILLIAMS

from *Colorado Quarterly*

When Walter Hubbard was a child, he ate Queen Anne cherries in heavy syrup for dessert. The pits would tell him his future, his calling, his place in life. He looked forward to the counting with great delight and great faith. His mother, however, had counted the cherries in the kitchen so that the boy would always be a richman, never a poorman and never a beggar.

W. O. (Walter) Hubbard had during the spring gone to the Kennel Club every Tuesday, Thursday, and Friday night to see the greyhounds run. He did not arrive home on those evenings until 11:00 p.m. He finished his job as a salesman on the floor of Kane Suburban Furniture at 6:00, ate shrimp boiled in beer at a nearby restaurant, and was out at the track by 7:30 in time to check the card and the green slip, rent a chair, and bet on the daily double. He was not a lucky man, but neither was he extravagant. The most he had won in a single night had been fifty-four dollars, the most he had lost was ten. His shy and tethered forays into gambling could, therefore, never be the basis or support of an argument between himself and Dottie. Not even in the worst arguments, when his wife would suddenly and irrationally become conscious of his heavy stomach, his pale eyelashes, and his complacent failure to rinse the soaped and clotted hairs of his razor down the drain, would it be mentioned. Not even at that point in a quarrel where the most aged and Lilliputian of grudges achieve billboard proportions would his consistent absence on Tuesday, Thursday, and Friday nights and his gambling be questioned.

The world of W.O. was limited but solid. He had never drunk Wild Turkey bourbon or worn Mezzo boots or speeded in his Chevrolet. No setter that he had ever owned had ever slammed into a point and starched at the edge of a clump of autumn bushes, nor had a boom ever slapped to leeward in his vision, nor had a woman ever approached him in a bar. He had had no extravagant camaraderie with men or dizzying relationships with women. His first attempt at seduction had met with immediate success, and happy and proud, he had married the girl. Now, every morning, he awoke to the same mail truck clattering over the same loose brick in the street and the hot water being made in the apartment's pipes and his wife's thin damp arm flung across his chest.

In the evenings that he wasn't at the track, he would sit in the kitchen—dark and checkered and smelling of whey—at the heavy mahogany table that he had got cut-rate, half-priced, slightly marred, and, with a dish full of cashews and several quarts of beer, play cribbage with Dottie and some friends. If the friends did not come over and if they did not go to the movies, he and his wife would play alone. Dorothy Hubbard's figure was full and her teeth were white and neat as little sugar cubes. Between the front teeth there was a small separation the width of a dime. It means, she had told him on one of their first dates, giggling, wriggling agilely about on the Naugahyde seats of his buddy's car—it means lust and wanderlust. Gazing lazily at her, drinking larger and larger quantities of beer, he would lust for her as softly and completely as he had then, his desire in his swimming eyes and the sweet swath of heat in his trousers. On such nights, he would take her early to bed and make gentle and self-effacing love.

Up until a month ago, Dottie had met him at work and had gone with him to the track, but the novelty had worn off, she said, and without betting it was no fun, and with betting she was too nervous even to watch her choice, she said, and she stood inside the clubhouse, staring into the stolid eyes of the sellers. So he went out there alone now, hung over the rail wailing his hopes home, beating the rail with his rolled program and scrambling to the window to collect his wins—alone now.

"C'mon you mutt! Hoof it! Hound that bunny!"

And he loved it.

He found the dogs a perfect outlet for his self-expression and geniality. He sat jammed against the fence in his folding chair, directly opposite the scales and the judges, there holding the tightest, most final view, his head veering towards the turn, round the oval, squashed by others, carried along by them and by the flight of the narrow, muzzled greyhounds flying so fast there were no legs, no muscles, no loins, just a static palette of blur. . . .

"Run you mess o'chops! Go you 8 dog! Don't get caught inside there. . . ."

And then when the canvas had been drawn before the galloping paws and the dogs had slid to a bewildered and whimpering stop, W.O. would sigh and smile and say to the dirt, the night, the winking board, anyone who would listen, "Why I almost bet on that little dog. I knew he looked good. I knew it. Oughta always play your hunches."

He was an excellent loser, and tore up the ticket as eagerly as he would cash it in. He wanted to share it all with the crowd—both his wins and his losses, both his wry grins of apology when screaming on an ambling brindle and his confrontation—with smiling deference to the ladies in line—with the cashiers. But on the Friday night that he received his raise, he wanted very much to win. He had expected a much larger check. He had been selling rosewood hutches, innersprings, and terrazzo coffee tables for five years and had personally sold, in the last year alone, nineteen stereo sets and twenty-eight tee vees. And yet that night the manager had only given him a bearish, presumably friendly sock on the shoulder and increased the slim pat of bills by a mere ten.

Walter smiled with the wan caution of a child uncertain as to what will happen next—a disaster or an Oreo—and unwrapped a stick of chewing gum. But nothing happened. The manager walked away with neither explanation nor admonition, leaving only the question of should he (Walter) or should he not throw the gum paper on the floor as a symbol of his voided allegiance to the establishment. He threw the paper down and kicked it under a rocking chair, a sprawling, heavily cushioned old maidish sort of thing which he had that day sold to a woman for the lobby of her aging hotel. The chair swayed frowning at the manager. In his more solitary moments, Walter believed he had a way with furniture. It was lonely, faithful, it tried hard to please. It knew, it suffered, it saw a great many things and it saw them as they were. He could tell at a glance if it could belong to a customer. For the happiness of all concerned, he believed, one had to be as careful as though one were running an adoption agency. He looked out for objects and they in turn buddied for him. The price of the rocker was $45—he saw it as an omen, he would wager on the good will of his surroundings.

Walter bought two hamburgers at a drive-in and stuffed them moodily into his mouth as he drove to the track. Once there he padded dutifully to the window and put $10 on 4 and 5 to win in the first two races and found upon examining the program that Judy's Nite, the big black 4 dog, had run a score of races and none of them well, though she had shown twice. Number 5 was Thistle, which the railbird had charted for a place finish. He returned to the window and bet the 2-3 for good measure, a good double combination in the past, bought a beer, and hauled his chair to the rail. Judy's Nite was pushed from the start into a fourth position, but she knowledgeably dropped back a fraction and swung around the pack, caught the lead the second turn and never lost it. The crowd moaned. Her odds were 20-1 in a race of heavy choices and the other high-odd dog drove to a place, allowing Judy's Nite to pay well over $40.

Walter thrust his fist heavily into the pocket where the ticket was and gulped down another beer. Number 5 was the solid favorite for the coming race; even the talisman, the legless man who sat on his wide skateboard in the men's room and collected tips, had raised one hand, fingers outstretched to Walter as he tossed him a quarter. Before the cages, the dog was eager to run and trotted a leash's length to and fro in front of the handler. He looked like a fighter pulling rings and Walter was almost calm with the certainty of a comfortable payoff. The race was a long one, three-eighths of a mile, and began on the opposite side of the track. A few minutes later, he was in an excellent position to see Thistle collide on the straightaway and take a scrambling flip in the air. He finished last.

During the next race, Walter sat up in the clubhouse and drank bourbon and ginger ale while the waiter made the bets for him. He had been going out to the track too long now to make the abrupt and flagrant wagers that brought in the big money. He had seen their sires race at other tracks, he knew the trainers, he remembered past runs, and his mind, when he seriously bet, was a cataclysmic checker-board of too much information. In the next half-hour he lost $35 including two perfecta tickets on a 4-8 combination. Number 8 stole a late lead and overtook the pounding 4 dog by an ear's length, and the tickets were worth nothing. With a quinella, he would have won several hundred dollars. He had lost over half a week's pay by then, and he began to drink without the ginger ale. He thought of Dottie sitting on a stool, the radio on the ironing board—waiting for him to come home so she could put the money in the budget envelopes: car, rent, insurance, entertainment, electricity, groceries and it was all gone, sucked up into little paper compartments. Then there would be a new supply of chicken breasts and hair spray, underwear and movie tickets. Another payment on the set of luggage would be made, another nibble at the drugstore's bill. He angrily beat the tabletop of simulated racing stubs and with studied extravagance pushed his empty glass away. It rocked to the edge and was scooped up by a passing waiter. He was relieved that it had not fallen. They would have thought he was tight. He ordered another drink, deciding grimly that he would spend every penny he had if he wanted to, and made another bet.

Good ol' Dottie sitting at home stroking those man-eating envelopes and typing out fantastic love stories for the confession magazines on a weak ribbon in an old machine. Would anyone ever read them? No, they would not. Basket-liners all, they were. Artsycraftsy ideas never added one whit to the world, he decided. Her sport, she says; well so, damn, he thought, this is *my* entertainment, a man's got to dare once in awhile, he's got a right to the joys of his own sweat. He took another sip of bourbon and his mind rocked to a fine conviction. Always being so good, always letting me come out here and do what I want 'cause she knows I won't do anything. It's not my nature she thinks, I bet. He rubbed his hand along his jaw. A man lives with a woman so long and she gobbles him right up, flattens his features, sometimes even makes him look just like her. Before he knows it, a man's got a big fanny and starts thinking about what he can get with green stamps and loses his jawline and his hair and his hard handshake. . . .

The lights fluttered on around the track and the lure sparked away, flung archly forward like an arm on a projecting steel rod. A man loses his personality, he thought, peering at the track. He gets all fouled up, he can forget what he was. You can't do that to greyhounds now. They're always the same for years and years. They can't help but straighten themselves out like that ol' great King Cob whose grand-daddy was a bulldog. . . .

The blue tic he had set on floundered in fourth. The race was over instantly. Even the mediocre blue was probably turning a foot in a tenth of a second.

It's her fault, he said, barely aloud, onct I was lucky. Onct I had a touch, why onct, fagadssake, I won a free trip to Florida in a supermarket drawing. He stood up, took off his jacket, rolled up his shirt sleeves, and ordered another bourbon neat. Two weeks in a Florida motel with a private beach and they gave me $75 for gas and such and all I had to pay for was food and I beat them there cause I used to make Spam sandwiches and eat them on that little beach. Ahhh, he giggled, burning the tickets with his lighter, I remember but I was alone, I can't deny that I was alone there though I had Dorothy waiting at home. I sent her all sorts of stuff from down there, some little glass earrings with seahorses inside and I know I'm sure she was dating others then but I was the one she sent the mail to. Five thick letters and I was gone less than two weeks in that light little straying handwriting of hers: gee baby I miss you you're probably all brown as cocoa, oh she has a nice way with words you can't deny that and those guys at the magazines don't appreciate a nice way with words, as cocoa except for where your trunks come of course and I bet you're so warm and it's so cowald up here Walt baby it's so cold up here alone without you it is the February of my heart, oh she had a classy way of saying things . . . and then we got married I snatched her right away from the others oh she liked my looks she said and my luck and the way I loved her and now though we don't have a private beach and that's all my fault now but she tries with those little picnics with the anchovies and the potato salad at the public on a blanket on the fishfoul peoplefull sand with her in that nice blue suit that shows off her figure . . . and I have no right to think poorly of her no right at all and it's real work to get up a mad at her it's all pretend because she sometimes likes a good fight, it cleans, she says. . . .

He glanced gloomily at the track where the boys were trotting back from the cages, jogging down the track, while the greyhounds in their boxes wept for their own running. Oh she's a lovely thing, he moaned softly. That's a nice summer job for those boys she said the first time she saw them. Aren't they cute in those bright shirts and caps and it's so much nicer and more interesting for them to be with animals than to be behind a cash register say or driving a truck she said.

He loved those sweet little, womanly little, wrong little thoughts. He saw the constant bunny on his interminable course spark off again. He had seen his dog take a leak on the grass before the race and that, he thought giddily again, would make him lighter and he might run faster. When Dottie had come with him, she would put his arm around her waist and whisper that it was the other way around, that the other dogs who didn't piddle (that coquettishly, girlishly) would win because they knew the faster they finished the race the quicker they'd get a biscuit and could. The logic of which, he nodded to himself soberly, was no worse than his own. All racing quirks were the same, they all carried the same no weight in the outcome, although he himself would never bet on a dog fawning about the handler, the kind who begged to have his ears rubbed. That made him weak like somebody's pet and he wouldn't run well. All of which just added up to the fact that you just couldn't tell about dog racing. You couldn't compare it at all to horse racing and it was even harder to handicap than the pacers.

The sixth race was suddenly over and Walter found himself still staring glassily at the starting gate. He bounced to his feet and trotted around the small table like a beleaguered bull, as if he had been lulled, against his wits, from emergency into catastrophe. "Hey," he said. "Hey, I missed that." The numbers were flashing on the board but they slipped over him without import. He knew he had made several bets, but he could not, for the life of him, remember the dogs they had been on.

"Here you are, sir"—a starched cuff waved in front of him. "Number 2 scored for you, sir"—and $46 passed between the waiter's cool and W.O.'s wet and uncertain hand.

He plopped back into the chair. "Whaty'ed I tell you," he said to his glass. "You can never tell, you just have to *bet* and think of those who love you and they're the ones who'll bring the luck." He looked cheerfully at the waiter. "My woman brought me luck. I don't even look at the races," he said, "I just think about my woman and *she,*" he ended vehemently, "is the winning force. Lemme buy you a drink."

"No thank you, sir," the waiter smiled. "You'd like another bourbon?"

"Why, yes," W.O. said.

A place like this, a few wins, can make a man feel pretty good, he thought. A little service, a little respect, a few drinks. . . . He flattened the bills out on the table and emptied his pockets. The latter held only one bill and some coins. He had been broke when the greyhounds were running—more than he realized. He had never really imagined that he would go home with nothing. Even now he had only a little bit more than half of his paycheck, including the raise, left. He regarded stolidly the scene of his homecoming—the anger, then the tears, then the silence, then the drawing upon the meagre bank account to get them through the week—the drawing upon the money saved for the trip that they would take with their new luggage when they finally got their new luggage. Number 2 had brought a new, though small, stake. Nothing was no worse than half. $83.20 take-home a week couldn't buy anything anyway. He would make a big bet. One might as well be hung for a—he couldn't think of how that went.

He looked around him at the bar, the crisp motions of the waiters, the lights, the track looping before and beneath him. W.O. liked it up there very much. He was tipping too heavily but he felt tall and able like he had when he was a kid and he had trotted to school on his springy dirty-white Keds. He had pole-vaulted a little in those years, too. Not much, just a little, but every time he had hung in the air, the instant before he let the pole go and he himself started to fall towards the sawdust, he felt good. He had not liked his books then but he liked his friends. He was a very friendly guy. It was always a good feeling to be O.K.—to know that you were squared with things and didn't have anything to worry about because you were tight right in with a group of buddies.

He settled back still further in his chair. It was fine at the track, classy and clear, and with his bourbon and the knowledge that he would soon shoot the small stake he had, he felt in control. He hadn't felt in control for years—not since he used to practice smiling and lighting a cigarette in a locked bathroom, fanning the effect, forcing the compliment, and then go out to a dance or stand in front of a movie theatre with a girl to find that it worked, that the shadows fell just right and the match didn't slip from his hands. And the night he seduced Dottie, he had felt perfect and he had driven her home later and kissed her goodnight with what he was certain was a gentle yet confident possessiveness. Only great self-control and a growing concern with gallantry kept him from offering a complete account of the evening to his friends. He counted instead upon their intuitive recognition of his allowed intimacy as he steadily dated her. The truth however was that he lay awake nights wanting after that, reliving in solitude the warm tangle of bodies, and satisfying himself instead with the wet and tonguing kisses and happy mauling that she allowed. But not for the world would he have exposed in brutish words her early and singular gift to him—for he had discovered that he was in love with her.

Walter turned the program to the new card with its collection of names. Had little Dottie ever been up to this fine clubhouse? Noooo, he shook his head sadly. Dottie had not. He wished that there were someone there he could talk to about her or even better, he wished for Dottie herself. He wanted to talk to her about her. Yes. The good times they had. He stood up and put his jacket back on again, smoothed his hair and swung his eyes, ragged as a horseshoe dribbling down a stake, back to the card. In the seventh it was Bama, Little Clem, Pinto Lee, Cracker, Whimpy, Jeanie Rocker, Wenger, and Dry Rob Roy. Oh yes they had had good times and still did but she deserved more than she got. He wished that he had taken her to Florida with him when he had won the contest, never mind what anybody would have said. He thought he had tanned real well in Florida but now he had trouble getting brown. He was no kid now on the beach. He was only two inches under 6 ft. but he looked shorter and he looked slightly older than 36 too as he sat under the sun in an unbuttoned shirt. He looked his best in a suit. He was getting to the point where he felt uncomfortable in anything but a suit and tie. He knew that she loved the weekends when they could go to the beach though. Her skin got the color of some lovely soft rich caramel candy.

Oh yes, he scanned the card listlessly, muttering. If he had taken her up here, she'd probably still be coming out to the track. She'd love it if she could just get a little dressed up and have things nice. No, poor little Dottie, poor kid had to stand downstairs by the rail with the bums tossing their paper cups on the ground. Once a coke had sloshed right over her ankle. Of course the people get excited down there. You can't blame them if they lose, and you sure can't blame them for being thoughtless if they win.

But he didn't want people sloshing cokes over his wife. What kind of a guy was he anyway. Walter punched his palm irritably. When they were going together, he was always watching out for her facryingoutloud. He never was much on muscles but he wore his teeshirts rolled high on his arms and he would have fought like a tiger for her fagadssake. They'd sit over at her house drinking golden ginger ale and listening to records in a cool dark living room. The shades were always drawn to save the furniture, and even now, holding his bourbon glass in a bar, he could feel the slick starchiness of the antimacassars under his fingers. He could even remember the books there—*We* and *The Wake of the Red Witch* and *Gone With the Wind* and all the knick-knacks perched dustless on the shelves. Walter sighed. He knew he was sentimental. He could remember everything. He couldn't remember great speeches or anything like that but he thought of things like furniture or songs or the food on a dinner plate and he could bring everything back. He could bring back a whole day. He saw Dottie in a chocolate-colored dress with her knees tucked beneath her, sorting records on the floor. "Ghost Riders in the Sky" and "There Goes That Song Again" and "At Last" and some funny little song about a pony and an Indian. She just loved that song. She'd play it over and over again, giggling and nodding and pretending to cry a little when the part that was supposed to be sad came along. Uuuuuuuu, he sang, tapping his foot—like a train see, ooh ooh

They were swishing, not looking
Ooh Ooh they never came back

Walter pounded his foot on the floor and smiled. Things were so simple then. The newspapers headlined 30 Million Kids Overseas Need Soap but that could be taken care of easy, and he and Dottie never fought then either. They'd sit in the dim, cool living room with the family pictures watching them from the piano and play records and kiss each other and when he touched her she shivered all over . . . oh yes and Mae West was saying, I used to be Snow-White But I drifted—and everything was a howl and uncomplicated. He felt so *right* with Dottie then. She was the one that made him feel big. He was never cool and poisonperfect like Kirk Douglas in *Champion.* He was no Widmark or Cagney. He knew a kid in school that looked just like Widmark, the same mouth and everything. He was never in with his friends like that kid was. Walter gripped his hands, still thankful after seventeen years. If he had told them about Dottie they would have just used it against him later or something. He was a real friendly guy but they hadn't always treated him like a friend.

Ooh Ooh . . . he remembered her sitting there, teasing him, pursing those pretty red lips. . . .

Walter looked down at the track again. The boys were just leading the dogs to the starting box. It was a grade T race with dogs of mixed class and the betting was erratic and the board top-heavy with known favorites. He snapped the program in his hands so sharply that it tore. Cracker, Whimpy, Wenger— she would like the seventh dog best because he was the best-looking.

Ooh Ooh sweet Dottie in her chocolate dress. She was very witty. She used to imagine the horse in that song trotting down the railroad track wearing trousers and a hat and holding a bottle of tequila. . . . And that was it. Walter gathered up his money. Just as clear as daylight. He would press this bet for Dottie and he would bet it all on a memory, on a sure thing.

Da-da-da-dee

> Across the Alley from the Alamo
> Lived a pinto pony and a navaho—
> Who sang a sort of Indian hi-dee-ho

It was a pinto pony that she loved and it was Pinto Lee in the seventh that would save them. Even if he lost he would go home and just tell her that and tell her that he loved her and that he was going to make everything nice for them again. He couldn't do anymore than that. She'd sure understand that. Walter could no more see her angry now than he could imagine himself unfaithful.

The number 3 dog, Pinto Lee, was standing still as shock in the midst of the yapping dogs and he was the largest and ugliest greyhound Walter had ever seen. He was primarily white and the few black spots he did have dotted just his hindquarters and one ear. His odds were 90-1. Walter rolled the dog up the track twice with two perfecta tickets which came to a total of $42. He did not want to chance the second place dog and anyway he felt that if Pinto Lee did not come in first, he would not be in the running at all. The waiter palmed the money neatly and walked away. Walter had never rolled a dog before. It cost too much money and the chances weren't that good. If you bothered to place every dog in a particular race against the number you were counting on to win and your constant failed to win you were wiped out and if your constant did win but pulled in a high favorite for second sometimes the payoff would be less than what you put down for the roll.

The odds remained deceptively, exhilaratingly high on the boards until after the dogs were placed in the boxes and then they dropped. Number 3, however, was still a healthy 50-1. Walter clutched the tickets and tried to pick up his thoughts about his wife again but all he could imagine was his dog running with two wooden legs covered with papier-mâché. When the lights at the far end of the track came on and the lure began its seventh inexorable swish along its rails, Walter forced himself to look into his brown drink and coax up the images that had tempted him into throwing away the only insurance that remained against an awful weekend of anger and tears. Her nice big warm body, he thought hysterically, the light glowing in the apartment hallway, the records, that movie *White Heat,* all the memories, all them boyfriends she tossed away for me.

"Please now," he said, the emotional vagaries of the evening tobogganing down into a pleading groan, "please dog. For us now."

To Walter's eyes, the dogs were no longer a blur. They seemed to be quietly, unhurriedly loping. Their legs didn't seem to be moving at all. They ran all in a knot except for one white dog in a white blanket whose bland and determined hulk galloped far along the outside, around the leaders who strained against the rail. Pinto Lee ran as if he had iron filings in his teeth and the bunny romped in a magnetic field. Bama closed fast, but there had been no question. It wasn't even a photo. In two minutes the board ran the perfecta into four figures. $1,717 for a $3 bet.

Walter gagged noisily on his drink and the bourbon coursed dully up into his nose. "I'll collect it myself," he shrieked to the waiter and in a running lope, spinning, bouncing, lurching from table to table, he finally gained the cashier's window. He stood there the solitary winner—watched, hated and envied, and trembling, he shoved his pack's two correct tickets under the grate. The bespectacled cashier gloomily counted out a stack of $100 and $50 bills and asked him if he cared to pay his tax on the money now or fill out a voucher. W.O. would be glad to fill out the voucher. He was going to let nothing subtract immediately from the $3,434 he was going to scatter before Dottie, amid the cribbage sticks and wrinkled laundry, over the budget envelopes and the confession magazines, on top of the Ritz crackers and the candy dish full of bobby pins and pennies. He was going to bring it all home to Dottie—he would buy her a beach and ten new bathing suits. They would eat steak and wild rice and baked Alaska. They would pay off the damn luggage and take a trip. They would use white wine for a mouthwash. They would, W.O. decided, swing.

He folded the money up and held it with a rubber band. He wasn't going to be a sucker and stay at the track and hope to maybe fatten it up to four thousand. He wished now though that he hadn't wanted to show off. He knew people had seen him at the perfecta window and he was afraid of thieves so he sent a boy to bring his car around. It wasn't quite ten o'clock and the streets were almost empty and Walter rolled the windows down and turned the radio up to clear his head. He was sure nobody had won that much all season. His name might be in the paper. "Beautiful ol' Pinto Lee," he crooned to the radio, "an' he didn't even look healthy." At a package store, he bought twelve bottles of heavy dark German beer which was the most expensive thing on the shelf and a tin of fancy nuts. The third and top floor of the apartment building was ablaze with lights as he pulled into the driveway and maneuvered into a small area between another car and a giant maple. It seemed to Walter that he was always squeezing his car in behind the maple, was always dangerously close to scraping the fenders, smudging the whitewalls and, in general, heavily wheeling himself into impossible escape. It seemed also that after seven years in the apartment house, it was tacitly understood that this was the parking space for the Hubbards of the third floor. He would chop down the tree. He would toss the landlord a fifty and tell him to go buy some dirt.

As he walked up the stairs with his beer and his fortune, he heard the television chatting and saw himself striding in and purposefully shutting off "The Man from U.N.C.L.E." or whatever—he would kick in the screen, he would buy a flashy new hooded console—and telling his wife casually that they now had about three thousand more dollars than they had when he left the house that morning. When he opened the door, he saw the television wasn't on and the voice he had heard belonged to Jimmy Ladd, who sat at the kitchen table eating a sandwich.

"Hiya, kid," Walter said. He liked Jimmy. He was a lousy cribbage player but he was a very nice guy. Walter called him "kid" all the time even though he was only two years younger than himself.

"Jimmy forgot that this was your track night," Dottie said. She was standing by the stove in a shift, heating water for the instant. "He came over to play some cards."

"I'm glad you came back," Jimmy said. "Maybe we can still have a game or two."

"It's funny," Dottie said. "He just came over about ten minutes before you walked in."

Walter put the paperbag on the table. "Have a beer," he said, taking out one of the dark bottles. "Only kind to drink. Imported. Hearty."

"I wasn't hungry tonight for some reason," Dottie said, pulling down two glasses from the shelf. "That's why I gave Jimmy my sandwich. Maybe I'd better take an aspirin."

"It's a very good sandwich," Jimmy nodded.

"Well," Walter said, sitting down. "What a night."

"Was it Be Kind to Animals Week?" the other man said. "Did you give all your money to the doggies?" Walter and Dottie laughed. He was a very funny guy. He had long hair and a midwestern stacatto. His wife was blond and mournful and everyone called her "Nat." They were both in the Neighborhood Acting Group who put on plays in churches and people's living rooms. They were always tossing out the lines for the next play between hands.

Walter did not feel that he could tease about losing with Jimmy there. Dottie might get upset. "Just a little evening's entertainment. I ended 'bout even. Hey Dottie," he said eagerly, "what was your favorite song when we were going together?"

"Oh, sweetie, I can't remember. There were so many of them." She turned to Jimmy. "I was crazy about records."

"Yeah," Walter insisted, "but your special favorite one." Her hair clung damply to her cheeks. She's got a fever, Walter thought. She looks flushed. They would get a maid. She wouldn't have to iron or cook for months.

"Probably something by the Andrews Sisters," she said. "They were pretty good."

"How 'bout the one with the pony?" Walter was grinning so broadly he thought his mouth would creak and he began to sing loudly. "Remember?" He took a thirsty gulp of beer and, closing his eyes, he saw himself in a dark pub, his arms around dozens of girls, singing college songs.

"You've got a horrible voice," she said laughing.

"Sure, I remember that one," Jimmy said. "'Across the Alley from the Alamo.' That was the Mills Brothers."

"That's right, kid." In his pocket, Walter worked the rubber band off the money with his thumb.

"I don't know. . . ." Dottie said slowly.

"Dee dee dee," Walter crowed.

> The pinto spent his time aswishing flies
> And the navaho watched the lazy skies
> And very rarely did they ever rest their eyes
> On the people passing by

"Wouldn't you like that, baby? No cares—just watch the lazy skies."

"Oh, Walt," she giggled. "I want to do more than that."

"Anything," he said and flipped the bills onto the table.

Dottie squealed. "My god," Jimmy said.

"Baby," Walter grasped her shoulders, "tonight I rolled this mutt called Pinto Lee all because of that song, see, because I started to think about when we used to play it all the time and about the swell times and about how cute you looked singing and bouncing to all those records." He remembered Jimmy sitting at the table and his ears reddened. "More than three grand," he said.

"I can't believe it," Dottie touched the money. "That's terrific, Walt."

"It ain't too bad," he said.

"You did it with songs, huh," Jimmy said. "I'll see you later. I'm going to get a copy of *Variety* and get out there for the last race."

Walter laughed. He was a very funny guy.

"You seem to be more of the lucky type," Dottie chirped. "Walt was never really lucky before, were you, sweetie, but my goodness, just once like this is enough."

"Sometimes I'm lucky," Jimmy grinned.

"You're under a good sign for that sort of thing," she went on. "Libras are fortuitous." She turned back to Walter. "I've been studying up on astrology for my next story. You're a Piscean—'a man of great sensations and appetites yet delicately aware of psychic impressions.' You're supposed to be good at metal and mathematics, too."

"I feel pretty good at figures right now, I'll tell you," he said, making a circle around the sugar bowl with the bills.

Jimmy shoved back his chair. "I should go."

"Have another beer, kid. Stick around and celebrate." Walter began to rummage through the paperbag again.

"No, I'd better be going." He smacked his stomach with the flat of his hand. "I'll be putting on a belly with so much beer. I suppose you'll be a real addict out there now, huh, Walt."

"I don't think so. Hey, now, you come on over tomorrow night and we'll cook something up."

"O.K.," Jimmy said. "So long. Thanks for the sandwich, Dottie." He flicked his fingers across her arm. "Piece o' lint," he said.

"So long now," Dottie chorused.

The door slammed and Walter took another sip of beer.

"We should put this money away someplace," Dottie said, "so we won't misplace it. You know this plus your salary makes a nice little yearly income. They don't pay you enough at that store."

"Yeah," he picked up her hand to kiss it.

"I forgot," Jimmy shouted through the door, "congratulations."

"Hey, yah," Walter wheeled around but he could already hear footsteps going down the stairs. Suddenly he felt very tired and rather drunk. He patted the money again. "Baby, I'm kinda bushed. D'ya mind if we go to bed?"

"No," she said, "of course not. My stomach feels a little better now. It was probably the heat. Walt, do you think if we saved this money we could move to New York? We could use it while you were finding another job. Jimmy lived there for awhile and he just raves about it all the time."

"Sure baby. Anyplace you'd like to go. We should be hitting a big city by now." He walked towards the bathroom.

"Walt," she called to him. "I remember that song now. Sure. 'Across the Alley from the Alamo.'"

"God, what a dog," Walter said, scrubbing his face, rubbing the soap deep down onto his nails. "He just come in like a shot—that beautiful Pinto Lee."

The Bride

MARGERY WOOD from *Carleton Miscellany*

At breakfast, he told his mother and Lyn of his resolve. "No beer, nothing," he spread his hand in the air above the table and swept it sideways. "Absolutely nothing to drink until after she arrives." He placed his fair, freckled hand on the table and tilted back in the kitchen chair. "I'm going to be one hundred per cent sober when my daughter arrives. She's got to take me as I really am—cold sober, that's what I'm going to be because it is a big day for both of us, a re-union after all these years." He dropped the chair legs to the floor and nudged his wife's elbow. "I'm scared as hell, Lyn."

Stoop-shouldered, Lyn was mopping up egg yolk with a bit of toast. "She'll like you, Jack," she assured him quietly without looking up. Then, in her mild, Southern drawl, Lyn added, "Do you want to do something about those new pants? They sort of need fixing at the cuff." She blew out smoke from her freshly-lit cigarette.

"I'll do it!" his mother said promptly. "One trouser leg is almost an inch longer than the other. Looks terrible, Jack. You must have bought that suit in a cut-rate place with no care given to nice alterations."

"I'll start cleaning the turkey then, Mutha," Lyn placed her cigarette between her lips, and took up her dish and cup.

Dutifully, he stood while his mother fitted the trousers. She sat cross-legged on the floor. Looking down, he could see the beautiful valley between her laced-high breasts. The flesh was wrinkled, but she still had quite a pair, for an old lady.

"Hold up your head, Jack. Now hitch your trousers to the exact place you wear them."

Their eyes met. She smiled coaxingly. "I want you to look nice today, Jackie."

"God," he groaned. "I wish it was over. It's going to be so funny to meet her. Why, I wouldn't know her if I saw her. Does she look like me or Fran?"

His mother removed a pin from her mouth. "Both of you. She has blonde hair and our family's coloring, but she reminds me of Fran, too. She has a way of talking, mannerisms really, I guess you'd say, of Fran's. And she's got a cute figure like Fran had. Well, you'll see—"

"If Diana inherited her mother's temper, God help her husband."

"Hold still, Jack. Just a minute more," his mother admonished. "She seems to be a very sweet girl, a real nice child. Of course, I don't really know. Stand back a minute, dear. And she looked just beautiful in her wedding dress. You can take them off now, Jack. I think that's correct." Then she added reproachfully, "you should have gone to her wedding, Jack. I was the only one there from our side of the family. And the child is a real credit to us. You'll be pleased with your daughter."

His mother and Lyn were at the sink together when he came back from changing his trousers. He opened the refrigerator, looked longingly at the cold beer, and slammed shut the door. Then he sat down with his broad feet spread apart, and leaned forward, looking at his freckled hands. "What I still can't understand," he said to his mother, "is why this sudden interest in me after all these years."

"Hand me the stuffing, Marilyn, please. Well, I think after she was married and all, when she felt she was really free of her mother, then she wanted to see her father. At the wedding I promised her that I would get you two together after all these years. I wanted you to visit me, anyway, Jack. You never come to see me."

"Yes, he ought to come visit more often," put in Lyn.

Lyn was a great one for visiting kinfolk, and it was the only thing she could be insistent about. She had done the driving from Louisville to Dayton. He had sat in the seat beside her, drinking all the way. "Going to see my mother, going to see my daughter," had tipped the bottle.

Now, he was restless, sticky-hot, and scared. "I'm going to the drugstore for your cigarettes, Lyn."

On the sidewalk that ran beside the house, he passed the kitchen window, and he observed Lyn's profile as she held the turkey's legs for his mother to truss the bird. Lyn had the look of a patient, underfed coon dog. She had a large nose, plain brown eyes and sagging cheek muscles. But a more accommodating woman he had never known, and after living with his strong-minded mother and the spitfire, Fran, he had needed a woman who was quiet on the nerves.

His mother had always been nag, nag, nag. As soon as they arrived from Louisville yesterday, she had started right in, wanting to know if Marilyn still worked in the factory and if he had anything better than his stockroom job.

"Sure, sure, I was made president of GE just last week." He had glanced at Lyn, then. She had looked bushed with her wrinkled dress, her hair stringy and with caked lipstick in the corners of her mouth. She was tired from the long auto ride, but for one disloyal moment, he had been ashamed of her, seeing her with his mother's critical eyes.

He had told his mother about his dream of going in with Joe on the vending machine business. "If I could just get my hands on some cash—" he had said.

And what did she do, but put on a martyrish air and say she certainly hoped he hadn't come to visit her in hopes of any loan. Didn't he remember how he had lost all that money in the candy store business?

So then, he'd shouted at her and said, God how could he forget, especially with her to remind him, and he'd come to Dayton to see her and to meet Diana, for pete's sake. After that, his mother had been all lovey-dovey again and said she had been so *hungry* to see him and she was so glad that he had come for a visit.

On the way back to the house from the drugstore, he paused on the sidewalk to admire the neat, stuccoed houses with broad front porches, cheerful awnings, and the nice green lawns. People up and down the block were watering or mowing or trimming their front lawns. Back in Louisville their front yard was two tufts of wiry grass growing out of crunchy, cindery dirt. He and Lyn lived in a brown-shingled double which was darkened by a tavern on one side and a supermarket on the other.

But this year, the year he was forty-five, he was going to break out of the rut he was in. Someway, he was going to get going on a pile of dough, because by God, if you're over forty-five, you've had it.

His mother's kitchen was hot as blazes. Why did women cook turkey when it was ninety in the shade? He had taken a beer bottle out of the refrigerator, and had jerked open a couple of drawers, hunting an opener when he remembered. He had to stay sober for Diana's arrival. So he put the beer back and drank a glass of tepid water from the faucet.

Diana had sure been a cute little baby. Damp curls on the back of her neck, and when he held her, she had given him fat, open-mouthed, drooly kisses on his cheek. Her eyes were dark and big and bright as stars and how she had loved to snuggle against him and lay her head on his shoulder. He still remembered how it felt to have her cling to him and love him. But in this life you can't have everything, as his mother always said, and one day, after he and Fran had moved into her folks' house because he had lost his store manager's job, he had walked out and not told anybody where he was going. He had handed the baby to his mother-in-law—he had been swinging the baby in her canvas seat and she had shrieked with joy when he pushed her high—but he had handed her over and walked out the door. Fran was down the street, shopping. While he waited for the train he had had to hide his face in his hands because he was crying at the thought of never seeing his cute little baby again. But you can't have your cake and eat it, too. He couldn't live with Fran and her folks another day.

It was funny that Diana wanted to see her father after all these years. You could bet Fran had complained plenty about him. Yet the little kid probably had romantic notions about her stranger-father. He'd have to be careful not to disillusion her. Ha ha, what the hell? He'd just be natural. Have some laughs. She was twenty-one, a chick.

He thought they would never arrive. They were half an hour late. He waited for them, sitting on the davenport, with his hands on his knees. He was perspiring like a sponge and he worried about looking good when they came. In the dining room, Lyn, wearing a sleeveless cotton dress, was setting the table. Her bony arms were splotched with brown. She tanned unevenly. They went fishing together most Sundays in the summer. He wished he was down along the Ohio River right now instead of sitting here, dreading the visit and so thirsty he could spit cotton.

The sound of a car door slamming in front of the house made his throat constrict still further. He stood up, hitched up his trousers, and walked to the screen door and out onto the porch. They were coming up the walk.

Her husband was a beanpole which made the little figure beside him take two steps to every one of her husband's. She had a scrumptious figure with a small waist and good legs. He could see that in a minute. She was wearing a dark blue sheath dress and she moved with confidence and grace. She lifted a white gloved hand and called, "Hi!" gaily. He felt himself melt with pure joy. He was so excited that he went down two steps to greet them, then awkwardly backed up as they mounted the concrete porch steps.

"Well, well, well!" he cried. "How are you all? Glad to see you!"

His Diana smiled at him so sweetly and so naturally and said, "Hi, Dad!" with such an unself-conscious manner that he drew her slender figure to him and brushed the apple-firm cheek with his lips. His heart pounded in his ears until he felt that he was drowning. He held her at arm's length. "Let me look at you, kid," he said, and then he swallowed past the desert in his throat. There was a fresh delicate fragrance about her, like a sweet meadow in June. Her cute figure was sheathed in a dark-blue linen dress that felt crisp to the touch. Her eyes were greenish-brown and they were bright, young eyes full of dancing lights. She drew away slightly to introduce the tall young man. "This is Carl, Dad," she said.

"Glad to meetcha, Carl. Come in, come in—" He opened the screen. All he could think of now was a drink. Thank God, that first moment was over, and she was all right, he thought, seeing her trip over to her grandmother and kiss her, and then greet Lyn with a friendly smile after his mother introduced them.

"What'll you have, Carl?" he addressed the sober-looking young man. He decided he didn't like his son-in-law. He had a bored and arrogant expression. "Sit down, everybody," Jack cried. "What'll you have? Take off your coat, Carl. Let's be comfortable, eh? Damn hot day. We have vodka, bourbon, beer. What'll it be?"

Carl removed his jacket with a slight shrug as though to say, okay, whatever rules you have, I'll play. I'm only an in-law. This is Diana's party, not mine. I didn't expect her father to be much. After all, a runaway parent, a deserter—

Was he thinking that? Jack was uncomfortable with the guy, but Diana, now there was a doll! He wished he had her all to himself. She reminded him of Fran when she was that age, not in looks, but in mannerisms.

She began brightly, sociably, "We're sorry we're late. We got lost. We made the wrong turn off Main Street—"

Jack watched her, fascinated. He had started for the kitchen to fix the drinks but then he turned and watched the little hands wave as she talked, and the girlish voice with its merry lilt filling the room with brightness, gaiety, exuberance. She had seated herself on the davenport and the dark-blue sheath dress had crept above her knees.

He got to the kitchen and leaned against the sink. Whee! He mopped his face with his handkerchief and then drank two swallows of vodka straight.

His mother was right on his heels. She came out to the kitchen and asked him to lift the turkey so she could baste it. "How do you like her?" she whispered.

His voice was hoarse when he spoke. "Swell! She reminds me of Fran an awful lot."

"But she has our coloring. None of Fran's people were blonde, Jack."

He got out some ice cubes. Fran had had long black hair that fell around her shoulders at night and hung straight as a die, spraying out into fine ends in the small of her back. She had soft brown shoulders, but she would jerk away just as he put his head down to kiss her breasts so he used to feel like a baffled bull. She punished him by leading him on and then jerking away and brushing her hair so vigorously that he was afraid she'd hit him if he approached. Some days her anger ricocheted all over the house as she slammed doors and knocked pots about in the kitchen. One of the troubles between them was her cleverness. She was always correcting his English, trying to get him to keep his accounts better and suggesting ideas to spark up sales. When he came home and told her that he had lost his job, her face went so white that he thought she would faint with her anger.

A little voice behind him said, "Can I help?"

He turned around. Like a little girl, she stood before him, teetering on her high heels. She was smiling in her friendly, open manner. "I came out to help," she said. "Ooh, that looks good, Grandmother." His mother was grating cheese over a salad bowl. She asked Diana if she liked to cook and Diana said she was a terrible cook and then went on to chatter about cooking wieners, hamburgers and chocolate chip cookies.

After he had downed a vodka and tonic, he slipped an arm about that tempting waistline which was the neatest he had ever seen. She was so easy and natural with him that he couldn't get over it. She allowed him to embrace her as though he had been doing it all his life and as though there hadn't been all those nineteen years in between when he hadn't set eyes on her. "It's fun having you here, Diana," he said.

She tilted up her chin and replied, "I'm glad to be here, Dad," and he was so enchanted that he grasped her to him more firmly and with his free hand he drew a line along her chin from the delicate ear lobe to the soft throat.

"Look, Mother," he said, gazing into Diana's face, "what long, dark lashes she has."

"I noticed that myself," his mother replied.

Diana wiggled very gently from the pressure of his arm. "Is Carl's drink ready?" she asked. "I'll take it in to him."

She wasn't pulling away. She was as natural with him as a little kid would be. When you hold a child, he remembered from visiting Lyn's brother's folks, the child wiggles off your lap after a while. Well, that was the way with Diana. She wiggled free of his grasp and cheerfully smiling at him, picked up the vodka and tonic he had prepared for Carl and tripped out of the kitchen on her spike heels.

As fast as possible, he made himself another drink, but by the time he got to the living room, Diana was showing a packet of wedding photographs. She distributed them, and then flitted about like a darting bird, explaining who were the guests, showing Lyn the picture of her "weird Aunt Muriel. I mean, she's sweet and all that, but she wears these absolutely weird hats that are huge and came out of her attic, I swear. Here Lyn, this is Aunt Muriel here. Do you remember how funny she was, Grandmother? Whoever sat behind her in the church was unable to see a thing. Not a thing! No kidding, Dad," she paused in front of him and rocked on her heels as she held out those expressive hands of hers to two feet on either side of her head. "I want you to see the picture. You won't believe it."

She placed the picture in his hands, then perched on the arm of his chair. He had trouble focussing his eyes. "My arms are too short, ha ha," he said and shifted closer to that bundle of loveliness sitting so near him. Her gracefulness made him feel awkward and old. The sweet fragrance from her and her shapely arm tapering to a dainty wrist so intoxicated him that he only pretended to attend to the picture until she said, "Here's mother, of course."

By stretching his arm and holding up his chin, the glossy photo came in focus. Carl and Diana in wedding dress were in the center of a group of dumpy women and bald-headed men. Diana's neat fingernail was pointing to the figure standing next to Diana, the bride. Staring straight at the camera, unsmiling and aggressive, was a fat woman in a silky dress that was too long for her. Her bobbed grey hair was topped with a flowered hat.

"Christ!" he exploded. Surely, that couldn't be his fiery, beautiful Fran. This female looked like a dressed-up prison matron.

"I keep telling her to reduce," babbled Diana. "But she doesn't care how she looks. She and Eddie are getting a divorce. They hate each other."

She spoke with such charming honesty that he reached out to draw her down on to his lap. He would love to hold her like that, but she was swift as a humming bird, and was across the room showing the photograph to her grandmother.

Jack was beginning to feel his drinks and he grabbed up his glass and reached out a hand toward Carl's glass. "Sweeten it a little for you, Carl?" but Carl shook his head.

"We're going to eat very soon, Jack," his mother said and she and Lyn excused themselves to work in the kitchen. Jack made his drink stiff, and rushed back to the living room. He didn't want to miss a minute of being with her. He was beginning to feel really good, too, from the drinks and he could hear himself laughing frequently and loudly. "How about it, Carl?" he cried. "Diana doesn't have her mother's temper, does she?"

Carl finished his drink deliberately and then reached for his pocket handkerchief to wipe his hands and lips. What a slow, careful type character he was. Finally, with a small smile he said, "Diana is a good kid, a good girl."

Diana was wiggling about on the mohair cushion of the davenport. She was trying to get her skirt pulled down a little farther toward her knees. She glanced up, radiating her smile and shivering a little with remembered pleasure, and said, "Marriage is the most fun, ever."

For a delicious second, Jack saw two of Diana sitting on the davenport. Then his head cleared. As for Carl, he had picked up the latest copy of *The Reader's Digest* and was thumbing through it as though he was so bored with their company that he had to do something else.

"Except for dancing," Diana was saying. Jack's thoughts, skittering like water spiders, came back to his girl. "What?" he said.

"We do all the same things together and have lots in common except Carl doesn't dance and I love to dance."

A mist of tears filled his eyes. Boy, if he had anything to say about it, she would go dancing every night. He'd take that dream girl with the prettiest knees and legs in the world to any spot she wanted to go.

"I know one thing," Diana spoke with resolution and in a strong, clear voice. "I'm not going to let anything spoil our marriage. I'm positive of that."

Carl tossed *The Reader's Digest* back on the end table. A silence hung after Diana's words. Then Jack raised his glass and said drunkenly, "To my beautiful daughter whom I love very much, all the very best." He was at the crest of a full sense of intoxication, the crest really peaked, but then it passed away and he lowered his glass. "Hell—," laughing and coughing into his hand, "we're too serious. Let me get you a drink, Carl. We're too serious around here. Let's have some laughs."

"Dinner's ready," his mother called.

Quickly, Jack got his glass of vodka and tonic refilled and he brought it to the table, calling to Carl if he didn't want "another short one with his dinner," but Carl raised his hand, palm outwards and shook his dark head.

Jack stood at the table, behind the huge turkey, ready to carve it. His face, he knew, was hot and red. It always got like raw steak when he had some drinks like this. He really should have gone to the bathroom, maybe even changed his shirt; he wanted to look nice. But he was so excited and happy, anyway, that he snappily honed the knife and cried, "So you like to dance, eh, Diana?" She was sitting next to him and gazing up at him. "Well, you and I will try some steps before you go home. Bet you didn't know I was a Ray Bolger myself." He jabbed the fork into the center of the turkey and masterfully sliced down the breast meat.

He served himself last. He had no appetite. The thought of food gagged him. He gulped more of his drink, pulled his chair closer into the table and, as Diana was picking up her knife he imprisoned her braceleted wrist, covering it with his whole hand. She glanced up inquiringly. "About a wedding present for you, Diana, I've got in mind—"

Across the table Lyn stirred in her chair and Jack remembered foggily that they had sent something but what the hell was it? Diana chimed, "Oh, I love the tablecloth," and Jack, still holding the wrist and hand, said, "Oh, tablecloth nothing! You deserve at least a mink coat or a white convertible."

As though he had placed his hand over a small bird, the little hand moved under his grasp, and he let it go with a pat. "Yes sir, you'd look great in a white convertible, Diana."

She took up her knife to cut her turkey meat. "Oh, the tablecloth is just beautiful. Thanks ever so much, Dad and Lyn."

From the other end of the table his mother ordered him to eat. "Put something in your stomach, Jack, for goodness' sake!"

Was he acting tight or something? He had never felt better in his life because here he was with an absolute doll and she was his, all his! She belonged to him.

Halfway through the dinner, he went to the kitchen to refill his glass and saw that there was an inch of vodka left in the bottle, so he opened a beer. Returning to his seat, wiping his hand moist from the beer bottle on to his napkin, he kept his chair away from the table—who wanted food anyway?— and interrupted the talk at the table. "Tell you what, Diana, we'll cut a rug right after dinner. Where's that old stack of records, Mother?"

His mother's voice was prim as an old maid's. "On Sunday? Right after dinner? Really, Jack, it is too warm to dance."

"'Scuse me a minute," Jack cried, and went into the living room. In the cupboard beside the dark-bricked fireplace, he found his old phonograph and a stack of dusty records. Boy, he hoped the phonograph still worked. He lugged it out into the room and hunted for a wall outlet.

"Come have your peach pie," his mother called but he paid no attention. He finally got the phonograph plugged in. He picked up the black, clumsy-feeling, thick phonograph records and looked through them. His hands were trembling with eagerness. Boy, he hoped she wouldn't mind dancing to these oldies. He fitted a record on to the spindle, and as the phonograph warmed up, a tinny, scratchy music came out.

At the dining room table, Diana greeted him with a winsome smile. A half-eaten piece of pie was before her. Carl was shovelling in pie like a stoker filling up a furnace. Jack sang a few bars of the song, bowed low and asked her if he might have the honor of this dance.

She said, "After I help with the dishes," so he had to stand around, drinking beer and waiting while the women scraped dishes, and washed and rinsed and dried the dishes.

At one point, his mother said, "Go talk to Carl, Jack," so he forced himself to leave Diana's gay chatter about bridesmaids and to plod into the living room to see the string bean sitting there, comfortably settled behind the newspaper. Jack asked him if he wanted a beer and Carl said, "No thanks, not right after dinner." Jack went back to the kitchen. Why should he entertain Carl who was a stranger to him, when he had his own flesh and blood there, his petite daughter who was the sweetest, dearest child he'd ever seen. He decided that he had better get freshened up a little before dancing with her. He went to the bathroom and washed his face in cold water. He really was bloody-red in the face, but it was a hot day. He wet his hair and smoothed down the yellow strands over the balding spot. Now, he said to the mirror, I look pretty good for a date with my girl.

He hoped his breath wasn't too beery. He grasped her waist and propelled her a few steps across the living room carpet. Carl lowered the newspaper an inch and peered at Jack with his squirrel-round eyes. This guy, Carl, reminded him of somebody. Yeah, now he remembered. There was a young quality control engineer who was always bugging the guys in the stockroom for one thing or another. Never mind, thought Jack, looking away from the top of Carl's brushed hair to the front door standing opened back against the wall. He had his sweetie in his arms.

She broke from his embrace. "I can't follow you very well on the carpet, Dad."

"We'll dance in the kitchen." He turned up the volume on the phonograph as far as it would go and pulled Diana by the hand toward the kitchen.

There he wrapped his arm around the trim waist and pressed his temple against her soft golden hair. Her young body felt both taut and yielding, as he pressed her close. God, what a dear child she was, as full of fragrance as a spring flower, as sweet a disposition as one could ask for. He ached with the joy of holding her and closed his eyes, gliding back and forth to the music of regret and lost love as the refrain scratched itself out on the record player. At the Valley Lane Dance Pavilion twenty-some years ago, he and Fran had danced together like this under balloonsized colored light bulbs on the open air dance floor. Life was a funny business. He could imagine that he was young again and holding the body of a lovely young girl close to him.

Diana stopped dancing. "The music's not going anymore, hear?" She cocked her cute head sideways.

His mother spoke from the doorway. "It was too loud. We can't hear ourselves think. Why don't you stop now, Jack?"

He held his hands on the curve of her waist as he faced her. Her small figure was perfectly shaped, molded like Venus de Milo but this was warm, lovely girl, not any old marble. "One more dance," he said to Diana. "A fast one this time."

Past his mother at the doorway Jack said, "Okay, we'll quit after this dance, Mother."

Diana was dancing around, doing a twist when he came back. "Fraid I'm a foxtrotter," Jack said, grabbing her and whirling her around. This was fun. He swung her so fast that they bumped into the refrigerator and he bowed and said, "Excuse me," to the white enamelled door. Diana giggled and he squeezed her tight as a drum skin. "This place is crowded tonight," he gasped out. He was losing all the breath in his lungs but instead of slowing down, he speeded up, dancing faster and faster and her dainty feet were right with him all the way. His moodiness was gone. Hell, live it up. Life's too short to worry. Be gay. Have some fun. He wasn't so old. Not when you stopped to think about it. He had lots of fuel in the old engine, ready to go.

But he had to stop now. He fell against the sink, heaving for air like a fish. His head was flying around, spinning through white surfaces, bright linoleum, and red-dotted curtains. When he could see one spot steadily, he concentrated on her face where two lines of worry had formed on her brow. "Are you okay, Dad?" she said.

His legs ached like the toothache but he got to the refrigerator and took out a cold beer. He was as thirsty as if he had been lost at sea. "How about you, Diana, are you okay? We kinda cut a rug on that, didn't we, cutie?" He gulped several swallows of beer. There, that felt better. "Oh, excuse me, Diana. Let me get you a beer, dear, of course."

She shook her short blonde hair. "No thanks, Dad. We've got to be going. I promised Carl we wouldn't stay because it's a long drive back."

"To hell with Carl!" Her little face expressed such acute shock that he thought he'd die. "Oh no, no, Diana. I didn't mean it." He set the beer down and started to hug her but for the first time he sensed a rigidity to his embrace. "Oh forgive me," he grovelled, "I just want you to stay so much, honey, that's all. I didn't mean anything by it."

She patted his arm. "Sure Dad, I understand." She was smiling again, thanks be. He was so grateful that he grabbed her waist and propelled her toward the door. In the living room the faces turned toward the father and daughter. Jack hugged her and pressed her against him and brushed his lips against the flower-petal cheek. "This is my girl, folks," he said, "and she's a sweet one. Honey, you're my sweetheart." He was holding her at an awkward angle, but she allowed him to press her tight against his heavy body.

From Carl's chair came his bone-dry voice, "Time to go, Di."

Instantly she was away from him. He felt her easy, gentle movement as though she were a swan gliding away. He caught her hand and crushed it in his and he spoke urgently. "Look, Diana, stay. Just a little while longer. We can have a ball. Why, we're just getting acquainted, for pete's sake. Come on, don't go." He turned. "Carl, it's a snap to drive. The new freeway puts you there in no time. No sense in starting so early."

Carl didn't even answer. He picked up Diana's cloth purse and handed it to her. She turned to Jack and said kindly, "Thanks anyway, Dad, but we do have to go."

Light as a feather, fragile as a mote floating in the air, she was leaving. Jack watched her kiss her grandmother and take Lyn's hands and charm them both with her dear smile and gestures. Then she started for the front door while Carl went around with his cold, polite goodbyes. As he turned to Jack and before he could speak, Jack said, "I'll come out to the car with you," and he rushed to hold open the screen for Diana.

He held her arm as she tripped down the front steps. "When can I see you again?" he asked her twice.

"Oh, you'll have to come to Cleveland," she said. "Carl and I just love to entertain in our apartment," she chattered. "You and Lyn could come. Of course, we couldn't put you up all night but there's a motel near by."

Carl came up behind them and repeated, "Come on, Diana." He had the car key in one hand and he held out the other in a brusque, business-like manner. "Nice to have met you, Jack." His hand was as stiff and firm as the handle of a new fishing rod.

Carl first opened the door for Diana and then went around to the driver's seat. Diana started to kiss Jack goodbye when he wrapped both arms around her, squeezing her hard. She felt so good and huggable that he thought he was going to bawl all over her. A regular lake of tears was lying right in his throat. Some tears had sneaked into his eyes. He blinked and said, as he gazed into those young, beautiful, shining eyes, "Oh Diana, I love you so much."

She answered nicely, "Thank you, Dad," and gave him her most radiant smile. "Do come see us now. Don't forget."

She got into the car and then yanked at her sheath dress, trying to straighten out the skirt. Jack closed the car door. Carl waved his hand slightly and turned the ignition key. The engine started.

Diana's perky face was framed by the car window. "'Bye now," she said. Jack held onto the ledge a moment. "Goodbye, darling," he said. Then he let go.

He had to let go. Carl was easing the car forward.

Jack stood and watched while Carl turned around in a driveway across the street. Diana's short blonde hair blew in the breeze as Carl started up and she put her face out the window, waved merrily and was gone as the car went around the corner.

In his mother's living room, the air was dead, motionless and smelly. Lyn's cigarette smoke hung in the air and the food smells from dinner were nauseating. He sank down on the overstuffed davenport and laid his throbbing head against the cushion. Lyn glided over and sat down beside him. She asked him, in her quiet, Southern-accented voice if he was all right. He nodded once, painfully.

After a bit, he bent over and put his head in his hands. "God," he said. "God."

"She's a lovely girl, Jack. A girl to be proud of," Lyn said.

"I'm beat, Lyn, clean through."

His mother came into the living room. She was rubbing hand lotion into her hands. "That was a nice visit," she said. "And whatever is the matter with you, Jack?"

"He's just tired," Lyn said.

"You look green, Jack, and no wonder after all that vodka and beer. You drank too much. I didn't want to say anything while they were here, but I'm sure that they noticed, too. And the way you hugged and kissed Diana— honestly, Jack, it was too much smooching, if you want my opinion."

Lyn placed her oar in with the slightest of dips. "She is his daughter, Mutha. He was glad to be with her."

Jack straightened up and patted Lyn's bony thigh. Good old Lyn. He could always count on her. She had dumb brown eyes, mousy hair and razor blade shoulders, but she had a heart of gold. A good girl.

His mother was saying, "You know, Lyn, those trousers of Jack's still aren't the right length. One cuff hangs a quarter of an inch below the other. I noticed it when he was standing beside Diana. Here I thought I'd measured exactly—"

Lyn's cottony, soothing voice replied, "They look fine to me."

"Jack, stand up a minute, will you? I can fix them. You know, Lyn, I hate to see trousers badly fitted. Do stand up, please, Jack, and let me measure those trousers again."

THE TENNIS PLAYER

JOHN F. ZEUGNER from *Perspective*

HIT MOVING INTO THE BALL, AND OFF THE FRONT FOOT

The pro shop was small and he had to share it with golf bags. Each morning he pulled the bags out and set them along the white stucco wall at the back of the club house. He resented them more for smell than for space; by morning the stacked bags had transformed the scent of his room. At some point during the night the fuzzy, rubbery scent of Wilson tennis balls (he kept his lesson basket full—though he seldom gave lessons), the crisp tissue smell of Moody shirts and shorts, yielded to the greasy leather odor of the bags. He often wondered just when the transition occurred. He thought once of sitting in the room through the night and smelling every five minutes or so, trying to pinpoint when the change came. He was amused by that vision of himself. Balding, fattening, (from Moody 33 to Moody 36 in the last two years) and now at thirty-nine, he was constantly watching himself, projecting himself into various absurd poses, laughing and yet resigning to the present as an alternative to the seal of the future. That had been his great weakness: an ability to project all situations— failure to success, weakness to power, poverty to wealth, and then, having so projected, fully experience, fully reject as inadequate. Four years before, his wife had summed it up. "You're a waste."

He dragged the last two bags out, pulling them along the terrazzo, over the lip of the sprung, aluminum door, along the outside cement, scratching them.

So it had come to this, he thought—the quiet pro at Cape Revere Club, twenty miles south of Hane, Florida. Grand developers from the East Coast of Florida had come over to project Cape Revere on the discontented Haneites. Purchasing a solid segment of bay front (one of the last available pieces) they had begun the quick process of killing every living thing (thwarting the conservationists by releasing to the *Hane Tribune,* every now and then, the number of rattlesnakes butchered.) Pumping in the new land, beating it flat, white, arid, unfrustrating, and then moving back in a few cabbage palms here, one royal palm there to landscape, beautify, renature, the surface. And, most importantly, building the Cape Revere Golf and Tennis Club for residents. But not enough lots sold, and the *Hane Tribune* continually ran the contractor's advertisements exhorting Haneites to come down, join, enjoy the salve.

They had given him two courts, two hard surface courts because they needed no maintenance, or none beyond the sweeping that was the next job in his morning routine. If he could build interest, they would provide more courts, but they must have known he was not going to build interest. He was not a young, money-hungry pro. He had been that, made that projection, seen through it, and Peg and the two children as a result had left him. They went back to Westchester and he elected not to return for the lucrative summer. Once taken, the decision made everything fall into place.

He went back into the shop, checked his lesson book—one lesson with Brian when Brian got there after school. Brian the ambitious, prodded by his parents, one of whom always sat at the side of the courts and jotted down Brian's errors. He was free then til 3:30—a typical day. In May the club was vacant anyway, and there were continual rumors of not being paid.

He got the heavy stiff bristle broom out from behind his hydraulic stringer purchased in that moneyed interval when he had been the pro at the Hane Country Club. The stringer paid for itself there in six months, but he regretted the evenings when hours passed as he fitted first one clamp then another, one awl then another, waxed one set for crossing then another. But there were always people at the Hane Club. Even at 11:30 at night when he left his elaborate shop, someone sitting in the moonlight by the pool would offer to buy him a drink.

"Come on Frank, you can't work all night."

And then he got home later which made Peg madder. But the bills were paid, the house purchased, the car repaired. However, he played less and less, taught more and more. It was disappointing, so in a volley of self-will he vowed to reverse the process. That was not what they paid him for. It was an interesting struggle. He went to the mat with them. He fought, argued, insinuated, he got a tremendous kick out of that, but in the end they axed him—with surprisingly little severance pay.

He dragged the broom out along the walk by the pool. Mike, the lifeguard, climbed up to his chair, his plump tawny body glistening with oil. He nodded to Frank, who cranked the broom handle in acknowledgment.

His own body had been blessed once in that summit of his game at twenty-two. When to quit singles, twenty-five? Thirty? Certainly no later. At twenty-two his body, browned but not oily plump, had been as good a retrieving and attacking machine as he would possess. But the toughest muscles, the tightest sinews then were only strengthened for what? A local ranking that would go down, and down, and find a level below sea level (despite Cape Revere's filled land)—a level so nicely summed up by two courts in need of no maintenance, adjacent to a vacant golf course, near a vacant club house, in a vacant season that never ended, never began. With the end of the broom handle he flicked the gate latch up. He never missed it. He always forced the gate on the first try.

MEET THE BALL AT THE TOP OF THE BOUNCE, OR ON THE RISE

In the morning, dew sparkled on the link fence surrounding his courts, dew shimmered on the green background wind-break, clamped four feet from the ground and ending two feet from the top of the fence. To enter his courts was to enter, in the morning, a glistening pen of greens and rhinestones. Yet by 11:00 the irritant glitter was gone, sun scattered, traceable only in the coruscation on the galvanized wire. He stood at the east corner and plotted the brooming. The sweeping prevented boredom, so he thought. But it was not a matter of dragging the broom as on clay. On the hard surface the broom had to be lifted and stroke pushed, lifted, stroke pushed, and for all the effort not much accumulated before the bristles. Whoever used the courts? Brian in the afternoons—meticulously clean. Three old men on the weekends. On clay, at the Hane Country Club, he had liked to watch the ridge of claydust which ran before the broom and the even leveling after. Here, his strokes could not disturb the concrete surface and yielded no evidence of his energy. It was difficult, but a routine. And that was how to pass the days.

The rasp stroke of the stiff bristles dominated his courts. He worked quickly brooming from the back court to the net. On this surface that was the way to play, the way to broom. Get the fissures behind you. Get to net. Put the ball, the trash, away. And if at the end of the brooming, if you had, after the careful lift stroke pushing (the tedious overlapping of one lane of cleanliness on another), if then as you eased the bristles toward the final edge of grass, if then the steady broom delivered to the lawn only one gum wrapper brought all that way, what did it matter? An hour had passed—and the reward was the same for the keenest volley on the most crucial match point.

Beyond the fence, on the west side of the courts there was a white metal table and two aluminum chairs. He righted the broom, carried it out, flung it down so that in settling the long handle nearly whacked his leg, and then sat in one of the chairs. Just south of the courts there was a series of condominium apartments, offering he understood from Mrs. Silvern (whose apartment overlooked his courts) a paid-up initiation fee for the Cape Revere Club with each purchase. A widow and bored, lonely, well to do, she pestered him— waving, laughing, cajoling, on her way to lunch at 12:30 every day but Monday in the club dining room. He could sit for her arrival, but he did not want to. What else was there?

At noon the sky was a solid block of blue in which the bell of sun clanged and clanged, cringing the greens of his courts paler. Across the road which led to the main entrance on the west, Mr. Sweeting, the grounds keeper, atop a rotary tractor, was mowing the heavy lawn. There, at least, were lanes of cleanliness clearly marked. Sweeting slumped on the foam rubber seat, rippling with each jostle. He was an old man, a genuine Floridian, born in Hane and never beyond it. Frank did not think it possible for Mr. Sweeting to be outside of Hane.

There was the scent of fresh cut grass. Frank got up. He liked Sweeting. He never thought of him as hired help. He saw himself that way. Sweeting seemed, rather, a permanent structure in Hane who merely bent this way and that to let the recent Haneites flow by. Sweeting's face had apparently swallowed sunlight, was puckered in a myriad of needle thin wrinkles, crow's feet, furrows and freckles. His eyes, always squinting, always recessed in the sunlight, opened wider in the shade. They filled with surprise at how Hane had grown—what Hane had attracted.

"I can remember when there was nothing here but swamp." Sweeting stopped the tractor, but the rotary blade still clattered whirling.

"Turn it off will ya!" Frank shouted.

Sweeting smiled. The motor sputtered dying. "I'm supposed to finish this strip before lunch."

"Siroka tell you that?"

Sweeting squinted, adjusted himself on the seat, "Yes, sure did. Can't say that he can do much about it. I was thinking about how you could get more lessons."

Frank thought about turning away. He could feel himself dropping, dropping—landing on that solid green floor of pretense. "It's mainly the lack of members," he was appalled at the business-like tone he spoke in. "But the club will grow. I'll probably try to get a youth group going over the summer. It'll build. I'm on the job." He felt hungry. "Besides, I could always have your job."

"I reckon you could. Almost anytime you know." Sweeting leaned down from the rusted orange tractor. Frank anticipated a joke. He never quite knew what Sweeting's attitude was. "You know I'm not even supposed to be riding one of these. Course Siroka doesn't care. But my doc doesn't think it helps my stomach at all."

"You want me to finish the strip?"

Sweeting looked at him hesitating. Frank stepped up on the machine.

"All right, old man, get out of the seat. I'll finish your goddam work for you."

Mr. Sweeting got down. He arched his back bulging a stomach which looked as hard as the tumor it suggested. "I'll take your lessons," Sweeting said smiling.

So he knew. Frank answered, "No, you take the youth group." He laughed. Sweeting chuckled.

"How do you start it?" Frank asked, then pulled the correct knob. Sweeting stepped away. He waved his arm in a slow rectangle, indicating how to finish the strip.

WHEN OUT OF POSITION LOB TO THE BACKHAND CORNER, OR SLAM TO THE CENTER

He made the rough rectangle smaller and smaller, then double cut the cuttings. Fine particles, needles of grass, spewed out from under, at first pluming behind, then on the second cut, misting. Mr. Sweeting had settled by the white table. Now he rocked back and Frank saw him fall into his standard half-slumber.

What was better than the scent of grass? Orange groves? Perhaps. The thick lawns of Westchester. How green they were! How brownish flat, under-nourished was Hane! Yet there, as here, what were the options? To go round and round. At the Westchester club the trip from the back to the fore court, the fence to the net, retrieving balls, standing at the cord holding a pile of balls, locked to the elbow in fuzz, and blandly stating, "Take your racket back. See the ball hit the strings. Turn. Shift the weight to the front foot."—Was that not the same as the continual mowing of rectangles of grass? Around and around. Surely Peg could see why he did not go back. Surely. But no. She had gone back because that is what they had always done. That was the order of things—an order for things: cars and houses; clothes and dinners out—in short, the unwasted life. As if in purchase of movement or something they could avoid the freckling sun, the crow's feet and furrows. A southern girl she never tanned. She was always ashen. Her skin stretched so softly in eggplant smoothness. Oh Peg, nothing of the needle thin wrinkles of Hane.

He cut the motor. Mr. Sweeting, disturbed by the silence, leaned forward. "Lunch?" Frank shouted.

Mr. Sweeting unfolded his arms, shook his head.

"What's a matter, food not good enough?" Frank approached him, "Siroka give you indigestion?"

"Henph! I don't care about him. My wife's coming. She'll bring lunch."

"She drive all the way down from Hane?"

"It's her day off."

"Well, that strip's never been cut better. Try to do as well next time, eh?" Sweeting smiled, stroked his stomach, closed his eyes.

Frank went back through his pro shop—the scent of rubber and starch, normalcy. He paused. He was not hungry, but it was time. He knew after he tasted food his hunger would build. He thought about rearranging the shop, as if he would have traffic, congestion, sales. He laughed a little to himself, opened the inside door which led to the court before the dining room. The gravel was fresh washed. Willie stood in the corner, holding the hose, moving it back and forth limply from his hand, dangling it over the stones to give them the polish of moisture, the luster which dried out.

There were sliding glass doors to the dining room. Frank came through right at the center. In the season he would have had to come through the kitchen. Now only the three waitresses retained in May sat at the large round group table. There were, however, two drinks on the table near Frank's entrance. Women golfers he thought. He took a small table by himself, near the bar. He did not hold that kitchen was different from professional help. He did not see the gradation—Peg did. But he simply did not care for the three waitresses. Thelma he found sweet but aging and cloying. The others dirty, acid-tongued, demanding, what have you. He could not imagine marriage to any of them. Now, least of all Peg.

Thelma got his order. It was standard, no choice (Siroka's rules), today Welsh rarebit on toast with cole slaw and a swimming fruit salad. The plate was filled with white slosh soaking into the toast. He ordered a Budweiser. Thelma shook her head as she put it down. He smiled. In eating he did become hungrier. The two women golfers came back to their table. They wore slacks and metallic blue and red blouses, were tanned, frowzy, and slightly high. In the dining room black topped linoleum tables needed tablecloths, which because it was May, would not appear.

He piled all his food together. Because it was May. Because it was May, all the pros went North, all the pros who made a living went north, took their wives, their kids, their ball-boy machines, practice nets, and baskets of Wilsons, boxes of Moodies—all following the sun or avoiding it. He had not adhered. Just as he had applied, some days, a layer of white sun screen to his nose, so he had shut Westchester out. Shut Peg, the kids, the Wilsons and Moodies out. There would be no blisters, only the moistness of a meal clumped together, and a beer.

The big room was quiet. Once in a while he heard a glass slip into the soap-thick water of the stainless steel sink in the bar behind him—or the phone rang in the front lobby, and the short woman in the black sweater who had come to the waitress table shrugged, got up and ran back to the front. He chewed the soggy rarebit, smiled at the women golfers, felt himself grow bloated.

Then Siroka came in. The small chatter at the waitress table stopped. He was a tall, very stocky man with slicked black hair, a metallic brown suit, black shoes, and nervous eyes. He stopped at Frank's table.

"Look, you got lessons on this afternoon?" he said, slicking back his hair. The voice, gruff, urgent, utterly sincere, amused Frank. Could it be Siroka lived the myth that his club was successful. Would he stand now in the empty dining room and truthfully ask, "Do you have lessons on this afternoon?" Was success such a deception-prompted thing?

Frank wiped his mouth. Siroka leaned in, seemed about to pounce. "One at 3:30," Frank said.

"Oh good!" he straightened up. "You'll be free then. When you finish lunch?"

"In a while."

"When's that?"

"Ten, maybe fifteen minutes."

"That's great," he slicked his hair again. "Good. Good. Look, I'll meet you upstairs in ten minutes. O.K.?"

"What's wrong?"

"Wrong? Did I say anything was wrong? Wrong? Nothing's wrong. I just want you to help me, that's all. A little job."

"I charge $3.50 a half hour," Frank said.

Siroka looked down at him, hard, quizzically, then smiled. "Oh good! How come you're messing up another table?" He laughed, shrugged, and went on.

The rarebit was terrible but to live out his time Frank ate every bit of it. Siroka was waiting for him.

"I need to spray some of the rooms up here."

"What?"

"The rooms. My wife saw a couple roaches last night. She won't let the kids back in the rooms."

"Why didn't you have Willie or Sweeting spray them?"

Siroka looked at him incredulously. "Look, they're our rooms."

"But the club owns them. Certainly it's part of club business."

"Of course it's club business. Of course it is. But they're *our* rooms. You think I let just anybody in our rooms?"

"Oh, I didn't understand."

"Come in here. I'll get the spray."

They went into his office. He dragged a large tank shaped like a milk cannister from behind his desk. "This is a heavy son of a bitch. Grab hold will ya?" They carried it outside, then down the maroon carpeted corridor. Siroka stopped twice: once to rest and the second time to get a can of Raid from a closet at the end of the hall. They dragged the tank through a screen door, across an open porch, which overlooked the golf course, and then into another corridor.

"My wife is so damn finicky about bugs. Here we are." He opened the door. "My little girl's room. These rooms are supposed to be picked up."

The room was a narrow cubicle holding one spongy bed, a chest, and secretary with a flap down used as a desk. There were dolls on the bed and books and two broken toys. Shoes were just under the edge of the spread trailing on the floor.

"We'll shoot the baseboard first."

"How old's your daughter?" Frank said.

"Eight. How old's yours? Drag that closer."

"Nine I guess. Yes, nine."

"All right, pull up that handle. That's right, all the way up. Now when I give you the signal push it down real slow. I don't want to flood this place. Set?"

"O.K."

"Good. Oh good! Go ahead. Push!"

As gently as possible Frank eased the handle down, feeling the fluid give against him. Siroka grasped the tube from the tank firmly and directed the squirt neatly along the baseboard. There was the scent not of cut grass, nor orange blossoms, rather, a thick flour-ammonia smell which expanded.

"Stop. We gotta move the bed," Siroka smiled, embarrassed at how much work it had turned out to be. That Siroka could be concerned at all surprised Frank. They pulled the bed out from the wall, then the secretary and chest—each time spraying the baseboard. Finally they dragged the tank back out into the hall.

"We might not be able to finish this before my lesson," Frank said.

"Really?"

Frank didn't answer.

"Well, look, we'll skip my son's room. He's got to learn how to live with bugs anyway. We'll do Rita's room, ours. She's the one bitching anyway. She's the only one who could have got me doing this."

"Yes, I guess we can get that one done."

"Oh good. I kept saying, why cut myself off over a few bugs? Know what I mean?"

"Yes."

"If getting rid of the few bugs is all it takes, then get rid of the bugs. Why cut myself off? This is getting lighter, notice that?" Siroka seemed genuinely surprised.

The master bedroom was filled with religious statues. Several Madonnas stood on several corner shelves. Three crucifixes hung from the walls. And there were pictures and scapulars.

"Rita's very religious. We're Polish you know. Not much stuff to move in here." Siroka threw himself into pushing chairs. "I want to set it up so we can go right around. We gotta put it on thick, else Rita won't believe we did it."

This time Frank aimed the tube. The white bug spray trickled down off the baseboard, puddled on the green linoleum. He went right around the room, then right around the walk-in closet.

"Help me move the stuff back," Siroka said. "I appreciate this. It's not what you're paid for. I know that and I appreciate it. Look, while I drag the tank back, you seal up this place and spray with the Raid."

"Around the windows?"

"No, everywhere. I mean everywhere. Fill the whole room up. She won't be able to sleep in here tonight. She'll know we got the bugs—eh?"

"Close the windows?"

"Right. Good! I'll take this back to the office."

"O.K."

"Seal it up good and really spray it on." Siroka slammed the door.

After he had shut the two casement windows, Frank sat down on the bed. Ammonia scent and heat. The room was nearly stifling. Why cut myself off? He had to laugh at that. Fondling the Raid can he turned, looked at all the corners of the room and decided where to start spreading his film. He filled the closet with the gasoline-scented mist. Would it stain the clothes? He closed off the closet, sprayed the windows, then the hanging corner shelves, spreading an oily frosting on the blue statues of the Virgin. Then stepping back he aimed the can high, pressed down full, and waving his arm back and forth, plumed out a fine mist which fell too directly. He moved more quickly spraying thicker and thicker plumes. Some of the mist hung in the air, finally obscuring the view to the windows. He kept back stepping, still sending out arcs of spray. He made his cloud a delicate reticulation of mist and moisture, bulbous and stretched almost to eye level. Above it though, from three walls there was Jesus in iron, in plastic, in wood, watching as he eased out of the door. Why should I cut myself off?

IN SERVING TOSS THE BALL TO THE MAXIMUM OF YOUR REACH, AND FOR POWER, FORWARD INTO THE COURT

He had a ritual for preparing for a lesson. He bent down and slid the basket of balls out from under the shelf which held his hand stringer. He eased the basket around in front of the counter. He took his favorite Kramer racket from off the peg-board clamp. Brian could give him a game. The gut-strung racket would be appropriate. At the Hane Country Club he had given most of his lessons with a lesser Kramer strung with profected nylon. He brought the gut out, then, only for special games against excellent juniors, or prestigious members. The nylon stood up better. He had given lessons right after a rain—sometimes even in a mist that would have doomed the gut. Now Brian alone was his special case.

Today there was no mist, no breeze—sun-hammered sky, hot, forcing sweat, his favorite tennis weather. He banged the heel of his left palm into the strings, listening for the correct twang. He could string a racket by tone. 3:15. He put the racket down, clacking on the glass counter top. He picked up the tube of sun screen and using the plate glass as a mirror applied a careful layer to his nose. The cream was itchy, sticky. He felt momentarily like a warrior. His legs, he thought, took up a certain spring with the application. His shoulders felt larger, shoving at the Moody knit shirt. In deference to the May sun, he should have worn a hat, but today he didn't feel like it. He picked up the basket, wedged it awkwardly against his side, picked up the racket and went outside.

His dark glasses were still on the white metal table. He put the basket down. Usually Brian was early but not today. He put the glasses on, nudged the basket into the court, thought about hitting a few serves, but rejected the idea and sat down.

Then he saw Brian's mother. A short plump woman in tight Bermuda shorts and a green blouse, she waved to him and indicated by arm motion that Brian was in the locker room. She carried, as always, a large yellow pad.

"How'd Brian do in Orlando?" he said, "I didn't see anything in the paper."

"He got to the finals. Frank, how are you? But lost to a boy four years older." She firmly put the pad down, snapping it on the white table. "Lord, what a tournament! Mismanaged? I've never seen anything like it. And the finals in the rain. You know how rain bothers Brian. I, mind you, I got reprimanded for pointing out to the umpire—what a jerk—that the rain spotted Brian's glasses every time he looked up to serve. It seems to me that's pretty unfair to Brian. But the other boy was local. I told Brian he had to expect that. In the sanctioned tournaments things will be different. Mostly it was his low backhands. I've never seen him hit so many into the net. Of course the other boy was smart. He kept feeding them to Brian. But Brian couldn't seem to chip them up. He was picking up the tape all, I mean all, of the time. After the first set I told him, 'Forget about the corners. Try cross court with some top—anything. Get the ball back.' But that only rattled him more. I should have stayed quiet. His father's smarter that way."

"He probably wasn't getting down to the ball."

"Yes. That's it exactly. But he thinks he just had an off day. He could have beaten that boy. I guess too many things were stacked against him. You're right. I should have told him to get down, bend his knees. You know he's so lazy. Course all of 'em at that age are so lazy about anything, anything at all. He chokes up, stops stroking, then it's just a matter of time, but he'll learn."

"Listen," Frank said, "he's a fine tennis player right now."

"Oh, I know that, but it would please his father so if he could win one or two big tournaments."

"Like Wimbledon?" Frank laughed.

She looked at him quizzically. "What's he going to do today?"

"Well, I guess we better work on low backhands."

"I wouldn't do that. He'll think I put you up to it. Why don't you just play him some. Just games, or a pro set."

Penalty for the Wimbledon remark, Frank thought. She was skeptical of his playing ability, he knew that. And doubtless since she had not been able to join the Hane Country Club, she was hesitant about accepting its cast-offs. But ah, how she belonged at Hane! She drew a chair up to the table, brought out her ball point pen. It was all decided. Brian would humiliate him.

"Well, I suppose that would do. It's my kind of weather."

She nodded, apparently writing a box score up already.

Brian came out through the pro shop. Short and pudgy, though his fat portended elongation, he walked slowly toward the courts.

"Get us a can of balls," Frank called out. "No practice today, we'll play some." He pulled the basket of balls back out through the gate. He knew Brian was steady but no threat. At a moderate pace the boy could hit all day from the back court, but once the speed picked up, once Frank began rushing net, Brian's errors would multiply. He would begin to look pleadingly toward his mother. Frank swallowed, shook his head slightly. Had it come to this concern: how to clobber a fourteen-year-old?

Brian came back, "Mom tell you about Orlando?"

"Yes, that was great, just getting to the finals."

"I could have beaten him. But the umpire made us finish in the rain. It smeared my glasses. How come we're playing?"

"Seemed like a good idea."

"Brian," she said, "take a good long warm up." She smiled at Frank.

There came the usual hiss as Brian opened the can of Wilson balls. They went into the court. He took the north court, facing into the sun. He did not like to begin serving. The serve was the weakest part of his game. It fell apart in the tension of a match first. He preferred to work into it. Get a sweat up and then start serving. Would they spin to see who would serve first? He didn't think so. Ironically, as the older, as the pro, he could say to Brian, "You go ahead and serve." It would be taken as a gracious gesture, giving the boy the advantage. And changing on the odd game would get him out of the sun for his first serve. He knew he was plotting as if Wimbledon had come to Hane.

Brian began the rally. His balls were coming short, a foot or two beyond the service line. It was a poor way to practice. In a match, having warmed up this way, he might never find the range. But the boy was hitting smoothly, turning, stroking, nothing to suggest he was upset at the prospect of playing.

"Lift your sights," Frank called. "Hit deeper, aim higher over the net. Send a few out even. Get the feel of the court." He felt magnanimous, powerful, for he knew all he had to do was say a few more words and he could rattle Brian irrevocably. But he had limited himself. He could have suggested dropping a shoulder or changing a grip and then watched amused as Brian clumsily extricated himself from a new style. Brian's mother would have seen through it. So he had made the proper instruction. A good student, properly instructed, should excel his teacher. Wasn't that so?

And then he fell silent, lapsing into that pre-game euphoria somewhere between concentration and instinct, loping effortlessly, delighting in each shock of delivery as the ball leapt to his directing. He knew he hit with a mild slap motion. It was not a perfect stroke, especially on his forehand. He met the ball too far forward, compensated by cocking his wrist, flicking it at impact. But on a fast surface court, such as this, a slap stroke had its advantages. Hard-hit balls skidded off irretrievable. He could really put them away. The surface gave him percentages. The slap stroke wasn't steady, but on the concrete he would have to hit less of them. Besides he had always delighted in the speed, the thrust of tennis. He never cared to retrieve. A well-hit, a slammed fault, was more enjoyable than a cautious, well-placed serve. He had tried as a serious tournament player to correct that flaw in himself. It had cost him victories. But he could not entirely suppress the conviction that joy sprung from going down slugging. On grass he could win slugging. That was an almost overwhelming experience—enjoyment and victory in one match! Now, as if to drive home his feeling, he waited for a high forehand and when Brian sent one, slashed it away into the backhand corner. The boy, awed by the speed, did not even turn to run.

Frank felt Brian was somewhat comical: bulging stomach of early adolescence. Brian couldn't move very well, that would be his flaw, just as a certain power lust had been mine, Frank thought. But who could tell what the boy would grow into? Frank followed a short ball to net. His volley was always the strength of his game. He hung in on the top of the net almost by instinct and when his reflexes were sharp (as on days like this) his slap stroke rifled points away. At the net he never came out of a crouch. Even his low volley had a deceptive sharpness to it. But there was no rhythm in net play—at least not with Brian. The boy had too much difficulty returning his volleys.

"Try a few lobs please," Frank said. Brian nodded. The first one came too short to be hit as an overhead.

"Sorry," Brian said.

"That's normal. Get the range."

The next lob arched high but not deep. At the last minute, Frank had to bend to get his racket fully on it. The third was better—over his backhand, high, deep, unwobbling. He back stepped, remembered to turn, leapt up, watched white fuzz against the blue until the ball fused with the sun in a prickling, white blast of light, swung, felt the shock, landed blinking. He had pulled it into the alley, but there had been pace, terrific pace, on the shot.

"One more," he called out, though he could not yet see Brian clearly, blinded by periodic sunspots in his eyes. Brian's shot was short and on the forehand. Frank closed on the net, swung hard without turning, met the ball full. He slammed it into the forecourt. The ball bounced high toward the second court. Brian made a snap decision and went after it. He sprinted well, far into the other court, reached out and, though off the wrong foot, stroked the ball back up into the air. It was an excellent lob.

"Nice get," Frank said, catching the ball. "You look ready. Are you?"

"Yes."

He threw him the ball. "Go ahead and serve."

IN DOUBLES CHIP, IN SINGLES STROKE

His practice serves were all long, but he hit them smoothly. Brian didn't seem to tighten up.

"Ready," he called out, holding two balls up to indicate play was about to begin. He rocked back, came into the serve too quickly and faulted it in the middle of the net. Frank crouched down. The second serve would drop short. He instinctively shuffled forward waiting for it. There was no pace on it at all. Frank had time to turn, cock and slap the ball away cleanly into the backhand corner. He followed his shot to net but Brian didn't make a move to retrieve.

"Get the first ball in," Frank said sharply, "and deeper. Serves like that will get crammed down your throat every time."

Brian nodded. Out of the corner of his eye Frank saw Brian's mother jotting down notes. On the next point Brian double-faulted. Rattled already, Frank thought, the victory cheapening with each error. He won the game at love. When they changed courts he said, "You should have served more practice balls. Don't ever be afraid to take dozens of them."

There was no question of the outcome now. Frank felt himself relaxing. Once on top, the pressure eased. He could take more chances and that would demoralize the opposition even more. He could be magnanimous. He served easily and elected to stay in the back court. Brian returned deeply, rushed into position and they sparred at long range. There was the rhythm again. He hit easily, with the depth and loft, not so much of a stroke as a push. It was dangerous, but he was confident. Even with his experience such casual soft hitting could choke him up, force him into a pushing game which would favor Brian who could run all day. By prolonging the rally he knew he was building Brian's confidence. But if he built the boy's game up a little, wouldn't it be more enjoyable? Wasn't he paid for that?

Surprisingly, Brian chipped back one of Frank's short shots and closed toward the net. It was arrogant, but there he was, pudgy and determined, hanging in right on top of the net. Frank ran deep to the backhand, tossed up a lob. Brian backed up, eyed the ball carefully, but only half swung at the overhead. Frank was set for a slam. It was disconcerting. He had to leap back again, deeper this time to the backhand. He elected to go down the line, figuring that Brian would be set for another lob, but the boy had moved to the alley, outguessing him. He met the ball sharply, but was not far enough in front of it to get good cross-court angle. His volley was within reach. Frank wheeled, lunged, opening the face of his racket, spearing a short lob neatly down the backhand line. It would be a winner. Frank straightened up, elated, but Brian had sprinted after the ball, had reached it, and now, his back to Frank, actually managed a backhand high enough, deep enough, to keep Frank away from the net, keep the rally going. Frank, winded, disappointed, back-pedalled and stroked, adding a little pace. However, Brian, alert, crouching, was in position. He seemed ready to close on the net again. Frank was breathing harder. No matter how the point turned out he knew he would have to give away a few more just to rest. But it would be bad psychology to lose the point. He felt he had to stay in with Brian. And for the first time he felt he could not count on an error. He would have to force the win. His stroking steadiness would only keep him even. It was not enough to win. He would have to make the extra effort, take the extra risk. When had he first learned it?

He moved toward center court. Brian's shot had not been that short. Frank knew he should have stayed back but he hoped that by crowding in he might panic Brian. He hit soft and deep to Brian's backhand, then sprinted to net. Brian lobbed, short. Frank cocked, met the ball perfectly, put it away. He relaxed, panted. His legs felt dead.

"Good rally," he said. Brian nodded, took his position quickly, waiting for the next point. He's learning, Frank thought. He's trying to pressure me. Was it pressure or just the natural impatience of a youth who wanted to get on with the game—someone so utterly confident now that he wanted to speed time and the inevitable up. Frank was thinking back as he slowed, walking toward the baseline, of another match twelve years before. A match which seemed now his last effort in exhibition—against a 16-year-old who stroked flawlessly, relentlessly, and who burned to win. That dedication, that was the upsetting part. Frank expected to triumph but lost. He had fallen then, as now, into the natural sway of shots, but they had all come back. The exhibition had drawn well at the Hane Public Courts. A crowd, linesmen, ball boys, an umpire who was Chinese (former Davis cupper) and who shouted the score incomprehensibly: "Oddvontage Surva!" Against a lanky junior who hit all the balls back. The Chinaman perched aloft, hunched over his score card, like Brian's mother over her pad. A sky as pale as this one, as hard, unetchable as this. More sweat then—longer rallies—a clay court. But the same perception. Steadiness was not enough. He would have to force the win. But the boy was tireless.

Frank served and followed to net. He did not know where he found the energy. Brian, awed (he guessed), didn't turn for position, rather chipped to Frank's feet. The low volley worked, went deep and cross court. Brian was there, tried a slashing backhand which only bulged the middle of the net.

"Oddvontage Surva!"

Frank thought he would have to go to net each time, every time. The long run pulling out his legs. The long run working its cold fingers into flaccid thigh muscles, pinching off, for an instant, calf muscles. What if the boy lobbed? What if the run up was only the beginning of the run back? Frank served hard. Brian thrust his racket out, blocked the serve and surprisingly lobbed perfectly. At the service line Frank made a wrenching turnabout, watching the lob as it drifted almost eerily toward the forehand corner. For an instant he thought, hoped, it would go out. But no. He sprinted back, ran hard. He hit a half lob return—regained position. Brian hadn't moved to the net. That was stupid. Had the boy crowded in, the point would have ended there. Instead Brian loped easily to Frank's shot, returned it deep to the backhand and then followed to net. Frank tossed up a good lob, but Brian, went up on giraffe legs, cocked, slammed, angling the ball short to the forecourt, out of play. Frank was exhausted. Brian hurried back to position, not even breathing hard. So it was finished Frank thought. After a few points which experience might salvage, endurance would prevail. The longer the rallies the less chance of victory.

Frank rubbed his leg, bounced the ball before serving—letting breath slow down a bit. Not to this kid, he thought. From a private, desperate reserve he summoned enough energy to hit two blazing serves. Brian erred on both of them.

"Your game," Brian said.

"Yes," he answered. "Concentrate. My serve wasn't that hard. You shouldn't have missed it."

"It was the hardest serve I've ever."

"Oh, come on," Frank laughed.

"Well, it was. Do you know how hard you hit?"

"I'm a pusher."

Brian's mother laughed.

Not hard enough, not sure enough, not long or steady enough. The brittle, blue light sky astounding even through the dark glasses, and now not enough energy to last another set, not enough detachment to be amused at his own racking. And then too much detachment. The loser climbed right out of his skin, completed the stroking, rushed to net and was passed, leapt high and lost overheads in the sun, raced to the backcourt to face down drop shots, was continually lurching in the wrong direction.

The end always began when he started watching this loser, this alien mired in his own skin. It had to be somebody else—somebody else with aching, half-cramping legs and no desire to win. He drew further and further away, thinking: on that distant, green court there's a fellow in white shorts and tired legs who's going to lose. He thinks well enough, but he runs poorly and very probably he doesn't care enough about each point. In a way he is amusing, getting caught flatfooted and standing straight up all the time. But he is going to lose. Leave him to his own devices. It's not a team sport. Let him lose separately. Would that salvage pride?

Brian held two balls up—a summons to get ready to play within the lines and according to the surface. The loser apparently hated the boy but Frank did not. The boy's impatience, the loser's hatred were veneered with amusement. The little game going on below. The separate Frank, the observing Frank, two figures refusing to blend and hence causing disaster. But merge of course they did—delusions only of separation. He felt them hug, loser and observer, beneath the crisp, scratchy towel, felt them lock together in the ripple wave of cramp as he slumped against the fence. As he watched Brian lower his racket, all matches became one. He heard the Chinaman of that prior exhibition, heard him try to say the right thing, the right consolation for Frank's loss. But he had trouble with the language. He wanted to say "good match" but it came out, "goo motch." A thousand points gone by, a million balls hit. Legs pounding, knees rising, earth receding, and the perfect consolation for the wasted man—"Goo motch, Frank, goo motch!"

ON CRUCIAL POINTS DISGUISE YOUR SHOTS EVEN IF IT MEANS CHANGING YOUR STROKE

"Are we going to finish the set?" Brian said. "I'm hitting much better now. I'm getting down to the ball."

"Time's up," Frank said. "Besides, you were hitting too many balls back."

Brian's mother stood up, angry, thwarted. He expected her to offer payment for another half-hour, and he did not know how to answer this. He projected himself before her on his knees, saying. "I decided not to go back north this summer, not to try again, and lately I've been so tired, as if muscles holding, now released, have given up. I don't think I can play another game, another rally. Forgive. Put your sweet white fingers in my hair. Ah, hold me up, Brian's sweet mother." What would she say? The scene amused him especially now as she burned with frustration.

"We can try again tomorrow," he said.

"What time?" she asked.

"Oh, in the morning. I'm fresher then."

"So's Brian."

"Good then, how about 11:00?"

"Too late. I play golf then."

"Oh," he looked at her.

"Try 10:00," she said.

"I guess that will be all right. I'll get the sleep out of my eyes."

"Come on, Brian."

"Thanks," Brian said.

Frank nodded, picked up the stiff towel and raked it across his forehead, down his arms. All business, they walked away. He slumped beside the white metal table. The sky was darkening. The court greens grew richer, and for the first time the fence cast a shadow longer than itself. He heard splashing from the pool. For a good while the delicious exhaustion of the game held him—not that he had played that long or hard. Ten games or whatever would never have bothered him before. But now—no matter, physical tiredness was the purest joy he knew. If only such enervation could persist. Renewal was the enemy. Resumption the terror. His feet flat on the grass seemed to grow right out of the earth, his body diffused to the air. All of the coolness of the sky seemed to wrap him up, trading him for its currency: beads of sweat. To be so permanently tired as to be beyond pretense, illusion, ultimately care itself—that was the gift of the game. That and a good night's sleep.

Mrs. Silvern came out from the pro shop, stood hanging on the open door, her short yellow dressed body framed by the darkening aluminum strips. Then she saw him and came wobbling quickly at him.

"Is lunch just getting over?" he said.

"No, why no. It's bridge day. You know that!" her voice, as always, was high, rasping, somewhat phlegmy. "I looked for you when I came over. I thought we should have dinner tonight. I'm a damn good cook you know. And I thought with Peg away you might be getting tired of the fare." She pointed to the dining room. "Besides, you've never seen the apartment. It's scrumptious and I keep it just as neat as a pin—not that I'm a finicky woman. Harry used to say, 'Louise, you think dust undisturbed is no dirt.' Harry, ah now there was a finicky man. He was hell to live with but how I miss him. You hear me, Harry. I miss you. That's why I dust. Oh Harry, I do miss you so."

Frank was thinking, "I could have tried harder. I can try harder. If you can just stay with a junior—stay with him long enough, he'll fold up. They can't yet take the pressure. They will fold up, but you have to stay with them, keep the pressure on.''

"What would you like for dinner? Nothing too elaborate now. Are you listening to me? Come on now. That's not polite. Harry used to do that too. I used to say the most elaborate things to him, and suddenly I'd realize he was a million miles away. No come on. What do you want for dinner?''

"A martini.''

"Oh good! But you'll have to make it. I never mix the drinks. Harry always handled that, and well too. So well! You hear me Harry?'' She turned, addressed the fence, the segmented shadows of the court.

Frank wondered if he could stand dinner with her.

"When do you want to come over?'' she asked.

"Let me shower first.''

She smiled at him with infinitely knowledgeable coyness. It flabbergasted him, for an instant an actual message came from her. But she was hardly southern—tanned not ashen, rasping not soft-spoken, and easily to top it off, 68 years old. He shuddered internally. It had come to this. Exhausted by juniors, he had been left to fill the fantasies of seniors.

A meal at the club was no prospect. "About an hour,'' he said.

"Good,'' she answered, "that'll give me time to get the smell of cards off my hands. See you then. Apartment 10, right by the pool, on the ground floor. Oh, this'll be such fun.'' She made the move of kicking up her right leg. He had to laugh.

The shower smelled of sulfur. The soap filmed rather than lathered. Siroka must have cut the softener back. A typical move in May to reduce overhead. He resented it. Then he stood in the locker room, watching the grey asbestos walls. But there was a nice contrast. The evening sun had stroked the upper ventilation jalousies a rose color. Rose and grey—starchy concrete underfoot— and an ache the length of his body. He sat down on the blue green bench, rested his right arm on a locker handle. He thought about calling Peg. She never dusted well.

He got dressed, closed the shop, leaving the golf bags out till later. Dew would form. Manny, the golf pro, would be irritated but no matter. His anger might liven the day. He paused at the courts, noticed the broom, sighed, and brought it back, unlocked the shop and tucked the broom clumsily in the darkness away behind the stringer.

He had no trouble finding apartment 10. Reflected light from the pool, blue, shimmering, clearly lit the number. Would she meet him in a flimsy negligee? He shook his head, knocked, and went in. The air conditioning was on, rumbling.

"The bugs,'' she called out from the kitchen. She had not changed her dress, merely put a green apron on over it. "You know those no see 'ems—that's what Harry used to call 'em. Actually 'no see 'em' is a southern expression and Harry never really was in the South. I don't know where he picked it up. Where did you Harry? Eh, where? Where did a nice Chicago boy like you learn that southern expression? You didn't have a nice southern belle did you? Oh, but the martinis. The bar's in here.'' She pointed to the end of the kitchen. "I put the glasses in the freezer. Harry liked that. He liked that. Harry demanded that. Oh, he was hell to live with, but you go ahead."

"Do you want one too?"

"I certainly do. We're going to have a party aren't we?" She stroked his arm. "And it's getting cool in here."

"What's for dinner?"

"Oh now, don't ask that. Don't you! You let me take care of that. I want it to be a surprise. It's going to be wonderful."

He made the drinks. She took hers and said, "Now I want you to see the apartment. It's bigger you know than a lot of houses. Of course, I spent a fortune furnishing it, but I kept thinking. You know I'm not such a spring chicken, am I?" She slipped her arm around his. They walked out of the kitchen into a den which opened directly on the living room. "So if I spent a little more now on some things, who could care? All his hard money for frills like these." She pointed to the valence boards. "And wall to wall carpeting. The bedrooms!" She dragged him. He had finished his martini.

"Harry liked yellow of course, but not this much." She set her drink down, sat on the edge of the bed. "There's no view in here. All the windows are up, so people walking out front can't see in. You never met Harry did you?"

"No."

"Of course not. That was before I moved here—four years before in Chicago. And the bathroom." Abruptly she got up. "Small, just the right size. Do your business and get out. But cheery. So cheery. I like a bathroom to wake you up, start the day right."

"Yes, do you want another?" He held his glass up.

"Yes. Yes, of course. But take a look at the guest bedroom."

There was no view there either and they went back from the yellows and blues to the soft pale browns of the living room. He made a second martini.

"You ever hear the people upstairs?" They sat in green velvet chairs, drank, watched each other and noticed the silence thickening. Finally she said, "Eh?"

"You know, drop shoes or what have you upstairs."

"Of course they do. That's what an apartment's all about. Now the Mellows are moving out because the people above them have kids and the kids are always tumbling around, thumping. But I don't have to tell you that. How many children do you have?"

"Two."

"Mr. Siroka says you're going to stay the summer?"

"Yes."

"Now, you know there's no business here in the summer. It's hotter than blazes."

"Winter either," he said.

She smiled at him, held her glass up. He made two more martinis. Standing in front of the gleaming formica he felt himself relax, subside, under the velour of the gin, as if the props inside the skin had slid, part into part, like a telescope closing up. He could have stirred the pitcher for an hour, fascinated by the slosh-clack of the ice.

She took the drink and leaned back. The fluid lapped over the glass, down the stem.

"It is nice," he said. "The apartment I mean." Why had he forgotten to tell her that before? It was very dark outside. No trace of the sunset. Across the way the stucco of the condominium glowed bluely from the light of the pool.

Pointing at the pool Frank asked, "There any hours on that?"

"I don't care about noise you know. I'm used to it. I've lived in apartments everywhere. Evanston, Lake Forest, Winnetka, Everywhere. Here you can get more for your money. Thicker pile. Bigger rooms." She began looking about the room, motioning vaguely toward the bedroom. "More tile. Heavier drapes. Just more of everything."

"I was wondering about the pool."

"Would you like to swim? A swim! Say, that is an idea. That is a cracker jack of an idea. But it's so cold in here. I wouldn't want to come back in here in the cold. Besides," she leaned forward, crouching, "I haven't been swimming in ten years." She finished her drink. "Oh, don't you say it. Don't call me a killjoy. Why in my time. Don't you call me a killjoy. I haven't even thought about swimming in so long. So long. I love a party. Harry had to drag me home. Why, getting him to stay out til 10:00 was a feat. A real feat. Of course, he enjoyed himself more than he let on. Men are that way. I bet you do the same thing to Peg." She paused. He wondered if she recognized an impropriety. "But just to show you, I'm no killjoy. I, I, what do they say now?"

"About what?"

"You know when you enjoy yourself. A party, everything."

"Swing."

"Yes," she ate the olive and spoke across green particles which slurred her pronunciation. "Yes, I swing. One more and then I'll finish dinner."

He got up, thinking, well, at least dinner has begun. But he was not really hungry. The gin had spun the threads of his concern out and swirling like cotton candy. It was quite enough challenge to stir the pitcher, plunk the ice, pour the drinks. She was humming "The Lady Is a Tramp."

Slumped back in the chair she said, "Remember when they had that party for the young people at the club?"

"Yes."

"Ah, the parties. Harry was the best dancer and he never wanted to go home. My legs would ache and ache and, and. You dance?"

"Not the new ones."

"Oh I mean dance."

"Not now."

"Who said anything about now? To tell the truth I don't think I could get out of this chair. What d'ya think of that Harry Silvern? What d'ya think of them apples? Them apples. He always said that. Them apples. It was his favorite expression. He'd throw a bonus on the dining room table. 'What d'ya think of them apples.' Oh, Harry. Find that record. Put it on."

"Not now."

"Oh, you're worse than Harry. What a stick in the mud. How old are you? Come on, how old are you?"

"Thirty-nine."

"Thirty-nine and too old to dance. Of course, some men don't like to dance. Oh, this is good, so good. And fun." She took another swallow of the

martini. Closed her eyes. The long-stemmed glass in her hand tilted ominously. He would have said something, but he felt sadfully settled, swayed by the drinking. He stared at the pool, listened to the rumbling of the air conditioning. He was thinking of someone for her. Someone to marry her. But he could think of no one appropriate. There was a seventy-year-old Dr. Spanos who came down to the club, shuffled out on to the court, dumped an Abercrombie and Fitch traveling bag filled with tennis balls and then began practicing his serve. He stood hunched over in the backcourt, balls streaming away from his feet. "I had a game," he always said defensively, "but I guess he couldn't make it. I had a game coming." Her expression was the same as his—a game who couldn't make it, wouldn't arrive. In the late afternoon near light, the old doctor, rocking back, tossing the ball directly above him—no need of power forward—and mis-hitting the serve. Did he want to rally? No. Why had he come? To practice what? For what? Their expressions were the same.

"Should I go back north to Peg?" he asked wondering if Mrs. Silvern was asleep.

"Hell no!" she said, rasping, her face still against the velvet. "We're having too much fun right now. Why didn't you go back with her in the first place?"

Perhaps by keeping her eyes closed, her head turned, she's trying to say she doesn't care, Frank thought. "We had our problems. Maybe she was too religious. I don't know." He felt cornered, clumsy, angry.

"That's a problem?"

"Yes, it can be."

"Sure. Sure," she sighed.

Suddenly he felt very, very hungry—realized that she would not cook him a meal. He watched her raise herself enough to finish her drink, eerie blue lit, pale. She dropped back against the chair.

"Mrs. Silvern, I think I better put you to bed. I'll get something to eat over at the club." He got to his feet. The pool seemed to grow brighter, began to move. He shook his head. "Mrs. Silvern?"

There came a faint "Wha?"

"I think I'd better put you to bed." He paused, moved toward her.

"You're the doctor," she said extending her arms.

He held her close to him, walk-wobbling with her to the bedroom. He hoisted her up on the bed. She left one hand about his neck.

"Frank, Frank. Thanks for coming over."

"Mrs. Silvern, I've got to go back to the club."

She dropped her hand, let it reach for the other side of the bed. She patted the opposite pillow, then turned over.

ON SOFT SURFACES RETRIEVE AND RETRIEVE, ON HARD ATTACK AND ATTACK (EXCEPTION: GRASS)

He pulled the spread down underneath her, then brought it back, double folding it across her shoulders. He opened a closet, brought down a green blanket, spread it on the bed so that she could reach it later. She was out all right. He went back into the living room. The pool lights were off. He lit a lamp.

Then wondering about dinner he went into the kitchen. Sure enough there were two Stauffer dinners, chicken breasts, in their trays, sitting in the unlit oven. He thought about cooking them. It would take too long. Of course he could maintain the next day that she had cooked the meal. That might make her feel better. He was sure she wouldn't remember, but it would take too long. From a roller near the sink he got some foil, re-wrapped the trays of chicken and put them back in the freezer. Had she just forgotten about dinner? Who would take care of her? How often did she forget? He didn't notice any pictures of children or grandchildren around the place. How did she get along? It occurred to him that he might have been the very first caller in the new apartment.

He thought about leaving a note. Instead he left a full glass of ice water on the night stand by her bed and put a can of V-8 in the refrigerator to chill.

It was not a clear night. In the late afternoon in summer, clouds piled up from inland, cooled approaching the Gulf, and sent quick torrents on Hane, on the whole west coast. But May, though hot, though buggy, was still not summer. Evenings, afternoons, passed without rain. The threat was there, obscuring the moon. He could see a few stars and also, strangely, some low mist. It was moist but cool out. He breathed deeply. There was a little difficulty walking. He tended to lurch, his shoulders leading his legs. It amused him. Each time he was scared that his feet might not shuffle fast enough to catch up. He expected any moment to be staring face to face with the grass, but he kept on his feet.

He went through the pro shop, clattered through the darkened dining room, and made his way to the kitchen refrigerator. It was not locked. No one was around. Siroka had not made his final check. Frank eased the door open. Not much—two plates of chilled rarebit and five squat bottles of Budweiser, beading up beautifully as he leaned on the open door. He took a plate of rarebit out. Upstairs a door slammed. He listened. He was entitled to dinner, but he still felt thievish. Overhead Siroka was saying, barely audible:

"What d'ya mean? What d'ya mean, deliberate?"

"You know perfectly well I can't sleep in there. D.D.T. on everything."

"Oh that."

"Yes. That. Yes, that exactly. Deliberately."

"I can't win."

"Don't start that. Don't you dare start that."

Frank picked out three bottles, all he could hold in one hand, closed the refrigerator with his hip. He took up the plate and snuck back out through the dining hall. He put the plate down on top of the counter in his shop. There was an opener somewhere around the stringer. He stepped on the broom which snapped at him, and finally found the rusted opener. The rarebit clung to the soggy toast and he ate it like a sandwich, tough custard almost. He opened two beers. He gulped the first down. Cool, thirst quenching. The rarebit seemed much saltier in a gelatin form. Then he sprawled out on the floor in front of the case. He stretched his legs, reached up and brought down the second beer. After the first swallow it occurred to him his room was too large. "The golf bags," he thought. "They must be covered with dew." He took another sip, contemplated leaving them out all night, rejected it, got to his feet. He eased the door open.

They were still there all right, like headless animals on the dark ground. Irons like silver legs speared out in the grass. He drew a five iron out from the nearest bag.

Golf was a less competitive game—an older game. No enduring juniors. Terms only with the wind and grass. He put the beer down, unzippered the ball pouch and spilled three balls out onto the grass, kicked them further from the building—arranged them for blasting. He clasped the iron's handle firmly, locked his fingers, and took a few practice swings. The pressure was off his legs. Tension became more naturally located in his torso. The swing was easy, swooping through the rough. He addressed the first ball. Yes! He whacked the ball, pulling off a little as he started into the down stroke, seeing how it would go, waiting for an unused muscle to twinge. But it was natural right through the shock of collision and follow up. Not lifting his head, he delighted in the metallic clack of club on ball. It must have sailed 100 yards and though he couldn't follow it, he knew it had gone straight.

He let himself go on the next ball, flailed through, straining all the way. Harder shock. He connected lower. A longer wait til the click as it dropped on the distant fairway. If only he could have seen it. On the third shot he jerked his head up determined to follow the whiteness all the way. He topped the ball—laughed as it sluffed, tic-bounced out of sight. Perhaps in the morning he'd hit a few more. There was something to the game, some quality removing it from time, making it less demeaning than a set. Nobility, maturity. That was it. The game had a maturity, a certain maturity to it.

He put the iron back and one by one dragged the bags inside. He stacked them in an L shape, leaving him space to sit on the floor. He finished the second beer, tossed it in the waste basket. He uncapped the last Budweiser. He closed the shop door, and using the stacked bags as handles eased himself down onto the cold terrazzo. There was a terrible darkness. The chrome buckles and zippers barely flickered. He took a deep sniff—still rubber and starch, still Wilson and Moody—not leather, wood and iron. Not yet. He smiled, took a long swallow of the warming beer. Still fuzz and rubber—not leather. But some time the change would come. He sat back hopeful, but not confident, head against the glass of his display case, that the exact moment of transformation would be revealed to him.

Mr. and Mrs. McGill

GEORGE ZORN

from *Perspective*

The courthouse was like all old, small town courthouses. The ceilings were high, everything narrow and dim. Five feet up, the walls were green, the rest cream—old, soured cream that caught the dust on each belly and wave of the plaster.

Rosemary McGill sat drumming her gloved fingers on the scroll arm of the bench where the secretary had asked her to wait. It was on the second floor, in the corridor, and few people passed—a fat woman in a housedress looking up with sad, cow eyes at the slack-mouthed handsome boy she had by the arm. An old man with a cane, hawking, his grizzled chin pushed forth, moving along as if he owned the place.

She found herself thinking about the men again—she couldn't imagine why she kept coming back to that. The three of them standing on the great plateau of junk, the incinerator smokestack behind them, laughing, calling to her in the way they did. Then the youngest one—skinny, handkerchief around his neck, naked to the waist—raising his arm and making that gesture.

Finally the heavy door with the pebbled-glass panel opened and Lieutenant Goist himself came out. "Mrs. McGill," he said, his voice bright, almost jovial. He shook her hand and held the door for her. The secretary left them, moved back down the hall toward the reception desk at the top of the landing.

She had difficulty for a moment once she was inside the office because he surprised her. His voice on the phone that morning had suggested a different man—much older, thin and harried, with perhaps a flaw of some sort in his dentures. The man being kind to her, telling her which was the best chair, couldn't have been more than thirty—straight pale hair, big red face, bull chest that stretched the coat of his suit at the button. Nor could she detect anything wrong with his speech except a slight affectation, a fussiness, that went with neither his appearance nor his otherwise easy and friendly manner.

"I almost gave you up," he said when he'd settled behind the desk.

"I'm afraid I got lost."

"Out by the reservation?"

"I stopped at a little store."

"Koontz's," he smiled familiarly.

She didn't know.

The office was large and neatly kept, but the air was stale and the furniture heavy and old-fashioned. A glass-fronted bookcase. A coat tree. A brown leather couch, humpy, the curve of the arm worn. The pictures were long rectangular photographs, brown with age, of groups of men—policemen, she imagined. There was a large old photograph of a boxer, arms stiffly up, a silk sash about his waist. Behind the lieutenant's desk was a bay window, the Venetian blinds drawn against the sun. But she had a feeling that the tall windows they curtained were painted shut, that even if one wanted. . . .

"I imagine you've come to pay your husband's fine." He sat up, business-like, and leaned across the blotter.

He'd called her that morning—out of the blue—while she'd been killing flies. She'd been sitting on the sun porch looking wearily out—disappointed that among the advertisements in her lap there wasn't a letter from her daughter—when she'd become aware that there were more flies than usual. She'd thought nothing about it until one sat on her lip and in her disgust she'd gone to the kitchen and got the fly-swatter. She was almost through—she'd managed to swat four or five of them—when the phone had rung.

He'd explained that he was a lieutenant of the police in Parkersville and that he had reason to believe her husband was in jail there.

She couldn't think. "Has there been an accident?"

No, he'd been arrested on a drunk and disorderly charge.

And she'd felt immediate relief at that. "I'm sure you're mistaken. . . ."

"Your husband is there then?"

No, she'd explained, Dr. McGill wasn't there. But there wasn't any question about where he was. He was in Chicago, attending a medical convention. . . .

"The woman said he was a doctor."

"Woman?"

So he'd given her the rest of the story. The man had been picked up two nights ago at a motel just outside of town. He'd given an obviously false name—Hannibal Hoo-hoo, or something of the sort—but there'd been no other means of identification. He'd pleaded guilty in court the day before and been fined, but since he couldn't pay the fine he was in jail. He was taking that all right; he didn't seem to mind it at all. But this morning the woman he'd been arrested with had volunteered the information that his name was McGull or McGill and that he was a doctor in Remus.

"Where is this?" Rosemary had asked. "Where did you say you're calling from?"

"Parkersville."

She'd never heard of the town.

"It's about sixty miles from you there in Remus. Off 26. Just past Wace. . . ." And he began to give her directions. But she hardly listened. She was sure it was just one of those peculiar—sometimes chilling—little mix-ups, accidents: like when you hear your name called by a strange voice and turn—that odd moment—only to discover the person is calling someone else. . . .

"I don't know what to say," she said. "I'm sure the man isn't my husband, Lieutenant. He'd prepared this paper . . . to read. . . ." How did one end it? "Still I want to thank you for being so concerned, doing your duty. . . ."

"It wouldn't hurt to call him, Mrs. McGill. I'd suggest you do that. Just to make sure."

"Yes."

"And you have the directions?"

She'd called Stan's hotel immediately, but he wasn't in his room. Ten minutes later she'd called again. Yes, he was registered. No, he hadn't checked out. Yes, they would page him. Minutes of hollow deadness . . . she heard a coin fall into it . . . what sounded like the muffled roar of a lion far off in a cave. "I'm very sorry," the operator finally said. Once she'd got the convention headquarters and a woman told her yes, he was registered, oh just a minute, he might be right there. But that turned out to be Dr. *Frank* McGill. . . . She didn't know what to do . . . she kept trying . . . the telephone had never seemed so inadequate. Finally at one o'clock she felt she had to decide whether to wait until evening, when she was supposed to pick Stan up at the airport, or drive the sixty miles to Parkersville. . . .

And here she was.

"Well, we can settle it easily enough," Lieutenant Goist said when she'd explained her trouble.

"I'm sure it isn't my husband," she said.

He seemed hardly to hear. "I can have him back here"—he glanced at his watch—"in . . . oh . . . say half an hour."

"Isn't he in the jail?" He'd surprised and somehow disappointed her. She'd imagined it would be much simpler. She'd passed the jail—a new low brick building, modern, with thick glass doors like a bank's—on her way to the courthouse. She'd thought he'd just call up, have the man brought to the office . . . or they'd walk down together, across the shady courthouse square. . . .

"If I'd have known you were coming . . . ," he lifted his hands apologetically. As he did he hunched his shoulders in a peculiar way, as if there was a tag on his shirt that scratched his neck. She'd noticed it before. "As it is," he said, "he'll be out with the others. . . ."

"Out?"

"It's nothing," he shook his head. "The prisoners do odd jobs for the county. Not much, but it gives them exercise and takes their mind off their troubles."

"Do you mean digging?" she stared across at him.

And he laughed at that—a bright burst—as if he couldn't prevent himself.

"Sometimes," he said. "But not today. I think Charlie just has them picking up bricks and boards . . . cleaning up. Over on Wheeler Street. Where we tore down the old junior high."

He told her she was welcome to wait in the office—it might be more comfortable—but she stood up when he did. She didn't want to wait there. The office had continued to depress her. The dead heat. The silk flag behind the desk, for all its fancy gold tassels with a thick layer of dust on its folds. . . . The picture of the boxer—tilted irritatingly—the slicked gray hair, the proud, sharp-jawed face . . . standing like that. . . .

She told him that in her hurry she'd come away without lunch. The town was so close she might just walk to a restaurant and get something.

"Good idea," he said. "Well," he looked around the office, "are we ready? Oops!" He went back to the desk, took a gun from the drawer, and put it in his shoulder holster. "That's better." He seemed to feel almost as relieved as she did that the interview was over, suddenly so gay that she thought as they neared the door he might take her arm.

The courthouse was an old red brick structure with a slatted wooden cupola, built on a square just behind the town. The lawns were patchy, with ragged continents stepped away here and there, but the trees were great pillows of leaves that shaded everything pleasantly—the railed walks, the benches, the big-bowled iron drinking fountain. . . .

Rosemary's first response, when she came through the door with Lieutenant Goist, was to the light and air. It was so good to be outside she just wanted to breathe for a moment. Her second response was to him . . . Lieutenant Goist . . . to a slight halt and sudden quickening in him when he started down the steps. . . .

The woman was sitting on a bench just below them, full in the sun, sharing something from a paper bag with a girl of about five or six who looked as if she'd been crying. Both were thin . . . the same badly curled, stringy blond hair . . . the same small mouth, tight, pinched at the corners. The woman squashed something into the girl's lap, then whispered to her, hit her playfully on the back of her head, laughing, cajoling. . . . It was hard for Rosemary to guess how old she was—twenty-five, thirty. Pretty, with a wiry, wasted prettiness. Raw white sticks of arms. Ugly shoes . . . the brace on the left leg reaching to just beneath the rolled stocking. . . .

When they passed, the woman paid no attention to them. She'd got the girl to laugh. "That's my love," she said, smacking her lightly again.

Rosemary could see her car parked across from the square. She should go home, she thought . . . walk across the street, get into it, and drive home. Had it been someone else . . . a girl . . . young . . . fresh . . . she might perhaps have imagined. . . . But not a woman like that. . . . Still, instead of making any sign to leave, she found herself, when they'd stopped at the short flight of steps that led down to the street, asking, "What is she doing there?"

"I really don't know."

"Is she from here?"

"Her name's Mrs. Kline. Mavis Kline. Her brother's Artie Hooper. Hooper's their name. There's a whole flock of them around here . . . Hoopers . . . one as bad as the other."

People were passing on the street. She saw the mechanical-eyed door of the supermarket across the way flick open as customers went in. A dumpy woman in sun glasses and soiled red slacks walking a dog. Two old men standing a distance apart, one butting the other with the rubber heel of his cane. . . .

"I wouldn't worry," Lieutenant Goist said. He had a way of holding himself, tilted back on his heels, his hands in his jacket pocket, just the pink thumbs sticking out. "You might try your husband's hotel again . . . just to check."

She told herself it was nonsense . . . that she was beginning to imagine things.

"Well, say half an hour . . . ," he smiled at her.

She watched him move along a raw gravel path toward the jail. She stood for a moment . . . working her gloves . . . resisting looking back toward the courthouse. But when she did the woman still wasn't paying any attention to her. A heavy-set man had joined them, picked up the girl and swung her high in the air while she wriggled happily and kicked him in the stomach.

The town, when she'd walked the two blocks to it, tended to buoy Rosemary's spirits. The group of stores wasn't much—a railroad crossing at one end and at the other, down the hill, a grain mill. But it looked busy, thriving. . . . The bank had been recently remodeled—slick gray and pink marble decorating the front. The Penney's looked a fair size. A movie. Grant's . . . lawn mowers on the sidewalk, sale banners across the long windows.

She telephoned from the drugstore next to the bank. She sat there caught in the spell of the droning buzz until the operator finally interrupted it.

"I'm afraid there's no one there," she said.

"It's very important," Rosemary said.

"I can have him paged."

But nothing came of that.

"Well . . . ," Rosemary said. But she remained there, wanting the operator to do more . . . there must, she thought, be something else.

"Can I take a message?"

Rosemary said she'd call back.

It was nothing . . . there could be a million and one reasons . . . , she told herself as she moved through the store out into the street again. The sun was blinding and she raised her hand, shaded her eyes to look across the street for a restaurant. And when she glanced down she saw an Indian boy imitating her, black popped eyes staring out under ridiculously raised fingers. When he caught her eyes he said something she didn't understand, burst out laughing, and ran down the street toward a heavy, lank-haired woman who held another child by the hand and was looking into a store window.

What had he said? she thought, her brow wrinkling. She'd noticed a restaurant, down farther on the other side, a faded green awning over the front. What had . . . ? She stepped down from the curb and as she did felt a sudden coil of tension which released itself in a terrible shiver down her back. He'd reminded her of the other Indian. . . .

It had hardly been anything, and if she'd been prepared for it it probably would have been nothing at all. When she'd turned off the highway she'd got lost, and before she'd had sense enough to ask at a house there hadn't been any houses . . . or at least none she cared to stop at. The countryside was flat and poor, dotted here and there with uniform gray shacks, each with a weedy patch of vegetable garden at the side. Finally though, with a sigh of relief, she'd seen from a rise in the road three or four weatherbeaten stores at a crossroads clearing. . . .

But the place, when she'd driven the mile or two to it, appeared deserted. She'd had no luck at the garage she'd pulled into. "Hello!" Honk, honk. No one. So she'd pulled down farther, beyond the crossroad, to what looked like a grocery store. And that had been open . . . she'd been able to tell by the screendoor. So she'd picked up her purse. . . . And just as she did, from the side of the wooden building, she'd heard a soft burst of child's laughter . . . then another . . . and in the next moment a tubby little girl, curls flying, her hand cupped to her mouth, had come running around the front and disappeared inside the store. She was gone before Rosemary had been able to call her . . . she'd simply flashed past . . . so Rosemary had slid over in the seat, thinking to get out . . . when the Indian had stepped around the same corner and terrified her so she'd almost shrieked.

"You loss?" he asked from the distance, smiling.

He wore khaki pants and a T-shirt that didn't quite cover his barrel stomach. Neither young nor old. Flat nose, pale brown eyes, thick brown hair. . . .

"Hey, lady."

As he moved toward her he slid one hand under his belt, inside his trousers. . . .

"You loss?" He was almost at the car window.

And she'd sat there, frozen, gripping her purse . . . actually thinking, if he opened the door, how . . . where . . . to strike him . . . when the screendoor had swung open and a neatly dressed Indian woman had come out on the steps of the store. She'd spoken inquiringly to the man and walked down to the car. And it had been then that Rosemary had learned—with a hiccough of foolish laughter she hadn't been able to control—that by some accident she had got onto the reservation.

The two of them had been kind to her—gave her directions—the woman slapping the man's arm playfully when she thought he was telling her wrong. "Don't listen to him," she laughed. "They're all the same. Men. Jokers." Both were leaning toward the car door, and Rosemary realized now that what she was smelling was the man's hair scent. The girl had come out and was standing on the top step straddling an old broom. She couldn't be theirs, Rosemary thought . . . she was white . . . that's why he'd surprised her so. "I don't go in much," the woman said, ". . . just to pick him up once in awhile. But that's the best way . . . stay on Patterson . . . then left at the old grange." In the mirror as she drove off Rosemary had seen the man give the woman a familiar pat on the buttock and turn toward the store. The girl had disappeared. But the woman had remained on the clayey slope . . . her hand up . . . smiling . . . waving after the car.

In the restaurant Rosemary ordered a tuna fish sandwich. The waitress leaned across, cleaned something from the table Rosemary hadn't even seen. . . . "We'll get it, honey," she said, bright, friendly, when Rosemary told her she was in a hurry.

The restaurant was old—metal ceiling, a pattern of decorated squares, three large overhead fans still in place. But it had been air-conditioned . . . everything freshly painted. The tables were a recent addition—gray and rose speckled vinyl or whatever it was—but she hadn't seen anything like the benches in years: scroll arms, heavy as lead, with high backs framing narrow rectangular strips of mirror. The place reminded her of—what was its name?— an ice cream parlor she used to go to as a girl.

She drew off her gloves, laid them carefully over her purse. She was happy, for some reason, to see so many people about . . . a group at the counter . . . three men in a booth . . . shirtsleeves . . . cigars . . . probably businessmen, owners of the stores. At one of the straight tables she noticed two elderly women. The one had both hands bandaged, so the other had to feed her the ice cream, but it didn't seem to bother them at all. They pecked their faces at one another, talking a mile a minute. The bigger, blowzier one, the one doing the feeding, would wait until the little one had finished a sentence, pop the ice cream in her mouth, and then dive back to her own dish.

Rosemary touched her gloves, and suddenly wished someone was with her . . . she felt so alone. She hadn't been like this . . . alone in a strange place . . . since . . . she couldn't remember. Probably since before she was married. That seemed for a minute far too long a time, but when she thought about it she realized it was true. Because before they'd grown up . . . gone off . . . like Muriel this summer . . . there'd always been the children . . . one or the other along with her. She hadn't realized until now how much she'd counted on them. . . .

She saw she was looking into the mirror of the opposite bench and was struck by her face . . . how drawn it looked. And somehow her hat had got knocked slightly crooked. She immediately raised her arms to fix it, and as she did, staring at the faded image that gazed back at her, she suddenly wondered if Stan loved her. The idea for a moment surprised her . . . so much that she hardly knew what to do with it. She hadn't thought about it . . . Stan and herself in that way . . . in she didn't know how long. After twenty-three years . . . all they'd been through . . . raising children . . . she hoped that was something she could take for granted. To start thinking about love now. . . . But as it turned out she didn't have to, for almost immediately—from nowhere— she was flooded with the unalterable certainty that he *did*. There was no question. He'd always loved her . . . through all those years. . . . He loved her now.

"Your tuna, honey."

But if he did—she was still lost in the image in the mirror—what was she doing sitting here like this, her hat crooked, alone, in a strange town she didn't like. . . .

"Honey."

She hadn't realized, until she began eating, how hungry she was . . . probably that's what was making her so lightheaded. As she ate she noticed the two women were still at their ice cream. Gab, gab, gab—plunk, the ice cream in the little one's mouth. And then suddenly, as she watched, the big one missed. The little one had ducked to blow something from her breast, her companion didn't notice, and the whole spoonful went right into her nose. The small one was prettily dressed and had looked such a dignified little lady—and there she was with a blob of ice cream on her nose. Rosemary expected her, at least for the moment, to become indignant—she herself would have; but instead, to her surprise, the woman howled with laughter, her skinny neck creaking back, her bandaged hands flapping the air at the joke. When she caught Rosemary watching, she nodded to her, as if encouraging her to join the fun, but Rosemary, annoyed by the scene, turned her glance quickly away. Finally the waitress noticed the accident and smiling along with the two women brought a soft white cloth from behind the counter.

She'd only had time to call Stan's hotel once again, with no better luck. When she got back to the courthouse square the first thing she noticed was that the bench was empty—the woman and the girl were gone. She felt relieved at that. When she moved through the entrance, the smell inside the building seemed worse than before—like years and years, she thought, of one's painting over dirt. She didn't realize she was hurrying until, at a turn in the stairway, she stumbled and a woman coming down caught her arm: "Here we go," she helped her.

The broad second-floor landing was deserted now—not even the secretary at the desk. She saw a public telephone booth against the side wall—she hadn't noticed it before—but she immediately rejected the idea: There wouldn't be any sense . . . she'd just called. She fixed her purse under her arm and began walking down the corridor to the right. In the dimness all the doors looked alike and she almost knocked on one before she saw the flicker of a shadow on the pebbled glass and noticed a sign in the corner—small, in chipped black paint: MEN. It was the next one . . . ! In front of Lieutenant Goist's door she took a handkerchief from her purse and touched perspiration from her nose. Her jaws ached, but she didn't realize it was because her teeth were clenched so. She raised her hand and knocked.

But there was no one . . . her fear had been needless . . . the office was empty except for Lieutenant Goist, still in his jacket and tie despite the sweltering heat. "Ah, Mrs. McGill," he raised his hand. Before he stood up to come around the desk he made the hunching movement she'd become familiar with. . . .

"Did you reach him?" he asked. He actually touched her arm this time as he ushered her to the chair. "I'm afraid he isn't here either. Our man. I thought Charlie just had him out with the others, but he sent him over to Raceville with Sergeant Eberhardt to pick up some beds. . . . But I do have something that might help . . . I brought his things."

"Things?" From somewhere about the desk she caught the smell of a half-eaten apple. He'd probably put it away in a drawer.

"We take their personal belongings . . . wallet, keys, whatever's in their pockets . . . keep them in an envelope until they get out. Here . . . wait. . . ." But when he moved to the bookcase, looked on top, his brow creased. . . . He came back and looked over the top of the desk. He smiled, snapped his fingers. "They're downstairs . . . I left them on the table. . . . I'll just be a minute." And before she knew it . . . before she hardly had a chance to understand what it was about . . . he was out the door and she was left alone in the office.

She sat quietly, almost stiffly in the chair, hoping he'd be back right away. . . . When five minutes had passed, she thought of getting up and leaving . . . just leaving—it was what, more than anything in the world, she wanted to do . . . but then she considered how peculiar that would seem. She'd begun nervously clasping and unclasping her purse, and once when she looked down she noticed her hands . . . her gloves! . . . what had she done with her gloves? She looked under the chair, then stooped to look under the desk . . . until she realized she hadn't *had* them. The waitress back at the restaurant had picked them up to hand them to her when she was about to leave . . . put them on the tray when she'd given her her change . . . and . . . and they'd both forgotten. They were still back there on the tray. . . .

Now she'd have to stop back there . . . waste more time. . . . She felt her nerves pull. . . . She sat forward and brushed something . . . nothing . . . from her skirt. . . . Then, in her distress, she closed her eyes. And with that . . . as if waiting for just such a moment . . . the image of the men immediately focused: the three of them lined in the blazing sunlight, the incinerator smokestack behind them . . . laughing, poking one another, calling to her in that crazy way across the distance. . . .

She'd only been three or four miles from town . . . on the right road . . . so she needn't have stopped at all. But the Indian couple hadn't said anything about the deserted sugar beet factory she'd passed . . . or the incinerator that loomed ahead . . . and the three men working there seemed close enough for her to just call to. So she'd pulled to the side and turned down the window. There was a chain-linked fence, then a mound of rusted metal and ashes and junk stretching as far as she could see into the glare of the white sky.

"Parkersville!" she called again, louder, when they all cupped their ears as if they had difficulty hearing. Two of them were older—one fat, with a bush of black hair. The third one was only a boy, fair, skinny—in nothing but dungarees cut off at the knees, frayed ends hanging down . . . a handkerchief tied jauntily about his neck.

The fat one yelled something, but just before he did he turned his head toward the others, so she hadn't been able to hear clearly. Then the youngest one poked the others slyly, stepped out in front of them, and shouted, "Who's winning the game?" She guessed he meant some baseball game, but it left her bewildered because she didn't know anything about such things. Perhaps it was the look on her face . . . she didn't know what . . . but the next minute they were all in hysterics. The third one, hunched forward with laughter, tickled the boy so he jumped high in the air, and while they were chasing around the fat one shouted something like, "Open your eyes, lady."

She decided they were drunk and turned away. She started the car. But as she did, something light—a clinker?—struck the roof, and when she looked up, frightened, she saw the boy had thrown it. He stood out in front of the others as before, his eyes lowered against the sun, his mouth a bright crescent of gaiety. She thought he meant to say something kind. Then, before she could escape, he raised his arm like an axe and made a quick obscene gesture. She pressed the gas pedal so hard that the car jolted her against the wheel. Only minutes later, when the mound had disappeared into a punk swamp, did she find the courage to look into the rear-view mirror.

"Here we are!" Lieutenant Goist said . . . and she almost screamed. She hadn't heard the door, his steps, anything until he was behind her.

"Oopsidaisy," he said, picking up the purse she'd let drop to the floor. He handed it to her, seeming unaware that anything was wrong. "Got it," he said, waving a large manilla envelope at her as he walked behind the desk. . . .

It took her moments to recover . . . and by the time she did he was jiggling the mouth of the envelope and letting the things tumble to the desk. . . .

And it was *over.*

"Oh," she laughed into the side of her hand.

"Well?"

She got control of herself . . . allowed her eyes to move over the things again. A comb, a marble, a gold-banded watch, two or three keys on a cheap metal loop, a wadded handkerchief. . . . They weren't his . . . they weren't even *like* him. . . .

"They aren't Stan's." She was sitting up, laughing easily now.

He ran his hand over the things . . . picked up the watch. "No wallet. There isn't really very much," he said doubtfully. "Are you sure?"

"Yes."

He hesitated . . . then dropped the watch back on the blotter. It was as if he had decided to allow her the moment. "Well, who should know better than you?" he smiled brightly. The brown eyes almost winked at her. "Well,"—he tapped the desk with his knuckles—"I guess that's it . . . I guess that ought to settle that." He kept her for a few minutes to apologize . . . explain that mistakes of the kind happened. . . .

Once outside the office she blew her nose, dusted under her eyes with her handkerchief. . . . She felt the momentary giddiness that sometimes comes with relief, but shook it away. . . . Here she'd come all this way, she told herself . . . upset herself like this . . . when she'd known all along. . . .

There were people in the corridor now . . . the secretary back at her desk . . . a policeman, his shoe up, picking at a knot . . . a group of boy scouts—their knapsacks and half their clothes in a heap on the floor—fooling around at the water cooler. . . .

The point now of course was where *was* he? The question simply intruded . . . was suddenly there . . . and she wanted to close her mind to it . . . but her love of the certain . . . her distaste for the unknown, the disorderly, and the frayed . . . forced her to listen . . . to accept its simple truth. She *didn't* know where he was. She'd only come here . . . gone through this whole insane rigmarole . . . because she hadn't been able, all day. . . .

She noticed the telephone booth then across the landing . . . glanced at her watch and calculated something. . . . It hardly seemed likely, but it was just possible he hadn't left the hotel yet. . . . And two minutes later, with the surprise that comes from the totally unexpected, there he was at the other end of the line. . . .

"You're there!" She couldn't prevent the words from popping out melodramatically . . . she had to struggle for a minute against a catch of tears. It was the strain, she realized . . . the strain of the whole wasteful shattering day. . . .

"Well, where did you expect me to be?" he said. She saw the heavy figure, head tilted, crooking the phone the way he did . . . the serious face . . . the gentle, half-mocking eyes. . . .

"I've been trying to get you," she said.

"*You've* been trying to get *me*? *I've* been trying to get *you*. I've been calling home ever since I got your message. What's the matter? Where in heaven are you?"

And she was on the point of simply telling him . . . she hadn't considered for a moment *not* telling him . . . when she suddenly realized there was no longer any need. It was over. The whole unpleasant affair was over. It had had nothing to do with *them*. So why bother, go through the whole business of . . . .

She disliked lying, but in the end she made up a story about having had to drive—not to Parkersville, they knew no one *there*—but to Wassau City.

"That's *it?*" he said when she was finished.

She knew it sounded a little foolish . . . so she searched . . . found something to bolster it. "I thought this might happen. I'm just starting back now. I wanted you to know I might be a little late picking you up at the airport."

"What?" he said. "I can't hear you."

She made a face at the mouthpiece as if the trouble was there. She could hear *him* perfectly well. "Can't you hear me?"

"Now I can."

"I said I might be a little late picking you up."

"Oh. I couldn't hear you."

She frowned. He had a habit . . . he'd always had it but it had grown increasing over the years . . . of making fun of her in a way she didn't always understand.

"Will that be all right?" she said.

"No. Who wants to be left stranded. But what can I do?"

Then, luckily, he was through with his joking. He asked how she was . . . the children . . . whether she'd heard from their daughter Muriel. . . . In the end, the mask dropping completely away, he laughed, confessed that he'd missed her . . . that he was pooped . . . anxious, as always, to get home. . . .

When she stepped out of the booth she dug for her handkerchief and touched her chin. She was dripping. The booth had been stuffier . . . more dead-smelling . . . than the office. . . . And that in turn reminded her of Lieutenant Goist. Should she? . . . there really wasn't any necessity. . . . Yet at the recollection of something . . . some vague note of condescension . . . superiority . . . which seemed now to have marked his attitude toward her from the beginning . . . she felt suddenly swell in her—even against her will—a great rose bloom of final feminine triumph. . . .

It would be simply the decent thing, she told herself, to take the extra minute to let him know what had happened . . . that she'd spoken to Stan. . . .

She was riding so high in the new glow that when she passed the secretary she smiled at her . . . only to find it was another woman. In the dimness, seeing her at the typewriter, she had simply thought. . . . And there instead was this totally unfamiliar woman bouncing up from her chair. "Oy, those kids . . . they'll be the ruin of me," she rolled her eyes at Rosemary in comic exasperation. Then she beat around the chair and began clapping her hands at the boy scouts, who had come down to the landing and were shouting and running wildly over the benches lined under the long row of dusty windows. . . .

"Tell it to the marines!" Rosemary heard one of them yell.

She moved along . . . the corridor was empty again. Lieutenant Goist's door was open now, she noticed . . . she could see a pale wash of light filtering from it into the hallway. . . . She hoped he hadn't left.

Fortunately he hadn't . . . though when she got there the fact that the door was open presented its own little difficulty . . . where were you supposed to knock on an open door? He was still inside . . . sitting at his desk. Looking more relaxed now . . . less official-looking. Somehow—the thought came to her—more *real.* He'd taken off his jacket, loosened his tie, turned back the stiff white cuffs. . . .

She knocked on the side of the door, but he didn't hear. . . . So she leaned forward, touched her purse to her breast, and said, "Lieutenant Goist."

And what happened next happened so suddenly . . . came with such shocking abruptness . . . that she actually raised her purse to her face to protect herself. The pale blond head had come up, apparently startled . . . and the left arm had flown up . . . but there hadn't been a hand . . . only the swish of a white cord cutting the air with something chrome at the end flying wildly toward his head, almost catching his cheek. But the hand remained on the desk . . . cupped and pink . . . until he'd hastily caught it up and swung out of the chair, away from her. She'd seen the broad back make a precise hunching arc, the elbow jerk toward her twice. . . .

She stood there, her eyes wide, staring out above her purse. . . .

He managed the situation better than she did. When he had snapped the hand back in place, he turned around and said, "I'm very sorry. I wasn't expecting anyone. Please come in, Mrs. McGill. Just a minute." He brushed his shirtsleeves down, walked to the coat tree and quickly slipped into his jacket.

But she remained in the doorway . . . hardly hearing . . . her mind careening after a fantastic thought that had suddenly shot up, facing her . . . eyes going, large gapped teeth . . . only to immediately turn, bright rags flying, and begin chasing toward a landscape she had never seen. . . .

He had no hand . . . he'd lost it somehow . . . there was nothing, she realized, very unusual about that. But she'd been seeing it all day . . . it had been right there, in front of her eyes, all day . . . folded on top of the other on the blotter . . . the pink thumb poking out of the jacket outside there, under the trees . . . touching her when he'd led her to the chair . . . jiggling the mouth of the envelope over the desk. . . . It even seemed now, in her bewilderment, that all day he'd been using it like a magician, purposely doing tricks with it to tease her. . . .

"Please come in," he said again. And at the new brusque tone, the flush she noticed on his cheek, she woke up . . . came to herself. What was the matter with her? What was she thinking? It was nothing . . . he'd just been thought-less. And standing here like this she was merely embarrassing him further. . . .

When she walked into the office and explained why she'd stopped back, he said "No!" his face lighting up with surprise and pleasure. "Well can you imagine?" And that ended it . . . his bright gay burst . . . for both of them—all the awkwardness of the moment before.

She only stayed a minute.

"He's been calling me at home all afternoon," she said.

"And *you* weren't there."

They both laughed at the irony.

The things were still on the desk . . . he hadn't put them away yet . . . the marble . . . the keys . . . the wadded handkerchief. . . .

As he walked her to the door he apologized again for the trouble she'd been through.

"I knew it all along," she couldn't prevent herself from saying.

"Ho, women!" he laughed with a final easy informality.

They shook hands briefly and she heard him close the door behind her.

On the bench across from the office a girl was sitting with knees up chanting "Hoopers-ploopers!" but Rosemary hardly noticed. She did, however, recognize the blond woman talking to the secretary up ahead at the desk. There was no mistaking her—the frizzed hair . . . the greasy paper bag she'd held on the bench outside . . . the slack, wasted figure above the glinting brace. . . . But for Rosemary it was past. It was over. She was already feeling too apart from it all even to wonder what the woman was doing there . . . to care. . . . Now all she wanted was to get outside . . . back to the car . . . be on her way. . . .

And once outside, standing on the top landing of the courthouse steps, there before her—blowing away whatever cobwebs might have remained—lay the square, bright and clear in the late afternoon sun. She blinked. Jigsaws of bright sky through the leaves . . . the lawn softly freckled . . . people about, walking, sitting on the benches . . . pigeons fluffing themselves, pecking along the walk. A woman passed . . . stooped over to fix a mosquito netting on a carriage. . . . A boy doing tricks . . . no hands . . . curving away on his bicycle toward the street. . . .

The light . . . the air . . . fresh air. . . . She breathed . . . breathed. . . . She saw a handyman drawing a hose across the lawn, yanking the end, toward a flower bed. He chased some children and she saw them hop away, climb over the iron railing of the path. . . . If one of the children had been with her, she thought . . . just along to keep her company . . . there wouldn't have been any of this . . . the whole day would have been so much easier. . . .

The main path of the square led from the courthouse to the wide street behind the stores. As Rosemary moved down the steps she couldn't help seeing to the end. There was little to draw her attention. A peddler's cart with an orange and black umbrella . . . an old man attending it . . . a woman digging in her purse. Two men . . . one young, in limp suntans, thin and gawky, but somehow official-looking. . . . The other older, heavy set, in an undershirt, his topshirt hooked on a finger over his shoulder. They were eating ice cream bars and joking, the heavier one bouncing on his heels . . . roughhousing. . . .

She reached the bottom of the stairs and was about to turn toward the side path.

And at that moment the older one let out a sudden whallop of laughter and swung around, facing up the path . . . and she saw it was Stan.

She stood rooted to the pavement. . . .

His laughter echoed down the shaded path . . . the loose warm roll of it . . . expansive . . . free. . . . He tossed the ice cream stick in a wide baseball curve into the bushes. He pinched his nose and said something that set the others going, even the old man at the cart. Then he glanced up the path toward the courthouse . . . wholly at ease in his surroundings . . . wiping his neck with his shirt . . . enjoying the scene. When his eyes fell on Rosemary, he squinted . . . then cocked his head in comic, affectionate surprise. . . .

She stared. . . .

He raised the finger holding the shirt several inches . . . his eyes had grown welcoming, expectant . . . he stood there smiling away more happily than ever. . . .

And for a moment . . . for a curious lightheaded moment when everything seemed to fade but the man . . . when she seemed to rise out of herself buoyed by some hope . . . some promise she had never dreamed . . . Rosemary almost responded . . . almost raised her purse in a gesture of recognition. . . .

He flapped his hand at the group at the cart, dismissing them. He touched his belt and took a step up the path. . . .

And at that instant, with a cathartic sense of relief, she remembered the telephone call. . . . It *couldn't* be Stan. . . . She'd just *spoken* to Stan. . . .

The man seemed to notice some change in her expression. He hesitated . . . his eyes straining . . . his brow furrowed in a question.

But what could she do? It wasn't Stan. She made a formal face . . . nodded her head almost imperceptibly: No.

And with that he appeared to recognize the mistake too. He blinked . . . then suddenly smiled . . . an altogether different smile . . . quick and empty and somewhat shy . . . the smile of a stranger who finds himself, to his embarrassment, staring at the wrong woman.

But it wasn't his fault, she realized . . . she'd stared first. . . . And completely relieved now, wanting to make up for her share in the little error, she was about to smile back . . . when he suddenly spat . . . clipping one of the pigeons so it fluttered its wings . . . rose under the trees. . . . He swung his shirt from his shoulder . . . hallooing . . . turning as the bird flew over the street . . . among the cars for a moment . . . then up . . . disappeared behind the stores. . . .

But she was still seeing the abrupt, ugly gesture . . . it had surprised and offended her so. She kept looking at the heavy naked shoulders as he walked back to the group at the cart. Men . . . , she thought. But she shrugged the shiver away, turned, and moved hurriedly down the side path.

And in the car she dug for her keys. . . . You try to be decent . . . kind . . . , she found herself thinking as she fished beneath the checkbook, the handkerchief, the green stamps . . . and they abuse you . . . act as if you've done . . . she didn't know *what.* She'd done *nothing* to that man. . . .

When she found the keys she snapped open the small leather case. Then she patted the cushion of the seat . . . sat back. . . .

She could see across to the square . . . the handyman watering a patch of stalky marigolds . . . the modern jail with its glass doors . . . the old courthouse . . . the dusty trees. It looked—the commonplace thought washed up as if it were of actual importance—like every courthouse square she had ever seen in her life. And if with that she felt a sudden deepening sense of loneliness, it hardly lasted long enough for her to recognize, and quickly passed in more practical matters. She had to get gas. And there were her gloves . . . should she bother? . . . but it would just take a minute to swing around into town . . . pick them up at the restaurant. . . .

She jiggled her hand at a fly on the windshield . . . turned on the ignition.

As she was pulling away from the curb a driver stopped, gave her a friendly wave, let her pull out ahead of him. She had no trouble at the restaurant . . . nor in finding her way to the highway. And when she arrived at the airport, Stan of course was there. . . .

THE AUTHORS

THEODORE BLOOM was born in Boston. He now lives in Switzerland where he is working on a novel. "A Four-Day Wait" was his first published story.

BROCK BROWER, born in 1931 in Westfield, New Jersey, is currently a lecturer in creative writing at Princeton University. A former assistant editor of *Esquire* and staff member of the Breadloaf Writers' Conference, he has published *Debris*, a novel, and *Other Loyalties: A Politics of Personality,* a collection of journalism. He is working on a novel about a horror-film star—tentative title: *A Clown in the Dark*.

RAYMOND CARVER was born in Clatskanie, Oregon (population, 707), attended Humboldt State College in Arcata, California, the University of Iowa, and Tel Aviv University. His stories and poems have appeared in a score of little magazines. A collection of his poems, *Near Klamath,* has been published; another, *Drinking While Driving,* is soon to be published. He makes his living as a textbook editor.

DANIEL CURLEY since 1955 has taught English at the University of Illinois, where he was also an editor of the now defunct *Accent.* Some three dozen of his stories have been published, almost exclusively in little magazines. He has published *The Marriage Bed of Procrustes,* a collection of stories, and two novels, *How Many Angels?* and *A Stone Man, Yes.*

RALPH DENNIS has a B.A. and an M.A. from the University of North Carolina, where he now teaches television and film writing. He has attended the Yale School of Drama, written documentary films, and has had plays produced. Mr. Dennis has appeared in a number of literary magazines with both fiction and poetry and is currently working on a novel.

STANLEY ELKIN was born in New York City and raised in Chicago. He is married to the painter, Joan Elkin. Since taking his doctorate at the University of Illinois, he has taught writing and literature courses at Washington University at St. Louis. He is one of the editors of *Perspective: A Quarterly of Modern Literature.* He has two novels to his credit, *Boswell* and *A Bad Man,* as well as a volume of stories, *Criers and Kibitzers, Kibitzers and Criers.*

Washington University
Photography Service

J. M. FERGUSON, JR., was born in Lexington, Kentucky, grew up in New Mexico, and graduated from the University of New Mexico with a B.A. in 1957 and an M.A. in 1959. His stories and poems have appeared in half a dozen little magazines.

ANDREW FETLER   was born in Riga, Latvia, in 1925. His stories have appeared in *Kenyon Review, Antioch Review, Epoch,* and *Malahat Review.* He received a first prize for an *Atlantic* "First," and his work includes a novel, *The Travelers.* He teaches creative writing at the University of Massachusetts.

WILLIAM FIFIELD   is fifty-four years old and lives in Spain with his third wife, an Amsterdam fashion model, and two-year-old daughter. He has published more than one hundred short stories and the novels *The Devil's Marchioness, The Sign of Taurus,* and *Matadora.* For the past nine years he has been at work on a novel based on original materials about the Borgias, Machiavelli, da Vinci, Michelangelo, and Vitelli. "You have to work back through all the nonhistory to zero," he writes, "and that's what takes so long."

ROBERT FOX   was born in 1943, got his first encouraging word on a story from Gordon Lish, the editor of *Genesis West,* and has since appeared in a dozen little magazines. He has one novel, *Peter's Stride,* making the rounds of publishers; another is in progress.

CAROLYN GAISER,   a graduate of Swarthmore and the Yale School of Drama, lived in Rome two years on a Fulbright scholarship, and has worked as a translator, freelance writer, and promotion writer for New York City publishers.

WILLIAM GASS   was born in Fargo, North Dakota, in 1924. He has taught philosophy at Wooster College, Ohio, and Purdue University, and is now professor of philosophy at Washington University, St. Louis. He has published the novel *Omensetter's Luck,* a collection of stories called *In the Heart of the Heart of the Country,* and the short prose fiction *Willie Master's Lonesome Wife.*

PHILIP L. GREENE was born in Brooklyn, served in the Air Force in World War II, and graduated from Lowell Technological Institute with a B.S. in textile engineering, a profession at which he worked for several years. In 1962 he received a Ph.D. in English from New York University. He was editor of the little magazine *Venture* for five years, and since 1959 has taught English at Adelphi University. "One of You Must Be Wendell Corey" was his first published story.

JAMES W. GROSHONG was born in Corvallis, Oregon (as were his parents), where he still lives. Mr. Groshong is currently teaching English at Oregon State University. "The Gesture" has appeared in three anthologies to date and has also been published in Germany. He has had short fiction published in various literary magazines, and for the past three years has been working on a novel.

JAMES B. HALL, presently Provost of College V, University of California, Santa Cruz, was born in Ohio. After stints as a merchant sailor and as a soldier, he went on to a Ph.D. at the University of Iowa. His most recent collection of stories is *Us He Devours*. He has also published four novels, the latest being *Mayo Sergeant.*

JOSEPHINE JACOBSEN attended a private school in Baltimore for four years, her total formal education. She is married to Eric Jacobsen and has one son. Her poetry, fiction, and criticism have appeared in numerous little magazines and other periodicals. She is poetry critic for the *Baltimore Sun.*

Photograph by
André Snow

CONRAD KNICKERBOCKER, born in Berlin, son of the well-known correspondent H. R. Knickerbocker, died from a self-inflicted rifle wound at the age of thirty-seven. A Harvard graduate, he was married twice and had three children. He published in *Life, Esquire,* and the *New York Times,* and was particularly noted for his articles describing the "Black Humor" movement in American literature.

DENNIS LYNDS was born in St. Louis, has lived most of his life in New York City, and is now living in Santa Barbara, California. He was an infantryman in World War II and has been a chemist, farmhand, stagehand, and, for a number of years, an editor of chemical trade journals. To make a living he writes mystery novels under the pen names of Michael Collins and William Arden.

NANCY K. MacKENZIE, born in Michigan, has shuttled between England and America most of her life. She is now living in New York City where she is a freelance copy editor. She has published more than 150 essays and short book reviews in the *New York Times,* but prefers writing fiction. She is, at present, working on a novel.

DAVID MADDEN, writer-in-residence at Louisiana University, was born in 1933 and raised in Knoxville, Tennessee. He graduated from the University of Tennessee and from San Francisco State, and attended the Yale School of Drama. His stories, poems, plays, articles, and essays have appeared in a great variety of publications and he has taught in six colleges and universities, including Kenyon College, where he was also an editor of *Kenyon Review.*

Michael H. Abramson

JACK MATTHEWS was born in Columbus, Ohio, and teaches English at Ohio University in Athens. He has had more than eighty stories published and roughly the same number of poems. His stories have been collected in *Bitter Knowledge,* his poems, in *An Almanac for Twilight.* His most recent novels are *Hanger Stout, Awake!* and *Beyond the Bridge.*

LEONARD MICHAELS was born in New York City in 1933, attended New York University, the University of Michigan, and the University of California at Berkeley (where he is now teaching in the English department). He has received an appointment to the University of California Institute for Creative Art. His stories have appeared in publications ranging from *Audit* to *Playboy.*

Alexis Bespaloff

HOWARD NEMEROV was born in New York City in 1920 and graduated from Harvard in 1941. Before becoming professor of English at Brandeis University, he taught at Bennington College for many years and, in 1964, held the position of Consultant in Poetry for the Library of Congress. A poet, novelist, and critic, Mr. Nemerov has published thirteen books. His latest book of poems is *The Blue Swallows.* He is married and has three children.

Lloyd Studio
Bennington, Vermont

ALDEN NOWLAN, writer-in-residence at the University of New Brunswick, Fredericton, Canada, has published seven volumes of poetry, the most recent of which, *Bread, Wine and Salt,* won the Governor-General's Award for poetry. He writes a weekly column for the *Telegraph-Journal,* Saint John, of which he was formerly night news editor, and has published one collection of stories, *Miracle at Indian River.*

JOYCE CAROL OATES was born in upstate New York in 1938, educated at Syracuse University and the University of Wisconsin, and is now an associate professor of English at the University of Windsor, Canada, where she is also fiction editor of the *University of Windsor Review.* Her short stories have consistently been chosen for the O. Henry and Foley prize story collections. Thrice nominated for the National Book Award for Fiction, she received it in 1970 for her novel *Them.*

Joe McTyre

FLANNERY O'CONNOR was born March 25, 1925, in Savannah, Georgia. She died of lupus, an incurable disease, in 1964 in Milledgeville, Georgia, where she had passed the last thirteen years of her life with her mother on their farm. A graduate of the Woman's College of Georgia, she took an M.F.A. at the University of Iowa. Her publications include the novels *Wise Blood* and *The Violent Bear It Away* and two volumes of stories, *A Good Man Is Hard to Find* and *Everything That Rises Must Converge*.

HENRY H. ROTH has published more than fifty stories, chiefly in little magazines. Born in Brooklyn in 1933, he is married to the artist Sylvia Roth and has a son and twin daughters. At present he is living in South Nyack, New York, and working on stories and novels.

ABRAHAM ROTHBERG, a native New Yorker, was educated at Brooklyn College, the University of Iowa, and Columbia University. Following army service in World War II, he has been a teacher, journalist, editor, political analyst, and writer. He has published four novels, *The Other Man's Shoes, The Song of David Freed, The Heirs of Cain,* and *The Thousand Doors*.

DAVID SPRIGGS on himself: "I was born in 1936, raised and schooled near Montreal, Canada. Ten years of travelling about and working in several unrelated fields have led to the conviction that perhaps a better formal education was really best—the past five years of study towards the coveted B.A., and final attainment thereof have led to the conviction that perhaps it really wasn't. At present I am preparing to spend a year motorcycling about the continent with my wife. . . . Meanwhile I enjoy writing short stories." "The Autopsy" was published when he was a student at Sir George Williams University, Montreal. It was his first published story.

PETER TAYLOR, born in 1919 in Trenton, Tennessee, married the poet-novelist Eleanor Ross in 1943. He attended Vanderbilt University, Southwestern at Memphis, and Kenyon College (where he took his B.A. in 1940). He is currently a professor of English at the University of North Carolina. Among his many publications are *A Long Fourth, Happy Families Are All Alike, Miss Leonora When Last Seen* (short stories), *A Woman of Means* (novel), and *Tennessee Day in St. Louis* (play).

GORDON WEAVER was born in Moline, Illinois, in 1937 and grew up in Wisconsin, returning to the University of Illinois for college. A Woodrow Wilson Fellow in 1961–62, his stories have appeared in many little magazines and he has published one novel, *Count a Lonely Cadence.* Mr. Weaver is currently teaching at the University of Southern Mississippi in Hattiesburg.

H. W. Ellis

VICTOR WHITE was born in Vienna in 1902. Between the ages of eighteen and twenty he worked in Thomas Alva Edison's personal laboratory, then attended Rutgers University, Yale, and the Sorbonne. In 1941 he published the novel *Peter Domanig: Morning in Vienna*—and subsequently three more novels with Peter Domanig as hero, but with the setting in the United States. He has been a journalist and is presently teaching.

JOSEPH WHITEHILL was born in 1927 in Ohio and raised in Oklahoma. He was educated at Exeter, Harvard, University of Tulsa, Washburn College at Topeka, and The Johns Hopkins University, and has worked as a Navy seaman, machinist, design draftsman, accountant, and engineer. Married and the father of five, he has published a collection of short stories, *Able Baker and Others,* and two novels, *The Angers of Spring* and *Precious Little.*

JOY WILLIAMS lives on the west coast of Florida with her husband, a newspaperman, and a small menagerie of wild animals. Until recently she worked at a shark research laboratory. Her stories have appeared in many little magazines.

MARGERY WOOD grew up in Columbus, Ohio, and graduated from Ohio State University in 1940. She lives in Wellesley, Massachusetts, and has a daughter in college and a daughter in kindergarten. She spent the past two years in Africa where her husband, a consulting engineer, completed an assignment and she completed a novel. Her work has appeared in the *Minnesota Review* as well as the *Carleton Miscellany*.

JOHN ZEUGNER was born in New York City in 1938, grew up in Connecticut, and received a B.A. from Harvard College and an M.A. from Florida State University, where he is currently working on a Ph.D. in American History. "The Tennis Player" was his first published story.

von Guttenberg

GEORGE ZORN   was born in Brooklyn in 1922. After three years in the service in World War II, he attended Hofstra, Columbia, and Indiana Universities where he received a B.A., M.A., and A.B.D. respectively. Married, with three sons, Mr. Zorn has been at Central Michigan University for the past nine years. Two of his stories have been reprinted in O. Henry collections, and he is presently working on a book of "haiku-like" poems, some of which have already been published in the Tokyo literary magazine, *Poetry 15*.

DIRECTORY OF LITERARY MAGAZINES

The following North American literary magazines were consulted in the compilation of this anthology. Some of the magazines no longer publish; some are no longer active; some have changed addresses. For an up-to-date listing of names and addresses, consult the *Directory of Little Magazines* (DUSTbooks, 5218 Scottwood Road, Paradise, California 95969).

Abyss, Box C, Somerville, Massachusetts 02143

Activist, 27¹/₂ West College, Oberlin, Ohio 44074

Adept, Box 52927, Houston, Texas 77052

Aesop's Feast, 207 West Fowler Avenue, West Lafayette, Indiana 47906

Alaska Review, Alaska Methodist University, Anchorage, Alaska 99504

Alphabet, University of Western Ontario, London, Ontario, Canada

American Dialog, 32 Union Square, New York, New York 10003

Analecta, Box 133, Demarest, New Jersey 07627

Angels, 70 Snowberry Lane, Central Islip, New York 11722

Ann Arbor Review, 2118 Arlene Street, Ann Arbor, Michigan 48103

Ante, Box 29915, Los Angeles, California 90029

Antioch Review, Antioch Press, Yellow Springs, Ohio 45387

Ants Forefoot, Founders College, York University, Toronto, Canada

Appalachian Review, West Virginia University, Morgantown, West Virginia 26506

Approach, 114 Petrie Avenue, Rosemont, Pennsylvania 19010

Ararat, 109 East 40th Street, New York, New York 10016

Arizona Quarterly, University of Arizona, Tucson, Arizona 85721

Arlington Quarterly, Box 366, University Station, Arlington, Texas 76010

ARX, 12109 Bell Avenue, Austin, Texas 78759

Aspects, Box 3125, Eugene, Oregon 97403

Assay, University of Washington, Seattle, Washington 98105

Athanor, 151 West 25th Street, New York, New York 10001

Ball State University Forum, Ball State University, Muncie, Indiana 47306

Bay Podium, Box 9262, Berkeley, California 94719

Bennington Review, Box N, Bennington College, Bennington, Vermont 05201

Beyond Baroque, Box 675, Venice, California 90291

Blackbird, 6016 S. Kimbark Avenue, Chicago, Illinois 60637

Bluestone, Box 355, Woodstock, New York 12498

California Review, 280 East Mountain Drive, Santa Barbara, California 93103

Calumet Review, Box 65, Purdue University, Calumet Campus, Hammond, Indiana 46323

Carleton Miscellany, Carleton College, Northfield, Minnesota, 55057

Carolina Quarterly, Box 1117, Chapel Hill, North Carolina 27514

Chelsea, Box 242, Old Chelsea Station, New York, New York 10011

Cheshire, University of Wisconsin-Milwaukee, 3202 North Downer Avenue, Milwaukee, Wisconsin 53211

Chicago Review, University of Chicago, Chicago, Illinois 60637

Chimes, Saint Mary's College, Notre Dame, Indiana 46556

Cimarron Review, 203B Morrill Hall, Oklahoma State University, Stillwater, Oklahoma 74074

Coastlines, 471 Sycamore Road, Santa Monica, California 90402

Colorado Quarterly, Hellems 124, University of Colorado, Boulder, Colorado 80521

Colorado State Review, 360 Liberal Arts, Colorado State University, Fort Collins, Colorado 80521

Columbia Review, 317 Ferris Booth Hall, Columbia University, New York, New York 10027

Confrontation, Long Island University, Greenvale, New York 11548

Consumption, 53½ North East Ravenna Boulevard, Seattle, Washington 98115

Contact, Box 755, Sausalito, California 94965

Corno Emplumado, Apartado 13-546, Mexico 13, D.F., Mexico

Cottonwood Review, 118 Kansas Union, University of Kansas, Lawrence, Kansas 66044

Dasein, Box 2121, New York, New York 10001

December, Box 274, Western Springs, Illinois 60558

DeKalb Journal, DeKalb College, 555 Indian Creek Drive, Clarkston, Georgia 30021

Denver Quarterly, University of Denver, Denver, Colorado 80210

DePaul Literary Magazine, 25 East Jackson Boulevard, Chicago, Illinois 60604

Descant, TCU Station, Fort Worth, Texas 76129

Discourse, Concordia College, Moorhead, Minnesota 56560

Duel (formerly *Prism '68*), Sir George Williams University, 1455 de Maisonneuve Boulevard, Montreal 107, Quebec, Canada

Dust, 5218 Scottwood Road, Paradise, California 95969

Edge, Box 4067, Edmonton, Alberta, Canada

Eikon, Box 1144, Portsmouth, New Hampshire 03801

Entrails, 283 East Houston Street, New York, New York 10002

Epoch, 251 Goldwin Smith Hall, Cornell University, Ithaca, New York 14850

Esprit, 21-25 South Franklin Street, Wilkes Barre, Pennsylvania 18701

Evidence, Box 245, Station F, Toronto, Canada

Exit, Box 1812, New York, New York 10001

Fair, 1642 North 8th Street, Terre Haute, Indiana 47804

Fiddlehead, University of New Brunswick, Fredericton, New Brunswick, Canada

Foxfire, Rabun Gap-Nacoochee School, Rabun Gap, Georgia 30568

Fuck you, Box 193, Stuyvesant Station, New York, New York 10009

Gato, Box 654, Los Gatos, California 95030

Generation, 420 Maynard Street, Ann Arbor, Michigan 48104

Genesis West, c/o G. Lish, 307 E. 56th St., New York, New York 10002

Georgia Review, University of Georgia, Athens, Georgia 30601

Goodly Co., 724 Minor Avenue, Kalamazoo, Michigan 49001

Gooseberry, Studio 427, 5511 Euclid Avenue, Cleveland, Ohio 44103

Graffiti, 4228-45th St., N.W., Washington, D.C. 20016

Grain of Sand, Municipal University of Omaha, Omaha, Nebraska 68132

Grande Ronde Review, 1901 F Street, Sacramento, California 95814

Grecourt Review, Smith College, Northampton, Massachusetts 01060

Greensboro Review, University of North Carolina at Greensboro, Greensboro, North Carolina 27412

Grist, 1237 Oread, Lawrence, Kansas 66044

Hanging Loose, c/o R. Hershon, 301 Hick Street, Brooklyn, New York 11201

Harlequin, Austin College, Sherman, Texas 75090

Horseshit, Box 361, Hermosa Beach, California 90254

Hudson Review, 65 East 55th Street, New York, New York 10022

Human Voice, Box 1409, Homestead, Florida 33030

Husk, Cornell College, Mount Vernon, Iowa 52314

I • Kon, 78 East 4th Street, New York, New York 10003

Illuminations, 20 East King Road, Tucson, Arizona 85705

Inner Well, Box 274, Marion, Indiana 46952

Inscape, University of Ottawa, Ottawa 2, Ontario, Canada

Insect Trust Gazette, 5011 Baltimore Avenue, Philadelphia, Pennsylvania 19143

In/Sert, 3524 N.E. Alameda, Portland, Oregon 97212

Intermission, 3179 North Broadway, Chicago, Illinois 60657

Intransit, Box 1586, Eugene, Oregon 97401

Iota, Idaho State University, Pocatello, Idaho 83201

Jason, Williamette University, Salem, Oregon 97301

Jeopardy, English Department Western Washington State College, Bellingham, Washington 98225

Juggler, Box 185, Notre Dame, Indiana 46556

Kansas Quarterly (formerly *Kansas Magazine*), Room 358 Watson Library, Lawrence, Kansas 66044

Kenyon Review, Kenyon College, Gambier, Ohio 43022 (Now defunct.)

Lace Review, Box 7181, Roseville Station, Newark, New Jersey 07107

Ladder, 1005 Market Street, San Francisco, California 94103

Latitudes, 6102 Sherwood, Houston, Texas 77021

Laurel Review, College Box 47, Buckhannon, West Virginia 26201

Leprechaun Review, Box 2324, French Quarter, New Orleans, Louisiana 70116

Lillabulero, Krums Corners Road, R.D. 3, Ithaca, New York 14850

Limbo, Box 4193, Postal Station D, Vancouver, British Columbia, Canada

Literary Review, Fairleigh Dickinson University, Rutherford, New Jersey 07070

Little Review of the Pacific Northwest, Box 4046, Portland, Oregon 97208

Location, 16 East 23rd Street, New York, New York 10010

Love, 618 Channing Avenue, Palo Alto, California 94301

Macabre, 91 Westerleigh Road, New Haven, Connecticut 06515

Maelstrom, 310 East 12th Street, New York, New York 10003

Maelstrom, Box 688, Blacksburg, Virginia 24060

Maguey, Box 385, El Cerrito, California 94530

Malahat Review, University of Victoria, Victoria, British Columbia, Canada

Mandala, 818 Terry Place, Madison, Wisconsin 53711

Manhattan Review, 229 East 12th Street, New York, New York 10003

Massachusetts Review, Memorial Hall, University of Massachusetts, Amherst, Massachusetts 01002

Mexico Quarterly Review, Apartado 72–852, Mexico 10, D.F., Mexico

Michigan's Voices, 716 Holland Avenue, Saginaw, Michigan 48601

Middle R, Eastern Oregon College, La Grande, Oregon 97850

Midwestern University Quarterly, Midwestern University, Wichita Falls, Texas 76308

Mikrokosmos, English Department, Wichita State University, Wichita, Kansas 67208

Minnesota Review, Box 4066, Highland Station, Saint Paul, Minnesota 55116

Miscellany, Box 2455, Davidson, North Carolina 28036

Moonlight Review, Box 1686, Brooklyn, New York 11202

Mother, Annex A, SUNY at Buffalo, New York 14214

MSS, c/o John Gardner, Southern Illinois University, Carbondale, Illinois 62901

Mt. Adams Review, Box 6054, Cincinnati, Ohio 45206

Mundus Artium, Ellis Hall, Box 89, Ohio University, Athens, Ohio 45701

New American Review, 1301 Avenue of the Americas, New York, New York 10019

New Campus Review, Metropolitan State College, Denver, Colorado 80204

New Mexico Quarterly, University of New Mexico Press, Albuquerque, New Mexico 87106

New Renaissance, 9 Heath Road, Arlington, Massachusetts 02174

Nexus, Box 2854, San Francisco, California 94126

Niagara Frontier Review, Box 37, Kensington Station, Buffalo, New York 14215

North American Mentor, 5105 Ripley Street, Davenport, Iowa 52801

North American Review, University of Northern Iowa, Cedar Falls, Iowa 50613

Northwest Review, 129 French Hall, University of Oregon, Eugene, Oregon 97403

Notes from Underground, 1303 Rhode Island Street, San Francisco, California 94107

Now, Fairleigh Dickinson University, Teaneck Campus, Teaneck, New Jersey 07666

Oberlin Quarterly, Box 176, Oberlin, Ohio 44074

Occident, Eshleman Hall, University of California, Berkeley, California 94720

Out of Sight, 1642 28th Avenue, San Francisco, California 94122

Oyez, Roosevelt University, 430 South Michigan Avenue, Chicago, Illinois 60605

Panache, 153 East 84th Street, New York, New York 10028

Parallax, Box 519, Carbondale, Illinois 62902

Paris Review, 45–39 171st Place, Flushing, New York 11358

Partisan Review, Rutgers University, New Brunswick, New Jersey 08903

Pegasus, Ballantine Hall, Indiana University, Bloomington, Indiana 47401

PEN, University of Utah, Salt Lake City, Utah 84112

Per/Se, Box 2377, Stanford, California 94305

Perspective, Box 1122, Washington University Post Office, Saint Louis, Missouri 63130

Phoenix, University of Chicago, Chicago, Illinois 60637

Plainsong, 4174 University Station, Minneapolis, Minnesota 55414

Plaintiff, Mankato State College, Mankato, Minnesota 56001

Pluck, Assinboia Hall, University of Alberta, Edmonton, Alberta, Canada

Plume & Sword, Box 85, Newcomb Hall, University of Virginia, Charlottesville, Virginia 22904

Polemic, Western Reserve University, Cleveland, Ohio 44106
Prairie Schooner, 219 Andrews Hall, University of Nebraska, Lincoln, Nebraska 68508
Premiere, Box 252, Lexington, Massachusetts 02173
Prism, 250 Park Avenue South, New York, New York, 10003
Prism International, University of British Columbia, Vancouver 8, British Columbia, Canada
Prospero's Cell, Box G, Queen Anne Station, Seattle, Washington 98109
Provincetown Review, 108 West 76 Street, New York, New York 10023
PS, Swallow Press, 1139 South Wabash Avenue, Chicago, Illinois 60605
Pyramid, 32 Waverley Street, Belmont, Massachusetts 02178

Quarry, Box 1061, Kingston, Ontario, Canada
Quarterly, Montclair State College, Upper Montclair, New Jersey 07043
Quarterly Review of Literature, 26 Haslet Avenue, Princeton, New Jersey 08540
Quartet, 346 Sylvia Street, West Lafayette, Indiana 47906
Quest, Box 207, Cathedral Station, New York City 10025
Quixote, c/o Kaleidoscope, Box 881, Madison, Wisconsin 53701

R.C. Lion, 1519 Walnut, Berkeley, California 94703
Rebel Magazine, Box 2486, Greenville, North Carolina 27834
Red Cedar Review, 325 Morrill Hall, Michigan State University, East Lansing, Michigan 48823
Red Clay Reader, 6336 Sharon Hills Road, Charlotte, North Carolina 28210
Reed, San Jose State College, San Jose, California 95114
Riata, Drawer D, University Station, Austin, Texas 78712
Riverside Quarterly, Box 40, University Station, Regina, Canada

Sage, University of Wyoming, Laramie, Wyoming 82070
San Francisco Earthquake, 1562 Grant Avenue, San Francisco, California 94133
Sequoia, Stanford University, Stanford, California 94305
Sewanee Review, Sewanee, Tennessee 37375
Shenandoah, Box 722, Lexington, Virginia 24450
Signet, Queens College, Charlotte, North Carolina 28207
Silo, Bennington College, Bennington, Vermont 05201
Small Pond, Box 101-A, RFD 3, Auburn, Missouri 04210
Smith, 5 Beekman Street, New York, New York 10038
Smoky Hill Review, Fort Hays Kansas State College, Hays, Kansas 67601
Sortie, 2626 Milburn Avenue, Baldwin, New York 11510
Soundings, Box 202, South Hall, SUNY at Stony Brook, New York 11790
South Dakota Review, Box 111, University Exchange, Vermillion, South Dakota 57069
Southern Humanities Review, 210 Samford Hall, Auburn University, Auburn, Alabama 36830
Southern Review, Drawer D, University Station, Baton Rouge, Louisiana 70803
Southwest Review, Southern Methodist University, Dallas, Texas 75222
Sou'wester, Humanities Division, Southern Illinois University, Edwardsville, Illinois 62025
Spectrum, Box 11762, University of California, Santa Barbara, California 93107
Spero, 1850 North Orchard, Chicago, Illinois 60614
Spokesman, Box 1, Loras College, Dubuque, Iowa 52003
Statement, California State College at Los Angeles, California 90032

Talon, 1911 Acadia Road, Vancouver 8, British Columbia, Canada
Tamarack Review, Box 159, Station K, Toronto 12, Canada
Texas Quarterly, Box 7517, University Station, Austin, Texas 78712
Toucan, 1520 South Boulevard, Kent, Ohio 44240
Trace, Box 1068, Hollywood, California 90028
Transatlantic Review, Box 3348, Grand Central Station, New York, New York 10017
TransPacific, Antioch College, Yellow Springs, Ohio 45387
Trenton Review, Trenton State College, Trenton, New Jersey 08625
TriQuarterly, University Hall 101, Northwestern University, Evanston, Illinois 62201
Trumpet, 6400 Forest Lane, Dallas, Texas 75230

UMD Humanist, University of Minnesota, Duluth, Minnesota 55812
Unicorn Journal, El Paseo, Studios 126–27, Santa Barbara, California 93101
University Review (formerly *University of Kansas City Review*), 5100 Rockhill Road, Kansas City, Missouri 64110
University of Windsor Review, University of Windsor, Windsor, Ontario, Canada

Vagabond, 66 Dorland, San Francisco, California 94110
Virginia Quarterly Review, 1 West Range, Charlottesville, Virginia 22903
Voyages, 2034 Allen Place N.W., Washington, D.C. 20008

Wascana Review, Wascana Parkway, Regina, Saskatchewan, Canada
Waterloo Review, 17 Craig Street, London, Ontario, Canada
West Coast Review, Simon Fraser University, Burnaby 2, British Columbia, Canada
Western Review, Western New Mexico University, Silver City, New Mexico 88061
Western Humanities Review, University of Utah, Salt Lake City, Utah 84112
Whetstone, Box 2234 Sam Houston State College, Huntsville, Texas 77340
Works, 56 East 13th Street, New York, New York 10003
Writing Magazine, St. Edwards University, Austin, Texas 78704

Yale Literary Magazine, 165 Elm Street, New Haven, Connecticut 06520
Yale Review, 28 Hillhouse Avenue, New Haven, Connecticut 06520

Zeitgeist, Box 150, East Lansing, Michigan 44823

1 2 3 4 5 6 7 8 9 10 11 12 13 14 15 16 17 18 19 20 21 22 23 24 25   78 77 76 75 74 73 72 71 70